Texas

PIONEER HEARTS ARE OPEN TO LOVE
AND AT RISK FOR DANGER IN FOUR INTERWOVEN NOVELS

DEBRA WHITE SMITH

BARBOUR
PUBLISHING, INC.
Uhrichsville, Ohio

Member of the
Evangelical Christian
Publishers Association

Printed in the United States of America.

DEBRA WHITE SMITH lives in East Texas with her husband and two small children. She is an author and speaker who pens both books and magazine articles and has twenty-eight book sales to her credit, both fiction and nonfiction including *The Harder I Laugh, the Deeper I Hurt* (Beacon Hill Press) and *The Seven Sister Series* (Harvest House). Debra holds a B.A. and M.A. in English and has had nearly half a million books in print since 1997. Both she and her novels have been voted favorites by **Heartsong Presents** readers and the Texas Series was one of her earliest works that she began at age twenty-seven. You may visit Debra on the World Wide Web at www.debrawhitesmith.com.

Texas Honor

Dedication

To my mother-in-law, Mildred Smith,
for the many times she has kept my little boy, Brett,
while I pursue my writing.
Also dedicated to the memory of my late father-in-law,
Travis Smith

Chapter 1

Dogwood, Texas
August, 1885

R achel! Rachel!" Ella called in the high-pitched panic that usually preceded bad news.

Relaxing her grip on the cow's warm udder, Rachel Isaacs nervously peered across the graying barn. The lantern, Rachel's ever present morning milking companion, projected shadowed silhouettes across the spacious barn's closed door. *What could be wrong this time?* she thought.

"Heaven help us! Rachel, it be the storage barn!" Ella shoved open the squeaking barn door, and an unnatural glow from behind turned her frizzy hair into a dark halo around her swarthy face. "It be on fire!"

With a startled "Wuff!" Rachel's loyal coonhound, Tiny, jumped from his slumber in the barn's hay-lined corner.

Rachel could not move. For what felt like an eternity, she tried to comprehend Ella's words. *No,* she wanted to yell, *this isn't true. Not the storage barn! Not the hay and corn!*

But the crackling flames dancing behind Ella's plump frame in the predawn light were real. The sound of Ginger nervously neighing in her stall behind Rachel was real. And the horror rounding Ella's eyes was as real as if she had seen the bowels of hell itself.

"Child! I said the storage barn's afire!" Ella repeated.

Finally the words registered with Rachel. They registered and sent a rush of cold clammy chills down her spine, a twist of nausea to her stomach. She jumped to her feet, sending her milking stool toppling into the half-full milk pail. "The corn! The hay!" Rachel screamed as the warm milk soaked through the laces on her leather work boots.

"I know it, Child! Get the shovel and dig a ditch around the barn. I'll get as many buckets of water as I can!" Ella swiveled and lumbered toward the well.

Rachel, her pulse pounding in her throat, stumbled toward the old shovel, grabbed its worn handle, then bolted for the glowing barn. She squinted in disbelief, in horror at the red, spitting flames licking the whitewashed building's roof and the pall of smoke marring the sunrise. There was no use in even hoping they could put out the hungry fire. But if she hurried, perhaps she could begin a trench that would stop the fire from spreading.

Throwing her waist-length auburn braid over her shoulder, she attacked the ground around the smoking structure. With every shovelful of moist, fragrant soil she overturned, with every quiver of her knees, Rachel, for the first time in her life, wanted to curse. Lately she was having bad luck, and it seemed that everything she touched exploded into disaster. All her life she had heard and believed that God would protect her, would take care of her, but recently she had grown to doubt it. *Where are You now?* she thought in frustration. *Where were You when Pa died?*

"The hay and corn are gone," she spat at the mute soil as sweat beaded above her brows and trickled into her eyes.

Hopefully she and Ella could stop the fire from spreading to the sprawling gray barn or to Rachel's lifetime home, that is, if the bad luck swarming her did not decide that the other structures were also appropriate food for the ravenous flames.

What if the fire did spread? Ginger. . .how could Rachel have forgotten her? A lump in her throat, she threw her shovel to the earth and raced back to the ancient barn.

A chestnut mare, ears pricked, black glassy eyes rolling in fear, pranced nervously within her narrow stall.

"Everything's fine, Girl. It's all goin' to be fine," Rachel crooned in a shaking voice. She deftly opened the stall door, grasped the mare's leather halter, and led her across the hay-strewn dirt floor to the side door.

Ginger had been Rachel's last gift from her father before he died of consumption in July. "There's something for you out in the barn," her pa had said from his bed. Rachel, her curiosity peaked, never expected the soft-eyed beauty of a horse that had persistently nudged her hand for a treat. To Rachel, Ginger was her last link to her father; and if anything happened to her, she would not be able to bear it.

"It's okay," Rachel whispered again, knowing that the gentle mare sensed the danger as much as she did. Within seconds, Rachel secured Ginger, her other horses, and the milk cow inside the nearby pasture, then raced back to her vigil at the fire.

"Give me that shovel," a deep voice demanded from behind her.

Gasping, Rachel turned to stare into the clear blue eyes of a man she had never seen. His slim face seemed drawn with concern and fear. Her mind numb with terror, Rachel did nothing, said nothing.

Then his big hand wrenched the shovel from her grasp. "Go help with the water," he said. "Don't worry about trying to put the fire out. Just soak the ground 'round it the best you can."

Rachel, always cautious, would normally have been reluctant to readily accept a total stranger. But right now, she didn't care who he was or where he came from. He was help; perhaps her luck was turning.

"Thanks, Mister," she said, racing toward the well.

After thirty minutes of hauling water, Rachel watched as the flames devoured the barn and the acrid smell of black smoke burned her nostrils.

The stranger strode from the back of the barn, the faint dawn light illuminating the black smudges on his lean face; a face so angular it reminded Rachel of a collection of triangles and squares.

"I got a ditch dug 'round it, and the ground's soaked. Looks like the barn's gone. But at least the fire won't spread," he said.

Rachel swallowed against the nausea creeping from the bottom of her stomach and up her throat like a grasping bony hand.

"I'm awfully sorry, Ma'am," he said.

"I guess I'm in a streak of bad luck lately," Rachel answered as she looked up into the stranger's serious eyes that were surrounded by tiny, V-shaped lines. Who was he anyway?

"I'm afraid this is more than a streak of bad luck, Miss Rachel," he said.

Blinking, she fleetingly wondered how he knew her name. "What? If it wasn't an accident, then that means—"

"I found a broken lantern by the back door. Looks mighty suspicious."

"Oh, no," Ella breathed from close behind. "It's enough what we've been through, without somebody settin' fire to the barn."

Rachel, her arms numb with fatigue, threw her auburn braid over her shoulder. *Was the fire related to what had happened a fortnight ago?* she thought, nervously rubbing the bridge of her freckled nose. Rachel scanned the rolling piny hills and sprawling green pastures of her three-hundred-acre, east Texas ranch. Perhaps someone was trying to harm her by destroying her ranch.

"I tell you this one thing, I will. It be the Lawd that done sent us this here stranger to help us out. Yes it be. What be your name, Mister?" Ella asked, her capable hands propped on massive hips.

"Name's Travis Campbell," he said, tilting his straw cowboy hat to reveal a glimpse of wheat-colored hair.

Rachel's neck stiffened, her mind spinning at his name. "You came after all, did you? I was beginnin' to think you weren't going to show your face."

"Now, Rachel, don't you go being rude to Mr. Campbell," Ella advised. "I think it's good he's come. I told you already. You need some-body to help you—"

"Well, I don't need *him!*" Rachel said as she glared into the man's slim face.

"I assume my guess is right, then. You're Rachel Isaacs? I'm pleased to meet you, too," he said dryly.

"I'll draw y'all up some cool water," Ella said over her shoulder. "I tell you what, yes I will, that Rachel, I just don't know. . .I just don't know if I'll ever make a lady outa her yet. She only nineteen year old, and she be as plain spoken as a old man. . . ." Ella's voice mixed with the swishing of her olive green skirt as she neared the well.

"You might as well get on your horse and go back to El Paso because we don't need you here."

"But my pa promised your pa. I can't just haul off and leave."

"Your pa promised my pa something he shouldn't have. It isn't right. And I'm not going to have some. . .some meddler come in here and. . .and marry me just because my pa didn't trust me to run this ranch alone. I won't have it. I'd eat a skunk first!"

Oh, Pa, why did you do it? Rachel wanted to wail. *Didn't you know I could run the ranch alone? Didn't you trust me?*

"Well now, I ain't exactly proposed yet," he said.

"Well you can save your proposal, Mister, 'cause I'm getting married in two months anyway."

"That's fine with me. I aim to marry next spring, too."

"Well why. . .how. . .?" Rachel's speech sputtered to a standstill as pounding horses' hooves echoed from the tree-lined dirt road.

Rachel and Travis turned to see Samuel James, Rachel's nearest neighbor and future husband, ride toward them in a cloud of dust. Many a woman in Cherokee County thought Samuel James was a handsome catch with his near-black hair and eyes, long proud nose, and high cheekbones that testified to his grandfather's Cherokee Indian blood. For Rachel, though, Samuel was simply a steadfast anchor on whom she could always rely.

As he reined in his puffing palomino, Samuel's dark gaze scanned the smoldering barn. "I saw the fire's glow," he said, his curious gaze resting on Travis.

"It's too late," Rachel said, wearily rubbing her damp brow.

Samuel, Rachel's lifelong friend, shoved his black hat from his forehead and shook his head in disbelief. Then, his saddle squeaking, he dismounted his giant of a horse.

Rachel cleared her throat and laid a possessive hand on Samuel's muscular forearm. "This is my intended, Mr. Samuel James. Samuel, this is Mr. Travis Campbell. Mr. Campbell is. . .is. . ."

"A family friend who's come to help Rachel," Travis said, then extended his hand to Samuel.

Irritation welled up in Rachel's chest at his familiar use of her given name.

Samuel, his eyes glinting with suspicion, slowly shook Travis's hand.

"Mr. Campbell thinks someone set the fire," she said, trying to hide her annoyance.

"On your way here, you didn't happen to see anyone on the road, did you?" Travis drawled as he looked up at Samuel, who nearly dwarfed him.

"Nah. Sure didn't. Not even any fresh tracks." Samuel took off his hat and, in a frustrated gesture, ran a calloused hand over his black hair. Focusing on Rachel, he ignored Travis. "Do you think it was the same person—"

"I don't know," Rachel said.

"What?" Travis asked quickly, almost too quickly.

"I lost thirty head of cattle the week 'fore last to rustlers."

"That twister took your pear crop, too. And now this!" Samuel said, waving toward the smoldering embers. "I'll be glad when—" He stopped abruptly and cast a guarded glance toward Travis. "There's no need for you to stay in these parts, Mr. Campbell. Rachel and I are marryin' in October," he said, encircling her shoulders with his arm.

Travis's smile, slow and measured, resembled a pointed-faced possum. "Listen, I didn't come here to cause any trouble. It's plain and simple the reason I came. 'Fore he died, her pa wrote my pa and asked that I come and help Rachel run the ranch. I promised I'd stay till spring. I got a weddin' of my own to attend then."

Rachel's spine relaxed a fraction. At least Travis had not told Samuel the whole contents of that horrible letter. Rachel had known nothing of it herself until she found Clayton Campbell's reply letter in her father's dresser after his death. She wished Samuel had proposed before Pa had died because then Pa would have never written to Clayton.

Some of the mistrust left Samuel's dark brown eyes. "That's mighty good of you, Mr. Campbell. But Rachel won't be needin' you. I guess you can go back home and tell your pa—"

"Well, if that's the way it is," he said, peering about as if he were memorizing every inch of the sprawling ranch, "I guess I should head back. It's been such a long ride, though, it would be mighty kind of you to let me stay in that ol' barn till I get good and rested up. Maybe a day or two?"

Not knowing what to do, Rachel glanced at Samuel.

"You're welcome to stay at my place," Samuel said. "I got something a little more comfortable than a barn."

"Ah, I couldn't do that. This here barn of Rachel's will be fine." He peered at Rachel. "Besides, I'm sure her pa wouldn't want her to turn away the son of the best friend he ever had."

Travis was right. Rachel's pa would expect her to be friendly to Clayton Campbell's son. "Well, if you don't mind sharin' it with my mare, Mr. Campbell, you're welcome to stay in the barn," Rachel said.

As soon as the words left her mouth, Samuel's hand tightened disapprovingly on her upper arm and Rachel pulled away. They were not married yet, and she still had the right to do what she thought was best.

"Thanks," Travis said.

Chapter 2

The next morning at four o'clock, Rachel's eyelids fluttered open to stare at her bedroom's shadowed pine ceiling. The events of the previous day weighed heavily on her mind. Both Samuel and Ella had assured her that the community would probably replace her corn and hay as soon as word spread that she was in need.

She thought about praying for her need, then dismissed the idea. God, if He were listening, probably would not answer her prayer. He had not bothered Himself long enough to save Pa or stop someone from stealing her cattle and burning her barn, so why would He concern Himself over her lack of hay and corn?

Perhaps when she and Samuel married next month, things would calm and her life would resume its normal pace. Her chest tightened in something close to dread, and Rachel promptly suppressed the feeling, then told herself it was only nerves. But still, a small voice deep within whispered all kinds of doubts.

The faint crunch of footsteps from the backyard ended Rachel's musings. She tensed, pushed aside the cotton sheets, sat up in bed, and then peered out the open window. The full moon illuminated the yard, bathing the barn and trees with a soft, silvery light. In the distance two whippoorwills called to one another like lonely soul mates.

Nothing seemed out of the ordinary. Nothing—until she once again heard someone walking in her yard, prowling around the house.

Rachel's body stilled in paralyzed fear. *Pa. I have to go get Pa,* she thought.

She slid from the feather ticks, her bare feet silently touching the

13

cool, plank floor. She put on her housecoat and stole down the hall to her father's room. As she pushed open his door, though, Rachel knew she had made a terrible mistake. Her pa's rugged walnut bed was empty; the colorful Star Flower quilt that she and Ella had stitched last winter lay there, undisturbed.

"Oh, Pa," she whispered, "I forgot you're not with me anymore." Her lips trembling, her eyes misting with tears, Rachel stumbled back up the narrow hall. She was the one who must protect the ranch now.

But could she? Apparently Pa hadn't thought so, or he would have never sent for Travis Campbell. After a hard bite on her bottom lip, Rachel rushed back into her room to grab the Winchester rifle from the bedside. Yes, she determined, she could and she would protect the ranch.

Her heart palpitating like a captured eagle's, she tiptoed down the shadowed hall toward the back door. Reluctantly, Rachel grasped its cool, metal knob and wondered if she should alert Ella.

No, she decided, for that would take too long, and whoever was out there might escape before Rachel got a good shot at him.

Fearfully, she eased open the door and peered at the yard, bathed by the moon's glow. A man, tall and lean, held a lantern and stood beside the burned barn's ashes. He looked toward the giant weeping willow tree behind the house, then glanced at the tree's twin in back of the big barn.

Rachel stepped out the doorway. The dried grass pricked between her toes as she trotted across the yard. Her lips trembling, she stopped behind a big pine tree, propped the rifle's barrel against its trunk, and pulled back the gun's cool hammer.

"All right, Mister, hold it right there!" she demanded, then sucked in lungfuls of pine-laden air.

Jumping, the man looked around.

"Now raise your hands nice and easy," she instructed.

"Rachel? Is that you?" the man called.

Her heart slowed with relief. "Mr. Campbell?"

"Yes, it's me. I was just—"

Walking from behind the tree, Rachel approached the burned barn. "What are you doing out here in the middle of the night?"

Her big coonhound, Tiny, barked once from behind the barn, ran to Rachel's side, then licked her fingers.

"I couldn't sleep and came out to see if I could spot anything else in this here heap that might help you figure out who set the fire." Travis raised the lantern, illuminating the few feet between them, and he saw Rachel, standing there in her night clothes. A flicker of something dark, something wicked flashed in his eyes, and then he glanced down as if he were embarrassed.

Heat rushing to her cheeks, Rachel stumbled away from the light.

"Excuse me, Ma'am," he said like a shy schoolboy. "I just ain't never seen a lady in her night clothes before."

Rachel placed an unsteady hand against her chest as if to cover her already covered bosom. Pa would have skinned her alive for going outside clothed like this. Travis Campbell must think she was anything but a lady.

"I don't usually go outside dressed like this, Mr. Campbell," she said in the most matronly voice she could muster, "but I was so scared that I didn't think."

"Of course you were. Please forgive me, Ma'am. What must you think of me, acting like that." His voice was almost too kind, too thoughtful.

"Well, good night, Mr. Campbell," she said firmly, turning to hurry back into the safety of her home. Maybe she should have heeded Samuel's unspoken warning about letting Travis sleep in the barn. Travis's father and hers might have been friends, but he was not the kind of man her pa would have allowed near his daughter.

Rachel, locking the back door, leaned against it and hoped Ella had not awakened. Why did Travis Campbell care who had tried to burn down the barn? He would be gone in a day or two, and she would be glad of it.

After stealing back to her room, she replaced the Winchester and stared out her bedroom window. Travis was slowly walking toward the barn, the lantern swinging in his big fist and casting splashes of light in his pathway.

Suddenly a hand, firm and warm, gripped Rachel's shoulder. Her stomach clenching, she swiveled around, then stifled the scream surging up her throat.

"It's only me, Rachel," Ella said. "What you doing? You done woke me up."

Rachel placed a calming hand over her palpitating heart and took a deep breath. "You scared me. I was just. . .I. . .oh, Momma Ella, I. . .I think I made a mistake letting that Campbell man stay here."

Rachel expected a reassuring hand and encouraging words, but all she got was a hug and a moment of heavy silence. "Now don't fret none, Child," Ella finally said. "He'll be up and gone before you know it."

Pulling away, Rachel looked into big, dark, uncertain eyes whose whites almost glowed in the moonlit room. "You don't think I should've let him stay, do you?"

"Now I didn't say that. Seeing as I was the one who done told you to go and be nice to him, it don't seem fitting for me to go and say you done wrong by bein' nice to him."

"But. . .he isn't. . .he's so. . ." Rachel didn't know exactly how to express her feelings for, after all, Travis hadn't done anything that was out of the ordinary—except for that one second when his eyes had seemed so wicked.

"I knowed it, Child. And there's another thing I can't figure on."

"What?"

"Well, I remember little Travis Campbell when your pa and ma and his pa and ma was acoming from Tennessee twenty years ago, after that war."

A familiar, wistful expression flitted across Ella's face and then came the pause that usually followed and the faraway longing, yearning tilt of her full lips. Lately, Rachel had begun to suspect what might be behind Ella's fond memories, and she felt it was more than the Isaacs family.

Rachel's pa had never believed in slavery. When he had seen how cruelly Ella's master treated her, he bought her to set her free. In 1865 she traveled with the Isaacses from Tennessee to Texas. When a bull trampled Rachel's mama to death shortly after Rachel's birth, Ella stayed as part of the family and became Rachel's Momma. Rachel sometimes wondered why Ella had never married or never pursued a life of her own. She now suspected that the reason was laced with pain.

"You was just barely thought of on that long trip from Tennessee," Ella continued, the wistful moment gone, "and that there Travis Campbell was the spittin' image of his pa. He wasn't but eight years old, but everybody said he'd grow up to be just like Mr. Clayton Campbell."

"Well, does he look like him?"

"That be the problem, Rachel. He don't look nothing like no Campbell I ever saw."

"Oh." Rachel and Ella shared a contemplative stare.

"But his horse, it have the Campbell brand."

"You looked at it?"

Ella nodded. "After supper yesterday. I done sneaked out to that barn while Mr. Campbell was bathin' at the creek."

"So he must be Travis Campbell. But why was he. . .?"

"What?"

"Well, I heard someone outside, so I went to see who it was. And Mr. Campbell was standin' by the barn's ashes, looking around like. . .like. . ."

"Shh, Child." Ella, grabbing Rachel's arm, propelled her to the window. "There he goes."

Rachel observed Travis as he left the barn and tiptoed across the yard with a shovel in his one hand and a lantern in the other. He stopped to peer over his shoulder as if he were afraid the demons of hell were watching.

"What's he up to?" Rachel mumbled.

"I don' know. But I aim to find out." Ella turned for the door.

"No. . .you can't. He might. . .he. . .he looked at me just *awful* when I went out there. I. . .I. . ." Rachel swallowed, her cheeks warming. She and Ella had never talked about such unladylike things.

A quick turn from the door, then Ella slowly widened her eyes. "Has that man done tried to get. . .to get *ugly* with you?"

Rachel said nothing, but Ella's incredulous expression said she had heard all she needed. "I'll just fix him where he can't do that no more." With determination, she turned for the door.

"Oh, I wish Pa were here, or Samuel, or—"

"That man tryin' to get ugly with *my* child. I don't care whose son he be," Ella muttered to herself. "I'll fill the seat of his pants full of shot. Make him think again 'bout how he acts."

"Momma Ella! You can't!" Rachel hissed, rushing after her. "He's stronger and. . .and. . ." She started to say "bigger than you," but stopped herself. Travis might be taller than Ella, but he was not bigger, for she probably outweighed him by a good fifty pounds.

Ella entered the hall, rifle in hand. "I'm gonna see what he's up to. It ain't no good; I can tell you that. Then, I'm agonna tell him to get off this here property."

Her pulse pounding against her temples, Rachel grabbed Ella's arm. "What are you goin' to do if he tells you he won't leave?"

Tiny's low warning growl sent a spiral of chills down Rachel's spine, chills that felt like the icy brush of death's skeletal fingers. Then a loud shot resounded through the woods, and Rachel's heart skipped a beat to only race like the wheels of a careening carriage.

Another shot exploded, closer to the house, and this time someone yelled in pain as Tiny's growls escalated into wild barking.

"Did you lock the back door?" Ella asked.

Unable to force a reply from her tight throat, Rachel nodded.

"Stay in the hall." Ella rushed for the back of the house.

Running into her bedroom, Rachel grabbed the Winchester and followed Ella to the floor-to-ceiling kitchen window.

"I told you—" A soft and low moan, followed by a scraping sound cut off Ella's words.

"Help," a deep voice rasped, but a new shot silenced it. Then, a shadowed figure collapsed to the ground in front of the window.

Rachel, her upper lip beading in cold sweat, blinked against the terrorized tears flooding her eyes. Was Travis the gunman or victim? Were she and Ella next?

"Dear Lawd in heaven, we done got problems. You gotta get us outa this mess!"

Wishing she had consented to marrying Samuel last month when he had asked, Rachel clutched her rifle until her fingers ached; she was ready for whatever might happen.

But nothing did happen. An eerie long silence settled across the ranch yard like a visit from death. The only noise was the sound of Ella's short shaking breaths and the distant whippoorwills.

Like two wooden statues, neither Rachel nor Ella moved. . .and neither did anything else. The grounds were as still as if the shooting had never occurred.

Rachel fleetingly wondered where Tiny was and why he had stopped barking. She hoped he had not taken a bullet.

The next second accounted for Tiny, though, as a loud curse echoed from the woods' edge and mingled with a new onslaught of growls and barking. Then Tiny yelped, and there was silence again.

Ella dared to inch open the door. "I hear the man. He's runnin'."

Rachel, straining her ears, listened hard, finally hearing the crunch of retreating footsteps through the woods.

"Tiny," Rachel whispered.

"We gotta see about the man who been shot," Ella said urgently, then opened the door.

"What if there was more than one? They might still be out there."

"I imagine they gone now. I imagine they done what they came to do. Go get me a lamp, Child."

"Be careful," Rachel whispered as she turned toward the spacious dining room. With trembling fingers she removed a nearby lamp from its wall holder and lit it with one of the new brand of matches that Ethan Tucker carried at his general store.

"It be Mr. Travis," Ella said, glancing over her shoulder as Rachel descended the back steps. "And he be dead."

18

As she stared at the corpse, Rachel's veins went as cold as frost on cattails. Two bullet holes, perfectly round, oozed blood onto Travis's tan shirt just under his left shoulder. Only minutes ago she had talked with him and his eyes had seen her. Now, those same blue eyes stared in blank incomprehension as his right cheek pressed into the chilled morning soil. His corpse would soon be just as cold, a corpse whose arms and legs were sprawled as if he had been crawling seconds before his death.

"What are we goin' to do?" Rachel asked, peering at Ella through dawn's gray light.

"We gotta go get Mr. Samuel."

"I'll go."

"No. *We* gonna go. I ain't leaving you here by your lonesome, and I sure ain't lettin' you go by your lonesome. That man might be watching, and he might have friends."

Chapter 3

Ａnd you say the body was right here?" Samuel asked again, holding the lantern beside the back door steps.

Rachel's mouth was as dry as a west Texas trail. She couldn't speak. The body had disappeared. Vanished.

"Yes, Sir. He was right there," Ella said, pointing to the dark bloody puddle marring the parched grass.

"He's gone," Rachel muttered incredulously, finally able to speak. "He's just. . .just gone." She rubbed the bridge of her nose as a cool pine-scented breeze lifted her hair from her shoulders.

"Are you sure he was dead?" Samuel asked.

Ella's head bobbed up and down in certainty. "He was deader than a burned flapjack. Yes, Sir, that man was dead."

"Whoever shot him must've hauled him off," Samuel said.

"That means they watched us go get you," Rachel said.

"Possibly. Constable Parker oughta be here before too much longer," Samuel said. "I guess we should leave the figurin' to him."

Tiny ran toward them from the north woods. Whining, he sniffed the ground where the body had been and looked up at Rachel in canine query.

Relieved to see her buddy in one piece, Rachel dropped to her knees and rubbed his warm ears. "I thought you were a goner, ol' boy. You did a good job with all that barking."

Tiny, his black tail wagging, extended his tan paw toward her. "He must be cleared out by now, whoever it was. Tiny doesn't offer to shake hands unless he's ready to go to sleep, and he wouldn't go to sleep with a prowler around."

Matthew James, Samuel's nephew, and Constable Parker rounded the dusty road's corner with the sound of pounding horses' hooves.

In a matter of minutes, the prematurely gray-haired, wiry constable took a full report of the situation. Then he stared at Rachel, his keen brown eyes full of speculation.

"It's not that I'm tryin' to doubt your word now, Miss Rachel, but are you sure this man said his name was Travis Campbell?"

Rachel glanced at Samuel in the predawn light, then nodded to the constable. "Yes," she said.

"That's the name he gave," Samuel agreed.

"Shore is," Ella added. "That's what he said but—"

"But, what?" Parker asked.

"Well," Ella glanced at Rachel, "he didn't look like no Campbell I ever done saw. Them Campbells had green eyes, every one of 'em. What with the barn burnin' and all the uproar, I didn't think about that till after supper. So I gave a hard look at his stallion. It had the Campbell brand and I just figured. . ." She shrugged.

The constable narrowed his eyes. "What's his horse look like?"

"It's a big'un. Black as coal all over," Ella said, "except he has one white sock from the knee down."

"He's in the pasture beside the barn with Sue Girl. Want to look at him?" Rachel asked. The cow began to bellow as if on cue.

"It's milking time, isn't it?" Samuel asked.

Rachel nodded.

"Take care of Sue Girl, Matthew."

Matthew headed for the restless cow.

"Don't think I need to see the horse," Constable Parker said. "That white leg. . .it's his left back one, ain't it?"

Ella nodded slowly.

Rachel's pulse increased. Did Constable Parker know something he wasn't telling them?

"What are you gettin' at?" Samuel asked.

"Well, a man came limping into town 'bout one o'clock this morning. Says his name's Travis Campbell. Says he camped two nights ago with a man named Hubert Calhoun. They talked like campin' folks do. Travis told you pa'd sent for him, Rachel. Next thing Travis knew, that Calhoun man jumped on him while he was sleepin'. Beat him up real bad 'fore Travis had a chance to wake up good. And when Travis started fightin' back, Calhoun whacked him on the head with an iron skillet. Knocked him out cold. When Travis woke up, he was tied to a tree, left for the bears or starvation, whichever came first. Everything but his bundle of clothes was gone." Parker looped his thumb through his gun belt. "He sat there all day long. When night fell again, he went back to sleep. But sleeping tied to a tree ain't too awfully comfortable, so he woke up 'bout midnight or so, he seems to think. And would you believe it, somebody'd cut the ropes."

"Is he. . .is he all right?" Rachel asked, feeling partly responsible for his predicament. After all, her pa had sent for him.

"He's mighty bruised up. But accordin' to the doc, he'll be fit as a fiddle in a few days' time." Parker smoothed his gnarled index finger across his graying whiskers. "Seems the rope was wrapped 'round and 'round Travis and the tree. Mr. Campbell says it was cut in only two places."

"Just enough to help him get loose," Samuel said.

"Right," Constable Parker said. "And whoever did it was mighty sneaky about it, too."

Two weeks ago Constable Parker said similar words to Rachel. *Whoever stole your cattle was mighty sneaky about it.* Those words brought back the shock Rachel had experienced when one of her hired hands, David Cosgrove, told her that thirty head of her cattle were missing. She had been standing outside the barn that morning, preparing to groom Ginger.

"You mean they're just gone?" she had blurted.

David had nodded, his sandy hair disheveled from his search.

"They were here yesterday evening, weren't they?" Rachel had asked.

"Yes, Ma'am. But the south pasture's fence was cut. Looks like someone stole them."

Now the violation, anger, and helplessness washed over Rachel anew. She felt the same when Travis Campbell, or the man who said he was Travis Campbell, had told her he suspected that someone purposely burned the storage barn. Could he have been involved in both crimes?

Ella's voice shook Rachel from her reverie. "My, my. I ain't never seen so much go on in one day in all my life."

"Me, neither," Parker said. However, Parker, tougher than his late thirties, thin frame depicted, had stood face to face with one outlaw after another and won. "Mind if I look around your place, Miss Rachel?" he asked as if he planned to solve Rachel's dilemma.

"Go ahead," Rachel said flatly.

"The shots, they came from the north pasture," Ella said.

22

"The men are supposed to be here any time," Rachel said, referring to her four hired hands. "They can help you, Constable."

"Maybe the five of you together can find something," Samuel said with little conviction. "I ain't too sure what to think of all this. But I do know. . ." He trailed off, glancing at Ella, then at Constable Parker. "With all due respect, I'd like to talk to Miss Rachel alone for a minute."

"We can use the parlor," Rachel said, already knowing that Samuel was going to say they should go ahead and get married. Maybe he was right; but for some very good reasons, she had made up her mind a month ago that they should wait until October.

❖

Ella turned to watch Rachel and Samuel walk toward the house as Parker headed for the north pasture. Samuel placed his hand on the small of Rachel's back and opened the door for her. From the second Rachel had announced her engagement to Samuel, Ella had felt uneasy. The two looked downright handsome together, but Ella could not convince herself that they should get married. Rachel had never asked her opinion, though, and until she did, Ella would keep her thoughts to herself.

Then Ella remembered back to a time when she had a young man of her own, and she suppressed the latent desire twining its way through her heart. Lionel, an employee of the Campbells, had traveled with them to Texas and had stolen her heart.

Constable Parker said that the real Travis Campbell was in Dogwood now. Like a schoolgirl in love, Ella's heart skipped a beat. Mr. Campbell might have word of Lionel. Had he ever married, ever had children? Did he still remember her and her search for her daughter lost in slavery? If Ella got a chance, she would ask him.

"Pardon me, but I need to know what to do with the milk," Matthew called from the barn.

Ella turned to face Samuel's scrawny nephew. "I'll take it," she said, and with that, she began her day's chores. She could not think too much on the past because Rachel had troubles in the present, and Rachel's troubles were her troubles.

❖

In the parlor, Rachel stood only inches from Samuel. "Rachel," Samuel said, placing his hands on her shoulders, "I'm worried 'bout your safety. We don't need to put off gettin' married till October. I can take care of the details, and we can marry by the end of the week."

Rachel stared over Samuel's shoulder and thought about last night, when, during all the uproar, she had wished Samuel were there to protect her.

But last night had also shown her something. After Pa had obviously not trusted her to run the ranch, she wanted to prove her strength to herself and to her pa. If only for two months, she would like to know that she could take care of the ranch.

Well, Pa, I do plan to overcome all that's happened, and in two months this ranch will be runnin' as smoothly as it was the day you died.

A haunting doubt lurked behind her brave thoughts. What about the missing cattle? Perhaps the barn burning and the cattle disappearing were the end of her problems. But somehow Rachel sensed that the opposite was true. Perhaps her trouble had only just begun. Could her life be in danger? Would it be more practical to go ahead and marry Samuel now?

Then that same doubtful whisper from only hours before haunted her heart once more. Did she really want to marry Samuel? Or did she want to wait. . .to take her chances on true love?

She pushed such hopeless thoughts aside and, ready to nod her head in agreement, opened her mouth to speak. "No," she said, realizing for the first time just how strong was her desire to prove herself, "you've got a harvest to finish and so do I. And you know Matthew's parents aren't moving here till October. Who'll be there to run your ranch till they get here if you're over here protectin' me? And who'd be here to run my ranch if I moved to your place?"

Samuel, dropping his arms, clamped his mouth into a straight line. "You ain't changed a bit, Rachel Isaacs. In all the years I've known you—"

"Momma Ella calls it common sense," Rachel said, raising her chin a fraction, daring him with her eyes to say anything else. She did not add, though, that Ella called it *stubborn* common sense.

"Your hired hands should be here in a minute or two, Rachel. I'm gonna see if David or one of the others can stay—"

"I've been thinking on something, Samuel," she said, not adding that the thought had just come to her. "Pa wrote Clayton Campbell to send his son out here to help me. Well, he's here. He's in town. . .and I need help. And. . .and he's going to need a place to stay till he recovers from that beating."

"I don't like the idea of a stranger stayin' with the woman I aim to marry," Samuel argued.

"He won't be staying with me. He'd stay in the barn. And as soon as he gets better, he'll be protection." Rachel marveled at her own quick plan. This would be perfect. Mr. Campbell would be close if her life were in danger; and at the same time, Rachel could maintain sole ownership of the ranch. She would still be the one running things.

Samuel looked into her eyes as if he were weighing her every word.

"Besides, I can't ask David to stay here. You know his wife just. . . just recovered from an. . .encouchment." Rachel's cheeks warmed with the introduction of such a delicate subject as childbirth. "And the other three are married men, too. Would you leave your wife alone at night to go sleep in someone else's barn?"

"Common sense," he muttered in disgust.

"You don't have to say Mr. Campbell can stay 'til we meet him. Why, I. . . I might not even agree to it after we meet him. But it would be a good plan if he's as respectable as Pa thought his father was."

Rachel suspected she had reasoned Samuel into at least considering her idea. However, if he knew the letter Pa had written also included references to marriage, he would never agree to it. He would also never agree if he suspected what Rachel was reluctant to admit to herself: that she was a tiny bit curious about the real Travis Campbell.

"We'll go meet him," Samuel finally said, "then we'll decide."

Chapter 4

O ne hour later, Rachel and Samuel arrived at Dr. Engle's brick office in Dogwood.

"Dr. Engle, Constable Parker says there's a man staying here named Travis Campbell," Samuel said as Rachel stood beside him at the doctor's front door.

The short, portly, gray-haired physician nodded, peering up at Samuel through wire-rimmed spectacles. "Yep. Sure is. He took a good beating, too." The sounds of squeaking wagons and horses' hooves in the street seemed to punctuate the doctor's claim.

"Is he. . .may we see Mr. Campbell?" Rachel asked, adjusting her plumed conversation hat.

"Well, he was asleep again the last time I checked, but I can see if he's awake." Dr. Engle opened the door wider, and Rachel and Samuel entered his cramped quarters.

"Wait," Samuel said, removing his black hat, "do you know for sure he's Travis Campbell?"

"Well, he had a letter in his hip pocket. . ." The doctor looked at Rachel. "From your pa to his pa, Miss Rachel."

Rachel's face warmed. So Dr. Engle knew her pa had arranged their marriage. Clasping her hands, she peered down at the tops of her white lace gloves.

"And he had me wire his pa, Clayton Campbell, in El Paso first thing this mornin' to tell him he was all right and ask to send him some more money since all of his had been stolen."

A big man with green eyes and golden hair limped into the room from the hall and cleared his throat. "I'm Travis Campbell. You wanted to see me?" His voice contrasted with his rugged cowhand appearance and sounded more like someone from the East than from Texas.

He was dressed in denims and a tan pullover shirt that buttoned from midchest up. Rachel figured that because of his size, he had to have his clothes tailor-made like Samuel did. Dr. Engle's small kitchen and parlor seemed overcrowded with Travis on one side and Samuel on the other.

"Well, I'll be," the doctor said. "You woke up. Feeling any better?" the doctor asked.

With a smile, Travis winced and fingered the bruises under his left eye. "Yeah. Still sore though."

Rachel needed no other proof than his looks to decide that he was the real Travis Campbell. Ella had insisted on drawing a rough sketch of Travis's father so she could determine if there was a family resemblance. Her sketch of Clayton Campbell was almost identical to the handsome man who stood before her. Square jaw and chin, a nose that was just almost too large, wide-set, honest eyes that resembled emeralds. . .emeralds with a touch of fire, and full lips that naturally curved upward, giving him the look of a lad planning mischief.

He was the spit and image of his father and had the mannerisms of a gentleman who should wear handmade wool suits and sit in fancy parlors sipping tea instead of riding across Texas. He was the kind of man Abby Bishop, Rachel's best friend, would call a sight for sore eyes. Rachel had to admit, he was.

"Come on and sit down." Dr. Engle motioned to Travis, then to Rachel and Samuel. "Here's the man you were asking about. Travis, this is Miss Rachel Isaacs and her intended, Samuel James."

"Pleased to meet you," Travis said, his gaze lingering on Rachel in a way that made a tendril of fleeting restlessness ignite deep within her.

As they all seated themselves around the sturdy oak kitchen table, Travis glanced at Samuel and extended his hand.

Rachel watched the two men shake hands and size each other up. Knowing Samuel, she imagined he was disconcerted to finally meet up with a man who was slightly bigger than he.

"Pa didn't tell me about his sendin' for you," Rachel said slowly as they sat down. "I found your pa's letter of response to Pa's letter shortly after. . . after. . ." Rachel tried to control her shaking voice.

Attempting to compose herself, she stared out the streaked window as her best friend, Abby Bishop, drove by with her father in their black two-seater buggy. A hot tear splashed onto her round cheek. Abby still had her father.

Samuel laid a possessive hand on her shoulder and finished for her. "Mr. Isaacs died last month. Consumption."

"I'm terribly sorry," Travis said respectfully. "He mentioned something of his illness in his letter."

Rachel nodded.

"He went fast," Dr. Engle muttered. "Too fast. I. . .um, would you young 'uns like some coffee?" he asked, his gray eyes suspiciously red. Dr. Engle was like one of the family. He had delivered Rachel, watched her mother die, and then tried to stop her pa from dying.

Five minutes later, Rachel sipped a cup of hot, bitter coffee from one of Dr. Engle's chipped blue mugs and finally regained her composure. The town agreed that Dr. Engle made the worst coffee in Dogwood.

"As I was saying, Mr. Campbell," she started, trying not to choke, "I know about Pa sending after you—"

"That letter he mailed. . . He didn't seem to think you'd let me stay if you knew. . ." Travis trailed off and glanced cautiously at Samuel.

Rachel squirmed inside. Travis understood. He had just stopped himself from mentioning that awful arranged marriage. "Well. . .I, um, I seem to be in a little. . .a little predicament." Rubbing the bridge of her nose, she looked into Samuel's dark eyes, asking for support.

And he told Travis everything, concluding with Rachel's burned barn and the murder.

"It's a good thing your father sent for me, Miss Rachel. Looks like I got here just in time." Travis stroked his jaw thoughtfully.

"I ain't said you could stay yet," Samuel said, raising his chin.

"I guess I must not have made myself very clear. Please excuse me," Travis said, one side of his mouth lifting in a politely challenging smile, "but her pa was the best friend my father ever had. Mr. Isaacs wrote, asking that I come to help Miss Rachel. My father wrote back and gave his word that I would stay until spring. That's all I would agree to since I'm getting married in the spring myself. And well. . ."

Travis looked Samuel square in the eyes, his words measured. "My father is a man of honor. So am I. We promised a dying man I would help his daughter, and I am here to give that help whether anybody agrees to it or not."

Samuel tensed.

Rachel's stomach knotted.

28

A long silence as thick as cold honey filled the room. And the two men stared at each other like a pair of bulls trying to decide whether to butt heads or come to a mutual respect of the other's strength.

"Besides," Travis added, "I want to know why Hubert Calhoun tied me up."

Samuel nodded slowly. "He was on Rachel's property for a reason."

"I think we owe it to her pa to find out that reason," Travis said.

"I think you might be right," Samuel agreed.

Rachel relaxed. Maybe her plan would work. Travis Campbell's protection would help her prove to herself that she could run the ranch smoothly.

"Well, if I'm to be staying with Miss Rachel, I guess I should go on out to her ranch. But I need to replace my guns first. The only thing that Hubert Calhoun didn't steal was my clothing."

Within ten minutes, Rachel was enveloped in the smells of coffee and peppermint as she preceded Travis and Samuel into the general store. Through a clutter of horse plows and hand tools and fabric, she spotted her best friend, Abby Bishop, scrutinizing a bolt of blue taffeta. Instantly, Abby dimpled into a warm smile. "Rachel, look! Bess was just showing me their new fabric. It came in on the stagecoach this morning, straight from Dallas! I was thinking about buying these pieces." Abby held up the taffeta and a piece of rose-colored silk. "What do you think?"

"Mmm." Rachel fingered the fabric. Her mind, cluttered with her own problems, barely registered Abby's question. Instead of answering Abby, she turned toward Travis. "Abby, this is Mr. Travis Campbell, an old family friend. He's come to help me out at the ranch for awhile. Mr. Campbell, Abby Bishop, my best friend."

"Miss Bishop," Travis said, nodding his head.

"How do, Miss Abby," Samuel muttered respectfully.

Abby produced a strained, although polite smile.

"The guns are over here, Travis," Samuel said, and the two big men walked toward the counter in the back of the store, their hats in hand.

Bess, the buxom, red-cheeked clerk, was not far behind. "Just what kind of gun did you have in mind?"

With disgust, Rachel turned to Abby. She did not want to witness Bess once again throwing herself in the path of the gentlemen customers. "We need to talk," Rachel whispered. She desperately needed to discuss her recent turmoil with her dearest friend.

"Okay."

"Abby, I'm ready," Joshua Bishop said, walking toward the front door with a fifty-pound bag of cornmeal over his right shoulder.

"Oh, just a minute, Pa. I wanted to buy this material." Abby clutched the blue taffeta and pink silk.

"Make it quick. Your ma wants you back home to help plan next week's menu." The dark-haired, blue-eyed man turned to Rachel. "How do, Miss Rachel," he said with the usual chill. He had never really approved of Rachel as a friend for his daughter because of Rachel's association with Ella. "How's everything up your way?"

Rachel gazed at Abby. "Not too good, Mr. Bishop. Somebody burned down my storage barn yesterday."

Abby gasped.

"I'm real sorry to hear that," Joshua Bishop said, his deep voice cold. "Think you might know who did it?"

"We aren't really sure. But I had a visitor who lied about who he was. Then somebody shot and killed him, and his body just up and disappeared."

"Do you think he started the fire?" Abby asked.

"I don't know." Rachel swallowed hard against the lump in her throat, then recounted Hubert's tying Travis to a tree.

"Sounds to me like this might have something to do with that cattle theft of yours," Joshua said.

Rachel nodded. "That's what I'm afraid of."

"Oh, Rachel," Abby breathed, "how awful. Why don't you and Miss Ella come stay with us 'til you find out for sure who did it? Our house is big enough for half of Dogwood. I would just *die* if anything happened to you."

Joshua Bishop cleared his throat in objection, and Rachel did not have to look at his face to know that there was a granitelike gleam in his eyes. Abby's pa didn't think black folks ought to live in white folks' houses, and he had fought Abby and Rachel's friendship because of it. His pa, Abby's grandpa, had been one of the biggest slaveholders around before the Civil War. Joshua Bishop still honored the Confederate flag, and he believed black folks weren't any count unless they were slaves.

Both Abby's grandmother Bishop, a true saint of God, and Abby hadn't thought slavery was right, though. Rachel was thankful, for she loved Ella like her own mother.

"I've got to run the ranch," Rachel finally said. "I can't just haul off and leave it."

"But you've got hired hands," Abby argued.

"I still have to be there. Besides, Mr. Campbell will be protection." Rachel set her mouth in a line, a gesture that usually hushed Abby's argument.

Abby, her eyes still pleading, silently returned Rachel's gaze.

"We need to be going, Abby," her father said.

"Okay, Pa. Just a minute." A quick squeeze of Rachel's hand and then, gathering the material, she went to pay Ethan Tucker, who waited expectantly behind the counter.

"I'm sure the lucky man you ask to the turnaround picnic won't be able to eat for looking at you in your new dress," Mr. Tucker said as Abby handed him the money. "Who are you asking?"

Rachel, unable to ignore Abby and Mr. Tucker's conversation, pretended interest in one of the new Butterick patterns in a wooden box near the material. She so wished Abby would happily marry, and Ethan Tucker was a great prospect.

"I'll probably be going by myself," Abby said.

Ethan had been trying to court her for a year, but for some reason Abby had not encouraged him. Most young women in Dogwood thought that Ethan was an attractive man. His gray eyes, chestnut hair, finely chiseled mouth, and six-foot-tall frame had turned many a head. He also owned his own business and had money in the bank. But at thirty, he had yet to marry. Despite all that, the few times Rachel had mentioned Ethan to Abby, her friend had swiftly changed the subject. Perhaps Abby simply was not ready to marry; but at nineteen years of age, neither Abby nor Rachel had much time left if they wanted a husband. That was part of the reason Rachel had accepted Samuel's proposal.

Rachel stole a surreptitious glance toward Travis, who was fingering a Colt revolver. Had she acted too hastily?

Chapter 5

Travis, admiring the bejeweled sunset, relaxed against the porch's white post, his head still aching where the iron skillet had hit him. Glancing at Rachel's thoughtful profile as she gently rocked the porch swing, he wondered exactly what the relationship was between her and Samuel James. Sure, they were engaged, but they acted more like brother and sister than two people in love. And, unless he was badly mistaken, Miss Abby Bishop and Mr. Samuel James had eyes for each other. Today in the general store they had both seemed a bit too discreetly interested in the other.

But then, none of this was Travis's business. He had simply come to Dogwood to help out a family friend, and he would be gone in the spring.

"Where do you want me to sleep, Miss Isaacs?" he finally asked.

The last glint of warm light from the setting sun made Rachel's auburn hair glisten with a jewel-like life of its own. She rubbed the top of her nose and anxiously looked at him. "I don't think it would be fit and proper for you to stay in the house with Momma Ella and me. Folks in Dogwood would find out and start talkin'."

"We don't want that now, do we?" Travis smiled mischievously, and his left eye protested in pain.

Rachel, raising her chin, stared at him in matronly reproof. "No, we don't."

He cocked his head toward the yard. "So I guess that leaves that big oak tree or the barn."

"Take your pick."

"Well, I guess I'll take the barn."

Straightening her blue work skirt, she stood; her prim expression vanished and uncertainty took its place. "Don't get me wrong, Mr. Campbell. I. . .do appreciate your helpin' me with the ranch. I. . .it's just that a lady can't be too safe when it comes to her reputation."

Even in the dim light, Travis saw the faint rush of color to her cheeks. "Now, Miss Rachel, please don't think for one minute I would do anything to harm your reputation. The way I see it, our parents were such good friends that I have a responsibility to you. Why, I guess I'm more or less your guardian angel."

"My intended wouldn't appreciate your saying things like that." She raised her chin again.

"I didn't mean anything by it. You know I've got a lady back home. I came out here thinking of you like I would my sister. I—"

"I didn't have anything to do with. . .with what Pa. . .with. . ."

"About our arranged marriage?"

Rachel nodded curtly.

"I didn't have anything to do with it, either. I guess when you were born, your pa and my pa just got carried away and decided we should get married. Well, nobody bothered to ask either of us about it, and it's very clear we think otherwise. So I say we should leave it at that. You've chosen your husband, and I've chosen my wife."

"Samuel doesn't know about. . .about that part of the letter."

"I had already gathered that. No man worth his salt would let me stay here if he knew." He stroked the side of his jaw.

"Well, you told Samuel you were stayin' whether anybody agrees or not. Didn't sound to me like you gave him much choice."

"I did promise your pa, and a gentleman always stands by his word."

"You're right. I imagine Samuel would do the same."

"Yes, I'm sure you're right. I think you've got a fine man."

"Yes, he is. Well, I'll get you some blankets, Mr. Campbell," she said, bustling through the front door.

Travis picked up a nearby match, lit the lantern sitting on the porch railing, then stepped off the porch, lantern in hand. His worn boots scuffed against the rain-deprived grass, and the lantern's hinges squeaked with every step he took. As the whippoorwills and pond frogs sang in synchrony, he reflected over the day's events.

When Travis had arrived this morning, all four of Rachel's hired hands, David Cosgrove, Gunther Peterson, Tyrone Burks, and Mac

Dixon, had been out branding cattle. Travis met them when they came in for lunch, and he strongly suspected that one of them could be involved in Rachel's theft and arson.

However, he had not revealed his thoughts. Instead, as long as his aching body allowed, he had tried to clean up around the burned barn. He sensed that Samuel was not very happy about his staying with Rachel. What man would be? But maybe the two of them working together could come up with some answers to Miss Rachel's problems. He wondered if Samuel also suspected Rachel's hired hands.

Travis, entering the sprawling barn, raised the lantern to illuminate the building. The loft was well stocked with fragrant hay; six occupied horse stalls lined the back wall. A tin milk can sat against the barn's side door, which led out to the cow pasture.

The harnesses. The saddles. The smell of cow manure and horse flesh. Travis smiled in derision. *And I'm going to be sleeping here.*

When the door creaked open behind him, Travis stilled in fear. Out of instinct, he whipped his new Colt Peacemaker from its holster, spun around, and had the weapon cocked before he stopped.

Rachel stared back at him like a startled, golden-eyed kitten.

Smiling tightly, he let out a pent-up breath and placed his gun back in its holster. "Sorry. I'm a little jumpy with all that's gone on. You startled me."

"Pulling guns on people can be dangerous," Rachel clipped.

"You're right. But *not* pulling guns on people can be dangerous, too."

"I guess I'll call out your name from now on. You'd have a hard time explaining to Samuel—"

"I don't shoot carelessly, if that's what you're implying," Travis snapped. Anger tightened his chest as a horrifying memory washed over him, the same memory that had been his bedfellow, his tormentor for one solid year. He would never forgive himself, and he knew God wouldn't, either.

"Here are your blankets," she said and then walked toward him.

Teeth clamped, he took the bedding.

"I didn't mean to imply. . . It's just, you scared me."

Travis nodded and took in the smells of hay and leather.

Would he ever recover? Would the guilt ever end? "It's okay. I guess we're both a little on edge."

"I guess." She glanced around the barn as if she wanted to say something else but didn't quite know how to say it.

"Did you notice the moon is full tonight?" Travis asked. The rising moon's mellow glow spilled in from the open door, ignited Rachel's waist-length wavy hair, and softened her creamy cheeks.

Rachel Isaacs was not a blazing beauty such as the kind he had seen on the East Coast or even the kind his fiancée, Kate Lowell, was. "Fresh" was the word to describe Rachel. Fresh, like a cool tangy breeze wafting in from the ocean. He chuckled to himself—an ocean breeze with a stubborn streak. And Travis, a featherlike caution stirring his chest, imagined that Rachel's pristine charm could twist itself into a man's heart, into his very soul, and forever transform his world.

But Miss Rachel Isaacs's pristine charm was none of his concern for his obligation lay with Kate Lowell. Fate had decided that, and nothing or no one would ever change his pledge of duty. However, there were some things a man, regardless of his obligations, found hard to ignore.

"I. . .I hope the coyotes don't get too noisy for you. They sometimes get rowdy when the moon's full."

"I never minded a few coyotes. It's the panthers I don't care for."

"I haven't seen a panther in a good six weeks. But Tiny, my dog, doesn't like them, either. He'll let us know if one shows up."

"Where is Tiny?"

"On my way to the barn, I saw him sniffing around the west woods. Every night he makes his rounds, then settles down under the house."

"Good. I want him close. Sometimes a dog can save your life."

Nodding, Rachel hesitated. "Momma Ella seems to think it's an awful shame for you to sleep in the barn, but. . ."

A slow, easy smile tugged at his mouth. So she was at least slightly concerned about his well-being. Travis was beginning to think she didn't care whether he lived or died. "Don't worry about me, Miss Rachel. I've slept in a barn or two before."

He didn't bother to tell her that the last time he had done it had been when he was home for the summer from the boy's school he attended in Boston and his father had let him sleep in the barn. Until Travis was studying law at Harvard, he had never understood why his parents insisted on his East Coast education. But now he was thankful for the knowledge.

He smiled to himself. What would Rachel think if she knew his father was the wealthiest cattleman in El Paso? He didn't think that would make any difference with a woman like Rachel, and for some unexplainable reason, Travis was glad.

Rachel grinned, her relief obvious in her relaxing brows. "I hoped you wouldn't take it personally." She rubbed those freckles again, and Travis expected them to fall off any minute at the rate she was going.

"Nothing personal taken."

"Well, good night then, Mr. Campbell."

"Good night."

She walked toward the door.

"Oh, and Ma'am. . .?" he started.

Rachel turned back to face him.

"My name is Travis." Why did he say that?

"I don't think Samuel would—"

"Of course not. And we wouldn't want to do anything to make Mr. James mad now, would we?" And where had that come from?

Rachel, blinking once, peered at him in cold appraisal. "What's your intended's name?"

"Kate Lowell."

"Would you want Miss Kate Lowell gettin' too. . .too friendly with another man?"

"Of course not. I apologize. I shouldn't have said that. I guess I'm slightly irritable from being so sore."

Warm concern replaced the coldness in her eyes. "Are you going to be all right? Momma Ella said we could probably scare up an old tick for you to sleep on instead of these blankets."

"No, don't go to all that trouble. These blankets will be fine. I'll be fine. It's just going to take a couple of days for me to get over that beating. It seems the closer I get to thirty, the longer I stay sore."

"Well, all right," she said, then closed the squeaking door behind her.

Shaking his head, Travis wondered what had gotten into him. Seemed like every time he opened his mouth, he had said the exact opposite of what a gentleman should say. Maybe tomorrow would be a better day for conversation, but right now he was beat.

Travis spread one of the blankets on what he hoped was the softest pile of hay. Just as he was ready to remove his gun belt, the door slowly creaked open again.

Rachel stepped into the barn, her slender hand pressed to her heart. "Mr. Campbell, somebody's prowling around the burned barn."

All vestiges of sleep vanished. Travis double-checked his holstered Colt, then turned out the lantern. "You stay here, Miss Rachel," he whispered, then rushed outside.

Travis, fear in his gut, cold sweat trickling down his back, tiptoed in front of the barn. Did the intruder have a gun? He sucked in the smell of Texas dust and cherished what could be his last breath.

In seconds he reached the barn's corner, flattened himself against the rough wood, and quickly surveyed the yard. Just as Rachel had said, a shadowed figure lurked near the burned barn, digging. Like a ghostly gravedigger, a man rhythmically placed a shovel deep into the earth, emptied it, then methodically went back for more. Travis slowly pulled out his Peacemaker.

Scanning the yard, he searched for a better vantage point and found one: Ella's summer log kitchen, to the right of where the man dug. It was in the barn's shadow and was the perfect place from which to take aim.

With a quick breath, he inched around the corner. Then he heard something behind him. A sniff? Glancing back, Travis peered down into a pair of round eyes. "What are you doing here?" he hissed. "I told you to stay in the barn."

Rachel raised her chin. "This is *my* barn and *my* property. If I want to follow you, then I'll follow you," she whispered.

Just what Travis had suspected, obstinance. And if Miss Rachel Isaacs were as strong as her will, that would be a problem. But as things stood. . .

Without another word, he replaced his gun, grabbed her small waist, and picked her up with little effort.

Eyes widened and a mouth opened in shock. Those were the last things Travis saw before he threw Rachel over his shoulder like a bag of potatoes.

"Put me down!" she demanded, beating his back and squirming like a cornered feline.

In six easy, silent strides, Travis hauled her back into the barn like she was a half empty bag of corn, for that's about what she weighed. Then with equal ease he deposited her on her backside into a pile of hay.

"Just what do you think you're doin'?" she whispered, trying to scramble to her feet.

"I'm protecting you from *yourself.*" Travis reached for the long rope hanging from a nail and gently pushed her back into the hay. He jerked her wrists together and tried to place them at her ankles.

Rachel broke free and groped for the rope. "Give me that!"

Travis, gritting his teeth, regained his grip on her wrists and jerked them to her ankles. Then, one wrap, two wraps, and the knot, just as if she were a calf he had roped.

"You. . .you. . ."

"Shh!" he commanded. "And don't move."

37

Trying to suppress the fury gripping his stomach, Travis tiptoed back to the barn's corner. *She could have gotten herself killed,* he thought.

Once again, with his Colt ready, he peeked around the barn. Nothing. He blinked. No shadowed figure, no digging, nothing, just as if he had been dreaming only seconds before.

Breathing in uneven huffs, Travis slipped down the barn's shadowed side. Still, no one stirred. Then Tiny's muffled bark from the woods' depth shattered the stillness.

Doubling his fist, Travis hit the first oak he passed, glad for the punishing blow of flesh against unforgiving bark.

"Women!"

Knowing that tracking the man was fruitless, Travis went after him anyway. He followed the direction of Tiny's bark across the north pasture and toward the waiting woods. Scrubby dry grass and fragrant bitterweeds tore at his boots as Tiny's bark grew closer. A breeze wound through the thick evergreens, oaks, and hickories. Shadows, foreboding and suspicious, lurked among the foliage. Travis slowed his pace. No sense in taking any chances.

Then, out of nowhere, a small ball of fur raced past his feet. Tiny was close behind, his coonhound bellow proudly proclaiming that he was on the trail.

Travis rolled his eyes in frustration. *Some bandit is on the loose, and Tiny's chasing a rabbit.*

A quick scan around the woods and pasture, then Travis gave up on tracking the man, who was long gone. Besides, Travis didn't like the woods at night because of the shadows that brought back too many memories. Memories splattered with Zach's warm blood.

Oh, Lord, can You ever forgive me? His now-stinging eyes went blurry, but a hard, determined blink held the tears in abeyance.

He had not cried at the funeral; he would not start now.

Knowing he should go release Rachel, Travis trudged back toward the barn. *I don't imagine she's very happy with me,* he thought. But his father had promised her father, and Travis refused to let her get hurt.

❖

Rachel, her heart pounding out furious beats, struggled against the rope chafing her wrists. *When Travis Campbell comes back, he better be ready for a fight!* She scanned the dark barn, looking for something, anything with which to cut the rope.

Tiny, barking excitedly, neared the barn, and raced across the south field. Then a man's slow, crunching footsteps approached and halted outside the door. Rachel held her breath, hoping the man was Travis.

The barn door slowly creaked open to reveal an ominous shadowed figure who slowly approached with the brush of boots against hay. Rachel's stomach clenched in terror as she opened her mouth, ready to scream.

"I wasn't surprised when I didn't catch the intruder, but your staying quiet, Miss Rachel, now that's a surprise," the intruder said.

Relief, warm and comforting, flowed through her veins, but the indignation that followed annihilated that relief. "Travis Campbell, you untie me right now! Do you hear me? Right now!"

Chuckling, Travis bent over her bound arms and legs, and, with one quick jerk of the rope, she was free. But before he had a chance to straighten, Rachel slammed her open palm against his cheek.

Rachel gasped; Travis stilled. And the two stared at each other nearly nose to nose in dead silence.

She had never slapped anyone in her life, and now hot, accusing tingles spiderwebbed from her palm to her wrist.

"Maybe next time, you should double your fist so I might feel it," Travis finally said, a genuine, infuriating quirk to his lips.

"Oh, you. . .you. . ." Rachel stumbled to her feet. "I own this land you're standing on, and I'll have you to remember it! And if you ever, *ever* do anything like that again, I'll have Constable Parker throw you off this property for good! Do you understand me?"

"I was only trying to protect you!"

"Well, I don't need that kind of protecting!"

"Then why did you ask me to stay?"

"It wasn't so you could tie me up in my own barn!" Rachel's chest heaved with every churning breath, and she turned to stomp toward the ajar door. Then, with more power than she dreamed she possessed, she slammed it behind her with a resounding boom.

❖

Wincing, Travis whistled softly as he gingerly stroked his left cheek. Her slap had connected right under his bruised eye. He had tightened his gut to stop himself from yelling when she delivered the blow.

Yet now he laughed, a soft rumbling laugh that started deep and refused denial. Miss Rachel did have spunk, and that was something he admired in a woman. Earlier he compared her to an ocean breeze with a stubborn streak. Now Travis knew he had underestimated her. Rachel had *definite* hurricane potential. For the first time in his life, Travis felt a cold, coiling jealousy slither into the pit of his stomach. . .a jealousy of one Samuel James.

Chapter 6

Ella jumped away from the open parlor window and hurried down the hall to her bedroom. She had begun to wonder what was delaying Rachel and had walked into the parlor to investigate. Then she heard Rachel's awful screaming and the barn door slamming.

Chuckling under her breath, Ella crawled into bed and pulled the sheet under her chin. She reflected over her doubts that Rachel should marry Samuel and then she snickered. *One interesting autumn, that's what it's gonna be,* she mused.

Ella heard Rachel fling the front door open and bang it shut. She closed her eyes, tilted her head just right, opened her mouth wide, and started snoring.

Rachel's angry footfalls echoed up the hallway, stopping outside Ella's ajar door.

Not opening her eyes, Ella pictured Rachel, who probably stood with her hands on narrow hips, her chin high in defiance, and her full lips pressed into a narrow line. Ella tried not to smile. *That Mr. Travis is gonna keep things good and stirred up, yes he is.*

"Momma Ella, are you awake?" Rachel whispered.

Skipping a snore, Ella swallowed.

"Momma Ella?"

"Child? What you need?" Ella asked groggily.

"Oh, Momma Ella," Rachel wailed. Then she was on the bed, piled up in the middle, sobbing like she had at her pa's funeral.

"Here now, Child. It can't be all that bad." Pulling Rachel close, Ella stroked her mane of auburn hair, laced with the smell of lilacs.

"I. . .I miss Pa so badly," Rachel finally choked out. "If. . .if he hadn't died, he would know how to handle all this. . .this. . .the barn burning and the cattle missing and somebody prowling around."

"Prowling around?" Ella's eyes widened.

Through diminishing sniffles, Rachel recited the events of the last thirty minutes.

"Do you know what the man was digging for?" Ella asked.

"No. I didn't think to look. I was too mad at Travis. . .I mean Mr. Campbell. Oh, Momma Ella, why do you think God let Pa die?"

"Here now, Child. The good Lawd, well, He allows all sorts of things we don't understand. We just have to trust that He knows what's best."

Ella squeezed Rachel's hand, remembering being young and asking similar questions. Why did the Lord allow slavery? Why did He allow cruel, white masters to rape their defenseless slaves? Why did He let Ella give birth only to have the child ripped from her?

"Just you remember, Child. No matter what happens to you, the Lawd, He's gonna always be there for you."

"Then why do I feel like He's so far away?"

❖

Ten minutes later, Rachel took off her tan work dress and laid it over the straight-backed pine chair at her bed's end. Her talk with Ella had lessened her emotional tension. Her spiritual tension, however, steadily increased like a growing heap of bitter despair that seemed insurmountable.

God should have never let Pa die, she wanted to scream at the pine ceiling. She had been to church every Sunday of her life. Sang in the choir. Visited the sick. Took food to the poor. And this was the way God repaid her.

"Good night, Pa," she whispered, sitting on the side of her bed. They had always shared a Scripture at bedtime and sunrise. Ella had tried to keep up their tradition, but Rachel refused. She missed Pa the worst at those times and didn't want to deepen the pain.

Rachel thought of Samuel as she crawled beneath the soft, clean sheets. Pa would be glad Rachel was marrying Samuel. She so wished he had not written that letter to Travis's father. Even though Travis was going to be protection, Rachel was beginning to wonder if she would be better off marrying Samuel now and sending Travis home.

He was the most exasperating man Rachel had ever met. The thought of having to put up with his smug highhandedness another day made her want to slap him again. She rubbed her wrists, still stinging from that enraging, humiliating rope.

A thought—an explosion of curiosity—and Rachel sat straight up. The hole. She still did not know what that prowler had been digging for.

So Rachel made a quick decision. Out of bed, into the work dress, don't worry with shoes, grab the lantern, and down the hallway.

When she opened the back door, she noticed a lantern's soft glow from near the old stump, right where the man had been digging.

She gripped the metal knob tighter as terror likewise gripped her stomach. He was back!

Then another figure joined the first one: a plump, skirted figure—Ella.

"What you think, Mr. Travis?" Ella's clear voice pierced the night air while Travis's low tone was unintelligible.

Travis. Thank God.

Her hand relaxing on the knob, Rachel smiled. She had caught Ella in the act, just like earlier when Ella was spying on her from the window. But Ella had been spying on her ever since she was a little girl, and Rachel knew Ella did it because she loved her.

Placing her right foot out the door, Rachel stopped. The cool stone step against her toes seemed to awaken her fury. *I'd rather eat a skunk than face Travis Campbell again tonight!* With that, she decided to wait until morning to appease her curiosity.

Rachel, after haunting, sleepless hours, made a decision about marrying Samuel. With determination she donned her green gingham work dress and headed up the hallway to inspect the hole, then gather the eggs.

Ella had already risen and had neatly spread her multicolored patchwork quilt over her bed. That meant she was in the summer kitchen starting breakfast for the hired hands. Rachel's pa always made sure that his workers were fed well. "If we're gonna ask them to take three days away from their own farms, they'll get breakfast and dinner," he would say.

As always, Rachel's eyes misted with thoughts of her father, but a hard blink and a bite on the lip forced the tears away. She was through with crying but not with hurting. Her swollen eyelids felt tight, though, and the mirror had attested that everybody would know she had been weeping. The last thing she wanted was Travis Campbell feeling sorry for her.

When she got to the hole, Rachel lowered her lantern and peered into the two-foot-wide cavity. Nothing. Had Travis found something last night?

As the morning crickets shrieked in unison, Rachel felt as if she were stuck in the middle of a demoniacal tornado. Her whole life of late, everything around her, seemed to be chaos, and she hoped Constable Parker would end it.

"It looks like whoever dug the hole was barking up the wrong tree, or should I say digging in the wrong spot? I don't think he found what he was looking for," Travis said, walking from the barn.

Jumping, Rachel glanced his way. "Looks like it," she said in a cold, formal voice, then turned for the chicken coup. It was already after five o'clock; Ella would be needing the eggs.

A big, warm hand on her shoulder made Rachel stop. "Miss Rachel?" Travis mumbled.

She hesitantly turned to face him.

"I'm sorry for tying you up last night. I've been thinking about it and don't believe it was quite fair or something of which the Lord would approve. But I was afraid you would get hurt."

Rachel, shocked to her toes, wanted to drop her mouth open in surprise. Instead, she schooled her features into the blandest expression she could conjure. "It's okay, Mr. Campbell," she heard herself saying.

A hesitant smile. "I'm glad you feel that way because it's going to be a long fall and winter if we're angry with each other."

This was the perfect opportunity to tell Travis of her decision to marry Samuel this week, then send Travis on his way. But her tongue would not come away from the roof of her mouth. When it did move, she said, "I guess I shouldn't have slapped you. I've never slapped anyone before. It surprised me as much as it probably did you."

Chuckling, he rubbed his left jaw. "It was a surprise, I'll say that."

After her initial introduction to Travis, Rachel had not paid much attention to his looks, perhaps because she had been in an uproar over everything else. Yet here, in the morning darkness, with nothing more than the lantern's light illuminating his face, Rachel caught a glimpse of the man behind that mischievous smile. His glittering green eyes held a hint of compassion and pain and brawny tenacity. Travis Campbell was like the combination of a soft sunset and a lazy river with dangerous currents that ran deceptively deep.

He had even apologized, something lots of men would not do. Samuel never had. But then, they had never fought, either. *Do I really want to spend the rest of my life with Samuel James?*

Blinking at the disturbing question, Rachel realized she had been staring. "I've. . .I've been wondering about your accent. You don't sound like a Texan," she said, trying to make polite conversation.

44

He pushed his straw cowboy hat off his brow. "I guess that's because I went to school in Boston. Went to law school there, too."

"You've been to college?" Rachel had dreamed of attending college before her pa had become ill. Now, she would have to be satisfied with running the ranch.

"Yes. My father insisted on it. I think it's because he only finished the eighth grade. It hasn't made much difference in my job, though. I'm still just one of Father's ranch hands."

Rachel, for some inexplicable reason, suddenly wanted to know more about Travis's home, his family, his way of life. Instead, she suppressed the urge to ask anything else and said, "I. . .I guess I need to go gather the eggs for Momma Ella. I smell the smoke from the stove, so breakfast should be ready in an hour or so."

Tell him you're marrying Samuel this week, her common sense urged. But Rachel could not obey.

Chapter 7

Ella stared into the cooking stove's glowing coals and took in the smell of burning oak. She remembered another fire, a fire she could never forget, on the last night she had held her ten-year-old Daisy close. Little did she know the next day would bring a mother's sorrow that would torment her until death.

"Miss Ella?" The sound of Travis Campbell's voice from the doorway jolted her back to reality.

And with a smile, Ella turned to face him. Most other folks just called her Ella. And some like Joshua Bishop called her "that old nigger woman who lives with Rachel." It was mighty nice to feel respected.

"Yes, Sir?"

Travis walked into the kitchen and placed his hand against the rock fireplace. "I was wondering if you could answer a few questions about Miss Rachel's employees. I understand they're to be here for breakfast."

Ella studied him, trying to see past the bland expression masking his face. The lantern's light, dim and flickering, did not reveal his thoughts, yet he seemed to be up to something. Ella figured he was thinking what she already suspected, a matter she had not mentioned to Rachel, who was too loyal to think anything bad about her employees.

"Whatever it is you be thinking on, Mr. Campbell, I think you might be right."

"How do you know what I'm thinking?"

"I don't rightly knows how I knows. My momma used to be able to tell what a body was thinking just by his expression. And well, so can I. I don't knows how it works. I just knows you think some of them hired hands might be up to no good."

"And you agree?"

"Can't say I completely agrees." Ella took two massive iron skillets from their nails on the wall and set them on the stove top. "But I just thinks you might be right," she slyly added.

"Could you tell me what their names are once more? With everything that's happened, they seem to be jumbled in my mind."

"Well, there be Mac Dixon, David Cosgrove, Gunther Peterson, and Tyrone Burks."

Travis paused a moment to firmly establish their names in his mind. "Are they married?"

"Yep. Every one of 'em." Grabbing a large wooden bowl from the wall shelf, Ella walked toward the bag of flour in the corner. "They all own small farms 'round these parts. And Mr. Isaacs offered them a salary and a small part in his harvest if they'd help out 'round here 'bout three days a week. Plus we feeds 'em breakfast and dinner."

"That sounds like a pretty good deal."

"Yep. Mr. Isaacs, that was a fair man." Ella's throat tightened and her eyes blurred before she grabbed the tin cup and began dipping flour into the bowl.

She had not let on to Rachel because one of them had to be strong, but Mr. Isaacs's death had hurt her almost as much as Rachel. He had rescued her from that auction block twenty-five years ago, and only the Lord knew what would have happened if he had not come along. Certainly she would never have met Lionel, and she would have never fallen in love.

Travis discreetly cleared his throat. "Is there any reason you know that any of Rachel's. . .I mean, Miss Isaacs's hired hands might want to hurt her?"

"Nope." Ella turned from dipping the flour, her dark hands sprinkled in white. "That be the problem. None of them four men has ever been more than hard-working, honest fellows who wouldn't hurt a soul."

"Then why do you suspect them?"

"Well, who else be there?" Ella reached for the baking soda sitting on the wooden shelf, dumped some into her cupped hand, then sprinkled it into the flour.

"Mmm," Travis said thoughtfully. Standing straight, he crossed his arms. "I keep thinking that whoever was digging last night will probably be back. I don't know what he was looking for, but I've got a hunch he didn't find it."

" 'Bout last night," Ella said, glancing toward him from the corners of her eyes. "I wouldn't take too much offense to what Rachel does. That child be a little hot tempered at times. And I wants you to know that I'm mighty glad you be here."

With a chuckle, Travis turned for the door. "Rachel and I worked out our differences this morning. But I appreciate your concern."

Ella smiled. *There be something else I knows about what's going on in your mind, Mr. Campbell. And neither you or Rachel will admit it. One interestin' autumn it's gonna be.*

Just as Travis opened the kitchen door, Ella reached for the milk to find none. Then she realized she had forgotten to go to the springhouse.

"Mr. Campbell? Would you mind goin' down to the springhouse for the milk and butter? I done forgot it this morning."

"Okay," Travis said, stepping out the door.

Ella opened her mouth, ready to ask him about something that had plagued her memory since Rachel's birth: Did Lionel ever marry? Was he still alive? Did he even remember her?

But the heavy wooden door closed before she could form a question. *Maybe that be for the best,* she thought. No sense in stirring up the past. It was over. And, with a sigh of resignation, Ella locked away her desires, once again.

❖

One hour later, Travis thoughtfully chewed his salty bacon and secretly studied all four of the hired hands who sat around a crude oak table under the monstrous weeping willow tree behind the barn. Ancient barrels were their chairs, tin plates and cups, their dining utensils.

As Rachel and Ella served their breakfast of bacon, eggs, biscuits, and hot coffee, Travis had kept up light conversation with the four employees. So far, he had asked nothing personal. They all seemed honest enough, just like Miss Ella said. Yet, who else but an insider could be responsible for all that had happened?

"So, how long have you lived in Dogwood, David?" Travis asked the sandy-haired young man to his right. Ella had insisted that Travis sit at the head of the table.

"All my life. We were all born and raised here. . .all 'cept Gunther there." The small man pointed across the table. David had an intelligent gleam in his gray eyes that Travis wasn't sure he liked. The same sort of gleam that might be able to head up a cattle rustling scheme.

48

"Yep," Gunther said from Travis's left, his wide smile revealing a missing front tooth. "I was born out west. Moved here when I was ten. So I guess you could say I was half raised here anyway." Just plain dumb, that was the look Gunther had. Travis figured Tiny probably had more brains than Gunther Peterson.

Leaning over Mac Dixon's shoulder, Rachel refilled his coffee cup.

"My people go way back," Mac said. "Why, some of 'em were killed in the Killough Massacre of 1838." He scrubbed thick fingers through his short black hair. "And my pa was in the Confederate Army. Fought in the battle at Sabine Pass, matter of fact." Mac looked about like any man you would see on the streets of a small Texas town. Aside from his rather large hands, there was nothing distinguishable about him. Dark eyes, hair, and stubble; a scruffy red neck scarf; the usual gray suspenders.

"Hmmmmpf." Tyrone Burks's sarcastic grunt was the first thing he had verbalized all morning. However, his hostile blue gaze didn't miss much. Travis sensed that Tyrone was born the quiet sort and that life had intensified that trait.

"What's the Killough Massacre?" Travis asked as Rachel refilled his cup, her lilac scent mixing with the mellow smell of coffee. The scent, simple yet enchanting, matched Rachel's uncomplicated beauty; a scent that emphasized the difference between Rachel's honesty and Kate's sophistication. Nothing but the best for Kate; only the most exotic oils would please her dainty nose. Travis had often laughed indulgently at her discriminating tastes. Now, with Rachel's fresh smile lighting the morning, he didn't feel so indulgent.

David's gray eyes flashed with interest as he related Mac's massacre story. "A bunch of Cherokee Indians led by Chief Dog Shoot killed a bunch of white folks about fifteen miles from here. After all the smoke settled, eighteen people were missing. But they never found all the bodies. Only a handful escaped. Four women, two children, and one man, Nathaniel Killough."

"One of those women was my third cousin," Mac bragged. "Yes, Sir, I come from a sturdy lot."

Pushing his tin plate forward, Tyrone stood. "Let's see how sturdy you are at mending fences, then." The tall thin man trudged toward his chestnut gelding, crammed a straw hat over his blond hair, stepped into the stirrup, and rode across the north pasture.

Gunther's chuckle revealed a tooth missing on the bottom, too. "Don't take no stock by him."

"Yeah." Rubbing his protruding belly, Mac stood. "When the good

Lord made Tyrone, He made him a bit grouchy in the mornings. We just overlook him."

"He's a good hand, though," Rachel declared as she gathered Tyrone's empty plate.

Ella had said that Rachel was loyal to her employees. She was obviously right.

"Yep." David stood, his intelligent gray gaze taking in the rising sun. "It's hard to find a harder worker."

"Mmm." Travis stared into his steaming coffee. This conversation had not given him much information, but it had made him curious about Tyrone Burks, whose cold blue eyes said he was not friendly any time.

What about David Cosgrove, though? He seemed to have more intelligence than the other three put together, the kind of intelligence needed to be a successful outlaw.

"Well, Boys, looks like we gotta hit the fences," Mac said. And with that, the three men mounted their horses and followed Tyrone.

"Are you through with your coffee?" Rachel asked as she stacked the plates.

"Not quite. It's really good. The best I've had since I left home." Travis rubbed the sore knot near his right temple.

Her cheeks flushed with pleasure. "I made it."

"You could teach Dr. Engle a thing or two. I think muddy water would be better than his brew."

A musical giggle. "I know. Isn't it just *awful?*"

The morning sun, now highlighting a seeming explosion of crystal dew on the surrounding foliage, revealed Rachel's slightly swollen, red eyes. "Have you—" He stopped himself short of asking if she had been crying. A quick sip of coffee, and maybe she wouldn't notice his unfinished question. Her crying was none of his business, and he hoped his escapade last night had not instigated her tears.

"Yes, Mr. Campbell?" She stepped between the rising sun and him.

And Travis almost choked on his coffee. The sun turned her hair into a wavy mass of fire and highlights, like an angel.

"I. . .I was just wondering if you ever noticed anything suspicious about your hired hands."

"Are you implying that one of them could be responsible for what's going on around here?"

Travis squirmed internally. He didn't like the tone of her voice. "The thought had crossed my mind."

"Well, I think you're wrong," she said, scooping up the forks and spoons.

"Maybe you shouldn't be so quick to defend them. Any of the four could have had ample opportunity to steal your cattle. And that's a fact you cannot ignore."

Her amber eyes sparked with ire. "Mr. Campbell, where you come from, people might not trust each other. But here, we do. And what you're suggestin' is wrong, dead wrong. These four men have been working here for almost ten years. If they were going to do something illegal, they'd have done it before now."

"And I think you're wrong."

A raised chin. A clamped jaw. And Travis knew Rachel Isaacs resented being told she was wrong as much as he did. His chest tightened. What was it about this woman that brought out his argumentative side?

"Up until a month ago, there was a man around to see that things went right. And until I came along, you and Miss Ella were on your own. That's reason enough for someone who's been thinking about causing trouble to go ahead and do it."

"Well, then, what reason would you give for one of them to burn down the barn?" she demanded. "That doesn't make sense. What gain would they get from *that?*"

"I don't know. But—"

"No 'buts,' Mr. Campbell. If you think you can come in here with your education and your smooth voice and start throwing stones at innocent people, well, you're going to get a fight from me!" With that, she grabbed the five plates and marched toward the summer kitchen.

Your smooth voice. . .your smooth voice. The words echoed in his mind, his memory. Zachary. Zachary had been teasing Travis the night before it happened, saying that Travis could get any woman in El Paso with his smooth voice. "Any girl but Kate," Zach had bragged. Kate and Zach had been engaged, planning to get married a year ago in June.

Then the trip to the dark woods that fateful morning. . .*Oh, dear God, oh, Lord, how will You ever forgive me?*

"Mr. Campbell?" Ella called.

Travis jumped and stared at his shaking hands. Trying to calm himself, he wrapped his fingers around the warm tin cup and took a long swallow of Rachel's mellow coffee.

"Mr. Campbell, I be wondering if you could move my big washtub

51

for me. I's got to wash some clothes." Then Ella was standing beside him, her dark face beaded with perspiration.

"Sure. Where do you want it?"

And the day's activities for Travis began like every day within the last year. The same questions, the same guilt, the same haunting memories. Could God ever forgive him? Could he forgive himself? Would Kate ever forget?

❖

Later that afternoon, Rachel decided that if she were a man she would punch Travis Campbell right in the nose. The nerve of him suggesting that some of her hired hands might be responsible for her troubles!

From beside the hole the man had dug the night before, she listened as Samuel and Travis discussed last night's events.

Trying to break into the conversation was useless; the two men acted as if she weren't there. Somehow, that made Rachel feel as if Samuel were betraying her.

Rachel had been angry all day and was still determined to marry Samuel this week; and as soon as supper was over, she planned to tell him. Then, they could tell Travis to leave.

"All I can figure," Travis said, "is that Hubert Calhoun must have been working with someone else, because Rachel said he'd been trying to dig up something the night he got killed."

"Right," Samuel said.

"That makes me wonder how many of them there are."

"Yes. And did they kill Hubert?"

"Possibly, or I should say, probably." Travis unbuttoned the cuffs of his white work shirt and slowly rolled back the sleeves.

"But why burn the barn?" Samuel asked.

"And did the same people steal the cattle?" Rachel asked.

Samuel glanced at Rachel, his eyes glimmering with something new, something strange that puzzled her. Was it guilt? Why would Samuel feel guilty? Was there something he was hiding?

As if to confirm her conclusion, Samuel quickly switched his gaze to Travis. "Have you told Constable Parker about the hole?"

"Yeah. I rode into town after dinner and had a talk with him. He came out and looked things over. But he doesn't know any more than we do. I think Rachel's hired hands might—" Stopping in midsentence, Travis's gaze slowly moved to Rachel as if he knew he had stepped over an invisible boundary.

"Well, you're wrong, Mr. Campbell," she said firmly. "And I don't want you spreadin' untrue rumors about good, honest men." A new thought struck her. Her eyes widened. "You told Constable Parker, didn't you?"

"I did what I had to do."

"What you *had* to do?" Rachel shrieked.

"Now, Rachel—" Samuel started.

"I'll have you remember, Travis Campbell, that you're here to help and that's it. Nobody gave you permission to pass judgment on four innocent men!"

"I'm here to protect you because my father promised—"

"I know what your father promised!" she snapped.

This was the perfect opportunity to tell him she was going to marry Samuel soon and that he and his pa could forget that promise. She opened her mouth to do it, then stopped. A look at Samuel, a glare at Travis, a glance back at Samuel, and her mouth refused to utter the words.

"Listen, Rachel, I think Travis, here, might have a good point," Samuel said, tilting his wide-brimmed, straw hat off his forehead.

Rachel's mouth dropped in speechless fury. She never dreamed Samuel would take Travis's side over hers. The traitor! "And just who do you suggest might be involved? David, whose wife just. . .just recovered from childbirth?" Rachel's already hot cheeks flamed, but she kept right on talking.

"Or Gunther, who doesn't even have the mental capacity to read? Or Tyrone, who's so kind he nursed a half-dead fawn back to health?" Rachel placed perspiring palms on her slim hips. "Or, I know," she said sarcastically, "maybe it's Mac, the newest deacon at Dogwood Community Church!"

"Now, Rachel," Samuel said, stepping toward her.

"Don't you 'Now, Rachel' me!" With a glare that took in both of them, she stomped toward the summer kitchen. Flinging open the door, Rachel stormed into Ella's domain, slammed the door, and leaned against it.

Ella, glancing up from a pot of fragrant, bubbling beans, stared at Rachel in feigned surprise. "What's the matter, Child?"

As usual, Ella was playing dumb. Rachel knew she had heard every word through the glassless windows. This time, Rachel played along because she needed to stop leaning on Ella so much and start solving her own problems. "I. . .I just came in to help with supper," she said.

The men's voices outside mingled with a nearby bobwhite. "I think it's because she's still so upset over her pa's death," Samuel said.

"I can understand that," Travis mumbled.

"Yeah, that and the fact that she was practically raised with those men around. Why, come payday, they used to bring her licorice from the general store when she wasn't but that tall."

"She said they'd been here almost ten years."

"Yeah. All but Tyrone Burks. He's the youngest. Started, I'd say, 'bout five years ago."

Chapter 8

Zachary. His shadowed eyes full of shocked accusation. His blood-stained lips uttering, uttering, but no words forming.

Travis. Running through the woods, tripping over logs, clawing at vines that snaked after him like a menacing monster's evil arms.

Dear God, let me get to Dr. Henry before Zach dies.

Then, Zach's corpse lying among the vines in front of Travis.

Ashen cheeks, blue lips, dark red blood oozing from his stomach and chest. And the ever-open brown eyes, always accusing, always questioning.

"No, no, no! Zach!" Travis screamed, reaching for his best friend.

Then he sat straight up, his arms flailing in the morning's twilight. Sweat, cold and clammy, beaded his face and heaving chest as he peered around the barn, gulping in the cool, hay-scented air.

Only a dream. The same dream.

"Mr. Campbell?" Rachel hesitantly knocked on the barn's door. "Are you all right?"

Travis, his throat dry, tried to force his voice into a normal tone. "Fine. I. . .I guess I was just having a–a dream," he answered as Zach's funeral flashed before his eyes. How ironic that he, the very person responsible for Zach's death, had been one of the pall bearers. And Kate, that delicate, dark-haired beauty, had sobbed until she collapsed.

"Okay." Rachel hesitated. "Breakfast is almost ready."

"Thanks." He had overslept. Usually he was up an hour before now, making sure that Ella had enough firewood, helping Rachel by gathering the eggs, and milking Sue Girl so she wouldn't have to.

"Hard to believe I've been here three weeks," he mumbled. Standing, Travis stretched his sleepy muscles, then reached for his boots. *Hard to believe Zach's been dead fifteen months.* Or had Travis killed him only yesterday?

❖

Rachel walked toward the outdoor dining table, her mind occupied with what she had just heard. Who was Zach? This was the sixth time in the past few weeks that Rachel had interrupted one of Travis's nightmares.

She thoughtfully put the tin plates in their places and followed with the coffee cups, forks, spoons, and stained white napkins.

What past secret haunted Travis? Rachel could see it in his green eyes, like a shadowed apparition that refused to die. The times she had heard him call out in that horror-stricken victim's voice, Rachel wanted to wrap her arms around him, soothe him, tell him that all would be well. Baffled by her emotions, she watched Travis walk toward the cool stream for his usual morning "splash in the face" and drink of cool water.

Knifelike guilt stabbed her chest. Travis had been so helpful over the past few weeks, and Rachel still made him sleep in the barn while she enjoyed a comfortable bed. But what would the townspeople think if they learned he was sleeping in her house?

Travis kneeled beside the murmuring brook, then splashed water against his cheeks. And Rachel, ever the curious, wondered what Miss Kate Lowell was like, wondered if she realized how fine a man was her betrothed.

Admiration. That's as strong a word as Rachel would accept. But on that twilight morn, she admitted to herself that Travis Campbell was not an ordinary man. Why had she never felt such strong emotions for Samuel?

A hard bite on her full bottom lip, and she forced all thoughts of Travis from her mind. He would be gone soon. He was engaged to someone who was probably far more beautiful, more educated, and more sophisticated than Rachel could ever be.

Someone with distinguished speech who didn't waste time staring at the sunset.

"Mornin', Miss Rachel."

Jumping, Rachel turned to see Tyrone Burks walking toward the table, straw hat in hand.

"You scared me, Mr. Burks. I had my mind on something else."

"Sorry, Ma'am." Tyrone smiled and some of the chill left his blue eyes.

Ever since her trouble began, Rachel had wanted a word alone with her hired hands. She felt like they could see Travis's suspicion, and she needed to ease their minds.

"I've been meanin' to tell you that I want you and all my hired hands to know that I trust you completely."

"You don't know how much that means to me, Ma'am. To tell you the truth, I was beginning to wonder if I should quit and find another job."

She placed a flattened hand against the high neck of her green work dress. "No, please don't do that. I'd feel just awful if you quit because of my troubles."

David Cosgrove rode up on his white stallion. "Mornin', Miss Rachel," he called.

Was David thinking of quitting, too? Rachel rushed toward the intelligent man. "Mr. Cosgrove, Mr. Burks and I were just discussing what's been going on around the ranch. And I wanted you to know, like I told him, that I don't in the least suspect you. . .any of you."

"Didn't figure you did." David dismounted with the sound of a squeaking saddle and the smell of horse flesh and leather. "Way I see it, I've done an honest job all these years. Why would I up and start causin' trouble? And I figured you seen the same thing." David's gray eyes reflected a man who didn't stop thinking until he solved a problem.

"I did. . .do see it. It looks like the trouble's stopped, though. And you don't know how glad I am."

The last few weeks had been peaceful. Peaceful around the ranch. Peaceful between Travis and Rachel. Without saying a word, the two had called a truce, agreed to disagree, and stayed away from the subject of Rachel's hired hands. Travis had never stopped being polite to Rachel's employees at mealtime. For that, she was grateful.

Her pride had even quit smarting from his tying her up. She attributed that to his charming smile, a smile she secretly hoped he saved only for her.

The rapid sound of horses' hooves biting into the dusty road floated over the gentle breeze. Rachel knew her other hired hands were on their way and she should go make the coffee. But the man who rode the black mare into her yard was not a hired hand.

"Miss Rachel!" Caleb Singletary called, an alarmed expression filling his gray eyes.

Rachel's fists balled. "What happened?" she croaked before Caleb uttered another word.

As he reined in his mare, Caleb respectfully removed his straw hat. He was the kind of man who looked like a large little boy with his round cheeks and eyes, a cherub mouth, and white-blond hair. Shortly after he moved to Dogwood two months ago, everyone had been surprised that he was thirty-five and had ten children.

"It's Bess and Ethan Tucker," Caleb said. "Someone stole their steers and two horses during the night. And Preacher Jones asked me to ride through and tell everyone. He thinks this will be a good chance for the congregation to reach out to Bess and Ethan, seein' as they don't attend services regularly."

Ethan and Bess lived in their parents' old homestead on the town's outskirts. Because of their general store, they didn't have much time to farm. The only livestock they owned were some steers they raised and sold and their horses. Had the same person stolen Rachel's cattle? "What does Preacher Jones suggest we do?"

"Well, I figure the same we did for you. Take up an offering, stop by with a pie or something, and tell 'em we're real sorry."

David and Tyrone were watching, listening. Rachel felt it. "Are you collecting the money?"

"Yes'm."

"Okay. Just a minute." She walked toward her house.

"Oh, and Miss Rachel?"

She turned back to Caleb. "Yes?"

"Thanks a bunch for telling Trudy 'bout that servant's job opened at Mr. Bishop's mansion. They hired her yesterday, and it's sure gonna help the missus and me with the cost of raisin' the young 'uns."

"You're welcome. Glad she got the job." Rachel knew money was scarce with most folks, except Joshua Bishop, of course. And she hoped Caleb's oldest teenaged daughter could work many years for the Bishops.

Rachel went to get her money from under the loose rock in the fireplace. When she had lost her cattle, somehow the community had produced a sizable amount. Then, they had also pledged to replace her hay and corn at last week's church service, just as Ella and Samuel had said they would. Her pa always said, "Make sure to help those in need, 'cause tomorrow you might be in need." Lately, that was true for Rachel. Her turn to help had now arrived.

❖

As Caleb Singletary rode away, Travis trudged from the spring toward the summer kitchen and watched. Probably local gossip, he surmised. He was so tired he didn't even want to hear it.

However, this tired was a satisfied, mellow tired, the kind that left you feeling like a man with some worth. Travis had been working six days a week to get the new barn dried in. He was close to accomplishing his goal. Rachel's employees had helped some, but they were so busy planting the fall potatoes they hadn't been able to do much. Travis learned last week that most of Dogwood counted on Rachel's fall potatoes. Ethan Tucker at the general store bought them in October, then resold them to the townspeople. A nice arrangement for everyone.

Last week, Joshua Bishop sent a man to assist on the barn, and Rachel had been flabbergasted. "I never dreamed he'd do something like that," she had said one night over supper. "Joshua Bishop has never been known for his generosity." But even with Joshua's helper, all the work had left Travis bone tired.

Glancing toward the new barn's yellow timbers, Travis made a decision. The smell of crisp pines and damp earth were beckoning him to wander, and that's exactly what he was going to do.

Travis paused at the kitchen's log door. Yesterday, he had received a letter from his mother, but there was no news from Kate, no answer to the two letters he had already sent her. His mother had mentioned Kate was looking pale. Naturally, Travis hoped she was not ill. He wanted to take care of Kate and knew that was his duty. Some days, especially the ones when he forgot to think of her, brought guilt because he was actually enjoying himself for the first time since Zach's death.

"It'll do ya good to get away, Son," Travis's father had said.

Travis had doubted him, but time proved his father right. Nothing, though, could ever make him forgive himself for killing Zach. Travis, full of self-condemnation, knew God must likewise remain unforgiving and that was the source of his nightmares. God must be repaying him for the murder.

He opened the kitchen door. Along with news of Kate, his mother's letter also contained a message for Ella.

"Mornin', Mr. Travis. Ain't it gonna be another hot day!" Ella stood over a pan of sizzling bacon. "I thought that rain yesterday and the breeze would cool things down. But don't look like it."

From the time of Travis's waking until now, the sun had stretched its blazing arms over the horizon and promised yet another scorching day.

"Yes, it is. Too hot to work, that's for sure. I'm thinking about taking the day off and doing a little exploring. Would you mind packing a picnic for me?"

"Don't mind in the least."

He floundered for a way to broach the next subject. What went on between Lionel and Ella twenty years ago was none of his business. But leave it up to his mother to make it his business.

Attempting to sound casual, he cleared his throat. "Do you remember a Mr. Lionel, Miss Ella?" If she said no, then Travis would say no more.

Ella's hands stilled, her spine straightened, and her eyes took on a faraway, longing gleam matched only by Kate's eyes after Zach's funeral. "Sure, I do. Why you ask that?" she chanted in near reverent cadence.

"Well, when I went into town for the flour yesterday, Bess Tucker gave me a letter from my mother that had just arrived. I didn't get a chance to read it until last night. And Mother inquired about you, whether or not you ever married, and asked me to see if you remembered Lionel."

Travis's chest tightened with the tension flowing from Ella. He didn't want anyone asking him personal questions about Zach and therefore didn't like prying into others' pasts.

"Is. . .is Lionel still livin'?" she asked in a husky whisper while absently toying with the top button of her brown work dress.

"Oh, yes, Ma'am," Travis assured her. "I've never known Mr. Lionel to be sick a day in his life."

"Did he ever get hitched?"

"No."

Her stiff posture relaxed.

Since childhood, Travis had always assumed that Lionel simply was not the marrying sort. Now, he wondered what really prompted Lionel's lonely existence.

"Your pa was s'posed to give him his own house and plot o' land. Did he?"

"Yes. And Lionel has always been grateful."

"Your pa's a fair man."

Lionel had been in Travis's family ever since he could remember, the only slave his father had ever owned. Travis was not sure why he ever bought Lionel in the first place. All he knew was that Lionel had never been treated like a slave but more like a family member, the same as Ella.

Travis placed his right hand against the rock fireplace.

"Mother asked me to pass along a message for Mr. Lionel. He wishes to give you his regards, if you will accept them."

Ella swallowed hard. She opened her mouth to speak, shut it, then opened it again. "Yes. I accept them."

"Mother also wanted to know if you would like to return his regards with yours."

With little jerking movements, Ella turned over a thick piece of fragrant bacon. "Yes," she squeaked out.

Travis smiled slowly, indulgently. Maybe his mother's assumptions were correct.

The kitchen door opened, and Rachel walked in carrying a pail of water. "I guess it's time I started the coffee. They're all here and as hungry as four bears." She walked to the rugged table in the room's center and set the water on it.

Travis, swallowing hard, tried not to stare at her, but all he could think about was that angel image when the morning sun had ignited her hair with a halolike fire. What would it be like to wake up every morning to those shining auburn locks on his pillow? A constricting, jealous hand tightened around his heart. Samuel James was one lucky man.

He purposefully looked out the window. There was no sense in thinking of the unattainable. He had promised Kate, and a man of honor never violated his promise.

"Caleb Singletary just stopped by with news that Ethan and Bess Tucker's horses and steers were stolen last night."

"That be just awful. Whatever will be happenin' next?" Ella asked.

"Did he say what Constable Parker thinks?" Travis, not wanting to look into Rachel's eyes, glanced back out the window.

"No." Then Rachel repeated all that Caleb had told her.

"Maybe I'll ride in this afternoon and talk with Parker and see if he thinks this is the same person who stole your cattle. I'm going to take the day off, anyway," he said to the nearby weeping willow. "The barn is coming along faster than I thought, and I need the rest. I'm probably just going to laze around until eleven or so, then take a picnic over to that far west hill and relax some more."

"Oh, well, okay," Rachel said, a disappointed droop to her voice. Was it because he wouldn't be working on the barn or because he would be gone?

"Would you and Miss Ella like to go?" Travis heard himself ask, then wondered if he had lost his mind. Hadn't the purpose of this expedition been to get *away* from his problems, not take them with him? Miss Rachel Isaacs was definitely becoming a problem.

"We would love to go," Rachel said with a bright smile.

Chapter 9

"Would you like some pear pie?" Rachel asked, removing the beige cloth from a batch of Ella's half-moon-shaped, baked pies.

"You and Miss Ella are going to make me fat." Travis leaned forward, took the pie from Rachel, then settled back against an oak.

"With all the work you've been doing, we have to keep up your strength," she said, glancing toward Ella, who waded in the nearby spring's cool water. A canopy of oaks, hickories, and pines shaded the stream as well as the meadow where Travis and she sat. Rachel had yet to express her appreciation for Travis's work and she felt now was as good a time as any. "I. . .I wanted you to know how much I appreciate all your help with the barn. . .and everything else, too," she said, never taking her gaze from Ella.

Rachel's fingers tightened around her glass of lemonade. Would he ever suspect how desperately she had wanted to come on this picnic with him? Or how much she had grown to depend on him? What would life be like when he left? "I don't know how I would have made it through the last few weeks without you." A shy look his way.

His mouth turned into the lazy, teasing half-smile he hadn't used since she told him he had to sleep in the barn. "Well, I'm glad to be able to help, Miss Rachel. After all, my father—"

"Promised your father," Rachel finished and, with a mischievous grin, rubbed the bridge of her nose.

Travis glanced at his pie, then back to Rachel. "Miss Rachel, would you mind if I asked you a personal question?" The smile increased, revealing a row of white, even teeth.

"I don't mind in the least," she said and knew she meant it.

"Well, I've just, um, noticed that you rub your nose a lot. And sometimes I wonder if those freckles are going to fall right off! So I was wondering—"

"Why?" Rachel finished through a heartfelt laugh. She couldn't remember laughing so spontaneously since before her pa died. "Well, it's because when I was a little girl I hated my freckles. I always wanted to be like Abby. Tall and willowy, and no freckles!" A soft giggle. "I knew I couldn't be as tall as Abby, but I thought that maybe if I started rubbin' my nose, then my freckles would come off."

"And you've been rubbing it ever since?" he asked, his eyes full of indulgent amusement.

She nodded. "It turned into a habit after a couple of years, and I can't seem to stop!" Another giggle. "Are you through with your personal questions now, Mr. Campbell?"

Tilting his head to one side, he chuckled, and the tired lines from his nose to mouth relaxed. "Yes."

"Okay, then. Now I've got a personal question for you." Rachel threw her long braid over her shoulder and blotted the sweat from her upper lip with a white linen handkerchief.

"I guess I have to answer since I started this."

"Yes, you do," she said primly. Then, taking a quick cautious breath, she hesitated over the question she had been pondering the last week. "I've noticed that you sometimes have nightmares."

He never moved, but Rachel felt Travis erecting an invisible wall between them.

"I was just wondering. . . ," and she began the floundering, "if there's anything I could ever do." An embarrassed cough. "If you ever need to talk. . ."

Stonily, he stared at the picnic basket.

Rachel wished she had never opened the subject. What had possessed her? As the silent seconds stretched into heartache, Rachel grappled for anything to say. Travis was truly disturbed about something. She should have never interfered.

"I was responsible for the death of my best friend, Zachary Huntington, a little over a year ago." The words sounded as if he had plucked them from the tender flesh of an infected wound. "I'm just having trouble dealing with it, I guess. I've asked God to forgive me, but. . ."

"Oh." Had he murdered his friend or had it been an accident? Rachel peered deeply into his tormented eyes and knew the answer. Travis Campbell, a man she had seen earnestly praying in church, could never plan the death of another. And the whole wretched story only added to Rachel's growing fascination for him.

"Zach and Kate were engaged at the time."

"Oh?"

"I don't know if I'll ever be able to make it up to her. But I'm going to try." His face took on the set expression of a man who meant what he said.

"Oh," Rachel said again, feeling like a brainless parrot.

"What's Miss Kate Lowell like?" she asked, trying to quickly change the painful subject while her mind spun with what Travis had told her. If Kate Lowell had been engaged to Zach, did that mean Travis asked her to marry him out of duty? Did he love her?

Travis gazed toward the trees surrounding their haven, and the invisible wall he had erected between them seemed to crumble as he answered her question about Kate. "Well, she's about your height I guess," he started, his eyes half-closed. "Twenty-one, long black hair, and the most beautiful eyes you've ever seen. Some days they're green, others, they're blue. Milky skin and lips the color of peaches."

His cultured voice grew poetic, and Rachel thought of some of the Shakespearean plays she cherished.

"And, to tell you the truth," Travis continued, exposing Rachel to a measured glance, "there were a lot of men in El Paso who would have given their right arm for her hand in marriage. But she said 'yes' to me."

"Oh," Rachel said again, disappointment spreading its bony fingers through her midsection. *And I know why she said 'yes' to you.* "I. . .I guess it's mighty hard, your being here and her in El Paso." For some reason, Rachel had desperately hoped Kate was not every man's dream of beauty.

A faraway look, a slight nod from Travis, and Rachel learned more than she wanted to know. Even though she had been initially engaged to Zachary, Travis Campbell was deeply in love with Kate. From the sound of her, what man wouldn't be?

But Rachel had Samuel, and Travis's devotion to his fiancée was none of her concern. "As. . .as much as I've appreciated your help, Mr. Campbell, you're more than welcome to go on back home after Samuel and I marry in October. His brother and sister-in-law will be runnin' his ranch, and he'll be with me. I'd hate to think that I was the reason for your not being with your—"

"Do you *want* me to go back in October?"

As much as Rachel tried to look away, she couldn't. "I. . .I, well. . .I didn't mean to imply that at all. It's just that I. . .I. . ." Licking her lips, she twisted the linen handkerchief, "I just assumed that you would want to be with Miss Lowell."

"I promised I would stay until the spring." The same lazy smile. "And unless you chase me off with that Winchester rifle of yours, I'll be here until spring."

Some of the disappointment eased. "Well, if that's really the way you feel, I won't say anything else about it."

"That's the way I feel." He took his first bite of Ella's pie, and the subject was closed. "Before too much longer, we need to head back home. I want to have time to ride into town and talk with Constable Parker about the Tuckers' theft."

"I guess we won't ever see my cattle again?"

"Doesn't look like it." In three big bites, Travis finished the pie, then rose to his feet.

Rachel, gathering her green skirts, tried to stand with him, but her left leg had numbed, and it buckled under the pressure.

Travis's reaching out to steady her only caused Rachel to lose her balance all the more. She toppled forward, grabbing at anything with which to regain her equilibrium. That "anything" turned out to be his upper arms.

"Hold on," he said with a slight chuckle as his large hands softly gripped her shoulders. "I've got you."

Rachel's eyes were on the exact level as the top button of his white shirt. "Sorry 'bout that." Her heart raced in a disconcerting way. "My left leg went to sleep."

"Think you can stand on your own now?"

"I. . .I think so." Rachel wiggled her foot as hot tingles spiraled up her leg, the same hot tingles that were spreading from the heat of Travis's hands on her shoulders. She had never reacted to Samuel like this.

Pull away, a prim voice urged. Trying to pull away, however, was like trying to break the force of a gigantic magnet.

One hand tightening against her shoulder, Travis tilted her chin with his free hand. She had no choice but to encounter his gaze. Then that lazy half-smile again, and he traced the length of her nose with his index finger. "I hope you never rub these freckles off, Rachel," he teased, a green fire glowing in his eyes.

As new tingles spread across Rachel's cheeks, her reason finally overcame her emotions. She jerked from his grasp to take three stumbling steps backward. Confusion, conflict, and consternation rolled through her like the boiling clouds of a conquering hurricane. Her chest heaved with every breath as she stared at Travis in wide-eyed accusation.

He was in love with Kate Lowell and flirting with her. Well, Rachel Isaacs had never and would never participate in such two-faced behavior.

"Travis, I'll have you remember that. . .that I'm an engaged woman. And you're an engaged man. And even if you don't respect Miss Kate Lowell enough to behave so, I respect my intended."

"I thought it was 'Mr. Campbell,' " he said, his eyes half-closed in a speculative gleam.

"It is 'Mr. Campbell'! And you'll do well to remember that I'm 'Miss Isaacs'!"

Travis glanced at their patchwork quilt, then bent to pick up his wide-rimmed straw hat. "You're right," he said tightly. "I'm. . .I'm terribly sorry. I. . .I should not have behaved so. I guess it's just that. . ." He crammed the hat on his head. "I'm sorry." And with that, he turned for the buggy.

But he stopped in midstride and stared toward the horizon. Rachel followed his gaze to see smoke. Long, floating, menacing tendrils of smoke marred the eastern sky.

"Rachel!" Ella screamed. "There be smoke that look like it be acomin' from the house!"

❖

"Oh, Lord, help us," Rachel prayed as the work wagon rounded the last corner and she faced what she had feared.

The new barn was engulfed in hot flames that stretched their pointed tongues upward like laughing demons, licking the sky. All four of Rachel's employees were fighting the fire as if it were their own barn.

Rachel jumped from the buggy as Travis reined the horses to a standstill.

"Get more water!" Gunther Peterson yelled.

"What are we women folk agonna do?" Ella wailed.

"I'll get blankets!" Pulse pounding in her ears, Rachel raced for the house. Maybe if they worked hard enough, they could salvage part of the timbers.

Within minutes, Rachel beat at the flames in crazed desperation. The corn, the hay, where would they put it without this barn? Raise the blanket, beat at the smoldering grass. Who could be doing this to her? Why was God letting it happen? A deep breath of the acrid air, a dry cough, and try to beat out another flame.

The men's yells and calls were a fuzz of unintelligible words. Maybe if she got close enough to the barn, her blanket would smother the flames. Another breath of smoke. Another cough.

"Rachel, move!" But Travis's strained words meant nothing to her. She would not move until the flames were out!

"Rachel! Dear God, help her!" Then a hard body knocked her several feet from the barn as a falling, flaming timber crashed to the ground right where she had been standing.

The ground slammed into Rachel's back. "Mmmph." Then the taste of dirt, the feel of dried grass against her cheek as she rolled down the sloping yard with Travis close behind. In seconds, the world stopped spinning and Rachel tried to sit up. She had to fight the fire, no matter what. But Travis clamped his arm around her waist.

"Let me up!" she demanded.

"No! It's gone. We can't save it," Travis yelled.

"We've got to!" Arms flailing in reckless abandon, Rachel struggled upward and wrestled against his hold.

"You're going to get yourself hurt," he growled, shoving her back.

"Listen you. . .you overgrown bully! This is *my* barn and *my* land, and—"

"And your timber that almost killed you!" Travis rose to his knees and, with his hands, pinned her shoulders against the ground. "Rachel Isaacs, you've got to be the most obstinate woman alive!" His face, smudged with soot, was only inches from hers.

Then, his gaze roamed to her half-parted lips and for one second, time ceased to exist. The barn's flames, the hired hands' yelling, Ella's hauling water, they all dissolved in comparison to the intensity in Travis's eyes.

What would his firm lips feel like pressed against hers? Rachel's breath caught. Her heart raced in wild abandon. As his confused gaze met hers again, her common sense reappeared.

Wanton! That's what her friend Abby called women who had such thoughts. Rachel refused to tolerate Travis's playing with her emotions, his causing her to react like some saloon girl.

With a twist of her shoulders, she loosened his slack grip. With a roll to the left, Rachel was free to stand. Scrambling to her knees, she held his gaze. "If you ever touch me again, Travis Campbell, I promise right here before God that I *will* come after you with my Winchester!"

Chapter 10

So what do you think, Constable?" Travis asked as the fire still smoldered. Parker had questioned all of Rachel's hired hands, then sent them back to the potato field. Now he and Parker stood by the barn, trying to make sense of all that had happened.

"Tyrone didn't say he got a good look at the man he saw runnin' into the woods," Parker muttered to no one.

"Do you think he really saw anyone?" Much to Rachel's fury, Travis's suspicions had never waned, and he still thought that one of her employees was involved. Something told him that Tyrone or David were the most likely villains.

"Sounds suspicious to me." Parker removed his straw hat, rubbed his balding head, and scanned the nearby line of trees. "So Tyrone says he left the potato field to come back to the barn for another shovel. But how do we know he didn't leave to start the fire?"

"The only problem is that David, Tyrone, and Mac all say that Gunther left the shovel by accident. So how could it have been planned?"

"Yeah. Unless Gunther and Tyrone are in cahoots together. Gunther could have left the shovel on purpose so Tyrone could come back and get it, then start the fire."

"Well, that would be a possibility if Gunther weren't as dumb as an ox. I imagine that man has trouble getting his boots on straight. How could he have the brains to plan to burn Miss Rachel's barn?" Travis normally didn't speak so strongly of others less fortunate than he, but frustration was taking over his tongue. "Please forgive my comment about Gunther. He can't help it."

"No, he can't." Parker's lips twitched as he rubbed his graying whiskers. "But you're right."

"Do you think the same person responsible for Miss Rachel's problems is also the Tucker thief?" Travis asked.

"Don't know. But I hope we find 'em soon, whoever they are."

The sound of a galloping horse, echoing from the tree-lined dirt road, preceded Samuel's riding up on his palomino stallion, frothy with perspiration. "I was on my way home from town and saw the smoke. Where's Rachel? Is she okay?" The dark protective gleam in Samuel's eyes both comforted and challenged Travis. Didn't Samuel know that Travis would take care of Rachel at all costs?

"She's in the house," Travis clipped. "And she's as mad as a momma bear with a stolen cub."

"Well I would be, too!"

Travis placed his hands on his jean-clad hips and blotted out the image of his almost kissing her. "Yeah. But it's more than just the barn burning. Constable Parker here questioned her hired hands."

And I acted like anything but a gentleman. Travis had been raised to treat a lady with respect. In one afternoon, he had forgotten all his upbringing. That, however, was the way Rachel affected him. From the night of his arrival, she had caused him to react from instinct alone. If he had any sense, he would saddle his horse and head back to El Paso.

"I'll go in and see if I can calm her down," Samuel said, leading his panting stallion to the water trough near the barn. "But first, was this fire set, too?"

Parker nodded as Samuel reapproached. "Yeah, we think so. Tyrone says he saw somebody run into the woods after the fire was on its way up."

"I'm going to have a long talk with Miss Rachel Isaacs." Samuel crammed his hands into the pockets of his britches. "And if I have my way, we'll be married by the end of the week. Maybe with a man around, this craziness'll stop."

The hair on the back of Travis's neck prickled. "Exactly what are you insinuating?" he asked softly.

Samuel's eyes narrowed for a split second. "I wasn't insinuatin' anything. But apparently *you* aren't doing a very good job of protecting the property. Where were you, anyway?"

Travis had never in his life wanted to hit someone as much as he wanted to hit Samuel James. Perhaps the weeks of watching Rachel and knowing she would soon be Samuel's bride added to his frustration. "Rachel and Miss Ella and I had gone on a picnic," he said through clamped teeth. Even to his own ears the explanation sounded irresponsible.

"Exactly how often has this been goin' on?" Samuel asked, his eyes glowing with a protective, brotherly fire.

"It's the first and probably the last time. And it might be for the best that we were gone. How do you know the man wouldn't have tried to hurt Rachel if she had been here?"

Samuel took a step closer, then stopped, his jaw muscles working beneath his whisker-roughened face. "How do I know she was safe with you?"

Of its own volition, Travis's right hand curled into a fist. He knew Samuel had sensed what only one man can know about another. Then he felt Rachel in his arms, saw Rachel fighting the fire, fantasized about the kiss that never happened. But Travis would go down in flames himself before he admitted his real feelings. "Listen, you—"

"Hmm. . .hmm. . .hmm." Parker made a big job of clearing his throat. "I guess we've discussed this about all we need to. And there ain't no sense in two churchgoin' men as friendly as y'all to come to blows. Now, is there?"

Parker was right. Travis and Samuel had become friends in the last few weeks. Maybe because they were a lot alike, but different, too. And maybe the parts of them that were similar weren't enjoying each other at the moment.

"Sorry," Samuel muttered, looking over Travis's shoulder.

"Same here," Travis mumbled, yet wondered if either meant it.

"Now, Samuel, why don't you go on in the house and talk with Miss Rachel," Parker said, "I've done just about all I can do here at the house. Now I'm agonna go look around the woods." He glanced toward the smoldering barn. "Mighty sorry 'bout all that lost work."

As Samuel walked toward the house, Travis turned to stare at the burning embers. So much for his earlier feelings of accomplishment.

❖

When Samuel stepped in the front doorway, Ella went out the back. Rachel was mighty upset; Ella figured Rachel and Samuel needed some time alone.

She walked toward a nearby pine, leaned against it, then absentmindedly fingered the rough bark. Twenty years ago, she and Lionel had stood on this very spot, and Ella had promised him that when Mrs. Campbell gave birth and recovered, she would travel to El Paso to be his wife.

Oh, how the years had flown. Twenty of them. Just like yesterday, she could feel Lionel's light kiss, see his dark eyes full of love and a fore-shadowing of what would come.

"For some reason, I feel like I'm alosin' you," he had said, touching her cheek.

"Oh, don't you go on, Lionel. I'll be in El Paso afore you knows it."

Then he had smiled that special smile he used only with her. "Promise me, Ella."

Ella had stared toward the North Star making its first appearance in the evening twilight. "On that there star, I promise that I'll come, no matter what."

And twenty years later, she still had not gone.

Yet, how was Ella to know that Rachel's mother would be trampled by a bull and leave behind a defenseless newborn?

Little Rachel, her tiny fingers curling around Ella's finger, her soft, chubby cheeks dimpling when Ella picked her up. It was like having Daisy once more. Ella had fallen in love as only a mother can, and the thought of leaving little Rachel was like losing Daisy all over again.

Oh, Lawd, did I go and do the right thing? Even after all these years, a tiny part of Ella's heart still wondered. At first, she had thought that maybe Mr. Isaacs would remarry, then going to Lionel would have been easier. Of course, leaving Rachel at all would have been heartbreaking, but Ella could have left her if Mr. Isaacs had remarried. Then, Rachel would have a new momma.

But he didn't, and Ella had felt she owed it to him to stay and help raise Rachel. If he hadn't bought her from that slave block, Ella was sure she would be dead today. The man that Mr. Isaacs had bid against had the looks of the devil.

So she had written Lionel the first letter, telling him that she would be delayed. He had written back, pleading that she come, pledging his love, and promising his heart. Eventually, Ella realized she was the only mother Rachel would ever know, and she had written again, this time, tearfully releasing Lionel from their engagement.

"Oh, my gentle lion," she whispered as if Lionel were with her, "would you ever forgive me for a breakin' yo' heart?"

Hands trembling, Ella wiped her damp eyes and watched as Mr. Travis and Constable Parker scanned the woods and pasture. Had Mr. Travis delivered Lionel's regards only this morning? A lifetime of hoping, praying, and wishing seemed to have passed since then. The very idea that Lionel had not married, the very thought that he had sent his regards made Ella's palms clammy.

Please, Lawd, let him write me.

How many times had Lionel cradled Ella against his shoulder while she sobbed about her lost Daisy, sold to another master? She had been ripped from Ella when she was a tender ten years old. Just as Ella had thought she was healing from being torn from her own momma, their master had sold Daisy, as if she were nothing more than a dog. To this day, she had not stopped hoping that she would find her daughter.

Would Lionel remember this? Would he remember this and much more?

❖

Rachel, nervously chewing her lip, faced Samuel in the center of her parlor.

"All that's been going on around here has *got* to stop," Samuel demanded. "And I don't think it will until you and I marry, and there's a man around to protect you."

"You know we both have crops to finish," Rachel said firmly. Their wedding date, October 28, was only eight weeks away. After that she would spend the rest of her life with Samuel. An uncomfortable tendril of doubt curled its way through her heart. Is that what she *really* wanted?

"The crops can be taken care of. Your hired hands can manage yours or, if you want, Joshua Bishop mentioned buying your place last Sunday in church."

"I don't want to sell my land. Besides, Travis is here. He's a man. He's protection." *But who will protect me from him?* Rachel tried to blot out the embarrassing moment when she had longed for his kiss.

"I wonder," Samuel said, irony stirring his dark eyes.

"What's *that* supposed to mean?"

"It means I don't trust him!"

Rachel's mouth fell open. "I'm not really sure what you think you're implying, Mr. James, but I can assure you, I am a lady, and I would never—"

"I didn't say anything about you, did I?" Samuel's voice rose in agitation, and Rachel never remembered seeing him so frustrated.

"Well, if you really trusted me, then you wouldn't have to worry about Mr. Campbell! Besides, I detest him, and I'll be glad when he leaves!" Was that really true? Maybe the humiliation from wanting his lips on hers had forced those words, for her heart told her otherwise.

"Well, if you detest him, then why don't you tell him to leave, and we'll get married?"

Rachel stared into Samuel's dark eyes, wondering at the contradictory, confused light flickering there, a light that hinted that his thoughts didn't match his words. He had been withdrawn the last few weeks. Or had Rachel only imagined something that she had created herself?

"Are you going to answer me?" Samuel demanded.

"Excuse me," Travis said from the dining room doorway, the sound of cold, jagged rocks in his voice.

With a gasp, Rachel turned to face him. "How long have you been standin' there?" Rachel's heart pounded out steady, hard beats. Had he heard her say she detested him?

"Long enough," Travis said through clamped teeth. "And it's always been my experience that the most untrusting are usually the most untrustworthy."

"And what do you mean by that?" Samuel asked.

"You figure it out."

Rachel grasped the back of the upholstered chair sitting nearby. Travis had heard her.

"Listen, you—" Samuel stepped forward.

"I didn't mean to get involved in your *important* conversation," Travis said. "I came in to tell you that there's something outside you might want to see. Parker and I found a new hole that someone dug behind the barn. And this time, they got what they've been looking for."

Rachel rushed after him with Samuel close behind. Soon she was peering into a shallow hole near the weeping willow behind the barn, a hole with the imprint of a box. And the overturned dirt was dried as if the hole had been dug during the night.

"Looks like a small box of some kind had been here," Parker said.

"Probably a strongbox," Travis mused.

Samuel knelt beside the hole. "If it were large, I'd say maybe it contained gold or something. But as small as it is. . ."

All her life, Rachel had heard stories about gold buried in these parts. Sometimes it was Confederate gold, sometimes Union.

Other times, it was the dowry of a princess. No one ever believed the stories, but they did love to tell them.

Parker stroked his whiskers. "I wonder why they didn't re-cover the hole. Looks to me like they would want to hide that they finally found it."

"Reckon Tiny got after 'em?" Samuel asked.

"Probably," Travis said. "I faintly remember hearing him growling last night."

"And you didn't get up to see what was the matter?" Samuel asked.

Travis's eyes narrowed.

"I heard him, too," Rachel rushed, hoping Samuel and Travis wouldn't start arguing. She had already been through too much to listen to them go at it. "But the growling didn't last long, so I didn't think much of it."

"I 'magine it's because Tiny knew the person," Parker said.

"I still say you should've gotten up." Samuel's accusing expression dared Travis to deny his claim.

"Look, you two." Rachel stepped between them. "This childishness is goin' to stop or I'm goin' to throw you both off the premises."

Parker stifled a snicker as Travis and Samuel eyed each other like two restless stallions.

"If the person got what he was after, maybe this means my troubles are over," Rachel said, giving Samuel a meaningful glance. Perhaps now he would stop pushing about their marriage.

"Doesn't it bother you in the least that someone actually stole something from your property?" The hint of scorn in Travis's voice suggested his irritation did not stop with Samuel.

Rachel's spine straightened. "Of course, it bothers me, Mr. Campbell. Just as much as it bothers me that somebody burned the barn twice and stole my cattle and that someone was shot and killed, then disappeared. And that my pa just died!"

The worry, the pain, the tension of the last few months erupted within Rachel like a pulsating volcano. She wanted to cry but knew the time of crying had ceased. "And if the cost of peace is letting them have what they want, then I'm willing to let them have it!"

Wary silence cloaked them for an eternal second.

"I think you owe Rachel an apology," Samuel snapped.

"No," Travis said slowly, *"you're* the one who owes Rachel an apology." He strode toward the barn, saddled his ebony stallion, and rode away.

Chapter 11

"Where have you been?" Rachel asked later that night as she held up the lantern to illuminate Travis's face.

Without a glance her way, he dismounted his stallion.

For the last hour, Rachel had sat on the front porch, worrying about him, wondering if he were coming back. "Come on in, Child," Ella kept calling, but Rachel had refused.

Now that he had arrived, both irritation and relief tore at her. "Are you going to answer me?" she demanded, following him as he led the horse toward the water trough.

Still no words.

"Don't you know I was worried about you?"

"I didn't think women worried about men they detested," he clipped, then began removing the stallion's saddle.

Rachel winced. "I guess I deserved that," she whispered, wanting to apologize but unable to form the words.

Even a deep breath of the smoke-scented air did not help her courage. Maybe that was for the best. If Rachel started talking, she might tell the absolute truth, and that was something even she wasn't prepared to face.

"Well, I'm home. I'm fine. And you can go back in the house now and stop worrying," he said, a hint of dry humor wiping away his former clipped tones.

"Have you had supper?" Rachel ignored his implications.

"Yes."

"Where—" She stopped herself. His whereabouts was none of her business, but she still wanted to know how he had spent the evening.

"Miss Rachel, when I get married, I'll tell my wife where I am and when I'll be home. Right now I don't plan to start answering to you." He was toying with her, playing with her emotions again, and that lazy, half-smile said he was thoroughly enjoying it.

Rachel opened her mouth to retort, then snapped it shut. "I'm sorry if I was prying, Mr. Campbell. Please forgive me. It's just that Pa always taught me not to leave people worrying, and I've grown to expect the same respect from others. Good night." She turned and walked halfway to the house before he spoke.

"Miss Rachel?" This time his voice was soft, coaxing, unsure.

Rachel turned back around.

"I. . .I've been thinking about today. . .about the way I acted." He set down the saddle and took a step toward her, the moon's soft glow accentuating the hesitant tilt of his chin. "And I'd like to formally apologize and tell you it won't ever happen again. I'm not really sure what got into me. I guess being away from Kate has left me. . .I really don't know how to say it. I. . .I guess I. . ."

"It's okay, Mr. Campbell," Rachel said primly. "I'm sure Miss Kate Lowell is a deserving recipient of your steadfastness." Ella would be proud of her composure, but it penetrated only skin deep. Inside, she relived that pulse-stopping second when she had longed for Travis's lips against hers.

"I guess I also owe you an apology," she said to the few coals left glowing in the barn's ashes. "I. . .I never thanked you for saving me from that burning timber. I'm sure I could have been killed or at least burned badly."

Embarrassed silence settled about them like a dense fog, and Rachel sensed that he was also reliving that near kiss.

"I would have done it for anyone." Then as if he were as eager to change the subject as she, he rushed, "The turnaround picnic is coming up in a couple of weeks. And Miss Abby mentioned making a new dress. I don't think you've had time to shop for any material. Would you let me take you into town tomorrow? It would be like a peace offering."

"I hadn't planned on making a new dress for the picnic," Rachel said, rubbing her nose. Her sewing machine had always been in Pa's room. In the evenings after Ella went to bed, Rachel would often sew while Pa read, or they just visited.

He had bought her the machine for her twelfth birthday. Amongst an abundance of laughter and misshapen garments, together they had learned to use it. Now, the thought of sewing brought back a lifetime of haunting memories. Swallowing against the lump in her throat, she sniffed and tried to deny the tears.

"But Abby said everyone wears a new dress."

"Well, they do. It's just that. . .that Pa and I used to visit while. . .while I sewed. And I just can't. . ." Her voice cracked, and Rachel resisted the urge to scream out in fury, *Why, God? Why my father?* Then flashes of her father's lifeless form that summer morning. . .the funeral. . .the casket being lowered into the ground. . .and then the sound of earth hitting the lid.

Travis cleared his throat. "I'm terribly sorry I brought it up. I shouldn't have."

"You didn't know." Rachel, forcing her voice to normalcy, blotted out the image of her father's ashen corpse.

"Well, I noticed there's a seamstress in town. Would you consider—"

"I can't afford—"

"I would pay."

"No."

"Yes. It's the least I can do. Please. I have never in my life acted like I did today. It would make me feel more like the gentleman I truly am."

Rachel's cheeks warmed with a combination of pleasure and embarrassment. "What would Samuel say if he knew?"

"He doesn't have to know."

"I'll think about it." The way Samuel was acting lately, she hoped for both their sakes he would never know she even thought about it.

"Good. Shall we say we'll leave at eight, then?"

"I. . .yes." *How did he get me to agree?* But that thought was wiped out by another. "When did you talk with Abby?" Rachel never remembered seeing the two of them speak except at their introduction.

"I rode over to the Bishops'. Last Sunday Joshua extended a standing invitation for dinner, and I decided to take him up on it. It seems he's interested in buying your ranch."

"Yes. Samuel mentioned that, but I'm not interested in selling."

A pause. "I guess you're happy now. You finally found out where I spent the evening."

"That wasn't the reason I asked."

"I'm sure it wasn't." That same lazy smile.

And Rachel felt like a thirteen-year-old schoolgirl, swimming in a bottomless pool of chagrin. "Did you enjoy your meal?" she asked, wishing he would stop looking like a satisfied cat who had just outwitted a mouse.

"Yes, of course. From what I gather, the Bishops serve only the finest."

"That's true. Well, I guess I'll go on in now."

"Good night."

Rachel turned and left, wanting to put as much distance between them as possible.

❖

Grinning, Travis bent to retrieve the saddle, then stopped. *Kate.* Why did he feel as if she were a million miles away when he was with Rachel? *Oh, Lord, I've gotten myself into a mess, and this may be one that only You can get me out of.*

He took the saddle into the barn, then came back for the stallion. He had gone over to Joshua Bishop's for more than just a polite call. He had also wanted to visit with Miss Abby, to see if his growing suspicions were founded. Travis had seen all he needed to see. The very mention of Samuel's name brought a flush to Abby Bishop's cheeks and a glow to her eyes.

Travis felt sorry for her. The whole thing wasn't fair. If Rachel Isaacs were in love with Samuel, that would be one thing. But the way things stood. . . Well, it just wasn't fair.

What about you? a haunting voice questioned.

He led the stallion to the pasture gate, then removed his reins and bit. Was Travis any better than Samuel? He had convinced himself he was in love with Kate, but how much was brotherly concern and duty, and how much was love?

Grinding his teeth, Travis opened the barbed wire gate and led the ebony horse through. Whether or not he loved Kate didn't matter. He could never forgive himself for killing Zach. He owed her, and that debt was something that only a lifetime could repay.

Chapter 12

"Mornin', Mr. Campbell," Bess Tucker called from the store's rear. "Good morning," Travis replied.

Rachel, inhaling the smells of fresh coffee, horse feed, and leather, smiled tightly at the approaching Bess, who promptly ignored her. She wondered if Travis suspected that the plump, ruddy-cheeked redhead was throwing herself at him. Even in church, she had sat in a pew right in front of him every service.

Disgusting. If this were not the only place in town that sold fabric, Rachel would shop elsewhere.

"Can I help you find somethin'?" Bess, fluttering her eyelashes, smiled up at Travis as if he were a luscious lamb and she a ravenous wolf.

"Miss Rachel is looking for some fabric."

"Oh," Bess said, her smile fading.

"And I'll just look around while you wait on her," Travis said.

"I was thinking of somethin' in a gold, maybe," Rachel said pointedly and followed Bess to the material table.

As she fingered a piece of thick, pumpkin-colored cotton, she thought of how Travis might react to seeing her in this color. Then she wondered why her traitorous mind couldn't stop caring what Travis did or didn't think of her.

"I'll take this," she said, handing the pumpkin-colored cloth to Bess, who longingly gazed at Travis.

"Okay," Bess said absently.

"And this piece of chocolate brown," Rachel clipped, resisting the

80

urge to whack Bess over the head with it. *Jealousy?* That same offensive emotion that had gripped her heart last Sunday when Bess flirted with Travis gripped it once again.

No! Rachel refused to admit she could stoop to such base feelings. *But haven't you already stooped more than any lady should?* a haunting voice mocked.

And Rachel, as she had already done hundreds of times, relived that heated moment by the burning barn. If she were honest with herself, she would admit that her lips still tingled at the very thought of Travis's kiss, so promising, so forbidding.

"Oh, Mr. Campbell, I almost forgot," Bess crooned as she laid Rachel's material on the counter. "I have a letter for you from. . ." Her large hips swaying beneath her bustling floral dress, Bess turned to the myriad of postal cubbyholes behind her. "From El Paso, I believe."

Compulsively, Rachel stood on her tiptoes to read the return address neatly printed on the envelope's left, upper corner.

With that lazy, indulgent grin, Travis turned to face her. "It's from Kate."

"Oh," Rachel said in a small, prim voice and tried to act as if she didn't care.

They simultaneously glanced toward Bess, who was far too interested in their conversation.

"I'll wait outside," Rachel mumbled. Gathering her full pink skirt, she stepped through the doorway and onto the boardwalk.

"Mornin', Rachel," a familiar voice called.

She stiffened, and with guilty dread, watched as Samuel crossed the dusty, wagon-rutted street. Only last night, Rachel had hoped Samuel would not discover that Travis was buying her the material. A feigned smile, welcoming and surprised. A lead fist tight in her stomach. A hot rush of uncertainty overcame her.

Peace, something Rachel now craved, seemed to forever elude her of late. *Why, oh why, did I agree to Travis's gift?* After seeing Samuel and Travis almost come to blows yesterday, Rachel would have rather not faced them together again.

"Remember, Child, your sins will find you out," Ella had harped all through Rachel's childhood. This time, Ella was right.

"Samuel," she acknowledged as he stopped beside her. Rachel's following nod—cool, respectful, ladylike—was the same nod with which she had always greeted him. A nod with which she would never dream of greeting Travis. Funny, it didn't seem quite enough for Travis.

"What brings you to town so early?" he asked, his sincere, brown eyes smiling in brotherly query despite yesterday's disagreement.

The store's cheerful doorbell jingled as Travis, studying the cloth, opened the door and stepped out. "Here's the material, Miss Rachel. And I must say you picked some lovely col—" Travis stopped in midsentence as he glanced at Samuel.

Samuel's eyes, once bright and calm, clouded in agitated reserve. "Mornin', Travis," he said evenly.

"Good morning." A measured smile and Travis deftly handed the cloth to Rachel.

Silence, awkward, cold, and accusing, seemed to scream Samuel's suspicions as he studied the material, now in Rachel's hands.

With more willpower than she ever dreamed she possessed, Rachel resisted the urge to guiltily hide it behind her back.

"I. . ." "We. . ." She and Travis began in unison.

"Mr. Campbell. . ." "Miss Rachel. . ." They tried again.

Nervously, Rachel cleared her throat and her quick, beseeching glance to Travis changed to pleas for understanding when she turned to Samuel's brooding expression.

"Miss Rachel needed some material for a dress for the turnaround picnic," Travis supplied evenly, "so we decided to come get it this morning."

"I didn't think you wanted to sew anymore, Rachel," Samuel said, ignoring Travis.

"Well. . .I don't. I was going to get Miss Timms, the new seamstress, to do it for me." She pointed across the busy street, gradually filling with squeaking buggies and horse manure.

"Oh," Samuel said, his gaze seeming to bore into hers, to look into her very soul, to somehow sense who was paying the bill.

"I was walkin' that way when I saw you. Why don't you let me walk you over there? And I insist on payin' for it." His darting, triumphant glance at Travis dismissed the other man. "We could even eat dinner at Mrs. Cone's new restaurant after the fittin', and then I could drive you home."

"Oh, I don't want to intrude on your work at the ranch," Rachel said, the relief evident in her voice. Maybe there would not be a scene, after all. With that thought came new irritation with herself. Why was she so worried about what Samuel, or any man, thought?

"Intrude? How could a mornin' with the woman I aim to marry be the likes of intrusion?" He gently took her elbow and propelled her toward the street.

A hesitant glance over her shoulder, and Rachel smiled her apology into Travis's impassive face. Impassive? Or was that discouragement glimmering in his emerald eyes?

Clamping his teeth, Travis narrowed his eyes and watched as Samuel escorted Rachel into Miss Timms's establishment. A sinking disappointment replaced the anticipation of only moments ago.

"But maybe it's for the best," he mumbled as he removed Kate's letter from his chest pocket and examined the meticulous script, so like its creator. Each letter was perfectly slanted, perfectly round or straight, perfectly proportioned.

Without a moment of hesitation or anticipation, Travis opened the envelope and read the brief message. The words seemed to pierce his very soul, to singe his conscience, to insure his life's destiny.

The smell of her exclusive rose oil wafted from the letter, so carefully crafted. He rubbed the textured paper between his index finger and thumb. Closing his eyes, Travis touched the paper to his nose and breathed deeply. Only weeks ago that scent had inspired, enthralled, or so he thought.

Then he remembered Rachel's lilacs.

With an ironic twist to his lips, he folded the letter and placed it back in its envelope. *Oh, Zach, if only I hadn't killed you. If only you had lived to marry Kate. If only, if only. . .*

Then the same guilt that had plagued him, had accused him, had molded his life with its misshapen hands, once again chilled his heart.

"But that is not what God dealt us, is it?" he whispered.

Later that evening, Rachel walked toward the clothesline to remove the dried wash that Ella and she had hung before lunch. All during dinner, her gaze had been drawn to Travis's wary, haunted eyes. For some reason he had been awkward with Rachel. Was it Kate's letter? What had it said that made him so withdrawn? Only this morning, they had shared a pleasant ride into town and, although the tumultuous occurrences from the day before still chased through her mind, Rachel had managed to relax in Travis's company. Travis had relaxed, too. But now, he and consequently she were anything but relaxed. The only thing to which Rachel could attribute his actions was that letter.

As she neared the clothesline, Rachel noticed a white piece of paper lying on the dried grass. She automatically bent to pick it up, then stopped as she realized what it was: Travis's letter from Kate. He must have accidentally dropped it.

Rachel glanced over her shoulder; neither Travis nor Ella were anywhere to be seen.

He'll never know you found it, a devious voice hissed. *You could read it, then drop it where he'll see it. He'll never know.*

She picked up the letter and studied the feminine curves of the written address.

You should give it to him, another voice urged. *It's the only honest thing to do.*

But don't you want to know what Kate is like? the first voice parried.

Another glance over her shoulder, and Rachel slipped the envelope into her skirt's hidden pocket.

Chapter 13

R achel, lying in her bed, peered over her sheet at Kate Lowell's letter, propped against her dresser's mirror. She had deliberated all evening about whether she should read it or discreetly drop it outside the barn.

The trusty mantel clock in the living room struck midnight. Rachel counted each stroke and with each stroke she changed her mind. *I'll read it. I'll return it. I'll read it. I'll return it.*

By six o'clock in the morning, she still had not come to a decision. After splashing her face with cold water and rinsing her hands in the lilac water she so loved, Rachel picked up the envelope. Once again, she examined the graceful script. That's when the folded letter slipped out, sailed to the floor, and plopped open with the sound of paper against wood.

Biting her lip, Rachel bent to retrieve the note and tried not to look at the first line. But her gaze was drawn to it, despite her puny attempts to avert her eyes.

Dearest Travis,
I cannot tell you in mere words how much I miss you. Mother says I am pale, and I guess I am. You were the light of my life. Now, I seem to have no life. I keep thinking of Zach and how he was taken from me. Please do not assume I am trying to incriminate you. I know his death was a complete accident. Yet I feel that in spirit, you are farther away than the miles that sepa-

*rate us and that you, too, will perhaps be taken from me. Please
tell me I am wrong. I do not think I could live without you. . . .*

The letter then related trivial news of people Rachel did not know.
Her chest tensing, she replaced the letter in the envelope without rereading it. She couldn't. The words were, for some reason, too hard for her to
take.

Zach. The name that instigated a flood of grief and guilt in Travis's
eyes. Travis said he was responsible for Zach's death, but he had not
expounded, and Rachel had not pushed for details. She had deduced that
Travis could never purposefully kill another, and Kate's calling the incident an accident proved Rachel's assumptions about Travis.

Slipping the letter into her pocket, Rachel remembered Travis's
poetic description of Miss Lowell. Milky skin, blue-green eyes, peachy
lips, long, black hair. The near royal description matched her letter's soft
rose scent, and Rachel knew, despite her heart's latent longing, that Travis
would go back to the woman who first claimed him.

"I wish you would go home. Now. And I wish you would stay forever," Rachel whispered, dreading the months of seeing him and knowing
she could never have him and, at the same time, forever wanting him near.
Her stomach churned as a tide of nausea creeped up her throat. Rachel
could deny it no longer. She did want Travis, wanted him as her friend,
her sweetheart, her husband.

"Why, oh, why did you have to come here?" Through her open window, she watched Travis in the weak dawn light as he left the barn and
headed for the chicken coop. "God, if You had only let Pa live, I wouldn't
be in this fix. How could You. . .?

Perhaps, though, when she married Samuel, she would feel differently, especially if a little one came along. Pledging to keep this thought
foremost in her mind, Rachel rushed for the front door. While Travis
retrieved the eggs, she would drop the letter outside the barn door and
hope he never suspected she had read it.

I do not think I could live without you. Kate's words rattled in Travis's
mind like a chain, constricting his soul, his life.

"Oh, Lord," he breathed as he checked each warm nest for eggs, "do
You want me to marry Kate? Should I marry her when. . .when. . .? Is it
fair to any of us?

Travis had not slept all night. With each hour that passed, he had
gone from knowing his place was with Kate to doubting that very

assumption. At this point he knew only one person who could direct him. Even though Travis was still a murderer, even though he still doubted God's forgiveness, even though guilt still tainted his soul, he desperately needed an answer to his dilemma.

Just this once, Lord, please forget that I'm a murderer and help me.

That prayer, ever so humble, stayed with Travis as he delivered the eggs to Ella and started toward the barn to retrieve his Colt Peacemaker. He had forgotten to put it on. Not that he thought he would need it today, but he couldn't be too careful, especially with what had transpired of late.

Just as he rounded the front of the barn, he glanced up to encounter Rachel, her amber eyes widened in surprise. "Good morning, Miss Rachel," he said, grinning indulgently.

"Mornin'," she said, averting her eyes. "I. . .I was just um. . ."

Travis wrinkled his brow, wondering why she thought she had to explain to him. "This is your property, remember?" His mind flashed to his first night and her primly reminding him of that very fact. "You don't have to explain to me."

"I know, but—" She stopped herself as her cheeks flushed with guilt.

Puzzled, he stared at her. She was acting as if she were trying to hide something.

"Momma Ella needs me in the kitchen," she mumbled, then rushed past him.

Travis stared after her for several thoughtful seconds. Her hair, a cascade of fire, hung loosely down her back and swung with every sway of her hips. He rarely saw it unbraided, and the sight was a special treat. With a dismissing chuckle, Travis turned for the barn. There was no sense in trying to figure out Rachel or her actions. He had stopped that pursuit long ago.

That was when he saw it. The letter from Kate, lying outside the barn's door. Thoughtfully, Travis bent to pick it up. He had missed it yesterday, shortly after arriving home. He assumed it had slipped from his pocket on the way. He hadn't noticed the letter lying outside the barn last night or earlier this morning. Perhaps he had simply overlooked it.

Musing over the contents, Travis entered the barn, set the lantern on a wall shelf, and once again opened the letter. He so wished those constricting words were not there. Maybe he had imagined them. But as he scanned the first paragraph, every word said exactly what he remembered.

Then, something about the letter struck him odd. Kate's rose oil didn't smell the same. The oil smelled as if it had been mixed with— Travis held the note to his nose, trying to place the familiar scent.

Lilacs. . .*Rachel's* lilacs.

Suddenly, her strange behavior made sense. Somehow, she had managed to get her hands on his letter, his private, personal property, and had read it. Stunned, he stared at a nearby milk can while the audacity of her actions sank in. Then, the anger emerged.

How dare she! With a decisive turn, he stomped toward the summer kitchen.

Rachel, tin plates and cups in hand, hovered over the outdoor table and seemed to recoil at his swift approach.

"What's the matter?" he demanded. "Are you feeling guilty about something?"

She stiffened. "Exactly what is that supposed to mean?"

"This!" He threw the letter on the table and, even in the gray dawn, he could not miss the rush of color to her cheeks. "Care to tell me how it landed outside the barn's door?"

"What?" she rasped.

"The whole thing reeks of lilacs! What business is it of yours what my fiancée writes to me?"

Her nostrils flared; her jaw tightened; her lips quivered.

"What did you do? Go through my belongings until you found it?"

"No!" she said, slamming the tin plates and cups against the table with a resounding clatter. "I found it by the clothesline yester—" She stopped in the middle of incriminating herself.

Compulsively, Travis rounded the table to stand only inches from her. His mind whirled with new anger, new frustration, new attraction for this infuriating woman. "And I don't guess you ever considered returning it to me?"

"You have it, don't you?" She raised her chin in haughty determination, and her amber eyes never wavered.

"Listen to me, you little nosy—" Travis grabbed her upper arms, not sure why, but regretted the moment he did. For that mere physical contact stopped his words and filled his heart with the admiration he so wished to deny.

Silence—long, tense, and loaded with unspoken messages— engulfed them in a world of their own. The mourning dove's lonely, romantic call intensified their lack of words. And in that moment—so poignant, so fraught with expectation—Travis gazed into Rachel's eyes, into her very soul. What he saw there, a reflection of his own turbulent emotions, both elated him and conquered his anger. Then his betraying gaze moved to her lips, half parted, ever so expectant.

"Rachel. . . ," he muttered, his hand reaching to stroke the tendrils of auburn hair surrounding her face.

Then Kate's words pierced his mind. *I do not think I could live without you.*

With regret, Travis let his hand drop and then he deliberately stepped backwards.

Rachel, pressing her lips together, turned to the table and slammed each plate in place without another look his way. "I shouldn't have read your precious letter in the first place." Then, her green gingham work dress rustled as she marched toward the kitchen. She stopped in midstride and turned back to face him, her eyes narrowed in stubborn determination. "But I'm glad I did."

Chapter 14

"Rachel! Rachel!" Ella's high-pitched "emergency" voice floated from the front door.

Rachel's hands stilled as she finished buttoning her calico dress. Minutes before, when she had come in to change for supper, everything had been fine.

The front door banged shut and Rachel, her eyes widened in dread, rushed from her room to meet Ella halfway down the hall.

"What is it?" Rachel asked.

"It be Elmira Reeve! Her time be here."

"But she's not supposed to. . .to. . .for another month!" Rachel immediately pictured the youthful, frail waif of a woman who attended Ella's church.

"I knows it. That's why she done sent for me." Ella pushed past Rachel and, her brown skirts held high, ran toward her bedroom. "I got to go to her and see what I can do."

With the clatter of Ella's mysterious birthing equipment, Rachel stood in the hallway and anxiously chewed her lip. Any mention of giving birth left Rachel nervous and somewhat concerned. Once she and Samuel married, she might be the one in need of Ella's expertise. When folks thought there would be trouble during a childbirth, they often requested Ella, and Rachel was thankful that somebody close to her knew about such things.

A dilapidated carpetbag in one hand and her skirts in the other, Ella turned from her bedroom and brushed past Rachel. "I probably gonna be all night. You and Mr. Campbell needs to eat without me. The beans and ham bone is ready." And with that, she slammed out of the house.

Rachel blinked after her, a sinking feeling in the pit of her stomach. After this morning's embarrassing scene, she and Travis had not looked at or spoken to each other. Travis had mutely worked on the barn while Rachel groomed Ginger and washed their clothes.

When he touched her this morning, Rachel had once again longed for his lips against hers. This time, she knew the feeling would not die. She had never been so mortified as when Travis had confronted her with that horrible letter. She would have eaten a skunk before admitting to having read it, but Travis had somehow gotten the admission out of her. *It was for the best,* a little voice whispered.

As Rachel walked up the narrow hall, she knew that voice was right. Lying had never been something she enjoyed or was even good at. Besides, she didn't want to displease the Lord.

With that thought, Rachel stopped. Why worry about displeasing the Lord anymore? God certainly hadn't worried about displeasing her when He let her pa die. Then, a doubt so faint, so fragile, sprouted in her heart. Could she be wrong in her anger toward God?

Instead of going outside as she had planned, Rachel turned into her father's bedroom for only the third time since his death. Taking in the spicy smell of his hair tonic, she stared at his empty, rugged, walnut bed and tried to imagine him as he had been the morning he died.

His faded hair, once the color of hers. . .his blue eyes, already dulled by death's dreadful claim. . .his skin, gray and lifeless. "Lean on the Lord, Rachel, lean on the Lord. He will never forsake you." With those final words, he had gripped her fingers and rasped his last breath.

Rachel walked toward the bed and stroked the multicolored Star Flower quilt that she and Ella had created and given to him on his last Christmas. Could Pa's dying words have been true? Would the Lord never forsake her?

"Why, oh, why do I feel as if You have?" she prayed like a confused, defenseless child.

Not knowing the answer, not even sure she cared, Rachel turned from her pa's memory and headed for the summer kitchen. Perhaps she could eat her beans and ham and retire to her room before Travis quit working.

❖

"Something smells heavenly," Travis said five minutes later as Rachel filled a bowl with the beans.

Taken off guard, she glanced toward his voice before she had time to check herself.

He stood outside one of the glassless windows, smiling as if nothing had happened this morning, as if he had never even thought of kissing her.

Half relieved, half irritated, Rachel masked her features into their blandest expression, then feigned her own smile. "Yes. I've always said nothin' beats Momma Ella's beans and cornbread. The Reeves called her away because. . .because of Elmira. She's having some difficulties." Rachel, concentrating on the beans in their thick, brown soup, hoped she hid her sudden flush.

"Oh," Travis said meaningfully.

"So I guess it will be just you and me for supper. Are you ready to eat?" *So much for eating alone.*

"I am ravenous. Let me get washed up, and I'll meet you at the outdoor table. Unless you insist, I think it's too hot to eat inside."

"Me, too." Rachel pushed a damp tendril of hair away from her forehead.

With that, he turned away.

"Oh, Travis?"

He turned back to face her, his expression guarded.

"Could you please get the milk and butter from the springhouse?"

"I'd be glad to," he said as if she had just asked him to perform the most cherished of tasks.

❖

When he returned, they both sat down and ate in strained silence.

"Delicious," Travis declared after his third bowl of beans and ham.

"Momma Ella will be glad you enjoyed your supper," Rachel said, the setting sun glistening in her hair.

The nearby dove's haunting call brought back memories of this morning, of Travis's moment of weakness. So far, he had surprised himself at how composed he had been through supper. If Rachel knew what lay behind his polite façade, she would probably stiffly remind him that they were both spoken for.

Staring at a loose, rusty nail on the graying barn, Travis suppressed an indulgent smile. Grit. . .Rachel had enough for three men. He didn't know any woman who would admit to being glad she had read another's mail. And suddenly, what had angered him this morning only endeared her to him.

"I'm sorry I was so mad this morning," he said spontaneously and cast a sidelong glance her way.

She stiffened, sniffed, and then gripped her spoon. "I. . .it's quite all right. I should have never read. . .read your letter."

"Well, I can understand a certain amount of curiosity. Especially since. . ." Since what? Since the two of them were so attracted to each other? Since they were slowly falling in love? Since that love was hopeless?

Yes. Travis could see it in Rachel's eyes, see exactly what he felt. She might have told Samuel that she detested Travis, but after this morning he knew that that declaration was an attempt to cover what both of them wished to deny.

He cleared his throat and tried to clear his mind. "Since you have never met Miss Kate, I'm sure you're naturally curious."

"That's still no excuse." She stood, grabbed their dishes, and walked toward the kitchen, her spine stiff.

Balling his fists, Travis resisted the urge to follow her, to tell her that, regardless of the letter's contents, he did not love Kate, that his heart belonged—would always belong—to her. The cool evening breeze, laced with the calls of lowing cattle, fingered the surrounding trees and seemed to mock Travis's helpless state.

For the first time since Zach's death, Travis felt like a man, a whole man. Rachel, with her wit, her grit, and her charm had somehow sneaked into his heart and sweetened the waters, once so bitter. After spring, after Travis rode away and left her, he would be back to only half living, to being only half a man. He swallowed compulsively—if he could make it until spring.

How would he survive once she and Samuel married, and Rachel would bear Samuel's children instead of his? How would he go on, knowing his arms would be empty? Hollow. His heart, his home, his whole world would be hollow.

"Good news, Travis," Samuel called from nearby.

Travis, startled, glanced up to see Samuel reining his palomino. His thoughts had so absorbed him that he hadn't even heard the approaching horse.

"I've just come from the constable's. He thinks we've found our cattle thief." Samuel slid from the saddle.

"Who?" Travis asked, standing to meet his rival.

"Caleb Singletary."

Rachel gasped from close behind. "Surely not. He seems so—"

"Honest?" Samuel finished, a knowing gleam in his eyes. "That's what everybody thought, including Preacher Jones. He sent Caleb around a few days back to collect money for the Tuckers when their horses and steers came up missin'."

"Yes, I know," Rachel said. "I gave him three dollars."

"Well, I hate to tell you this. . . . ," Samuel laid a consoling, possessive hand on Rachel's shoulder, and Travis clamped his jaw, "but Caleb has left town. And he took your three dollars and everybody else's money, along with Joshua Bishop's new work wagon and two of his finest geldings."

The high-strung palomino snorted and pranced sideways, and Samuel removed his hand from Rachel and stroked the beast's neck. "Easy, Boy."

"Have they caught him?" Travis asked.

"No. Parker has sent me and two others to round up some men. We're gonna form a posse and go after him. We think he went north because he has relatives in Dallas." Eyes squinted in male speculation, Samuel challenged Travis. "Are you in?"

"Who would look after Miss Rachel?" Travis asked, not relishing the idea of leaving her alone.

"I'll be fine," Rachel said firmly. "If Caleb is behind all the crimes, then I have no one to fear."

"That's what I figured. And you're probably a better shot than either of us, anyway," Samuel said through a reassuring smile. "Why, between you and Miss Ella—"

"Miss Ella's not—" Travis interrupted.

"I'll be *fine,*" Rachel said, glancing pointedly at Travis.

And Travis immediately understood her plight. If Samuel learned that they were here alone, had shared supper alone, would be alone through the night, he would probably disapprove, and disapprove unpleasantly.

But what man wouldn't? Travis himself didn't like the thought of Rachel even riding to church alone with Samuel.

Suppressing his distracting emotions, Travis hesitated. Regardless of her expertise with a gun, he did not want to leave Rachel by herself. Caleb strongly appeared to be the cattle thief and arsonist. But what if he weren't?

"So are you in or not, Travis?" Samuel asked again, that same challenge in his eyes, his voice.

Travis recognized what Samuel's words didn't say: Do you have the guts to chase an outlaw or are you going to hide behind Rachel's skirts?

Clamping his teeth, Travis made his decision, made it swiftly, and hoped he would not regret it. "I'm in."

Chapter 15

Propping herself up in bed, Rachel opened the book of Shakespeare plays her teacher had given her at graduation. Before her father died, she mostly read the Bible. Now, she looked to Shakespeare, and although he was good, she could not deny that he did nothing to ease her soul like that worn, black book once did.

Pressing her lips together, Rachel suppressed the urge to reach for her Bible because it had lied to her by saying that God would take care of her.

Her shoulders protesting with an ache that only hard work can deliver, Rachel's eyes blurred before she finished the first act of *Antony and Cleopatra*. With a yawn, she closed the leather-bound book and gave in to the urge to turn out the oil lamp without changing into her nightgown.

As the wick's glow diminished, so did Rachel's sleepiness, and her eyes opened to stare at the pine ceiling. When Samuel tried to get her to marry him after her barn burned the first time, Rachel rejected him, telling herself she wanted to prove her ability to run the ranch alone. Now, she knew that had been a ploy to put off their inevitable marriage, because with Travis around, she had never really run the ranch alone.

The wedding date steadily approached, and Rachel could put it off no longer. In eight weeks, Samuel would be in bed with her. She nervously rubbed the bridge of her nose while contemplating their wedding night. All her youth she had overheard vague references to the relationship between men and women and having children, but Rachel had no idea what Samuel expected of her.

The thought of. . .of. . .with Samuel, of all people, and her stomach churned with nausea. Samuel had been there all her life. He was like the oak out front—steady, dependable, familiar. . .something like a brother. When she had agreed to marry him, having a partner to help run the ranch had appealed to her, and Samuel was the most likely choice. Rachel, caught up in her worries, had never contemplated the physical side of their relationship. Now, if Rachel were engaged to Travis, she would have thought often about. . .

Her cheeks flaming, Rachel covered her head. *A wanton woman,* that was what Abby would call her. What would Momma Ella think? Or Samuel? Or Travis? Her cheeks flamed anew until the clean snap of a broken twig left them cold.

I'm alone, Rachel realized.

Travis had gone to join the posse, and Rachel was a woman completely alone on a big ranch—or so she hoped. Rachel strained to hear any new sound. Another broken twig, perhaps? Or footsteps? *It's probably just Tiny,* she told herself while trying not to remember seeing Tiny trotting toward the south field only moments before she had settled onto her bed.

Soon, Rachel could deny her fear no longer. Footsteps—slow, steady, sinister—approached her bedroom window. Panting, she instinctively reached for the Winchester propped near her bed, but her hand groped air.

The cautious footsteps grew closer, more threatening.

Rachel, her heart hammering, frantically glanced around the room for the absent gun. Then she remembered cleaning it yesterday morning and propping it near her dresser. She had meant to move the gun to her bedside later but had forgotten.

The footsteps continually neared and became faster and more ominous. Then they stopped outside her open window and a shadowed figure leaned forward as if he planned to crawl in.

"If. . .if you touch that windowsill, I'll. . .I'll scream," Rachel croaked, her voice quivering with every word.

A laugh, low, wicked, and knowing. "What good will it do ya?" he growled. "Ain't nobody here but you." His voice, evil, slurred, and distorted, violated the clean, summer air. A hot bolt of lightning seemed to punctuate his words while illuminating his image. A tattered, straw hat, pulled low over shadowed eyes, a neck scarf, covering the rest of his face, and hands, large, powerful, and menacing gripping the windowsill. "See, Miss Rachel, I been watchin' ya. I been plannin' this. You ain't gonna fool me."

Rachel, in a pathetic attempt to breathe, panted like a winded stallion.

This invader had been watching her, and she had never known, never even sensed his presence. Could he be Caleb?

"What. . .what do you want?" she pleaded, imagining the worst.

"Now we're agettin' somewhere." He raised his hand—a dark silhouette against the flashing, low clouds—and cocked the hammer of a handgun. "If you'll just tell me what I want to know, I won't even have to come in there and get. . .well. . .rough."

Gulping, she mentally calculated the distance to her Winchester. If she could somehow catch him off guard.

Then, he pointed the gun at her head, and her plan dissolved. "Now, I want you to tell me where all that gold is buried."

"What gold?" Her heart pounded in her temples as she remembered the stories about a buried treasure that she had heard of since childhood. Could they be true?

That same, wicked chuckle. "Don't play stupid with me. I found the box with what was supposed to be a map in it buried behind your barn, but all it said was 'hard spot.' Tell me what 'hard spot' means or I'll shoot."

"What?"

"Hard spot. That's all that no count piece of paper said. What does it mean?"

"I have no idea what you're talking about."

Dear Lord, please protect me. Please don't leave me to die like. . .like Pa. Please.

A universe-shaking clap of thunder accompanied a fierce gust of cool, humid air that seemed to mock Rachel's prayer. As if it were a twig, an ancient, rotting pine swayed, and Rachel remembered the unexpected twister from only weeks before.

"Stop lyin' and tell me where the gold is. Now!"

She jumped. "I—"

A cracking noise, slow, deliberate, escalated into the empty moan of a tree losing a limb. And the dark invader, covering his head with his gun hand, turned to look behind him just as a black, swooping limb crashed around him.

The curses followed his fall. Rachel dove for her Winchester. Cold metal had never felt more assuring. She cocked the hammer and, without aiming, pulled the trigger, then dropped behind the dresser for cover. The lightning, now resembling a million, flickering lanterns, created an eerie backdrop for the shattering window that the whirling wind forced inside.

"If you don't get off my property," Rachel screamed during a brief pause in the thunder, "I'll kill you!" *Would I really?*

Never having taken the life of another, Rachel didn't know if she could truly kill. But he didn't have to know that.

"I mean it!" she said. A quick cock of the hammer, then Rachel leaned out from the dresser and, with trembling fingers, pulled the trigger for added emphasis.

No answer. . .nothing but the patter of raindrops on her windowsill as the heavens slowly opened. A gradual crackle of lightning, a resounding boom, and the deluge followed.

Biting her lip, her legs wobbling, Rachel gathered her skirts, scrambled onto the bed, and leaned toward the window to hesitantly peer out. Had the limb killed the intruder?

Then she saw him, running from the barn toward her front porch.

A new scream pressing against her throat, Rachel dropped the rifle, grabbed her work boots, slipped them on, gripped the Winchester, and crunched across the broken glass to brace the gun barrel against the window frame. Through the blinding rain, Rachel carefully aimed over his head and pulled the trigger once more.

He dropped, just like a dead duck, and her heart skidded to a standstill. "I've killed him," she gasped.

But the next streak of lightning dispelled her fear, for it illuminated the man, hunched over and running, as if uninjured.

New fear enclosed her like an icy tomb, and Rachel stood motionless while footfalls pounded the front porch. The door banged open as a roll of receding thunder testified to the storm's swift passing.

Gulping against her churning stomach, she rushed for the bedroom door and braced her gun's barrel against the frame. He might be coming after her, but he was going to get a fight.

"All right, drop your gun and come out. Now!" Travis called from the parlor.

"Travis?" Rachel shrieked, her legs almost buckling with relief.

"Rachel?"

A sob of anguish, of fear, of release poured from her as she dropped the Winchester and ran up the hallway. "Oh, Travis!" Another sob, and Rachel collapsed against him, clinging to his soggy frame as if he were her lifeline. "Thank God you came back."

"Rachel, Rachel, Rachel, you're alive!" His lips, ever so tender, brushed her hair. "When I saw that man running from your window and

then the shooting, I thought. . .I thought someone had you and. . .and. . ."
He squeezed her tighter. "Thank the Lord you're alive."

She pulled away to look up into his shadowed face. "Oh, no," she
gasped, "I almost killed you. I. . .I thought you were. . . I'm so sorry."

His cold, damp hands, on either side of her face, assured her that he
readily forgave her. "It's fine. It's fine. I'm just so glad. . ."

Rachel realized what she had done. With his face only inches from
hers, with his damp, masculine smell filling her nostrils, with his every
breath fanning her cheek, Rachel realized she had thrown herself in his
arms.

I do not think I could live without you. Kate's words, so pleading, so
pathetic, tortured Rachel's mind, her soul. She had thrown herself at
another woman's man.

Taking a deliberate, although regretful, step backward, she hurriedly
told him of her "visitor" in an attempt to cover her humiliation. What
must he think? *Wanton.* The word from her earlier musings still accused.

The story had no sooner left her, than Travis rushed to her bedroom
to light the oil lamp and examine the mess. With the storm now a dripping
memory, he leaned out of the shattered window and held the lamp over
the broken limb.

Rachel, hovering close behind, clasped and unclasped her hands in an
attempt to control the shaking that steadily increased. She had been
threatened; she had almost been killed; she had nearly killed Travis.

"That limb fell at just the right time, didn't it?" he said. "I'd say
Somebody was looking out for you."

Rachel didn't answer. Had that limb been an answer to her heavenly
appeal for protection? If it were, did that mean God really did care for
her? Too distraught to further contemplate such musings, she rushed
headlong into words, any words. Words that she soon regretted. "I'm so
glad you came to protect me. What made you decide to come back
home?"

Home. The word seemed to echo off her bedroom walls.

With heavy silence stretching into an aching eternity, Travis slowly
turned to face her. The lamp's flickering flame revealed his confusion, the
same confusion that was Rachel's bedfellow. This wasn't Travis's home,
but she felt as if he belonged, had always belonged, with her, on this ranch.

"You're glad I came to protect you?" he finally teased, a slow grin not
matching his churning, haunted eyes. "The way I see it, *I'm* the one who
needed protection."

Rachel giggled nervously, glad the tense moment had passed.

"Believe it or not," he continued, "I was getting ready to leave town with the posse when I had this overwhelming urge to come back to the ranch."

"Well, I'm glad you did."

"Me, too." He crunched toward the bedroom door as if their conversation were over, then thoughtfully turned back to her. "I guess we now know there *is* gold on your land."

"I can hardly believe it. If that. . .that horrible man hadn't been so serious, I wouldn't believe it still." Stiffening, Rachel crossed her arms as she remembered that man's distorted, gravelly voice.

"Are you all right?" Travis took a step closer.

Rachel stumbled backward. "I'm fine," she said primly, wishing she could forget the feel of his arms around her, wondering if she would long for them when Samuel held her in eight short weeks. "I was just scared, that's all."

"Well," he said, that lazy half-grin tilting his lips, "so was I. I don't get shot at every day."

Chapter 16

M r. Reeve?" Ella called from the doorway of Elmira's tiny bedroom. "You have a healthy little girl." The newborn's screaming punctuated her words.

"A girl! A girl!" Adam Reeve jumped from the rickety, pine chair, his massive frame filling the shabby, shadowed parlor.

"Can I see her. . .her and Elmira? How be Elmira, Miss Ella?" His dark eyes, full of apprehension, pleaded for a positive answer. "Her screamin'. . .it was just somethin' awful. I. . .I just didn't know—"

"Elmira's just fine, Son." Ella, her shoulders aching from her night's work, gave his hand a reassuring squeeze. "You can come on in shortly. Just as soon as her ma gets her situated." Another encouraging smile, and she turned back toward the mother and her newborn.

"Thank you, thank you," Elmira whispered weakly, the flickering candle accentuating her hollow cheeks and exhausted gaze. "I'd a done died without you."

"Ah, now, don't you go on," Ella said with a rush of pleasure.

"We can't pays you much," Elmira's plump mother added, holding the whimpering newborn.

"Oh, yes, you can," Ella said, smiling into the face of the new arrival. "Just you let me hold this little angel, and that'll be worth every bit a my work."

A beaming grandmother extended the baby. "I'll go an' tell Adam he can come on in."

Ella, humming a lullaby in her deep, rich voice, neared the candle

101

and cradled that tiny scrap of humanity to her chest. "Daisy, Daisy, my only Daisy," she crooned, then kissed a cheek, ever so soft.

Dear Lawd, please tell me she wasn't ever taken away. Please tell me it was all just one of them terrible dreams. Please tell me I still has my Daisy.

Then the silent torment from the past. "Momma, look at this here frog. Momma, how did the stars git a way up there? Momma, see the pretty rock I found today? Momma, Momma, please don't let 'em take me. . . Please. . . stop 'em, Momma! Momma, tell 'em, Momma, tell 'em I belongs to you. Momma. . . Momma. . .Momma!"

Oh, my little Daisy, where are you? Dear Lawd, please, please, please let me find her.

But for the first time in her search of a lifetime, Ella sensed that it might never be. She would probably never see her Daisy again. Should she accept the reality that so many slave families had likewise accepted? The reality of never again seeing her daughter. Had the time come for Ella to release her grip on the past?

A still, small voice affirmed her thoughts. As she looked into the wrinkled face of that precious infant, Ella felt a knot unraveling within her. No, she probably would never find Daisy. She knew that now. Knew it on a deeper level than she had ever accepted before. The time had come for Ella to stop the mourning and start the accepting.

God, in His mercy, had given Ella Rachel to love. And Ella had loved her with all the love a mother could pour upon her daughter.

"Thank You, Lord," Ella breathed. "Thank You for my Rachel."

❖

"I'm atellin' you straight, Constable, I don't know nothin' about no cattle thieving." Caleb Singletary stood behind iron bars in Constable Parker's office, his blue eyes as cold as the Atlantic in winter.

Travis, entering in the middle of their conversation, closed the door behind him. After Ella arrived back at the ranch, he had ridden into town to see if the constable and his posse were back and, if so, to tell Parker about Rachel's "visitor." It looked as if the posse had accomplished its mission.

"Mornin', Travis." Constable Parker turned from his prisoner; his lips were clamped in a grim line.

"Good morning." Travis, removing his straw hat, nodded toward cherub-faced Caleb, who responded with a retreat into his cell. As Parker closed the door that blocked off the prisoners from his office, Travis felt an unexpected surge of sympathy for the poor farmer behind bars.

"Glad you came in," Parker said. "I've got some news for you."

"It looks as if the posse was successful," Travis said.

"Yeah. I looked for you after we got started, and Ethan Tucker said you'd gone on back home." The constable rubbed his whiskers and turned toward a pot of fragrant coffee. "Everything okay?"

"If only it were." Travis seated himself in the tattered cowhide chair near Parker's gnarled desk. "Miss Isaacs had an unexpected visitor—or should I say intruder—last night."

"And. . .?" The wiry constable, his expression never changing, plopped a tin cup full of steaming coffee in front of Travis.

"And he threatened to kill her if she didn't tell him where the gold was buried."

With a low whistle, the constable settled into his chair, his graying brows raised. "I'm supposin' you got there in time to stop any injury?"

Remembering that bullet whizzing over his head, Travis chuckled and examined his worn work boots. "You've known Miss Isaacs longer than I have, what do you think?"

"She didn't kill him, did she?"

"No, but she came close to killing him *and* me, and by the time I was able to make sure she was all right, the man had run away."

A soft, knowing laugh. "That Miss Rachel would probably fight a bear if she had to. Sometimes when I think about her and Samuel gettin' hitched, well, I just have to have myself a good snicker. I wonder if Samuel James knows what he's gettin' himself in for."

Wishing to hide the rush of irritation, Travis leaned forward to pick up his hot coffee and reminded himself that Parker meant no harm with his comments. Still, a man just naturally wanted to defend the woman he loved.

Travis could almost feel her heart racing as it had last night when she had fallen into his arms. How right that moment had felt. How ironic that the very woman Travis's father had planned for him to marry was the very woman forbidden him.

"So I guess that old tale about the gold is true," Travis said in an attempt to redirect his wayward thoughts.

"Sure does look that way." Parker absently toyed with a cracked button on his faded, blue, pullover shirt. His confused gaze reflected Travis's own thoughts. "I don't guess Miss Rachel recognized the man?"

"No. But whoever he was, he knew her and knew she would be alone."

"Makes me wonder." Parker leaned forward, placing his elbows on the desk cluttered with dirty cups, stained papers, and an array of spent candles. "You're not the only one with news. It seems Tyrone Burks lied about where he was the mornin' Miss Rachel's barn was first burned."

"Oh?" Travis pondered Tyrone's sullen disposition. His interest peaked, he sipped the steaming, acrid coffee, then forced himself to swallow against a threatening gag. Dr. Engle's coffee tasted like heaven compared to this bitter brew.

Parker, without a blink, drained his cup with three gulps. "Yep." Still sitting, he turned for the coffeepot and refilled his cup with the thick liquid, then extended the gray pot toward Travis. "More coffee?"

"No, no thank you."

With the sound of metal against metal, Parker replaced the pot on his small, corner stove. "Anyway, Tyrone swore he was with a drinkin' friend. Well, it took me awhile to find that friend. To tell you the truth, I don't think Tyrone much thought I would, seein' as this friend lives in Rusk, a good twenty miles away. But I did, and once I found him, he said he didn't even see Tyrone the day of that fire. Says he was out of town that whole week."

"Interesting," Travis said. Setting his cup back on the desk, Travis pictured the sullen face of Rachel's moody hired hand. "What does Tyrone say now?"

"Nothin'. Can't find him."

"This is starting to sound rather incriminating, don't you think?"

"I think a lot of things. Like maybe Tyrone and Caleb," he said, pointing toward the cells, "are in cahoots with a third somebody. While we were out lookin' for Caleb last night, cattle was stolen from another ranch, and the ranch owner was out with the posse."

"What?"

"That's right. Now don't you think it's kinda peculiar that we were all out lookin' for Caleb?" A new light flickered in Parker's keen brown eyes. "And that Miss Rachel's visitor just happened to show up then?"

"Do you think it was all planned to—"

"Yep. And I don't care what that Caleb Singletary says." The corners of his mouth turned down as he spoke through gritted teeth. "I think he's up to his skinny little Adam's apple in this business. Joshua Bishop does, too, by the way."

"He would probably know Caleb better than anyone, I guess. Doesn't Caleb rent from Joshua?"

"Yes."

"What about Caleb's wife and family? Where are they staying?"

104

"Magnolia Alexander, Dr. Engle's nurse, you probably ain't met her. Anyway, she's talked her uncle into lettin' them stay at their house."

Travis thought of Mrs. Singletary as he had seen her during worship. A thin woman with a disillusioned, disappointed demeanor and a wardrobe to match. Travis wondered what the large family would do without Caleb. At the very best, a thief spent his future in prison. For some unexplained reason, Travis hoped things would be better for Caleb and hoped with equal fervor that he was not part of the cattle rustling.

❖

"Once again, we can't tell you how glad we are to have you as our customer." The smiling bank president, Mr. John Rothschild, escorted Rachel to the small bank's front door and toyed with his gold watch chain, dangling from his pliable leather vest.

"You're quite welcome." A warm smile. As Rachel turned to leave the busy bank, she hoped her smile hid her misgivings. Her pa had never trusted the bank, but he had never been held at gunpoint in his own home, either. And right now, Rachel felt as if her pa's small savings would be safer in a bank vault than behind the rock in her fireplace. She hoped she was right. Another polite smile, waves of good-bye, and she stepped outside.

"Rachel!" Abby gasped.

"Oh, hello, Abby," she replied, closing the door on the bank and facing the busy street. "What brings you out so early?"

"I. . .I was just in town to pick up my dress for the turnaround picnic. I had Miss Timms make it." Abby looked everywhere but in Rachel's eyes.

While tense, silent seconds stretched into awkward minutes, Rachel tried to remember the last time she and Abby had talked, the last time Abby had come over for her traditional Saturday dinner. When had Abby stopped? Rachel had been so caught up in all her problems, she hadn't even noticed until now.

"I had her make my dress, too," Rachel said in an attempt to end the silence.

"I was terribly pleased with her work," Abby said as if they were two strangers at a tea party.

"I'm sure you'll be the most beautiful one there," Rachel said, meaning every word. All the women in Dogwood faded when compared to Abby's dark hair, striking blue eyes, and milky skin. Rachel absently rubbed her freckled nose.

"Only second to you." Was that a twist of envy in Abby's clear, soprano voice?

Rachel blinked, not sure how to take the compliment, not sure it was a compliment. More tense silence. Had Rachel unknowingly offended Abby? She had never known her to act so distant, especially not with her very best friend. They had always been like sisters.

"I. . .I guess I need to go." A tremulous smile, a whisk of her scarlet skirts, and Abby turned toward her distinguished carriage waiting nearby.

Her brow wrinkling in confusion, Rachel stared after her best friend, her best friend ever since she could remember. Abby had never hidden anything from Rachel. Why now?

Chapter 17

"M y, my, Rachel! I ain't never seen you look so pretty!" Ella said. Twirling around the room, Rachel felt like a royal princess attending a ball instead of a Texas girl about to go to a country town's picnic. She stopped in front of her dresser mirror. "Didn't Miss Timms do a lovely job?"

The pumpkin-colored cloth had been transformed into a work of fashion art. The rich, chocolate bustle contrasted against the full, russet skirt and complimented Rachel's hair and eyes to perfection.

"Miss Timms is going to be one busy woman, yessiree," Ella said, bobbing her head emphatically. "You don't see this kinda work just every day."

I wonder what Travis will say, Rachel started to say, then stopped herself. In the past four weeks, she had refused herself the pleasure of musing about him. In mere weeks, Rachel would be Mrs. Samuel James. Rachel must resign herself to the inevitable. But was that possible?

"I'm sure Samuel will be pleased with the dress," Rachel said.

"If he ain't, Child, he ain't ever gonna be." Then Ella left to put the finishing touches to Rachel's picnic basket.

Picking up the cameo lying on her dresser, Rachel tied it around her neck with the piece of brown velvet ribbon that Miss Timms had supplied. The cameo had been Rachel's mother's, and she wondered, as she had wondered hundreds of times, what her mother had been like. "You must have been something special to have captured Pa," she said to the cameo. "I wish you could both be at the weddin'."

But God did not will it, a bitter voice whispered. *Maybe you should accept it,* another voice parried. *Now they're both with the Lord.*

"But I still miss them," she whispered, no longer certain which voice was right.

Pondering these thoughts, Rachel glanced toward the boarded-up window, ever the reminder of that near fatal night only four weeks ago. Ethan Tucker had ordered some more glass, but it hadn't come in yet. Rachel wasn't sure she wanted to replace the window, anyway. She felt much safer with the boards in place.

Then the questions that plagued her through the night. *Who was that gunman? Is it the missing Tyrone? Is he still watching. . .waiting to find the gold?*

❖

"You look lovely today, Miss Rachel," Mac Dixon said.

Rachel tore her gaze from the quaint white church where Abby, in seeming distress, tripped down the steps. What was wrong with her dearest friend? She had barely spoken to Rachel during the whole picnic. Rachel forced herself to concentrate on the conversation with Mac.

"Thank you, Mr. Dixon," she said with a ready smile. "You're looking well yourself."

Surprisingly, Mac had shaven his dark stubble for the picnic, and a black neck scarf and crisp, white shirt replaced his ever present red scarf and gray work shirt.

"I think this is the best spread of food we've ever had at one of these here picnics." He rubbed his protruding belly with his large hand.

"It was scrumptious," she said while further studying his hands. The shadowed man who had stood at her window seemed to have large hands. Could it have been Mac? Rachel blinked as the first featherlike caution stirred her chest. Was the man Mac or one of her other hired hands? Rachel glanced over the mumbling crowd and tables of fragrant food toward another of her hired hands, David Cosgrove. Was he somehow involved?

Again, Rachel looked at Mac, who eyed the nearest plateful of mincemeat cookies. Then she glanced back to David. As discreetly as possible, she stole a glimpse of her third hired hand attending the picnic, Gunther Peterson. Sitting at one of the many tables created from barrels and wooden slats, he threw his head back and laughed at something the pastor said. His missing teeth seemed to speak of his missing intelligence. Another look at Mac, a quick glimpse to Gunther, one more to David. An uneasy tendril of fear coiled through her stomach.

Travis and Samuel had repeatedly warned Rachel to tread cautiously around her hired hands, and all this time she had heatedly defended them. But that was before the sullen Tyrone lied about where he was the morning of the first fire and before he disappeared. Was he her harasser? Was he the person who had murdered the man who rode onto her ranch claiming to be Travis?

If so, was David or Mac or Gunther his accomplice?

"Have you heard anything more 'bout the cattle thievin' in these parts?" Mac asked.

Rachel, palms moist, smiled stiffly. "No, no I haven't."

"Hard to believe Caleb Singletary might be involved," Mac said absently, his gaze wandering back to the plate of mincemeat cookies.

"I know," Rachel said, wondering if Caleb was capable of such widespread theft.

❖

Travis thoughtfully sipped a cup of apple cider and watched Samuel James exit the white country church. Five minutes ago, Travis had noticed Abby rushing from the church as if she were running from a fire. His gut stirred. What had transpired between the two in the shadowed sanctuary?

Any time Travis had seen Abby and Samuel together, the tension between them was poignant, to say the least. Travis sensed it the first time he met Abby at the general store. Then he had suspected, now he knew, the two of them were in love. Why Samuel James had ever proposed to Rachel was beyond Travis's wildest imagination. They were obviously nothing but friends. Samuel's heart belonged to Abby Bishop and Abby's to him.

Narrowing his eyes, Travis scanned the crowd for Samuel. There he was, talking to Rachel, his head bent toward her in brotherly respect. Travis suppressed the urge to go punch that two-faced Samuel James in the gut and tell him to be decent and honest and tell Rachel the truth.

Then he remembered his own dilemma. Was Travis any more honest than Samuel? Wasn't he engaged to one woman and in love with another? Desperately, he tried to conjure up the image of Kate, but all Travis could see was Rachel. Rachel, her hair afire in the sunset. . .Rachel, her eyes alight with laughter. . .Rachel and her soft lilac scent. His own predicament left such a foul taste in his mouth that Travis gulped the remaining apple cider and turned his back on the crowd. Absently, he walked away from the picnic and toward Dogwood's main street.

"Excuse me," a soft feminine voice said from behind.

Travis turned to see Abby Bishop, smiling timidly. "Yes, Ma'am?" He returned the smile.

"I. . .there's something. . .is there someplace where the two of us might speak in private?" Her voice quivered over every word.

"Yes, of course." Travis hesitated, wondering why Abby would need to talk with him. The two of them barely knew each other. "Would you like to step into the restaurant?" He pointed toward the street corner where a large window spanned the front of a spacious eating establishment. Red-and-white checked tablecloths donned the tables, and bold red letters across the window announced the name: DOTTY'S.

"No," Abby insisted, casting a worried glance over her shoulder. "That's too public." She swept her lashes downward to study her lacy gloves. "I'll step behind the church. You follow in a few minutes."

"All right," Travis said slowly.

Without another word, Abby blended back into the crowd to wind her way toward the church. Travis, his curiosity aflame, nonchalantly set his tin cup on one of the makeshift tables and headed toward the church from the opposite direction. Within three minutes, he faced Abby, who seemed as shy as a hummingbird.

"I. . .I have a request for you," she whispered, then cleared her throat. "The money that everyone thought Caleb Singletary stole?"

"The money he went around and collected for Ethan and Bess Tucker when their livestock was stolen?"

"Yes. Well, um, well, I have it. Here." Her hand shaking, she shoved the bills forward like a school truant caught in a heinous crime. "Would you please give this to Preacher Jones for me? Trudy Singletary, Caleb's daughter, just gave it to me in the church."

"Trudy Singletary?" Travis had never met her but had a vague memory of a sixteen-year-old who looked more like a washed-up rat than a young woman.

"Yes. She says her pa told her to give it to the preacher, and she decided to keep it for herself."

"So Caleb didn't steal it like everybody thought?"

"No."

Slowly, Travis accepted the bills. "I guess that clears him on the money, but Caleb also stole your father's horses and new work wagon, from what I understand."

"Yes, but there was a good reason," Abby blurted as she clamped her hands together.

"There was?"

"Yes. Mr. Campbell, promise me you won't tell where you heard this."

"Well, Abby, I. . ." Uncertainty clouded Travis's thoughts, the kind of uncertainty that makes a man wonder what he has gotten himself into. Of all the men at the picnic, why had Abby chosen Travis as her confidant?

A step forward, and Abby gripped his hand. "Please. I've simply *got* to tell someone, or I'm going to explode."

"Why me?"

"Because nobody will suspect who you heard it from. As far as the community is concerned, you and I barely know each other."

"We do barely know each other."

"I know. And that makes this perfect. I've seen you enough to know you are a man of honor, and I know you won't tell anyone where you got your information, but you will do the right thing with it." She nervously rubbed the sides of her blue taffeta skirt.

"All right," Travis said, hoping he wasn't getting himself into more than he could get out of.

Like a small child, Abby took a gulping breath. "Caleb was renting an old shack and some land from my father. The deal was my father got a cut of Caleb's crop."

Travis nodded, knowing the setup all too well.

"Well, my father cheated Caleb out of so much of his crop that there was no way the Singletarys could make it through the winter. Caleb Singletary took the horses and wagon out of desperation. He was trying to get his hungry family to some relatives in Dallas. It was either that or starve."

"Trudy told you all this?"

"Yes."

"And you believe her?"

"I don't have a reason not to believe her."

"Even though it's against your own father?"

Abby studied the toes of her pointed, black ankle boots. "I know my pa," she uttered.

Travis remembered Rachel's surprise when Joshua Bishop sent a workman to help with the barn.

Apparently Joshua Bishop was not the giving sort. "Who am I supposed to tell?"

"Like I've already said, I want you to give the money to Preacher Jones. Then, tell Constable Parker about the rest."

"Okay." Travis, deep in thought, studied the diamond broach fastened to the neck of Abby's taffeta and satin dress. Had Samuel been in the church during this discussion between Abby and Trudy? Travis had seen him leave the sanctuary shortly after Abby left, but Travis had never seen Trudy enter or exit. Where was Trudy, anyway?

"There's one more thing I need to tell you," Abby continued, her face beginning to relax. "Trudy Singletary helped her pa escape from jail about an hour ago. She took him a pie, and when the constable stepped out, she unlocked the jail cell, and they left through the back doorway."

"What?" Travis's eyes widened.

"Caleb is supposed to be trying to get to his relatives in Dallas on his own, and Trudy and her family are going to follow him next month."

"Why did Trudy tell you all this?"

"I found her crying at the altar. She was worried sick that God was going to strike her dead after her stealing the money and helping her pa escape. Even though he is her pa, he's still a prisoner. She wanted me to give Preacher Jones the money and tell the constable everything. She thought that if Parker knew about what my pa did that he would be kinder to Caleb. But I can't be the one to tell the constable. If my pa found out. . ." Abby trailed off, anxiety filling her pale blue eyes.

"How does Samuel James fit into all this?" The words escaped Travis before he could check them.

Abby's pale cheeks flamed.

"I saw him leaving the church shortly after you left," Travis said.

"Trudy had left before Samuel came in. He doesn't know about what Trudy told me. I. . .I had gone in there for a quiet time of prayer when I discovered Trudy weeping at the altar."

Abby averted her eyes. Travis, ever the gentleman, didn't push for more information about Samuel's intent. The answer was already obvious, too obvious.

"Like I've already said, I would be much obliged if you could please speak to Constable Parker about what I've told you. From what I understand, they are putting off Caleb's trial until they discover whether he's involved in the cattle theft. But even if he isn't, the constable suspects a hard sentence because Caleb stole my pa's horses. And now that Caleb has escaped, it will make him look even worse."

"I'll talk with Parker," Travis said, "but I'm not sure it will do any good."

"Well, all we can do is try."

"Yes, and you've done your part."

❖

Thirty minutes later, Rachel collected her leftover steak and pear pies and placed them into her oversized basket. Discreetly, she watched Abby, who sat beside her mother in their expensive carriage. In a few minutes, Rachel and Samuel would go to McKee's Lookout with the rest of the courting couples. Abby, however, had chosen not to invite anyone to the picnic. Rachel wondered why Abby had not asked Ethan Tucker. The tall, brown-eyed store owner was obviously enamored with her, and many women longed for the adoring smiles he bestowed on Abby during the whole picnic. Rachel tried to remember who Abby had invited to last year's picnic, but she couldn't. So much had happened in the past year that that detail had slipped Rachel's mind.

Abby had barely spoken to Rachel all afternoon, and Rachel repeatedly asked herself what she could have done to offend the best friend she had ever known. Still lacking an answer, she cast one last, longing look to Abby and walked toward Samuel's waiting buggy.

Out of the corner of her eye, she saw Travis exiting the constable's office across the street from the church. Constable Parker, close behind, rushed from the office and toward the crowd surrounding the church. As Travis crossed the street full of wagon ruts, Rachel wondered what business had led Travis to the constable's office and why Parker was in such a panic. Then, Bess Tucker descended on Travis like a lioness after an unsuspecting gazelle. And Rachel dismissed her musings about the constable.

"Well, Mr. Campbell, I must say you're looking like a man who's eaten his fill." Bess's high-pitched voice floated across the few feet separating them.

Gritting her teeth, Rachel resolved not to look toward Travis as he acknowledged Bess, then scanned the picnic crowd. But Rachel's traitorous eyes were drawn to him despite her flimsy resolve. As she had imagined, the plump, red-headed Bess, dressed in glaring green, looped her hand through the crook of Travis's arm.

"You're right. I ate entirely too much." A distracted smile.

Doesn't the man have eyes? Can't he see what Bess is up to?

"Well, now, did you happen to eat any of that buttermilk pie sitting on the very end of the third table?"

Her eyelashes are fluttering enough to fan him!

"Yes, as a matter of fact I did."

A delighted giggle. "That was mine." She placed a proprietal hand on his arm. "I was hopin' you'd like it!"

Rachel narrowed her eyes, gripped the basket, and bit her bottom lip in an attempt to hold her tongue.

"Rachel," Samuel said from nearby.

She turned to see him only inches away; Constable Parker was right behind him. Bess had so distracted Rachel that she had failed to hear their approach. "Are you ready to go?" she asked, purposefully turning from another of Bess's tasteless giggles.

He hesitated. "Would you be disappointed if we didn't go to McKee's Lookout? Something. . ." He broke eye contact. "Something has come up, and I'm not even gonna be able to take you home."

"Oh," Rachel said, not half as disappointed as she sounded. She had consumed too much fried chicken, and the corset she tolerated when she donned her pumpkin-colored gown now ate into her waist like a restricting, iron chain. "I don't mind at all." Besides, her and Samuel's going to McKee's Lookout with the host of "in-love" couples somehow seemed a mockery. But what had suddenly called Samuel away? This was not like him.

"I'll see Miss Rachel home," Travis said from behind her.

Schooling her features into a bland mask, Rachel swallowed against her pulse's sudden jump and forced herself not to cast a triumphant glance toward the stunned Bess Tucker. "That won't be necessary. I'm sure the Bishops wouldn't mind takin' me home."

Samuel quickly looked toward Constable Parker, who had taken Pastor Jones aside for an intense conversation. "Good. Travis can see you home, then," he said absently, ignoring Rachel's words. "Why don't you take my buggy, Travis? Mind if I borrow your horse?"

"No. That's perfectly fine," Travis replied.

Rachel felt like a bag of mute cornmeal being hauled from one destination to another.

"My horse is tied with the rest of the horses." He pointed toward the long hitching post near the white church. "It's the black stallion with the white sock."

"I'll return it later," Samuel muttered, then rushed toward the hitching post.

With a deep breath of the crisp, autumn air, Rachel suppressed the retort ready on her lips. Samuel had a way of treating her like a dense child when he chose, something she was not looking forward to for the next twenty years.

"I wonder what's going on?" Rachel muttered, watching as Parker rounded up several more men.

"I'll tell you on the way home."

"How do you know?"

"Can't answer that question," he clipped. "It's confidential."

"Oh," Rachel said primly.

"But I can tell you that the problem has left Samuel James confused at best."

"What's that supposed to mean?"

"It means, my dear Miss Isaacs," Travis said precisely, his eyes glittering, mocking emeralds, "that Samuel James would never leave me to take you home if he were thinking straight."

Chapter 18

Rachel, staring straight ahead, watched the two white mares pulling Samuel's covered buggy. As the horses *clop-clopped* along the worn, tree-lined road, the setting sun created a maze of mottled shadows on the dusty trail; mottled shadows that seemed to fill Rachel's thoughts. She wondered once again why Travis had made that detestable statement. Rachel had immediately blushed and turned her stiffened back to him. She had not even graced his uncouth remark with a reply. But at the same time, her pulse had not slowed since they left the picnic. Despite her need for propriety, she reacted to Travis on a very deep, very scary level.

"Feels like it's going to be cool again tonight," Travis said practically, as if to dismiss those terrible words hanging between them.

"Yes, and I'm glad," Rachel responded. Perhaps they could simply pretend he had never said those words. "I was tired of all the hot weather."

More awkward silence, and Rachel searched for another topic, anything to ease the tension between them. Then she remembered the mystery surrounding their departure from the picnic. "What was the constable up to when we left?"

Travis briefed her on the whole story.

After he was through, Rachel scrutinized his expression. "So, as a lawyer, do you think Caleb Singletary should go to trial?"

"Well, he has broken the law. Twice, now," Travis said.

"Yeah. But it sounds like he had a good reason. After all, his family was going to starve, thanks to Joshua Bishop."

116

"It might be a reason, but it's not an excuse. He could have gone to Preacher Jones and asked for help."

"Since he's so new to the community, maybe he didn't think he could get much help."

"You've got a point," Travis said. "To tell you the truth, I've run into more situations like this than I would like to admit. A rich man takes advantage of a poor man, then out of desperation, the poor man retaliates. And the poor man is the one who lands in jail. Sometimes, life just isn't fair."

Rachel thought about the death of her pa, about Travis's being involved in the death of his best friend, about Travis being engaged to another when Rachel was in love with him. No, life was not always fair.

On the rest of their silent, homeward journey, Rachel almost wept for Caleb. She so wished she could have somehow assisted him. She so wished he had come to her or another neighbor in the first place. She so hoped he would not have to endure a hard prison sentence. As the declining sun's slender, gold fingers reached across the horizon, Rachel's heart reached out to the man who had been her neighbor.

After twenty minutes of silence, they rounded the last curve in the road, and with that slight change in direction came a full vision of the setting sun and its bejeweled horizon.

"Nice sunset," Travis muttered as her ranch came into view. "It reminds me of that first night I was here."

"A lot has happened since then," she said wearily. The day had been a long one, and her unforgiving corset seemed to grow tighter with each of the horses' rhythmic steps.

"Yes," he said as if he were recalling every moment of his stay.

While a new silence, tense and expectant, stretched between them, Rachel glanced toward Travis's large, capable hands, gripping the reins. Then, of its own volition, her gaze traveled to his face and those green eyes, sometimes gentle, sometimes troubled, sometimes filled with a mysterious pain. Those lips, tilted in a boyish grin that sometimes teased, sometimes grew hard or determined or mocking. That strong, straight, prominent nose that balanced his features and seemed to speak of his strong character. Every fine line etched at the corners of his eyes, his every tone of voice, his every gesture, Rachel knew she would always remember, always cherish.

Yes, much had happened since Travis first arrived. Rachel had gradually depended less and less on Ella, had developed more self-discipline with her emotions, had fallen in love.

She looked toward the sunset, feeling as if that sinking, flaming ball were her heart. In four short weeks, she would marry Samuel and bury her heart in the horizon of a loveless marriage. The sun, Rachel knew, would be back tomorrow, but she didn't think her heart would ever be exhumed.

Oh, how complicated life had grown. The man she truly loved belonged to another woman; a woman who could not live without him.

"We're home," Travis said, bringing the horses to a stop near the barn.

Rachel's long, slow sigh spoke of her physical, emotional, and even spiritual exhaustion.

"You're tired," Travis said, touching her elbow, his considerate voice soft and low. "Stay here, and I'll help you out of the buggy." He rushed to her side, and then he was reaching for her with his hands, his arms, his eyes.

She stood, feeling as if they had been transported to another world, a world without Samuel or Kate or the duties society imposed. His hands were on her waist as he deposited her to the ground. His gaze longingly caressed her eyes, her cheeks, her lips.

Pulse pounding, Rachel held her breath. Twice before she had seen that look in Travis's eyes. Both times, neither she nor he had followed their instincts. This time seemed different. This time, Rachel desperately wished to pretend that Kate could indeed live without him and that Rachel was to marry Travis and not Samuel. She recalled his forbidden comment before they left the picnic. Even then, had he been planning to kiss her?

Sensing that Travis craved any sign of her consent, Rachel swayed toward him. Her eyes fluttered shut, and she prepared herself for the gentle brush of his lips. *Just this once. . .just this tiny kiss. Samuel will never know.*

"Rachel," he breathed, then crushed her to him in an impassioned embrace that culminated in an equally passionate kiss.

As her heart raced, she caught her breath in surprise—surprise at the pressure of his lips, surprise at the strength of his arms, surprise at her own abandoned response. The kiss lengthened, deepened, and some voice of caution told her to run. Her first reluctant efforts to break the embrace only heightened Travis's resolve, which in turn increased her response and her alarm.

Flee! a voice urged.

Balling her fists against his chest, turning her face, she managed the two words her heart resisted. "No, stop!"

"Rachel," he breathed against her ear, then sought her lips once more.

"No, no, let me go," she rasped against his persistent kiss.

She shoved harder, and this time he loosened his hold. When she stumbled away from his arms, she didn't expect to see what clouded his eyes—cold regret.

"Forgive me, Miss Isaacs," he said in his most precise, most proper, East Coast voice. "I thought you wanted me to kiss you."

"I didn't want *that*," she said, a churning, heaving sea of anger boiling through her chest. Anger with him for holding her so closely, anger with herself for enjoying it so much.

"Oh, I see. I guess you're used to Samuel's cold pecks and expected the same from me?" His eyes narrowed in speculation. "Or has he even kissed you?"

The hot, churning sea rushed from her chest to her cheeks. "That's none of your business!"

A step toward her. "You just made it my business."

The frustration of the last weeks culminated in that moment—life's unfairness, the mockery, the love denied— and Rachel felt the overwhelming urge to lash out. Gritting her teeth, she raised her hand, ready to—

His calloused hand grabbed her wrist in midswing, his eyes glittering like hard, icy spikes. "I don't recommend your slapping me again," he growled through his own gritted teeth.

With a determined, painful wrench, Rachel freed her wrist and stumbled backward. "You. . .you overgrown bully!"

"Tell me you didn't enjoy it, Rachel," he muttered, his soft, mocking tone stunning her to silence.

That's when she saw the pain, the disappointment, the regret cloaking his every feature. But not regret that he had held her, but regret that he could not hold her for life.

The only words that would come were the words so trite that Rachel hated voicing them, but she did. "I'm sorry," she whispered, staring toward the glorious sun, now half buried in the horizon.

"Me, too."

❖

Travis watched as Rachel rushed toward the house, her shoulders slumped, her head bent, her hand on her mouth, and he felt like the biggest cad in Texas. He should have never said what he said before leaving the picnic. It was beyond uncalled for. He had desperately wanted to apologize but had not known exactly how to word the apology. Then, when he thought he had figured out exactly what to say, she had been leaning toward him like a spring rose awaiting someone to drink in its heady fragrance. Well, Travis had done much more than that.

Would Rachel ever forgive him? The disgusting part was that Travis was not exactly sure he even wanted forgiveness. He had enjoyed her in his arms more than he ever dreamed he could.

With a grimace, he pulled on the halter of one of the horses and led them toward the barn. Travis knew deep in his heart he would never be able to hold Kate without having Rachel tormenting his thoughts.

Chapter 19

With the midmorning sun spilling a blush across the countryside, Rachel clenched her bouquet of mums as if it were her last breath. The crisp, autumn air lifted the tendrils of hair from her neck while Ella brought their buggy to a standstill outside the church. As planned, Rachel and Abby were to arrive minutes before the wedding ceremony. Even now, Samuel and Preacher Jones probably awaited Rachel's descent down the aisle.

Her wedding. . .the event that most women dream of. But Rachel wasn't sure that her dreams weren't nightmares. Samuel, she was marrying Samuel, not Travis. But wasn't it for the best? Travis was attached to a woman who could not live without him and, as she had told Ella only that morning, Rachel did not want to become an old maid.

Pressing her lips together with new resolve, Rachel tugged the veil over her face, gathered the skirts of her mother's off-white wedding gown, and then she stood up and stepped from the buggy.

"Rachel," Ella said, uncertainty glimmering in her large, dark eyes, "is you sure you're adoin' the right thing?"

"Yes," she said, surprised at her own firm tone. But, regardless of her tone, she could not meet Ella's eyes. The woman who had been like her mother knew much more than Rachel wanted to admit.

"And you're still sure you want me. . .?"

"Yes, you're coming in," Rachel said calmly, tilting her chin in defiance. This time she met Ella's gaze. "You're the closest thing to a mother I've ever had, and I don't care what anybody thinks. I'd rather have you here than the whole town!"

Samuel and she had extended verbal invitations to nearly everyone in the Dogwood area. When word got out that Miss Ella was expected, too, over half the guests had supplied a limp excuse. Like Joshua Bishop, most of them did not think black folks ought to tread in a white folks' church and refused to go where that happened. However, Rachel did not care what they thought. This was her wedding, and Ella was her "mother." By the sight of the numerous buggies, though, Rachel was delighted that many people decided to come anyway.

She glanced around for Abby's exquisite, black carriage, then noticed it approaching from the main street. Abby, her blue eyes avoiding Rachel's, brought the lone horse to a halt, then stepped to the ground.

Ella gasped. "Miss Abby, I ain't never seen you look so lovely."

Rachel, smiling tremulously, nodded her agreement. "I'm glad you chose the green," she said, admiring Miss Timms's masterpiece trimmed in black fringe.

"I decided on it because it seems I always choose blue because of my eyes." And, for the first time in weeks, those incredible, haunted eyes peered at Rachel, and raw, ravaging pain and envy stared from them.

Stopping the reflexive flinch, Rachel started to entreat Abby to please stop this silence, this death of their friendship, and confide her feelings, however negative they might be. But she could not. This was her wedding day, and people were waiting for her, and they expected her to smile, be radiant, be happy. She could not let the problem between her and Abby mar the guests' expectations.

Ella extended a carefully crafted bouquet of mums to Abby.

"I'm agoin' on in, now," she said, turning for the church. Then she turned back to Rachel, her eyes full of tears, and the two, acting from their hearts, embraced. "I can't believe you're all growed up," Miss Ella said, followed with a tender kiss on the cheek.

"I. . .I. . ." Rachel swallowed against her own tears, not feeling grown up at all, feeling like an uncertain child, not the bride-to-be. "Oh, Momma Ella, I'm so nervous."

"You gonna be just fine." With a squeeze of Rachel's tightly clasped hands, Ella abruptly turned and walked toward the church, sniffling all the way.

Is this really what you want to do? an inner voice asked Rachel.

Rachel thought of Travis as she had left him, standing near the new barn, watching her ride away as if he would never again see her. They had barely spoken since that shameful kiss. He had not even wished her well this morning. Instead, he had sat brooding over his breakfast, then worked on the nearly finished barn, his face set in stony, grim lines. With each new board he erected, though, it seemed he demolished Rachel's heart.

It's still not too late to back out, the voice urged.

But the voice was drowned out by the chorus of whispers from the church door as Ella entered. "She's here. . .she's here. . ."

"I guess this is it, Abby," Rachel said brightly as the organist's wedding march filtered from the church.

Abby, nodding curtly, trudged toward the door with Rachel close behind her.

As they entered the church, Rachel gasped at the crowded sanctuary and was so glad that most of her friends had chosen to come. The mousey Trudy Singletary, Caleb's daughter, bestowed a winsome smile upon Rachel. Word had it that Caleb was never found. Samuel seemed to think Parker didn't try terribly hard to hunt him down. Rachel hoped for the sake of the Singletary family that Caleb could somehow be exonerated.

The cattle thieving had seemed to stop, and Rachel had not encountered any more intruders on her property. She was also beginning to doubt she would ever learn the reason for the murder of Hubert Calhoun, the man who had claimed to be Travis. Nonetheless, Rachel was thankful for the peace. Perhaps the Singletary family would likewise experience peace if Caleb were found and forgiven.

As more grinning, excited faces greeted her, Rachel shoved Caleb Singletary from her mind and focused on the moment. Mrs. Hawthorne increased her volume on the organ, and then Abby began her slow descent down the aisle to take her place near Preacher Jones. The whole while, Rachel stared at Samuel, dressed in a stiff black suit, patiently standing at the altar, hands folded in front of him, his eyes fixed on Abby, walking down the aisle. He watched Abby with regret. He watched Abby with uncertainty. He watched Abby with *love.*

And it finally all made sense. Abby's reticence, her pain-filled eyes, her weight loss. Abby and Samuel were in love, but Samuel was marrying Rachel. Rachel's mind replayed several instances over the last few months when she had noticed Abby and Samuel talking politely: at church, in the general store, at the restaurant. Rachel had assumed they were simply friends. Now she saw they were much more than that.

The realization punched her in the stomach like a doubled fist. Her knees weakened, and she collapsed against the closed church door. She swallowed against her stomach's flutters and tried to take a cleansing breath despite her corset's confining choke.

No, no, no. This can't be! I can't do this to Abby, to Samuel, to myself.

Samuel leaned toward Pastor Jones to whisper something in his ear. Rachel stumbled forward, and the church door banged open.

"I can't let you do it, Rachel!" Travis growled from behind.

As one, the crowd gasped. Stunned, Rachel spun to face the granite-eyed Travis.

With one step, he diminished the space between them, picked her up, threw her over his shoulder like a bag of flour, and headed back out the door.

Speechless, furious, Rachel watched the rapidly passing ground. Warm blood drained to her face with every crunch of his boots against the earth. At last, the words came. "Travis Campbell!" she screamed, beating his lower back. "You put me down, you overgrown bully! Do you hear me? Put me down!"

With a disrespectful swoosh, she landed on a pile of hay in the back of the worn work wagon, her bouquet of fresh mums scattering to the ground.

"There. You're down now. Happy?" he challenged as he jumped onto the seat and cracked an impatient whip over the horses.

The wagon's sudden jerk jarred Rachel's teeth and filled her mouth with a handful of sweet hay. Spitting, she struggled to sit up as the hay pricked and poked her neck and face and hands. Her pulse pounding in anger, she gripped the sideboard as they careened up the road.

"Help!" she screamed to the aghast congregation who spilled from the church. "Somebody do somethin'!"

The squeaking wagon rounded a dusty curve, and the congregation disappeared.

Unceremoniously, she ripped the furling veil from her tumbling hair and clawed her way to the seat. "Travis Campbell!" she spat. "I'll never forgive you for this, do you hear me?"

His shaking shoulders spoke of his mirth.

"This is not funny!" The overwhelming fury surfaced in hot, helpless tears. Not caring that her knees showed, Rachel gripped the seat and hoisted herself up next to Travis. "Give me those reins!" She jerked them from his unsuspecting hands with more strength than she ever thought she possessed.

"Oh, no, you don't," he said before she could pull the horses to a stop. With one powerful wrench, the reins were back in Travis's hands.

Blindly flailing her arms, Rachel scrambled to recover the strips of leather as dust from the pounding horses' hooves boiled under their feet.

"You little spitfire." He wrapped his free arm around her shoulders and clamped her to his side.

In immobile rage, Rachel squirmed and panted and cried. "Let go of me! I hate you! I hate you! I hate you!" Finally, one fist broke free, and she impotently beat against his broad chest. The tears turned into a flustered deluge, and she helplessly sobbed against his chest.

Minutes passed before his calloused thumb caressed her cheek.

"Ah, Rachel, don't. . .don't—"

"Stop it!" She shoved his hand aside and scooted to the seat's farthest edge. "And don't you ever touch me again!" Like a child, Rachel scrubbed her cheek, the cheek he had touched, the cheek that betrayed her with its expectant tingles.

She glimpsed a movement from the corner of her eye and turned to see Samuel, leaning from his galloping palomino, riding parallel with Travis. The next second found him jumping toward Travis, who unsuccessfully tried to beat him off. As the two toppled into the bouncing hay, Rachel lunged for the reins that had fallen from the bench.

Her mind spinning, she secured the leather strips in her sweating palms. The men rolling in the wagon's swaying bed caught her off balance, and as if she were in a time-warped nightmare, the reins slipped from her grip to the tips of her fingers. Screaming, she pictured the wagon's crashing demise and grappled with the slithering reins to eventually come out the victor.

Pulling her excited gray mares to a halt, Rachel tugged on the wagon's brake as Travis's accusations rose above Samuel's voice.

"Why haven't you told Rachel, you spineless, weak-kneed—"

"I'll tell her what I want, when I want!"

Rachel, breathing like the winded horses, turned to watch the two fighting men. "Stop it!" she yelled, feeling more and more foolish by the second. "You two just stop it!"

A bloodied nose. A swelling eye. Hay in ears, in shirts. Boots flailing. Another roll, and the buggy shuddered.

The sound of approaching horses, the sight of Abby's carriage, left Rachel sighing. "Do something!" she pleaded toward Pastor Jones, Abby, and Ella. "They're going to kill each other!"

One last punch. One final grunt. And the two big men collapsed against each other in the cloud of hay.

"This is amazing, just amazing," the pale pastor muttered, rushing forward.

"Abby?" Rachel said, gazing uncertainly at her friend, who softly wept as she stepped to the ground.

"In all my born days, I ain't never seen the likes," Ella muttered, hoisting her large frame from the black carriage. "Two churchgoin' men acting like this in broad daylight!"

Rachel awkwardly jumped from the wagon as Travis and Samuel struggled to sit up.

"If you don't tell her right now," Travis growled, apparently more ready to fight than his battered appearance depicted, "I'm going to—"

"Tell me what? That he's in love with Abby?" Rachel blurted compulsively.

A collective gasp.

"How. . .how did you know?" Abby whispered, gripping the wagon's sideboard until her knuckles turned white.

Samuel, his inky eyes full of regret, chagrin, and apology, held Rachel's gaze for several, silent seconds. And with a cool breeze shimmering through the autumn leaves, everyone turned to Rachel.

"I didn't. Not until I walked into the church. Then, I saw. And. . ." Glaring at Travis, she gritted her teeth. "I was about to tell Samuel we shouldn't go through with the wedding when—"

"Samuel had just whispered the same thing to me." Preacher Jones shook his head, and his brown eyes brimmed with laughter. "He said, 'I can't marry her,' and there I was, panicking, wondering how I was going to break it to Miss Rachel and the congregation, when. . .when. . ." He covered his mouth, his eyes pools of bottomless hilarity.

Travis's soft chuckle broke the dam on the pastor's mirth, and the two burst into laughter.

"This is not funny," Rachel said, her fury igniting anew as more tears streamed Abby's face. Ignoring the rest, she rushed to Abby, wrapped her arms around her dearest friend, and wept with her. "I. . .I'm so sorry, Abby. I didn't know. I would have never. . .never. . ." Rachel compulsively turned to Samuel, finding a new target for her anger. "Why did you ever propose to me in the first place?"

"I did it out of. . .out of honor to you and to your pa." Samuel studied the towering trees lining the road. "Also, at the time, I. . .I didn't know of Abby's feelings. I had felt a fondness for her for some time." With a silent plea, he looked at Abby. "But I had no idea she loved me or that my fondness would grow into love." As if they were the only two present, Samuel continued in a soft, intimate voice. "I kept telling myself that Rachel needed me more than Abby. And even though I loved Abby, I couldn't back out on my promise to Rachel. But when it came right down to it, I just couldn't go through with the weddin'." He turned his attention to Rachel. "I'm sorry to have put you through all this—"

The sound of a nearing carriage cut off Samuel's words, and the group turned to acknowledge the approaching people. Rachel, momentarily forgetting her dilemma, stared in instant admiration at a woman of the most enthralling beauty she had ever encountered. And beside her sat a middle-aged black man, proud, erect, distinguished.

"Kate," Travis gasped. "What. . .?"

"Lionel?" Ella whispered.

Chapter 20

The giddy joy that produced Travis's relieved laughter turned into astonishment as he gaped at his fiancée. "What. . .what are you doing here?" he finally sputtered, rushing to her carriage to assist her descent.

"I sent a letter telling you I was coming. Didn't you get it?" Her high-pitched voice, so cultured, so refined, reminded him, had always reminded him, of the voice of an angel. As usual, that voice made him feel as if he must protect her, but Travis couldn't say he had actually missed her.

Rachel's guilty glance told Travis more than he wanted to know. "No, I didn't get the letter," he said evenly as Rachel mouthed, "I'm sorry. I forgot to give it to you." He wondered if Rachel had read this letter as she had read the other one. He would soon find out.

Gritting his teeth, Travis tried to control the irritation, but it would not be controlled. Lately, his life had been full of such annoying surprises. Like the fact that mere weeks ago he had almost lost his head with the feel of Rachel's warm lips against his. Or the fact that every night since that kiss he had dreamed of her. Annoying. Yes, these things were very annoying to an engaged man. Annoying, because he had tasted heaven and knew it would be misery to live without Rachel Isaacs.

And Kate. There stood Kate, secure in his presence, looking as if she expected him to take control of the whole uncomfortable situation and escort her to her visitor's quarters, wherever that might be. A quick glance to the rest of the crowd told him everyone else awaited introductions.

"Excuse me," Travis said with a tight smile. "I've forgotten my manners." He proceeded with the introductions as quickly as polite society allowed.

The latent curiosity lighting Kate's almond-shaped hazel eyes reminded Travis of his disheveled appearance, of his stinging, swelling eye and lips, of the hay prickling his scalp. As he glanced at Rachel's hay-strewn wedding attire, Travis could feel Kate's curiosity growing to tidal wave proportions. How must the situation appear to an outsider?

Samuel, hay in his pockets and his nose swollen, was consoling a sniffling Abby. Pastor Jones, dressed in solemn black, was holding a Bible, his astounded expression that of a man who had just experienced the strangest wedding ceremony of his life. Rachel, whose mussed hair looked like that of an angry eagle's nest, was standing there with her hands on her hips. And Ella, gripping the side of Abby's black carriage, was staring at Mr. Lionel as if she were hallucinating.

Biting his lip, Travis suppressed another round of laughter. The giddiness was back. Never had he felt such relief that accompanied his knowing that Samuel would not be marrying Rachel. The overwhelming impulse to wrap his arms around Rachel, to swirl her in celebration, coursed through him.

Then he remembered Kate, and the impulse faded.

❖

Three hours later, in the summer kitchen, Rachel sat, gritting her teeth, smashing her curled fists into cool, pliable bread dough, turning it over and kneading again. Her initial anger with Travis had tripled since the wedding. Kate Lowell's perfect smile, perfect teeth, perfect complexion had not contributed to decreasing her anger.

"And she's staying *here!*" Rachel muttered to the bread dough as she unmercifully pressed it against the wooden mixing bowl. Rachel had felt that the only civilized thing to do was insist on Kate and Lionel's staying at the ranch. Another punishing blow to the mute dough. "Who cares about being civilized?" she asked, berating herself for falling victim to propriety.

Travis Campbell, the man with whom she wanted to share her life, was out on a picnic with his fiancée, probably planning their wedding, and Rachel was powerless to stop it. If he were the devoted fiancé that he had acted like from the second of Kate's arrival, why had he hauled Rachel away from her wedding? Why had he needed to avoid Rachel the last few weeks? Why had he held her in his arms and kissed her in abandon?

The memory of that scorching moment sent the blood racing to Rachel's face in hot accusation. If Kate only knew. Should Rachel tell her? A twisted smile. Now that would be an interesting way to pay Travis back for humiliating her in front of the whole town.

Squinting her eyes, Rachel peered out the window toward the weeping willow and recalled that abashing moment when Travis had hauled her away from the church as if she were a truant schoolgirl. A new rush of blood heated her cheeks, this time in embarrassment. How would she ever face her friends, or even the whole town? Rachel imagined herself at church next Sunday, the faint whispers, the hidden smirks, the thinly veiled questions. Biting her lip to stop the sudden rush of tears, she pounded the bread dough and wished it were Travis.

Yes, his disgusting deed did deserve vindication. Even though Rachel loved him, that did not give him the right to abuse that love. Perhaps a little chat with Kate would indeed be Rachel's way of getting even.

"Child, I don't know what you aplanning, but it ain't no good, I can tell you that much."

Jumping, Rachel turned from staring out the window to face Ella, standing in the doorway. Lionel was close behind, a radiant glow lighting his sparkling ebony eyes and softly lined face.

"You startled me," Rachel said, laying a sticky hand against her chest.

"And it was probably a good thing I did." Ella looked at Rachel as she had when Rachel was planning childhood mischief.

Rachel diverted her attention back to kneading the bread dough and took in the smells of yeast and flour and the essence of autumn. At times Ella was almost clairvoyant, and Rachel's recent thoughts were something she did not want Ella to know.

"I done finished getting your pa's room ready for Miss Kate," Ella said evenly. "She's a right sweet girl."

"Yes, she is," Rachel replied, meaning every word. That was part of what was so aggravating. Rachel should despise Travis's fiancée. Instead, the brief time she had spent with Kate had proven her a woman to be admired, respected, and loved. "I imagine Kate Lowell seldom makes an enemy."

"I 'magine you're right."

With a smile of chagrin, Rachel glanced back to Ella. No, Rachel wouldn't tell Kate about that kiss, for in paying back Travis, she would hurt one of the sweetest women she had ever met. Miss Kate Lowell did not deserve Rachel's scorn, but Travis was a different story. Never had

Rachel's pride been so bruised, and the man responsible seemed oblivious to her pain. Yes, he must pay for his brusque treatment.

"If it's all the same with you, Mr. Lionel and I are agoin' into town. He needs to return Miss Kate's rented buggy, and I'm agonna follow him in the wagon. We'll return together."

"Go on," Rachel said, thrilling at the silly grin that had claimed Ella's face since the hour of Lionel's arrival. Ella had definitely been keeping secrets from Rachel. "I'll see to supper."

"Thanks," Ella said, her dark eyes twin pools of expectation.

Barely hearing Kate's nervous chatter, Travis stared across the lazy, gray pond by which they had taken their afternoon meal. Before their picnic, he had briefly held Kate, had kissed her soft, rose-scented cheek, had looked deeply into her eyes. She told him she came simply because she missed him. But sadly enough, Travis was in no way moved. Sad, because he felt sorry for Kate. She had lost one fiancé to death. Now, the man responsible for that death was repaying her loyalty with betrayal. The whole thing was not fair.

Despite his heart's desire, though, despite his turbulent longings, he would keep his promise to Kate. Even if Travis couldn't control his wayward heart, he could control his choices. Travis had taken something very precious from Kate, and he was honor bound to repay her. And repay her he would, with a lifetime of devotion.

Once Travis left, once he went back to El Paso, he hoped, he prayed he would forget about Rachel. Perhaps her memory would fade in the face of his new life with Kate. Perhaps Kate would bear him a child. Perhaps Travis would learn to love Kate with the same passion that Rachel had awakened in him. Perhaps. . .perhaps. . .perhaps. How often would he "perhaps" before he realized Rachel would never fade from his memory?

Sighing, he scrutinized the clump of cedars on the opposite bank and felt as if a giant chain encompassed his heart, enslaved his soul to an unforgiving burden.

"You're in love with her, aren't you?" Kate's sudden question exploded into his musings.

Speechless, Travis stared at downcast eyes, creamy cheeks, rosy lips. "What? Who?" he sputtered, not expecting Kate to ever suspect his love for Rachel, and especially not after mere hours in his and Rachel's company. Was he *that* obvious?

"You don't have to pretend, Travis." She looked up from the fried chicken and potato salad and lemonade to peer into his eyes, her own eyes the sad orbs of a lone owl, too wise for comfort. "I saw the way she looked at you. . . us when you introduced her. And. . .and the way you looked at her when she handed you my letter. You were angry and amused and. . .and. . .something else all at once. Then, when we left for the picnic, she watched us drive away."

Kate toyed with the red velvet reticule lying in her lap, her elegant neck and head like the melancholic droop of a weeping lily. She rushed on as if the words, left too long on her tongue, would cause unbearable pain. "I don't think she knew I saw her, but she was crying, and. . .and then there was that. . .that episode that Mr. Lionel and I stumbled onto which you never. . .never explained." Here, Kate halted as if to incite him to please expound on her final subject.

Swallowing against a throat tightening in accusation, Travis had never been so speechless. Silently he resumed his spot on the picnic blanket. Educated in the classics, an expert orator, a student of the law, and he could find no words to deny or acknowledge her claim. Instead, he looked helplessly into her eyes brimming with tears and reached to touch the dark tendril of hair escaping its restraint. How, oh how had life become so complicated?

"You are the most beautiful woman I have ever met, Kate. I—"

"But I'm not Rachel." Pressing the tips of her trembling, gloved fingers against unsteady lips, Kate held his gaze. Her hazel eyes begged him to refute her words.

But he could not. "I'm so sorry," he breathed, taking in the smells of dried grass and earth and Kate's rose perfume. "I didn't mean. . .I didn't intend. . .I never wanted to hurt. I—" A compulsive swallow.

"Were you even going to tell me?" she asked through a haze of tears. "Or were you just going to. . .to pretend and then marry me anyway?"

Blinking, Travis marveled at her perception.

"Why?" she demanded, her fists tightened in angry knots.

"Because. . .I couldn't, I won't abandon you, not after all that's happened."

"What do you mean, 'All that's happened'? What are you talking about?" The questions fell between them like a stifling pall. Questions that Travis didn't want to answer.

As he held her challenging gaze, autumn's cool breeze scampered across the brittle grass to tease Kate's hair and lace collar, then mock him in accusing whispers. God knew Travis didn't want to hurt her any more than he had already hurt her. But Travis sensed that Kate Lowell would expect him to reveal the whole truth.

"You're talking about Zachary. . .about his death, aren't you?"

More silence.

"Why did you propose to me, Travis?"

He gazed toward a lone, gray fish that flipped its tail against the pond's smooth surface. "Kate. . . ," he began, wishing to remove the note of pain in her voice, wishing she would accept his devotion without questions. Another glance her way and Travis knew he must reveal his heart. "I loved. . .love you, but I also felt. . .feel responsible for you because of Zach. . ." A choke, misty eyes, and his mind replayed that horrible morning when he had witnessed his best friend's demise. The pepperbox, that defective little pistol with all its barrels. Travis would have never let Zach shoot it if he had known it was going to backfire and kill him.

"But it wasn't your fault!"

"Yes, it was. . .it was. You, yourself, called me a murderer," he groaned as an agony ripped through his soul, heaving like a storm-tortured ocean. Then came the tears that he had refused to release since Zach's death. Tears that could no longer be imprisoned in his distressed heart.

"But I. . .I. . ." And she was at his side, gripping his arm. "I didn't mean it. You know I didn't mean it. I was overreacting. I. . .that was right after you came and told me that. . .that he was. . .was dead. . .that. . .that you had killed him. I didn't mean it," she said again, her voice cracking on a new sob.

"I didn't want him to die." Wrapping his arms around her, Travis buried his head in the rose-scented locks of her hair, and the barrier around his emotions collapsed, leaving him the shaking victim of overdue grief. "It was that pepperbox. . .that defective pepperbox. It misfired, and the next thing I knew, Zachary was lying in a pool of his own blood."

"I know. . .I know," she whispered, stroking his hair like a mother comforting a child.

After several minutes of uncontrolled grief, Travis released a shuddering sigh and began to gain control of his emotions. He pulled away to grip her upper arms. "There's no way I can ever replace Zach, but at least I can try."

There, he had finally revealed the real reason he had proposed. And in the light of that truth, all glistening and penetrating, Travis also saw that he had never really loved Kate. Oh, he loved her as a brother might love his sister but not as the woman of his heart. That place was reserved for Rachel.

With her face so close to his, with her tearful eyes boring twin points

133

of doubt into his mind, Travis saw for the first time that Kate's feelings for him shrank in the shadow of her feelings for Zachary.

"Why did you agree to marry me?" he blurted, suddenly needing to know her reasons.

"Because. . .because I. . ." Now it was her turn to flounder. "I needed someone so desperately," she rushed, "and. . .and I felt that you needed me, and. . .and I knew that after Zachary, after my love for him, that I would. . .that it wouldn't matter that. . . Then I grew to care so deeply for you, Travis. Don't think that I don't love you, because I do. As I told you in my letter, I have begun to depend on you so much that I have felt that I cannot live without you."

"And I love you, too," he muttered, kissing her forehead.

"But not the same way you love Rachel."

"And not the same way you loved Zach."

"No."

Reflective silence. The kind that reveals a truth, long hidden.

Standing, Travis walked through the scruffy grass and aimlessly kicked a loose rock into the pond's placid face. The silent moment hung about his shoulders. What should they do from here?

"Exactly what *did* happen before my arrival?" she asked from close behind.

A chuckle, soft and low, tumbled from him as he remembered the look on Rachel's face when he deposited her in that wagonful of hay. "I had just kidnapped a bride," he said to the cedars.

"You mean Rachel?"

A sly glance. "Yes. She was about to walk down the aisle, and I—"

"Travis, you didn't! No wonder she kept glaring at you."

Another chuckle, and his soul's confining chains were loosened.

"That's completely unlike you," Kate continued, so like a scolding sister. "What has gotten into you?"

Love. It has made me crazy. Another shrug, more laughter, and Travis was beginning to feel like a carefree schoolboy. Or was this the way he had felt before Zach's death?

It wasn't my fault. Zach's death wasn't my fault. It was that crazy little gun with all its misfiring barrels. The gun. . .the gun was defective. The thoughts whirled through his head like the refreshing winds of spring, ushering in new life, a new life for Travis. For the first time since that fateful night, Travis could face himself in the mirror without the accusing nausea. Travis knew the nightmares would no longer be his bedfellow. They were gone, and the overwhelming guilt was gone.

Thank You, Lord, for showing me the truth.

"Travis. . .Travis!" Kate's urgent voice broke through his reverie. "Look at this strange gold piece I just stepped on. It looks like some of the gold pieces Father has collected. And look! There's another one."

Chapter 21

Gritting her teeth, Rachel ferociously swept the front porch, her faded blue skirt rustling with each stroke. The bread was made. The linens were washed. The wedding dress was put away. The chickens were fed. And now Rachel attacked the porch, glad for yet another chore to expend her mounting emotions.

She hoped, oh, how she hoped, Miss Kate Lowell would convince Travis to return to El Paso with her. Rachel didn't think she could bear his presence until spring.

With Ella gone, the house seemed so terribly lonely. Would Lionel take Ella away as Kate would take away Travis? Wanting to run from the aching loneliness, Rachel turned for the parlor but stopped herself.

Only minutes ago, she had almost felt Pa's presence in that room. How she still missed him, especially today, when she felt so far away from the little girl he had known. Somehow that girl had vanished, and there was no way to retrieve her. What would Pa think of Rachel now? What would he say? Probably something like, "My girl is all grown up."

How she wished he were not dead. *Maybe he isn't. Maybe this is all a nightmare that will end, and. . .*

A horse's lone canter penetrated her turbulent thoughts and found her squinting against the autumn sun. A pine-laden breeze, so characteristic of October, lifted the wisps of hair from Rachel's neck and promised yet cooler days ahead. Propping the broom against the porch railing, Rachel watched as Constable Parker rode his dappled gray gelding into the yard.

"Miss Rachel," he said, tilting his straw hat.

"Won't you come in?"

"Can't. Old man Linkenhoker's done lost a hundred head of cattle. I'm headin' out that way to check things out."

"So the thieves are still at it. It's been so long since anyone lost cattle, I was hopin' the thieves were through. Do you think it's the same person who stole my cattle?"

"Don't know, but it sure seems that way." Thoughtfully, he rubbed his whiskers.

"Have you heard anything more about the whereabouts of Caleb Singletary?"

"Uh, not lately." Parker averted his eyes.

"I understand his family left for Dallas last week?"

"Did they?"

Silence, a silence that found Rachel relieved for the poor farmer. It looked as if Constable Parker, the man who had built an iron reputation with outlaws, was also a man with a big heart. He had obviously allowed Caleb enough room to escape.

"I came to tell you I found your hired hand, Tyrone Burks."

"Really?"

"Yep. Seems he's been on a drinking spree. His wife got tired of waiting for him to come home and found him 'bout thirty miles north of here."

"I had no idea he was a drinkin' man. He always took care of his chores here. Maybe that explains his moodiness. You never could tell with Tyrone whether you would get snapped at or smiled at."

"According to his wife, he's got a real problem with whiskey. Or should I say, whiskey's got him."

"He must be in bad shape to just go off and disappear like that. I was beginning to think maybe he was the cattle thief or maybe the one who visited me that night." The thought of that dark, sinister form, outlined by sporadic lightning, sent a foreboding shiver through Rachel's very soul.

"I'm glad you're finally seeing some light concerning your hired hands, Miss Rachel," Parker said, his restless gelding prancing beneath him. "I don't have nothing against neither a one of your men, but you just can't be too careful."

Rachel nudged a clump of damp earth with the toe of her work boot. "I know," she muttered, hating to admit that her earlier support of her employees might have been wrong. But, they had each shown up for work as usual the last few weeks. Each had done his job and done it thoroughly.

And there had been no more digging, no more threats, no more mention of gold, no more cattle rustling. . .until now.

❖

Ella, her spine erect, sat next to Lionel as the two gray mares pulled the wagon with a steady *clop, clop, clop* of their hooves against the damp earth. The cleansing autumn rains of late seemed to have penetrated Ella's heart to wash away all the pains of years past and fill it with new hope, the same hope that was reflected in Lionel's eyes, in his smile.

"Lovely day," he muttered.

"Yes, it is," she returned, reveling in the feel of his arm brushing hers. "Nice day for fishing."

They continued in the elusive, small talk that had plagued them since the moment Ella had recovered from the shock of seeing him. His smile, the light in his eyes spoke so much. There was so much Ella wanted to say and ask, but she didn't quite know how to form the words.

"There's lots of nice fishing holes in El Paso," he said casually.

"Are there?"

"Yes. And the fish are just waiting for somebody like you to catch them."

Hot blood rushed to Ella's face. What was he trying to say? After all these years. . . Could it be? No, it couldn't. He wouldn't, not so soon after arriving. She averted her face, refusing to allow him to see her trembling lips.

Only after Lionel's calloused finger stroked her cheek and an explosion of delicious tingles raced down her neck, did Ella realize they had stopped beneath a towering oak, waiting to shed its golden leaves.

"Oh, Ella," he breathed, his bass voice raspy, "I was going to wait awhile, but I can't."

Gripping her fingers until they ached, Ella kept her gaze firmly attached to a red bird, frolicking in a nearby mud puddle. "Whatever are you agettin' at, Lionel?" She dared not look at him, dared not say more. What if she misread his intentions and embarrassed herself? What if he had come to Dogwood only to escort Miss Kate? But then there was that light in his eyes.

Another stroke of her cheek. More tingles and more emotions that had been buried beneath years of pain, of longing, of waiting. Placing his hands on her cheeks, he gently turned her face to his.

"I think you know what I mean." His rich, mellow banter was that of a man sure of his own feelings.

"But. . .but it's abeen so long, and. . .and. . ." She thought of the girl she once was, of the buxom woman she had become. "And I ain't the same. . ." She thought of how educated he sounded, of how distinguished he had grown, of the marked differences that said he deserved a finer woman than she. "And you ain't the same."

His chocolate brown eyes clouded with disappointment. "Are you saying you no longer feel anything for me?"

Ella averted her gaze back to the red bird. The old pride. She had almost forgotten what a proud man Lionel was. All she had to do was act politely cool, and he would never mention the subject again.

New doubt suffocated the elation she had felt since his arrival. Was he really in love with her, or was it the young woman she had been? In all these years, he had never written, never pursued their relationship. He had simply accepted her decision to free him. If his love had been true, would he have let her go? Or was that also due to his pride?

Plagued by questions, Ella, who had lived a lifetime of agony, suddenly wanted to protect herself against new heartache.

"I see," he muttered slowly, sadly. A derisive chuckle. "I guess I have just made a fool of myself." With a "tch-tch" he snapped the horses' reins, and the wagon lurched forward.

"No, stop!" Ella blurted, unable to bear the sorrow in his voice. Her heart pounding like a captured sparrow, she instinctively grabbed his hands and turned a beseeching gaze to eyes full of pain. "I *do* care. I cares a great deal. But—"

"But you don't want to marry me," he said flatly, his hands never leaving the reins. His eyes, now masked in coldness, seemed to peer through her.

Swallowing, she gulped for air, amazed that she had not noticed the deep lines around his mouth before now. A mouth, which had been tilted in an expectant smile. Then she also saw the lines between his brows, on his forehead, near his eyes. Lonely lines that spoke of sorrow. Was she responsible for part of that sorrow?

"I should have never agreed to escort Miss Kate. I thought—"

"I still love you," Ella heard herself whisper. "I. . .I never stopped. Over all them years, I never stopped."

A faint flicker of surprise cracked his eyes' cold mask. And Ella held her breath as his gaze slowly caressed her every feature.

"What are you trying to say?" he asked.

"I. . .I guess I'm atryin' to say that if. . ." A swallow. "If you was to ask me to. . .to marry you, I'd have to say, 'yes.' "

"Well, Ella Isaacs, I think *you* just proposed to *me*."

His indulgent grin left Ella spinning in a whirl of chagrin.

She had proposed, although indirectly. What must he think of her?

As if in answer to her silent question, Lionel wrapped his arms around her and pulled her against the musty warmth of his leather jacket. "Ah, Ella," he breathed, "all these years I've prayed to hear you say you still love me."

❖

Rachel opened her swollen eyes to the sound of someone moving about in the next room, her pa's room. Was it Pa? Was he back? Slightly disoriented, she stared at the afternoon shadows, shifting across her bedroom's wall. Exhausted, she had lain down for an afternoon nap. Silently, Rachel swung her legs to the floor and sat up.

No, the person in the next room was not her pa. Like her mother, he had gone to be with the Lord, and he was not coming back. For the first time since his unexpected death, Rachel felt an unexplainable calm seeping into her soul.

Then the day's events all tumbled in upon her, and Rachel's musings about her father were ended. When Lionel and Ella returned from their trip to return Kate's rented buggy, Ella had gently explained to Rachel the twenty-year-old story of her relationship with Lionel. Then, she announced she would be at long last marrying Lionel, and the two planned to go back to Lionel's home in El Paso as soon as possible. "But I ain't about to leave you here alone, Child," Ella had assured. "Mr. Lionel say you can come with us, and if that don't agree with you, we'll stay here awhile."

That was the reason Rachel's eyes were swollen. She had been crying, selfishly crying because her Momma Ella wouldn't be here much longer. But Rachel would never let on to Ella, even though she dreaded the thought of letting Ella traipse across Texas. She might never again see the woman she had called "mother." Their only communication would be through letters. Could Rachel live with that separation? But Rachel had no desires to move to El Paso, for Travis and his wife, Kate, would be there. On the other hand, how could she not allow Ella the freedom to pursue her own life? The dear woman had poured out herself for Rachel. The least Rachel could do was give her the freedom to follow her heart.

So Rachel had cried. Like a small child, she scrubbed at her eyes, wishing she could scrub away her turbulent emotions. Another bump from the next room switched her attention back to the present.

Standing, Rachel squared her shoulders and prepared to face Travis's fiancée, face her and offer friendship. The poor woman obviously had no idea what a two-faced man she was marrying. Despite her earlier musings, Rachel would never be able to enlighten Kate to Travis's true feelings.

Putting aside her aching pride, Rachel adjusted her braid, rubbed her eyes a last time, and walked toward her pa's room. But just as she entered the hallway, so did Travis, carrying Miss Kate's trunk. Rachel stopped. Speechlessly, she stared at the man who had humiliated her in front of the whole town.

"Good afternoon." With a hesitant smile, he deposited the trunk on the floor between them.

"Good afternoon."

"I was just retrieving Kate's things. She seems to think it would be better for her to spend the night at the hotel in Dogwood and catch the morning train for home. She's waiting for me now in the buggy."

"Oh?"

"Yes."

Rachel refused to ask the question about to leap from her lips: *Why is Kate leaving so soon?*

"I think it's only fair to tell you that Kate and I found some gold coins near the big boulder by the pond. Someone had managed to overturn the rock and dig underneath it. There was a square, boxlike imprint in the dirt beneath it." Awkwardly, Travis removed half a dozen coins from his britches pocket and extended them to Rachel. "The coins are U.S. gold, dating from 1859. Kate says her father has some pieces just like these."

As she took the cool gold pieces, Rachel relived the night the man had threatened to kill her if she didn't tell him what "hard spot" meant. "Hard spot," she muttered.

"What?"

"The man who was here the night of the storm wanted to know what 'hard spot' meant. Remember, I told you he said he had dug up a map and that was all it said."

Travis nodded.

"Well, 'hard spot' must have been a reference to the boulder."

"Must have."

"Now that they've gotten what they were after, maybe they'll leave me alone."

"Don't you want to know who took the gold?"

"Yes, I'd like to know, but I like my peace better." Rachel handed the coins back to him.

"Well, I'm going to take these coins by to Parker as soon as I see

Kate settled. Maybe they'll help him trace the thieves. The person who took the gold is probably a lot closer than you want to believe."

Rachel didn't respond. She didn't want to admit that Travis might have been right in suspecting her hired hands. Parker had already cleared Tyrone Burks because of his drinking. But that still left David Cosgrove, Mac Dixon, and Gunther Peterson. Had one of them betrayed her? Were they also involved in her barn's burning and the cattle thefts that plagued the community? Rachel had the haunting feeling that she would soon learn the truth, whether she wanted to or not. If one of her hired hands had taken the gold, he would have no need of money and no need to work tomorrow. Tomorrow would tell.

Feeling Travis's gaze, Rachel appraised the tips of her work shoes peeking from beneath her worn everyday dress. Why didn't he just take the trunk and go? Perhaps with Miss Kate returning home, Travis would likewise consider leaving for good. Part of Rachel embraced the idea, but another part wanted to weep all over again.

"You might be interested in knowing that Kate and I won't be getting married after all."

Rachel quickly looked into his smiling, emerald eyes. "Really?"

"Yes. We. . .um. . .had a long talk. Neither of us believes it's the right thing to do. It wouldn't be fair to—" Cutting himself off, Travis averted his gaze. "To either of us," he finished. "That's why she is going home. She feels it's for the best."

"And how do you feel?"

"Me?" He rounded the trunk, his gaze never leaving her. "I think you know how I feel, Rachel."

Not expecting this turn of events, Rachel stumbled away from his approach. "Whatever do you mean?"

"I mean that if it's obvious to Kate, then it's got to be obvious to you." He steadily approached her.

"What? What's so obvious?" She bumped into the wall at the end of the hall.

"Need you ask? After the way I kidnapped you from your own wedding?" His lips twisted derisively.

The fury of the morning assaulted her once more. Who did Travis Campbell think he was? He acted as if he could march into her life and take over like some trail boss and expect Rachel to bow to his every whim. "I have never been so humiliated in my life, if that's what you mean."

"Neither have I. I have never acted like that, Rachel. Back home, I'm known as a gentleman." His steady approach diminished the distance between them to mere inches.

Rachel pressed herself against the wall. "They must not know how good you are at tying defenseless women up in barns. . .or. . .or taking advantage of engaged women after picnics when. . ." Rachel trailed off as his gaze descended to her lips and she relived the moment he had kissed her soundly. If the truth were known, Travis had not really taken advantage of her because Rachel had shamefully fallen in his arms. She wouldn't dare admit that to him now.

"You have a way of making me lose my head, Rachel." He reached to caress the tendril of hair escaping her braid.

"Don't touch me," she rasped, her voice sounding more like a plea than a command, but all the while her traitorous heart longed for his embrace.

His eyes clouded.

"If you think I'm going to. . .to let you. . .with Miss Kate Lowell waiting on you outside, then you're crazy."

Travis chuckled. "I guess you befuddled me again. You're absolutely right. My duty lies with Kate for the present. I'll save my proposal for later."

"You can keep your proposal," she ground out. "I wouldn't marry you if you were the last man in Cherokee County. How could you be so arrogant? After what you did this morning, I'll never forgive you."

Travis flinched. "You can't mean that."

"I *do* mean it." But something inside Rachel recoiled at her own words. Words that settled between them like a gaping chasm and left her feeling empty, desolate, alone.

His lips twisted bitterly. "Then please excuse my assuming that your feelings were the same as mine."

"*My* feelings? Since when do you care about *my* feelings?" she accused, sounding far more sure than her trembling heart felt. Should Rachel retract her hasty refusal? Should she readily forgive Travis's rash behavior and embrace life with the man she truly loved?

He clamped his teeth; his nostrils flared; his eyes narrowed. "There are some days, Miss Rachel Isaacs, when you make me very angry."

"And I guess you presume you have *never* made me angry?"

"I'll be back. We aren't through with this conversation."

"We very well are." She raised her chin in defiance.

Travis's challenging gaze descended to her mouth, and Rachel feared he would take her in his arms whether she agreed or not. A bittersweet longing writhed in her midsection.

A light tap on the front door preceded Kate's timid call. "Travis?"

A frustrated growl, and he glanced over his shoulder. "Yes, coming." Then he turned, picked up the trunk, and stomped down the hallway.

As his boots scuffed across the porch, Rachel felt she would explode. Travis Campbell was *the* most infuriating, presumptuous, high-handed man she had ever met. She would be glad to see him out of her life!

Chapter 22

S omething was wrong, terribly wrong. Travis had been gone almost two hours. Plenty of time for him to settle Kate at a hotel, talk to Constable Parker about the gold, and return home. Rachel paced the front porch, looked toward the dusty road, basking in the golden beams of the setting sun. Within an hour, darkness would wrap its ebony arms around the countryside. Would Travis make it home before nightfall?

"Miss Rachel," Ella called from the doorway. "Do come in and eat. I's got cold ham and cheese and bread." Ella and Rachel had agreed on a quick, light supper because of the day's hectic events.

Lionel, walking onto the porch, offered his assistance for the third time. "Rachel, if it would be any comfort to you, I would be glad to go and see if I can find Travis." Three times Rachel had refused his offer. This time, she hesitated over it.

"Let's just all of us go." Ella nervously eyed the road.

Rachel, glancing toward Ella, nodded her approval. "I think that would be for the best." What would she ever do if something awful had befallen Travis? Rachel's last words to him had been unkind. She had told him she would never forgive him for humiliating her. Now Rachel wondered if she could forgive herself. For the first time since her pa's death, Rachel prayed earnestly. All the while Lionel harnessed the horses to the work wagon. All the while Ella chattered about her and Lionel's plans to marry and move back to El Paso. All the while they began their journey toward town, Rachel prayed.

Dear Lord, I've really been hard to get along with lately. I know that. I'm sorry. I'm sorry for being mad at You for lettin' Pa die. You must have known what was best for me. . .and for Pa. He's with Momma now. I'm not goin' to pretend like I understand it all. I know there's no sense in that. But if You could please forgive me for being so mad and help me to do better, I'd be awfully grateful. And Lord, I. . .I don't know what's become of Travis. But please let him be safe. Oh, Lord, if there's any way You could just let him be alive, I would be sure to treat him with the respect I know he deserves and to tell him how I really feel and to. . .

"Oh, no," Lionel groaned fifteen minutes into the trek toward town. "It's what I feared the most."

As the wagon halted, Rachel was snatched from her prayerful reverie and plopped back into reality. Ella's gasp preceded Rachel's by only a heartbeat.

Travis was sprawled on the pallet of auburn leaves blanketing the roadside. He was face down, arms askew, a patch of oozing blood marring his left shoulder.

The horses had pulled the buggy Travis had been driving under a nearby clump of trees. Ears pricked, the gray mares watched Mr. Lionel and Ella rush toward Travis.

And Rachel, sickened by her own actions, by her own selfishness, vomited. Clutching the wagon's side, trembling against another heave, she remembered a similar scene mere months ago. Hubert Calhoun, claiming to be Travis, had come onto Rachel's property and begun the mysterious digging. Soon, he had been murdered. Today, Travis and Kate had discovered more digging and then the coins. Had the person responsible for killing Travis been the one who killed Hubert Calhoun and eventually dug up the gold? Why would that evil person kill an innocent man?

As Lionel gingerly turned Travis's limp form onto his back, Rachel's heaving subsided. She grimaced against the burning bitterness on her tongue. That bitterness seemed the gall from her very soul. How could she have treated Travis so despicably?

He had all but confessed his love, something Rachel had dreamed of, and she had allowed her wretched pride to interfere. Could God ever forgive her?

"He ain't dead!" Ella shouted. "He ain't dead, Rachel."

A groan, low and pain filled, escaped Travis's lips.

Rachel, her heart leaping, scrambled from the buggy and raced toward the man of her heart. With a sob, she collapsed onto the carpet of leaves, clutched the front of his pullover shirt, and buried her head against his chest. "Oh, Travis. . .Travis. . .I. . .I'm so sorry. If there's any way you can ever forgive me. . . Please, please, please don't die. Please. . . I love you! I *do* want to marry you. I *will* marry you. Tomorrow. . .today. . .whenever. Just don't die." More sobs and enough tears to drench the skies in grief.

"Rachel?" Travis said groggily.

"Miss Rachel, you need to give the poor man some room to breathe," Lionel gently chided.

"Here, Child, here," Ella crooned. "Mr. Travis, he gonna be just fine. Just fine." She pulled Rachel into her arms. "We're agonna get him to that doctor, and he's agonna fix Mr. Travis up, right and good."

Barely hearing Ella's words, Rachel clung to the woman who had been her mother. "Oh, Momma Ella, I'll never forgive myself if he dies. You just don't know what I've done."

"Mr. Travis. . .he ain't gonna die, now. The Lawd, He gonna take care of him."

"I'm going to need help getting him into the back of the buggy," Lionel said. "This young'un has been bigger than me since he was a strapping teenager."

"I'll help; 'course I'll help," Ella said.

Travis released an agonized moan.

"We should put him in the work wagon instead of the buggy. There's hay in the back." Rachel sniffled. "It'll be more comfortable on him. He can put his head on my lap."

"That's right good thinkin'." Ella patted Rachel's back.

Within minutes, the three had managed to maneuver Travis into the hay-lined wagon. Surprisingly, Travis had regained consciousness enough to hobble a bit, then collapsed against the hay. While Lionel drove the work wagon and Ella drove Travis's buggy, Rachel lovingly cradled his head in her lap and gently stroked his forehead and temples. Once, during the brief, bumpy drive into town, Travis opened his groggy eyes and produced a half-smile in her general direction. Rachel choked against another sob.

Mere minutes seemed to stretch into hours, but eventually they entered the streets of Dogwood and left the horses outside Dr. Engle's small brick home that doubled as his office. Then, the bustle of activity—moving the moaning Travis onto a narrow bed in the office, Dr. Engle's concern, Ella's consoling assurance, Lionel's brief snatches of prayer, and Travis's groaning.

"He's taken a bullet wound to the shoulder," Dr. Engle muttered after cutting away Travis's tan shirt. "Lucky for him, it passed right through, but I believe he's lost plenty of blood. I think whoever was aiming meant it for his heart."

"Joshua Bishop," Travis croaked through dry lips.

Dr. Engle's snapping blue eyes widened. "What's that you say, Son? Joshua Bishop's the one who shot you?"

A weak nod. "He told me. . .He held me at gunpoint and told me. . . Wants Rachel's land. Wants to expand cattle thieving business. Burned her barns." A dry cough. "Stole her cattle. . .all the cattle in Cher. . .Cherokee County. Wanted to buy Rachel's land after. . ." A moan. "After she married Samuel. But no wedding, so. . .so Joshua. . .Joshua. . ." Another cough. "Kill me. Then, R. . .Rachel would have to sell." As if relating this story cost him his last ounce of energy, Travis slipped back into unconsciousness.

The nausea crept up Rachel's throat once more. She swallowed. Joshua Bishop, the father of her very best friend. He was the one who had burned Rachel's barns? *He* was the one who had stolen the cattle across Cherokee County? *He* was the one who had shot Travis? Had *he* also been the one digging for the gold?

"Miss Rachel," Dr. Engle clipped, turning to face her, "go get Constable Parker and tell him to come *now*. Miss Ella, I'm going to need your help." He turned to Lionel. "And maybe yours, too. And, Miss Rachel. . . ," a surreptitious glance passed between the doctor and Ella, "after you leave the constable's, go get Magnolia, my nurse, then go to the general store and get some coffee."

"But it's almost dark. Are they opened?"

"Yes. Ethan Tucker opens at dawn and closes after dark. Tell him to charge the coffee to me. I'm all out, and we're going to be needing some."

"But. . ." Rachel had no desire to leave Travis's side. She still clung to his hand as if it were her last contact with sanity.

"Now, don't you go arguing with the doctor, Rachel," Ella scolded. "You go and do what he need you to be a doin'."

Rachel knew all too well what Dr. Engle was up to. He wanted her out of the way. He did not trust her not to become hysterical if. . . If what? If Travis cried out or writhed in pain? If Lionel had to hold him down while the doctor sewed him up? Or worse, if he died? "I'm not leavin'." Rachel pressed her lips together and raised her chin. It was time Dr. Engle saw she was all grown up and did *not* need to be protected against the realities of life.

148

"*Somebody's* got to get Parker," the doctor snapped. With a gleam in his eyes, he looked up from the bandage and antiseptic he was preparing for Travis's shoulder.

She opened her mouth to tell him Lionel could go.

"*Now!*" Dr. Engle demanded.

Rachel jumped. "All right, then," she muttered. Feeling as if she were betraying Travis, Rachel reluctantly released his cold, calloused hand and scurried from the office. Within minutes, she had alerted Parker, who rushed toward the doctor's office. With the sun taking a final peek of the rutted, dusty streets, she traipsed toward the general store and prayed all the way. Prayed that Parker would catch Joshua Bishop. Prayed that she would not harbor hatred toward Joshua. Prayed that Travis would recover completely.

Impatiently, Rachel entered the general store and was immediately assaulted by the familiar smells of licorice and coffee and new fabric. With the tap, tapping of her work shoes against the wooden floors, Rachel approached the counter, peering around the store for some sign of Ethan Tucker or his sister Bess. But the store seemed empty. Quickly, she rounded the counter, calling an impatient, "Hello."

Still no answer.

This had happened to Rachel on more than one occasion. Often, Bess sat in the office lost in one of her dime novels and didn't bother to acknowledge a customer until the customer made enough noise to alert the plump redhead. Today, Rachel didn't have the time or patience to go through the usual steps of that game. Not considering propriety for one second, she swept aside the blue floral curtain that substituted for the office door.

But Rachel didn't find Bess. Instead, she found a revolver aimed right at her nose. And on the other end of the revolver, her hired hand, Mac Dixon. As usual, he needed a shave, a haircut, and a bath. But his normally smiling brown eyes now glared at Rachel in sinister appraisal. "Fancy meeting you here, Miss Rachel," he sneered.

Her heart leaping into her throat, Rachel glanced around the austere room. Behind a worn oak desk, Ethan Tucker sat in front of a wall-to-wall bookcase. In the center of the desk was a mound of gold coins. "Bess was supposed to be watching the front," Ethan clipped. "I told her not to leave and not to come back here. Isn't she out there?"

"N–No," Rachel rasped. "But I could go find her—"

"Don't even think about it," Mac growled. "It's too late. You done seen our little find."

"You. . .you were the person who came to my window that night," Rachel whispered on trembling tongue.

"Yes."

"How could you? I trusted you, just as much as I trusted my other employees. I even defended you to Travis when he—"

"I know it. And Ethan and me, we're particularly grateful." Mac produced a mocking bow. "I was hopin' your other hand's innocent look was rubbing off on me."

Her heart pounded out hard, even beats. Rachel's panicked mind raced for a means of escape.

"We were just about to split the gold," Ethan said, his voice not as sinister as Mac's. The tall, auburn-haired store owner had never treated Rachel with anything but respect. Furthermore, he was greatly revered across the countryside. How could he stoop to being an outlaw?

"If you'll let me go safely, Ethan, I won't mention a word of this to anyone," she pleaded.

Ethan, his uncertain eyes shifting to the older Mac, seemed to weigh Rachel's request.

"Now, Miss Rachel," Mac drawled, "you and me's been knowin' each other for many a long year. I know you well enough to know you'll be down there fillin' Parker's ears full the minute we leave town. The two of us, me and Ethan here, we've done too much outside the law to expect you to go and stay quiet."

"You're the one who killed Hubert Calhoun," Rachel muttered, starting to piece together the whole story.

"Had to," Mac replied, lowering the revolver a bit.

"I didn't have anything to do with that," Ethan claimed. "I never wanted any part of murder."

"Well, I couldn't let Hubert double-cross us, could I?" Mac challenged, daring Ethan to speak.

Ethan silenced.

And Mac turned his scheming eyes back to Rachel. "The plan was, you see, that I was gonna get Hubert hired on your place, and the two of us could work together on the inside with Ethan on the outside. Instead, Hubert accidentally stumbled onto Travis Campbell camping out and decided to sneak on the property, pretendin' to be him. I guess Hubert thought he could dig up the map and find the gold in one night, then be gone by the time the real Travis was able to escape." Mac crudely scratched his belly protruding against his gray work shirt. "After we seen what Hubert was up to, Ethan, here, found Travis and cut them ropes so he could go free."

All the while, Rachel developed more and more confidence in Ethan's honesty. The longer she observed the two of them, the more she saw that Mac was the one in charge. Ethan was not nearly so committed to the crime as Mac seemed. Perhaps Ethan had been sucked into a situation he really wanted out of.

"How did you know there was gold in the first place?" Rachel queried, still desperately seeking a means of escape.

"Our fathers," Ethan calmly supplied. "The three of them robbed a Confederate stagecoach right at the end of the Civil War. Then my father and Mac's father buried the gold on what's now your property." He absently fingered one of the coins.

"They also buried a map," Mac growled, "right behind where your barn is."

"But all it said was 'hard spot,' " Rachel mused.

"You have a good memory, Miss Rachel," Mac mocked, cocking the menacing revolver.

Her throat tightened. Travis lay in Dr. Engle's office with a bullet wound. Would she soon join him? She desperately searched for anything to keep Mac diverted from thoughts of killing her.

"Is Joshua Bishop involved in this, too?"

"What?" he replied, genuinely confused. "I don't know nothing about Joshua Bishop's doin's. And he sure ain't no concern of mine."

Rachel was astonished. She had been the victim of two separate ploys.

"Why. . .why haven't you tried to find the gold before now? If it's been there all these years?" she asked, still stalling.

Standing, Ethan rounded the desk to stop near Mac. "We didn't know about it until Hubert Calhoun came to town with the story." Stealthily, he eyed the revolver.

Rachel's hopes soared. Perhaps Ethan would protect her.

"Like Ethan done told you," Mac said, "our three fathers robbed a stagecoach together. Ethan, here, was just a baby at the time. Anyway, my pa and Ethan's pa was the ones who buried it and then buried a map between two weepin' willow trees. Then they up and killed each other over that gold before tellin' Hubert's pa where they'd buried it. All he knew was the map was buried out in the country between two weeping willows. The whole thing must've upset Hubert's pa real bad 'cause after his partners killed each other, he decided to live like a honest man. Hubert said he found religion and moved his family out west, far away from the place where he was a thief."

"I thought you found religion, too," Rachel said. "You're a new deacon and—"

Mac laughed bitterly. "God ain't never done nothin' for me. Why would I go and stick by Him when somethin' like this comes along?"

Ethan silently inched his way toward Mac, and Rachel tensed all the more. What was Ethan planning?

"Hubert Calhoun's father was stupid to leave that gold sittin' on your property all them years," Mac growled. "Hubert says his pa told him the whole story right 'fore he died. Seems that old man wanted Hubert to try to find the gold and give it to the government. But Hubert had other plans. He came to Dogwood and found me and Ethan. He told us all he knew about the gold's whereabouts and the map leadin' to it. I knew enough about your place, Miss Rachel, to see right quick like that it was somewheres on your property. Hubert promised me and Ethan we'd split that gold three ways. Then, he got greedy. He shouldn't have done that."

Rachel nervously chewed her lip as Mac's sinister appraisal lengthened. "Now we've got to decide what to do with you. What do you think, Ethan?"

Ethan stood nearby, and Rachel prayed he would do something to stop Mac's devious schemes. *And Lord,* she continued praying, *please don't let him kill me. I want to live to marry Travis and have a family and—*

"I don't want to go and kill you, Miss Rachel," Mac said, shaking his head with regret, "but I really don't see no other way. If I'm gonna live the life I want to live, I can't have nobody knowing what I've done."

"What's going on here?" Bess asked from the doorway.

Mac cast a quick glance toward Ethan's sister, and that was the second of diversion that Ethan needed. Rachel never remembered seeing anyone move so swiftly. He whipped a book from behind his back and slammed it against Mac's gun hand. The cocked revolver flew toward the bookcase, discharging a bullet into the books with a resounding bang.

"Why you double-crossin'—" Mac returned Ethan's attack with a blow of his own, and the two crashed onto the desk to send glittering gold coins scattering across the room.

Rachel, feeling as if she had been delivered from a lion's den, stumbled past the awestruck Bess and raced for the front door. By now Parker would be at Dr. Engle's. Before he went after Joshua Bishop, he could arrest Mac Dixon, as well.

❖

By ten o'clock, Constable Parker had both Mac Dixon and Joshua Bishop behind bars. Rachel pleaded with Parker not to arrest Ethan Tucker, and he complied. When it was all said and done, Ethan's only crime had been digging up some stolen gold. He admitted that he had been forced into that by Mac Dixon and Hubert Calhoun. He had tried to get them to alert Rachel, find the gold, and turn it in to the government, but Mac had threatened to kill him. After Mac murdered Hubert, Ethan was terrified to cross him.

Once Parker was through questioning Rachel, she insisted on staying with Travis at Dr. Engle's. He planned to keep Travis all night for observation, and Rachel didn't want to leave Travis's side.

Upon her arrival, she found him teetering on the brink of sleep. Lovingly, Rachel supplied sips of water and answers to questions he had regarding Mac Dixon and Joshua Bishop, including the land-hungry Joshua's running a million-dollar-business selling stolen cattle out west.

As if Travis could not completely rest until he knew the whole story, he had awakened every quarter hour with a new question. Rachel would talk to him until he slipped back into dreamland. Eventually, Travis understood that Rachel was now safe, and he slept.

Chapter 23

The next morning, Rachel awoke to a horrible pain in her neck and back. Disoriented, she blinked in confusion, taking in the smells of antiseptic and freshly washed sheets. Eventually, the tiny room's rugged surroundings took on a familiar appearance in the dawn's mellow light. Dr. Engle's spare room. The room in which he put any of his patients whom he wanted to observe throughout the night.

Stiffly, Rachel sat up from her slumped position. At midnight, Dr. Engle insisted she quit fussing around the sleeping Travis. Rachel, persisting in keeping a vigil, finally settled in a chair at Travis's bedside. Within minutes she had placed her head against his uninjured shoulder just to "rest." Rachel had not moved since.

"Did you sleep well?" Travis asked.

Startled, Rachel looked into his glittering eyes, full of mischief.

"You're awake!"

"I've been awake about an hour." A teasing smile. "I was enjoying having you so close."

Her face heating, Rachel stood and jerked several wrinkles out of the blanket covering Travis. Last night he had been conscious but groggy. Now it looked as if he was back to his infuriating, endearing self. "If Momma Ella knew you said something like that, she'd fill the seat of your pants with shot." Rachel stifled an exuberant giggle. Despite his improper remark, she was so relieved to see that spark back in Travis's eyes. Eyes that had haunted her dreams throughout the night. Could he ever forgive her for brutally refusing his attempts at proposing? She hadn't dared broach the subject last night. He had been too ill and too distracted by all

154

that happened. Did he now remember her impassioned pleas when they found him on the side of the road?

"I don't think Miss Ella would interfere between a man and his wife," Travis said.

She caught her breath. "But I'm not your wife."

"You will be before the day's over if I have my way." A lazy smile. "I seem to have a faint remembrance of your saying something about marrying me immediately." He hesitated and an uncertain gleam chased the sparkles from his eyes. "Did you mean it?"

"Oh, Travis." Rachel plopped back into the chair and gripped his arm. "I'm. . .I'm so sorry for the way I acted yesterday. I was just awful. It was nothing more than a case of hurt pride and childishness. If you could ever forgive me, I *will* marry you today. *Now,* if that's what you want."

"Well, I think it might be best to give me a chance to eat some breakfast and wash up, don't you?"

Another giggle. "Yes. And me, too. I think I'll go back home and change into something a little more suitable for a wedding."

Rachel wondered if she had died and gone to heaven. Could she actually be going to marry the man of her heart? The man with whom she had fallen so desperately in love? The man who had captivated her undivided attention from the moment she saw him in Dr. Engle's tiny parlor?

"What about that dress you wore to the picnic? I've never seen you look so lovely." Gently, he stroked her braid while his eyes caressed her face. "It's the color of your hair."

Rachel swallowed against her tightening throat. "Okay," she rasped, thinking that she would wear an old curtain if that was what he wanted.

With a painful twist of his lips, Travis pushed himself up in bed. Rachel slipped two feather pillows against the simple oak headboard, and Travis relaxed against them.

"How long have you wanted to marry me, my little spitfire? How long?"

"Almost since the first time I saw you, I think."

An indulgent laugh. "I must admit I started having thoughts in that direction after I tied you up in the barn."

"That was uncalled for," she said with feigned indignance.

"Yes, it was." He sobered. "I promise to never do it again. I deserved that slap you delivered."

Her thoughts flew to the second time she had attempted to slap Travis, after that eye-opening kiss. A new rush of heat assaulted her face.

"I guess I owe you another heartfelt apology for the first slap. . .and. . .and the second one."

"I don't recall your slapping me a second time," he teased. "Would you care to remind me?"

"Travis Campbell, you full well remember the second time. I didn't quite get to complete it because. . ."

"Ah, yes. Now I remember. It happened after that shameful kiss." With a painful grimace, Travis tried to lift himself from the pillows.

Rachel gently pushed him back. "Dr. Engle told me that if you woke up to keep you down."

A dry chuckle. "Well, Dr. Engle didn't have a pair of inviting lips to kiss." He tugged on her braid. "I'd really like to repeat that first kiss."

Her quivering heart pounding, she willingly leaned toward him. This time, no guilt tainted their united lips. Neither was there a Kate or Samuel in the background, waiting to claim first priority. Rachel felt as if she were in heaven.

"Pa would have been thrilled," she whispered.

"My father will be, too. He never tried to talk me out of marrying Kate. But to tell you the truth, I think this trip was his way of giving me the time I needed to sort through a few things."

"Travis, is Kate terribly upset about your not marrying her?" She hated to be the cause of breaking the heart of such a lovely woman.

He smiled. "To tell you the truth, I think she's relieved."

"Relieved?"

A nod. "Yesterday, when she and I first agreed to break our engagement, she seemed disturbed. But by the time we arrived at the hotel, she acted as if she felt light as a feather. I think Kate and I were simply two people who turned to each other after a tragedy. We both loved each other, but not in the way a husband and wife should love. Not in the way I love you." Once again, he stroked her braid, and Rachel reveled in his open affection.

"Kate is leaving on the first train this morning, isn't she?" Rachel asked.

"Yes."

"If I have time, I'd like to call on her before she leaves. I never did get to say a proper good-bye."

"That would be very nice."

"Well, she's a terribly sweet woman. I hate it about Zachary's death. I hope someday she'll be able to find someone she'll love as much as she did him."

A trace of guilt flittered across Travis's face.

"I'm sorry," Rachel said. "I shouldn't have—"

"It's okay. Believe it or not, I think the Lord has helped me see it wasn't really my fault. It was really a matter of my new pepperbox pistol misfiring. But even so, I still felt responsible. I don't guess I've had a chance to tell you, but Kate and I talked about it yesterday. She doesn't blame me in the least. Just hearing her say that helped me tremendously."

"I guess life doesn't always work out the way we seem to think it should, does it?"

"No, it doesn't." Travis's eyes drooped drowsily. "But then the Lord has a way of bringing good out of the bad."

Rachel thought about her pa's death and all that had happened because of it. She had met Travis, Travis had not married Kate, Rachel had not married Samuel, and Ella had reunited with Lionel. Most of all, Rachel had fought the greatest spiritual battle of her life. Fortunately, she had survived the battle, and her faith increased.

Yes, God did allow her pa to die, but He had never stopped loving her. As Rachel embraced her new life with Travis, she vowed to lovingly embrace her Lord.

Texas Rose

Dedication

To my sister, Rebecca White.

Prologue

(Taken from *Texas Honor*)

Barely hearing Kate's nervous chatter, Travis stared across the stagnant gray pond by which they had taken their afternoon meal. Before their picnic, he had briefly held Kate, had kissed her soft, rose-scented cheek, had looked deeply into her eyes. She told him she came simply because she missed him. But sadly enough, Travis felt no emotional tug. Sure, he felt sorry for Kate. She had, after all, lost one fiancé to death. And now, as the man responsible for that death, Travis was repaying her loyalty with betrayal. The whole thing was not fair.

Travis had taken something very precious from Kate, and he was honor bound to repay her. And repay her he would, with a lifetime of devotion. Despite his heart's desire, though, despite his turbulent longings, he would keep his promise to Kate. Even if Travis couldn't control his wayward heart, he could control his choices.

Once Travis left, once he returned to El Paso, he hoped. . .he prayed he would forget about Rachel. Perhaps her memory would fade in the face of his new life with Kate. Perhaps Kate would bear him a child. Perhaps Travis would learn to love Kate with the same passion that Rachel awakened in him. Perhaps. . .perhaps. . .perhaps. How often would he "perhaps" before he realized the indelible impression that Rachel had left on his memory would never fade?

Sighing, he scrutinized the clump of cedars on the opposite bank. Travis felt as if a giant chain encompassed his heart, enslaving his soul to an unforgiving burden.

"You're in love with her, aren't you?" Kate's sudden question exploded into his musings.

Speechless, Travis stared into Kate's downcast eyes, creamy cheeks, and rosy lips. "What? Who?" he sputtered, not expecting Kate to ever suspect his love for Rachel, and especially not after mere hours in his and Rachel's company. Was he *that* obvious?

"You don't have to pretend, Travis." She looked up from the fried chicken and potato salad and lemonade to peer into his eyes, her own eyes the sad orbs of a lone owl, too wise for comfort. "I saw the way she looked at you. . .us when you introduced her. Then, when you left for the picnic, she watched us drive away."

Kate toyed with the red velvet reticule lying in her lap, her elegant neck and head like the melancholic droop of a weeping lily. She rushed on as if the words, left too long on her tongue, would cause unbearable pain. "I don't think she knew I saw her, but she was crying, and. . .and then there was that. . .that episode that Mr. Lionel and I stumbled onto which you never. . .never explained." Here, Kate halted as if to incite him to please expound on her final subject.

Swallowing against a throat tightening in accusation, Travis had never been so speechless. Silently he resumed his spot on the picnic blanket. Educated in the classics, an expert orator, a student of the law, and he could find no words to deny or acknowledge her claim. Instead, he looked helplessly into her eyes brimming with tears and reached to touch the dark tendril of hair escaping its restraint. How, oh how, had life become so complicated?

"You are the most beautiful woman I ever met, Kate. I—"

"But I'm not Rachel." Pressing the tips of her trembling, gloved fingers against unsteady lips, Kate held his gaze, her hazel eyes begging him to refute her words.

But he could not. "I'm so sorry," he breathed, taking in the smells of dried grass and earth and Kate's rose perfume. "I didn't mean. . .I didn't intend. . .I never wanted to hurt you. I—" A compulsive swallow.

"Were you even going to tell me?" she asked through a haze of tears. "Or were you just going to. . .to pretend and then marry me anyway?"

Blinking, Travis marveled at her perception.

"Why?" she demanded, her fists tightened in angry knots.

"Because. . .I couldn't, I won't abandon you, not after all that's happened."

"What do you mean, 'All that's happened'? What are you talking

162

about?" The questions fell between them like a stifling pall. Questions that Travis didn't want to answer.

As he held her challenging gaze, autumn's cool breeze scampered across the brittle grass to tease Kate's hair and lace collar, then mock him in accusing whispers. God knew Travis didn't want to hurt her any more than he had already hurt her. But Travis sensed that Kate Lowell would expect him to reveal the whole truth.

"You're talking about Zachary. . .about his death, aren't you?"

More silence.

"Why did you propose to me, Travis?"

He gazed toward a lone, gray fish that flipped its tail against the pond's smooth surface. "Kate. . . ," he began, wishing to remove the note of pain in her voice, wishing she would accept his devotion without questions. Another glance her way and Travis knew he must reveal his heart. "I loved. . .love you, but I also felt. . .feel responsible for you because of Zach. . . ." A choke, misty eyes, and his mind replayed that horrible morning when he had witnessed his best friend's demise. The pepperbox, that defective little pistol with all its barrels. Travis would have never let Zach shoot it if he'd known it was going to backfire and kill him.

"But it wasn't your fault!"

"Yes, it was. . .it was. You, yourself, called me a murderer," he groaned as an agony ripped through his soul, heaving like a storm-tortured ocean. Then came the tears that he had refused to release since Zach's death. Tears that could no longer be imprisoned in his distressed heart.

"But I–I. . ." And she was at his side, gripping his arm. "I didn't mean it. You know I didn't mean it. I was overreacting. I. . .that was right after you came and told me that. . .that he was. . .was dead. . .that. . .that you had killed him. I didn't mean it," she said again, her voice cracking on a new sob.

"I didn't want him to die." Wrapping his arms around her, Travis buried his head in the rose-scented locks of her hair, and the barrier around his emotions collapsed, leaving him the shaking victim of overdue grief. "It was that pepperbox. . .that defective pepperbox. It misfired, and the next thing I knew, Zachary was lying in a pool of his own blood."

"I know. . .I know," she whispered, stroking his hair like a mother comforting a child.

After several minutes of uncontrolled grief, Travis released a shuddering sigh and began to gain control of his emotions. He pulled away to grip her upper arms. "There's no way I can ever replace Zach, but at least I can try."

There, he had finally revealed the real reason he had proposed. And in the light of that truth, all glistening and penetrating, Travis also saw that he had never really loved Kate. Oh, he loved her as a brother might love his sister, but not as the woman of his heart. That place was reserved for Rachel.

With her face so close to him, with her tearful eyes boring twin points of doubt into his mind, Travis saw for the first time that Kate's feelings for him shrank in the shadow of her feelings for Zachary.

"Why did you agree to marry me?" he blurted, suddenly needing to know her reasons.

"Because. . .because. . .I. . ." Now it was her turn to flounder. "I needed someone so desperately," she rushed, "and. . .and I felt that you needed me, and. . .and I knew that after Zachary, after my love for him, that I would. . .that it wouldn't matter that. . . Then I grew to care so deeply for you, Travis. Don't think that I don't love you, because I do. As I told you in my letter, I have begun to depend on you so much that I have felt that I cannot live without you."

"And I love you, too," he muttered, kissing her forehead.

"But not the same way you love Rachel."

"And not the same way you loved Zach."

"No."

Reflective silence. The kind that reveals a truth, long hidden.

Standing, Travis walked through the scruffy grass and aimlessly kicked a loose rock into the pond's placid face. The silent moment hung about his shoulders. What would Kate do if they did not marry?

Chapter 1

Dogwood, Texas
October 1885

Y ou misled me, Mr. Adams! You never once told me your son was
an. . .an *Indian*." The petite blond stubbornly stared toward the
empty train tracks, avoiding eye contact with the tall, bearded man
standing nearby. "My Christian convictions simply will not allow me to
tutor such a child!"

Kate Lowell turned her back on the arguing man and woman. Arranging her royal blue skirt, she lowered herself to the hard bench outside the
train station's ticket office. She hoped to avoid further eavesdropping on
the troubled pair but wondered if that were possible, given their close
proximity. Just a few days ago, Kate had come to Dogwood, Texas, to
visit her fiancé, Travis Campbell. She arrived in Dogwood an engaged
woman. Now, she was returning home to El Paso and a future devoid of
matrimony.

"How exactly do you perceive that my son's heritage goes against
your Christian convictions?" the man demanded.

"The Good Book says we aren't to associate with. . .with things that
are *dirty*, and. . .and. . ."

Forgetting all propriety, Kate's head snapped up. She peered into the
face of the bearded gentleman who appeared to be on the brink of losing
all control. A red flush slowly crept up his neck toward his forehead. His
dark eyes virtually shot bullets into the blond. His hands coiled and
uncoiled like twin cobras ready to assault their victims.

Kate's stomach churned with the obvious emotions pouring from the man. Her gloved hands, chilled with autumn's breeze, trembled when she recognized the petite blond's attitude. Kate's own mother recently displayed this same attitude when a poor Tigua Indian girl asked Kate for a few coins.

"Ignore her," Kate's mother insisted. "You'll only contribute to the problem. She needs to get a job."

But who would hire her? Kate wanted to ask. The only place the unfortunate creature could hope to find work would be in one of the dance halls or saloons or houses of prostitution that lined El Paso's main street. The sleepy little town of Kate's childhood was certainly not the El Paso of the present. The coming of the railroad had transformed the city in many ways, some of them for the better, some for the worse. Kate understood all too well that an orphaned Indian girl stood little chance for more than a life of hardship and early death. Kate's fingers had ached to reach into her reticule and give the unfortunate beggar all the money she carried. But her mother insisted, and Kate turned her back on the young girl. She blended in with the El Paso pedestrians, and Kate never saw her again.

But her image was emblazoned on Kate's mind. Every time she tried to pray, the Indian girl's forlorn face still tore at her heart. The girl's pleading eyes pierced her soul when she attended church alongside El Paso's prominent citizens. Many of them proudly wore their Christianity like a new suit that mustn't be sullied with those who participated in the vices now so prominent in town.

What would the bearded stranger think if he knew I had refused to help a girl who shared his son's heritage? Kate pondered. Presently, the man seemed so busy grappling with self-control that he had few other concerns. At last, he turned away from the blond and stomped toward a farm wagon harnessed to a black gelding.

"Drew! Let's go!" he snapped as he boarded the wagon. A dark-haired, dark-eyed lad ran toward the wagon from across the street. He looked about fourteen years old—all legs and arms. The boy clambered into the wagon with a question on his lips. The man cast a troubled glance toward the haughty, erect woman, then produced a soft smile for his son. "She wasn't the right one," he said.

As the curious lad peered around his father toward the blond, Kate was thankful he had obviously missed the woman's tirade. Drew's skin, the color of coffee mixed with heavy cream, his high cheekbones, and prominent nose, all spoke strongly of his mixed heritage.

The boy needs a tutor. Mr. Adams's plight echoed in Kate's mind as a westward bound train whistled in the distance. Kate looked toward the east to see the steam engine's pillar of smoke billowing atop the autumn-hued trees. The 10:40 would soon arrive to carry Kate back to El Paso—back to the place where nothing awaited her—nothing but an empty future and rounds of meaningless social activities.

The boy needs a tutor. Kate had served as her niece's tutor last year when the dear girl had been so sick. She glanced toward the man and his son. Mr. Adams picked up the reins and tapped them against the horse's back. The young Indian girl in the streets of El Paso trailed through her mind once more. As her thoughts raced, Kate worried the brown train ticket, which she clutched like a lifeline.

The boy needs a tutor. Why not you? The thought was a whisper in her spirit, a nuance in her soul. Nonetheless, it sent her heart racing with possibilities. She started to jump up but stopped herself. Kate Lowell had never made an impulsive decision in her life. Her mother trained her from birth to exude an aura of reserved dignity. "There is simply no room for impulsiveness among the well-bred and upper class," she could hear her mother say.

But apparently, neither was there room for compassion or charity. Could it be that God was giving Kate a second chance? She had refused to help once before; could she dare refuse again?

Mr. Adams turned the horse toward the rutted street.

Kate jumped up, her legs quaking beneath her. "Excuse me, Sir!" she called, rushing toward the departing wagon.

The man continued his journey.

"Excuse me!" Kate yelled again. She had never raised her voice in public before. Now she felt the gaze of every waiting passenger penetrating her back. But the haunted eyes of the Indian girl in El Paso proved a stronger motivator.

Still, the man didn't acknowledge her call.

With renewed determination, Kate clamped her plumed hat down with one hand and lifted her skirt with the other. She ran off the wooden walkway and onto the dried grass, attempting once more to gain the man's attention. "Mr. Adams!" she called. "Please, wait!"

He abruptly pulled on the horse's reins and turned around, his face dark with anger. Kate didn't let his expression stop her. *The boy needs a tutor!* By the time she stood beside the wagon, Mr. Adams observed her with surprise. Kate received the distinct impression that he thought the blond had been calling him.

Now that his attention was hers, Kate was immediately plagued with doubts. Had she taken leave of all her senses? She had never even seen Mr. Adams until minutes before. Nervously, she eyed his revolver, ensconced in its holster. The man might be a gunfighter or a scoundrel at large. But, as Kate peered up into soft brown eyes that reflected a deep compassion, she knew at once that Mr. Adams could never be an evil man.

"Was there something you needed of me, Ma'am?" he asked in the soft voice of a cultured gentleman. A voice that strongly contrasted with the angry tones he used with the blond. A voice that didn't match his worn denim shirt, scruffy boots, and the dusty wooden wagon. He gracefully removed his hat to reveal a shock of light brown hair, a shade fairer than his beard and brows. Kate recognized the traces of upper society in his every move. Who was this gracious gentleman, dressed as a farmer? And what was he doing in a small east Texas town?

Kate strained to breathe against her corset's snug fit. "Did I understand you to say that you are looking for a tutor for your son?"

"Yes." Mr. Adams cast a troubled glance toward the train tracks where the 10:40 hissed to a stop with metal screeching against metal.

"It's possible that I might be interested in the position," Kate supplied.

Mr. Adams's brows rose sharply. His son leaned forward to scrutinize her with questioning, dark eyes. Suddenly, Kate felt like a heifer under examination on the auction block. Adams briefly glanced at Kate's tailor-made traveling frock and the ivory brooch pinned to her lapel.

"While the position is honorable, Miss. . ."

"Miss Kate Lowell," Kate said firmly, sounding much more self-confident than she felt.

"Miss Lowell." A spark of recognition registered in the stranger's eyes—eyes surrounded by tanned lines that attested to long hours in the sun.

Kate wondered how he could possibly know her.

"I am McCall Adams, and this is my son, Drew."

"Pleased to meet you."

Drew produced a ready smile as the horse shifted restlessly from one hoof to another.

"While I appreciate your interest, I cannot imagine the position would in any way pay enough to support your current standard of—"

"This has nothing to do with money," Kate interrupted. She glanced over her shoulder toward the train and hoped it would maintain an appropriately long layover—long enough for her to make a decision.

"Oh?" Mr. Adams said, his kind brown eyes assuming a hint of surprise.

If only Adams could have felt her compassion for that unfortunate Indian girl. If only he could sense her sensitivity to God's will or her anguish over the choice of staying in Dogwood rather than returning to the safety of home and family. "There are things more precious than money," she answered.

"Well, in that case, I think perhaps we should discuss the situation."

"Yes, that would be nice."

"Can you meet me in about twenty minutes at the cafe on the corner?" He pointed toward an eating establishment with "Dotty's" painted in red across the large front window. "I will make arrangements for Drew to visit with a friend while you and I discuss the position."

"Yes. Yes. That will be fine. Thank you."

"And thank you," he returned, a wisp of relief teasing the corners of his mouth.

❖

How could Kate have failed to notice just how handsome Mr. Adams actually was? Perhaps the distraction of making such a quick decision had clouded her thoughts. Furthermore, the hurried moments when she rechecked into the hotel and rushed to Dotty's didn't allow her time to reflect on the man's appearance. But as they settled into the straight-backed chairs at the homey eating establishment, Kate, at long last, realized what she had initially failed to recognize. With Mr. Adams's contemplative gaze on her, she was taken aback by the strong angles of his square jaw, the aristocratic lines of his straight nose. Once again, she peered into eyes full of compassion and something else, something Kate recognized all too well. Pain.

"I can't imagine that you didn't overhear the whole conversation at the train station between Miss Pimberly and me."

"Yes, I heard." Kate chose to look across the cheerful room at the collection of rough oak tables covered with red checked cloths, at the bare pine walls, at the half-opened kitchen door—at anything other than Mr. Adams. Had she been thinking clearly when she agreed to this meeting? Her mother would be aghast, to say the least. But her mother wasn't present, and Kate was now a young woman—almost twenty-two. She could make her own decisions.

"Does it not bother you that my son is of mixed heritage?" he asked in a deceptively soft voice that riveted Kate's attention.

"Not in the least."

Mr. Adams's guarded eyes softened to reveal an unconditional love for Drew. "He's all I've got," he rasped. "My wife died soon after she bore him. And when I hear someone say something like. . .like. . ." His hands curled on the table.

Once more, Kate saw the pain in his eyes. A pain that went deep. A pain that touched her heart of hearts. Kate knew that kind of pain. Intimately. She understood the agony of losing that special person, the one most beloved.

Zachary. Zachary. Zachary. His memory echoed within her soul like tormenting midnight thunder. Would she ever free herself from him?

Already, she felt a kindred spirit with this stranger, a common understanding of what it means to have loved and lost. Suddenly, the feeling scared her beyond reason. Why in the name of common sense had she chased him down and expressed an interest in the tutoring position? Was this encounter indeed of God? Or, was it nothing but a product of her own guilt over not helping the girl in El Paso?

"I'm a horse breeder. I own a farm three miles east of Dogwood. If you agree to the tutoring position, we have a schoolroom set up in our summer kitchen there at the homestead. It has everything you would need to facilitate your teaching.

"Drew is a good boy," Mr. Adams continued as the plump waitress placed aromatic coffee and homemade cinnamon rolls on the table before them. "He is intelligent and strong and should give you very little trouble.

"From what I understand, you have been educated at an eastern university? Am I correct?"

Kate blinked in amazement. How did Mr. Adams know of her background? "Yes. You're right. I—how did you know about me?"

"This is a small town," he supplied with a slight smile. "You can't stay here two days without the whole place humming with every detail of your life. I also have heard that you live in El Paso and were here to visit an. . . acquaintance."

"I see," Kate said as her face warmed. He must be referring to her broken engagement with Travis Campbell. The very idea that this man would bring up something so intensely personal left her astounded. Had living in a small country town completely removed all vestiges of propriety from him? "I guess that means I'll know all your secrets by tomorrow," she snapped in defense.

"Don't count on it," he challenged. Kate felt the verbal slap as keenly as any physical one. Furthermore, his guarded, hostile expression warned her not to get any closer.

What could he be hiding that left him so wary? Some haunting mystery seemed to cloak his every feature.

Suddenly, Kate decided not to accept the tutoring position. Within the few minutes she had been in this man's presence, she felt as though she were being drawn into a tangled web of past pain and secrets of the heart. Kate's own wounds since losing Zachary were still gaping sores of agony. She was still unable to burden herself with the heartache of another.

Then she remembered that Indian girl in El Paso. Would those dark eyes never cease to haunt her? As that girl had needed money, Drew Adams, also, had a need. If Kate rejected Drew, she would be rejecting that poor beggar all over again. Thus, her thoughts vacillated from one wave to another like an unanchored ship in a tempestuous sea.

"I'm sorry," Mr. Adams said at last, a gentleman's smile tilting his lips. "I didn't mean to snap at you."

"Nor I, you," Kate returned, responding to his kind expression with an apologetic smile of her own. Despite her former pondering about Zachary, Kate could not deny her heart's stirring response to this man's smooth charm. She wondered how many women had lost their hearts without his ever knowing it.

"Excuse me, Mr. Adams," an attractive blond lady called from the doorway.

"Yes, Miss Alexander?" Mr. Adams replied, his brow furrowed in alarm. "What's the matter? I left Drew with you and Dr. Engle—"

"The doctor sent me for you. There's a terrible altercation with Eugene Wilcox's son in the street. Dr. Engle seems to think you better stop it before Eugene finds out."

Mr. Adams stood, his chair toppling behind him. "Please excuse me," he stated curtly as he ran toward the doorway.

Chapter 2

McCall raced down the boardwalk toward the circle of shouting boys who had congregated on the dusty street in front of Dr. Engle's office. The sounds of intermittent punches and grunts mingled with juvenile yelling. Over the din, Dr. Engle's voice shouted, "Stop it! You two, stop it now!"

In a matter of seconds, McCall broke through the rowdy ring of boys to see his son, covered in dirt and his mouth bleeding. The young Adams straddled the blond Calvin Wilcox, who wriggled face-down beneath Drew's weight. Gritting his teeth, McCall grabbed his son under the arms and dragged him off his adversary. Calvin, his faded overalls soiled with dirt and blood, gasped for air.

"Calvin's the one who started it. I saw the whole thing," Dr. Engle growled as he glared at the wiry bully. Just then, Calvin rolled over, jumped to his feet, and dove headlong toward Drew's midsection.

McCall, still gripping his son, sidestepped Calvin. His move sent Calvin hurling into the travel-hardened road. Calvin sputtered against a mouthful of dirt as he scrambled to regain his footing.

The huffing, angry Drew struggled against McCall's grasp. "Don't you ever jump me like that again, Calvin Wilcox," he yelled. "I didn't do one thing to you! You. . .you. . ."

"What's goin' on here?" an angry bearlike voice boomed from down the street.

"That's Calvin's father." Dr. Engle's nurse, Magnolia Alexander, worriedly gazed down the street.

"He's nothin' but trouble," Dr. Engle urged. "You two need to get out

172

of here. *Now*." The graying Dr. Engle had been a second father to McCall, a grandfather to Drew. From the moment McCall bought the horse farm thirteen years ago, the doctor had been a mainstay while the younger man raised his adopted son. Dr. Engle, the only person in Dogwood who knew the story behind Drew's parentage, had recommended an excellent nanny who was not a gossip. Thus, McCall was able to guard his and Drew's privacy. At this point, Drew himself didn't even know the whole story of his parentage.

McCall dragged the flailing Drew toward their wagon, parked near Dotty's. "I'm gonna beat the stuffin' out of that Calvin Wilcox," Drew protested.

"Looks like you already have to me," McCall said sarcastically. With a grunt, he hefted Drew onto the bags of flour, sugar, and cornmeal in the back of the wagon.

Drew sat up.

His father shoved him back down. "Stay flat, and don't get up until I say you can. You've already caused enough of a scene. The less Eugene Wilcox sees of you, the better."

"I didn't cause a scene," Drew said, his bleeding bottom lip stubbornly set. "Calvin did. I was just defending myself."

"We're gonna get you for this!" Eugene Wilcox bellowed from the crowd of boys.

McCall climbed onto the bench seat and glanced over his shoulder to see Eugene holding a sagging Calvin, nose bleeding, eyes swollen. Grinding his teeth, McCall released the wagon's brake and snapped the reins over the horse's back. He looked toward Dotty's to see Kate forlornly staring at him from the boardwalk. With a groan, McCall realized he had completely forgotten about the new tutor. What should he do?

Spontaneously, he pulled the horse to a halt and jumped from the wagon. Without preamble, he scooped the petite Miss Lowell into his arms.

"Oh, *please* Mr. Adams. What are you *thinking*?" she protested, while firmly gripping her oversized, plumed hat.

"I'm thinking you and I need to talk some more, and Drew and I need to get out of town as fast as we can," he said, plopping her onto the wagon seat.

She landed with a muffled gasp.

Her rose perfume's delicate fragrance clung to his denim shirt, and McCall tried to produce a gentlemanly smile. He was certain he came closer to a grimace. With the sound of Eugene Wilcox's unedited expletives in their wake, McCall once more cracked the reins over the ebony gelding's haunches and the wagon jerked.

"Mr. Adams, I find this *highly* unsuitable," Miss Lowell protested as the buggy jarred over the ruts formed during the last rainstorm. "I hardly know you. Please, Sir, I think it would be much better if you would just allow me to return to my hotel room, and—"

"Of course," McCall said over the sound of the horse's pounding hooves. "I agree with all you've said. And you'll have to forgive me. Under normal circumstances, I would have never behaved so. But given my son's recent. . . escapade, I think it would be much better for me to avoid town for a couple of weeks." McCall paused to allow Miss Lowell to contemplate the aspects of Drew's parentage, which could easily guarantee a conviction, even in the face of his innocence.

"You will agree that the two of us need to discuss the arrangements for your tutoring position. I could hardly have left you waiting at the hotel indefinitely. And given the mood of Eugene Wilcox, I could hardly have taken the time to assist you into the buggy properly." McCall produced a smile, hoping to assure the beautiful young woman that he in no way intended to harm her. But the trembling, uncertain twist of her lips left him feeling like a cad.

As they sped from the streets of Dogwood and down the wooded lane to his farm, McCall wondered what had possessed him to scoop this immaculate lady into his arms and plop her onto the wagon seat. Had the situation truly called for such cavalier action? Or had McCall simply responded to the impulse that had urged him to get closer to Kate Lowell from the moment she sat across from him at Dotty's? If he were completely honest with himself, he would admit that she was the first woman he had met since Melody's death who awakened more than a passing interest. Something in Kate Lowell's eyes hinted that the two of them shared a similar way of thought. But despite the attraction he felt for her, McCall knew he could never be unfaithful to the memory of his Melody.

"Exactly how do you propose that I return to the hotel? I *cannot* stay at your farm," Miss Lowell stated.

"Of course not. Dr. Engle will come out later to check on Drew. You can go back into town with him." McCall said, concentrating on the hardened path before him.

"You are certain the doctor will pay a visit?"

"Absolutely. He'll want to take a look at Drew's lip. He's like a second father to me."

"Well, in that case. . ."

McCall felt Kate relaxing and was relieved that she no longer worried about her predicament.

The thick, barren woods produced a wall on each side of the lane, shading them from the bright autumn sunshine. As McCall slowed the horse's rapid pace, the piney forest's cool, earthy smell seemed to awaken the common sense that Miss Lowell's blatant beauty had momentarily defused. McCall made a personal vow, then and there, to never make eye contact again with his son's tutor. The effect practically mesmerized him. He had been a man alone too long, and she was simply too lovely for her own good.

"Can I sit up now, Dad?" Drew asked from behind.

"Sure, Son."

"Hi!" Drew exclaimed as he pulled himself onto the seat beside his new teacher. "I'm Drew." He produced a swollen smile that made McCall want to groan. Was he so wise to hire such a pretty lady for his son's educator?

But you don't have a choice. The reality of their desperate situation settled around McCall's neck like a harness on a weary plow horse. He really didn't have a choice. Up until recently, McCall had tutored Drew. But the cares of the ranch pulled McCall away from Drew's increasing educational demands. Now, he desperately needed a tutor. It was out of the question for Drew to attend school in town. Today's fight with Calvin Wilcox proved just how unaccepting the townspeople were of Drew. McCall simply wasn't ready to see his son live through the misery that one human being can force upon another because of blind prejudice.

As a last resort, McCall had placed an ad for a tutor in the Dallas paper, hoping to attract some applicants who were open-minded enough to willingly tutor a child of Drew's heritage. Of all the applicants, only Miss Pimberly had obtained a college education, one of McCall's definite requirements. When she refused, McCall had despaired of ever hiring a tutor. But to have Miss Lowell appear from nowhere following Miss Pimberly's despicable rejection. . .the likelihood of such an occurrence being anything more than divine providence surpassed McCall's comprehension. *Miss Kate Lowell must be an answer to my many prayers.*

McCall simply hoped he understood all of God's motives. Something within him cringed at the thought of fully releasing his hold on Melody, even for God. True, she had been gone fourteen years, but she still lived in McCall's heart. The thought of betraying her memory filled him with nothing but guilt. He fervently hoped that God wasn't placing the stunning Miss Lowell into his life for a purpose other than tutoring Drew.

Anything more than an employer/employee relationship left McCall wanting to run in the other direction.

However, he could not deny that the woman sitting next to him did appeal to his masculinity. He repeated the vow to never again make eye contact with her. Once McCall showed her the schoolroom and observed her bonding with Drew, he would confirm his wish to hire her. From that point forward, he would maintain his distance, at all costs—for Melody.

❖

Eugene Wilcox watched as McCall Adams rode out of town with that woman beside him. He hadn't seen where that stinkin' Indian boy had gone, but Eugene would bet his last steer that Drew Adams was lying in the back of the wagon, like the lowlife coward he was. He turned to his son, who held his right wrist and whimpered and moaned like a chewed-up mutt. Calvin's friends, who moments ago cheered for him, now snickered under their breath as they went in search of excitement elsewhere.

"Get in the wagon," Eugene growled, pushing Calvin toward their horse and wagon, tethered across the street. "How many times have I told you not to get into a fight you can't win?"

"I didn't have no choice," Calvin whined. "That Injun boy tripped me, and I had to defend myself."

"He's lying!" Dr. Engle called. "He's the one who started it. He jumped Drew from behind for no reason. I saw the whole thing myself."

Hiking up his baggy work pants, the wiry Eugene turned toward the doctor's establishment, which served as both his home and office. He looked the elderly man square in the eyes and dared him to refute his next words. "I believe my son. And you need to stay out of this."

"There's nothing to stay out of. It's over." The doctor pushed up his wire-rimmed spectacles as that saucy nurse of his nodded her agreement. "And you'll be wise to drop the whole thing."

"I'll drop it when that stinkin' Injun pays for humiliatin' Calvin in front of his friends." For added emphasis, Eugene spit a stream of sweet tobacco juice onto the sandy road.

"Calvin is the one who humiliated himself when he jumped Drew from behind. That's no way for a young man to act. Calvin deserved every punch he got."

"Yes. He's right," Magnolia added.

The thin Eugene, now rigid with anger, doubled his fists and glared at the interfering doctor and his nurse. "I didn't ask for no report from you!

176

I know my son. And I know those stinkin' Injuns. There ain't a one of 'em alive who's worth his keep!"

Wilcox observed Dr. Engle as he clamped his lips together in that uppity way of his. The man acted like he knew everything. Truth of the matter, Eugene thought he knew far more about Indians than that haughty doctor ever would. His grandpa had told him story after story of the way those Cherokees had tried to steal everything from chickens to Wilcox women. Eugene grew up hating Indians. He still hated Indians. And he would make doubly certain that Indian of McCall Adams's suffered for beating up Calvin.

Deciding to ignore Dr. Engle, Eugene grabbed Calvin's arm and marched toward their worn wagon. He'd get the boy home and wear him out for letting the likes of an Indian beat him up.

"Don't go so fast, Pa," Calvin whined, hobbling beside him.

"Just get in the wagon," Eugene demanded. "I'm just hopin' no one I know saw you get whipped. It's a shame and disgrace!"

Calvin, still nursing his right wrist, struggled to pull himself into the wagon.

Eugene gave him a quick shove, and the boy stumbled forward to collapse onto the seat.

"I think I need to take a look at Calvin's wrist," Dr. Engle said from behind.

New rage twisting his gut, Eugene spun and grabbed a handful of Dr. Engle's woolen shirt in his calloused fist. "Stay out of our business," he growled, only inches from the physician's wrinkled face.

"When I see someone who has an injured wrist, it's my business!" the doctor growled.

Eugene couldn't believe the pluck of the old man. Didn't Dr. Engle know Eugene could knock him flat with one blow? "I'll tend to my boy. If he needs doctorin', I'll take care of it!"

The doctor looked past Eugene, toward Calvin. "Tell your mother I'm here, if you need me."

Eugene shoved the doctor away from the wagon, untethered the horse, crawled up to the bench, and snapped the reins over the dappled mare's back. If it took him a solid year, he'd see that sorry Drew Adams punished for what happened today.

He hadn't seen Drew more than a dozen times in the last decade. Drew and his pa stayed pretty much to themselves. But the whole town knew the boy's ma must have been nothing more than a rotten squaw.

What a clean white man like McCall Adams would have ever wanted with a squaw went beyond Eugene's understanding. As he encouraged his tired mare out of town and down the tree-lined dirt road, Eugene ground his teeth and determined to see the day when McCall and Drew would both wish they had never moved to these parts.

Chapter 3

Two weeks after accepting her teaching assignment, Kate Lowell stood gazing out her hotel window across the rolling hills, now ablaze with autumn's splendor. Occasionally, she looked up the busy, rutted streets for the familiar sight of Dr. Engle's black, hooded buggy. As Mr. Adams had predicted, the doctor did indeed pay a visit to check on Drew the evening of his unfortunate encounter with Calvin. Then, the kind physician had escorted Kate back to the hotel and provided transportation to and from the horse farm every school day since. Dr. Engle had agreed with Mr. Adams that he should avoid town indefinitely due to Eugene Wilcox's livid temper.

Kate closed her eyes and reflected over the last two weeks. She hadn't seen Mr. Adams more than three times. During those few occasions, he had remained aloof and seemed to look past her rather than at her. Kate had the disturbing impression that the man was taking extra pains to ignore her.

Drew, on the other hand, did nothing but look at her. Kate sensed, almost from the beginning, that the boy held an immediate fancy for her and she responded in an appropriately cool and professional manner. The handsome lad was nothing short of brilliant, far above his age in intellectual capacity and achievements. Kate felt a deep sense of satisfaction in knowing that she opened new doors to Drew's knowledge. At long last, thoughts of the Indian girl from the streets of El Paso were put to rest. However, new thoughts, just as disturbing, plagued her. She was overcome with curiosity about McCall Adams and his former wife. Strangely, Drew didn't favor his father in the least.

A soft tap at her door arrested her reverie. "Miss Lowell?" a hesitant feminine voice called.

Kate walked across the faded floral rug and opened her door to the smiling face of the hotel owner's timid, plain daughter. "Yes?" Kate asked.

"There's a Mr. Adams waiting for you downstairs," the girl said, and with a quick curtsy, she was gone.

Kate compulsively gripped the doorknob as her throat tightened. Thoughts of sitting next to Mr. Adams during the thirty-minute ride to the horse farm left Kate with a multitude of tremors flitting up and down her spine. *Nonsense*, Kate scolded herself. *You're being unreasonable,* she thought as she retrieved her black velvet reticule from the poster bed's quilted coverlet. The man had no interest in her whatsoever, as attested by his obviously ignoring her the last two weeks. He had even paid her by sending an envelope with Drew that held her biweekly salary of twenty dollars. As she stepped into the hallway, Kate decided she would simply treat the father in the same manner she treated the son—with the same cool dignity her mother had long since taught her.

Schooling her features into a pleasant mask, Kate descended the flight of steps at the end of the musty, narrow hallway. She saw Mr. Adams long before he saw her. McCall leaned against the modest reception desk, chatting with the hotel's plump owner. Not quite understanding her motive, Kate paused halfway down the steps to examine the tall, lean man. The man of many walls. The man of shadowed corridors.

What dreadful pain from his past caused him to shut out the world? Essentially, that was what he had done. He had shut out everyone, except Drew, of course, and Dr. Engle. He didn't even attend Sunday services, although Kate knew beyond a doubt that the Lord was vitally important to him. The fact that he had emphatically requested that Kate teach Drew from the Word of God underscored his belief in a holy creator. Kate was momentarily overcome with a raging curiosity about her employer, who carried himself like a handsome prince. A nagging little voice made her wonder what it would feel like to have his strong arms wrapped around her.

Kate's face heated at the very thought, and much to her dismay, Mr. Adams looked straight at her. His brow quirked momentarily. His nostrils flared. And under his unwavering gaze, Kate sensed that he knew she had been examining him. Her hands produced an annoying film of sweat. Her legs trembled. Her stomach clenched into a tight knot. Then, something she hadn't felt since before Zachary's death swept through her soul—the fire of attraction. Never had she known such an attraction for Travis Campbell, her former fiancé. Kate thought she would never feel it again. Never, for anyone except her beloved Zachary.

Oh, Lord, help me! Kate pleaded. She should board the next train to El Paso and leave this town, leave McCall Adams's web of mystery, which daily seemed to enclose her all the tighter.

As their gaze lengthened, she was further dismayed to see reflections of her own turbulent emotions shimmering in the depths of McCall's eyes. The unwavering attraction. The dismay. The urge to bolt. Her stomach lurched, and Kate wondered if his avoiding her stemmed from an intent to escape such an encounter as this. *Why did you ever agree to this tutoring position,* she questioned herself.

But which was better? Life in El Paso, trapped in a round of meaningless social activities and haunted by that poor Indian girl—or being here, in this tiny east Texas town, pouring herself into a worthy occupation?

At long last, she forced herself to look down and slowly descend the stairs. On the last step, the heel of Kate's ankle boot tangled in the hem of her gingham dress. She had arranged for the dress to be made just a few days earlier. Nothing in her trunk seemed appropriate attire for a tutor on a horse farm, but the new dress was proving her tormentor. She hadn't realized until this morning that it was a bit too long for her. Now, she was forever tripping over the skirt. Feeling as if she were in a dream, Kate stumbled forward, but her firm grip on the banister stopped her fall.

She felt Mr. Adams at her side before she saw him. His steady hand on her elbow did nothing but increase her lack of equilibrium *and* her pulse.

"Are you all right?" he asked softly.

"Yes, fine. I'm fine. Thank you," Kate squeaked out, refusing to look at him.

"The buggy is out front. I thought you might prefer it to the wagon."

"Yes. That's thoughtful of you," she supplied, stubbornly keeping her focus on the lobby's faded floral rug, a larger version of the one in her room. All of Dogwood's quaint establishments paled in comparison to some of the ornate structures in the east where Kate had attended university or even those in El Paso. Nonetheless, Kate had grown increasingly fond of the friendly atmosphere that Dogwood offered. The simplicity of its people, their amiability and charm, only added to Kate's growing fancy for the town.

However, Kate could not deny that a dark, dark streak of something sinister and evil slithered through the streets of this charming community.

There was a reason Dr. Engle had been emphatic about McCall and Drew staying out of town for awhile. There was a reason Mr. Adams was forced to hire a tutor. Kate could never deny the ugly truth, no matter how delightful the residents appeared.

Silently, McCall assisted Kate into the hooded buggy, which looked a lot like Dr. Engle's. Silently, he took the seat beside her. Silently, they began the short journey toward the horse farm and another day of school-work for Drew. The lack of words only added to Kate's overwrought emotions. Her stomach twisted in nervous nausea.

"I shall escort you back and forth to town from now on," McCall said, his breath a cloudy mist in the cold, morning air.

Any reply stuck in Kate's throat. She shivered with the breeze as the cantering mare pulled them away from Dogwood and down the familiar, tree-lined lane. Impulsively, she tugged her woolen, black cape closer around her shoulders.

"Are you cold?" McCall asked.

Kate, feeling his gaze on her, shook her head. "I'm f–f–fine," she stuttered in reply, her teeth chattering.

"You *are* cold." He pulled the chestnut horse to a halt, and with one swift motion, removed his coarse, leather jacket. "Here."

Kate attempted a protest, only to have him brush aside her resistance. "This is the coldest morning we've had yet," he said. "And I forgot to bring any kind of quilt. We can't have you catching cold."

The heavy coat, several times too large for Kate, draped around her shoulders and seeped warmth into her. Warmth, and the smells of well-groomed horses. The smells of a man who spent many hours outdoors. "Thanks," she said, glancing up with a shy smile.

She should have never made that mistake. For that quick glance into McCall Adams's soft brown eyes turned into a long gaze, fraught with admiration.

❖

For two weeks, McCall had watched her. For two weeks, he had felt as if he were being drawn to Miss Lowell like a moth, fatefully flirting with a candle's flame. *God help me, she's beautiful. Too beautiful*, he mused, as their gaze lengthened. He had thought. . .McCall honestly had thought he could escort her to and from the farm and maintain his distance. Had he been fooling himself?

He wanted to kiss her. Here. Now. He wanted to feel her in his arms.

But those feelings were far, far, far from appropriate. Miss Kate Lowell was truly a proper lady. McCall, always the gentleman, would never violate the laws of propriety. Never. No matter how much his heart urged him to respond.

Plus, there was Melody. How could he have forgotten her? He hadn't thought of her all morning. The realization made him mentally scold himself with a stream of invectives. How could he forget the woman who had borne Drew? How could he forget the pain she had endured? Was he so weak that one pretty face swept aside all former loyalty to the memory of his wife?

Nonetheless, like a man under the hypnotic gaze of a sorceress, these thoughts immediately blurred as he basked under the spell of Kate's lovely, blue-green eyes. Eyes much wiser than her years. Eyes that testified to seeing substantial pain. Eyes that seemed to peer into his very soul and understand McCall's own agony. No one except his grandfather and Dr. Engle had ever offered that kind of understanding. Even McCall's own family turned from him in his hour of deepest need. Only McCall's relationship with Jesus Christ had stopped him from falling into the pits of despair.

Perhaps God put Kate Lowell into your life for more reasons than tutoring. The thought echoed disturbingly as McCall continued to helplessly gaze into her limpid eyes. With the forest full of birds, cheerfully singing about starting their day, McCall wondered why God would fling him into the throes of a romance. Didn't the Lord know McCall wasn't ready for any kind of relationship? He still clung to Melody. His dear, sweet Melody. She may be gone from the earth but certainly not from McCall's heart.

At long last, Miss Lowell tore her gaze from his and looked at her hands, tightly clasped in her lap. "Don't. . .don't you think we sh–should continue our j–journey?" she rasped, turning her attention toward the woods.

"Certainly," McCall barked. Disgusted with his own reactions, he gripped the reins and slapped them against the horse's haunches.

Within half an hour, their reticent, strained journey ended. McCall stopped the carriage next to the massive, hay-strewn barn, which sat close to the log cabin he built with his own hands thirteen years before. The vast expanse of rolling, east Texas hills, ablaze with autumn, seemed to close in on him and only intensified his need to distance himself from the lovely tutor.

McCall couldn't help but notice the swiftness with which Miss Lowell disembarked the carriage. She didn't even tarry for his assistance. That was quite all right with him. The fewer encounters they shared, the better.

Furthermore, McCall would soon ask his hired hand, Bob Mosely, to provide transportation for Miss Lowell to and from the farm. McCall could not risk another experience like this morning's. His heart was in no way ready to be involved with a woman, regardless of God's plans.

❖

Kate rushed toward the summer kitchen, her heart pounding so furiously she could hardly catch her breath. With a muffled sob, she stumbled into the log structure, full of shadows, and collapsed at the rough-hewn, pine table where she taught Drew. Fortunately Drew was not present, and Kate seized the opportunity to regain her composure.

During those heavy moments when she and McCall Adams stared into each other's eyes, Kate wanted so much more from her employer than a mere friendship. God help her, McCall might as well have kissed her. She felt nothing short of emotionally shattered from the incident. Though they had never even touched physically, their hearts had indeed touched. Did this signal the beginnings of love? If so, Kate should board the next train home. She was not ready, in any fashion, to commit to loving a man as she had once loved Zachary. Kate had experienced the consuming grief of a broken heart once. That was enough for a lifetime.

Pressing her lips together, she removed the dainty handkerchief from the hidden pocket in her blue gingham dress. She dabbled at her damp eyes and firmly pressed her lips together. She must focus on the task at hand and turn her mind from Mr. Adams's beseeching brown eyes. Otherwise, she would have no peace.

Determinedly, Kate squared her shoulders, took a deep breath, stood, and began rolling up and tying the oilcloth that covered the kitchen's numerous windows. With the bright autumn sunshine now streaming into the room, Kate lit only one lantern. She noticed the trace coals in the rock fireplace and wondered why Drew had not finished his list of chores, which included keeping the fire ablaze.

Where is Drew anyway? she mused, turning to look out one of the windows, toward the log cabin. But a glance toward the cabin meant another glimpse of Mr. Adams. Like a man on a mission, he briskly walked onto the long front porch, whipped open the door, and stepped into his home. Abruptly Kate whirled from the window. Even the slightest glimpse of Mr. Adams brought to mind those tense moments when their spirits had touched.

Her hands trembling anew, Kate noticed a slip of paper in the spot where Drew normally sat. On it was a message scrawled in his familiar handwriting, a script that should belong to a grown man, not a fledgling boy. "I have gone for a walk. I will be back soon. Yours, Drew."

Kate tossed the note back onto the table. He had done it to her again. The third time in two weeks. But this time, not only had Drew disappeared before the day even started, he had also left without feeding the fire. Kate had refrained from mentioning Drew's frequent morning wanderings to his father. She had hoped that by reasoning with the boy she could convince him to postpone his exploratory hikes until after school. At once, Kate turned toward the door. She must report Drew's repeated tardiness to his father.

But she stopped. No. She couldn't report anything to McCall Adams. Kate was not prepared to face him again. Not now. Not after that moment when she had ached to feel his arms around her. Kate recalled her mother's recent telegram in which she almost demanded that Kate return to El Paso. But Kate had firmly stood by her decision to tutor Drew. Should she have listened to her mother? Kate could go home even today, if she chose.

With great dread, she contemplated Mr. Adams escorting her into Dogwood this very afternoon. With great dread, she wondered what would transpire. Yet, despite her dread, a flame of anticipation flickered. No, she would not assent to her mother's demands and return to El Paso. She would continue as Drew's tutor.

After some deliberation, Kate decided she would search for Drew herself. On the two previous occasions that he had "conveniently" disappeared before her arrival, she had seen him coming home from the same spot—an opening in the wood's thick thatch, across the pasture full of horses. With ample effort, which cost her a broken fingernail, Kate placed two large logs on the dying coals and hoped they would blaze before her return. She wrapped her black shawl closer around her chilled arms and opened the door. Setting her lips, Kate marched from the summer kitchen toward the pasture's wooden gate. Nervously, she eyed the numerous mares grazing with their half-grown offspring. Kate's experience with horses had been limited to sitting in an exquisite buggy while a well-groomed steed pulled her along. As she began timidly picking her way across the frigid, dew-laden pasture, Kate wished she had taken more pains in equestrian pursuits.

However, the gentle horses never pursued her, and Kate arrived at her destination in a matter of minutes. Hesitantly, she stepped from the open pasture and into another world. A world full of pines and maples and oaks. A world full of underbrush and the damp scent of decaying leaves. A world full of birds and squirrels and deer. The haven of nature.

"Drew!" Kate called as she picked her way across the path he had obviously taken, a path that looked like it had been in use for several years. "Drew!" she called again, determined to find the boy and demand that he postpone his walks until after studies.

Kate, continuing strict adherence to the pathway, walked for what felt like hours. At long last, she came upon a scene that stopped her in her tracks and left her startled beyond words.

Chapter 4

McCall rushed into his sparse bedroom and closed the door. There was so much he needed to do this morning. A buyer was coming from Dallas this afternoon with the intent of purchasing stallions. McCall should be grooming the stallions instead of reliving his past, but he had left the chore to Bob Mosely, his hired hand, who really should be mending fences in the east pasture. Still, McCall's past beckoned him like a siren that he could not ignore. The log walls of his tiny room seemed to open their arms and draw him into another world where Melody still lived.

He stumbled across the braided rug toward the walnut dressing table in the corner—Melody's dressing table. McCall lowered himself onto the stool she had once used. He picked up her hairbrush by its whalebone handle. A hairbrush that still held strands of his wife's silky dark hair. Tenderly, he stroked the tarnished silver picture frame that protected the aging photo of the woman who had stolen his heart. The daguerreotype's gray tones hid the mahogany hue of her soft hair, the sparkle of her pale blue eyes, the sun-kissed freshness of her skin.

Fourteen years. Had fourteen years actually lapsed since the horrible events that led to her death? That fateful day seemed but hours removed. . . .

❖

McCall was long overdue to leave his father's bank in Dallas. He had been negotiating a loan for a prominent citizen who was opening yet another store, and the whole thing took hours longer than he anticipated. When he left, the sun was gradually descending in the western sky.

Nightfall was imminent. McCall was supposed to have met Melody at Devenport's Fine Restaurant thirty minutes before he left. He hated to keep her waiting, so he decided against going home to his parent's mansion in order to change into one of his formal evening suits. His business suit would have to do. Melody would understand. She always understood. That was one of the things McCall liked most about her. She had the looks *and* disposition of an angel.

When McCall arrived at Devenport's, he expected to see Melody waiting in the receiving room. A quick scan of the ornate room, decorated in plush red velvet, Persian rugs, and brass mirrors, revealed no sign of Melody.

Supposing that Melody had already been seated, McCall approached the host, dressed in a black tuxedo. "Excuse me, Appleton," he said, nearing the tall, cherry table. "I am to meet Melody Graham. Has she been seated?"

"Ah. . .Mr. Adams! We were wondering if you and your lovely fiancée would be keeping your reservations." He produced a smile and eyed McCall over his wire-rimmed reading glasses. Many times, McCall had seen the host's long face take on a haughty air, especially if the guests weren't at the top of society. "Miss Graham has yet to arrive," Appleton continued. "Would you care to be seated until she arrives?"

"No, thank you. I'll wait in the receiving room." At first, McCall had been relieved that his sweet Melody had not been kept waiting. But once the relief assuaged, a new concern came over him. Where *was* Melody? She had never, absolutely *never*, been late for any of their appointments. As the top of the hour neared and guest after guest entered with no sign of Melody, McCall experienced a case of full-fledged panic.

Something was wrong. Dreadfully wrong. He knew it in the deepest recesses of his heart, now pounding with fear. McCall rushed from the restaurant and into his awaiting carriage. In no time, he maneuvered the horse onto Melody's street, lined with the ostentatious homes of the well-to-do. Within ten minutes of his hasty exit from the restaurant, McCall pounded on the door of the Graham's three-story, pillared home. The usually cheerful doorman, Jim Lowery, met McCall with the troubled look of tragedy.

McCall, strangely certain that some grave adversity had overtaken his beloved fiancée, grabbed Jim's arms. "Where is Melody? Do you know? Is she all right?"

Jim lowered his distraught eyes and floundered for any words. Seconds later, Melody's assigned maid, stricken and tearful, rushed down the massive, curved stairway. McCall released the doorman and rushed toward the tall, slender woman. Her wrinkled dark face seemed set with grief. Now believing the worst, McCall swallowed against the bile rising in his throat.

"Melody. . .is she. . ." He grabbed Mrs. Thedford's trembling hands.

"She's in her room, Mistah Adams." A guarded sob.

McCall tackled the stairs two at a time. He had no idea which room was Melody's room, but he would find her. She must surely need him. Need him in a desperate manner.

"Oh. . .but you can't. . .you mustn't. . .she isn't in any kinda shape to be acceptin' callers. . . ."

He ignored the maid and continued opening and closing the doors that lined the massive, ornate hallway. At long last, he came to a room from which uncontrolled sobbing echoed like bursts of agony, held long at bay. By this point, Mrs. Thedford, ever the timid lady, had reached him. She desperately grabbed at McCall's arm, begging him not to enter. "You mustn't see her now. She will never forgive me if'n I allow you to see her—"

McCall turned the brass doorknob and pushed against the door, which refused to budge.

"Her mother musta locked it," Mrs. Thedford sighed.

"Melody!" McCall yelled, now frantic to see his shattered fiancée. He relentlessly pounded the door. "Melody! It's McCall!"

Melody produced no answer, only renewed sobbing, more intense, more tragic.

Growing increasingly desperate, McCall gritted his teeth, turned the doorknob, and slammed his shoulder against the door.

"No!" Mrs. Thedford wailed. "You mustn't! You can't! You're heapin' trouble on top of trouble. Can't you wait 'til tomorrow?"

McCall whirled to face the wrinkled maid. "She will see me now! I must see her. I must know what has happened to her. Why do you insist on keeping me in such suspense?" Perspiration now rolled down McCall's back, a product of his agitation and the heat of a summer night.

The doorknob rattled. A lock clicked. The door sighed as it swung inward, and Melody's mother, Lydia Graham, stood before him. Nothing but an older version of Melody, Mrs. Graham was known about town as an angel of light. Unlike many of the wealthy, who sought only to please themselves, Melody's mother made certain her inherited fortune fed the poor and clothed the needy. Even though McCall had seen her cry with the distress of the destitute, he had never seen her so broken as now. The genteel lady appeared to be mourning a death. Was Melody indeed dead? Were those sobs actually the wails of her mother?

McCall, now crazed, brushed past Mrs. Graham to see his beloved Melody, a crumpled, broken heap on her majestic, canopy bed. Her face buried in a pillow. Her body shaking with sobs. Her dress, torn and sullied. Oblivious to the codes of propriety, McCall rushed to Melody's side, sat on the edge of her bed, and pulled her into his arms. When she turned her face to his, McCall gasped at the sight of her swollen eyes and bleeding lips.

"Oh no. . ." McCall groaned, gathering Melody into his arms. "Oh no. . .no. . .no. . ." He held her tightly, and she clung to his lapel as a new onslaught of weeping wracked her thin body. "Have you sent for the doctor?" he demanded.

"Yes. Mr. Graham left only seconds before your arrival." Mrs. Graham choked back her own sob as she lowered herself to the end of Melody's bed. "I had just sent Mary down for some warm water."

As if on cue, Mary Thedford stopped hovering uncertainly near the doorway and dashed down the hallway.

"What happened?"

"I believe she. . .she. . .I cannot say it." Mrs. Graham covered her face while Melody clung to McCall as if he were her only link with sanity.

And McCall's worst suspicions were at last confirmed. Externally, he soothed Melody by gently stroking her hair and singing the love song he had written especially for her. Internally, McCall hurled every expletive he could conjure at the man who had done this to his beloved. Dashing all thoughts of biblical principles to the wind, McCall even plotted to kill the man if he found him.

The next few hours passed in a whirlwind of activity. After the doctor's examination and treatment, Melody was given a heavy sedative, which induced a sound sleep. While she slept, McCall requested an interview with Mr. Graham. The grim, stately gentleman ushered McCall into the shadowed library, which smelled of dried roses and musty books. Turning his back to McCall, Mr. Graham gazed out the floor-to-ceiling window, which opened onto the fragrant garden.

"I will understand if you feel that you must break the engagement with my daughter," Mr. Graham said, never taking his gaze from the garden, bathed in the full moon's light.

McCall choked on his own frustration and rushed to Mr. Graham's side. Didn't Melody's family understand just how desperately he loved her? "I was going to suggest just the opposite, Sir," McCall said respectfully. "Melody and I had planned to marry in the spring, but given the current circumstances, I–I wanted to suggest that perhaps the two of us should marry immediately."

Mr. Graham whirled to face McCall, his reddened eyes wide with astonishment. "Do you think your parents will support you in your decision once they know the truth?"

"They need not know."

"And how do you propose to keep it from them?"

"By requiring silence from everyone who knows of the situation. Who in your household knows?"

"Only the doorman and Melody's personal maid."

"Fine. We can tell them that if they tell a soul, they will lose their jobs. Furthermore, by marrying Melody now, if. . .if by chance there is a child. . ."

"Then everyone will think it was simply a product of your marriage."

"Yes."

The gentleman, who only yesterday appeared youthful enough to be Melody's elder brother, now looked old enough to be her grandfather rather than her father. The effects of grief upon the carefree man's demeanor struck McCall. "And this in no way affects your love for her?" Mr. Graham asked.

"If this were to affect my love, it is indeed no love at all. . . ."

❖

McCall, still sitting at Melody's dressing table, wearily pressed his fingertips against his forehead. This time, there were no tears in reliving the memory, only a dull ache where there had once been an opened, gaping hole. He looked into the mirror and gazed into his own eyes. Eyes that only an hour ago had drunk in the beauty of Miss Kate Lowell—cheeks red with the cool autumn breeze, lips tilted in a pleasant smile. Those eyes seemed determined to betray Melody's memory. Some part of him demanded that he continue to cling to Melody while another part of him seemed resolved to think only of Kate. Her dark hair, her gentle spirit, her obvious devotion to God, her eyes—the color of the sea. Something in McCall had urged him to take her in his arms, to feel her lips against his.

Deeply disgusted with himself, McCall fell to his knees beside the bed, gripping the homemade patchwork quilt in his clammy hands. In the last few years, with the help of God's Spirit at work in his life, McCall moved from wanting to kill the man who assaulted his beloved Melody to recognizing his need to forgive. Although McCall still periodically struggled with bitterness, God seemed forever patient as He gently led McCall toward a forgiving heart. Furthermore, God had begun to heal the pain caused by McCall's family disavowing him when he chose to raise Drew. McCall often prayed that his heart would be filled with unconditional love for those who should have supported his decision. Part of the answer to that prayer manifested itself in the restoration of the relationship between McCall and his elder sister, Rebekah, who now resided on the East Coast. But during all his struggles to try to be the man God wanted him to be, McCall never imagined that God would be pleased if he forgot Melody.

"Oh Lord," he pleaded. "Please take these detestable desires from me. I know, beyond any doubt, that you sent Miss Lowell here in answer to my prayer for a tutor. Please, Lord, *please,* end this torture within my soul. Oh God, help me to look upon Kate Lowell as a sister and nothing more. Surely, I could never truly love any other woman but Melody. That makes these feelings I'm having for Miss Lowell all the more abominable. . . ."

But in the midst of McCall's heavenward cry came a strong thought that left him distraught: *Release the past.* McCall blinked in stunned disbelief. How could McCall ever relinquish all that had happened? He couldn't. He wouldn't. No. This thought was not of God. It could never be of God. But he recalled his prior musings about God's intent in placing Miss Lowell at the ranch. Could the Lord actually be encouraging a romance that involved a man who was in no way ready for romance? The thought left McCall dismayed. Standing, he stiffly walked toward his bedroom door. He would not entertain these thoughts any further. McCall simply was not ready for another woman in his life, and God knew that.

But what if it were God's will for you to fall in love with Miss Lowell? Would you be willing to follow such a plan for your life?

The disturbing question stopped McCall as if he had slammed into a wall. With his mind still reeling from this emotional blow, McCall dashed from his log home and back toward his horse-grooming chores in the barn. McCall could, in no way, fathom that God would ask him to relinquish his feelings for Melody. He might as well put to death a part of his soul.

Chapter 5

Not believing her eyes, Kate blinked against the bright streaks of sunlight filtering through the thick trees. She had followed the path in the woods to a river that rushed along a wide, sandy bed. The smell of cold, fresh water wafted toward her senses as she examined the massive fallen tree trunk that spanned from one bank to the other. On that fallen tree tottered Drew, his arms extended for balance, as he followed another boy, dressed in faded overalls, who likewise walked across the fallen tree. Kate had seen this boy only once before—a boy with white-blond hair, a pug nose, and a stubborn set to his lips. Kate was certain this was none other than Calvin Wilcox, the boy with whom Drew had fought the day Kate agreed to the tutoring position.

As Kate studied them from her unobserved post, the two boys laughed companionably, as if they had been friends their whole lives. Deliberating her options, Kate chewed her lower lip. Should she reveal herself and demand Drew's return to the schoolroom? Or should she simply go back to the room and await his return? Should Kate report this incident to Mr. Adams? She couldn't imagine that he would want his son playing with Calvin, not after Wilcox had so blatantly disclosed his hostile intent. Furthermore, why wasn't Calvin in school himself?

"Calvin! Calvin Wilcox! Where are you, Boy?" a bearlike voice growled from the other side of the river.

Kate impulsively stepped behind a massive oak. Her heart pounding in dread, she peered around the tree to see both boys scramble from the fallen log. Calvin urgently pointed toward a hollow spot along the river's tall bank, much like a shallow cave. Drew skidded down the sandy bank on his backside and scrambled toward the concave hiding place.

"Calvin! Where are you?" Wilcox demanded once more.

"Right here, Pa," Calvin bellowed, his nonchalant walk matching his carefree voice. Kate marveled that only seconds before Calvin had urgently instructed Drew to hide. He casually bent to pick up a cane pole, a wooden bucket, and a basket full of fish. "I've been fishing," he said as his father appeared from amongst the thick thatch of trees on the opposite bank.

"Fishing?" The angular Wilcox, who carried a rifle, looked down at his son in such a critical, scornful manner that Kate pitied young Calvin. Next, Eugene scanned the river as if he were looking for someone. "Did I hear you talkin' to someone?" he barked.

"See! Ma can cook 'em for dinner." Calvin proudly held up the basket full of fish as if he were trying to divert his father's attention. "I found a school of minnows and dipped 'em out of the river, then used 'em for bait." He sloshed the bucket of water for emphasis.

"I kept ya home from school today to help me in the fields, not fish!" Eugene greedily grabbed the basket of fish. "Now go dig those sweet 'taters like I told you to."

"But Pa, Ma said we didn't have no meat for dinner today. I thought you'd be glad I caught so many—"

Eugene slapped Calvin on the side of his head and shoved him forward. "Just shut up and get to work."

Kate's stomach twisted in pity for Calvin. The Wilcoxes obviously needed the fish for their dinner. Why couldn't Eugene praise his son's efforts instead of treating him so harshly?

As Calvin picked his way through the underbrush, Eugene turned and examined the river again. "I coulda sworn I heard you talkin' to someone," he growled as he fell in behind his son.

Calvin maintained his silence and a startled buck instantly distracted Eugene. He dropped the fish basket, aimed, and fired his weapon.

Kate jumped as her ears rang with the gun's explosion.

A long stream of expletives followed as Wilcox watched the deer bound into the woods' thick underbrush. Eugene pulled a bottle of whisky from his pocket and took a long swallow, then he picked up the basket full of fish and silently followed his son. Kate released her pent-up breath as she realized the deer had so distracted Eugene that he forgot to further question Calvin about the person to whom he had been talking.

She watched until the father and son were nowhere to be seen or heard. At last, Drew scrambled up the river's bank, sand and fallen leaves softly crunching under his boots. Kate stepped from behind her hasty hiding spot. Her arms folded, she silently watched her pupil cautiously pick his way back over the fallen tree trunk that spanned the river. Tongue between his teeth, he hopped onto her side of the bank. Drew bent to brush the damp sand from his fresh denims before starting toward the path on which she stood. Drew casually glanced up to see Kate and stopped, his eyes round.

"Miss Lowell! What are you—"

"I came to find you, Drew Adams! What do you think you're doing, wandering off in the woods when it's time for school?" Kate said in her firmest voice. She had never found it necessary to discipline a tardy boy before. The authoritative tone of her own voice amazed her.

"Ah, Miss Lowell. . ." Drew, hanging his head, kicked at a protruding root with the tip of his boot. "I get so bored sitting in that room all day long, I just—"

"And what in the world has transpired between you and Calvin Wilcox?" Kate interrupted.

"We're friends now!" Drew said, his dark eyes bright with expectation.

"How did that happen? Two weeks ago, if I remember correctly, the two of you weren't on the friendliest terms."

"Oh that, Calvin just needed somebody to call his bluff, that's all. Once I showed him he couldn't bully me, he came around."

Kate often curiously mused that Drew didn't resemble his father, but she couldn't deny that he possessed McCall's mannerisms and turns of phrase. "I'm assuming the Wilcox's land must meet yours along here somewhere?"

"Yes Ma'am," Drew said, moving past Kate to walk along the path.

Kate fell into step behind him.

"Calvin says they just bought the land from Mr. Parker. They used to farm the land for him. Now they own it."

"Well," Kate continued, glancing up at the back of Drew's head, "do you think it's wise to develop such a friendship with Calvin, considering his father's recent outburst?"

"I'm not afraid of his father," Drew said bravely. A dove's gentle cooing filtered through the expanse of trees and wrapped its call around them.

"Does your father know of your friendship with Calvin?"

"No Ma'am." Drew spun to face her. "And please don't tell him. Dad never lets me have friends. I get so tired of. . .of being all alone. Calvin is the only friend I have right now."

Drew's dark, pleading eyes touched the very bottom of Kate's heart. She had silently observed Mr. Adams's protective tendencies toward Drew. Considering Drew's mixed heritage and the reactions of folks like the tutor at the train station, Kate couldn't say that she blamed Mr. Adams very much. Nonetheless, the impact of such shielding must be tremendously stifling to a free-spirited fourteen-year-old boy.

"Please promise you won't tell Dad," Drew pressed again.

Kate swallowed against a throat as dry as the autumn leaves, falling one by one from the surrounding trees. At once, she felt torn between allegiance to the boy she had grown extremely fond of and his handsome father who employed her. At long last, a thought struck her, and she spoke. "I won't tell your father if—"

"Oh, thank you, Miss Lowell!" The exuberant Drew grabbed her hands.

"I won't tell your father *if* you promise not to come to the woods any more until *after* lessons and *if* you promise to use the utmost discretion in your friendship. I do not believe it would be wise for Wilcox to discover that Calvin and you are friends."

"I promise! I promise! I'll just tell Calvin to meet me in the afternoons. That'll work out better anyway since he has to go to school most mornings. And we wouldn't dare tell his father. . .or mine." A thoughtful glimmer danced through Drew's eyes. "I wish Dad would let me go to school with Calvin," he muttered.

A stab of disappointment entered Kate's chest. Was Drew not happy with her as a teacher?

As if Drew could read Kate's mind, he interjected, "Oh. . .not that I don't like you, Miss Lowell. I–I–It's just that I would so like to know what other boys my age are up to." His voice squeaked on the final words, attesting to his emerging manhood.

"I understand," Kate said, squeezing Drew's arm. And the truth was, Kate understood too well. So well that she ached for the boy who seemed to have no idea that his mixed heritage would stalk him for life.

As they walked back through the dense trees and toward the pasture full of horses, a new thought struck Kate. A new thought that spawned raging curiosity. What was Drew's mother like? She must have been a beautiful, gracious woman to have stolen McCall Adams's heart. Kate pondered how McCall had come to know and fall in love with an Indian woman. His wife must have been full of charm and wisdom. Absently, she wondered if Mr. Adams possessed any photos. Perhaps there were some in the log cabin.

Immediately, Kate put an end to such thoughts. Mr. Adams had never once invited her into his log cabin. She and Drew usually shared their noon meal in the summer kitchen or they picnicked under a tree. If she did find a valid reason to be in McCall's home, Kate would not become a snoop in order to satisfy her inquisitive interests. As she followed Drew through the pasture's gate and toward the schoolroom, Kate couldn't deny her deep curiosity concerning the kind of woman whom McCall Adams would love. If he were ever to invite Kate into his home, she would certainly not decline the opportunity to view any photos that were in clear view.

Amazingly, the opportunity to see a photo of McCall's wife presented itself, with no effort from Kate, within a matter of weeks.

❖

By early December, Kate realized Mr. Adams's determination, at all costs, to avoid her. While Drew silently calculated his math equations, Kate watched out the window as Mr. Adams masterfully broke in a gray dappled stallion. After that one morning when McCall had escorted her from the hotel to the ranch, he had arranged for his hired hand, Bob Mosely, to drive Kate. From that day until now, Kate only caught momentary glimpses of her employer. Despite herself, she began to greedily consume those glimpses. His square jaw line. The aristocratic nose. His close-set dark eyes and heavy brows. The lean form of his powerful frame.

Today, Mr. Adams wore his usual pullover denim shirt and worn leather jacket, dark riding pants, the ever present black hat, and frayed working gloves. As the stallion repeatedly lowered his head, kicked his feet, and stirred clouds of dust into the cold, morning air, McCall rode in rhythm, seeming to second-guess the angry horse's every move. The stocky Mr. Mosely stood on the wooden fence that encompassed the corral, whooping as if McCall were a hero of war. At long last, the stallion calmed, snorting as he ran the circumference of the corral until he stopped and haughtily raised his head, ears pricked. McCall stroked the horse's pale gray neck; his concentration focused solely on the task at hand.

Then, as if he felt her watching him, Mr. Adams glanced toward the summer kitchen and directly into the window where Kate stood. Her stomach felt like it dropped to her feet as she was once more entranced by McCall Adams's warm appraisal. They might as well have been in the carriage all over again, reliving that moment when he placed his coat around her. The coat he wore now. Kate's arms warmed as if he had indeed placed it around her shoulders, and she could almost smell the odor of leather mixed with horses once more.

Their gaze continued, and the emotions Kate had suppressed for weeks would no longer be stifled. She felt as if the man might as well have kissed her. There was no denying the attraction Mr. Adams held for her. Even at this distance, his expression burned with open admiration. Kate, certain she was just as transparent, could do little to hide her feelings. Kate's mother had painstakingly taught her the art of maintaining a cool demeanor, during any circumstance. But since the moment she met Mr. Adams and Drew, Kate had somehow stepped out of that upper society style of conduct.

She should go home to El Paso. Now. Before this. . .this senseless hopelessness between her and Mr. Adams escalated into something neither of them wanted. Kate was not prepared to ever lose her heart again as she had with Zachary. His death had almost devastated her. Kate remembered, day after day, returning to his grave and sobbing until she collapsed. She remembered her irrational anger at Travis Campbell, who took Zach's accidental death as hard as Kate did. She didn't know if she could mentally survive another deep loss. There were times in the midst of her grief that she wondered if she were, indeed, going insane.

Kate had nothing against the possibilities of marriage. A marriage of convenience would suit her nicely. Nonetheless, she could not and would not ever give her heart to another man the way she had given it to Zachary. The prospect left her shaking in dread of what new pain that might involve.

As her legs trembled and she continued to be held captive by McCall's steady appraisal, Kate recognized, once and for all, that this man presented a dire threat to her need to forevermore withhold her heart. Not that she had, by any means, fallen in love with him. But Kate could no longer deny that too much time with McCall Adams would prove emotionally fatal.

The flames that crackled in the fireplace might as well have been the sounds of Kate's own emotions, stirred by the fire pulsing within her veins. McCall Adams was exactly the kind of man who arrested Kate. A man of strength and dignity. A man of strong faith. A man who would never turn his back on one in need. Over the last weeks, she had seen McCall give meals and a strong horse to two different, weary families, down on their luck, crossing the country on foot, in search of work and a place to call home. McCall was a stark contrast to the refined men in El Paso who wore their Christianity like a fine suit. McCall Adams lived his faith. He was genuine. And Kate was, without question, mesmerized.

A light tap on her shoulder stirred Kate from her reverie, and she spun to face Drew, his dancing, dark eyes full of questions. "What has you so distracted, Miss Lowell? I've asked you the same question three times." Drew glanced out the window in the very direction where Kate had been looking.

"Oh, I'm so sorry, I just. . ." As she trailed off helplessly, her cheeks grew exceptionally warm, and she nervously stepped toward Drew's desk.

The boy watched her, a speculative gleam in his eyes, and Kate knew, with a sense of dread, that Drew understood more than she ever wished.

"What was your question?" she asked, leaning over the page full of math equations that Drew had meticulously solved.

"I was just asking you to check over my work and wondering if I might go for a walk now. I thought I'd see if I could add to our leaf collection." He moved toward the fragrant fire, grabbed a poker, and jabbed at the flaming logs.

As she had suspected in recent weeks, Kate realized with certainty that Drew had grown at least an inch since her arrival two months ago. His ever-present denims, now much too short, attested to his growth spurt.

And Drew's keen eye for detail attested to his brilliance. While Kate had joyously embraced the opportunity to tutor such an intelligent lad, she now wished he weren't quite so astute in his powers of observation. Kate forced herself to examine the math problems, finding only one small error.

"You may go, if you like," she said, wanting more than anything to be left alone. Alone for prayer. Kate desperately needed to seek God's guidance concerning the possibility of her leaving Dogwood. . .soon. Out of the corner of her eye, she saw Drew hesitating, and she cringed with the tension that had sprung between them.

"Dad likes you," Drew said at last.

Kate looked up. "What?" she gasped.

"Dad likes you," Drew repeated in a very practical tone.

She produced a shaky, polite smile, while her heart whispered confirmation of Drew's admission. "Whatever would make you say something like that, Drew Adams?" Kate said in a fondly scolding tone.

Drew shrugged. "Just because I catch him watching you off and on, especially in the morning when Mr. Mosely arrives with you. It's like he waits at the kitchen window while I finish my breakfast until he sees you arrive. Yesterday morning, he even called me 'Kate' instead of 'Drew.' " The boy produced a dry cough.

Nonplussed, Kate glanced toward the dark, wooden floor and made a monumental job of examining the shadows from the flickering fire as they danced hither and yon.

"And I can't say that I blame him. . .for. . .for watching you," Drew continued in a halting voice.

Kate once more was compelled to look into Drew's eyes, now churning with emotion.

"Miss Lowell. . .you're so beautiful," he announced awkwardly, his face flushing.

She swallowed against the lump in her throat that threatened to choke her as she recognized a full-blown case of puppy love. "I. . .I don't know what to say, Drew. Of course, I'm. . .I'm flattered by your. . .your admiration, but. . .but. . ."

"Oh, I know I'm much too young for you," he continued helplessly. "But Dad isn't."

Truly stunned, she blinked and began a desperate, silent plea for heavenly deliverance from this awkward moment.

"I don't think he's even looked at another woman since mother—except you."

"Do you remember your mother, Drew?" Kate asked, relieved to grab onto a subject that would deliver her from the present line of conversation.

"No, of course not. She died when I was born."

"Oh."

"All I have are a few photos of her."

"Oh?" Kate's ongoing curiosity about McCall's wife resurrected itself in oversized proportions.

"Yes. Would you like to see her photo? I keep it in my desk."

"Well, I. . ."

With no encouragement from Kate, Drew walked toward the pine table, which served as his desk. He pulled open the bottom side drawer and extracted a picture frame that looked to be fine pewter, much like the ones her mother purchased from the silversmith.

"There she is. She was beautiful, wasn't she? Dad says I take after her."

Kate, trembling with expectation, took the extended photo and looked into the face of a woman who held no traces of Indian heritage. Kate's mind whirled with questions as she glanced from the photo to Drew and back to the photo. There was a marked resemblance between Drew and the woman, who possessed a sweet, candid tilt to her fine-boned face. She and Drew shared the same forehead and generous mouth. But Drew's obvious Indian traits varied greatly from any other facial features that his mother possessed, or that McCall possessed, for that matter.

"Yes. . .yes, I think you do take after her," Kate said gently, astounded at the implications of this photo. She continued to silently stare at the picture's varying shades of gray until they blurred. Vaguely, she acknowledged Drew's repeated request for a walk in the woods and gave him permission to leave.

When the door opened minutes later, Kate glanced up from her perusal of the photo, expecting to see Drew. Instead, she encountered the questioning eyes of McCall Adams. The pewter frame seemed to burn in Kate's hand, and her face warmed far past comfort.

"I noticed Drew going toward the woods. Did you give. . .him. . .permission. . .to. . ." McCall's words trailed to a stop as he glanced toward Kate's hands.

She resisted the urge to hide the picture behind her back.

Chapter 6

Despite his personal pledge to avoid Kate, McCall continued to look for an excuse—any excuse—to approach her. The last several weeks of watching Kate without speaking to her had been something close to torment. When he saw Drew traipsing off to the woods, McCall knew he had found his excuse to speak with the lovely tutor.

But seeing her holding Melody's photo left McCall's insides churning in rage. He felt as though Kate had somehow violated his privacy and his memory of the wife he still loved. "How *dare* you snoop in Drew's desk!" McCall accused. Closing the distance between them, he jerked the photo from her hands.

"I didn't snoop! I didn't even ask to see the photo. Drew retrieved it and asked me to look at it. How dare *you* accuse *me* of snooping!"

"You could have declined the offer!" McCall demanded, his face only inches from Kate's.

"He gave me little choice!" she said in a voice just as challenging as his. "Drew pulled the picture from his desk and placed it in my hands before I had the chance to decline."

McCall fully expected Miss Lowell to back down from him. Yet her flashing eyes, flared nostrils, and firm lips showed no signs that her retreat was even a remote possibility. Her strong will both shocked and perplexed McCall. He never anticipated this much determination from such an exquisite lady.

Thoughts of apologizing flitted through McCall's jumbled mind. But those considerations had precious little opportunity to mature into words as other disturbing reflections muddled his mind. Reflections of Kate's flushed cheeks and the soft contour of her narrow nose. Reflections of the silvery spokes that darted from her pupils to add a hint of intrigue to her eyes. Reflections of how her dark hair, glistening in the dim firelight, would feel under his touch. Reflections of the weeks and weeks and weeks he had silently watched her disembark Bob Mosely's wagon. Reflections of the moment that left him as weak as a newborn colt when he caught her watching him from the window.

McCall hadn't held a woman in fourteen years—not since he clutched Melody and watched her slip into a coma. But standing here in this schoolroom, McCall couldn't even remember why he was angry. All he could think was how much he wanted to feel Miss Kate Lowell's lips kissing his.

The room seemed to shimmer with the force of McCall's emotions. Kate's determined expression softened to one of mystique and attraction. McCall, reacting from the moment, did what he had wanted to do when he caught Kate watching him. He stroked her cheek with the back of his fingers. Her quick breath, her bottom lip caught between her teeth only added to McCall's own reactions. Kate's skin was as soft as he had ever imagined. The sweet scent of her rose perfume propelled him to move all the closer and brush his lips ever so gently against hers.

McCall half expected Miss Lowell to pull away. When she didn't, he reached for her arms with the intent of lengthening the kiss. But McCall, mesmerized by the moment, forgot about the treasured photo he held. When he clasped Kate's arms, the frame fell from his hand and crashed against the floor.

The jarring sound of shattering glass seemed to awaken McCall's common sense. *Melody. . .Melody. . .Melody.* He had forgotten all about her. And, in the forgetting, he had destroyed the glass that protected her precious photo. McCall abruptly stepped away from Kate, now disgusted with his jagged breathing, with his thoughtless reaction to this exquisite lady.

She immediately stooped to pick up the shards of broken glass. "I'm so sorry," Kate muttered, as though she had been the one who broke it.

"It wasn't your fault," McCall heard himself say, feeling as if he were still trapped under the spell of Kate's beauty. He bent to assist her, only to have their hands descend upon the frame in exactly the same spot. Kate's pliable, warm hand stilled under his and trembled against his calloused palm. Once more, the room seemed to fill with his raging emotions. McCall's stomach churned with the warm response he had worked so hard to deny since the first time he set eyes on Kate. As hard as he had prayed, as much as he wanted to remain loyal to Melody, as disgusted as he was with himself, McCall still found Miss Lowell fascinating.

Realizing the horrid irony of his present situation, McCall observed their hands, touching over Melody's photo. The sight gave him the strength to release Kate's hand, grab the pewter frame, and stalk toward the door.

"You're still in love with her, aren't you?" Kate whispered. Her voice sounded like the faint rustling of dry leaves stirred by a chilling winter breeze.

McCall, angered by her observation, whirled to face the woman who only seconds before he had kissed. Her crestfallen demeanor did little to calm his churning stomach and raging soul. "That's none of your business," he snapped, his voice sounding tormented, even to his own ears. "I didn't hire you to question my feelings."

"And did you hire me with plans to kiss me?" she demanded, her fists clenched at her side.

"I hired you to tutor my son. Period!"

"Is he *really* your son?" Kate blurted. Immediately she covered her mouth with the tips of her shaking fingers as if she were as shocked by her own words as McCall.

"How dare you." McCall growled, his paternal protection making him despise the idea of Kate's understanding the truth that no one in Dogwood but Dr. Engle knew. "That is none of your business."

"And what about Drew? Is it *his* business?" She rushed to a straight-backed chair near the fireplace and gripped the top rail until her knuckles were white.

"Drew—"

"How much longer do you think you can keep the truth from him? Do you honestly think the boy will continue on, blissfully thinking he just takes after his mother?"

McCall's face chilled. While he knew he couldn't indefinitely hide the truth from Drew, McCall had hoped to postpone that inevitable day of reckoning for a few more years.

"Were you ever even married to her?" Kate continued, as if the question were wrenched from her.

New fury churned through McCall's veins. His forehead beaded in sweat. "How can you suggest. . . You never even knew her!" He took several deliberate steps toward Kate and lowered his face to within inches of hers once more. Her responding flinch was barely discernible. "I will tell you one time, and one time only, and you'd better listen closely," he said in a menacing, measured tone. "Melody was forced into something she never wanted; I arrived at her house and found her beaten and sobbing in her mother's arms. She never even got a good look at the man's face—we didn't even know he was an Indian until Drew was born. She was my fiancée at the time. I could have very easily broken our engagement and no one—*no one* would have blamed me. I married her two days later because I *loved* her." A knot formed in McCall's throat. "And given the slight chance that there was to be a child, I wanted to do everything in my power to protect Melody's dignity."

Kate's eyes widened in dismay as the full force of the truth struck her. "I'm—I'm t–terribly. . .t–terribly sorry," she stammered, her face growing pale. "I should have never. . .I have been dreadfully. . ." With the swish of her forest green skirt, Kate turned from him and approached the rock fireplace. She crossed her arms and kept her back to him, her shoulders hunched.

McCall, gritting his teeth, whipped open the door and stalked onto the yard. With a rush, the cool afternoon air met the perspiration on his neck and forehead and produced an icy shiver down his spine. McCall paused, observing the winter sun proudly projecting its bright afternoon rays across the expanse of his property. The sun bathed McCall's world in golden light. The corral. The pasture full of horses. The massive barn. His small log cabin. But the sun had not shone on his heart for fourteen years. Not really. Oh, Drew had brought him an enormous amount of joy, and McCall had done everything in his power to be a good father. . .for Melody's sake. . .for his own sake. But deep inside, McCall was as cold as ice.

Release the past.

Just as that thought had intruded his mind and disturbed his quiet times over the last few weeks, it once more seemed to come from nowhere. McCall wanted to rend his hair with the anguish this thought delivered. How could he ever release his hold on the past? How could he ever release his love for Melody?

He rushed across the expanse of the yard that separated his home from the summer kitchen. Taking huge, determined strides, he stepped up onto his rough-hewn porch. McCall whipped open the door, slammed it behind him, and crashed onto the horsehair sofa. He tossed the shattered frame onto the sofa and threw his hat across the room. In despair over his wretched situation, McCall placed his elbows on his knees and grabbed his head in his hands. He curled his calloused fingers into his hair until it felt as if he were pulling the hair out by the roots.

Melody. . .Melody. . .Melody.

He tried with all his might to conjure her image, but all McCall saw was the wide-eyed beauty he had just kissed. With a groan, he leaned back, closed his eyes, and desperately tried to pray. But no words would come.

As if his heart were bent on tormenting him, he at long last *did* recall Melody's image. Melody, shortly after Drew's birth, clutching at McCall's shirt as if she were clutching at life. After the forty-hour labor, the doctor had sadly shaken his head and said she had begun to hemorrhage and had lost entirely too much blood. McCall, choking on his own sobs had begged Melody to stay with him. Up until the baby was born, McCall had respected the delicacy of her emotional and physical condition, never touching her in the way a husband knew a wife. But he had hoped, desperately hoped, that perhaps Melody's broken heart would mend, and they would be able to begin a true marriage after she recovered from giving birth. Now he watched all his hopes, all his dreams. . .his Melody weakly clinging to her last breaths.

Just before she went into the coma, she gripped McCall's shirt and said, "Promise me you'll. . .you'll keep little. . .little Drew. P–Promise me. I. . .I cannot explain it to you, b–but I love. . .love him. H–He is a part of. . .of me. . . even. . .even though. . .I would have never. . .never wished it. . .so. . . ."

"I promise. I promise. I promise," McCall had repeated like a mad man. He desperately wanted to deny the significance of Melody's request. He wanted to beg her to fight for her life. Instead, McCall had promised and then watched her slip away, into a coma, and from the coma into the arms of death.

During those following days, McCall was so numb from pain, so consumed with the funeral and the family gathering, so caught up in the task of finding a wet nurse, that he was blind to the intents of his immediate family. Melody's family was honored that he would even consider raising Drew. They offered both financial and moral support. McCall's family reacted in the opposite manner. Once they actually saw baby Drew, McCall's parents demanded the truth of his conception. Shortly thereafter, Mr. and Mrs. Adams arranged a private, surprise meeting with McCall and a woman who ran an orphanage. She grudgingly said she would take the baby off his hands for a substantial fee. When McCall refused, his parents were aghast that their son would risk the family reputation for a child who wasn't even his.

McCall relived that moment with vivid clarity. He stood in the ornate library at his parent's mansion, glaring at both of his elite parents and that plump, greedy redhead who wanted to take little Drew away.

"I promised Melody I would raise Drew myself, and I *will* raise him," McCall growled. "He might not be mine. But he is Melody's. I loved her. And I *will* love him." Out of the corner of his eye, he saw the library door inch open and his grandfather's wrinkled face appear in the opening. The sight of that face of character only increased McCall's determination. Pa Adams, who had been like a father to McCall, had been the only one in the Adams household who, from the onset, knew the whole truth of Melody's tragic circumstances. The kindly retired doctor had been nothing but a source of strength through the whole ordeal.

As the tense silence continued, the mantel clock ticked off the seconds, sounding more like a death toll than a timepiece.

At long last, his father spoke, slowly and deliberately. "If you do not release this. . .this. . .illegitimate. . .we will be forced to ask you to leave. For good."

McCall, rigid with rage, had stomped from the room to be greeted by his pale grandfather. "I will help you," Pa Adams said, gripping McCall's arms. And he did. Within the week, the dear, sickly saint had signed over every penny he owned to McCall and Drew, and the three of them moved into quarters of their own. A year later, Pa Adams went to meet the Lord, and Drew started his horse ranch in Dogwood.

The whole horrid story, fourteen years removed, still seemed as fresh in McCall's mind as if it had happened yesterday. He kept these events locked tightly within his heart's cold corridor, where the sun never shone. In that icy chamber, the story remained preserved and fresh; the pain, although dulled with the years, still lived to be recalled at any given moment.

Release the past.

"How? How? How?" he roared heavenward. McCall stood. With a vengeance, he retrieved his hat from across the room, crammed it back onto his head, and left the cabin, deliberately walking toward the spot in the woods where he had seen Drew disappear.

McCall would focus on the practical necessities of the moment and once more ignore that disturbing thought that suggested he put the past behind him. And the practical necessities of *this* moment involved finding out why his son was wandering through the woods when he should be studying.

Chapter 7

K ate scurried from one corner of the summer kitchen to the other, retrieving the few pencils and books that belonged to her. Once she arranged her possessions in a neat pile, she began straightening Drew's papers and books. At last, she grabbed the straw broom from its spot in the corner and swept up the last shards of broken glass.

She was leaving. She was leaving and not coming back. Kate would go home, back to El Paso. Never, absolutely never, would she return to Dogwood. For any reason.

After Mr. Adams's recent behavior and obvious love for his deceased wife, Kate fully realized the futility—yes, the blind stupidity—of continuing on as Drew's tutor. The situation was beyond volatile. Furthermore, Kate was well on the road to completely and irrevocably losing her heart to this tall, lean man, with his captivating eyes and hidden heart. And that was one loss she simply could not risk.

"Now!" she said aloud, gazing around the room to see if she'd left anything out of place. Satisfied with the neat appearance, Kate grabbed her reticule and light shawl, both hanging from a peg near the door. She wrapped the shawl around her arms, picked up her books and pencils, and reached for the doorknob.

As the cold metal contacted her already chilled palm, an equally chilling thought left her spine tingling. *You have not once stopped to pray about your hasty decision. What if it is God's will for you to stay? What if it is God's will for you to give your heart to Mr. Adams?*

Kate gripped the doorknob. She stared into the smoldering fire. She pressed her trembling lips together. At once, Kate felt as if she were involved in a battle of wills. Some still, small voice in the bottom of her soul whispered for her to stay, but her mind demanded she behave rationally and leave immediately. She should go this instant, find Mr. Mosely, and ask him to take her back to the hotel.

Her contemplative gaze fell upon Drew's desk and his pile of graded papers. Kate's heart twisted with thoughts of leaving the boy. Every day her fondness for Drew had grown. She was one of a precious few connections he had to the outside world. He would be so disappointed if Kate left.

She should at least leave him a note, explaining that her decision was in no way a product of her feelings for him. Kate, rushing to his desk, plopped down her books and reticule. The top book, Kate's Bible, toppled over and plunked open to release a dried red rose. The last rose Zachary gave Kate before his death. She slowly picked up the fading flower and held it to her nose, inhaling the faint, sweet odor. With the rose, Zachary had bestowed a gentle kiss upon Kate's waiting lips. Immediately, she compared that kiss to the one Mr. Adams and she had shared. Her face heated with the drastic difference in her response to Mr. Adams and her response to Zachary. Regardless of her love for him, Zachary had never stirred her as Mr. Adams had stirred her. This realization only heightened Kate's determination to leave. She placed the dried rose back into the Bible and firmly shut its pages.

Trembling anew, she grabbed a sheet of the coarse paper she found in the top drawer. Kate positioned her pencil over the empty page, bit her lips, and debated about how to begin. But she could never get past "Dear Drew." After several frustrating seconds of racking her brain, Kate's eyes began to sting. What a horrid predicament to be in, feeling as if she must flee the father, yet knowing her fleeing would betray the son in the deepest sense.

The determined pounding of boots against firm ground diverted her attention. The footsteps neared the kitchen's doorway and stopped only long enough for the door to fling open. McCall, his face dark, stepped into the room, followed by Drew, his head lowered, his eyes downcast.

McCall opened his mouth to speak, only to hesitate and briefly glance at the shawl Kate wore and her posture. A momentary expression of understanding flashed across his face before he narrowed his eyes and spoke.

"I just found Drew playing with Calvin Wilcox. Drew tells me you gave him permission to befriend Calvin," he growled as if Kate were guilty of the most heinous of crimes.

Kate looked from the downtrodden Drew, to his father, and back to Drew. "Yes. I did," she said defensively.

"How dare you go behind my back and allow a friendship you knew full well I would never approve!"

She deposited her pencil on the desk and turned to fully face McCall. "The child needs a friend," she said evenly. "I'm not going to tell you I wasn't concerned about Mr. Wilcox's attitude, but I admonished Drew to use discretion. How long do you think you are going to be able to keep him under lock and key, Mr. Adams? He is starved for friendship!"

"That is none of your business!" McCall walked across the room until he was once more standing within inches of Kate. "And furthermore, you have no right to approve such things. You should have referred him to me."

"Why? So you could tell him 'no' and keep him isolated his whole life?"

"I'm trying to protect him."

"Or trying to control him!"

"He's my son. I *should* control him."

"No! You should *lead* him. There's a *huge* difference!"

"For a woman who has no children, you are amazingly astute on the subject, Miss Lowell," he said sarcastically.

"I know enough to know you are gripping Drew so tightly the poor boy can hardly breathe!" she yelled. "And you're becoming a slave to your own control."

"What's that supposed to mean?"

"It's supposed to mean that it's an all-consuming job to hang onto someone to the degree you're hanging onto Drew. You don't have time for a life of your own because you're spending every spare moment making certain Drew is protected."

"Listen, Woman." He grabbed her upper arms, his eyes the glittering orbs of an angered panther.

"No, you listen, *Mr. Adams*." Gritting her teeth, Kate jerked away from his grip. "You might be able to intimidate every other woman you've ever known, but you *will not* intimidate me. So you might as well stop trying." Kate, her stomach churning, her legs about to collapse, could not believe the firmness, the self-assurance with which she uttered those words. She felt far from the bravado she claimed. But Kate would never let McCall Adams know that.

"Furthermore," she continued, narrowing her eyes once more. "I admonished Drew from the onset to take extra precaution in his dealings with Calvin. He understood that if Mr. Wilcox found out—"

"Let's not discuss Wilcox right now, especially not in front of. . ." Pressing his lips together, McCall trailed off as if he were frustrated with his own words.

"Why not, Dad?" Drew asked. "Do you think I don't know why Mr. Wilcox doesn't like me?"

Kate, stunned by what Drew might say, joined McCall in silently studying him.

"I know he calls me a 'stinkin' Injun.' And I also know that's because I am. . .am part Indian." Drew studied the tips of his boots.

"How do you know that?" McCall asked, his face ashen.

"A few months ago, I asked Dr. Engle some. . .some questions." Drew's intense dark eyes now scrutinized his father.

"And?"

"And he told me that. . .that you. . .you adopted me."

Silently, McCall rubbed a tired hand over his weary face. "And what else did he tell you, Drew?"

"That was all. That's all I know. But. . .but. . ." He shuffled his feet uncomfortably. "I'd certainly like to know the whole story. . .sometime."

"Why didn't you ask me in the first place?"

The boy shrugged and helplessly looked toward Kate.

"Perhaps he simply wasn't. . .wasn't comfortable with that prospect," she supplied with an encouraging note.

McCall produced a weary sigh, stuffed his hands into his pockets, and walked toward the fireplace. He placed his arm along the rugged mantel and rested his forehead against his arm.

"May I. . .may I go now?" Drew asked.

"Yes. That's fine. Go do your chores," McCall said in a tight voice.

Drew silently left the summer kitchen and closed the door behind him.

Kate braced herself for another outburst from her angry employer but determined to remain calm.

"You were leaving and not coming back." He turned to face her. "Am I correct?" His measured words surprised Kate more than any amount of yelling would have.

"You are correct."

"Why?"

She suppressed a sarcastic snort. "Why do you think, Mr. Adams?"

Lips tightly together, he silently appraised Kate until she felt more than uncomfortable. Nevertheless, she refused to flinch from his scrutiny.

"Would it make any difference if I apologized?" he said at last.

Kate blinked. Once more, the man had completely taken her by surprise. "For what do you contemplate apologizing?"

He walked toward the window and silently stared toward the rolling, east Texas hills, full of barren trees and evergreens. "I think you know full well," he said at last.

"You mean for everything?"

"Yes, everything."

So much had happened this afternoon that Kate's mind whirled with the events. Not only had Mr. Adams kissed her, he had also stormed away when she brought up the subject of Melody and Drew. Moments ago, he angrily confronted her with her decision to allow Drew to befriend Calvin.

A tendril of guilt twisted through Kate's heart. If the truth were known, she owed Mr. Adams an apology as well. She should have never allowed him to kiss her. She should have never broached the subject of Drew's parentage after the kiss. That was none of her business, just as he had so skillfully pointed out. No wonder McCall stormed away. Kate probably would have done the same. And she really *didn't* have the authority to approve Drew's friendship with Calvin, even though she believed it was in Drew's best interest to have a friend.

Kate looked down at her fingers, tightly intertwined. "You aren't the only one who should be apologizing," she whispered. "I'm sorry for everything, too."

She heard McCall turn from the window but didn't dare look up. She felt him staring at her but didn't dare meet his gaze. She understood his amazement but didn't dare express her own. For despite their quarrels, Kate still felt dangerously drawn to McCall. She didn't trust herself not to run into his arms, place her hands on either side of his face, and tell him she would do her best to make the pain in his life go away. That danger, coupled with the knowledge that she shouldn't leave, no matter what her common sense demanded, would make looking at McCall emotionally hazardous.

"Does that mean you'll stay? Drew likes you so much. He would be disappointed if you—"

"And would you be disappointed?" For the second time that day, Kate covered her lips with trembling fingertips and studied the tips of her black ankle boots, peeking from beneath the hem of her green skirt. Why did she persist in saying things she shouldn't? How many times in one day would her face heat?

This was beyond unreasonable.

She was beyond mortified.

If her mother had witnessed Kate's behavior today, she would faint from embarrassment. Actually, her mother would not be pleased with Kate's behavior since her arrival in Dogwood. Perhaps part of Kate's straying from her mother's instructions stemmed from the fact that her mother was not present. Kate, for the first time in her life, was feeling free. Free to be herself. Even Zachary himself had admired Kate for her cool restraint. Kate thought that was simply who she was. But given a few weeks as a tutor, a few weeks in the presence of this man who looked like an aristocrat, who rode horses like a prince, who had known enough grief for two lifetimes, the man who still scrutinized her, after but a few weeks in the presence of McCall Adams, Kate was learning she was far from a woman of cool dignity. She was a woman of deep passions.

Without another word, McCall stepped out of the room and snapped the door shut behind him.

Kate released a pent-up breath and collapsed in the desk's chair. Her cold hands shaking, she covered her equally chilled face. At first, the hot tears silently trickled down her cheeks. But at last, she broke with the intensity of her emotions to produce a cross between a cough and a sob.

Once more, Kate heard the door open, someone step in, and the door closing behind him. Assuming Mr. Adams was returning, she stifled her cries, part from dread, part from expectation.

"Miss Lowell?"

Drew's hesitant voice produced a wave of relief in Kate that left her slumping. She nervously fished in her skirt's hidden pocket for the ever present lace handkerchief. Gently, Kate dabbed away the tears and turned to face Drew. "Yes, Drew?" she said, producing a wobbly smile she was far from feeling.

"Is everything. . .are you—Dad. . .was he terribly mean to you?"

A new tear trickled from the corner of Kate's eye as she took in the deep concern cloaking Drew's every feature. The boy truly cared for Kate. How could she have ever thought of leaving him? He needed her. God had called her to this place at this time to minister to this Indian boy, just as He had called her to help that Indian girl in El Paso—the girl on which she had turned her back. Kate could not repeat that act, regardless of her differences with Mr. Adams.

214

"Your father apologized, Drew."

"But the whole thing was *my* fault." Drew hurried to Kate's side, gripped her hands, and knelt beside her.

"Oh Drew. . ."

"I should have never made you promise to hide my friendship with Calvin," he rushed. "I did it because I knew Dad would never approve, not after my fight with Calvin and the things his father said in town that day."

With a weary sigh, Kate stroked Drew's shiny, dark hair. "It's all right."

"Miss Lowell, please tell me you aren't going to leave. I would miss you so much!"

"Drew. . .Drew. . .Drew. . . ," Kate crooned, standing and tugging on the boy's hands. He stood with her, and she was once more stricken by how much he was growing. Drew was now as tall as Kate. "What makes you think I'm leaving?"

"It's obvious," Drew said, turning his intense gaze toward her shawl and the note she had barely started.

"You don't miss a thing, do you?" Kate said on a dry chuckle.

"No. Does that bother you?"

She turned to grip one of the straight-backed chairs near the fireplace and gazed out the window, toward the horse pasture. There, Mr. Adams trudged as if he were dragging one of the surrounding Texas hills behind him. "No. It doesn't bother me in the least," she said absently. "I'm thrilled to know I have such a keen student."

"So are you going to leave?"

"No, Drew. I'll be staying."

He remained respectfully silent, and Kate watched Mr. Adams until he was beyond her view. For the first time she realized just how much Drew needed a mother, just how much Mr. Adams needed a wife, regardless of what he said.

And Kate was forced to ask herself a question. Why had God placed her, a socialite, on this remote horse farm outside a tiny east Texas town? Did He have plans for her that went far beyond tutoring Drew?

Well, Lord, if You do, she prayed silently, *You are going to have to make some changes in me. . .and Mr. Adams.*

For Kate truly saw herself in that reflective moment in a way she never had before. McCall Adams wasn't the only one who needed to put his past pain behind him. She had told him only moments ago that he didn't have time for a life of his own because of his hold on Drew. The irony of Kate's own words haunted her, for she was guilty of the very thing of which she accused Mr. Adams. Kate was so busy holding onto her memory of Zachary that she was afraid to move forward in her own life.

Surely, Kate believed that God Himself was faced with a challenging task. For in her human view, she saw no way to remove her hold on Zachary, or Mr. Adams's hold on his deceased wife. . .and Drew.

"What do you know about my mother and my true. . . true father?" Drew muttered.

Kate, lost in her own thoughts, was jolted back to the present. She turned to face Drew, her eyes wide. "Wh–what?" she stammered, more as a means to stall for time than a need for Drew to repeat the question.

"I was wondering if you knew about. . .about my birth." Drew, his face flushed, crammed fidgeting hands into the pockets of his blue jeans.

Speechless, Kate grappled with any words she might say. She had only that day discovered the truth herself. She knew only the barest details. How could she explain the delicate situation to a fourteen-year-old boy? Furthermore, admitting to Drew that she knew his circumstances only heightened her growing embarrassment. At long last, she said, "Drew, I. . .I think your father would be the best one to. . .to answer those questions. Don't you?" She laid an assuring hand on the boy's arm.

Silently, he nodded. "Ah. . .I guess," Drew said in resignation. "I just feel. . . uncomfortable. . . ." With a shrug, he helplessly looked into Kate's eyes.

"I understand," she reassured. "I think he feels the same way."

❖

"So why is it that you keep on bein' late finishin' your chores?" Eugene Wilcox paced the plank house's narrow front porch. He wasn't sure whether to beat the boy or give him a tongue-lashing. Calvin stood on the edge of the porch, his head hanging like a guilty dog. Eugene, arms folded, paused beside the rickety porch swing and brooded about Calvin's lack of responsibility. For the last three days, Nadine hadn't been able to start supper on time because Calvin was so late with the afternoon milking.

"I've been playing at the river," Calvin muttered.

"By yourself?"

Silence. The kind of silence that tells a father that there was someone else at the river. Eugene started thinking about all the neighboring farms and which property owners had children. At last, he remembered that the river served as a boundary between his land and McCall Adams's land. The possibilities of his son meeting an Indian turned Eugene's stomach.

"Have you been sneakin' off to see that stinkin' Injun boy?" Eugene demanded, hoping Calvin would deny the question.

"Yes, Sir," he muttered, fidgeting with the snap on the front of his overalls.

"I don't know what to think of you!" Eugene exploded.

Calvin jumped.

"One minute that Injun attacks you and smears the Wilcox name, and the next minute the two of ya are as close as twin pups."

"But Drew didn't start that fight in town," Calvin mumbled. "*I* started it."

Eugene's stomach burned with new anger. "Now you're startin' to lie to me! I saw that fight! I know that Injun started it!"

"No, Pa." Calvin looked up. "*I* did. Drew was just defendin' himself."

With the sound of a woodpecker furiously hammering against a tree, Eugene silently observed his son. The sincere tone and honest gleam in Calvin's eyes confounded him. Usually, when the boy rebelled against Eugene's word, he did it with underhanded meanness. The last few weeks, there was definitely something unusual about Calvin. He had been more truthful and less rebellious. More kind and less hostile, even when Eugene himself had been hostile.

Eugene's thoughts of beating Calvin for befriending that "stinkin' Injun" left him. He was so stricken by his own son's blatant honesty, even in the face of punishment, that his anger slowly turned to amazement.

"Go on and finish your chores," Eugene growled. "And you won't be goin' to that river no time soon. Do you hear me?" Eugene yelled the last few words, right in the boy's face, to emphasize his earnestness. Even if he didn't beat the boy, at least Calvin would know he was close to getting a good one.

"Yes. . .yes. . .I hear ya, Pa," Calvin said, cringing as if he suspected a blow to follow.

"Please. . .please, don't. . . ," a whiny voice said from the doorway.

Eugene turned to see his scrawny, blond wife. Her weak, blue eyes pleaded with him to leave the boy alone. Nadine's interference almost made Eugene want to reverse his decision not to take the boy to the woodshed. "Get back in that house and take care of the baby, Woman!" he snarled.

The door instantly snapped shut.

"And you. . ." He turned back to Calvin. "Go milk the cow like I done told you to do."

Calvin rushed from his spot on the edge of the porch and ran toward the cow pasture where one of the cows bellowed about her need for relief.

After a long day's work in the fields, Eugene's back ached. He slumped onto the ancient porch swing and its weathered slats creaked with his weight. His eyes narrowed as he watched Calvin, milk pail in hand, scramble through the rusty barbed-wire fence and then lead the restless cow toward the barn. Something was mighty different about that boy of late. He was even gentler with the cows. It was enough to make Eugene want to ask him a few questions. But he could never afford to do that. *He's the boy, and I'm the man. That's the way it's gonna stay.*

But respectful or not, if Calvin ever met that "stinkin' Indian" again, Eugene would beat the living daylights out of his son. Then, he would go find that Indian boy and beat the living daylights out of him as well. That Drew Adams had yet to pay for whipping Calvin in front of all of Dogwood. No matter who started the fight, Calvin got the worst end of it, and Drew had it coming to him.

Eugene smiled as a new thought struck him. *Just supposing Calvin tried to meet that Indian again at the river. . .and just supposing I were to find them together. . .that would give me the perfect opportunity to give both the boys a good thrashing.* Eugene rubbed his fist against his palm. He would start with the Indian. When Eugene got through with Drew Adams, he'd never again think he was good enough to associate with white folks.

Chapter 8

December marched on, and the chilly days became frigid. By mid-January, a light snowfall covered all of east Texas and kept the countryside frozen for one day. On the morning of the snow, Bob Mosely failed to appear to escort Kate to the horse farm. This in no way surprised Kate. By the next morning, Kate had developed a slight cold and sent word to the hotel receptionist to explain to Mr. Mosely that she was ill and would not be accompanying him to the horse farm.

After several hours in bed, Kate at last arose to discover that, perhaps, her cold would be a light one. Now bored and restless, she wondered if she should have gone with Mr. Mosely today after all.

Nonetheless, the snow and her slight illness had given Kate a much needed break. As she stood at her hotel window and looked over the surrounding hills, lightly dusted with the melting white powder, she breathed deeply and relaxed—truly relaxed—for the first time in weeks. She wasn't at the horse farm yesterday. She wouldn't go today. Tomorrow was Saturday. That meant by Monday, Kate would have four days away from the inner tension that surfaced each time she saw McCall Adams.

Since the day he kissed her, Kate felt as if her nerves were on razor's edge. Monday through Friday, the whole time she was at the horse ranch, Kate spent every spare moment looking over her shoulder or out the schoolroom's window. Part in fear. Part in expectation. She desperately wanted to see McCall—yet desperately wanted to avoid him. Drew, seemingly oblivious to her plight, had turned into a model student. Other than occasional distant glimpses of the boy's father, Kate would have assumed she and Drew were alone on that expansive ranch. Nevertheless, she felt as if McCall were standing behind her each second, investigating her every move.

Absently, Kate turned her attention toward the streets of Dogwood. At daybreak yesterday, the streets had seemed covered in a magical, white veil. Today, the rutted roads appeared to be full of muddy, trampled cotton, marred beyond use. Yesterday few people came in from the countryside, but today the town teamed with people. The weak sunshine filtering through gray, blotchy clouds promised to warm the temperatures enough to completely melt the dissipating snow by noon.

Yesterday, Kate had stayed the day in her hotel room to begin reading *Pride and Prejudice*, sent by her mother. She also caught up on her correspondence with her mother and two sisters, who all begged her to return to El Paso. Kate could never explain to them why she continued to stay. Certainly, it wasn't for the forty dollars a month McCall paid her. Given her family's financial security, they would never understand her very deep need to help others, and Kate wasn't even sure if helping Drew was the only reason she was staying. Therefore, she simply ignored her family's written pleas and responded with news of the good time she was having.

After finishing yesterday's correspondence, Kate had even spent the afternoon napping, but a recurring, disturbing nightmare kept waking her. Kate had once more been dreaming she stood on the middle of the tree trunk, fallen across a river. Zachary, in ethereal form, hovered on one side of the riverbank. McCall occupied the opposite bank. A ghostlike beauty, sobbing uncontrollably, clung to McCall and placed a newborn baby into his arms. Kate's heart pounded in sympathy for the crying woman. Wanting to comfort Melody, she ran across the tree trunk, planning to wrap her arms around the broken girl. Kate almost reached the bank when she lost her balance. She began waving her arms, flailing in the air, feeling the tug of the rushing river beneath her. Kate repeatedly screamed for McCall's help, but he never even acknowledged her cries. He only clung to Melody. She twisted to beseech Zachary's assistance, but he faded from view. At last Kate tumbled toward the river to be caught by Drew, who asked her why he was part Indian, then he immediately begged her to become his mother. At this point, Kate awoke with a start, just as she had every night for the last month. As always, she had been drenched in sweat. Her heart beat furiously, and she gasped for air.

Wanting to expunge the troubling dream from her mind, she turned from the window and peered across her small room. Already, the morning was half over, and Kate felt as if the walls were closing in on her. With a delicate sneeze, she plopped onto the bed's blue and beige patchwork coverlet and looked toward the wardrobe's half-opened door. In that cedar closet hung her few dresses, which Kate wore over and over again while tutoring Drew. When she came to Dogwood, Kate never anticipated she would be here so long. She had purchased only one gingham dress, which she now wore. Her few other dresses were much too formal, but Kate had been forced to wear them.

Kate drew a decisive breath. Suddenly, she stood and reached for her reticule and shawl, which lay on the end of the bed. Kate would make another trip to the dressmaker's. She could certainly use two more work dresses, and today presented the perfect chance for her to place her order.

But first, she would stop by the general store to mail the letters to her mother and sisters. She grabbed the envelopes lying on the small, oval table in the corner and whisked into the hallway. Within minutes, Kate picked her way across the street, full of muddy slush, and opened the door to the Dogwood general store. The smells of coffee, peppermint, and new material greeted her. Kate glanced around the store, lined with horse plows, bags of cornmeal, sugar, flour, and the ever present wall of postal boxes behind the counter. Immediately she was drawn to the material table and began examining several bolts of heavy cotton, exactly the kind of material she needed for an all-purpose work dress. Out of the corner of her eye, Kate noticed the buxom Bess Tucker about to approach her, but she stopped to help another couple, buying supplies for their kitchen.

At closer observation, Kate noticed the couple was Travis Campbell and his new wife, Rachel. Never in her life had Kate wanted so desperately to disappear as that moment. She suppressed the urge to crawl under the material table but decided to simply keep her back to them in hopes that they wouldn't notice her. The last time she saw Travis and Rachel, she and Travis broke off their engagement, and she rode away, leaving him to marry the woman of his heart, Rachel Isaacs. That was the day before Kate met Mr. Adams and Drew at the train station.

To encounter Travis and Rachel now was highly awkward and embarrassing. Kate didn't even know if they were aware she was still in Dogwood. At last, she decided to simply turn around and leave without mailing the letters. She would go to the dressmaker's, who usually kept material in stock, and return to mail the letters after ordering her dress. Kate whirled around to bump squarely into Rachel.

"Oh excuse me," the young redhead said politely. "I didn't realize you. . ." She trailed off as she recognized exactly who she had bumped into—her husband's former fiancée. "Miss Lowell!" she said with faint surprise.

"Mrs. Campbell," Kate said calmly, feeling anything *but* calm. She stole a glance toward Travis, tall and fair, as he neared. The last time she saw him they were on friendly, although strained, terms. Kate was very much at peace about their mutual decision to break the engagement, but she hoped Mrs. Campbell in no way thought she was pining for Travis.

"Hello, Kate," Travis said as he neared. "We heard you were still in town; it's a delight to see you."

"Yes. . ." Kate cleared her throat and produced a shy smile. "I suppose there isn't much that goes on in Dogwood that everyone doesn't know about."

Rachel released a spontaneous giggle, and Kate eased a bit. Perhaps the flush on Mrs. Campbell's cheeks was an indicator of her happiness *and* security in her marriage.

Helplessly searching for any topic of conversation, Kate opened her mouth and heard herself say, "The snow must have made you as restless as it did me. I decided that after being trapped inside yesterday I needed to get out today."

"Actually, we—Rachel needed to see Dr. Engle," Travis said, placing an arm around his wife's waist as if she were a fragile doll.

The glowing, adoring gaze Rachel threw Travis left the rest unsaid. She was most likely expecting their first child. Kate shot a furtive glance toward Rachel's waistline only to find it unaltered. Perhaps Mrs. Campbell was very early in her pregnancy. Kate furtively hoped there were no problems.

Rachel turned her attention back to Kate. "Travis and I were thinking of sending you an invitation to dine with us one evening if—"

"That is so thoughtful of you," Kate interrupted. "But I'm so busy with the tutoring that I—"

"We understand," Travis said. And Kate knew Travis well enough to interpret the gleam in his green eyes. Such a meeting would be as uncomfortable for him as for Kate. Surprisingly, his young wife seemed the most at ease with the whole situation.

"Well, it was extremely nice to see you again," Kate said in her most refined tone.

Fully prepared to gracefully exit the store, she curtsied and began walking toward the front door. But it would appear that Kate had no room for escape this day, from any situation. For when she was no more than ten feet from the doorway, it swung open and McCall Adams walked into the store. Kate trembled in astonishment. Behind her stood the man she had once agreed to marry, and in front of her stood the man she would probably dream about the rest of her life but would never marry.

Kate would have loved to pretend she didn't see McCall, but that proved impossible, for he looked straight at her. The purposeful gleam in his dark eyes proclaimed that he had found the person for whom he was looking.

"Miss Lowell," he said with a slight smile. "The hotel owner mentioned that you might be here. May I have a minute of your time, please?"

"Yes, of course," Kate said quietly. She cringed, imagining that every eye in the store must be fixed on her as she stepped onto the boardwalk with Mr. Adams. Yet a quick glance over her shoulder proved no one watched her departure. Bess Tucker hovered near Rachel and Travis as they joyfully examined a tiny bonnet, just the size to fit a baby. The two most certainly were expectant parents.

As Mr. Adams shut the door behind them, Kate's heart twisted with a longing she thought had been obliterated by Zachary's death. The longing to be a mother. To hold a helpless infant in her arms and know the tiny baby belonged to her and would one day return her love. A stab of envy, as quick as a sword, passed through Kate's heart. Would she ever know the kind of joy Rachel exuded?

She seemed forever destined to love men who could never return her love. Zachary now lay cold in his grave. And McCall Adams—was she falling in love with McCall? Kate had guarded herself against the possibility from the onset of their acquaintance. Yet standing here beside him on this cold January day, looking up into his velvet brown eyes, so full of pain, soaking in every detail of him, Kate began to wonder if she was on the road to forgetting Zachary and losing her heart to McCall. Their kiss—that earth shattering kiss—she had relived it a million times. And each time, her heart pounded as if she had run to west Texas.

Still silent, McCall gently took her elbow and steered her out of the door's way. Kate resisted the urge to jerk her tingling arm out of his grasp, and simultaneously she resisted the urge to fall into his arms. Wondering why he had come for her, Kate stole another glance at McCall and found him appraising her. Before she realized what she was doing, Kate reached up with the intent to stroke the featherlike lines around his eyes and the softness of his dark beard. But she stopped herself and, instead, covered her lips with her fingertips.

Why was he even here? He seemed somewhat unsure of himself, and Kate almost exploded with the mounting tension. Unable to withstand another second of his probing gaze, she spoke at last. "You wanted to see me for something, Mr. Adams?"

"Yes. Actually, I did. I. . ." He stopped to clear his throat. "I came into town after Mr. Mosely informed me that you were unavailable this morning to ride to the ranch with him. He seemed to be under the impression that you were going to. . ." McCall trailed off meaningfully, as a glimmer of relief danced through his eyes.

Did he think that she had plans not to return to her tutoring position? The thought barely had time to form before Kate produced a high-pitched sneeze. "Excuse me. I seem to have developed a slight cold." She dabbed the end of her nose with her lace handkerchief.

"I'm so sorry. I didn't know. Is this the reason you left word for Mr. Mosely that you wouldn't be coming?"

"I told the hotel maid to tell the receptionist that I was ill. That apparently was not the message Mr. Mosely received. Please forgive me."

"You have nothing to apologize for. There simply must have been some miscommunication. Mr. Mosely was under the impression that you. . .well. . . that you wouldn't be coming back *ever*."

"Mr. Adams, do you honestly think I would do such a thing without notifying you?"

"Were you planning to notify me before?" One dark brow arched in an almost flirting manner, and Kate's heart palpitated despite herself.

"I. . .I. . .was at least going to leave a note for Drew, and you would have understood from that note. . . ." She examined the top button of his pullover denim shirt as pedestrians bustled around them and horses and wagons sloshed through the muddy streets.

"I hope you understand, Miss Lowell, just how much I have come to depend on you on behalf of Drew."

"Only for Drew?" The words seemed to have been snatched from her tongue, and Kate covered her lips with her gloved fingertips. Her heart felt as if it dropped to her feet. Kate longed to race back to her hotel room, bury her face in the depths of her feather bed, and die from embarrassment. "I'm so sorry," she rushed. "I don't know what comes over me when I'm speaking with you, Mr. Adams." She refused to look into his eyes. Instead, Kate addressed the door to the dressmaker's just across the street. "I seem to be forever saying things I don't. . .I shouldn't. . ." Another dainty sneeze. "If you'll please excuse me, I think I should return to my room now."

Kate whirled away from McCall and hurried along the covered boardwalk. At the corner, she began running across the street, almost tripping as her skirt dragged against the mounds of mud and snow that the wagons had created as they sliced through the slush. Only when she reached the boardwalk in front of her hotel did she hear Mr. Adams calling.

"Miss Lowell! Miss Lowell, wait!"

Pretending she didn't hear, Kate whipped open the hotel door, stepped into the quaint lobby, and rushed to the receptionist's desk. "I must b–be alone," she said, panting for breath. "Please tell any c–callers that I–I'm unavailable." Another sneeze punctuated her request.

"Of course, Ma'am," the elderly lady replied.

Kate, hearing the door open behind her, hurled herself toward the dark, wooden stairway.

"Miss Lowell, we must talk!"

McCall's voice stopped Kate midstride. How could she ever pretend she didn't hear him now?

Chapter 9

Eugene Wilcox noticed Calvin missing a good hour before he went looking for him. The boy was supposed to be doing his chores, not playing at the river. Eugene crunched through the woods, noticing that the last of yesterday's snowfall was melting. Deep in his gut, he knew Calvin had disobeyed him and had gone to meet that worthless Indian at the river again. He gripped the horsewhip all the tighter. Once Eugene got through with that Indian, he wouldn't be fit to meet the devil himself. He spit a stream of tobacco against the trunk of a stately oak, and his breath formed a white mist around his moist lips each time he exhaled.

This stupidity on Calvin's part really surprised Eugene. The boy had been exceptionally good of late, even good enough to make Eugene suspicious at first. But during the last week, he had begun to wonder if Calvin's recent church attendance at that church up the road had anything to do with his good behavior. Last Sunday, he had even asked Eugene and Nadine to go with him. Eugene had growled that Nadine was busy with the baby and he needed the rest. Calvin had silently left their three-room home, and Eugene felt as if the boy had touched his heart.

The odd moment left Eugene wishing he could handle his son the way he saw other men treating their boys. The truth was that Eugene couldn't quite do it. He didn't know what to do with Calvin other than give the boy the same treatment he had received as a kid. Grabbing a bare vine, Eugene angrily ripped it away from his path. If the truth were known, Calvin got far fewer beatings than Eugene ever got. He remembered after one particular beating, he could hardly walk for a week. And his right ankle had never been the same since his pa kicked him so hard that day.

Eugene's stomach turned with the memory. By the time he left home, he hated his father. Thinking of beating Calvin today almost made Eugene wish he had not been disobedient. Lately, Eugene had heard Calvin praying for him. Even though Wilcox had no desire to be affected, he could not deny the influence.

Despite those bothersome prayers, somebody needed a beating over this business of Calvin meeting that Indian even if it was only the Indian who got it. From the little he knew of God, Eugene supposed He didn't take too kindly to a couple of scheming boys.

At last, the roar of the narrow river met Eugene's ears. Next, the smell of fresh water. Eugene crept closer until he saw the frothy water, fifteen feet below, rushing across the protruding, flat rocks. A canopy of trees blocked out the weak, winter sun, and the air around the river was somewhat colder. Just as Eugene figured, Calvin and the Indian sat side by side on a big rock not twenty feet away. Eugene cringed with the thought of his clean, white son allowing a nasty Indian to even breathe close to him. He wrinkled his nose in disgust and poised to jump on that no-account kid and give him the beating of his life.

But the words those two boys shared wafted toward Eugene over the sound of the river and stilled his attack.

"You've done told me so much, Drew," Calvin said. "If it weren't for you, I'd a never gotten to know God, not for real. Why *can't* you come to church with me?"

"Because my Dad says I can't. We don't go to church. We worship at home on Sundays by ourselves."

"But the Good Book says you're supposed to go to church!" Calvin held up the black book that Eugene had seen him reading the last few weeks.

"I know." Drew stood. "But Dad says it's best for us to stay home mostly."

"Do you think it's because of what you said the other day—that you found out you're part Injun?"

Drew, turning his back on Calvin, shrugged his shoulders. "Your father doesn't seem to like me too much because of that. I guess maybe there's more like him." The sound of the river almost blotted out Drew's words.

Eugene knew now was the time for him to jump in the middle of those boys and teach them a lesson. He gripped the horsewhip, raised it, and prepared to rush forward.

"Well, I guess I really need to get back to my chores," Calvin said, standing. "I don't want to disappoint my pa. I've been doin' what you said and praying for him and trying to be good. . .even when he's mean."

Eugene's stomach twisted in guilt. What Calvin was saying was absolutely true. Why was Eugene constantly, compulsively, treating Calvin just like his father treated him? Deep, deep inside, Eugene sometimes wanted things to be different. But it seemed the harder he tried, the meaner he got with Calvin, and that only made Calvin meaner—until lately. Did that black book Calvin held have anything to do with the change in the boy? If there really was a God, *did* Calvin know Him like he said he did?

His thoughts spinning, Eugene silently watched as the boys exchanged a series of handshakes and ended with a little childish chant that mentioned brotherhood and God. Then Drew rushed across the fallen tree to jump onto the opposite bank, and Calvin turned to race up the pathway leading toward their home.

Eugene, deep in thought, barely noticed when the whip slipped from his grasp.

❖

McCall momentarily thought Miss Lowell was pausing long enough for him to approach her. But he no more than took two steps forward, when she began running up the stairs as if another moment in his presence would choke her. Yet McCall knew beyond doubt that wasn't the case. The open admiration flowing from her eyes only moments before, the instant he had been almost sure she was going to stroke his face, even her own words attested to Miss Lowell's growing attachment to him.

The truth of the matter was that McCall's heart had almost stopped the instant Mr. Mosely relayed his erroneous message that Kate would not be returning. McCall had tried to maintain his distance from Kate over the past weeks. He had tried to guard his heart against any threat of her influence. He had desperately tried to maintain a grip on his memory of Melody. He had pleaded with God to release him from his growing feelings for Miss Lowell. But only one thought circled through his mind in answer to his prayers:

Release the past.

As he watched Kate ascend to the top of the stairway, McCall decided to go after her. Taking the steps two at a time, he called her once more. "Miss Lowell. . .*please*. . .may I have a few more moments of your time?"

"Excuse me, Sir!" the aging clerk called in a squawking voice. "We don't allow male callers upstairs with our lady guests. It isn't appropriate!"

Ignoring her, McCall reached Miss Lowell's side and gripped her upper arm. "Please give me a few more moments," he whispered.

Kate muffled a broken sob, and McCall saw rivulets of tears dampening her cheeks. "Please allow me the honor of going to my room and dying of embarrassment in dignity, Mr. McCall," she mumbled. A furious sneeze followed her tearful words, and she refused to look him in the eyes.

With a fond chuckle, McCall removed his handkerchief from his pant's pocket and gently stroked away her tears.

"I don't know what possesses me to say the things I do when I am with you. Please accept my most humble apologies and my pledge to never speak to you again as long as I live."

The clerk, now standing at the base of the stairs, cleared her throat meaningfully.

McCall shot an impatient glance toward her, then turned back to Kate. "I can accept your apology, but I must resist your pledge to never speak to me again. That would be highly impractical, don't you think, considering your position as my son's tutor?"

"Sir, I'm afraid that I must demand your returning to the lobby," the old lady insisted. "Or I will be forced to send for my son, who happens to be the owner."

Kate looked toward the clerk, and McCall followed suit. He felt Kate's indecision, whether to return to her room or go to the lobby with him.

"Please," McCall said, not certain of the wisdom in insisting upon Miss Lowell's company. He certainly was in no way ready to begin a long-term relationship with her. It wouldn't be fair to her. Melody still held him too tightly. Perhaps he should be completely honest with Kate and tell her that there was no hope in a relationship between them.

Nevertheless, McCall could no longer deny that Miss Lowell was more of a distraction for him than his will-power could endure. Proof of this stood in his rushing to town to insist she not leave her position, only to discover she had no intentions of doing so. If he were honest with himself, McCall would admit that he had begun to hunger for the briefest glimpses of her. The last time they spoke, she had asked him if he would be disappointed if she left. Only minutes before, she had asked him if his dependence on her was only for Drew. McCall should answer both of those questions and hopefully put to rest some of the torment in her eyes.

But regardless of his feelings for Miss Lowell, his heart would always belong to Melody. He needed to make certain Kate understood this. The time had come to be completely honest. If she were willing to share his heart, perhaps McCall would. . .what? This line of thought left him blinking in surprise.

At last Kate silently turned and began to descend the stairs.

Satisfied, the wrinkled clerk stiffly returned to her duties at the front desk. McCall, his heart pounding out expectant beats, followed Miss Lowell and joined her on one of the green velvet settees in the hotel lobby. He glanced over his shoulder to see the clerk watching them. He boldly held her gaze, and she abruptly turned to busy herself with paperwork.

"Please understand, Miss Lowell," he said softly, "that I in no way scorn your questions and feel that, given my own behavior, they are most certainly appropriate."

"Really?" she said, tormenting the handkerchief in her hands.

"Of course. When a man. . .kisses a woman. . .it implies. . .and I most certainly feel that I have implied. . .and that you most certainly have every right to ask. . ." McCall groped for new words but found nothing except his own heightened emotions. Was he falling in love with Miss Lowell, despite his opposition? Desperately, he tried to recall the name of Drew's mother, long carved upon his heart, but his mind was so jumbled at the sight of the lovely Kate Lowell that her name momentarily escaped him.

"And when a woman allows a man to kiss her without. . .without so much as. . .as a commitment. . .it. . .it implies. . ." Still refusing to look at McCall, Kate stood and hurried to the floor-to-ceiling window that provided an expansive view of the streets of Dogwood.

McCall slowly followed her and stopped within inches of her back. His stomach churned as her hair, caught into its meticulous bun, glistened in the sunlight pouring through the window. What would it be like to awaken to her every morning of his life? *God save me, I am drowning!* he pleaded heavenward, feeling as if this situation with Miss Lowell were rapidly growing out of his own control. He lambasted himself for following the impulse to ride into town when Bob Mosely supplied the misinformation. McCall should have relied on logic and realized Miss Lowell wouldn't leave without bidding Drew good-bye. But he hadn't. He had acted on blind instinct and chased after the woman who—

"It implies. . . ," Kate whispered haltingly. "You know exactly what it implies. And. . .and given that, plus my humiliating questions, Mr. Adams, I have no other recourse but to believe you must think. . .y–you must think. . ." She gulped.

"I think nothing but. . ." He placed his hand on her shoulder. "Would you marry me, Miss Lowell?"

"*What?*" She spun to face him, her cheeks decidedly paler than they had ever been.

McCall couldn't believe he had blurted such a question. He hadn't even prayed about it. But if the truth were known, McCall understood in the deepest recesses of his heart what God's will was on this subject. God was beckoning him to release the past and embrace the future with this lovely woman before him. But he had resisted the Lord, was even *now* resisting. For he knew with sickening truth that even if Miss Lowell did agree to marry him, she would also have to assent to sharing his heart with Melody. What woman would ever consent to such a proposal. But would Kate have to know he still harbored a secret love for his former wife?

"What about Melody?" she whispered, as if she could read his thoughts.

"What about her?"

"You're still in love with her." Kate spoke the words as if she hoped he would refute them.

McCall helplessly stared into her eyes and knew he couldn't lie.

"Do you honestly think I would ever marry a man who was in love with another woman?" she asked, her whisper much louder than before, her cheeks now flushing.

He instinctively glanced toward the nosy clerk to find her attention riveted to them as if she were straining to hear every word of their intense conversation. Caught in the act of eavesdropping, she guiltily rushed from the desk and through the nearby office doorway.

"Besides," Kate added with a weary echo to her words. "Even if you weren't still. . .still in love with Melody, I have my own misgivings." She studied her fidgeting, gloved hands.

"Are you talking about your experience with Zachary?" McCall asked gently, not certain if he was disappointed or relieved that Kate hadn't immediately accepted his spontaneous proposal.

Her head snapped up. Her eyes widened. Her lips parted. "How do you know Zachary's name?"

"Dr. Engle told me about Zachary the first day I met you. If you remember, I dropped off Drew with him before you and I talked at Dotty's, and he mentioned. . ."

"That's something incredibly private. How would he know such about me?" she demanded, a frustrated note to her voice.

"He's like a father to Rachel Campbell, and she has shared with him the struggle her husband faced in forgiving himself for your fiancé's death."

"Dr. Engle certainly does know about everyone, doesn't he?" Kate snapped spitefully.

McCall narrowed his eyes and immediately jumped to the doctor's defense. "He never had any children, but he is like a father to several people in town, me included. The man is as good as gold."

"Yes, and as nosy as. . .as. . . ," she sputtered to a stop and whirled to once more gaze out the window.

"He meant well," McCall said.

"Well, it's none of his business!"

"Or mine?" he asked, at last deeply aware that he wasn't the only one with a former love that still haunted him. At once, McCall remembered Kate's urging him to release his own past and his hold on Drew. His gut twisted in irritation as he clearly saw what Dr. Engle could never know. Kate Lowell was still in love with her dead fiancé. How dare she preach to him when she harbored her own ghosts. "Miss Lowell," McCall said evenly, a note of aggravation in his voice. "I find it highly inconsiderate of you to point your finger at me about my. . .my feelings for Melody when you. . .you are guilty of the exact same predicament."

"How dare you!" she gasped, turning to face him once more. This time Kate's eyes snapped with abundant ire.

"I dare because *you* have dared!" McCall gripped her upper arms and wanted to kiss her again—kiss her until both Melody and Zachary were expunged from their hearts and Kate agreed to marry him. These new thoughts left him breathless. McCall, now within inches of her, peering deeply into her eyes, felt as if he would live forever in torment—desperately wanting to give his heart to Kate, yet unable to release Melody.

"Stop it! Stop it! Just. . .just stop it!" Twisting away from his hold, Kate raced toward the stairwell once more. This time, she hovered at the top, not because McCall beckoned her but because she had one last, surprising message to hurl toward him.

"I'm leaving. I'm going back home to El Paso. I cannot, I *will* not continue like this. Tell Drew I will not be back!" With a broken sob, she ran from sight.

Chapter 10

Three months later, Kate settled onto her chair in the ranch's school-room and reflected over the weeks since she had proclaimed her decision to leave Dogwood. Her resolve to leave had lasted until the Sunday after she hurled the words toward Mr. Adams. That Sunday in church, she had bowed her head and truly sought the Lord's guidance concerning her hasty decision. During those quiet moments on the church pew, Kate felt in her spirit that leaving her tutoring position would mean direct disobedience to God. Once more, God brought to her mind the incident with the Indian girl in the streets of El Paso. Once more, Kate felt that turning her back on Drew would be like refusing that helpless adolescent all over again.

So Kate had hired a driver to escort her to the horse farm Monday morning. Although she never saw Mr. Adams that morning, Drew bounded out of the log cabin like a young buck and embraced her with his engaging smile. Once they settled in the schoolroom, he industriously turned his mind to studies. Later, Drew made only one vague reference to her supposed resignation, and Kate had simply stated the truth: She felt she had spoken too hastily and that, after praying about it, she knew resigning the position was not God's will. Whether or not Drew ever told his father this was still a mystery to Kate; she and McCall had not spoken since that day in the hotel lobby when he blurted that unexpected proposal.

Thoughts of that moment still left Kate speechless and appalled. The man must be half-crazy to think she would *ever* marry him when his heart still belonged to Melody! The fact that Mr. Adams found Kate attractive was not hidden. He had obviously expressed his attraction to her, but a marriage must be based on much more. Nevertheless, despite her astonishment at McCall's proposal, from that fateful moment when he proposed, Kate mused about what life would be like as McCall's wife, as Drew's mother. For God had already shown her that Drew desperately needed a mother. And McCall—McCall, despite his lingering love for Melody, desperately needed a wife.

But was Kate the one? The prospect left her reeling in confusion.

The schoolroom's door opened, and Kate swiveled, expecting Drew. An hour ago, she had sent him on a venture to gather the final bugs that would finish their spring collection. But instead of Drew, Kate encountered McCall's bland scrutiny.

Her heart pounded.

Her palms moistened.

Her lips trembled.

"Mr. Mosely and I needed another helping hand with the west fences. Where's Drew?" McCall asked as if they were on perfectly amiable terms.

"He's finishing the bug collection," Kate rasped in a strained voice. "He should be back in a few minutes."

"Thank you." He hesitated. "Are you certain he is no longer playing with Calvin Wilcox?"

"As certain as I can be," Kate said, a bit defensively. "When I allow him to explore the woods, he always comes back with the things for which I sent him within the allotted time. I haven't discussed it with him, but I assumed he understood your view on the subject."

McCall produced a curt nod. "How is your afternoon progressing today? Are the two of you on schedule?"

"Yes. We're actually ahead in our schedule by a few days," Kate said, her defensive tone increasing. She felt as if the man were interrogating her. Why would he arrive after a three-month silence and accost her with a barrage of questions?

"Good. Then if you don't mind his missing the afternoon, I'll go see if I can find him. We really need his help on the fences."

"He's your son, Mr. Adams," Kate said pointedly. "That's perfectly fine with me."

McCall narrowed his eyes.

Kate, determined to maintain a demeanor of wide-eyed innocence, didn't dare flinch away.

"I was simply trying to be polite. I in no way intended to offend you," he stated.

"I never said I was offended."

"No, but your words—" He took an impatient breath. "Never mind. If you would like Mr. Mosely to drive you back into town while I find Drew, I'll be perfectly happy to tell him."

"Am I in your way?" she asked, not knowing why she was suddenly bent on needling him.

"No. That was the farthest thing from my mind." He pushed his dark hat back from his brow as if his irritation were growing.

"Good. Then I'll stay until my normal hour of departure. I have several things to do here before leaving today."

"Fine," he snapped.

"Fine, then."

He turned as if to leave, then swiveled to face her. "Miss Lowell," he said deliberately. "We haven't spoken in quite some time, but I must say that I think the same of you today as I thought of you the last time we spoke."

Automatically assuming Mr. Adams referred to his spontaneous proposal, Kate's face heated. "Mr. Adams, *please*, I—"

"You are beyond doubt the most exasperating woman I have ever met!"

Gaping, Kate stood, ready to do verbal battle. "Well, thank you for your kindness, Mr. Adams. I am certainly glad Drew doesn't agree with you."

"This has nothing to do with Drew."

"But my presence does."

"Undoubtedly! And if it weren't for Drew, I'd. . ."

"You'd what?" she challenged.

He eyed her silently.

"You'd send me back to El Paso? Is that it?"

"I never said that!" McCall stepped outside and slammed the door before she had a chance to form another thought.

Kate plopped back into her chair, resisting the urge to run after McCall Adams and explain to him that *he* was the most exasperating man *she* had ever met. And she wanted to make certain he understood that the only thing keeping her in Dogwood was Drew. Kate furiously counted the weeks until school would be over. Exactly six. If she could last six weeks, she could return to El Paso for the summer. From there, she could decide whether or not she would return to Dogwood in the fall. If McCall requested her decision now, Kate would deliver a firm "no."

But would that be God's will?

With a groan, she rested her elbows on the desk and covered her face with her hands. It always came back to that one conflict. Her human side wanted to bolt, while God consistently tugged her back to tutoring Drew.

"Why are you doing this to me?" she prayed, but received only silence.

Wanting to ease her frazzled nerves, Kate reached for her Bible and scooted the oil lamp closer. The bright spring sunshine flooded through the windows, but Kate still needed the extra lamplight to read the fine print. The time she allowed Drew to explore in the woods was usually the time she spent in the Word of God. She desperately needed a soothing Psalm today. But the Bible plopped open to the spot where Zachary's dried red rose resided. She encountered the rose every time she opened her Bible. Up until a few weeks ago, Kate always paused to ponder the man of her heart. But this afternoon, with the kerosene lamp producing fluttering shadows across the pages of her Bible, she realized many days had passed since she reflected over her time with Zachary. She picked up the flattened flower and studied it. Her nerves still scattered from her encounter with McCall, Kate stroked the lifeless petals, and one flaked away to float toward the Bible's opened pages.

Kate reflected over her last evening with Zachary.

She thought about his funeral.

She recalled the hours she had grieved his loss.

Surprisingly, no tears formed in her eyes. Only a dull ache remained in her heart. A sweet, dull ache. A nuance of the love Kate had once cherished, then lost. She glanced down at the pages of her Bible, now marked by the pale traces of the rose. And one verse from Luke, the words of Jesus Himself, sprang up at her: "The Spirit of the Lord is upon me, because he hath anointed me to preach the gospel to the poor; he hath sent me to heal the brokenhearted, to preach deliverance to the captives, and recovering of sight to the blind, to set at liberty them that are bruised."

"Oh Lord," Kate whispered as her eyes misted. "Can it be that You are healing my broken heart? Are You trying to set me at liberty?"

Release the past.

As those three words whisked through Kate's mind, she yearned for the strength and ability to embrace her future. No more hanging onto the memory of a man she could never again touch. No more living in fear of once more losing a love. No more resisting the divine will of God for her life.

But could Kate truly do it? Could she truly obey God's bidding and release the past?

With new determination, she pressed her lips together, picked up the rose, and walked toward the fireplace. Now that April was in full bloom, Drew seldom built fires. However, this morning had proven cool enough for a fire, but there was now no sign of live coals. Kate reached for the poker and stirred the gray ashes. A few coals glowed to life. She replaced the poker and brushed the dried rose petals against her lips.

Dare she burn the last flower Zachary had given her?

❖

McCall stormed across the north pasture toward the path that Drew always used when scouting the woods. Even though McCall searched for Drew, his mind remained with Kate Lowell. She knew how to goad him as no other woman had ever goaded him. McCall had thought, he honestly thought, that there would be no harm in simply opening the door of the summer kitchen and inquiring after Drew.

He hadn't spoken to Miss Lowell in the three months since their tense conversation in the hotel lobby. And for three months McCall had wanted to rip out his own tongue. How could he have ever proposed to her? Several times he had hoped that the whole episode was nothing more than a bad dream, only to discover the dreadful truth. McCall had not been dreaming. He had indeed proposed to Miss Lowell.

Nonetheless, when Kate declared that she would not return to tutor Drew, McCall felt as if a part of him were dying. So convinced was he of her intent, he even told Drew she would not be back. When Kate arrived as usual that next Monday morning, McCall didn't know whether to sing with glee or groan with embarrassment. But from the moment he saw Miss Lowell step from the hired carriage and into the schoolroom, McCall had vowed to avoid her.

Why, oh why, did he break that vow? If not for Drew's love for Kate, McCall would politely dismiss her. She only brought misery to his already tortured heart. One part of him declared lifelong allegiance to Melody while something deep within urged him to release the woman who had clung to him unto death. But McCall had determined it was impossible to release Melody. He was but a mere human being, and some things were unfeasible for a man to do.

With these thoughts plaguing him, McCall entered the woods, which were filled with wild dogwoods and the sounds of spring. He had precious little time to think of Miss Lowell. He needed to find Drew and head back to the fence line.

During the last months, Drew had seemingly adhered to McCall's request to avoid Calvin Wilcox, but McCall had a tiny doubt in the back of his mind. Drew was normally a good, obedient boy, but lately he seemed to be testing several of the rules that McCall had set for him. Why would the rule about Calvin be any different?

As he continued to crunch through the woods, McCall began calling his son. His heart was truly troubled with the battles the two of them had faced of late. It would seem that something very deep was troubling Drew, and he would not tell McCall. This was so strange to McCall, for Drew and he had always been the best of friends. McCall had, by some miraculous design, been able to keep the balance between his authority as a father and Drew's need for a friend. But lately, Drew seemed miles away from McCall. Several times, he wanted to approach Miss Lowell about the issue but had refrained. McCall hated to draw her any closer to the family than she already was. As things stood, McCall was just barely able to keep her at arm's length. Any further interaction and he couldn't trust himself not to collapse at her feet and again beg her to marry him.

But what insanity! She would never marry him as long as he loved Melody. McCall had begun to think the love for his deceased wife would haunt him until death. For the first time, he entertained the longing to release it.

"Drew!" he called again through his cupped hands. "Drew!"

McCall continued traipsing through the woods, instinctively winding his way toward the river. He truly hoped he didn't find Drew and Calvin together. McCall had not punished Drew when he first found out about the friendship. But at this point, if Drew were willingly disobeying McCall, he would have no choice.

"Drew!" he bellowed again as the sound of the river skipped along the newly budding trees.

"Dad! Dad! Come quick!"

The faint, panicked call, almost indiscernible, left McCall's heart racing in dread. He hurled himself forward, racing toward the sound of his son's troubled voice.

"Drew! Where are you?"

"Down here!"

With the river now in clear view, McCall looked over the steep bank and toward Drew's voice. The boy stood beside a body crumpled limply at his feet—the body of Calvin Wilcox.

"It's Calvin, Dad! It's Calvin! He fell off the log, and. . .and. . ."

His stomach churning, McCall glanced toward the fallen tree, which he had warned Drew about when he found him and Calvin walking across it in December. Beneath the fallen tree, the river swirled at one of its deepest levels. Even though he had assumed Calvin could swim as well as Drew, McCall had insisted both the boys stay off the precarious log.

He skidded down the sandy bank, not knowing what to expect. Was Calvin drowned?

Chapter 11

Eugene Wilcox, plowing in the north pasture, stopped in his tracks when he heard Nadine's distraught cries.

"Eugene! Eugene! It's Calvin! Eugene! Something terrible has happened!"

His heart felt as if it dropped to his knees. Forgetting the mare attached to the plow, Eugene abandoned his duties and ran toward his pale wife, who clambered across the clods of dirt that would soon be their spring garden. "What is it? What's happened?" he demanded, grabbing the panicking woman by the arms.

"It's Calvin!" she sobbed. "Oh my poor, poor baby boy. He's almost drowned!"

"What? Where is he? Tell me what's happened, Woman! Tell me!" Eugene shook his wife until her head rolled around like a rag doll's.

"He's–he's in the house with–with Mr. Adams," she said at last.

Eugene dashed toward the plank shack, his heart twisting in fear. If Calvin were to die. . .Eugene didn't even want to imagine the possibility. Calvin wasn't dead. Nadine said he was *almost* drowned. There must be hope for him. There must!

He burst into the three-room hovel to see McCall Adams gently placing the soaked boy on his bed.

Enraged, Eugene stomped toward McCall, grabbed his shirt in both hands, and looked into the face of a man at least six inches taller than he. "What have you done to him?" he screamed. "What did you do to my son?"

"I didn't do anything." McCall tore Eugene's hands from his shirt. "It was an accident. He fell into the river and hit his head."

"He was with that rotten Indian kid o' yours, wasn't he?"

McCall narrowed his eyes.

Eugene's stomach clenched in fury. His heart pounded in aversion. His mind whirled with hatred. He castigated himself for allowing the boys' talk about God the other day to distract him from beating Drew.

"I'm going for the doctor." McCall turned toward the door.

Collapsing beside his pale, drenched son, Eugene gripped the narrow bed's wooden frame. "I'm going to kill that Indian for this!" He turned to see McCall stepping from the earthy home's shadows into the light of day. "Do you hear me, McCall Adams! That Indian has done pushed my Calvin around for the last time. I shoulda stomped him already for beating up Calvin in town. Now that. . .that. . . ," he inserted a number of expletives, "has done tried to drown him. I tried to tell Calvin not to trust him, but—"

When McCall turned around, he looked like the devil himself. Eugene, momentarily silenced, stared at the man as he stalked back across the plank floors. Before Eugene could comprehend McCall's intent, he grabbed the sputtering man's shirt, lifted him, and slammed him against the wall. The blow reawakened an old back injury from Eugene's past—an injury caused by his father's brutal blows.

"I already told you, Eugene Wilcox," McCall snarled within an inch of his nose. "This was an *accident*. The truth is, Drew saved Calvin's life. And if you lay one hand on my son, I'll see that Constable Parker skins you alive! Now I'm going for Dr. Engle, and I'm taking one of your horses to get him!"

McCall released Eugene as quickly as he had grabbed him, and Eugene resisted the urge to jump him. McCall Adams was half again Eugene's size, and Eugene decided to leave him be for the present. He would get his revenge when he saw Drew dead.

Eugene once more collapsed at his son's side. Calvin's wet, blond hair was pitifully plastered to his forehead. In the dank room's shadows, he looked as if he were already caught in death's claws. Eugene's heart pounded hard, even beats behind his eyes. His labored breathing seemed to fuel his fury. He gritted his teeth, and amidst a collection of expletives, uttered an oath of death.

"Don't think I'll let a rotten Injun push you in the river and get away with it. I will make sure that Injun *dies* for this, Calvin."

❖

"Miss Lowell! Miss Lowell!"

Kate turned from straightening her desk to see a shattered Drew, ashen and panting, stumble through the doorway.

Her first thought was for McCall, and Kate's heart leapt. In a flash, she remembered their final words. Tense, argumentative words, spawned by Kate herself. How could she have treated the man she loved with such contempt!

The man she loved. The man she loved. The man she loved.

Kate was in love with McCall! The realization hit her like a stallion's kick. She was in love with him. Was he, like Zachary, already snatched from her before her love could know full bloom?

The lunch of cold ham and potato salad crept up her throat, and Kate swallowed against a heave. She stumbled for Drew, damp and shivering, who had slumped inside the door.

"McCall. . . ," she choked out. "Is he. . ."

"No. It's n–not D–Dad." Drew rubbed his violently shaking hands over his stricken face. "It's–It's Calvin!" He clutched at Kate. "Oh, Miss Lowell! He almost drowned!"

Kate, collapsing with relief and horror, pulled the sobbing boy into her arms. "Drew. . .Drew. . .Drew. . .calm down and tell me what happened."

"I–I—oh, Miss Lowell, I know. . .know I w–wasn't supposed to meet Calvin. But–But we didn't m–meet much. Only. . .only about twice a month, and–and he j–just h–happened to be at the r–river today. . . ." Drew paused for a hiccough and attempted to catch his breath. "We were racing back. . .back and forth across the—that fallen log–g—*the log D–Dad told us to stay off of*!" he continued, his face contorted.

"Drew. . .Drew. . .calm down," Kate soothed.

"I can't! I can't! Don't you see! He fell off the log and hit his head. I had to go in after him, or he would have drowned. The whole thing is my fault. I should have minded Dad, but–but—"

"Drew! Listen to me!" Kate grabbed him by the shoulders and gently shook him. "Did you force Calvin onto that log?"

"N–No."

"Then you can't blame yourself!"

"Oh, Miss Lowell! I just feel so–so *horrible* about the *whole thing*!"

"Well you shouldn't, Drew," Kate soothed as she began gently rocking him. "Sounds to me like you saved Calvin's life."

These words seemed to float around them and gently settle into Drew's mind to calm his nerves. As he clung to Kate, she continued rocking him in her arms and eventually began humming "Amazing Grace." At long last, Drew's weeping stopped, and Kate continued to simply hold him.

❖

McCall arrived home long past the time Bob Mosely usually departed. He steered Eugene Wilcox's worn-out mare onto the horse farm and decided to return the animal in the morning. After alerting Dr. Engle to Calvin's situation, McCall had debated whether or not to follow the doctor and his nurse, Magnolia Alexander, to the Wilcox's or return home. He chose to return home. McCall wanted to make certain Drew was safe. The look in Eugene Wilcox's eyes left him far from comfortable.

If he had to leave his whole ranch for the sake of saving Drew, he would. Recently, Bob Mosely had hinted that he would buy the horse ranch should McCall ever decide to sell it. At first McCall had dismissed the whole idea. But lately, he began to reconsider. In recent correspondences, McCall's elder sister, Rebekah, wrote that she and her husband would love for McCall to move near them in Boston. If he and Drew were to move to the East Coast, McCall most likely could arrange for his son to attend a school whose teachers and students would better accept him. As Miss Lowell had clearly pointed out, Drew desperately needed friends. He was desperate enough to actually place himself in danger by associating with the son of a man who hated him.

Perhaps the solution lay in McCall's moving. Maybe a close proximity with his only sibling would also begin to somehow heal the relationship with McCall's parents, still in Dallas. If his mother and father realized McCall and Rebekah were growing closer, perhaps that would instigate their rethinking former decisions. However, McCall also had Drew's future to consider. The boy did not deserve the danger that Eugene posed. If Eugene were alone in his notions, McCall would not be as concerned. However, other people in Dogwood felt as strongly as Eugene, even though they might never express their prejudice to McCall's face.

Wearily, McCall dismounted and gently cared for the old horse by settling her in a stall with a fresh bucket of oats and plenty of water. As he gently stroked her nose, he wondered how Eugene treated her. Probably in ways McCall didn't want to know.

Sighing, he shoved his hands in his riding britches and crunched across the hay-strewn floor. He savored the smells of horses and leather and straw, which were the essence of his life. A life he never thought he would be living. McCall had assumed in his younger years that he would spend his days in his father's bank, preparing to accept the reins from McCall Adams, Sr. But life had taken a different turn. In some ways, that turn had been tragic. In other ways, McCall enjoyed his existence with the horses. He had learned much about himself in the last fourteen years, including the fact that he would rather be outside with the horses any day than cooped up in an office. If he and Drew moved to the East Coast, McCall would undoubtedly glean his livelihood from another horse ranch, not the bank office where his brother-in-law presided as president.

If only Melody could have shared it all with him. A nostalgic chord echoed through his soul, and McCall's mind turned to another young lady who had been virtually dropped into his life. If only McCall could release his hold on Melody. He clenched his jaws and shook his head in defeat. The freedom to love again seemed an impossibility. McCall would most likely spend his life married to a ghost of his past.

He closed the barn door and walked across the dusty yard toward his log cabin. A lantern burned in the kitchen window, and McCall assumed Drew was either reading or in the process of eating everything in the pantry and everything from the spring house. That boy was beginning to devour enough for two grown men.

Thoughts of his son left him smiling fondly; then he sobered. Somehow he couldn't get Eugene's threat off his mind. He breathed a prayer and hoped Calvin recovered soon. He also debated how to handle the disciplinary aspect of Drew's blatant disobedience. Had he been "disciplined" enough by the realization that his friend almost drowned?

With a whippoorwill serenading the cool twilight, McCall stepped onto his porch and opened the cabin's door. Smells of freshly baked cookies and companionable laughter greeted him. McCall's mind whirled with the implications. He would recognize Kate Lowell's voice in a howling blizzard. She must have stayed with Drew for companionship. The thought left McCall thankful and agitated. He didn't think he had the strength to face Kate again. Not tonight. Not after Calvin's accident and all the worries that stirred.

McCall silently closed the door and made certain the metal bar latch was securely in its place. As he studied the sparsely furnished, shadowed room, he entertained the notion of tiptoeing into his bedroom, closing the door, and not coming out until Kate was gone. But that was impossible. She would need a ride back into Dogwood. Bob Mosely had undoubtedly already left, and McCall would assuredly be the person to escort her.

Stifling a groan, he lambasted his awkward predicament. Only one choice presented itself as appropriate. He would walk into the kitchen, face Miss Lowell, politely thank her for her companionship to Drew, and offer an immediate escort back to town. Setting his lips in a determined line, McCall removed his hat, hung it on the peg near the door, and resolutely walked toward the kitchen.

The sight that greeted him left an ache in the center of his soul. Miss Lowell and Drew hovered over the kitchen table examining a cookie sheet filled with fragrant, beige cookies. The kitchen, warm from the cooking stove, seemed to extend invisible arms and draw McCall into its heart. A heart that held his son and the woman who would make a perfect mother for Drew. Her dark hair, pulled loosely into its usually meticulous bun, was a bit disheveled and sprinkled with flour in spots. Her cheeks bore a faint flush, most likely from the heat of the stove. Her full lips turned upward in appreciation for the delicious smell. McCall knew the simple gingham dress she wore was a far cry from the fine gowns that must await her in El Paso. What made such a woman want to tutor his son?

"Drew, I believe we have been successful!" she said with triumph.

The boy broke off a piece of cookie and popped it into his mouth to gingerly chew it. He produced an instantaneous grimace and immediately removed the cookie from his mouth before Kate saw him.

"Isn't that too hot?" Kate asked.

"No. No, it. . .it was fine," he stammered as he reached for the clay water pitcher near the basin. Drew grabbed one of the thick mugs hanging under the cabinet, filled it with water, and took a huge gulp. Apparently the taste of Miss Lowell's cookies did not match their looks.

McCall stifled a chuckle at his son's attempts to hide his aversion from the teacher he so desperately wanted to please. And their companionable conversation dimmed in comparison to the thoughts now bombarding McCall. He had been so busy fighting his own internal battles regarding Miss Lowell that he had given precious little thought to Drew's needs. McCall had thought he had done a good job raising the boy alone. A job Melody would be proud of. But he saw now, more than ever, that Drew needed feminine influence in his life, evidenced in this homey scene before him as well as the weekends when Drew anxiously awaited Miss Lowell's return on Monday mornings.

He was so engrossed in his thoughts that he didn't realize their conversation had stopped and both Drew and Kate were anxiously staring at him as if they awaited an answer.

"Excuse me," he said, stepping into the room. "Did you say something to me?"

"Yes," Kate replied.

"We were wondering about Calvin," Drew said, his eyes now downcast.

"Dr. Engle should be seeing him now. I believe he's going to live, but. . ."

"M–Mr. Wilcox, was he. . ." Drew trailed off as Kate placed a supportive arm around the boy.

"Wilcox is. . .disturbed." McCall chose his words carefully and exchanged a meaningful look with Kate.

Drew nervously drew a circle in a bit of flour beside the wooden mixing bowl. "Is it just because I'm part Indian that he hates me so badly?" he asked at last.

McCall desperately wanted to deny his son's words. He abhorred the thought that this child would go through life scorned for something over which he possessed no control. Although he would have never wished Drew into existence the way he came, this adopted boy had been a source of joy from the start. McCall saw traces of Melody in him every day. At first, he had loved Drew because he was a part of Melody. But then he grew to love Drew just because he was Drew.

"Do you know who my real father was?" Drew blurted, staring at McCall as if he were terrified of his own words.

Blinking in surprise, McCall glanced toward Miss Lowell, who looked shocked herself. The question had come from nowhere and at a most inopportune moment. But looking back at Drew, McCall knew this was a question that continually haunted the boy. A question that very likely served as the source of Drew's recent distance from his father. A question that must be answered for his peace of mind.

Chapter 12

Eugene Wilcox paced across the porch of his humble home. The doctor and his nurse had been with Calvin for the better part of half an hour. The boy awoke right before the doctor arrived and didn't much recall what had happened. Well, Eugene knew what had happened. That stinkin' Indian had tried to kill Calvin. Once the doctor left and he knew Calvin was fine, Eugene had a score to settle.

He wasn't the only man in Dogwood who hated Indians. He wasn't the only man who wished McCall Adams would never bring Drew to town. He wasn't the only man who would be ready to hang Drew for trying to kill Calvin. All Eugene needed to do was show up at the saloon, announce what had happened, and lead the way to the Adamses' farm. Then, it would only be a matter of time before Drew hung from a rope.

The door rattled, then opened. Eugene stopped his pacing to turn and face the elderly doctor.

"Your son's going to be all right," Dr. Engle said as he scrutinized Eugene. "But he took a hard blow on the head. Magnolia is instructing your wife in caring for his head injury. I want him to stay in bed a couple of days. That means no chores or school."

"Fine. We'll see to it," Eugene said, anxious for the doctor to be on his way.

But the doctor wasn't finished. He pushed up his spectacles and continued to eye Eugene.

For some reason, making eye contact with the doctor left Eugene uneasy. So he looked across the west pasture toward the line of woods. The thick trees hid the setting sun from view, but the sky, ablaze with the hues of rich gold and rubies, proclaimed the sun's gradual descent. In the distance, a quail called out "Bob White" and another quail answered in return. Eugene wished he could whistle out a message to the Dogwood Township and have them just meet him at the Adamses' farm.

"I hope you understand that what happened was an accident," Dr. Engle said firmly.

Squinting, Eugene leveled a steady gaze at the interfering doctor. "Why do think you know so much about it?"

"Because McCall Adams—"

"I know what McCall Adams says, and I don't believe him."

"Calvin even says he believes it was an accident. He says he and Drew are best friends and that Drew wouldn't—"

Eugene snorted. "What does Calvin know? He don't even remember what happened."

"I'm sure Drew does."

"Yeah! Like he *remembers* who started that fight in town last fall!" Eugene raised his hands in disgust. "Do you honestly think I'm gonna believe anything an Injun would say?"

"He's a good, honest kid. And yes, I think you should believe him!" Dr. Engle barked, his mouth tight.

"And I think it's high time for you to go back home and leave us be." Eugene stabbed an index finger in the middle of Dr. Engle's chest.

"I'm going nowhere," the doctor declared. "My nurse and I are staying here to watch Calvin. He took a mighty hard blow to the head and—"

"*I'll* watch my son!" Eugene spit a well-aimed stream of tobacco near the doctor's boots.

The doctor narrowed his eyes, pressed his lips together, turned, opened the front door, and entered the shack.

Eugene debated whether to force the nosy doctor from his farm or to momentarily ignore him and ride into Dogwood. Forcing Dr. Engle to leave would certainly eat into the time that Eugene could use to round up the group of men who would help with the hanging. He decided to ignore the doctor for the time being.

That Indian had beaten up Calvin in front of the whole town. Now he had tried to murder Calvin. He should pay. The sooner, the better.

As Eugene strode toward the pasture to retrieve his horse, he cursed himself for not beating Drew the day he discovered him and Calvin near the river. Eugene had allowed all their talk about God to distract him from his purpose. Perhaps if he had used his whip as he had intended, Calvin would have never been injured today.

Only one solution remained to the problem. These parts didn't need the likes of Drew Adams.

❖

Kate watched the various expressions flit across McCall's face when Drew posed the unexpected question about the circumstances of his birth. McCall first appeared surprised, then uneasy, and eventually resigned, as if he realized he could no longer put off the talk with Drew. Kate felt as if she wanted the kitchen floor to open and swallow her. She certainly did not need to be present when McCall told his son the truth.

"If you'll excuse me," she said discreetly as she stepped toward the doorway. Glancing over her shoulder, Kate wondered if either of them even heard her. They were both so engrossed in the moment that everything else seemed to have faded from their view.

Within minutes, Kate had walked onto the cabin's front porch, into the cool evening, and toward the summer kitchen. Her shoulders sagged with the weight of the day. Until today, Kate had not spoken to McCall in three months. Until today, Kate had not realized she was fully in love with McCall. Until today, Kate had been able to bar even Drew from the inner sanctuary of her heart.

She stepped into the dark summer kitchen and immediately lit the oil lamp sitting on her desk. Then she noticed Zachary's dried rose, still lying on her Bible, exactly where she had left it when Drew stumbled in to announce Calvin's accident. Kate picked up the rose and glanced toward the cold fireplace. Earlier today, she had almost burned the memento. Should she now?

Kate settled into the straight-backed chair, propped her elbows on the desk, and placed her face into opened hands. "Oh, Lord," she breathed. "Somehow, I feel as if I've come to a sort of crossroads here. I can no longer deny my love for McCall. Oh, dear God, I think I love him more than I even loved Zachary."

Kate's own words shocked her. She removed her hands from her face and stared at the rose until it blurred in the lamp's flickering shadows. How could it be that she loved McCall more than Zach?

Perhaps because you have revealed more of your real self to him.

The thought left her blinking in surprise. It was true. With Zachary, Kate had been the person that her mother had taught her to be. Cool. Refined. Proper. With McCall Kate had done nothing but say the wrong thing at the wrong time and allow him the most inappropriate privileges, such as kissing her and suggesting that they should get married when he still loved Melody. Nonetheless, for once in her life she had spoken her mind.

Thoughts of McCall's proposal left Kate's stomach twisting in uncertainty. At the time of his hasty question, she had scorned the idea of marrying a man who harbored love for his deceased wife. Now, months later, with the full realization of her own love filling her heart, Kate considered the possibility.

Drew desperately needed so much more than a tutor. He needed a mother. He needed a strong woman who would step into his life and tell him she loved him unconditionally. At this crucial time, he needed the prayers of a godly mother. Even as she knew McCall was speaking to Drew, Kate wanted to be there for him, wanted to assure him that the circumstances of his birth in no way determined his worth.

And McCall—McCall needed someone with whom he could share his life. He needed someone to snuggle up to on cold winter evenings. Someone to experience his joy in the sight of a newborn colt. Someone to give him more children to love. And perhaps in time, Kate could somehow help him forget Melody.

With renewed purpose, she picked up the rose—Zachary's rose—and stood. Kate lifted the glass globe from the burning oil lamp on the desk. Holding the dried rose petals over the flame until the flower ignited and blazed on its own, she then tossed the blazing emblem from her past into the cold ashes of the fireplace.

In those moments, watching the fire devour her once-cherished rose, Kate felt as if God Himself entered her heart and, with the flames of His presence, purged the pain, the scars, and the heartache from her. Slowly, gently, with the utmost patience, the force that created the universe had been performing a work of healing within Kate from the time she agreed to the tutoring position. In the place of all her fear, all her pain, all her haunting memories, He delivered Kate into a glorious freedom, allowing her to embrace the future.

As the warmth of the Lord's presence enveloped her, Kate's eyes brimmed to overflowing. Warm tears splashed to her cheeks and trickled to her chin.

"Oh, Lord," she breathed. "Give me the courage to embrace the future. And McCall, Lord. . .I pray the same for McCall."

As if her prayers conjured his presence, the door opened, and Kate turned from the fireplace to see McCall stepping from the night and into the dimly lit room. He silently observed her for several seconds, and Kate didn't avert her gaze. McCall Adams had seemed a man of shadows when Kate met him. A man of walls. A man of many secrets. The oil lamp's dancing light only made the shadows, the walls, the secrets, all the more prominent. He wearily rubbed a hand across his bearded face and glanced out one of the windows.

In the distance an owl called out, "Who cooks for you? Who cooks for you?" Kate bit her tongue to stop herself from telling McCall that she would cook for him.

"Your cookies were terrible," McCall said, never taking his gaze from the window.

"What?" Kate hadn't exactly known what he would say to her, but she had never expected an evaluation of her cookies.

"The cookies. . ." He tossed a mischievous, sideways glance her way. "They smelled delicious, but. . ." McCall shrugged. "Drew and I were wondering if maybe you substituted salt for sugar or something. Have you ever made cookies before, Miss Lowell?"

Suddenly the day's worth of tension seemed to spew forth from the internal bottle in which Kate had desperately tried to contain it. Moments before she had shed tears as a result of the presence of God. New tears stung her eyes. Tears of frustration, aggravation, and exhaustion. "If you must know, Mr. Adams, I have never made cookies before tonight. And I did it in an attempt to. . .to try to distract Drew. I thought I was f–following. . . ," she sniffed, ". . .f–following the recipe Drew found in the kitchen drawer. I'm t–terribly sorry. . . ." She walked to her desk, shut her Bible with a snap, and picked it up. "I'm terribly s–sorry that they didn't meet your. . .your. . ." Her voice cracked, and she grew angry with her own crying. Whirling to face him, she challenged, "Did you come out here for the sole purpose of delivering a report of my cookies? If so—"

"No. That wasn't even a part of the reason I came. I'm sorry that my teasing has so upset you. I never intended—"

"Then what exactly *did* you intend?" Kate would never admit to him, or even herself, that a large degree of her escalating ire stemmed less from his comments and more from the dire situation in which she found herself: She was madly in love with McCall Adams. Madly in love with a man who could never fully return her love.

Kate knew McCall well enough by now to understand what his narrowed eyes meant. *Good!* she thought to herself. *Serves him right if he's angry, too.*

"I came out here to tell you that Drew and I are prepared to escort you back to the hotel now."

"Wonderful." Kate walked toward the peg where her reticule hung, retrieved it, and turned to face him. "I'm prepared to leave now, if you like." She desperately wished she weren't standing so close to him. She desperately wished she couldn't see the blatant admiration stirring the depths of his eyes. She desperately wished she could somehow reach into his heart and pluck the memories of Melody from his mind.

But only God could do that. Only if McCall would let Him.

Kate, snared by the moment, tried to gaze past McCall but couldn't. Instead, she greedily drank in his nearness. The magic the two of them shared since the moment they met now held her spellbound. As if he were as entranced as she was, McCall gently stroked her damp cheek with the backs of his fingers.

"Ah, Kate," he said softly. "I'm sorry. I didn't really want to tell you about those cookies. I wanted to tell you how lovely you looked, almost like an angel in the shadows."

She fought to swallow against her tightened throat. All vestiges of anger vanished in the tide of new, overwhelming emotions. Not only had McCall expressed his admiration, he had also called her by her given name, a name reserved for only the most intimate of acquaintances. As he stopped caressing her cheek, a cascade of tingles spread from her cheek, down her neck, and Kate fought to speak.

"I, too, am sorry. I'm. . .I'm s–sorry that I grew so agitated." To her own ears, she sounded as winded as if she had run a mile. "And. . .and I'm sorry about earlier today as well. I should have n–never been so snappy when you inquired of Drew's availability to work."

His silence only heightened the tense moment. Kate felt as though she might melt in the nearness of him. A part of her prayed that he would take her into his arms. The other part prayed that he wouldn't.

McCall, at long last, spoke. "I guess I should likewise apologize for some of the things I said this afternoon as well as. . . ," he cleared his throat nervously, ". . .when we spoke at the hotel."

His proposal sprang up between them and seemed to beg to be discussed. Kate, looking down at the reticule she clutched, chewed her bottom lip, and refused to mention the proposal.

"I should have never asked you to marry me," he said gently. "It was an insult to you and thoughtless on my part. I deeply regret many things about that day."

The pain in McCall's voice made Kate want to step into the circle of his arms, stroke his dark beard, and lay her head on his chest. She wanted to promise him she *would* marry him, and together they would work through the ghosts of his past. But she couldn't. Kate looked toward the fireplace where lay the ashes of Zachary's rose. McCall must burn his own roses before he could embrace her. Even if Kate were willing to marry him while he was still in love with Melody, she knew McCall would never expect her to share his heart with another woman, regardless of his hasty proposal.

"How did the talk go with Drew?" Kate asked, desperate for any other topic of conversation. Much longer on the existing subject, and she was certain she would explode from grief.

"Better than I thought. Actually, I think this has been bothering the boy for quite some time. He hasn't seemed himself of late."

"Yes. I agree. I think it was time to tell him."

"I would be lying if I said he wasn't disturbed at all. But I think knowing the truth was better for him than being left in suspense."

"And you?" Kate dared to look once more into McCall's eyes. "How do you feel about. . .about everything?" Her question, though it sounded innocent enough, seemed as innocuous as a coral snake. Kate reeled in the torment from his eyes, glittering in the lamp's dancing light. That was one question he answered without a word. It was as though someone slammed the door on any hopes she held for McCall's complete, total love.

"Dad!" Drew's faint call echoed from the yard. "Dad!" This time the call was closer.

McCall turned to the door and opened it. "In here, Drew. I was just preparing to escort Miss Lowell back into town."

"Mrs. Wilcox is here to see you," Drew said.

"Mr. Adams, Mr. Adams," an urgent, feminine voice cried.

Alarmed, Kate turned toward the nearby window and looked out onto the yard, illuminated by the moon's faint glow. A slight woman ran from the log cabin toward the summer kitchen as if she were terrified.

"Yes, Mrs. Wilcox," McCall said. "Is everything okay? Is Calvin—"

"The doctor says that Calvin is going to be fine. But Eugene—oh, Mr. Adams, Dr. Engle told me to come as soon as we suspected. I'm dreadfully afraid that he has gone to town with plans to bring a group of men here for–for—" She turned terror-filled eyes to Drew as the faint echoes of galloping horses wafted across the winds of the night.

Chapter 13

The sounds of those horses chilled McCall's blood. He glimpsed the momentary flashes of torches through the trees that lined the lane. In terror, McCall wondered how many men Eugene had managed to enlist in his crusade. At once he pictured Drew hanging by his neck from a nearby tree, and McCall swallowed against a stomach that threatened to unload its contents. Yet he had precious little time for anything but action.

He stepped from the summer kitchen and grabbed Drew's arms. "I want you to go into the woods and do not come out until we come for you. Do you understand?"

"Wh–what? Wh–why?" Drew's wide-eyed expression twisted McCall's heart.

An approaching cacophony of whooping and jeering seemed to mock the boy's innocent question.

"Just do what I tell you!" McCall barked. "There's no time for reasons." How could he ever explain that Wilcox was using the accident with Calvin as an excuse to kill Drew just because he hated Indians?

A flash of understanding crossed Drew's features. Next, a hint of bewilderment. Finally, a deluge of horror. Without another word, Drew turned and raced toward the woods, his second home.

"Mr. Adams, I'm so sorry I didn't get here sooner," Mrs. Wilcox said, her voice trembling. "But Dr. Engle and I were tendin' to Calvin, and I was a takin' care of the baby, and we didn't realize Eugene was gone for the longest. Then. . .then. . .I just had this most awful, sick feeling in my stomach, and the good doctor, too, and. . ."

255

"Drew Adams. . .Drew Adams!" a drunken voice bellowed across the night. "We're comin' a callin'." A burst of raucous laughter punctuated the absurd claim.

McCall ignored Mrs. Wilcox's well-meaning chatter as his heart pounded with dread. If he had to, McCall would lay down his own life for Drew. He utterly hoped that, in his doing so, the boy could escape. Only when a soft, warm hand slipped into his did he remember Kate's presence.

"You need to go into the cabin," he demanded, looking down at her. "You and Mrs. Wilcox both."

"I'm going nowhere," Kate said firmly. Her face set in determined lines, she refused to relinquish her grip on his hand.

"Me neither," Mrs. Wilcox said, crossing her arms.

The dastardly group's torches now glowed in clear view. McCall touched the Colt Peacemaker that he had strapped on that morning before repairing the fences. Since the days were growing warmer, he never took a chance on snakes. Looked like the snakes slithering up the road on horses were the ones his Peacemaker would meet.

At last the trio of men on restless steeds came to a collective halt about fifty feet in front of McCall and the women. McCall, having expected more men, was relieved he must face only three. Nevertheless, the relief did not blot out his caution. As he suspected, a tipsy Wilcox, worn rope in hand, took the leadership position. The other two men carried torches, which lit their hate-filled faces and made them appear more demonic than human. Kate's hand trembled in McCall's, and he wished she and Nadine Wilcox had gone into the cabin. Considering the trio's seeming lack of sobriety, McCall truly expected them to thoughtlessly shoot at anyone who crossed them.

Silently, he began to pray. To pray as he had never prayed before. To pray for a miracle.

"We come to hang that Injun!" one of the bearded men proclaimed.

"Yeah!" The wiry Eugene dismounted. "He done tried to kill my boy."

"It was an accident," McCall said evenly. His gut's quaking drastically contrasted his firm voice. "And you have no right—"

"You listen to me, Eugene!" Nadine called in a stern voice that belied her mousy demeanor.

"Woman! What are you doing here?" Eugene peered toward his wife as if he only just saw her.

She closed the distance between them by half. "I'll tell ya what I'm a here for. I come to warn Mr. Adams 'bout what you were up to. It ain't right, Eugene!"

"Sounds like you're havin' trouble keepin' up with your own woman," one of the men sneered while the other produced a perverse laugh.

"You shut up!" Eugene snapped, glancing over his shoulder.

McCall began to wonder just how committed Eugene's cohorts were to their murderous task. He wondered if they had simply come along for the thrill of the whole wretched ordeal.

"I'm not gonna shut up," the petite, blond woman said. "You've shut me up for the last time, and I aim to stand my ground this time." She placed her hands on her hips in a stance that said she meant it. McCall had to admit he was astounded at her bravado. The few times he had seen them in town, Eugene obviously maintained a dictatorial upper hand in their marriage. "I ain't about to let you murder an innocent boy!"

Eugene, overwrought with fury, marched to within an inch of his wife as if he thought she would recoil. But Nadine, head held high, stood her ground.

"That boy ain't innocent!" Eugene snarled, waving the worn, gray rope for emphasis. "He beat Calvin up in town, and now he's tried to kill him."

"Calvin started that fight, Eugene. He told me so! And I don't for one second believe Drew tried to kill our boy. He saved Calvin's life, that's what he done!"

"Sounds like your woman's got the best of you," one of the men scoffed.

As if the ridicule fueled Eugene's arrogance, he sluggishly raised his arm and delivered a backhanded blow across Nadine's face. With a cry of pain, she fell to the ground.

McCall's mind whirled with images of Melody, her face bruised from similar treatment, her cries of pain. Like Nadine, she had been a victim of masculine cruelty. Enraged, McCall stepped forward to defend the help-less woman whom Eugene mercilessly kicked twice to the leering cheers of the tipsy men.

But thoughts of Kate momentarily halted him. He whirled back to face her, picked her up by the waist, and plopped her back into the sum-mer kitchen. "You stay in here. There's a pistol on the mantel. The bullets are in the wooden box beside it."

"Yes. I have seen them."

"Do you know how to use it?"

"Yes. My father made certain of my abilities with a gun."

McCall hesitated but a second and desperately hoped he wasn't about to make a dread mistake. "Good. Lock the door. Get the pistol. And wait by the window. If you need to shoot, do it."

Her face pale, she mutely nodded, and McCall slammed the door. With the sound of the metal bar lock sliding into place, he ran toward Eugene Wilcox. Pulling his Peacemaker from its holster, McCall shot twice into the air. Not only did Eugene cower in fear, but his cronies also ducked in their saddles.

"Get up, Mrs. Wilcox." McCall stepped between her and Eugene and lowered his gun straight at Eugene's head. "Now you listen and you listen closely, Eugene Wilcox. I want you and your cronies off my property *now*."

"You're mighty brave for just one man," Eugene slurred.

"There's a woman in the summer kitchen with a pistol," McCall shouted loud enough for the men and Kate to hear him. "Kate!" he continued. "If anyone draws, you shoot them." *Oh dear God*, McCall prayed as the words left his mouth. *Please God, give Kate the guts to do what she needs to do.*

An unexpected shot, accompanied by the sound of shattering glass, exploded from the summer kitchen. McCall jumped, and Eugene covered his head and dropped to the ground.

"Get off my property!" McCall yelled. "Now! All of you!"

Although the men's horses pranced a bit, no one showed signs of retreat. McCall, praying like a mad man, decided on an alternative tactic. "Do you want to land in prison?" he reasoned. "What you're doing is against the law. It's wrong. And when you're through, Constable Parker will hunt you down and lock you away!"

Dead silence filled the yard. The only sounds were the chirping of crickets and that same, lone owl hooting at the night. Such peaceful sounds. Such a contrast to the deadly deeds on the verge of expression.

Eugene, still on the ground, looked behind him as if he expected support. Instead, a tired voice called, "Ah. . .let's go home."

"Yeah! What kinda man is afraid of a woman? He's probably lied to us from the start."

"That's right."

"I never did put much stock in what Eugene said no ways."

"Why'd we listen tonight?"

"Ain't no sense in hangin' a innocent boy."

The mumbling men turned their horses and, amidst more indiscernible discussion, began retracing their path.

"Hey, wait!" Eugene bellowed. Looking over his shoulder, he crawled toward his horse like a dog, and McCall resisted the urge to deliver a hard kick to the seat of his pants.

Another shot rang out from the kitchen. McCall derisively chuckled as Eugene flattened himself against the ground and the two horsemen urged their mounts into a gallop.

"Hold your fire, Kate!" he called, a note of approval ringing in his voice. "Eugene, get up and go home. *Now!*"

The half-drunk scoundrel stood, mounted his unsettled horse, and followed the retreating men.

From the ground, Mrs. Wilcox produced an agonized groan. McCall, still watching the group, helped the beaten woman to her feet. "Are you all right?" he asked.

"Yes. . .yes. . .I think," she rasped, leaning on his arm for support. "This ain't the first time he's done beat me. I've lived through worse."

"You were exceptionally brave." McCall placed a supportive arm around Nadine and once more observed the trio of men, now heading up the tree-lined lane. The tension in his chest began to ease.

"McCall, is. . .is it safe for m–me to come out?" Kate softly requested.

A certain sense of intimacy rang in Kate's voice. To McCall's knowledge, this was the first time she had ever used his first name. But then, he had naturally used her given name earlier without even so much as a thought. The two of them were certainly progressing in their relationship, despite resistance on both parts. What was to become of them? Would McCall ever be able to lay aside his past?

"Yes, it's safe," he answered, casting another glance toward the men whose torches now only occasionally glittered through the dense trees. "Come on out, Kate. Let's get Mrs. Wilcox into the house and make certain she's all right."

"I'll be fine," Nadine protested. Her right eye already appeared swollen, even in the shadows.

"You'll need to lie down for a bit," McCall said as Kate joined them. She, too, continued to watch the road in concern.

"I must g-get back to the baby and Calvin and Dr. Engle." Nadine made a feeble attempt to stumble toward the doctor's hooded carriage, parked near the barn.

"They'll be fine for the moment," Kate said, steering Nadine Wilcox toward the humble log cabin.

As she assented to Kate's urging, McCall could not resist the impulse to squeeze Kate's cold hand. "You were wonderful," he whispered.

She turned admiring eyes on him. Eyes that, in the moon's soft glow, seemed all the larger. Eyes that brimmed with love. At that moment, there was no question in McCall's mind that Kate Lowell loved him with her whole heart. With her *whole* heart. Several months ago in the hotel lobby, she had admitted the ties that bound her to Zachary. McCall now wondered if she had somehow released her hold on her former love.

A gentle spring breeze sprinted across the fresh foliage and promised yet another cool night, which contrasted with warm afternoons. The divergent spring temperatures seemed a metaphor for McCall's own feelings. At times, he warmed to the point of believing he could truly put Melody from his heart and embrace Kate. At other times, McCall remembered that cold chamber in his soul where those memories remained forever preserved in their chilling closet.

But tonight, with Kate's admiring gaze bathing him in love, McCall wondered if he were a fool for clinging to the past. Clearly, he needed to decide once and for all what he would do with his life: continue as a slave to the past or embrace a new future.

Chapter 14

Within an hour, Kate had settled Mrs. Wilcox into McCall's bed and encouraged her to rest. McCall, who had insisted that Nadine relax in his room, went in search of Drew. He promised to escort Nadine home upon his return. Kate supplied the scrawny, weary woman a cloth, soaked in cool spring water, to place on her swelling eye. Nadine uttered her thanks and shortly thereafter drifted into a shallow sleep.

Kate reached toward the oil lamp, sitting on the chest of drawers, and turned down the wick. The room seemed to shrink as the shadows closed in. Kate, her heart swelling in pity, watched poor Mrs. Wilcox as she flinched in her sleep. Only the Lord knew what the woman was dreaming. Undoubtedly, she had lived a harsh life with Eugene.

Stirred in sympathy, Kate breathed a prayer for Mrs. Wilcox. Much to her own surprise, she also found herself praying for Eugene. He desperately needed the Lord. For his own sake. For the sake of Nadine. And especially for the sake of his children. But he seemed so hardened, and Kate wondered if he would ever truly turn his life over to the Lord.

She turned to leave the room, which smelled of hair tonic and lye soap, but the dressing table in the corner caught her eye. Other than McCall's austere bed and chest of drawers, the feminine dressing table was the only other piece of furniture. Kate, noticing three photos on the dresser, picked up the lamp and slowly walked toward them as if a magnet were drawing her. Other than the three photos, only a yellowed, lace doily, a brush, hand mirror, and a bottle of perfume graced the dressing table. Kate leaned closer, extending the oil lamp toward the tarnished, silver picture frames. Just as she suspected, the photos were of Melody, and one included McCall as well. Perhaps their engagement photo. Kate set the oil lamp on the dresser and picked up the hairbrush by its whalebone handle. Dismayed, she examined the dark hair, which still clung to it.

Despair all but drowned her soul. Even from her grave, Melody clearly held McCall's love. Kate's eyes stung with fresh tears as she, at long last, comprehended just how difficult a battle McCall faced if he hoped to relinquish his past. Even though Kate had struggled to release Zachary, she had never been married to him. She had never known Melody's type of pain—a pain that had bound McCall and Melody even closer to each other. She had never raised his child.

Kate replaced the brush. With fear and trembling, she opened the tiny, square perfume bottle. Kate not only discerned the true depths of McCall's ties to Melody, but she also grasped anew the magnitude of his raising Melody's child—the child that many men would have rejected with their family and peers' approval. Truly McCall Adams was a man of unusually deep character. And love. Nothing with McCall probably ever ran shallow. Once he loved, he loved for life. Once he committed, he committed for life.

If only he could love, could commit to Kate.

She momentarily held her breath before delicately sniffing the perfume. When the light floral fragrance filled her nostrils, she sighed in relief. She had desperately hoped Melody's chosen perfume was not of roses. If McCall ever could completely love Kate, she didn't want it to be because she reminded him of Melody, not even in the choice of perfume.

A soft knock at the door left Kate jumping. Guiltily, she replaced the perfume's stopper, deposited it onto the dresser, and whirled to face the door.

"Kate?"

McCall's kind, concerned voice left her feeling all the more culpable.

"Yes. You may come in," Kate said, walking to the bedside as nonchalantly as possible.

McCall opened the door and hesitantly stepped into the room.

"Were you able to find Drew?" Kate asked.

"Yes. He's in the kitchen now. He never had any supper. And even in the face of death, the boy is starving." McCall rolled his eyes and produced a slight smile.

Kate returned the smile but could not ignore the tired lines around McCall's eyes. "Do you think Eugene will be back?"

"I have prayed that he won't until I can't pray anymore. As soon as I escort Mrs. Wilcox home, I will escort you back to the hotel and alert Constable Parker to what Eugene tried to do. I am hoping the constable will invite him to a few days in jail."

"Me, too," Kate said as Melody's perfume lingered on the air and grew stronger with each passing moment.

Seconds later, an odd look covered McCall's face, and he glanced toward the dresser.

Biting her bottom lip, Kate sneaked a peek toward the perfume bottle to have her worst fears confirmed. When she had hastily replaced the bottle, it fell to its side, and the stopper toppled off. The yellowed doily upon which the square bottle sat now bore a damp circle, which filled the room with a sweet smell.

Kate stole a glance back to McCall, who now looked at her. Obviously he understood that she had been meddlesome. This was evidenced, not only by the perfume bottle, but also by the strategic location of the oil lamp, still dimly burning on the dresser. She braced herself for the anger, certain to follow.

But McCall simply walked toward the dresser, righted the bottle, firmly replaced the stopper, and removed the soiled doily.

"I'm–I'm sorry," Kate stuttered.

McCall kept his back turned, and she wondered what on earth he must think of her. Certainly, the worst. "I'll. . .I'll wait in the summer kitchen until you are ready to escort me to the hotel," she rushed, forgetting about Mrs. Wilcox. Compulsively, Kate lifted her skirt and hurried toward the door.

"Kate," McCall whispered.

She stopped. Her legs shook. Her heart pounded.

"I understand."

Kate pressed her hand against her chest and fought to breathe evenly. Never did she expect such a response from McCall, especially after the way he reacted when he caught her looking at Melody's photo the day he kissed her.

"I guess. . .I have felt the same way," he continued.

Kate whirled to face him. "You mean about—"

"About Zachary."

She swallowed against her tightened throat. "I burned. . .burned his rose today," she rasped, wondering why she felt the need to tell McCall.

"Oh?"

263

"It was the. . .the last rose he gave me. I. . .I had kept it in my Bible."

"Are you saying it's time for me to burn some roses?"

"Not necessarily. I just thought. . ."

What had she thought? That perhaps McCall would like to know she had been able, at long last, to release her relationship with Zachary? Or perhaps by telling him of her release he would be motivated to find release himself? Even though Kate had not contemplated those exact words, she realized her motive had been exactly that. "Well. . .I just thought you might be able to. . ." She intertwined her fingers so tightly they ached.

A sad, strange mixture of sorrow, love, and regret poured from McCall's eyes. "You have no idea how much I wish. . .but I cannot seem to get past. . ."

Kate knew his words would haunt her the rest of her life. She knew this pathetic expression cloaking the fine face of character would be etched on her heart until she died. She knew, at last she *deeply* knew, that perhaps McCall could not, truly *could not*, release Melody. But before Kate accepted defeat, she chose to whisper one last request.

"I found a verse in the Bible today that I think might be some comfort to you."

"Oh?"

"Yes. In Luke." She struggled to remember the chapter and verse but could not recall the evasive numbers.

"The Spirit of the Lord is upon me, because he hath anointed me to preach the gospel to the poor," McCall calmly quoted. "He hath sent me to heal the brokenhearted, to preach deliverance to the captives, and recovering of sight to the blind, to set at liberty them that are bruised. Luke four verse eighteen." He paused. "Is that the verse, Kate?"

Speechless, she stared at the man of her heart and experienced an overwhelming sense of panic. If McCall knew this verse and other verses and still could not release Melody, that could mean only one thing. Indeed, his heart would never be free of his deceased wife. "Yes, that's the verse," she said, as despair sank into her spirit.

Nadine's tired cough reminded Kate that they were not alone. Immediately, she wondered how much of their conversation Nadine had overheard. Her face heating, Kate looked toward the beaten soul in McCall's bed, but she continued in a light, troubled sleep.

"You should awaken her," McCall said. "Tell her I will take her home now. Dr. Engle and his nurse cannot remain at her house indefinitely, and I'm sure her baby must need her."

"What if Eugene is there?" Kate asked. "Do you think he will beat her again?"

The two shared a pensive gaze.

"I hope he *is* home," McCall growled. "I'll tell him I'll be back tomorrow, and if he has laid a hand on his wife, I'll make certain Constable Parker holds him in jail twice as long."

"But what about their crops?"

"I'll help with their crops or arrange for someone who will."

"You would do that for a man who threatened to kill your son?"

McCall produced a twisted smile. "If only I *were* so holy. No. At this moment there are several things I would like to do for Eugene. None of them promotes long life." His scowl spoke of continued fury. "Nevertheless, I will do all I can for Mrs. Wilcox and the children. They are innocent in all this. Just as innocent as Drew." He brushed past Kate with a mumbled, "As soon as you can get Mrs. Wilcox awake, I'll be waiting with the horse and buggy."

❖

The next morning Kate arrived at the horse farm at the usual time. As usual she went into the summer kitchen and prepared for the day's schoolwork. As usual Drew stepped into the room and produced a cheerful greeting. But both of them understood there was nothing usual about this day. The shadows of the former evening draped themselves over every word, over every task, over every thought.

And Kate knew that Drew completely comprehended his predicament for the first time in his life. She desperately wanted to discuss everything with him, but she didn't know where to begin or even *how* to begin. Instead she cheerfully talked with him about *Romeo and Juliet* and hoped her smiles somehow comforted him.

By the end of the day Kate felt as if she had worked three days without sleep. Drew, unusually sober, likewise appeared exhausted. Even though McCall reported Eugene's escapade to Constable Parker the night before, all day Kate looked over her shoulder to see if Eugene was once more plotting senseless revenge. With every creak of the summer kitchen's floorboards, with every breeze, with every distant whinny, both Kate and Drew worriedly glanced out the window. By the day's end they had received no report from Constable Parker, and that could mean Eugene was still at large.

Wearily, Kate straightened up her desk and prepared for Mr. Mosely to return her to the hotel.

"Dad and I spoke last night about our moving to Boston where Aunt

Rebekah lives." Drew listlessly stared at his math papers, propped his elbows on the desk, and placed his chin in his hands.

Kate stilled from her task. Her heart dropped. "Is this your father's sister?"

Drew nodded. "I've never met her, but Dad says she looks just like him, without the beard." He grimaced.

Under normal circumstances, Kate would have smiled, but she presently felt far from a grin. The reasons behind the father-son discussion were obvious. In the East McCall most likely would find a school in which he could safely enroll Drew. This would undoubtedly be advantageous for Drew. But once they moved they would no longer require Kate's services.

"When would you be moving?" Kate asked.

"As soon as Dad sells the ranch. He said Mr. Mosely might be interested in buying it."

A surge of anger, frustration, and bitterness swept over Kate. *McCall Adams*, she wanted to yell. *Why are you running? Why not stay and fight?* Kate glanced out the window to see Bob and McCall casually chatting by a corral that held a mare and newborn colt. From what Kate understood, this colt had come into the world with great difficulty. Both mother and colt received nothing but McCall's most tender treatment. He obviously loved this ranch. He loved the horses. He had built a solid reputation for the quality horses he produced.

Why leave what he had worked so hard to achieve?

As McCall and Mr. Mosely continued their chat, Kate wondered if they might even now be discussing the sale of the horse ranch. New waves of fury splashed upon her. How could McCall do this? Or better yet, how could he do this to *her?*

Even after their disheartening conversation last night, Kate found it nearly impossible to sleep. Instead, she desperately prayed that God would perform a miracle in McCall's heart. Now, as she watched McCall and Bob Mosely's earnest interaction, a haunting realization struck her. God was more than willing to perform a miracle within McCall. But McCall had to *choose* to let Him. As long as he clung to his past, God could not do the work He desperately wanted to do. Just as Kate had to be compliant in relinquishing the pain caused by Zachary's death and embrace the healing that God generously extended, so McCall must likewise release the old heartache and embrace a new life. But McCall was not inclined to do that, demonstrated by his clear knowledge of the very scripture that spoke of healing. Obviously, the man knew the God-inspired words but had never applied them to his heart.

As Mr. Mosely ambled toward his horse and wagon, Kate placed hands on hips and stomped from the summer kitchen.

"Miss Lowell?" Drew's faint, confused call barely registered.

McCall, still gently stroking the mare's nose, didn't notice Kate's approach.

"Excuse me, Mr. Adams," she said firmly.

He glanced up and studied her face. "Yes, Miss Lowell, is there something wrong? Drew. . .is he—"

"Drew is perfectly fine." She crossed her arms and narrowed her eyes. "But he tells me that you are thinking of selling the horse ranch to Mr. Mosely and moving out east. Is it true?" Kate scrutinized his expression to properly gauge his response.

"Yes, it's true," he said simply, turning his attention back to the mare who nudged his hand for a treat. McCall, his back to her, placed his boot on the plank fence's bottom rail as if to dismiss Kate completely.

In the face of McCall's obvious unwillingness to discuss the matter, Kate's bravado significantly abated. She scanned the rolling pastures, the lush trees, the dogwoods dotting the countryside, the numerous horses, all of which belonged to McCall. How could he sell such a beautiful ranch? The sweet smells of fresh clover and a clean spring breeze seemed to taunt Kate's very question.

At long last, she spoke again. "I never thought you'd run," she said simply, a note of disillusionment in her voice.

He spun to face her, a spark of ire in his dark brown eyes. "So what would you rather I do? Stay and see Drew possibly lose his life? Or see Drew facing a hopeless future with no friends and eventually no prospects of matrimony?"

"Surely you can't believe everyone in Dogwood holds Mr. Wilcox's opinion."

McCall quirked one brow. "I have lived here thirteen years. And yes, I can believe that the majority of the citizens of Dogwood are not fond of the idea that I am the father of a *half-breed*," he said with mock disgust. "I can guarantee that if a child who was totally white had dragged Calvin out of the river that Wilcox and half the countryside would have made him a hero. Instead, Drew has been turned into a murderer."

"Dr. Engle and Mr. Mosely *certainly* don't think that."

"They are exceptions to the rule, Kate. And while I know others exist who agree with them, they are by far the minority."

"So you're just going to run? Is that it?" she challenged. "You're just going to tuck your tail and—"

His face darkened. "I'm trying to make the best decision for my son! *You're* the one who told me he needs friends!" he said, waving his hand in agitation. "Now look what's happened since he made a friend!"

"I think Eugene Wilcox is an extreme case."

"Oh yes, Miss Lowell, you have been in Dogwood the grand total of six months, and you have the whole citizenry figured out."

"No, I cannot boast of that, but—"

"While Eugene Wilcox might very well be one of the few who would blatantly try to harm Drew, there is a countryside full of those who breathe a sigh of relief because Drew has not tried to befriend *their* children." McCall pointed his finger directly at her nose. "Now you listen to me and listen closely," he said evenly. "Yes, I could do what you're saying and stay and fight, but what would it cost Drew? If I were the only one involved, I might do exactly that. But I'm not the only one involved. There's one other person to consider. And Drew's best interest must be the priority. I have weighed it. I have prayed about it. I have made my decision. Bob is going to the bank tomorrow to inquire about a loan. By the time Drew finishes his studies with you in a few weeks, he and I will move to Boston near my sister and hopefully begin a new chapter in our lives."

"So that's it?" Kate asked, tears stinging her eyes.

"That's it."

"Well, I must tell you then, Mr. McCall Adams, that you are dreadfully wrong on one count. Dreadfully, *dreadfully* wrong." A tear splashed to her cheek, and she angrily dashed it away. "There is more than one person to consider in this d–decision!" Kate's voice broke as her heart itself was breaking.

The dark shadows chasing through McCall's eyes attested to the fact that he accurately grasped Kate's meaning. However, he made no attempt to respond.

She stamped her foot in fury. "Do you know why you can't let go of Melody?" she demanded, so incensed she cared precious little that she was treading in deep, troubled waters.

"That is none of your—"

"It's every bit my business," she declared, her voice rising. "You haven't let go of her because you don't *want* to. You've set up a shrine to her in your heart, and you'd rather live in the past than—"

"Stop it! Stop it! Stop it!" he yelled.

Kate felt as if every ear on the ranch must have heard McCall's outburst. She cast a furtive glance toward the yard to see both Bob and Drew, who had been hitching the horses to Bob's wagon, now staring toward them in astonishment. Kate, breathing the fumes of disillusionment, looked back at McCall, whose stormy expression forbade her to push another inch. Silently, she wheeled away from him and stomped back to the summer kitchen.

Chapter 15

McCall turned his back on Kate and concentrated on the chestnut mare's gentle eyes, her twitching ears, her silky mane. He listened as Kate eventually boarded Bob's wagon. He listened to Bob's predictable "tch, tch." He listened as the wagon squeaked and quaked toward the lane that would lead them into Dogwood. Gritting his teeth, McCall deliberately dismissed Kate's heated words from his mind. Exhausted from the tension of the last twenty-four hours, he propped his arm on the fence's top rung and rested his forehead on his arm. All he wanted was a warm bath, a good meal, and an early, soft bed. At the moment, McCall had no desire to dissect his feelings.

He would take his son and move to the East Coast. He had survived fourteen years without a woman in his life. Drew would be fine once he developed some friendships. And Kate. . .Kate would find another love.

But what if God intended for you to be her love?

The tormenting thought twisted McCall's heart. If the truth were known, he *did* love Kate. He *did* think about her every morning when he awoke. He *did* pine for glimpses of her during the day. But every day McCall also encountered another woman who still lived in his heart. Kate said Melody was still there because McCall didn't really *want* to relinquish her.

Release the past.

That gentle whisper in his spirit disturbed him once more. Could Kate have been simply reinforcing what God had been nudging McCall to do for quite some time? She was right. McCall did know all the appropriate Bible verses. But somehow, he couldn't seem to make them com-

270

pletely work for him—not the way they were supposed to. Perhaps it was because McCall was so busy gripping the memories and holding onto the pain that he couldn't accept the healing God was freely offering.

These thoughts took McCall exactly to the point he didn't want to be. He was simply too exhausted to examine his feelings. A bath. He needed a bath. . . and a meal. . .and the bed. He looked toward the western horizon to see the sun still a few hours from setting. However, McCall's body and mind didn't care about the sun's activity at the moment. He had been awake most of the night, alert, listening for any signs of Eugene's return. McCall needed some sleep.

"Dad?"

He turned to see Drew only inches away, his questioning expression asking for an answer concerning McCall's explosive reaction to Kate.

"Hey, Drew." McCall fondly placed a hand on his son's broadening shoulder and urged him to his side. The boy was undoubtedly on the verge of manhood, and McCall certainly was proud of him.

Drew mimicked his father's stance and placed a booted foot on the fence's lower rung. "We haven't–haven't had much time to talk since last night. I. . .hmm. . .but I just want you to know that I. . ." He swallowed hard as his eyes reddened. ". . .I love you."

"I love you, too, Son." McCall blinked his stinging eyes and gazed across the pasture, bathed in late afternoon sunshine.

"After last night. . .after. . .after we talked. . ." Drew cleared his throat. "I never realized until last night. . ."

"I know," McCall said simply, at a loss for more words. McCall and his father had shared much less of a relationship than he now enjoyed with Drew. Nevertheless, there were often moments when McCall simply did not know how to communicate all he was feeling.

"And–and I want you to know that–that. . . ," Drew stuttered to a silent impasse.

"I understand." McCall once more squeezed the boy's shoulder, and the two stood in companionable silence. A dove's distant cooing seemed an echo of the years of love that had passed between McCall and the adopted son for whom he would give his own life.

"Will it be okay for me to attend school in the East?" Drew asked.

"Yes. I was planning that for you. Do you like the idea?"

"Yes," he said eagerly. "But what about Miss Lowell?"

McCall sensed that Drew was sizing up his reaction, and he refused to look at the boy. Instead he fixed his features into a bland mask and focused on a red bird, perched on the corral's opposite fence. "Miss Lowell will go back to her home in El Paso, of course," McCall said evenly. However, McCall's heart seemed to wither at the sound of his own words, despite his resolve that her leaving them must be for the best.

"Don't you want to marry her?" Drew asked.

Pressing his lips together, McCall bit back a reflexive, defensive retort. Drew in no way deserved to be snapped at. But then, Kate didn't deserve McCall's yelling at her either. She had simply expressed her true feelings, and he had responded by demanding her cessation.

"I wouldn't mind if you did," Drew continued hopefully.

"Oh?" McCall turned to him, wondering once again if he should propose to Kate for Drew's sake.

"I think she's wonderful." The dreamy look in Drew's eyes left McCall suppressing a tired smile.

"Let's go in and scrounge up something to eat." McCall punched Drew in the arm, and the boy returned a light punch to his father's midsection. They began their companionable walk toward the porch, but the sound of a horse galloping up the lane stopped both of them.

"Go on into the house," McCall ordered as he peered through the trees to see if perhaps the horseman were Eugene. Drew immediately obeyed his father, and McCall touched the Colt Peacemaker strapped to his leg. He had slept with the gun under his pillow and strapped it on first thing this morning.

Within minutes McCall clearly identified the horseman as Constable Parker. His worries alleviated, McCall slowly walked toward the wiry lawman. The constable wore his hard-as-nails reputation proudly, like a knight wore armor. However, McCall had long since seen beneath the constable's tough demeanor into his heart of gold.

He reined in his puffing palomino, and the high-strung steed stopped within a few feet of McCall. The men exchanged obligatory pleasantries, then Parker said, "I came to tell you I've got Eugene in jail. I was also able to nab those other two characters with him. Seems they haven't been in these parts long and spend most their time at the saloon. I'm gonna keep 'em locked up awhile. Make 'em think about what they did really hard." He narrowed his keen eyes and rubbed his mutton-chop sideburns.

McCall felt as if a dark shadow was lifted. *Thank the Lord*. The last twenty-four hours had been nothing short of torture, constantly looking over his shoulder, never certain whether he should actually let Drew out of his sight.

"Thanks for letting me know. I've been nervous, to say the least. Did you mention to the Preacher Eakin about Eugene's wife and children needing assistance while he's in jail? I can help them a few days but after that. . ."

"You *did* decide to sell the ranch to Bob Mosely then?"

"Yes." McCall had made a vague reference about moving to the East the night before when he reported Eugene's threats to Parker.

"I really wish you'd reconsider. There's a number of folks that's gonna miss you. Might do you good to know that Eugene tried to round up a whole bunch a support for his scheme but couldn't seem to get anybody to agree. I think it's 'cause they respect you, McCall."

"But what about Drew? Do they respect him as well?"

Parker rubbed his sun-dried, wrinkled face and stared at the horn of his saddle. "I do. And I know the doctor does. He's a good kid."

"Yes. And I'm hoping that in Boston I can find a community and a school who will agree with you."

"Well, good luck," Parker said reluctantly as his mount began its usual prancing.

"Why don't you come in and join us for dinner? Might be awhile before it's fixed, but we'd most certainly enjoy your company."

"I appreciate your hospitality." The constable gazed toward the north pasture. "But I'm headin' over to the Wilcox place to tell Nadine where her husband is."

"Tell her I'll try to be over tomorrow to help with the planting," McCall said.

"That's mighty Christian of you." The constable produced a faint smile.

"Don't start admiring me." McCall touched his Peacemaker. "I was tempted to use this last night to settle this problem once and for all."

"I'm sure anyone would feel that way."

"I just hope Eugene can get a dose of what Drew tells me Calvin has."

"You talkin' religion'?"

"Yeah."

"That'd do him more good than all the jail time in the world."

"I'll pray for him if you will."

Constable Parker smiled slyly. "You know my rule. You stay in my jail, you get a helpin' of the Good Book and a round of prayin' with every meal."

McCall smirked. "I like the way you manage your jail."

"Yep. I believe the Lord likes it, too." Parker reached toward McCall, extending his hand for a shake. "Good luck to you."

"Thanks." McCall firmly gripped the thin, calloused hand.

Parker tilted his straw hat, nudged his stallion with his spurs, and headed back up the lane.

McCall crossed his arms and savored the feeling of freedom. Freedom from worrying about what that vindictive Eugene might be going to pull next. Before Constable Parker's arrival, McCall had felt as if he were in bondage. He breathed deeply, relaxed, and savored the smells of horses and fresh spring foliage. As he turned to go into his home, he glimpsed the first pink blooms on the climbing rose bush that grew at the end of the cabin. McCall hadn't even planted the bush there. Before she died, Dr. Engle's wife had insisted the cabin needed a rose bush. McCall feigned a resigned compliance but secretly enjoyed the bush from the first day of its planting. Now, the bush served as a memorial to Mrs. Engle.

It also reminded him of Kate.

McCall stepped toward the bush and bent to inhale the roses' sweet aroma. The aroma filled his senses with the remembrance of Kate's perfume. He stroked the velvety petals and felt as if he were once again stroking Kate's soft cheeks. With the usual whippoorwills beginning their evening songs, McCall remembered Kate telling him she had burned her last rose from Zachary. He had asked her if she were implying he needed to burn some of his own roses.

At long last, McCall admitted that perhaps he did.

He retrieved the ever present whittling knife from the front porch and cut one of the bush's blossoms. Holding it to his nose, McCall slowly walked toward the cabin's door and contemplated the last few months. The months since Kate. They had been troubling. They had been overwhelming. They had been. . .exhilarating.

McCall walked into the cabin to find Drew in the kitchen, the room darkening with the lengthening shadows. The boy was sitting at their small dining table, finishing off the leftover venison from lunch and the remains of the day's supply of milk.

"I'm assuming you saw our visitor was the constable?" McCall asked.

"Yes, Sir. What did he say?"

He briefly related the news about Eugene. "I think it would be good for us to go over and help Nadine around the place sometime tomorrow."

"That would be great!" Drew said enthusiastically.

McCall grabbed a few pieces of the tough, salty venison and thoughtfully chewed it. He studied the rose, still in his hand and knew the time had come, whether he felt like it or not, to do some serious praying.

McCall's back ached. His head ached. But most importantly, his heart ached.

"I'm going to be in my room awhile, Drew."

"I sure hope you and Miss Lowell can work. . . ," Drew cleared his throat and stared into the empty milk mug, ". . .work out your differences. I really think she loves you."

McCall studied his son. "What makes you say that?"

"The way she looks at you," Drew said with an assured smile. "I see her looking at you all the time when you don't know it. Every time you cross the yard to the barn or come in from the horse pasture, she gets really still in front of the window. I usually tap her on the shoulder to get her attention. I'd say she watches you in about the same way I see you watching her in the morning when she arrives."

Speechless, McCall stared at his son. Convinced that Drew was a matchmaking schemer, he at last found his voice. "Have you by chance told Miss Lowell that I watch her arrival every morning?" McCall said, already knowing the answer.

"I'd bet if you asked her to marry you, she'd say 'yes.' " Drew barely paused for a breath. "Then she could go out east with us." His wide-eyed honesty left McCall reminiscent of the years he had watched the boy grow up.

"Thanks for letting me know your thoughts on the subject, Son," he said with a fond smile. If only Drew understood there was much more involved than McCall simply asking for Miss Lowell's hand in marriage. Kate would marry him if he, like she, had burned his roses.

"After you have your bath tonight, draw me up a tub full, too, would you?" McCall asked, turning for his room. "Until then, I need some time alone."

"Sure, Dad," Drew said, a note of discouragement in his voice.

McCall walked the short distance into his bedroom, shut the door, and collapsed to his knees beside his bed.

Release the past. Release the past. Release the past.

In the last few months, those three words had become a chant in McCall's soul. He remembered Kate's words from only hours ago. *You haven't let go of her because you don't want to. You've set up a shrine to her in your heart and you'd rather live in the past than. . .* At that point, McCall had rudely cut her off. He rehearsed the scripture that he had quoted from memory. The words of Jesus Christ Himself, *The Spirit of the Lord is upon me, because he hath anointed me to preach the gospel to the poor; he hath sent me to heal the brokenhearted, to preach deliver-*

ance to the captives, and recovering of sight to the blind, to set at liberty them that are bruised.

To set at liberty them that are bruised. McCall was certainly one who had been bruised. One who had been brokenhearted. One who needed healing. The time had come for him to release his pain and embrace that healing. The time to remove the shrine to Melody. The time to burn his roses.

Drew needed a mother. Kate needed a husband. McCall needed—*desperately* needed—Kate. He wanted her lying beside him in the morning when he awoke. He wanted her smile to brighten his every day. He wanted her love to fill his heart, *all* his heart.

"Oh, dear God," McCall prayed. "Please deliver me." The words felt as if they were pulled from his soul like an embedded, rusty chain that had held him captive. "Take my dreams of life with Melody, oh, Lord. Heal me. Free me from the wounds of the past. Teach me, dear God, to embrace Your healing. Forgive me for thinking I had to hold onto my pain when I know You wanted to free me. Oh, Jesus, my deliverer, heal my broken heart."

McCall wasn't certain how long he stayed on his knees embracing the presence of Jesus Christ, allowing the Lord to enfold him. But, at long last, McCall felt as if he were truly communing with his Heavenly Father. He realized that, in the years following Melody's death, he had somehow allowed the pain of that situation to create a wall between him and everyone, including God. True, God had dealt with him and had empowered him to forgive those he found most difficult to forgive—including the man who raped Melody and his own rejecting family. But McCall had stopped at the point of fully committing his whole heart to God.

When the long shadows turned to dusk and the last glimpses of gold stretched across the sky, McCall stood and lit his oil lamp. He turned to the dresser, Melody's dresser, and began to burn his roses. Piece by piece, he removed Melody's cherished mementos—the photos, the perfume, the brush and mirror—and laid them on his bed's patchwork quilt. He opened the dresser drawers and extracted the few pieces of her clothing to which he had clung, including the gown in which she died and a blue lacy shawl. He spread the shawl on the bed and filled it with the belongings he once had hoarded. With a shuddering breath, McCall secured the shawl into a tight knot and purposefully walked to Drew's room. The boy would one day be glad of these few possessions, a reminder of the woman who self-lessly bore him.

Chapter 16

The next morning, Kate busily packed her trunk and arranged for transportation to the train station. She was scheduled to catch the westbound 8:10 for El Paso. Six months before, Kate had planned to take the same route back home. But this time, she would get on that train, no matter what. Once more she wore her meticulous blue traveling frock, her ivory brooch, and the plumed hat.

Before sitting down to pen her good-bye notes to Drew and McCall, Kate glanced at her reflection in the round mirror that hung over the dressing table. She was appalled, truly appalled, at the young woman who stared back at her. A woman with puffy, red eyes, marred by dark circles beneath them. A woman with pale cheeks. A woman who looked as if she had sobbed all night.

Yet that was exactly what Kate had done.

By the time the morning's weak light eased onto the horizon, Kate had made her tearful decision. She was going back home to El Paso. This time, she meant it. She would no longer submit herself to the humiliating fact that McCall Adams knew she loved him while he was unable, or perhaps even unwilling, to fully return her love.

She sat down at the small correspondence table and snatched a piece of paper from the drawer. After much deliberation, Kate decided to simply write a note to Drew. He would tell his father she was not returning. That would be sufficient communication for McCall. Up until she started writing the brief note to Drew, Kate mistakenly assumed she was out of tears. But for every word she penned, a new tear seeped from the corners of her eyes.

She told Drew that she would not be back. That she did care very deeply for him. That she wished him the best on the East Coast. And that she would always remember him.

Within a matter of minutes, Kate's trunk was taken downstairs to await her in the hired carriage. She arranged for the letter to be delivered to Drew, and she rode the short distance to the train station. Although her heart felt as if it were being wrenched from her chest, Kate was certain she had no other choice in the matter. She had done everything she knew to do in relation to McCall, short of throwing herself at his feet and begging him to love her. That was the one thing Kate was not prepared to do. He had chosen to go to the East Coast without her. Therefore, Kate would behave in the way her mother had instructed. She would preserve her own dignity. She would quietly return home.

❖

"I am here to speak with Miss Kate Lowell," McCall said as he stepped up to the hotel clerk's desk. He clutched the bouquet of pink roses he had clipped from the trellis beside the cabin that very morning.

"Good morning, Mr. Adams," the aging clerk said. She eyed McCall with the same curiosity she had on the day she eavesdropped on his and Kate's conversation in the lobby. "I'm sorry, but you've missed Miss Lowell. She has checked out."

"Checked out!" McCall's shocked reply resonated off the lobby walls. A nauseating knot of nerves tightened in the pit of his stomach.

"Yes, I'm afraid so," the clerk said as if she were immensely enjoying this drama. "And I believe she hired a carriage to take her to the train station."

"The train station?" McCall echoed in bewilderment. He thought he had planned the whole proposal to perfection. He had dressed in one of his banking suits and arrived in Bob Mosely's place to pick up Kate. He had intended to meet her at the base of the stairs, roses in hand. He had arranged to have a special table set up at Dotty's for an early morning tryst. Just the two of them. With hot coffee and cinnamon rolls, the very thing they had eaten that first day they met. McCall had even rehearsed the words he would say to Kate until he had them memorized to perfection.

Now she was gone!

"What time does her train leave? Do you know?" He pulled his pocket watch out of his formal vest to see that it was about 7:55.

"I believe she mentioned leaving on the eight-ten." As if the train had been awaiting that exact moment to announce its arrival, a faint whistle sounded in the distance. "That should be it." The clerk's wrinkled cheeks seemed to glow with the intrigue of the moment.

"Thanks." McCall rushed toward the beveled glass doors.

"Oh, Sir! Mr. Adams! The young lady left a note, I believe for a Drew Adams. Isn't that your son?"

McCall wheeled around, raced across the polished wooden floors, grabbed the note, and whirled back toward the door. Within seconds, he jumped into his buggy and urged his trusty gelding forward. After but a few minutes, the train station came into view. McCall parked the buggy in front of the tidy, red building, tethered his horse, and rushed to the back where the passengers were ready to board the 8:10 as it swiftly approached.

Still clutching the bouquet of roses, he scanned the small crowd until he spotted Kate sitting on the bench outside the ticket window, her head lowered, her gloved hands clasped tightly in her lap, her shoulders drooped.

McCall wanted to rush forward, wrap his arms around Kate, and pour his heart out to her. But with the westbound train chugging into the station, he hesitated. What if she rejected him?

Kate stood, her head still bent as if she were ready to collapse with a load of sorrow. McCall knew the sorrow was a direct result of his cold treatment the day before. Could she ever forgive him? Whispering a prayer for courage, he silently approached her.

❖

Her eyes stinging anew, Kate watched the hammering, squeaking train wheels as they slowly churned across the tracks. She felt as if those steel disks were smashing her heart, and Kate fought the urge to reverse her decision, race back to the hotel room, and continue tutoring Drew until he and McCall moved. Leaving now allowed Kate to salvage her pride. But was that worth the irrevocable separation from the man she loved and his charming son? Perhaps if she continued praying for McCall, he would be able to put his past behind him and fully embrace a new love for Kate.

The idea of prayer marred Kate's thoughts with guilt. During the long, shadowed hours she had lain awake and sobbed, Kate never once sought God about whether she should go back home now or stay. As she reflected over those dismal hours, Kate admitted that her soul had wailed to God for comfort while purposefully avoiding the subject of whether she should go now or stay. For in past weeks, every time Kate asked God,

He impressed upon her to stay. Still, McCall's recent rejection proved much too painful for her to remain in Dogwood, regardless of what that gentle, persistent voice within her said.

Amidst the hissing of steam, the train finally came to a complete stop and several of those waiting on the boardwalk began waving wildly at passengers who peered out the numerous windows. Kate knew that, many hours down the tracks, her mother, father, and sisters would await her. But Kate would be forced to feign her pleasure at arriving back in El Paso, for deep in her heart she wanted to stay. She wanted to embrace McCall. She wanted to arrive on the East Coast as his new bride.

Her stomach clenched. Her chest tightened. Her mind whirled with possibilities of staying. No one was forcing Kate to leave. Only her own pride.

Impulsively she turned to rush into the ticket office and reclaim her trunk. But she only took three steps and stopped. For standing only a few inches from her, McCall Adams offered a burgeoning bouquet of pink roses and an apologetic smile.

❖

Awkwardly McCall extended the roses. Kate stared at the flowers for what felt like an eternity. At last, she lifted her swollen eyes to McCall. Eyes that looked as though they had shed enough tears to fill an ocean. McCall knew nothing to say. He simply bathed her in the warmth of his loving gaze and hoped Kate could see that she now held his *whole* heart in her hands.

The fragrance of these first spring roses mixed with the soft scent of Kate's perfume and teased McCall's senses. "I'm–I'm sorry about yesterday afternoon," he said at last. "I should have never yelled at you. You were right in what you said. Absolutely right."

Her lips trembling, her eyes filling with unshed tears, Kate covered her mouth with the tips of her shaking, gloved fingers and produced a mute nod.

"And. . .and I hope you understand that I–*I love you*," McCall whispered, his heart pounding.

Another silent nod. A wobbly smile.

"I've burned my roses, Kate," he said, his own throat thick. "And we can create fresh, new roses together. . . ," McCall raised the bouquet for added emphasis, ". . .if. . .if you will marry me."

"Yes," she blurted, her smile turning to laughter. "Yes, yes, yes!"

McCall, oblivious to the curious crowd, bent and kissed her damp cheek, then pulled her into the circle of his arms. "Ah Kate," he whispered in her ear. "Promise me you won't ever leave again."

"I promise." She placed quivering hands on either side of his face and gently stroked his beard. "Till death do us part."

Texas Lady

with Susan K. Downs

Dedication

For my friend, Susan K. Downs.

Prologue

(Taken from *Texas Rose*)

K ate Lowell picked her way across the street full of muddy slush
and opened the door to the Dogwood general store. The smells of
coffee, peppermint, and new material greeted her. Kate glanced
around the store lined with horse plows, bags of cornmeal, sugar, flour,
and the ever present wall of postal boxes behind the counter. Immediately
she was drawn to the material table and began examining several bolts of
heavy cotton, exactly the kind of material she needed for an all-purpose
work dress.

Out of the corner of her eye, Kate noticed the buxom Bess Tucker
about to approach her, but she stopped to help another couple, buying
supplies for their kitchen. At closer observation, Kate realized the couple
was Travis Campbell and his new wife, Rachel. Never in her life had
Kate wanted so desperately to disappear as at that moment. She suppressed the urge to crawl under the material table but decided to simply
keep her back to them in hopes that they wouldn't notice her. The last
time she saw Travis and Rachel, she and Travis broke off their engagement and she rode away, leaving him to marry the woman of his heart,
Rachel Isaacs. That was the day before Kate met Mr. Adams and Drew at
the train station.

To encounter Travis and Rachel now was highly awkward and
embarrassing. Kate didn't even know if they were aware she was still in
Dogwood. At last, she decided to simply turn around and leave without
mailing her letters. She would go to the dressmaker, who usually kept

material in stock, and return to mail the letters after ordering her dress. Kate whirled around to bump squarely into Rachel.

"Oh excuse me," the young redhead said politely. "I didn't realize you. . ."

She trailed off as she recognized exactly who she had bumped into—her husband's former fiancée. "Miss Lowell!" she said with faint surprise.

"Mrs. Campbell," Kate said calmly, feeling anything but calm. She stole a glance toward Travis, tall and fair, as he neared. The last time she saw him they were on friendly, although strained, terms. Kate was very much at peace about their mutual decision to break the engagement, but she hoped Mrs. Campbell in no way thought Kate was pining for Travis.

"Hello, Kate," Travis said as he neared. "We heard you were still in town. It's a delight to see you."

"Yes. . ." Kate cleared her throat and produced a shy smile. "I suppose there isn't much that goes on in Dogwood that everyone doesn't know about."

Rachel released a spontaneous giggle, and Kate eased a bit. Perhaps the flush on Mrs. Campbell's cheeks was an indicator of her happiness and security in her marriage.

Helplessly searching for any topic of conversation, Kate opened her mouth and heard herself say, "The snow must have made you as restless as it did me. I decided that after being trapped inside yesterday, I needed to get out today."

"Actually, we—Rachel needed to see Dr. Engle," Travis said, placing an arm around his wife's waist as if she were a fragile doll.

The glowing, adoring gaze Rachel threw Travis left the rest unsaid. She was most likely expecting their first child. Kate shot a furtive glance toward Rachel's waistline only to find it unaltered. Perhaps Mrs. Campbell was very early in her pregnancy. Kate hoped there were no problems.

Rachel turned her attention back to Kate. "Travis and I were thinking of sending you an invitation to dine with us one evening if—"

"That is so thoughtful of you," Kate interrupted. "But I'm so busy with the tutoring that I—"

"We understand," Travis said. And Kate knew Travis well enough to interpret the gleam in his green eyes. Such a meeting would be as uncomfortable for him as for Kate. Surprisingly, his young wife seemed the most at ease with the whole situation.

"Well, it was extremely nice to see you again," Kate said in her most refined tone. Fully prepared to gracefully exit the store, she curtsied and began walking toward the front door. But it would appear that Kate had no room for escape this day, from any situation, for when she was no more than ten feet from the doorway, it swung open, and McCall Adams walked into the store. Kate trembled in astonishment. Behind her stood the man she had once agreed to marry, and in front of her stood the man she would probably dream about the rest of her life but would never marry.

Kate would have loved to pretend she didn't see McCall, but that proved impossible, for he looked straight at her. The purposeful gleam in his dark eyes proclaimed that he had found the person for whom he was looking. "Miss Lowell," he said with a slight smile. "The hotel owner mentioned that you might be here. May I have a minute of your time, please?"

"Yes, of course," Kate said quietly. She cringed, imagining that every eye in the store must be fixed on her as she stepped onto the boardwalk with Mr. Adams. Yet a quick glance over her shoulder proved no one watched her departure. Bess Tucker hovered near Rachel and Travis as they joyfully examined a tiny bonnet, just the size to fit a baby. The two most certainly were expectant parents.

Chapter 1

Dogwood, Texas
June 1886

"Maggie!" Constable Parker shouted. "Magnolia Alexander!"
Maggie's spine tensed at the note of alarm ringing in the constable's voice. What could the constable possibly want? The bell hanging on the heavy wooden door of Dogwood's general store tinkled softly as the door closed behind her. Squinting into the sun, Maggie stepped onto the boardwalk and watched while the town's lone lawman tightened the reins of his gelding. The panting horse came to a halt amid a flurry of dust. The strong smell of leather and horse flesh swirled with the dust as Maggie waited for the constable to state his business.

"Doc Engle needs you right away," he announced. "I just brought in some fella who found himself on the wrong side of a gun during a train holdup five miles outside of town. Looks like he's been beat up pretty bad, too. I think he was throw'd from the train while it was still movin'. I've got to round up a posse to try and find—"

"I'll hurry right over," Maggie interrupted with uncustomary abruptness. Juggling the numerous packages and her worn reticule, she clutched her heavy skirt and darted down the boardwalk in an unladylike sprint.

In seconds, the young nurse stepped into the doctor's office, heavy with the scent of kerosene and antiseptic. As warm perspiration trickled down her temples, she dropped her packages on a nearby table and untied the sash of her calico sunbonnet. With a flip of her wrist, she tossed the headpiece atop the packages. Instinctively, she grabbed that forever defi-ant strand of blond hair and shoved it under the confines of her bun.

"Of all days for a good ol' Texas heat wave," Maggie complained into the stifling air. Leaning against the door, she paused to catch her breath and prepare herself for the task ahead.

As her eyes adjusted from summer sunshine to the dimness of oil lamps, she noticed Dr. Engle in the examination room. The dedicated physician, intently tending to his motionless patient, paused for a brief glance of Maggie as she stepped to his side.

"It looks like he's taken a bullet to the shoulder," the good doctor whispered. "From the looks of him, this man's gonna have a fight on his hands just to stay alive. He's already lost quite a bit of blood. Maggie, bring me some fresh water. Then gather as many clean bandages as we have around here. I'm afraid we'll need them all."

Maggie peered over the doctor's shoulder for a glimpse of the uncon-scious patient. Her stomach lurched as she turned away from the nauseat-ing sight and smell of fresh blood. In exasperation, Magnolia wondered how long she would be a nurse before growing accustomed to blood. As usual, she fought off feelings of inadequacy, of doubt, of anxiety. After two years as a nurse, Maggie was losing patience with her own queasi-ness. Suppressing her stomach's churning, she scurried off to fulfill the doctor's orders.

She was en route to deliver a second tray of bandages when the front door burst open. An anxious Travis Campbell and his expectant wife, Rachel, stepped over the threshold.

Oh, dear Lord, Maggie pleaded silently as she took in Rachel's pale face. *Rachel's baby can't be coming now. It's much too early*. But her prayers were interrupted as Travis bolted forward.

"Constable Parker told me I should look here for my brother. Is he here? Is he hurt? How bad is it?" As the barrage of questions continued, Travis paused just long enough to politely pull the wide-brimmed hat from his head.

A sense of relief flooded Maggie. The Campbells were not here regarding Rachel or her unborn child. However, a whole new set of con-cerns replaced Maggie's short-lived relief. Could the unconscious man be Travis Campbell's brother? Should Magnolia be the one to report his grave condition? What if the patient were someone else? She certainly did not want to bring undue stress upon the expecting Rachel.

Attempting to display an air of composure, Maggie motioned for the distraught couple to sit on the muddled-brown horsehair sofa that filled one wall of the office. Feigning nonchalance, she walked to the examination room's open door and pulled the handle until she heard a firm click. Thankfully, the Campbells had been too preoccupied to notice the activity in the next room. Positioning a chair in front of the troubled couple, Maggie sat facing Rachel and simply raised her eyebrows questioningly. With no further prompting, Rachel launched into a detailed explanation of the day's tragic events.

"We were waitin' at the station for Travis's brother, Levi, to arrive on this morning's ten-thirty train from El Paso," Rachel began, her pale brown eyes wide with worry. "But it didn't come, and it didn't come. Of course, you know the train is often delayed, so we weren't all that concerned—especially when we finally heard it coming down the tracks around noon or so."

Maggie nodded as Rachel forged ahead. "Then when the train stopped, passengers began to climb off and run to their family members. They were all visibly shaken. The women were cryin'. And we heard someone mention a holdup. We were anxious to get the news firsthand from Levi, but he never got off the train. Just as Travis was going in search of the conductor, Constable Parker approached us."

Maggie. Magnolia Alexander. The constable's intimidating shouts replayed in Maggie's mind as she thought back to their earlier encounter. She could easily imagine the Campbells' growing sense of fear at the approach of the constable's imposing figure.

She wondered if a constable ever got to deliver good news. From Maggie's perspective, every time Parker arrived, bad news usually trailed close behind. Maggie reached over and patted Rachel's hand in a heartfelt gesture of sympathy.

At last, Travis was able to add to his wife's vivid recollections with a reasonable degree of composure. "The constable said that, according to the accounts given by other passengers, a male passenger attempted to thwart a holdup. But the bandits shot him and threw him from the moving train. And, believe it or not, the robbers were apparently two women. Can you imagine that? What kind of a woman would hold up a train?"

Rachel flipped her auburn French braid over her shoulder and nervously rose to pace toward the window. Maggie, assuming the low couch was uncomfortable for a woman with child, stood to offer her straight-backed chair. Rachel merely waved her hand in protest. However, her fidgeting left Maggie all the more tense. She crossed the room and poured them each a glass of spring water from a crockery pitcher as Rachel continued.

"Some cattlemen who saw the man bein' thrown from the train went after Constable Parker. By then, the train had stopped a ways down the track. When the constable realized how bad off the man was, he prepared to rush him here. The constable told the train conductor that he'd meet up with him at the station. He asked that no passengers be allowed to leave the station platform once they arrived in town."

Maggie handed Rachel and Travis the mugs of water and waited as they gulped the liquid.

"The constable sought us out at the station as soon as he'd had a chance to go over the passenger list with the conductor," Rachel said. "Evidently, the injured man is Levi. All the other passengers have been accounted for. We rushed over as soon as we—"

"Can we see Levi?" Travis stood and gripped his hat all the tighter. "If he's here, we simply must be allowed to see him! Can you tell us his condition?" He nervously grabbed a handful of his wheat-colored hair as though attempting to extract the mental torment from his brain. "Where's Dr. Engle? Can we talk to him?"

Typical for such a hot day, Maggie's head began to throb with the beginnings of a blinding headache. The added pressure of handling this situation only added to the pounding in her temples. Part of her wanted to tell the Campbells the injured man was most likely their relative. But a professional voice, honed by Dr. Engle, cautioned her that he might very well not be the man for whom they searched. "Dr. Engle *is* with a patient right now," she replied as she backed toward the examination room. "If you will excuse me for a moment, I'll ask him when he thinks he'll be available to see you." She slipped quickly into the room and closed the door before either of the Campbells had time to respond.

Maggie turned toward the grandfatherly doctor in time to catch him smiling at her. "I overheard snatches of your conversation," he said, walking to the basin of clean water and washing his hands. "You did a superb job of maintaining a level head under pressure. Handling distraught family members can sometimes be the most difficult assignment of the medical profession."

"Thank you," Magnolia said, assuming she must have sounded much more controlled than she felt.

"As for my work in here," Dr. Engle continued, "it appears that I've done about all I can do for the patient. We'll have to leave the rest in the hands of the Great Physician. Why don't I go out and speak to the Campbells while you stand watch over our fallen hero?"

Maggie hoped her enthusiasm over relinquishing her duties with the distraught Campbells wasn't too obvious. While Dr. Engle left the room to greet Travis and Rachel, she settled herself onto a chair next to the patient.

After the upheaval of the last hour, she enjoyed the room's serenity. With a cleansing breath, Maggie rubbed her temples and prayed that the pounding would diminish as she watched the gentle rise and fall of the blankets covering the unconscious man. She reflected on the extent of his injuries and each new breath seemed to whisper the arrival of another miracle. Magnolia surveyed his bruised, swollen face, trying to imagine what he had looked like before the beating. No matter how hard she tried, she couldn't see a resemblance between Travis Campbell and this tall, thin man. Except for his weathered, bronze skin, Maggie's imagination placed her patient behind the desk of an East Coast lawyer's office rather than herding cows on the Texas range.

Travis Campbell was a big man, well suited for a rancher's life. This man's straight brown hair, matted with dried blood, looked nothing like Travis's thick shock of tawny blond. Of course, she couldn't tell if his eyes sparkled with the same emerald green flame that jumped in Travis's eyes. Were they really brothers?

Maggie chuckled softly as she recalled the time that Travis burst into the church and put a halt to Rachel's impending marriage to Samuel James. She wondered if this man had inherited his brother's tendency toward impulsiveness. That might explain his quick and gutsy reaction to the train robbery.

Dr. Engle's voice just outside the door stirred Maggie from her reverie. In lighthearted banter, the good doctor teased, "Travis, I seem to recall that my first introduction to you came in this office—and under similar circumstances."

Maggie remembered now. She had been home in bed with a bad cold and of no use to Dr. Engle when Travis Campbell limped into town battered and bruised. Apparently, a man intent on stealing Travis's identity had beaten him up, tied him to a tree, and left him to die. Were *all* the Campbell men destined to jump, feet-first, into trouble?

"Now, I'll let you in for just a moment, Travis," Dr. Engle warned. "But remember, you are not to utter a sound. We *cannot* allow you to disturb the patient. He desperately needs his rest. Just give me a quick nod if this man is definitely your brother. Do you understand?" Dr. Engle opened the door, and Travis entered the room alighted with lanterns and sunshine.

Leaving her seat, Maggie allowed Travis to tiptoe next to the bed. He took one look at the injured man, then immediately nodded his affirmation to Dr. Engle. At this signal, Dr. Engle motioned for Maggie to meet him at the door. "I'll stay here with Travis for a minute," the physician whispered. "Why don't you go out and sit with Rachel. I think she could use your company." Maggie quietly eased out of the room.

"It is Levi, isn't it?" Rachel asked as she adjusted her summer shawl to cover her expanding figure.

"Rachel, I'm. . .I'm sure he's going to be. . .be all right," Maggie sputtered. "You couldn't ask for a better doctor to look after him than Doc Engle. And I would be surprised if the reverend didn't already have the ladies' prayer circle on their knees."

"Levi was to be the first of Travis's relatives to visit us," Rachel said, fretting with the tangled tassels on her shawl. "I've yet to meet any of Travis's kin. And I so wanted to make a good first impression. We didn't offer him much of a welcome, did we?"

A flurry of activity out the front window caught Maggie's attention. Dust clouds rose in front of the jailhouse as a dozen or more men on stomping horses circled the constable. Maggie jerked her head toward the window. "Looks like Constable Parker has a great welcoming committee lined up for those women robbers—if they can find them."

As she spoke, Maggie scanned the faces of the gathering posse in hopes of catching a glimpse of Uncle Cahill, her only living relative. Perhaps he was out in the horse pasture and hadn't heard the news of the train holdup. One thing for sure, he would be hoppin' mad when he learned he missed a chance to hunt down and capture a couple of female outlaws.

Dr. Engle's firm footfalls distracted Maggie and Rachel from their observation of the gathering posse. "Maggie, I would appreciate it if you would stay with our patient while I walk over to Dotty's Café with the Campbells. They never had a chance to eat lunch. Regardless of the circumstances, Rachel must eat and take proper care of herself if we want this baby to be as strong and handsome as its papa."

Out of the corner of her eye, Maggie noticed Rachel's heat-flushed face turn a dark shade of crimson. *Surely Dr. Engle knows he should never refer to a woman's delicate condition in mixed company*, Maggie thought as the two men ushered Rachel out the door. *Has his wife been dead and gone so long that he has forgotten how to handle a lady's sensitive nature?*

She scurried back to the bedside of her unconscious charge and noiselessly set about the task of tidying up the mess Dr. Engle had left behind. With an armload of bloodied towels, Maggie headed for the hallway that led to the doctor's adjoining home. She needed to immediately set these things to soak in the kitchen's large washtub if there was to be any hope of removing the stains.

Just as Maggie reached the door, a low moan filtered from the bed. Dropping the towels where she stood, Maggie gingerly made her way back to the bedside. Although his eyes remained closed, his arm twitched. Well, the towels would simply have to stain. She certainly couldn't leave the room now.

Maggie positioned her chair no more than a foot from Levi's pillow so that she could observe his every move. Almost afraid to blink, she intently gazed at his face. *He certainly must be quite handsome without the swollen cuts and bruises*, she determined as she studied him. *I wonder what his eyes look like. I just hope and pray that he lives to see from them again!*

As if on cue, Levi blinked. His eyes sparkled with the same emerald green fire that danced in his brother Travis's eyes. Startled, Maggie simply held his gaze.

"Are. . .you. . .my guardian angel?" he rasped.

"Excuse me?" Maggie replied, not at all certain what she had heard.

"Are y–you my guardian angel," he whispered, this time a bit stronger.

"Why, no," Maggie stuttered, "I'm Magnolia Alexander."

"I. . .I am c–c–certain. Certain you m–m–must be an angel," Levi replied. "And I. . .I am undoubtedly in. . .in heaven." His weak, stammering speech halted just long enough for him to draw a deep breath. "A face as beauti–beautiful as yours doesn't be–be–belong on earth." Levi managed a weak smile, then winked at his angel of mercy as though he were a flirtatious schoolboy at a barn dance rather than a man freshly snatched from the jaws of death.

Chapter 2

Maggie's face heated as she groped for a proper response. She might have slapped him if he weren't already beaten and bruised. *What gall!* Apparently Dr. Engle wasn't the only man who didn't know the proper thing to say in the presence of a lady.

"Sir," Maggie impulsively responded, "with manners like yours, it's unlikely you would find yourself on heaven's shore. Consider yourself fortunate that you are still on this earth! I shall choose to assume that the morphine Dr. Engle administered must be wearing off and has left you a bit delirious. Surely under normal circumstances you would keep such comments to yourself!"

Despite her stern countenance and harsh words, Maggie couldn't stop the giddiness from washing over her. This brave man with his penetrating eyes thought she was beautiful! Maggie dared not look at him again for if she did, he might easily see the rush of pleasure his unexpected, flagrant flirtation had caused her. Mr. Campbell smiled drowsily. She rose and crossed the room, where she began to once again gather the soiled towels.

"Mr. Campbell, unless you have any pressing needs, I will momentarily excuse myself and put these things in the washtub." Her pale blue skirt swishing, Maggie glanced over her shoulder only to see the patient once more in the deep throes of slumber.

Upon reaching the kitchen, Maggie gave the soiled towels a cursory scrubbing with a bar of homemade lye soap, then dunked them in the washtub full of cool well water. "Mr. Campbell is sure to be hungry soon," she said to herself while she dried her hands on her starched apron.

A skillet of cornbread sat on the table next to the cast-iron stove, and Maggie cut a generous butter-smeared triangle.

The sound of rattled snoring greeted Maggie as she neared Levi's bedside. Frankly, she was glad that she didn't have to look Levi in the eyes again. Although her head's pounding had indeed subsided, she relished the chance to relax and think through the day's events. Easing herself into the bedside chair, she gently smoothed her patient's covers.

Allowing the room's peaceful ambience to embrace her, Maggie once more puzzled over not seeing Uncle Cahill among the posse. She resolved to soon travel out to the farm and check on him. Missing out on a posse wasn't like him. She really hoped he wasn't ill.

Before Maggie had a chance to further worry, Dr. Engle and the Campbells rattled at the door as they returned from their meal. The moment Maggie stepped into the outer office to greet them, the wafting aroma of Dotty's corned beef and cabbage assailed her senses. Maggie detested cabbage and the offensive smell left her stomach in knots. Excitedly, she whispered the news of Levi's waking, leaving out the details of their embarrassing conversation. "He seems to be resting as comfortably as can be expected now," she concluded.

Dr. Engle patted Maggie on the shoulder. "You've had a busy day. I'll stand watch over our patient. You head on home and get some rest. You can relieve me in the morning."

"Well," Maggie replied, "I *was* thinking that I should look in on Uncle Cahill. Mr. Campbell, would it be too much of an imposition for you and Rachel to carry me as far as his farm? That is, if you're goin' home now."

"Yes," Dr. Engle said, checking the brass watch tucked in the pocket of his ebony vest. "I insist they go home. The afternoon is waning, and Rachel *must* maintain her rest."

"But Levi—" Travis said.

"Will be fine." Dr. Engle laid a calming hand on Travis's arm.

Rachel, her face less agitated than when she left for Dotty's, nodded her agreement. "If you really think so, Doctor. I believe I am in need of some rest." Wearily, she shoved her braid over her shoulder.

"Of course. Of course," Travis said like a doting knight. His somewhat relaxed countenance attested to Dr. Engle's gift for soothing the relatives of his injured patients. "We pass right by your uncle's farm, Miss Alexander. Gather your things while I take one more look at Levi. I'll meet you and Rachel at the buggy."

After scooping up her belongings from the table, Maggie held the door for Rachel and they stepped into the steaming afternoon heat.

As Maggie assisted Rachel into the black runabout, she caught sight of the stately Sarah Baker, the boardinghouse mistress who owned the home where Maggie resided. "Oh, Mrs. Baker," Maggie called toward the boardwalk, "I'm glad you happened by. I won't be joining you for supper tonight. The Campbells have graciously agreed to drive me out to visit Uncle Cahill on the farm. I should be home before dark, though."

"That will be just fine, Maggie," Mrs. Baker replied, her refined voice barely reaching louder than a whisper. "Our gentlemen boarders are all out with the posse in search of the train bandits. I had planned to just dish up a bowl of bean soup with johnnycake anyway. It will keep another day. Besides, I need to pay a call on an acquaintance this evening." The cultured Mrs. Baker, dressed in a tailored, navy blue suit, hurried past the doctor's office in the direction of the Dogwood saloon.

Rachel leaned toward Maggie, her expression full of questions. "Maggie, you are close to both Doc Engle and the Widow Baker. Surely you have some idea why they haven't spoken to each other in over three years!"

"I wish I *did* know. But neither of them will discuss the matter. It's a cryin' shame that those two can't settle their differences and get together. Miz Baker is much too young to be alone for her remaining years. And when Dr. Engle's wife passed away, I think we all agreed that he and Miz Baker would make a perfect couple."

Travis joined the women in the buggy and stepped into the conversation. "I'm just a newcomer to Dogwood, but a man would have to be blind not to notice the sparks that fly between those two," he said in his well-bred voice. "I guess you are in quite a predicament, Miss Alexander, working for one and living with the other."

Maggie shrugged. "I've just learned which subjects to avoid." She smiled.

As the bay mare pulled the buggy past Main Street's last frame house and onto the tree-lined lane that led to the Alexander and Campbell farms, Travis and Rachel once more discussed the train robbery. However, Magnolia's mind rested less on the subject of the robbery and more on the victim, Levi Campbell, with his sparkling emerald eyes and flirtatious tongue. She forced her lips not to turn up at the improper delight his outlandish words stirred within her. In the morning, Dr. Engle fully expected her to sit with the patient. Perhaps Maggie would pay a "casual" visit to the office tonight "just to see if she could be of use."

At last, Travis pulled onto the earth-packed circle drive leading to the farmhouse. The fragrant pines filling the yard obscured the view of the white frame homestead until the buggy pulled around to the porch. A sense of nostalgia and anticipation swept over Maggie at the sight of her one-story childhood home. At the porch's east end, the green swing creaked gently on its chains as a soft breeze suggested the coming of evening. Magnolia knew without looking that notches in the doorpost charted her childhood growth.

"I do appreciate the lift, Mr. Campbell. There's no need for you to escort me in. Just drop me off right here at the door." Greeted by the deep bark of Uncle Cahill's coonhound, Ruff, Maggie climbed out of the buggy.

But as she ascended the two steps onto the covered porch, she noticed the front door standing wide open. At once, Magnolia revisited her earlier nagging worries, worries that her beloved uncle might be ill. Could those worries have been more than unfounded apprehension? A pall of precognition seemed to drape itself around her shoulders as she stepped through the open door. "Uncle Cahill, are you home?" she called in a trembling voice.

❖

Somewhere in the distance, a woman urged, "Wake up, Maggie! Maggie, you must wake up." The cool cloth on her forehead broke through her stupor, but her eyes refused to open. "Oh, Travis," the woman's voice came through again, "what are we goin' to do? The constable is out with the posse, and Dr. Engle has his hands full with Levi."

"Unfortunately, Dr. Engle's skills aren't needed here. Cahill Alexander is dead. We might as well head back to town and bring the undertaker. But we can't leave Maggie. We'll have to get her up and take her with us. It appears that whoever killed her uncle is long gone. Still, we can't be sure—and I can't take the risk of leaving either of you behind."

"Now, get up from the floor, Rachel. I worry about you. You're in no condition to be down there. Given time, Maggie will wake up on her own. She's received a terrible shock, but she'll be all right."

The words filtering into Maggie's consciousness brought a renewed sense of terror as she remembered the moments just prior to her fainting. *Murdered. Uncle Cahill has been murdered.* Maggie blinked and looked past the vigilant Rachel to see Travis in her uncle's bedroom, gingerly placing Cahill Alexander's body on his bed. Without warning, waves of nausea crashed over Maggie. Her stomach could no longer contain its contents. She turned her head away from Rachel just in time.

When her heaving stopped, an extended groan of pure agony escaped from the depths of Maggie's soul. Grief overwhelming her, she began to sob. Her uncle Cahill was the only family she had in this world. What was she going to do? How could she go on living? Why would anyone want to kill this kind, gentle man? At this moment, Maggie wished she could die, too. *Dear God, Why? Why? Why?*

Maggie lay on the floor and sobbed until her head began to pound anew, until her throat ached, until her heart felt as if it had been twisted in two. When her initial mourning began to fade, the sniffling Rachel gently dabbed her mouth with the cool washcloth. "Oh, you poor, poor dear. You poor, poor dear."

❖

Over the next several days, word spread throughout the county of Cahill Alexander's murder. As Maggie tended to the myriad of details and decisions that accompany any death, she must have heard Rachel's words repeated at least a thousand times. "You poor dear. . .you poor, poor dear." Maggie was surrounded, day and night, by well-meaning, sympathetic townsfolk, each one expressing their own variation of the same theme, "You poor, poor dear."

After a week of listening to the entire town's commiseration, Magnolia had a compelling urge to scream—not out of anguish and grief, but from a sense of being smothered. She was thoroughly tired of being pitied. She had been condolenced to death.

Three days after her uncle's funeral, Maggie decided her status of mourning must be altered. Before climbing out of bed, she had planned her entire day. In the afternoon, she would slip out to Uncle Cahill's farm alone and sort through his things. But first, she desperately needed a diversion from these prevailing thoughts of death and sorrow, and Maggie knew just where to go to soothe her frazzled nerves. She would head over to Doc Engle's and tend to Levi Campbell. There she could avoid this oppressive sympathy and focus her attentions on someone other than herself. A shiver of excitement raced through her thoughts as she considered seeing the convalescing Mr. Campbell again. But Maggie quickly squelched her improper contemplation with a forceful reminder: *You are supposed to be in mourning. . .and you are very vulnerable right now. Guard your heart!*

Afraid of disturbing the sleeping boarders, Maggie slipped into her black mourning clothes as quietly as possible and tiptoed from the boardinghouse onto the rain-soaked boardwalk. The gray weather matched Maggie's mood. Her violent inner storms of grief had subsided, leaving her spirits surrounded by a heavy haze.

Am I doing the right thing by coming here this morning? Maggie questioned as she paused outside Dr. Engle's office. But the prospect of seeing Levi Campbell again compelled her inside.

Dr. Engle, his shoulders drooping with exhaustion, appeared genuinely startled at the sight of Maggie as she shook the rain from her umbrella and hung her reticule on the peg beside the front door. "Maggie, my dear. Why are you here?" He stroked his white mustache and pushed the spectacles up his nose, closer to his bloodshot eyes. "I can handle the responsibilities. Really, I can manage just fine for at least another day or two," he insisted. "You must take as much time as you need to recover from your recent tragedy."

"Now, let's be reasonable, Dr. Engle," Maggie asserted, trying her dead-level best to resist the urge to cry in the face of the doctor's kind demeanor. "I can certainly help out for an hour or two. I know without asking that you at least need to make a house call out at the Williamses' farm. I insist that you run along and let me care for things around here. Might not hurt for you to lie down when you get back as well. You look like you need the rest. Besides. . ." She clutched the book she had brought for Levi's enjoyment. "I think it will. . .will do me. . . do me good to focus on something else for. . .for awhile." Magnolia blinked against her stinging eyes.

"Of course, Dear," the kind doctor said, his voice oozing with fatherly understanding. In respectful silence, he began preparing his black bag.

Maggie approached Levi's door, her palms moist as she touched the cool brass knob. Only days ago, she had said her final good-byes to Uncle Cahill, the man of her past. Could Levi Campbell be the man of her future? The thought sent a tremor along her spine. In her state of mourning, Magnolia should not be experiencing such improper emotions. But even *if* Uncle Cahill had not been murdered, Levi Campbell's blatantly flirtatious references to Maggie as his angel of mercy should be enough to curtail a proper lady's interest. Nonetheless, her heart gently pounded in anticipation of seeing him again. Immediately, another thought struck her. Would Mr. Campbell even remember her? Perhaps the effects of morphine had produced his disgraceful words, and Magnolia would be a stranger to him.

With a faint click, she opened the door, fully expecting to see Levi in the arms of sleep. Instead, she encountered those sparkling green eyes, a gaze of admiration, and a welcoming smile. "Well, if it isn't my angel of mercy, come to comfort me in my hour of need!"

Her face warming, Magnolia's question of whether or not he would recognize her fled through the window, opened for the morning's cool breeze. That same sparkle of mischief still stirred in his eyes, and Maggie sternly inserted her bottom lip between her teeth to stop the inappropriate smile now pushing against the corners of her mouth.

At last, she mustered an offended scowl. "Mr. Campbell, I've simply come to relieve Dr. Engle so that he can make some house calls," she said primly. But deep inside, Magnolia shamelessly reveled in the attention. What would Mrs. Baker think of her? Yet despite the landlady's disapproval, Mr. Campbell certainly offered Maggie a needed respite from her real-life nightmares.

As she smoothed the covers around her patient's shoulders, Levi nodded his head in acknowledgment of her curt rebuff. "Please forgive my insensitivity, Miss Alexander." Maggie gazed into his suddenly solemn eyes and, without warning, a warm rush of affection flooded over her. Could the man behind the mischievous eyes and flirtatious tongue also possess a tender heart?

"I don't know what came over me," Levi continued with a tone of sincerity that could not possibly be feigned. "Dr. Engle shared the circumstances of the terrible tragedy you have suffered. May I offer you my most heartfelt sympathies? I'm afraid I am not too skilled in the art of conversing with a lady. You see, while my brother chose to attend college in Boston, I decided to stay on the ranch. I spend most of my days talking to the cows on my father's spread in El Paso. In all honesty, I owe you a great debt for your good care, Miss Alexander, and I shall try to behave myself from now on."

"Apology accepted, Mr. Campbell." The surge of affection increased in potency to firmly wrap Maggie in its inviting embrace. "And there is really no need to thank me. I'm just doing my job." She should not— *should not* be experiencing such emotions about a man so recently in her acquaintance. Nevertheless, the emotions continued to flow, and her knees increased their traitorous trembling with his every word.

"I'd be much obliged if you'd just call me Levi," he said, his brows arched hopefully.

Magnolia swallowed hard and made a monumental job of walking across the room toward the simple table to fill his cup from the crockery pitcher. Astounded at her ability to maintain outward composure when, inwardly, she reeled with unexpected reactions, Maggie hesitated over his request. His asking for such a familiarity so early in their acquaintance bordered on improper. However, try as she might, she couldn't keep her lips from curving upward into the faintest of smiles as she placed the thick mug in his good hand.

"I know we only just met," he said with a measure of soft triumph. "But. . ."

The bruises and scrapes still marred his face, but his freshly washed brown hair now shimmered with sun-streaked highlights. And his chiseled features suggested a lineage of nobility. He was more than your run-of-the-mill Texas cowpoke. Despite his claims of not going to college in the East, the cadence of his words suggested a man well read.

"Everyone calls me Maggie," she said, amazed that she fell into his plan so readily. But nothing in her life the last few days was "as it should be." Why should her acquaintance with Levi be any different?

"Yes. . .Maggie. I've heard the doctor refer to you by that name. Is it by chance short for. . ." He winced with pain as he tried to scoot up in the bed.

"Magnolia. It's short for Magnolia." Instantly, she added an extra pillow behind Levi's head, and he relaxed against it to slowly raise the mug to his lips.

"Magnolia is such a beautiful name. It would be a shame to shorten it," he said, eyeing her over the rim of the stoneware mug.

Her heart now palpitating wildly, Maggie stood speechless, not really knowing the appropriate way to react. Levi's unexpected tenderness caught her completely off guard. *Is God sending Levi into my life at a time when I need someone the most?* Maggie transformed this fleeting thought into a silent prayer. *Oh, Lord, could it be?*

Although more than one suitor had strongly pursued Maggie's hand in marriage, she had never been in a hurry to find a husband. She enjoyed her work too much to trade it for life as a wife just yet. Besides, not a single one of her previous beaus had created the inner turmoil now overwhelming her.

This is ridiculous, Maggie scolded herself. *Absurd. I've only seen this man twice, and here I am practically tying the knot.* By force of habit, she pushed at the wayward lock of hair that constantly aggravated her.

"Have they caught the villain who committed this heinous act, Magnolia?" Never breaking eye contact, he extended the mug to her.

Maggie slowly shook her head. "I'm afraid not. Constable Parker suspects that the same women bandits who shot you might well have been responsible for my uncle's murder. The fact that they are still on the loose makes us all mighty uneasy in these parts. But I guess I needn't tell you. I imagine you won't really rest well at night until they are safely behind bars."

"Humph." Levi grimaced in agreement. "I suppose you're right about that. I am curious to know just what would make any woman turn to such a violent life of crime. Those two scoundrels just prove once again—women will always be a mystery to me!" The fiery sparkle of impishness returned to Levi's eyes. "One thing's for sure, they may be women, but they are certainly no ladies. They don't deserve the same respect afforded one as genteel as you."

Maggie's face heated at his blatant flattery, but she didn't feel compelled to make him stop. In fact, she swallowed a rising giggle and secretly wished he would continue. Levi was only too happy to oblige her unspoken desire.

"Magnolia, judging from my first impressions, your uncle must have been a very special man to have reared a lovely lady such as yourself. If you feel up to the task, I'd be honored if you'd tell me about him."

These words were the only prompting Maggie needed to launch her into a lengthy litany of her uncle's attributes.

❖

Captivated, Levi simply nodded his encouragement for Maggie to continue. *I wonder what it would be like to have someone as beautiful as Magnolia Alexander so deeply devoted to you?* If Levi had stopped to analyze his feelings, he would have recognized a slight twinge of jealousy over the fierce loyalty Magnolia held for her deceased Uncle Cahill. *What would it take for her to transfer such devotion to me?*

Every minute that ticked off the mantel clock wrapped him deeper in enthrallment over the beauty before him. Her peach-colored lips. Her expressive blue eyes. Her ladylike manners. Undoubtedly, Magnolia Alexander was a woman of integrity. An overwhelming urge to gently brush a strand of blond hair out of Magnolia's eyes was squelched only by his injuries and his earlier promise of propriety.

Never had Levi so blatantly flirted with a lady, but something about Miss Magnolia Alexander unleashed his tongue and filled the air with the sweet, poetic words he had often written or read but had never voiced. No one except his parents knew he read poetry while on the cattle trail. But at last, all those lines of iambic pentameter, long locked into his heart, seemed to be finding expression with this angelic creature before him.

An hour later, Dr. Engle's return ended Magnolia's sweet reminiscences. And Levi fought to mask his disappointment. In those sixty short minutes, Levi had received a succinct summary of Maggie's life history and a clear understanding of the important part her dearly beloved Uncle Cahill had played in her upbringing. With Dr. Engle attending Levi's wound, a startling supposition consumed his thoughts. *Just suppose. Could it be? Dear God, is Magnolia Alexander the answer to the countless prayers I've prayed under the prairie stars?*

"I know it's a lot to ask of you at this sad time, Magnolia," Levi blurted as Maggie prepared to leave. "But, would you mind coming back for a bit tomorrow? I truly enjoy your company. This visit has done me more good than any of Doc Engle's medicines."

Dr. Engle gently applied a clean bandage and produced a halfhearted grumble as his bloodshot eyes widened in speculation.

"No disrespect intended, Doc, but. . ." Levi eyed the flushing Maggie and didn't attempt to hide one ounce of the admiration flowing from his soul.

Maggie, smiling in pleasured reserve, nodded her agreement.

Chapter 3

Even as Maggie agreed to Levi's request, she scolded herself for her brazen openness with this virtual stranger. She had never revealed so much about herself to such a recent acquaintance. What had gotten into her? Surely it was her grief, expressing itself in this unexpected way. Still, she couldn't help but look forward to another opportunity to sit with the convalescing "fallen hero," as Dr. Engle had dubbed him. With a gentle sweeping motion, Maggie smoothed his sheets one last time and gave Levi's pillow a little pat as she turned and walked toward the door.

"Our patient appears much improved," Dr. Engle commented as he escorted Maggie to the outer office and she gathered her things. His teasing tone suggested that the doctor was baiting her to disclose her private thoughts. Had her attraction to the patient been as obvious as Levi's admiration for her?

Maggie refused to take the bait. "Why, yes, Dr. Engle," she said practically. "How could Mr. Campbell help but improve under your good care? Now, if you don't mind, I really must excuse myself until tomorrow. I have an important errand to run."

"You know, Maggie," Dr. Engle chuckled as she stepped out the door and opened her umbrella against the drizzling rain, "laughter and love are the best medicines for any injury, whether of the body *or* soul."

Averting her gaze, Maggie feigned a deaf ear to his sage advice. But inside, her broken heart, still palpitating with pain from the loss of her uncle, hungered for more of Levi's laughter, and perhaps. . .his love.

❖

A gentle shower continued to fall as Maggie hitched her wagon to the front porch where she had spent many long hours sipping lemonade. The old homestead seemed to open its arms to her as it had in years gone by. She had informed no one of the nature or destination of her errand. Had anyone known, they would have surely stopped her or insisted on coming along. But this was a job that Maggie simply must do alone.

Uncle Cahill's farm would be sold. Jed Sweeney, who owned the Dogwood saloon, as well as a string of saloons throughout the frontier, had been passing through town in order to check on his business. He approached Maggie about possibly buying the farm, making a solid offer. Respectfully offering his condolences, the saloon owner asked if he might return in another week or two to inquire of her decision.

The vices promoted through Sweeney's saloons repulsed Maggie, and she didn't relish the idea of someone like him taking over the place. But Maggie possessed neither the skills nor the desire required to run the farm. Unlike Rachel Campbell, who ran her father's ranch after his death, Magnolia simply lacked the spunk to undertake such an endeavor. Her strengths lay in comforting the sick, not managing an estate. Therefore, if no other buyers appeared, she would consider Mr. Sweeney's offer. Fortunately, God had granted them a wet summer so far, so Magnolia had turned all the livestock out to pasture, where they would find plenty to eat and drink from the fertile countryside and the farm pond. For now, they would survive. Besides, Uncle Cahill's hired hands had agreed to continue their usual chores and Travis Campbell graciously offered to keep an eye on the neighboring Alexander farm. But soon, the property and livestock would need the care someone like Jed Sweeney could provide.

In order to get the house ready for sale, she needed to clear out all of Uncle Cahill's personal possessions and those few items of her own that remained in her childhood home. Her uncle had been a man of little material wealth, so the task wouldn't take long.

Maggie was eager to finish this unwelcome chore and put her life back in order. Still, her emotions boiled to the surface as she walked through the door into the front room. Blood stubbornly stained the wood floors where Uncle Cahill had lain. Magnolia skittered as quickly as she could across the room and into her uncle's bedroom. She preferred to save the front room cleaning for last. Perhaps by then she could handle the ominous task.

Surely, she had made more decisions in the past three days than in all her previous twenty-three years. At every turn, well-meaning friends surrounded her, giving her advice and counsel, whether she had asked for it or not. Today, despite the heart-wrenching pain of the task, Maggie desired solitude.

The stiff skirts of Maggie's borrowed black moiré dress rustled around her as she knelt and opened the lid to the chest at the end of the pine bed. Maggie inhaled deeply, drawing in the pungent aroma of cedar from the open chest. Sighing, she lifted out the first item. Maggie knew before looking what the satin-wrapped package contained. The Alexander family Bible. Her mother, using meticulous penmanship, had recorded their brief family history in its front pages prior to her death. The first page recorded the marriage details of Maggie's parents, Jeremiah Taylor Alexander and Rose Marie Simpson Alexander on January 29, 1860, in Canal Town, Ohio.

Under the heading "Births," three entries were inscribed: *Twin sons, Curtis Jeremiah Alexander and Taylor Cahill Alexander, born November 10, 1861.* And *Magnolia Marie Alexander, born May 1, 1863.*

On the tear-stained page entitled "Deaths," Maggie's finger instinctively traced over the names written in her mother's delicate hand: *Curtis Jeremiah Alexander, died November 11, 1861. May his sweet, innocent soul rest secure in Jesus' arms. Taylor Cahill Alexander, died November 19, 1861. We shall understand it better by and by.*

The words were few, but even twenty-five years later, her mother's grief seemed to seep from the page. Surely Maggie's mother had loved her with the same fierce devotion she had heaped upon her firstborn twins. Maggie couldn't really remember her mother's love, yet her heart ached at the loss of the relationship she never experienced. All Maggie's knowledge of her mother sprang from this chest of mementos: the Bible, a diary, two photographs, and a threadbare, china-faced doll. Rose Alexander's journal chronicled their short-lived journey as settlers headed for the western frontier. The two faded photographs hinted at the strong resemblance Maggie now shared with her mother: one of Jeremiah and Rose Alexander on their wedding day; the other of a two-year-old Maggie and her mother. The same light hair. The same fine-boned features. The same petite frame.

Magnolia pulled her mother's suede-bound journal out of its hallowed space in the chest. As a teenager, she had practically memorized the crinkled pages. From the reading and rereading of its now familiar scrawl, Maggie had fallen in love with these people whom history recorded as her parents. The words written there were not profound or particularly insightful. Her mother had written mostly of the challenges and hardships of their frontier travels. Yet her words provided Maggie with a sense of connection to her heritage. The handwritten accounts gave life and breath, flesh and blood to the mother and father who died before Maggie's memories began.

Maggie flipped to the last entry, dated May 1, 1866.

Our precious Magnolia now sleeps in the wagon with the new doll we presented her in celebration of her third birthday. At such a tender age, she is only beginning to understand just what a "birthday" is. But she clapped her hands and squealed with delight when her papa brought out the package containing her gift. We had kept the precious birthday surprise carefully hidden since purchasing the doll on the day of our departure from Westport.

I do regret that neither my own parents nor Jeremiah's lived long enough to know our little angel. Maggie possesses such a gentle disposition. She brings joy to our difficult journey. I often think back to the time when we lost the twins and how I begged God to give us more children. Now, like Samuel's mother, Hannah, I can say, "For this child I prayed; and the Lord hath given me my petition which I asked of him."

I must close and get some rest, for we must start out early tomorrow morning. Sometime during the night, Gertrude, our milk cow, wandered off. We had to remain behind and search for her when the rest of the wagon train broke camp. Cahill and Jeremiah found the wayward animal within a few hours, but we need to travel a good many miles tomorrow if we hope to catch up with the others again before they leave Fort Dodge, as is our plan.

Despite our hardships, when I consider my good husband, his kind brother, Cahill, and our little Magnolia, I give thanks to the Lord for His many gifts to me. My heart echoes the verse I read today in the Psalms, which says, "The lines are fallen unto me in pleasant places; yea, I have a goodly heritage."

"Yea, I have a goodly heritage," Maggie said out loud. Long ago she had claimed this verse of scripture, Psalm 16:6, as her life's motto. The claim had proven true. For, despite the fact that her parents were killed in a calamitous accident the day after her mother wrote of this psalm, her uncle Cahill had provided a strong Christian example and stable home. Though he, too, was now gone, he had left her with a rich heritage of faith.

"Oh, Lord, may I do nothing to disgrace my family's name," Magnolia prayed as she gently sorted through the chest's remaining clothing that had once belonged to her parents.

By the time she finished going through her parents' things, dust-laden spears of sunlight shot through the bedroom window, dispelling any vestiges of the day's rain. *I must work faster if I hope to finish this job today,* Maggie thought, ignoring the hunger pangs assailing her. She hadn't culled a single item from the contents of the chest. Somehow she would find a place in her room at Mrs. Baker's for the cedar box and all its treasures.

Maggie turned her attentions to the desk adjacent to her uncle's bed. The rolltop compartments held a hodgepodge of papers: livestock bills of sale, receipts for farm supplies, and letters, all yellowed with age. Expecting to find more of the same in the forever stubborn desk drawer, she gave it the usual yank required to ensure its opening.

Instead of aging receipts and letters, she found a wax-sealed parchment package tied in blue ribbon with "Magnolia Alexander" emblazoned on the front. Maggie lifted the package from the drawer and held it to her nose. The paper still held the scent of her uncle's work gloves, and her eyes stung with the memory.

Suppressing the urge to cry, Maggie untied the ribbon, then broke the wax seal. The stiff parchment fell open to reveal a tattered "Wanted" poster and a thick letter, written in her uncle's unmistakable staccato script. *My Dearest Magnolia,* the letter began.

Puzzled, Maggie turned her attentions first to the poster. The sketch of the wanted man bore a striking resemblance to a younger Uncle Cahill. But the poster announced a one-thousand-dollar reward for the dead-or-alive return of a stagecoach bandit by the name of James Calloway. As Maggie studied the poster's fine print, her heart began to pound wildly.

Wanted:
Dead or Alive.
James Calloway, stagecoach bandit,
wanted for the armed robbery of a stagecoach in
Ford County, Kansas, on May 2, 1866.
If you have information that might assist in the arrest
of this armed and dangerous criminal,
contact the nearest U.S. Marshall.

May 2, 1866. The day her parents' Conestoga wagon overturned on the steep bank of the Arkansas River, killing them both instantly. Her uncle Cahill had retold the events of that fatal day to Maggie on countless occasions, yet not once had he mentioned anything about a stagecoach holdup. May 2, 1866. Was it just a curious parallel that the date of the holdup was the date of her parents' death—and in the same Kansas county? Could the familiar face on this wanted poster have had anything to do with the tragic events of that day? Surely it was all just a strange coincidence that the featured criminal resembled the man who had raised her. To her knowledge, Uncle Cahill had never been one to keep secrets. Even so, a sense of foreboding blanketed Maggie like a stifling cloud, bent on snuffing out her very breath.

Visions of the careening Conestoga wagon played in Magnolia's mind. She still bore a slight scar above her right eye to prove that she had been there. Yet as graphic as her mental images, Maggie realized that her memories of the fateful accident did not all come from first-person recollections. At age three, Maggie had been too young to truly remember the tragedy. But at Maggie's insistence, Uncle Cahill had recounted the story so many times that his memories eventually became her own.

The beloved uncle's oft repeated accounts corroborated with Maggie's mother's journal. Jeremiah and Rose Alexander had decided to pick up their Ohio roots and head for the western frontier. When Jeremiah invited his younger brother, Cahill, to accompany them, he jumped at the chance. He was always on the lookout for a new adventure. The Alexander boys used every cent of their inheritance from their parents' estate to prepare what they needed for the journey and a new life out west. They had a sturdy wagon built especially for rugged travel. Together, they planned to homestead a piece of the untamed West. They would simply set out on the Santa Fe Trail until they came to a place that felt like "home." Kansas. Colorado. New Mexico. Or points beyond.

When they reached Westport, Missouri, the Alexanders joined up with a wagon train in hopes of minimizing the dangers they would meet along the way. But one night on the Kansas plains, their milk cow, Gertie, wandered off. The Alexander family had to pull their wagon out of the train in order to search for the wayward bovine.

"Your momma insisted on our searching for that confounded cow!" Maggie could hear her uncle's booming voice echoing through her mind. "Your momma, she'd say, 'my little Magnolia needs her milk, and I won't go another mile without ol' Gertie.' " Uncle Cahill's voice would always soften about then, and he'd say, "But Maggie, you needed a mother a heap more than you needed milk. I wish we'd ajust kept on agoin' that day."

According to Uncle Cahill, the accident occurred just after they'd broken camp and were setting out onto the trail, skirting a deep embankment on the river. Rose sat beside Jeremiah on the buckboard as he drove the mule team; three-year-old Maggie still slept in the canvas-covered wagon behind them. Uncle Cahill said he had been riding his horse alongside the wagon when he saw a water moccasin fall from a willow tree. The poisonous snake landed on the back of the wagon's lead mule, instantly sinking its fangs into the mule's tender neck muscles. The startled mule bolted, and the entire mule team took off down the trail in a dead run, the wagon bouncing wildly in their wake. Uncle Cahill had been powerless to stop the panicked mules before the wagon hit a rut and toppled over the edge of the embankment.

The wagon flipped over and over before coming to rest in the shallow waters of the Arkansas, pinning Rose and Jeremiah under its weight. Maggie had been thrown clear of the tumbling Conestoga near the top of the embankment, suffering only minor cuts and scrapes. But her parents were dead, gone before Uncle Cahill could descend the slope and come to their aid.

I am an orphan now. The thought left Maggie with an overwhelming sense of loneliness. Even though she had been orphaned at age three, this reality had never settled into her soul for Uncle Cahill had filled the gaps. But now, without Uncle Cahill, she felt truly alone in this world, an orphan in every sense of the word.

Tears sprang afresh in Maggie's eyes, yet she once more refused to vent her grief. Once the sobs started, they often lasted hours. She would survive this somehow, by the grace of God. What was the psalm that Reverend Eakin had quoted her yesterday? Something along the lines of, "A father of the fatherless, and a judge of the widows, is God in his holy habitation."

Well, Lord, this fatherless child needs You desperately now. One lone tear slid down Maggie's cheek and spattered onto Uncle Cahill's unread letter. Carefully, she blotted the tears that smeared the ink in their miniature puddles.

"*My dearest Magnolia,*" Maggie read, through blurry eyes. She tenderly clutched the letter and eased herself into a straight-backed chair.

> *In all likelihood, if you are reading this letter, I am either behind bars or have gone on to meet my maker. Precious Maggie, let me begin by saying that no parent could love a child any more than I love you. You brought only joy and happiness into*

*my life. There was never a moment when I was not proud of you.
Your momma and papa would have been proud, too, to see the
beautiful young lady you have become. I have done my dead-
level best to bring you up like they would have wanted. If you
don't mind me sayin so myself, I think I done a pretty good job
of it, seeing how you have turned out and all. But, I figure you
already know how I feel bout you. I've got another reason for
writing this letter. You see, dear child, I have a confession to
make. Many times over the years, I tried to come clean with
you, but I would always chicken. I just could not face hurting
you or disappointing you in any way. Even now, as I write, I am
beggin God to help you understand.*

*My precious Maggie, it is with a heavy heart that I must tell
you that I am not your real uncle. The dark secret I have carried
with me these many years must now come to light. I pray that
you will forgive me for not confessin sooner.*

*Your real uncle, Cahill Alexander, died alongside your par-
ents on that fateful day in May. As you have probably already
guessed from the enclosed poster, I was nothing more than a
scoundrel and a thief in those days. My real name is James Calloway.*

*Now, before you get the wrong idea, let me hurry and say
that I did not mean to harm or kill your family that day. They
truly did die when their wagon rolled down an embankment into
the Arkansas River. But it weren't no snake that frightened the
mules that day. It was me—making my getaway after holding up
that stage.*

Chapter 4

M aggie! Magnolia Alexander!" Maggie jumped in surprise as
Constable Parker's familiar voice broke through her reading.
She stood horrified as she stared at the remaining pages of
Uncle Cahill's letter and the incriminating wanted poster.

She could not let Constable Parker see this now. Not until she had a
chance to sort it all out herself. She simply was not prepared to answer
any questions. Maggie sprang into action. Rolling the documents into a
scroll, she shoved them to the bottom of the open cedar chest and
slammed the lid shut just as the constable's shadow darkened the bedroom door.

"My dear Miss Alexander," the constable said as he removed his
straw hat. "May I ask just what on earth are you doin' out here all alone?
The Widow Baker is nearly beside herself with worry. Why, she was so
concerned, she even went ahuntin' you at Doc Engle's, and you know
how those two avoid each other like the plague." His weathered face
shone with compassion as he stroked his mutton chop whiskers. "Your
uncle's killers are still on the loose, remember. You can't go traipsin'
around the countryside by yourself. You're just askin' for more trouble."

"Constable Parker, I assure you, Sir, it was never my intent to alarm
or worry anyone. Please forgive me for causing you to come all this way.
Actually, I didn't expect to be here this long. I lost all track of time."

"Now, Miss Alexander." The constable's leathery countenance softened all the more as Maggie's eyes burned with unshed tears. "I'm not
aimin' to be unkind. I know you've suffered more in these past few days
than a soul ought to suffer in a lifetime. It's just that I'd feel so awful if

somethin' were to happen to you. I understand your need to be alone. But you'd best be waitin' until I have my hands on those no-goods who killed your uncle and left that Campbell fella for dead before you venture out here by yourself again. Remember, there are criminals runnin' around these parts."

He's worried about protecting me from criminals around these parts? Maggie thought as the lawman finished his gentle scolding. *Constable Parker doesn't know I've spent most of my life under the same roof with one!* She masked her disillusioned thoughts behind a sad smile. Despite her attempts to lighten her countenance, she couldn't achieve more than the melancholic grin. "I suppose you are right, as always, Constable. I promise you—I won't venture out of town alone again until the murderers are in your custody."

"Well, all right, then. Is there somethin' I can help you do since I'm here?"

Maggie enlisted the constable's help in dragging the cedar chest from the bedroom, and, with a good deal of effort, they managed to lift it onto the wagon's flatbed.

"My goodness, Girl," Constable Parker exclaimed as he wiped the sweat from his brow with a soiled bandanna. "What are you totin' in here? Gold bars?"

"Just a box of memories, Constable," Maggie replied listlessly as she contemplated Uncle Cahill's revealing letter beneath the layers of her parents' treasures. The cedar box held memories, all right. Memories of love. . .memories of respect. . .memories of deceit. The beginnings of slow-burning anger ignited within Magnolia. Anger and frustration. Bitterness and shame.

Preoccupied, the constable didn't even acknowledge Maggie's disturbed demeanor. Instead, he pointed to the coonhound, Ruff, who lay dreaming under one of the yard's pine trees. "Say, Magnolia. What plans do you have for that there huntin' dog? I could use a good sniffer like him."

"Consider him yours, Constable, as payment for your kind assistance to me today. Perhaps ol' Ruff can help you find those felons before they do any more harm."

Stepping back inside the house, Maggie rushed from room to room, filling a crate with the remaining items she felt were important to keep. Still stinging from the disturbing revelations of her uncle's letter, she forced herself to pack the framed photograph of the two of them at Maggie's eighth-grade graduation. *He's not my uncle, this impostor named*

Calloway. He's no kin to me at all! Nonetheless, her traitorous heart cried out for the man who had showered her with love and spoiled her as if he were her grandfather.

Dragging the packed crate onto the porch, Constable Parker jerked his head over his shoulder toward the front room and said, "I'll bring the missus by tomorrow, and she'll clean up them stains, Miz Alexander. Don't you give it another thought."

"You are too kind, Sir," she responded. "I'm near exhaustion, and I simply don't think I could face that dreadful task today. Plus, I promised Doc Engle that I'd sit with Levi Campbell tomorrow."

Immediately, unexpected doubts assailed Magnolia. Just the chance to speak Levi's name sent Maggie's heart racing. But if one man had betrayed her, would another? Could she ever place her confidence in the word of any other man? She sensed her spirit's very core of trust crumbling. Uncle Cahill's treasonous secrets robbed Maggie of her previous naiveté and left only suspicion and mistrust in its place. Still, a yearning for someone to disprove her cynicism bubbled to the top of her thoughts. She longed for Levi to dispel the blackness now saturating her soul, but the blackness even tainted her longing.

The freshly rooted shame sprouted to produce a malignant weed that began, even now, to eat away at Maggie's soul. Could someone as upstanding as Levi care for a woman raised by a criminal? Immediately, she recalled Preacher Eakin's sermon text from a fortnight ago: "Therefore if any man be in Christ, he is a new creature: old things are passed away; behold, all things are become new." If that verse were true, then Maggie knew she should focus on her status with Christ, not on her family origins. But what she was "supposed" to do somehow got lost in the hurricane of insecurity now attacking her soul.

With her spirit in tumult, Maggie reached for the open door. Originally intending to pull it shut, she stopped with her hand on the loose knob. "Constable, if you don't mind, I'd appreciate your patience for just another minute or two. I think I'd like to say 'good-bye' to this ol' place."

"Of course," he replied respectfully.

Maggie's footsteps on the wooden floors echoed throughout the house as she made her way to the kitchen. At last, she stopped and stared out the window over the drysink. She had watched her uncle Cahill from this spot on countless mornings as he headed toward the barn to begin his workday. Never again. She would never see her beloved uncle again. But the feelings Maggie expected to flood over her at this life-changing moment of farewells never came. Only numbness claimed her. Numbness, left in the wake of the hurricane of insecurity. There were no tears, no what-might-have-beens, no ache in her soul. . .only the numbness. Feeling as if she were ninety, Magnolia retraced her steps back onto the front porch. The youthful girl from last week seemed to have vanished, and in her place was a weathered woman, ready to embrace death. Without the slightest desire to look back, she climbed into her wagon, followed the constable onto the road, and headed for town.

When Maggie and the constable pulled up in front of the boarding-house, she fully expected Widow Baker to meet her on the porch ready with a tongue-lashing. Instead, Maggie had to go in search of her land-lady. The door to the kitchen had been pulled shut, and Maggie recognized the widow's gentle voice as she conversed with another woman. From the tone of the garbled conversation wafting through the closed door, Maggie formed the distinct impression that the woman with the unfamiliar voice was terribly distraught. Not wanting to interrupt, Maggie returned to the stoop alone to assist Constable Parker in carrying the cedar chest and crate up to her room.

With Maggie's things safely deposited in her room, she watched from the front steps as the constable mounted his high-spirited gelding and prepared to lead Maggie's sagging mare and wagon back to the livery stable. Ruff sat in the hay-strewn wagon barking into the humid air as the lawman tipped his hat and took off down the muddy street.

Weary in body and soul, Maggie dragged herself up the stairs to her bedroom. She should do the polite thing and offer Widow Baker her assistance with supper preparations. But the muffled voices floating from the kitchen suggested that Mrs. Baker's attentions weren't focused on supper anyway.

I can't face another person right now—and I certainly don't feel like meeting someone new. Maggie hung a hurriedly scribbled "Sleeping, Please do not disturb" note on the hook outside her door. Without even bothering to pull back her goose-down comforter or remove her shoes, she collapsed across the bed.

❖

The chiming mantel clock in the parlor jarred the fully clothed Maggie from her fitful, dream-filled sleep. One. . . two. . .three times the clock rang. Three o'clock in the morning, yet she didn't even remember lying down. In those fuzzy moments between sleep and consciousness, Maggie struggled to separate reality from her vivid dreams. Was the convalescing knight in shining armor, Levi Campbell, with his sparkling eyes and captivating smile, just a figment of her midnight imagination?

Maybe it's all been a horrible nightmare. Uncle Cahill couldn't have possibly been murdered. He can't really be dead. For a fleeting moment, Maggie convinced herself that only her wildest dreams could conjure up a story so surreal. How preposterous to even dream a tale that turned Uncle Cahill into a stagecoach robber wanted by the law. But as her eyes adjusted to the soft moonlight streaming through her window, her mind accepted the wrenching reality. Real life can be worse than the most awful of apparitions.

The rumble of her stomach reminded Maggie that she hadn't eaten since lunch yesterday. The only sound that greeted her when she opened her bedroom door was the rattled snoring of the rotund peddler, Mr. Winsek, on the third floor. With an outstretched hand, she felt her way through the darkness and down the staircase to the deserted kitchen. Turning up the kerosene lantern, Maggie surveyed the available possibilities that might appease her hunger. Widow Baker had hidden one of her wonderful pound cakes inside the Dutch oven, where mice couldn't and Mr. Winsek *wouldn't* find it. Maggie topped a thick slice with several hand-picked blackberries and gobbled the sweet meal down in a matter of seconds. Her mental list of things to apologize to Widow Baker for was growing ever longer, but Maggie was certain that the kind-hearted woman would understand.

Lighting another kerosene lantern, she carried it to her room so she didn't have to stumble around in the dark. Accompanied by the smell of burning kerosene, she crossed the room to the cedar chest. The wooden lid creaked softly as she inched it open. Thrusting her hand to the bottom of the chest, she immediately felt the scrolled packet she had hastily hidden at the constable's surprise interruption.

The soft lamplight threw eerie shadows across the "Wanted" poster and cast a sinister aura around the sketch of the man she had always called Uncle Cahill. Holding the paper close, she placed the lantern on the nightstand and settled onto the bed. Before reading, she studied the pen and ink drawing again, and the inner battle began raging once more.

Is there anyone around me who is who they seem to be? Is there no one in this world I can trust? If someone like this impostor James Calloway could dupe and deceive me for a lifetime, how can I begin to believe a stranger like Levi Campbell? Take care, Girl. She warned herself, *Guard your heart. Don't be duped again!*

Maggie held Uncle Cahill's letter and contemplated whether to finish reading it now or wait for a day when she was not so emotionally fragile. At last, she convinced herself to read the letter through to the end. No matter what other shocking revelations she would be forced to face, she decided to meet them head-on. Maggie skimmed her uncle's letter and found the place where she had been interrupted earlier.

Now, before you get the wrong idea, let me hurry and say that I did not mean to harm or kill your family that day. They truly did die when their wagon rolled down an embankment into the Arkansas River. But it weren't no snake that frightened the mules that day. It was me—making my getaway after holding up that stage.

Where do I begin to explain the events that led up to this fateful day? I suppose I could sum up my life prior to that day in just a few brief words. As a Federalist soldier, I was captured by Rebel forces during the battle at Spotsylvania in 1864. They were marching us to a prison, when I was able to make an escape, along with another fella. Being pretty well fed up with war and politics altogether, we decided to head off toward the new frontier and put our past behind us. I didn't have anything to go home to Pennsylvania for, anyway, as my mother had died of the cholera a couple of years earlier, and my papa had deserted us both before I was even borned.

Well, I'm sorry to say that I fell into some mighty bad company when I settled in Kansas. Hangin around the saloons and gamblin halls, it weren't difficult to find ways to get into trouble. Even so, I had not ever done nothing really terrible, until one day when I lost all I had to a mangy scoundrel at the poker table. Obliged to either pay my debt or face the killin end of a shootin iron, I was forced into service as what they call a road agent in an express mail heist. Out in the wide-open spaces of the Kansas prairie, it weren't too hard to hold up the mail carriers and stagecoaches in those days, and after I paid off my gamblin debt, I just kept on in that line of work. I never did have to kill nobody, though. Most of those folks I robbed seemed more than happy to turn over money that weren't their own to begin with if it meant breathin for another day.

That terrible morning in May started out as just another workday for me. I landed enough loot in that stage job that I figured I would lay low for a good long while. I even thought about giving up thievin altogether and maybe headin for California.

Well, I had made a clean getaway and was several miles

down the trail, but I wanted to put a safe distance between me and the stage I'd just robbed, so I kept on driving my horse as fast as she would go.

Your folkses wagon seemed to spring up from out a nowhere. There was nothin none of us could do to stop their startled mule team before they went headlong off the trail and into the soft sands of the riverbank. By the time I could scramble to the bottom, all of your kin had breathed their last. They had been crushed to death under the weight of the wagon and mule team. I heard you cryin up towards the top of the hill and hurried to find you. You came right to me, throwing your arms around my neck. I knew I couldn't just leave those bodies for the animals or Indians to find. Even a fella as rotten as me couldn't do a thing like that. So I settled you down and started in diggin one big grave in the best spot I could find. I did not have the time to go and fix em each a grave. After that, I started collectin the things that had been scattered about, and I came across that big family Bible and your mama's diary. That evenin as you slept beside me in front of a campfire, I set in a readin your momma's stories. Each page seemed to be written just for me. She told about how Jesus Christ had come into her and your papa's hearts, changin em for the better. She told about how useless and pitiful life had been before they knew God. She didn't see how anyone could face life without Christ.

I read from that Bible and your momma's diary most of the night. And, the more I read, the more I could see what an awful person I was. How much I needed forgivin. I didn't know if I did it right, but I asked God to forgive me and help me to give up my wicked ways. I decided then an there to turn in the loot from my robbin and take whatever punishment came my way.

I planned to fix up the wagon and carry you with me to turn over to the nearest lawman. That lawman happened to be a fella by the name of Dallas Blankenship. I walked into his jail with you in my arms, piled my money and you on his desk, and said I wanted to turn myself in.

Before I could even say who I was, he offered to strike a deal. He said I could go a free man if I would just leave the money and take you with me. He had no way of handlin a baby in the middle of Kansas, and all he cared about was recoverin the money.

I suppose if I'd stopped to think about it awhile, I'd a knowd somethin wasn't right, but I figured it was just God givin me a break. I drove out of town and set beside the Arkansas River for a good long while tryin to figure out what to do next. It just come to me that there weren't nobody that knewed your family was dead. And it wouldn't do anybody no harm if I was to take on the name of your uncle and start a new life somewheres far away. Seein as how I was the one responsible for your folks dyin, I figured God woulda wanted me to take care of you. Well, my sweet little Magnolia, that's how you and me came to settle here and how I took to raisin' you.

It weren't til today that I found out that I was still a wanted man. That crooked lawman, Dallas Blankenship, showed up at my door. I'd remember those beady eyes anywhere. He was a wavin this wanted poster under my nose and threatenin to turn me in for the reward if I didn't give him some gold he thought I had. But there ain't no gold. Said he'd give me a day to either get the gold or pay him the cash before he would go to the law. That was just four hours ago, but Maggie, I don't have to think any more. I know what I have to do. He can turn me in to the law, but I can't go back to those connivin old ways. Tomorrow when he shows up, I'll refuse to pay. If he does turn me in, I hope you'll find it in your heart to come and visit me, and let me explain, face to face, the rest of the story that I just couldn't put down on paper. If this Blankenship fella is as crooked as I think he is, tomorrow he may kill me for refusing to give in to his demands. I think he's got more reason to run from the law than I do these days, and I don't suppose he's going to run to the constable and turn me in.

The good Lord will see to it that justice is done. Don't take this matter into your own hands, as I know you'll be tempted to do. Show this letter to the constable and let him track down Dallas Blankenship—or whatever name he's usin these days.

Dearest Maggie, I know it was wrong of me not to tell you all this before. I've begged God every day to forgive me for bein dishonest with you. I'm not much of one to give advice, but Maggie, please always remember that I love you dearly, and God loves you, too.

> *All my love and devotion,*
> *James Calloway,*
> *alias Cahill Alexander.*

Maggie let the letter fall to the floor as she fell backward onto the feather pillow, her head throbbing with too many new thoughts and mysteries. While answering many questions, the letter had also posed a new mystery. Who was the ex-lawman who had murdered her uncle? Was he, even now, a part of Dogwood's citizenry? With Uncle Cahill dead and buried in the churchyard, Magnolia didn't know how she would ever discover the man's identity. The very thought of taking the letter and "Wanted" poster to Constable Parker humiliated Maggie beyond measure. She could never face the constable or anyone else in this town if Uncle Cahill's crooked past were known. But was she willing to let his murderer roam free because of her shame?

In a matter of hours, Maggie's foundation of trust in mankind, and in God Himself, had been severely shaken. *Nothing is as it seems to be. No one is who he says he is.* These thoughts played over and over through her mind. Already the night was giving way to the soft light of morning. But Maggie wasn't ready to face a new day.

If Levi Campbell expected her to sit with him today, then he would be sorely disappointed. At once, her former reaction to Levi mocked her. She could no longer allow her heart to be ensnared by a man, even one as charming as he. She had only just met him. How could she be sure he was as upright as he seemed? Even if he were Travis Campbell's brother, that guaranteed nothing. On the other hand, if he were as upright as his older brother was, what could Magnolia, an orphan raised by a common criminal, possibly offer the well-bred cattleman?

Chapter 5

Maggie bathed and changed into a comfortable cotton gown, then lay absorbed in her thoughts until the familiar rattling of breakfast preparations mingled with the smell of freshly brewed coffee. Expecting to find the Widow Baker alone, Maggie donned her house robe and walked toward the kitchen. She called a raspy, "Good morning," just before opening the creaky door. To her surprise, two female voices echoed, "Good morning."

Next to Widow Baker stood a dark-haired woman cracking eggs into a bowl. The ruddy-cheeked stranger wore one of the widow's favorite silk brocade dressing gowns. Several sizes too small, the elegant fabric stretched across her abdomen to reveal the young lady's impending motherhood.

"Oh, you poor dear," the soft-spoken landlady expressed the oft-repeated sentiment and pulled out a chair from the kitchen table. Deftly, she motioned for Magnolia to take a seat. "You look worn out before the day's even begun. Sit down here, and let me fix you a cup of coffee and a plate of these nice eggs."

Widow Baker poured coffee from the steaming pot into her favorite porcelain cup and saucer and handed the warm beverage to Maggie. "You gave me quite a scare yesterday, Miss Alexander," the doting widow said as she overflowed Maggie's coffee cup with the addition of fresh cream. I'm glad to see that you made it home safe and sound."

Relieved that she couldn't find an appropriate place to comment, Magnolia allowed the genteel Mrs. Baker to continue. "I know you must be exhausted. I understand about grieving. Even when you sleep you find no rest.

"Oh my, where are my manners? You two haven't been introduced." Widow Baker turned to the expectant mother. "Magnolia Alexander, I'd like you to meet Miss Louella Simpson. She's going to be staying with us for awhile."

Maggie had tried to surreptitiously study the young woman. *Miss, not Mrs. Simpson?* She only hoped her overwhelming curiosity wasn't blatantly apparent. "I'm so very pleased to make your acquaintance, Miss Simpson. I know you will be quite happy here at Miz Baker's boardinghouse."

The new tenant cast Maggie a weak and sympathizing smile, revealing yellowed, crooked teeth. "Miz Baker told me about your loss, Miss Alexander. I'm so sorry. I understand your uncle was a wonderful man."

For the first time in her life, Maggie found it impossible to agree with a positive comment about Uncle Cahill. Even though she could not ignore the twist of agony this realization brought to her soul, she chose to not address the statement. Instead, she watched as Widow Baker skillfully dumped the eggs into an iron skillet atop the cooking stove and grappled for a change in subject. With the eggs' telltale fragrance increasing Magnolia's appetite, her muddled mind finally stumbled upon a topic that needed to be addressed.

"Miz Baker, I know this is a great deal to ask of you, but I'm wondering if you would deliver a message to Dr. Engle's office for me this morning. You see, I agreed to sit with his patient, Levi Campbell, today. But I am simply not up to the task. I believe I am going to spend the entire day in bed, if you don't mind." Wearily, she rubbed her temples.

"Oh, Miss Alexander," Louella interrupted before the widow had a chance to respond, "please allow me to deliver your message for you. I had planned to stop in and speak with Dr. Engle today, anyway."

"Well, all right, then," Maggie agreed. "If you're sure you don't mind. I'll just run upstairs after breakfast and prepare a note. And thank you, Miss Simpson."

"Louella, call me Louella, please."

"I'd be honored if you'd address me as Maggie from now on as well," she replied before partaking of the mountain of scrambled eggs that Widow Baker had set before her.

❖

"Well, it's been quite a number of days since your injury, and I believe it won't be long before you are strong enough to travel out to Travis and

Rachel's ranch," Dr. Engle announced as he entered Levi's room, rattling a breakfast tray.

Levi turned from the window as the comment hit him like a rock between the eyes. Whatever had possessed him to let Dr. Engle catch him out of bed? Levi knew his brother and sister-in-law were anxious to have him in their home and under their care. And he couldn't impose on the good doctor indefinitely. Still, he wasn't prepared to think about leaving. Desperately, he wondered how he would ever see Magnolia again, if he were sentenced to the ranch.

"When do you think I should go?" Levi nonchalantly tossed the question toward Dr. Engle, his voice disguising the turmoil raging within.

Levi had wrestled with sleep most of the night, but he couldn't blame his restlessness on physical discomfort. Rather, his insomnia was due to the anticipation of Magnolia's arrival and the fleeting, few hours he would spend in her care. As the circumstances appeared, those hours would be a precious few, indeed.

"There's no hurry, but when Miss Alexander comes in this morning, I'll ride out to Travis's and see what day works out best for him. Maybe you can go as early as tomorrow or the next day if you're up to the trip. I need to check on Rachel, anyway. I wasn't happy about her coloring the last time she was in. She looks mighty peaked."

Levi hoped Travis didn't hurry to rescue him. This was one time Levi didn't want his big brother rushing to his aid! Levi's irrational resentment toward his older brother boiled to the surface as he frowned toward the red-doored saloon across the street.

All of his life, Levi had been hounded by comments like, "Why can't you be more like your brother?" "Your brother would never do such a thing!" "Aren't you Travis Campbell's kid brother?"

But Levi wanted to just be himself. When their father insisted that Levi attend the same Boston law school where Travis studied, Levi adamantly refused. He wasn't meant to be a lawyer. His home was wide, open fields. So he had taken his poetry and his stallion and spent his days with the livestock.

Travis had never really done anything to deserve Levi's rancor, and Levi was beginning to feel like a cad because of these negative feelings. Something insisted the time had come to grow up and put this childhood pettiness behind him.

His older brother had never been more than a gracious help, were Levi to ask his assistance. And he could certainly use Travis's advice in regard to Miss Magnolia Alexander. Before Travis married Rachel, he had his choice of El Paso's maidens. Levi, on the other hand, rarely enjoyed the company of one from the female persuasion, unless he counted cows. Now, Levi found himself blundering through the beginnings of a relationship with Magnolia Alexander. Hopefully, his lack of skill in dealing with ladies would in no way push her away.

Oh, Lord, give me wisdom in my interactings with Miss Alexander. And. . . and help me with this absurd jealousy, Levi prayed silently. *I know I should be thankful to have a brother like Travis. I reckon the reason I've been so irked is because I figure I can never measure up to him. That's probably not fair to him or me. Still, Lord, if you could work it out that I could find a woman like. . .like Magnolia Alexander to fall in love with, I'd never need to be jealous of Travis again.*

Levi sealed his silent bargain with an "amen" and absently watched the saloon's swinging red door open and close with the arrival and exit of patrons. *It's mighty early to be drinking,* Levi thought as he caught sight of a scroungy pair rushing onto the boardwalk.

The grimy men wore tattered, filthy clothes and shapeless hats. The pair, both clutching whiskey bottles, untied the reins of their horses, tethered at the hitching post. In one fluid motion, they mounted their steeds and spurred them into a full gallop. The resulting jolt sent one man's hat toppling to the side, and he grappled to retrieve it as a cascade of matted red hair spilled forth. *A woman! One of the men was really a woman! A woman with hair the same color as that bandit who had shot him.* At once, Levi's knees buckled as though they were made of jelly. "She's the one," he muttered and grasped the windowsill for support. He would have recognized the frizzled red hair in a crowd of a thousand.

"Doc, I. . ."

Dr. Engle immediately stepped toward Levi, guiding him to the bed. "Boy, you look like you've seen a ghost. You'd better lie down. I was afraid you were overdoing it. Maybe I was a bit hasty in assuming you were ready to leave—"

"No, Doc. You don't understand," he rushed. "It's one of those lady bandits—riding with that fella down the street."

By the time the doctor crossed the room and looked out the expansive window, Levi strained to see any sign that the two had been in the muddy street.

"I'll see if I can stir up the constable." The physician jumped into action. "I hate to leave you, but I don't see that I have any other choice since Maggie hasn't arrived yet. Now, get yourself back to bed. I'll hurry back as soon as I can."

Levi sank onto the pillow and eyed his breakfast tray sitting on the nearby table. As the outer door closed behind Dr. Engle, Levi's sense of helplessness particularly frustrated him. He was accustomed to handling whatever situation might come, no matter how challenging or difficult. But Levi was quickly learning that a gunshot wound had a way of turning a capable man into a weakling.

What would he do if someone intent on doing him harm were to enter after seeing the doctor leave? Levi was certainly in no condition to stand and fight, and he had given Travis his Peacemaker for safekeeping.

"A cowboy can do without a lot of things in life, but he should never be caught without his gun!" his papa always said. And those words proved true more than once out on the range. Why had he not remembered Papa's constant admonition? He should have kept his gun with him.

His stomach growled, and Levi sat up with plans to settle in the chair near the table holding those mellow-scented strips of bacon that now tormented his appetite. But all hunger vanished as the front door banged shut and an unfamiliar, feminine voice called out, "Hal-low, is anyone here?" He had hoped the slamming door would signal the arrival of Magnolia Alexander. But Levi had heard the gentle lilt of Magnolia's musical tongue enough to know that the woman calling out was not his angelic nurse. The mystery intruder's being a woman did little to dissuade the apprehension overwhelming Levi. He tried to tell himself that his fears were irrational. But his stomach clenched at the memory of that redheaded bandit he had just seen.

You coward! Afraid of a woman. Despite his mental castigation, he noticed the iron bar propped beside the cold fireplace and stood to retrieve it.

"Oh, hello. I wasn't sure if anyone was around." The feminine voice took on the face of a woman with blotched skin and dark, plaited hair. Her eyes guileless, she peered at him from around the door. "I do hope I didn't disturb you. I'm searchin' for the doctor. Is he in?"

Levi sighed and settled back onto the bed as the woman stepped through the doorway. Obviously heavy with child, she seemed as harmless as Levi's grandmother.

"No, he had to step out for a short while. I'm not any help as far as doctoring is concerned. But I'd be more than happy to pass along a message."

"W–Well," the unidentified visitor stammered with reluctance, "I. . .I did need to see him about a p–personal matter, though it's nothing urgent. Nothing that can't wait. Then, I also promised to deliver a note of explanation for Dr. Engle from his nurse, Magnolia Alexander. I suppose she wouldn't mind if you gave it to him instead. She's not going to be able to come to work today."

Levi took the perfumed note from the stranger's extended hand and stared at the envelope with downcast eyes, hoping to mask his profound disappointment.

Magnolia's not coming today. Magnolia's not coming today. Magnolia's not coming today. The words began a melancholic chorus in his mind, which seemed to dim the sunshine pouring through the window. Levi held the sealed letter under his nose and breathed deeply of Magnolia's lavender perfume. He longed to touch the hands that likewise bore this fragrance. Magnolia's hands. Did she suspect the power she slowly gained over him? For hours, his thoughts had dwelled on nothing else but being in her presence once more. *She's not coming. Was it something I did or said?*

The temptation to tear open the envelope and read Magnolia's note, addressed to Dr. Engle, was almost more than Levi could bear. The impropriety of such an act would be inexcusable. Still, he felt he had a right to know why she wasn't keeping her word. Magnolia's expressive face certainly bore witness to the fact that she felt the same overwhelming tug of attraction now drawing Levi to her. If she were holding back on her emotions, he understood. She had just suffered a terrible loss. Furthermore, she was a gentlewoman with a lady's sense of propriety. Certainly, Magnolia's absence today represented more than truancy from work. She was avoiding him, or his name wasn't Levi Jacob Campbell.

As the expectant mother stirred, Levi realized he had forgotten her very presence. "I guess I should be going now," she said as she backed away.

"Please, wait," Levi called before she stepped across the door's threshold. "I'm wondering if you could be so kind as to deliver a return message to Miss Alexander for me."

"Why, certainly," the woman replied as she hovered near the doorway.

I'm not going to make it easy for you to brush me off, Magnolia. Levi frantically racked his brain for the appropriate words as he reached for paper and pen on the nearby nightstand. Choking down a grimace, he painfully grasped the pen in his right hand, extending from the sling. In a barely legible script, he scribbled, "Be an *angel* and come back as soon as you can. I'm anxious to hear you read *Huckleberry Finn*." Upon her last visit, Magnolia had placed a book on the nightstand—a book she never read due to their lengthy conversation. Upon perusal, Levi discovered the book to be penned by one of his favorite authors, Mark Twain. Even though he had read *Huck Finn* at least three times, Levi longed to hear Magnolia's musical voice pose the words on his ear.

Folding the paper over once and once again, he passed it to the waiting woman and said, "Thank you, Ma'am. I really appreciate your kindness in delivering this message for me. I do hope Miss Alexander is well."

"I'll see that she gets it first thing after she wakes up. And I'll tell her of your concern. I'm sure she's going to be just fine. I have a feelin' she's just tuckered out. That's all. Now, if you'll excuse me, Sir. . ." The meek messenger turned and hurried out the door.

❖

When Dr. Engle clamored back in the door a short while later, Levi had finished his breakfast and turned his mind solely to the unread contents of Magnolia's note. However, Dr. Engle, whirling with the thrill of the chase, bounded to Levi's bedside, his eyes sparkling with excitement.

"I found the constable." The doctor set straight his twisted coat collar and removed the bowler from atop his well-greased hair. "He took off, hot on her trail, as soon as I told him about your sighting of that redheaded bandit and her male sidekick. I tell you, Levi, I think he's got a good chance of catching them, thanks to our quick work. I wonder just what they are up to, sneaking around town. If we're lucky, they'll lead the constable to the other female rascal as well."

"Great!"

"Say, are you feeling any better?" he asked, scrutinizing Levi. "I'm surprised Maggie's not here yet."

Levi held up the sealed note. "She sent this. Evidently, she's not coming in today. Her messenger said the note would explain," he said and attempted to hide his raging curiosity.

Gazing at the envelope, Dr. Engle drew his brows into a puzzled frown. "Did the Widow Baker bring this by?" he asked, a thinly veiled note of expectation in his voice.

"Well, I haven't met a Widow Baker, and this lady didn't give out her name, but she was about twenty years old, and I'd guess about eight months along in the motherly way. Said she needed to speak with you about a personal matter as well, so she'll be back."

"No, that's definitely not Sarah Baker." The doctor's ironic smile held a twist of mystery. "Oh, well, let's see what Maggie has to say. If it's all right with you, I'll just read it aloud." Dr. Engle's impish remarks suggested Levi's interest in the nurse's letter had not gone unnoticed.

"Whatever you prefer," Levi replied coolly and inwardly scolded himself for being too transparent.

Dr. Engle positioned his spectacles on his nose and, ignoring Levi's counterfeit indifference, began reading what she wrote.

My Dear Dr. Engle,

I do sincerely hope and pray that my absence today does not present too grave a hardship on you or Mr. Campbell. I had every intention of honoring my commitment when I left there yesterday. However, I now find myself weary to the point of exhaustion. Let me try to explain. When I departed your company in the morning, I set out for Uncle Cahill's farm in order to prepare the house for a new owner. I fear that I attempted to undertake more than I was capable of at this time of deep sorrow. For as I set about the task of sorting through my uncle's things, grievous emotion overwhelmed me. Now I feel that the best remedy is a day in bed. I believe I know you well enough to ascertain that this is also what you would prescribe. I am confident that I will be up and about by this time tomorrow, and I shall greet you in your office then.

Please extend my regrets to Mr. Campbell and convey my promise to begin reading from Twain's "Huck Finn" when I return.

Yours most sincerely,
Magnolia Alexander

"Well, there you have it, Levi. She'll be back on the job first thing tomorrow. I know Miss Alexander. She's not one to let life's troubles get the best of her."

Unconvinced that Magnolia's actions were not meant as a snub, Levi tried to analyze the words he had just heard. *Her note seems entirely too stilted to me. What is it that she's left unsaid?* He would just have to wait until she walked into his room tomorrow to know for certain if his fears were false or confirmed. One look at her candid countenance would answer Levi's dilemma. In the meantime, he would double his efforts to win her heart. *I'll replace your uncle Cahill as the man you can depend on, Magnolia. Just you wait and see.*

As Levi pondered what new approach he would take to solicit the affections of his charming nurse, the doctor's outer office door flew open again. He started and wondered what it took for an ailing fella to get any peace. But his complaints stopped short of vocalization when he recognized his brother's voice. "Doc. Dr. Engle. Are you here?"

"Yes. Yes, in here," the doctor replied, quickly shoving Maggie's note into his coat pocket as he turned to leave the room. Before Dr. Engle could manage to close Levi's bedroom door behind him, Travis Campbell had bounded across the hardwood floor and grabbed the doctor's shoulders in his muscular hands. Without so much as a glance at his brother, Travis launched into a frantic plea.

"Sir, please." The elder Campbell tugged at Dr. Engle's sleeves, practically dragging the physician from the room. "You've got to come to our place. And hurry. There's something terribly wrong with Rachel. She's in dreadful pain." Agony seemed to ooze from Travis's eyes. "I think the baby's trying to arrive. I told Rachel I'd come for you and get back to her as soon as I could." The frenzied husband implored his skilled friend to follow him as he rushed out the door. "Doc, can you? Won't you? You must come!"

Dr. Engle grabbed his black leather bag from the wall peg and hastily prepared to follow the already departed Travis. Halfway over the threshold, he called out to Levi, "I'll be back as soon as I can. Just do your best to manage things around here."

The jealousy that had plagued Levi earlier now haunted him. *Oh, Lord. You know I would never wish harm or ill on Travis or his family. Please, dear God, help them now! And forgive me, Lord. Forgive me. Help me to relinquish these feelings of inadequacy to You.*

Chapter 6

Throughout the morning Maggie tried in vain to sleep. The more she pursued relaxation, the more her fretfulness grew. "Idle hands are the devil's workshop," Maggie could still hear her uncle Cahill say. She wasn't accustomed to the life of leisure some championed, and she was beginning to doubt its merit. Magnolia found that, in the absence of productivity, her mind filled with dark thoughts, bitterness, and rage.

In an attempt to blot out the sun streaming through the window, she covered her head with the pillow. As the smells of Mrs. Baker's rose-scented sheets enveloped her, she desperately wanted to mourn her uncle's death by remembering all the good about him. During the wee hours of the night, she had determined that she could never think of him as James Calloway. To her, he would always be Uncle Cahill, regardless of his legal name. But thoughts of his twenty-year deception stubbornly replaced her wonderful memories. Even when her mind turned to Levi, rather than fantasizing about any wonderful possibilities, Maggie wondered if she could ever trust him—or any other man—*ever*. After all, the one man in this world she had completely believed in, in the end, had proven himself untrustworthy.

By midday, the early summer sun had sufficiently heated her room to such a degree that perspiration dampened her hair. *I've got to get out and make myself useful somewhere.* With hands skilled through years of experience, she captured her rebellious, frizzled hair into its usual chignon. After pouring cool water from the dressing table's porcelain pitcher into a matching bowl, she splashed her face. Chagrined at her reflection in the gilded mirror over the bowl, she pinched her cheeks and hoped to give them color. Yet even her most meticulous grooming tricks failed to mask the dark circles underscoring swollen, bloodshot eyes.

She removed the light cotton gown she had donned in the morning's wee hours and put on one of the two mourning dresses the Widow Baker had so thoughtfully lent her. Smoothing the stiff skirt, Maggie reached for her bedroom door's white enameled knob. Just then, she caught sight of a sloppily folded piece of paper that had been shoved under her door. Magnolia picked up the note and shook it open with a quick jerk. *This looks like it was written by a child.* Her eyes darted to the bottom of the page in search of an identifying signature. Finding the note unsigned, she focused her attentions on the brief message.

"Be an *angel* and come back as soon as you can. I'm anxious to hear you read *Huckleberry Finn.*"

Levi Campbell. The note came from Levi, not from a child. She winced as she considered the obvious pain Levi had endured to pen this simple message. Maggie chuckled to herself as she reread Levi's thinly veiled reference to their first verbal exchange. But a sense of foreboding scurried behind the chuckle. Obviously, Levi wasn't the type to let their new relationship die simply because Magnolia chose to distance herself. Perplexed with her dilemma, Magnolia frowned, refolded the note, crossed the room, and opened her mother's Bible on the bedside table. Tenderly, she tucked Levi's message inside, then hesitated. Sternly pressing her lips together, she removed the note and dropped it into the nearby wastebasket. Her spine stiff, she retraced her steps and left the room.

Tiptoeing noiselessly down the stairs, her traitorous heart beat with regret over discarding Levi's note. Would Levi think her heartless? He must have been terribly disappointed by her absence to have written a note despite the pain it caused him.

But before she reached the kitchen door, Maggie's common sense had once more overruled her heart. She simply could not allow herself to trust any man, not even one as sweet-talking as Levi Campbell. Stubbornly, she decided she would show no more concern over disappointing him. Furthermore, if he learned the truth about her upbringing, Levi might very easily decide Magnolia was not the breed of woman that would interest him.

"Hello," Louella Simpson greeted Maggie as she came through the swinging kitchen door. "I was just fixin' to make us a lunch tray," she said, pointing toward a wooden tray laden with two glasses of lemonade. "I didn't expect that you'd leave your bed today, and I figured the two of us could share the noon meal in your room. That is. . .if you didn't mind," she hedged. But before Maggie had a chance to answer, Louella rushed on, "Oh, before I forget it, I slid a note under your door. Did you notice it?" Her speculative gaze suggested Louella had already conjured a number of scenarios regarding the handsome patient.

"Yes, I found it." Maggie purposefully walked toward the loaf of thick-crusted bread on the kitchen counter. "Thank you for all the trouble you've gone to for me today." With a stained butcher knife, she cut a wide slice of the bread and doggedly changed the subject.

"You needn't bother with a lunch tray, Louella. You really are too kind. My room is so sweltering it's impossible to rest. And this heat has robbed me of much of an appetite, especially after eating the huge breakfast that you and Mrs. Baker prepared. Can you imagine what August will be like if June is this hot? Anyway, I'll just munch on this bread and a piece of cheese." She removed the glass dome, which rested atop a wooden cheese plate and helped herself to a wedge of mellow cheese. "I thought I might as well see if I could be of some assistance to Widow Baker. Is she around?" Maggie looked through the kitchen's screen door and scanned the backyard, expecting to see Sarah Baker hanging clothes on the line.

"Miz Baker had to do some shopping at the general store, so I offered to help her by peelin' the potatoes for tonight's soup. I've just finished the job, and it's hotter than blazes in here. Why don't we both take a glass of lemonade out to the back porch and sit a spell?"

"I'd like that, Louella. Let's do. It will give me a chance to get acquainted with you." Magnolia pulled open a nearby drawer and retrieved one of Mrs. Baker's red checked napkins.

" 'Tisn't likely that I'm the kind of folk you'd want to get to know." Her eyes downcast, Louella gazed forlornly at her thick waistline. She picked up the two tall glasses of freshly poured lemonade and started toward the screen door leading to the back porch.

Maggie set the bread and cheese atop the napkin and insisted on relieving Louella of one of the glasses. At once, Magnolia felt a certain kinship with the bereft young woman. She identified all too well with the hopelessness clouding Louella's eyes. The insecurity. The worries that no one would accept her when they found out the bitter truth. After reading her uncle's note, Magnolia had experienced every one of those emotions. By no means was she carrying an illegitimate child, but she did bear an illegitimate past. A past based on lies. The lies of an outlaw.

"Please don't feel that way for one minute," Magnolia said, sipping the tart, cool lemonade as she paused between the slat-backed rockers.

"You've been nothing but helpful, sweet, and kind to me all day." She held one of the chairs steady so Louella could slowly ease herself into it. A gentle breeze rustled the leaves of the oak tree that shaded the east end of the covered porch and both women breathed deeply of the markedly cooler air. Louella pushed her rocker into motion and Maggie soon matched her rhythm. As they tapped out a syncopated cadence on the gray slat floor, Maggie gazed intently into Louella's hazel eyes. Her eyes were obviously her best feature.

"If you'd allow me the chance, Louella, I think we could become good friends." Maggie pinched off a bite of bread and cheese and nibbled them.

"But, Miss Maggie, you obviously don't understand. I'm the kind of woman that a lady of class such as yourself would *never* associate with."

"I wouldn't be much of a lady at all if I looked down my nose at you," Maggie insisted, dusting the bread crumbs from her lap. "Whatever problems you're facing right now, given time and the Lord's help, they will all work out."

Louella began to blink rapidly as she fought back tears. Once again she eyed her protruding abdomen. "My life is such a mess, Miss Maggie. I don't think there's any fixin' it now."

Magnolia's nursing instincts took over as she sympathetically patted the back of Louella's hand. "Sometimes it helps just to share your burdens with another. Why don't you tell me all about it? Perhaps you could start by telling me where you call home. I know you're not from around Dogwood. I'm acquainted with pretty near all the folks in these parts."

"No, I'm not from around here," Louella offered. "I grew up in Pine Bend. Pine Bend, Arkansas, that is. My pa and ma raised chickens and farmed a little land about five miles west of town. My folks, they were good Christians, even though we couldn't make it into church but every now and again. I was reared on the Good Book, and my life was pretty normal back then."

Louella's eyes took on a faraway glaze as though she had transported herself back to happier times. Shaking her head slowly from side to side, she started in with her story once again.

"But, a couple years ago, my pa took sick and died. Poor Ma grieved so hard I thought I might lose her, too. That's why I know a little about the sufferin' you're goin' through." Maggie only nodded her head in agreement as Louella spoke.

"After Pa died, Ma and me, we didn't know how we would manage with the farm and all. But, somehow, we struggled through. One day, though, about this time last year, a smooth talkin', good lookin' Yankee by the name of Silas Turner showed up at our door. He was peddlin' some kind of elixir, swearin' it would cure whatever ailed you. Well, Miss Maggie, just starin' at Mr. Turner cured what ailed *me!* I had been so busy on the farm, I hadn't had time to bother with courtin' any beaus. Besides, the good Lord didn't bless me with an abundance of beauty, and I never had any boys bangin' down my door. But this Mr. Turner, he was somethin' different. He showed me attention like no fella had ever done before. He made me feel really and truly purdy for the first time in my life."

Just like Levi makes me feel. Maggie couldn't stop the words from invading her mind.

"Miss Maggie, lookin' back on it now, I realize that Mr. Turner was slicker than snake oil. He said so many sweet things to me, makin' me feel like I was the most beautiful thing he had ever seen. He told me he was goin' to look for work so he could stay close by me. One thing led to another, and, before summer's end, I was for sure that he was the man of my dreams and the answer to my prayers.

"My ma tried to tell me that I was rushin' into things, and it was all movin' too far, too soon, but I wouldn't listen. I was just sure that Silas Turner and me were meant for one another. It was the first time in my life that I can remember being at real odds with my ma. From that first feud with Ma on, I avoided her, and she steered clear of me. I figured I'd best just keep quiet and let time prove that I was right."

Louella rubbed her eyes, heavy with dark circles. "Things happened quick between Mr. Turner and me. I wasn't used to bein' fawned over and adored. He treated me like a queen, singin' me songs and bringin' me flowers. When he first kissed me, I found myself wantin' more, but I did the respectable thing and pushed him away.

"But one day, when Ma was gone to a quiltin' bee, Silas and I were out doin' chores in the barn, and he started sayin' such sweet words to me. He kissed me again. Only this time, I kissed him back. I'd never felt such wonderful feelin's in all my born days. I figured that we were goin' to be married soon, the way he was talkin' and all, and I wanted him to be happy, too. I didn't see how somethin' that felt so good could be all that sinful and bad. I am ashamed to say it now, Miss Maggie, but since I thought we were goin' to be husband and wife quick enough, I just let Silas do whatever he wanted to that day.

"After that day in the barn, it was next to impossible to tell Silas 'no.' He looked for more and more chances for us to be alone together. Each time, I'd try pushin' him to set a weddin' date, and he always hedged.

Finally after 'bout three weeks of that, I told him we *had* to get married or all of it was gonna stop.

"The next afternoon, I waited on the porch for Silas to show up for supper as we'd planned, but he never came. I went into town lookin' for him the following mornin', and the hotel clerk said he had checked out and said that he was headin' west. It was all I could do to keep from bustin' into tears right there in the hotel lobby, but I saved my tears for the journey home.

"With the trouble between Ma and me, I wasn't about to admit that she had been right all along. I didn't want to 'fess up to lettin' him love me the way only a husband should love a wife. I don't think I coulda ever looked my ma in the eyes again. I never felt so all alone as I did that day."

I know all about consuming loneliness and secrets too terrible to share with another living soul, Maggie thought as Louella took a long drink of her lemonade. *But maybe someday I'll be able to share with someone in the same way Louella is sharing with me.* Levi's face flashed through Maggie's mind. Would she ever dare to reveal her true self and deepest secrets to him? A desperate longing for such a relationship swept over Maggie and new tears stung her eyes. But what if Levi was nothing but another smooth-talker like Louella's Silas Turner? Could she be sure she could trust him? Too choked with emotion to even speak, Maggie deposited her uneaten bread and cheese on the nearby table as Louella continued.

The expectant mother brushed aside her own silent tears. "The only thing I could think to do was to run away from home. I think I was hopin' to find Silas and convince him to take me with him. So, when Ma was in the vegetable garden picking beans, I took what money she had stashed in her hatbox, left her a note tellin' her good-bye, and snuck off into the woods.

"Even though I was already plumb worn out from cryin', I walked all that afternoon and through the night. The next day, I was lucky enough to catch a westbound stage that had stopped off in some little Arkansas town. By the time the stage driver stopped to water his horses in Dogwood, I'd just about given up all hope of running into Silas and I figured that, even if I did, I couldn't convince him to come back with me. It was then that I saw a "Help Wanted" sign in the window of the Dogwood saloon.

"Dogwood looked pretty good to me right about then." She rubbed a thin film of perspiration from her upper lip and sipped her lemonade. "I was so tired. I just didn't feel like I could go another mile. Before the stage left town, I was standin' behind the saloon counter pourin' whiskey for the local men.

"Now, I knew it wasn't respectable work for a Christian girl to do, but I figured I had already fallen below my station by what I'd done with Silas Turner, and I didn't deserve any better. I reckon I wasn't thinkin' too highly of myself right then." Louella threw a shy grin to Maggie.

"And you've been in Dogwood ever since?" Maggie asked.

"Yes. Mr. Wentworth, who was managin' the saloon for Sweeney back then, put me up in a room over the bar, and I hardly ever left the place," Louella replied. "In fact, I stayed behind that counter as much as I could. You see, after a bit of time passed, I realized the full consequences of what Mr. Turner and I had done when we were alone." Louella's hand dropped to her stomach, and no further words needed to be said.

Maggie sadly shook her head.

"That explains why I've not seen you before. I don't think I've even looked inside the doors of a saloon. Uncle Cahill used to tell me that a saloon was nothing but a den of iniquity and I should stay as far away as I possibly could." As the words left her mouth, Maggie pondered the irony of her uncle's wisdom. Undoubtedly, he had learned that truth by firsthand experience.

"Your uncle must've been a pretty wise man, Miss Maggie. There weren't much that went on in there that was any good. But I'd probably still be there today if Jed Sweeney hadn't showed up to check up on Mr. Wentworth and his saloon last week. Sweeney took one look at me and sent both me and Wentworth packin'—and without our due pay. He said Wentworth might have been soft, but he sure wasn't gonna be. Said he didn't need any liabilities like a barmaid in the 'family way' workin' in his saloon. That Mr. Sweeney had me so frightened and flustered that I just grabbed what I could carry of my things and I skedaddled from there.

"You know, Miss Maggie, I should be glad Sweeney gave me the boot. I don't think I could bring myself to work too long for that man."

Louella's words sent the image of Jed Sweeney flashing across Maggie's mind. His inky eyes. His thin frame. His offer to buy Uncle Cahill's ranch. Should Magnolia sell the estate to a man who would throw out Louella without hesitation?

"So how did you happen to end up here?" Maggie asked.

"Well, when I left the saloon, I didn't know where to go. I wandered through town until I found myself sittin' in Dotty's Café with my head between my hands. I guess I was cryin'. I don't really remember, but I musta looked a sight, 'cause Miz Baker stopped to ask if there was anything she could do to help me. I tell you, Miz Baker's been nothin' but wonderful to me ever since. When she found out that I had no place to sleep and no money to pay, she took me in and said she'd give me free room and board in exchange for help around the house."

The two women sat in silence for several long moments as Maggie pondered the overabundance of life's heartaches. She patted Louella's hand once again as she softly asked, "What are your plans for when the baby comes?"

Louella shrugged and sighed deeply. "I haven't wanted to think about it much, but I know I need to sort it out soon. I don't mind tellin' you, Miss Maggie, I'm plumb scared. Miz Baker said I really ought to be checked over by the doctor, and I intended on talkin' with Doc Engle when I delivered your note today. But he was out, so I guess I'll have to try again."

"He was out?" Maggie abruptly stood from her chair. "Dr. Engle was out? Why? Where did he go? Who's caring for Levi Campbell?" The questions tumbled from her lips faster than Louella could respond to a single one.

Louella stammered as she struggled to climb out of her chair. "Well I . . . I don't rightly know. I . . .I assumed that the bedridden fella had addressed these things in his note."

"I think I might be able to answer at least one or two of your questions," Sarah Baker interjected as she opened the screen door and stepped out of the kitchen. With short, precise jerks, she removed her white gloves and held them in a blue-veined hand.

"It appears that Dr. Engle's been called out for an emergency at the Campbell place. I happened to run into Rachel's cousin, Angela Isaacs, outside the store. She said she'd just met Travis running into Dr. Engle's office and that he beseeched her to pray for Rachel. He came tearing out of the doctor's office a few seconds later, jumped on his horse, then galloped off toward his farm. Dr. Engle came out right behind him, carrying his black bag. I hope and pray Rachel's not having troubles with her unborn child."

Maggie grasped her throat, feeling as though she had been thrown into yet another perplexing predicament. Clearly, her duties as a nurse rested with caring for Dr. Engle's patients. Part of her insisted she rush to her medical responsibility. Yet another side of her, the wary side, bade her to avoid Levi Campbell at all costs. Her professional obligations finally overrode her emotions, and she muttered, "I. . .I really must go check on the injured Mr. Campbell."

"Have you heard?" Widow Baker asked, her eyes snapping with interest in all the latest stories. "Your patient spotted one of those women bandits with some man coming out of the saloon. Constable Parker is scouring the countryside for them now."

"No. I didn't know that either, but thank the good Lord. I hope Constable nabs 'em. Now, if you'll excuse me," she continued. Maggie spun into action. She raced to her room to retrieve her reticule, gloves, and parasol. Then she hurried past Widow Baker and Louella at the base of the stairs. Brows raised, they silently watched Magnolia rush through the front screen door. "I won't be home for supper," she yelled over her shoulder as the screen door slammed behind her.

Hastening from the porch steps and along the rutted road to Dr. Engle's, Magnolia firmly resolved to remain aloof and inexpressive in her dealings with Levi Campbell. *You are going to stay with him out of duty. Nothing more*, Maggie repeatedly admonished herself, refusing even the slightest flutter of excitement. Yet she betrayed her own covenant within seconds of stepping into Levi's room.

Chapter 7

M agnolia left her gloves, parasol, and reticule in the front office and entered Levi's room as nonchalantly as her pounding pulse would allow. Despite all her mental vows on Dogwood's Main Street, her heart insisted on palpitating at the sight of Levi Campbell. She had caught him in the act of sitting upright, intently reading the Word of God, like a man in near-perfect health. His attempts to scramble into a reclining position left Magnolia stifling a smile.

"Hello. I hoped you'd come." Levi reached for her hand, his emerald eyes dancing with anticipation.

As if her instincts were bent on betraying her, Magnolia found herself extending her hand toward his, expecting the feel of his calloused fingers as they closed around hers, reveling in the warm affection Levi so freely offered. However, a dark cloud of misgiving descended upon her soul, and Magnolia jerked her hand to her side. She balled her fist into a tight knot, firmly set her lips, and turned to the pile of soiled linens stacked in the corner. She didn't dare look at him. She didn't dare ponder the smoldering passion so blatant in his eyes. She didn't dare hope that a man like Levi would continue in his warm regard upon learning the truth of her upbringing.

Once more, the passage from Preacher Eakin's message several weeks past abruptly interrupted her thoughts: *Therefore if any man be in Christ, he is a new creature: old things are passed away; behold, all things are become new.* This time, the Bible verse seemed to breathe a wisp of hope upon Magnolia's soul, a hope that was short-lived. For even if she embraced the verse as truth, that did not mean Levi Campbell or anyone else would.

Magnolia pondered the plight of Louella Simpson. She weighed the reaction of most of Dogwood once they learned she was giving birth to an illegitimate child. Regardless of Louella's repentance, regardless of her worth in Christ, Maggie knew that most of the township, most of the church, would scorn her.

Likewise, Maggie's situation would evoke disdain from those who discovered the truth. The hard facts of human nature left Magnolia feeling as if she were sinking into the depths of a dank and dreary pit of despair.

Levi awkwardly cleared his throat.

Refusing to look at him, Magnolia picked up the soiled linens. Loaded with the laundry, she stiffened as his contrite words seemed bent on melting the barriers of her heart.

"Have I. . .in some way offended you, Magnolia?" he pleaded.

She bit her lip as tears of bitterness stung her eyes. *No!* she wanted to yell. *No. You have done nothing! Only Uncle Cahill, the man I thought I could trust. Now I don't know if I can trust a soul. Now I don't know if anyone will even want to associate with me.*

Instead, she hunched her shoulders, muttered a quick "No," and rushed toward the door without a backward glance. In an effort to regain composure, Magnolia occupied her time with household chores and early supper preparations. Levi was visibly gaining strength and no longer needed constant care. However, she could not indefinitely avoid him. Her professional obligations insisted she prepare the patient an evening meal. Desperately trying to harden her heart, Magnolia took a shaking breath before entering his room, holding the tray filled with ham and beans and cornbread.

However, this time her patient no longer claimed the bed. Instead, he sat in the armchair by the opened window and had somehow managed to change from the nightshirt into the stiff jeans and denim shirt that Dr. Engle had provided from the general store. At the sight of Levi's freshly shaven face, Magnolia glanced toward the bowl and pitcher stand to see signs of lather and water.

"I feel like an invalid lying in that bed all day," Levi answered Magnolia's unspoken question.

"It's good to see you gaining some strength." With an air of cool indifference, she refused to meet his gaze. However, the fact that Levi could actually dress himself and sit in the chair suggested that Dr. Engle would soon be releasing his patient. The very idea left Magnolia spinning in disappointment—a disappointment she squelched. As she bent to situate the tray on the nearby table, Maggie felt Levi studying her. At this close proximity, she smelled the lye soap he had used for shaving. Lye soap, and the odor of starch on new garments. Once again, her pulse insisted upon its telltale fluttering, and she determined to remove herself from his presence as soon as her professionalism allowed.

Setting her face like a stern spinster, Magnolia handed him his fork and desperately tried not to look into his eyes. But despite her valiant attempts to avoid peering into his soul, her gaze slowly traveled from the fork, to his arm in the white sling, past the buttons of the denim shirt, across his lips and aristocratic nose, and at last met his questioning scrutiny. The faint attraction that Magnolia initially felt for Levi had gradually grown into the fires of longing. Longing, which his own tormented eyes revealed. Only the lazy, summer sounds of an east Texas town broke the wordless communication that flashed between them—neither could hide the reciprocal fascination.

At once, Levi's earlier inquiry seemed to bounce between them, demanding an answer. *Have I. . .in some way offended you, Magnolia?* The question posed itself so strongly in Maggie's mind that she found herself ready to answer once more.

"Magnolia?" he whispered, again reaching for her hand.

Nervously, she pushed the fork into his opened hand and rushed from his presence. Her own vacillating emotions forced her to exercise a firm self-control of mind over emotions. She could no longer predict what she might feel or what words might spill from her lips. The task of stifling her feelings for Levi was the most difficult assignment she had ever attempted, and it grew more and more impossible as the hours passed.

Like a woman obsessed, Magnolia attacked the dirty dishes stacked on the kitchen counter. In a matter of minutes, she had washed and dried all but one plate. With the evening shadows lengthening, she furiously rubbed the last plate with a cup towel. Whether she wanted to or not, Magnolia sensed Levi's magnetic presence as if his very spirit were draping itself around her shoulders. No chore, regardless of how frenzied, could blot out Levi. His endearing smile. His open admiration. His obvious devotion to the Lord. In short, Levi Campbell was everything Magnolia would want in a husband. A tremble of yearning rippled through her.

The gentle tinkling of Levi's bedside bell sent a shock of dread through Magnolia. Dread and anticipation. She shouldn't enjoy every second she spent with him, regardless of her yearning. She shouldn't. . .for their potential relationship represented nothing but an impasse. An impasse weighted with heartache. The bell sounded again, and Magnolia set the plate in its spot in the cabinet and walked toward the room. Pausing on the threshold, she raised her brows in silent query.

From his spot by the window, Levi studied her, a spark of mischief in his eyes. "You never read *Huck Finn* to me," he said, lifting the book from his lap.

"Considering you had the strength to dress yourself, I assumed you were perfectly capable of reading to yourself as well," she said stiffly.

"I am, but. . ." The teasing smile suggested. . .invoked. . .promised.

Maggie's mind whirled with the pleading gleam in his eyes. Her mutinous heart once again began its pounding. Her outrageous imagination wondered what Levi's lips would feel like against her own.

"Please. . . ," he whispered.

And Magnolia could no longer remember why she was even avoiding him. On trembling legs, she walked forward, pulled the book from his grasp, and settled into the straight-backed chair near the bed. Deftly, she opened the book as the last spears of light from the scarlet sunset filled the room. Clearing her throat, she began reading chapter one.

"Uh. . .I was on chapter four," Levi said, that spark of impishness in his eyes igniting to laughter.

Once more, Magnolia reveled in a shameless, improper thrill that this injured cowboy was blatantly flirting with her. Despite her resolve to remain stoic, she inserted her bottom lip between her teeth in an attempt to prevent a smile. Her attempts failed miserably. Hurriedly, Maggie swished the pages to chapter four and began reading,

> WELL, three or four months run along, and it was well into the winter now. I had been to school most all the time and could spell and read and write just a little. . . .

But after her evening meal, after the shocking news of Uncle Cahill's letter, after enduring the heat of an exhausting day, Maggie found it necessary to stifle several unexpected yawns. Levi's magnetic charm faded as if he were wrapped in a veil of fog. The drowsiness she so wanted to earlier claim her now settled upon her with an undeniable heaviness. Gradually, her vision blurred, her speech slurred, and Magnolia decided to close her eyes for only a few seconds of respite from the long day. . . .

❖

Maggie started from her sleep when *The Adventures of Huckleberry Finn* slipped from her hand and hit the wooden floor.

"The sleeping beauty awakens," Levi whispered as her eyes adjusted to the soft glow of a flickering candle in a room darkened with the shadows of night.

"What happened? How long did I sleep?" Maggie pushed at her loose bun, attempting to regain a modicum of dignity and composure. The last thing she remembered, she had been reading to Levi and sunlight filled the room.

"I suppose Huck Finn's adventures seem pretty lame compared to ours these past days." The candle's soft glow only intensified the gleam in Levi's eyes as he playfully teased Maggie. "Ol' Twain flat-out put you to sleep."

"And you didn't have the decency to waken me?" Maggie shot back, her face warming at the thought of Levi watching her nap.

"Magnolia, you were exhausted. You needed rest. It would have been cruel and selfish for me to disturb your slumber. Besides," he said with a grin, "if I had awakened you, I wouldn't have had the privilege of listening to you snore."

"I do *not* snore!" Maggie vehemently denied, her face heating all the more. She moved to the window and pulled back the curtain. The only other light she could see came from the saloon across the street. Surprised again at the late hour, Maggie's tone of voice switched to serious concern. "Just what time is it, anyway? Is there no news from Dr. Engle concerning Rachel?"

"The last time the mantel clock chimed, it was nine o'clock. That's nine in the evening, Magnolia, just in case you've lost all track of time. And, no, there's been no word from Dr. Engle as of yet. I don't know whether to interpret his sustained absence as a good or bad sign. What do you think, Nurse?"

"It's hard to say in situations like this. We may very well not see Dr. Engle for another day. I know he won't leave Rachel until her condition is stable."

"I've been praying all day that the Lord would watch over them. It will break their hearts if this baby doesn't live. And I can't help but think that I might have brought on Rachel's suffering, with the worry and trouble I've been."

"Levi, don't," Maggie interjected, vaguely recalling her earlier attempts at indifference. "Don't say such things. You mustn't blame yourself. These kinds of problems happen to women all the time. Your situation has nothing to do with it."

Stop it, Maggie, she fiercely scolded herself. All day, Maggie had managed to keep her distance from Levi. . .until he had somehow talked her into reading to him. Now here she was showing too much interest, too much concern, too much familiarity—*again*.

"The hour is late, Levi," Maggie said firmly as she stooped to pick up the book from the floor. "And, while I am now rested, I'm certain that you need your sleep. I will retire to Dr. Engle's parlor until morning, if you don't mind. You know to ring the bell—"

"Wait, Magnolia," Levi caught her arm before she turned to go, and his tender touch left Magnolia trembling. "There's something I feel I must ask you while I still have the chance. You've left me in a quandary, and I want to get things straight."

The sudden seriousness in Levi's voice sent Maggie's thoughts spinning in a dozen directions, but she maintained a calm demeanor, diminutively studying her hands as he spoke.

"You've seen me at the most vulnerable time of my life and now, well, I might as well jump into this with both feet. I can't begin to tell you how many nights I prayed under the prairie stars of west Texas and asked the Lord to lead me to the woman He means for me. But never before, not until I met you, have I ever come across a woman I felt could be that special one." His gentle grip on her arm increased in fervency. Likewise, Maggie's quivering increased.

"Despite my torments and teasings, I believe that you are aware of my growing affection for you. Earlier, as you slept, I practically held my breath for fear of breaking that enchanting spell. Throughout your repose, your loveliness filled the room. I wanted to etch your beauty indelibly in my mind and I could have watched you sleep for countless hours on end."

Maggie desperately wanted to look into Levi's eyes and study the face of this man whose words had lost the cadence of a west Texas cattleman and taken on the nuance of a poet. But as Levi continued to speak, she stubbornly concentrated on her fingernails instead of basking in the warmth of his direct, admiring appraisal.

"The first moment I saw you, despite my delirium, you looked like an absolute angel to me, and my appreciation of your beauty has only deepened with each passing day. But it is more than just your loveliness that attracts me to you.

"Magnolia, you and I are kindred spirits. You put your faith to work and your compassionate heart is expressed in all you do." Levi released her arm and reached toward her face, softly stroking her cheeks. His light touch sent chills exploding throughout Maggie.

"Now, I may be totally wrong. Could be I've been alone under the stars one too many nights. Still, I feel pretty certain that you are having these same kinds of feelings for me. If I am wrong, then just look me straight in the eye and deny it.

"Look at me, Magnolia." Levi tenderly took her chin in his hand and tugged her face toward his. "Would you have me leave you alone?"

"Levi, I. . .you. . .you and I. . ." As hard as she tried, Maggie could not face his gaze. She focused on the window, just behind him instead. "We are not as alike as you seem to think. Actually, we are not anything alike. We come from two different worlds. There are things about me that, if I were to tell you, would send you running the other way."

"You can't do it, can you, Magnolia?" Levi defiantly interrupted, tugging at her chin again. "You can't honestly say that you aren't drawn to me."

"In the long run, Levi, we have to look beyond. . .beyond how we feel. We must be practical. For me to even consider encouraging a relationship—with you or anyone right now—would be absurd."

"All right, Magnolia. I won't fuss with you about it anymore tonight. But don't expect me to give up on winning your heart just yet."

"Listen, Levi," Maggie stepped out of his reach. "If you insist on pinning your hopes and dreams to this relationship you want with me, I can't very well stop you. But I'm afraid you're headed for a big disappointment."

Fear gripped Maggie's heart as she swiftly turned away and scurried from the room. He definitely knew too much regarding her feelings, although he had no knowledge of the fresh secrets this week's cataclysmic events dropped into her life.

Crossing through the short hallway that separated Dr. Engle's professional rooms from his private quarters, Maggie noticed too late that she had neglected to carry a light with her. She passed by the dark parlor and felt her way to the kitchen, where a smoldering fire cast a red glow across the walls. After lighting a kerosene lamp, Maggie returned to the ornate parlor, careful to lock the door between the personal and professional quarters—not that she suspected Mr. Campbell would attempt any manner of ungentlemanly conduct. However, Maggie forever considered appearances. She in no way wanted a sick citizen to arrive in the night only to find the door between the quarters unlocked. More than one night she had slept on Dr. Engle's couch when he was out and a patient needed care. The township accepted this fact of Maggie's position, but Uncle Cahill had taught her to take no chances on marring her spotless reputation.

The rarely used parlor still bore the distinctive decorative touch of the deceased doctor's wife. Maggie removed her high-topped shoes and eased herself onto the red velvet sofa, thankful that the size of Widow Baker's mourning dresses did not require that Maggie wear a corset. She covered her legs with an embroidered linen lap blanket used by Mrs. Engle in the months preceding her death. A portrait of the frail, yet stately lady hung over the stone fireplace. In an attempt to shove images of Levi from her mind, Magnolia turned to the one in the portrait.

Mrs. Engle had always treated Maggie with such kindness during her childhood, and the doctor's wife had been one of a precious few motherly influences upon Maggie. Without fail, Mrs. Engle delivered a large basket of pies and breads and sweets to the Alexander home each Christmas. Always tucked inside the basket was a package just for Maggie, containing some uniquely feminine thing that Uncle Cahill would never think to give. Delicate lace handkerchiefs. Real French perfume in a cut-glass bottle. A cameo broach. Tortoise-shell combs for her hair. Mrs. Engle seemed to delight in pampering Maggie, treating her like the child she never had.

As a little girl, Maggie loved visiting the Engles' home. She still cherished the memories of sitting on this very sofa, her feet dangling off the edge while she tried to behave like a little lady. Magnolia studied the portrait of the graceful, elegant Mrs. Engle, and her heart twisted for the doctor. With fresh insight, she related to the grief and despair he endured at his companion's death. How many sleepless nights since her death had Dr. Engle looked up at this portrait and longed to feel her, to speak with her once again—just as Maggie longed to speak to Uncle Cahill and feel his strong, warm hand on her shoulder.

When Mrs. Engle died, the poor doctor surely must have born an insufferable loneliness. Maggie cringed as she thought back to the comments folks all over Dogwood were making after Mrs. Engle was laid to rest. The whole citizenry seemed certain that Dr. Engle was the kind of man who simply couldn't survive without a wife. Even Uncle Cahill had said, "It's only natural that he and the Widow Baker get hitched." Maggie knew from recent experience that, despite their good intentions, the smothering compassion of the Dogwood townsfolk often oppressed rather than uplifted.

The local matchmakers were undoubtedly in their heyday after the doctor's mourning period, when he actually began to call on the middle-aged widow, Sarah Baker. Bess Tucker, the buxom, red-cheeked clerk at the general store, had immediately stocked a bolt of exquisitely patterned silk in anticipation of a wedding dress for Widow Baker.

But the good people of Dogwood were sorely disappointed when Doc Engle's courting of the Widow Baker came to an abrupt end. Within hours of the apparent breakup, speculations began to fly all over town as to what had caused the lovers' feud. The tension between Luke Engle and Sarah Baker could hardly go unnoticed. They deliberately avoided one another, despite the inconvenience of doing so. No matter how hard their friends and neighbors pried, neither would reveal the root of their dispute. Both the doctor and the widow refused to even discuss the other party. Quite obviously, they didn't want their private lives to continue as a topic of public debate. Even Maggie, who found herself in close association with both Dr. Engle and Widow Baker, was unable to broach the subject for fear of offending them.

"I wonder if Dr. Engle even shared with *you* the reason for their feud?"

As Maggie addressed the portrait of Mrs. Engle, the finely etched lips seemed to curl upwards into a hint of a grin.

And I wonder what drastic measures I'll have to take in order to squelch the rumor now circulating about me. Undoubtedly, eyebrows all over town were already raised in question concerning the prospects of a deepening relationship between Levi and Maggie. Whenever Maggie walked through town, she sensed that her life was the most popular discussion around.

The dear folks of Dogwood apparently saw the time of mourning as the perfect opportunity to find romance. In all likelihood, nosy Bess at the general store had already charged an order for a bolt of silk brocade to Maggie's account.

Magnolia grimaced at the thought before breaking into a calculating smile. She, too, would put into practice the tactics of Dr. Engle and Widow Baker. She could turn a deaf ear to the town gossips' comments just as skillfully as they. Her Dogwood audience was just one more reason to sidestep any sort of a relationship with Levi. If they ever learned about Uncle Cahill's past, the township would certainly associate any breakup in a relationship with Levi as a logical consequence of Mr. Campbell's disdain for a woman of Magnolia's upbringing. But if there were no relationship to end, that would give the citizens of Dogwood one less avenue of gossip.

With fresh resolve, Maggie pledged to scorn all of Mr. Campbell's advances. She picked up her book and stared at the pages of *Huckleberry Finn* until the words blurred together like a newspaper in the rain. Despite the fact that she had napped for several hours under Levi's watchful care, the exhaustion of the week once more evoked a pall of drowsiness upon her mind. Magnolia slept soundly throughout the night's remainder.

❖

The next morning, Maggie rubbed her cheeks in an effort to rouse herself from her deep sleep. Natural light overpowered the pale glow of the kerosene flame as she folded the lap blanket and began the task of washing her face, combing her hair, and freshening up. She was certain that she had heard the floorboards in the entryway creak under the weight of Dr. Engle's heavy boots as he walked toward the kitchen.

Convinced that the well-meaning doctor was planning to make some of his infamously awful coffee, Maggie hurried into the kitchen, determined to take over before everyone was forced to drink the acrid liquid.

"Good morning. Glad to see you made it home." Maggie laid her hand on the doctor's stooped shoulders as he gripped the sides of the drysink and stared blindly out the window.

"Hello, Maggie. I didn't expect to see you here. How's Levi?" he asked listlessly.

Magnolia stiffened against the pleasure the very sound of Levi's name evoked. "I haven't checked on him this morning, but he appeared much stronger when I saw him late last night. From the looks of things, he's doing better than you are." A certain dread rushed upon Maggie. She had seen the doctor this grim many times. . .many times when he had lost a patient. Magnolia swallowed against the lump in her throat. "Rachel. . .is she. . ."

Dr. Engle appraised his nurse through tear-reddened eyes. "You know, Maggie, I brought Rachel into this world, and it pains me somethin' fierce to see her suffering so. She lost the baby. And both she and Travis are taking it pretty hard."

Chapter 8

Furrowed lines of worry shadowed the doctor's face, making him appear older than his sixty years. "Maggie, would you mind running out to their farm later today and checking up on Rachel? I think she could really use another woman to talk to right about now."

"Certainly, Dr. Engle." Magnolia's heart wrenched with the agony Rachel must be facing. Perhaps Maggie's own recent loss would bond them together as only grief can bond. "You know I'll do whatever I can to help Rachel. It's all just so sad." She flipped the latch on the window above the drysink and pushed against the two wood-framed panes. With a faint squeak, they swung outward to allow fresh air into the already stuffy room. The gentle morning breeze that cooled Maggie's cheeks brought a welcome relief to the kitchen's fire-warmed air. Nonetheless, the bright sun promised to produce yet another hot Texas day with a heavy blanket of humidity. Her black moiré dress absorbed heat like a cast-iron stove, and Magnolia could feel her hair already curling against her temples.

"There's more to it than I had the courage to admit to Rachel and Travis today." The doctor absently toyed with the watch chain hanging from his vest pocket. "I couldn't bear to bring any more bad news, but I suspect that Rachel will never be able to carry a child to full term. She seems terribly small."

Maggie turned to Dr. Engle, shaking her head. "Life just doesn't seem fair sometimes, does it? When folks like Rachel and Travis long for a child and would make wonderful parents, yet are deprived of that privi-

350

lege, and then young girls like Louella Simpson, who have no husbands and no hope of providing a stable home, are strapped with the heavy burden of an impending child."

Dr. Engle raised an eyebrow in question. "I'm afraid I'm not familiar with a Louella Simpson."

"Oh, I'm sorry. I guess the two of you haven't met." Maggie busied herself in stoking the fire, then filled the coffeepot with well water from the wooden bucket beside the drysink. "Louella will be in to see you very shortly. She's a kind, gentle spirit with a good many problems. Louella's going to need some assistance in delivering a child very soon. I'll let her explain her situation. I don't want to betray any confidences. But I do think you'll find her delightful despite her compromised position."

"Ah, yes, she must be the messenger Levi spoke of yesterday morning," Dr. Engle recalled as he reached for the coffee tin. "But since we're talking of young women needing help, how are you doing, Maggie?"

Gently, Maggie removed the aging blue coffee tin from the doctor's weary hands. "As good as can be expected, I suppose, Dr. Engle. Really, that's one of the reasons I've kept myself busy around here. I can't let myself stop and think about all that's gone on this week. I'm afraid I'd go crazy."

"I know it's not much comfort now," Dr. Engle said, "but the pain does subside. Take it from me. I know. I have to tell you, though, I'll never get over missing my wife." He rubbed his jaw, covered by a day's gray stubble, and settled at the kitchen table. The doctor propped his elbow on the table and rested his forehead against his hand.

Dreading the resulting heat, Maggie inserted a couple of small sticks onto the glowing coals, then scooped two heaping spoonfuls of coffee into the pot and set it on the metal rack over the crackling fire.

"I'm so tired, I almost forgot," Dr. Engle said. "Travis insisted on sending me home with a basket full of fresh eggs and a slab of bacon from the hog he butchered last week. Do you think you could fry some up and feed our patient a hearty breakfast today? Your fine cookin' might do me good as well."

"Just leave the breakfast to me, Dr. Engle." Maggie crossed the room and uncovered a large wicker basket sitting by the back door. "You rest a spell. You've been working much too hard."

"I'm beginning to think that I'm getting too old for this business. I had always planned to retire when I started delivering a second generation of babies, and Rachel's baby would have been the first in that category. Now, it looks like I'll have to wait a little longer to take down my shingle."

Dr. Engle's shoulders heaved with the weight of a heavy sigh as he continued. "It seems like our work comes in spurts, doesn't it, Maggie? Remember just a couple of weeks ago, we were sitting in my office playing checkers for lack of anything better to do? Now we're hoppin' to stay on top of things.

"I suppose we'd better organize our day. After breakfast, before you head out to see Rachel, I'd like to see the constable and find out if he was able to track down those bandits. I'm committed to finding those scoundrels who murdered your uncle. If Constable Parker can't find 'em, I'm tempted to go on a manhunt—or a womanhunt—myself.

"You have heard, haven't you?" The doctor's eyes widened with question. "Yesterday, Levi spotted one of those women bandits leaving the saloon with some scroungy man."

"Yes, Widow Baker gave me the word. But I'm curious to hear if the constable's search has met with success. Does he still believe that the train holdup and Uncle Cahill's murder were the work of the same team?"

"The constable thinks maybe they left the train robbery and fell upon your uncle's house, bent on taking more money. That old homestead isn't very far from the place where the train stopped after the robbery, you know."

Flashes of panic, fear, and uncertainty skirted through Maggie's mind. She had been so consumed with her uncle's lifelong deception that she had given little thought to the fact that his murderer—or murderers—were still at large, despite the constable's warnings. She wasn't quite sure which would be worse, allowing a killer to go free or sitting in a murder trial, telling all regarding the questionable circumstances surrounding her uncle's death. Could the crooked ex-lawman, mentioned in her uncle's letter, have joined forces with the women bandits who robbed the train? No other suspicious stranger had been seen in town. She shuddered to imagine the spectacle of their trial. The whispered gossip around Dogwood concerning her and Levi would drastically dim in comparison to the buzz created by the revelations about her "upright" uncle.

"Have I upset you with all this talk, Maggie? You're looking pale," Dr. Engle asked as he grabbed a potholder and carefully removed the coffeepot from the rack over the fire.

"No. . .no, I'm fine. Just fine. I'm just thinking about those outlaws running free and all. Can I get you some sugar for your coffee?"

"No thanks. I think I'll have it black, if you can call this coffee," he grumbled, filling a stoneware mug to the brim. "It's more like water if you ask me."

Out of politeness to her employer and her elder, Maggie remained silent. However, a noise in the hallway dashed away all vestiges of the former conversation. Both Maggie and Dr. Engle turned toward the sound to see Levi pushing against the kitchen's swinging doors.

"You know, I'm pretty handy around a kitchen. And folks say that my coffee tastes mighty good."

Maggie gaped at the sight of him, decked out like a cowboy in the new jeans and denim shirt, with a sun-faded red bandanna around his neck. His arm still rested in the sling, and he looked every bit the wounded hero. Furthermore, his tanned skin spoke of good health rather than the sickly complexion of an invalid. At that moment, Maggie thought she had never seen a more handsome man. The embers in Levi's emerald eyes blazed when he playfully winked at Magnolia. The good doctor produced a humorous grunt, and Maggie quickly concentrated on the eggs she planned to scramble. Despite her pledges to remain distant with Levi, a delicious tremble passed through her midsection.

Levi passed her to approach the doctor, and Maggie's fingers shook as she cracked several eggs into a wooden mixing bowl. "You're right. That *does* look like water." Magnolia glanced toward the pair to witness Levi scrutinizing the doctor's steaming coffee mug. With his left hand, he took the coffeepot from the exhausted doctor. "Do you mind if I make a fresh pot? I like my coffee strong enough to hold a spoon upright."

"I knew we must have something in common, Boy," the doctor said with a tired smirk. "If Maggie had her way, I'd be sippin' watery coffee 'til my dyin' day."

"I'll take a cup of that before you throw it out." Magnolia hurriedly wiped her hands on a dishtowel before relieving Levi of the pot.

The men chuckled.

"Looks to me like you need to be moving along to your brother's ranch now, Levi," the doctor said as Maggie filled a mug with the fragrant coffee.

She felt Levi's observation as he reluctantly agreed with the doctor. Instinctively, Magnolia glanced toward him to see desperation and longing flitting across his features. If Levi left, when would the two of them ever see each other again? He might very easily complete his visit and return to west Texas without so much as another word with Maggie. *So let it be*, she thought. *The less I'm with him, the less likely I'll be to get hurt.* Regardless of the delight his audacious winks created, regardless of her growing attachment to him, the sad reality remained: Magnolia was afraid to trust, and he would be afraid to love once he learned her background.

"Well, I can see my assistance in the kitchen is no longer required," Dr. Engle said a bit too sagely. "I believe I'll try to catch a few minutes of shut-eye if you two will excuse me for awhile."

"No, Dr. Engle," Maggie rushed frantically. "You can't leave until you've had your breakfast. Sit down here and wait for just a minute while I scramble these eggs and fry up the bacon." Reaching for the cast-iron skillet hanging on a hook beside the fireplace, she intensely hoped her employer would take the hint. Maggie could have hugged him when he returned to his chair and said, "I guess my ol' stomach is grumbling a bit."

While Maggie turned her attention to the eggs and bacon, Levi settled across from Dr. Engle. "I'm afraid to ask, Doc," Levi said seriously. "But, how is Rachel doing?"

"Levi, I. . ." The doctor hesitated, and his voice grew thick. "I've got sad news to report."

"Is Rachel—"

"No, no. Rachel's fine. But the baby. . .the baby didn't make it. She just came too early."

The three of them remained silent as the fog of death seemed to settle upon the room, forever banishing any attempt at cheerfulness. Magnolia completed the breakfast, and the kitchen filled with the mouth-watering aroma of fresh bacon. At last, she heaped plates with the scrambled eggs and bacon, but even the scrumptious feast couldn't abate the despondent mood that had settled upon them. Levi stared in stunned silence at the candle, sitting in the middle of the table. Dr. Engle rubbed his eyes. And Magnolia blinked rapidly against tears, feeling as if she had lost Uncle Cahill all over again.

As she prepared to serve the breakfast, Maggie bumped the coffeepot, left sitting on the kitchen counter. With resignation, she grabbed the gray-specked pot and turned toward the back door, intent on discarding the mellow brew. On second thought, she just reached for the blue coffee tin and dumped an obnoxious amount of grounds into the

existing liquid. She grabbed the dipper from the well bucket and measured more water into the coffeepot. For the kind of concoction the doctor and Levi liked, it would make little difference if part of it were
warmed-up leftovers. With the sound of metal against metal, Magnolia
deposited the coffeepot on the cooking rack and picked up the breakfast
plates.

"Well, I haven't had much of a chance to get to know Rachel," Levi
said somberly. "But I think, by all Travis says, that I'll like her. She's
been through a pretty rough year—not unlike you, Magnolia, both of you
losing a parent and all." Levi and the doctor nodded their thanks as Maggie set the plates in front of them.

But before she could turn away, Levi's sympathetic appraisal bore
into her very soul. The rivulets of perspiration down her back seemed
more a result of the warmth in Levi's eyes than her work at the fireplace.
Magnolia held her breath as their gaze lengthened. She wondered what
life would be like, sharing breakfast with this man every morning. She
pondered the possibility that one day they might marry and, like Travis
and Rachel, would discover their love had blossomed into another life.
Terrified that Levi would perceive the shameful direction of her thoughts,
Maggie abruptly walked back to the fireplace to remove the bubbling coffee.

As Dr. Engle blessed their food, she closed her eyes and delayed the
task of pouring the inky liquid into two thick mugs until his "amen" freed
her to proceed.

"Doctor, I must confess," Levi said, "that my brother's loss now
leaves me in a quandary about what I should do." He cut a heel of bread
from the ever present loaf on the table, then filled his mouth with a fork-
ful of eggs.

"I understand," the doctor replied as Magnolia set a cup of the
detestable brew in front of each man.

"Like you said, it's time for me to move along, but I don't want to
intrude on Travis and Rachel at this delicate time. Can you direct me to a
good hotel in town?"

Dr. Engle looked at Maggie with questioning eyes. "Does Widow
Baker have any extra room to spare at her place right now?"

As she floundered for a reply, Magnolia's earlier, frantic musings
about never seeing Levi again now haunted her. What was worse? Never
seeing him again or having him in the same boardinghouse. . .always in
contact with him but forever keeping her distance. For a fleeting moment
she considered the possibility that the two men had previously plotted

this subversive scheme. Had Levi confided to Dr. Engle his intentions to win Maggie's heart? Immediately, she dismissed the notion. Dr. Engle, forever the tease, would have undoubtedly leaked any such information to the young lady whom he treated like a daughter.

She steeled herself against the temptation to lie about the widow's vacancies. That would do nothing but hinder the kind lady's livelihood and grieve the Lord. "Yes, Doc Engle. I think Mrs. Baker does have an opening," Magnolia said with resignation. "That fella Slim Rogers left to go back east last week. His room is still available as far as I know." Shoulders drooping, Maggie stepped back toward the kitchen counter with intent to place her own plate on the table and eat. But her churning stomach rejected the very sight of the food she had labored to prepare.

Gripping the kitchen counter, Magnolia debated what to do. She pressed her lips into a decisive line and determined to fill the drysink with the breakfast dishes. Magnolia would douse them with the water now boiling in the iron pot that hung over the cooking rack and leave the mess until later. While the men enjoyed their meal, she busied herself with the myriad of other chores a kitchen demands and sipped her coffee.

Finally, the men finished, and she began the task of clearing the table. "As soon as I finish here, Levi, I'll get my things and accompany you to Widow Baker's," she mumbled, frantically attempting to hide her desperation.

"Maggie, would you also inquire of Constable Parker any news of the bandits?" Dr. Engle said. "I certainly would like an update, as I'm sure you and Levi would." He glanced from her to Levi and back, as if he were contemplating much more than the status of the outlaw chase.

"Of course," Maggie said mechanically.

"Well, if the two of you will excuse me. . . ," the doctor said discreetly. Maggie could only imagine what he must be thinking. "I'll retire for a spell." His chair scraped against the floor.

Squelching the desire to run after the wise doctor, Maggie hopelessly watched him push his way through the swinging doors and vanish into the hallway. Like a woman on a grievous mission, she gathered the remaining dirty dishes from the table and piled them in the drysink, just as planned. But she hadn't planned on how to deal with Levi's non-plussed appraisal. Her legs trembling, Magnolia grabbed a thick towel, stepped to the fire, and struggled to retrieve the kettle of boiling water from its hook. Although manning the iron pot was usually the doctor's chore, Maggie's own weakness left her exasperated. The more she struggled to maneuver the kettle, the more frustrated she became. The last thing she wanted was the close proximity of Levi's assistance. But the sound of his chair scooting away from the table preceded his presence by only seconds. With his free left hand, he effortlessly took the kettle from Maggie and poured its contents over the dirty dishes in the sink.

Refusing to look at him, she said, "If you'll gather your things, I'll meet you at the front door."

"Would you prefer I find another place to stay?" he asked quietly. "I certainly don't want to burden you."

His words demanded Maggie's full attention. She looked upward to find him only inches from her, and his unexpected grin left her speechless.

"Y–You are–aren't a–a burden," she stammered as her mind spun with his nearness. For the first time in Maggie's determination to keep Mr. Levi Campbell at arm's length, she wondered if she could actually succeed. Would her tattered, lonely heart override her common sense? Would she find herself swept away by this charming man's obvious attempts to woo her, despite her better judgment?

"Well, in that case. . ." He paused to meaningfully clear his throat, his smile taking on the nuance of victory. "Would you mind if I tagged along when you go to my brother's? I'd like to visit with Travis while you're tending to Rachel's physical needs."

"Of course. That's understandable. But I'm afraid that you may overdo. You're not that strong yet. You still need plenty of rest." Maggie attempted to sound coldly professional in hopes of masking the quiver in her voice. But the thought of sitting next to him in a buggy left her feeling anything but coldly professional.

"I'll be fine," he said, that flirtatious grin ever in place. "What man wouldn't be with a lady like you at his side?"

"Levi—" She gripped the counter once again and watched the steam rising off the breakfast dishes. "*Don't*," she said firmly. "I already told you. . . I–I. . .there are things you don't know—things better left unsaid. Please honor my request to keep our interactings professional." Doing her best to present him with a stony stare, she silently demanded he discontinue his pursuit of her.

A gray disappointment washed across Levi's features, snuffing out the glow of expectation, molding his grin into a disheartened wilt. "Of course," he said as if she had slapped him. "I'll abide by your wishes, Miss Alexander."

"Thank you, Mr. Campbell," she replied stiffly, although her heart ached with the pain so evident in his eyes. "I'll retrieve my things and head over to the livery for Doc's horse and buggy. All I have is an opened wagon, and we'll need his covered buggy for protection against the sun. I'll meet you out front in, say, ten minutes. Does that sound agreeable to you?"

"I'll be there," Levi said solemnly.

Chapter 9

Within thirty minutes, Levi had settled his belongings at the boardinghouse, much to the pleasure of Mrs. Baker, whom he fully delighted. Magnolia and Levi then rode in silence to the constable's office, where she tethered the horse to the hitching post. As Maggie surreptitiously observed Levi climbing from the carriage, her heart beat with regret. Regret that her circumstances prevented the slightest chance of a relationship with the poetic cowboy. Even now, as he stepped onto the boardwalk, Magnolia knew she would never forget him. Never. Even if she lived to be ninety and the whole frontier separated them. Levi Campbell would be indelibly etched upon her memory. He hadn't so much as looked her way since those tense moments in the kitchen. And even as he pushed open the lawman's door, Levi maintained an impassive face and emotional distance. But wasn't that what she wanted?

The temperature inside the windowless building was significantly cooler due to its thick concrete walls. With the smells of mildew encompassing her, Maggie felt as if the cool air penetrated straight to her heart. Levi was indeed giving her what she had insisted upon for their relationship, but Maggie ached with his conformity to her demands. Part of her much preferred the dapper winks and adoring smile to this indifference. Nevertheless, her common sense demanded that the more formal their relationship, the safer.

Levi cleared his throat in an attempt to awaken the dozing constable, who leaned back in his chair with his feet propped on the desk. Uncle Cahill's old coonhound, Ruff, jumped up from a worn rag rug beside the constable's desk and woofed an excited greeting to Maggie, his familiar friend. The hound's tail flipped furiously as he barked. Startled from the catnap, Parker jumped. Rubbing his eyes, he slowly stood and produced a sheepish smile.

"It's been a long night," he said through a yawn.

"Do you have word on the bandits?" Levi asked.

"Word? Son, ain't you heard? We nabbed 'em last night!" The constable broke into a grin. "That's what they get for dependin' on the bottle too hard. Best I can figure, they came into town durin' the night because they had to have some whiskey. And that stuff made 'em lose all good judgment." The wall lantern's flickering shadows only increased the intensity of the lines, etching his weathered face.

A sense of both expectation and dread engulfed Magnolia. Were these the bandits who killed her uncle?

"Thanks to the keen nose of ol' Ruff here. . . ." The constable stooped to give the panting dog a scratch behind his ears. "I not only caught me the two women who we suspect held up the train, but I nabbed a third suspicious character as well. I figure he's the man you saw leaving the saloon with the redhead, Levi. He was holed up with those gals in a cave along White Woman Creek. Believe it or not, he used to be a deputy in Dallas, and I've got a "Wanted" poster for his return. Seems he used his influence as a lawman to help himself to some of the bank's money. I wouldn't be surprised if he was the mastermind behind all their evil schemes."

Maggie reeled with the implications. Her mind racing, she stared at the hodgepodge of "Wanted" posters lining one of the whitewashed walls. Uncle Cahill's murderer was an ex-lawman. This could very well be the beginnings of the process that she dreaded. The trial of her uncle's attacker. The revelation of Cahill Alexander's true identity. The loss of her good standing among the community. Her empty stomach twisted in nausea.

With the toe of his boot, the constable slid a tray full of dirty dishes from his path and approached Maggie and Levi. "I tell you what, those three put up quite a fight. I waited 'til they were sleepin' and took their guns away. But even unarmed, it was like corallin' bobcats to capture 'em." All traces of exhaustion left the lawman as he recounted the thrill of his most recent chase.

"I believe that," Levi said dryly. "Those two women are about the toughest two females I've ever met in my life."

"You feel up to identifying them?" The wiry constable paused to scrutinize Levi. "I didn't think for one minute to ask how you're doin'. Has that doctor turned you out now?"

"Yes. And I'm well on the mend. Enough that I'd like to take a look at those bandits. The sooner I make sure you've nabbed the right ones, the easier I can rest."

Grunting his approval, Constable Parker grabbed a brass key ring from its peg on the side of his desk. Motioning for Levi and Maggie to follow, he walked to the locked ironware door separating the jail cells from the outer office.

"Maggie, you can come along, too. I'd like you to see if you recognize any of 'em. I have a hunch you might of seen 'em around your place before."

Reluctantly, she joined Levi behind the constable as he inserted the key and turned the lock with an abundance of squeaks and clatters. "You know, it's a good thing the folks of Dogwood had enough sense to build two jail cells instead of one. This isn't the first time I've had 'em both filled," the lawman announced as he shoved open the creaking door and led the way into the dimly lighted quarters.

Immediately, Maggie's nostrils flared with the invasion of a repugnant stench. She looked to Levi, whose repulsed expression matched her own reaction. Two creatures bearing only a slight resemblance to females sat on the cots in the first cell. Neither bothered to look up as the trio entered the corridor in front of their cubicle.

Someone had hung a curtain to provide a modicum of privacy between their cell and the next one, where a solitary man lay on his cot, staring at the ceiling. Intent on examining the prisoners, Maggie crunched across something that felt like gravel and glue under her high-topped shoes. She glanced down to see shards of a shattered pottery bowl mixed with lumps of drying, gray oatmeal.

As distasteful a sight as the oatmeal presented, Magnolia turned her attention to the man. Her knees trembling, she attempted to find one thing familiar about him. But the lean angles of his granitelike face were those of a stranger. The only evidence against him would be her uncle's claim that his murderer was once a lawman.

A new rush of nausea assaulted Maggie. Nausea, accompanied by panic. She would be forced to read Uncle Cahill's letter in court. There would be no other way to convict the man who murdered him. And in convicting the murderer, Maggie would also be stating her own sentence. A sentence of shame. A sentence of scandal. A sentence of solitude.

"Whatcha botherin' us for?" one of the female creatures snarled. Her flame red hair, an unkempt mass of tangles, cascaded down her back as she glared at them. She tilted her head and spit a stream of tobacco on the floor near the iron bars. Her mud-crusted shirt and jeans looked as if she had been wearing them a year. "You'd think they ain't never seen the likes of a lady before," she mocked.

Her grimy cell mate produced a sarcastic snort and shoved a handful of dark, oily hair from her face.

"I wanted to give these folks a chance to see if y'all are the ones who've done 'em such harm," Constable Parker barked, looking toward Levi for confirmation.

Levi produced an affirmative nod.

"The gentleman here, you may recall, is the guy you shot and threw from the train. And his lady companion, why, her only livin' relative was murdered, and I suspect one or all of ya were in on it."

"We ain't no murderers," groused the redhead. Her companion cast a snake-eyed stare at Maggie as her partner in crime continued. "I told you before, we don't know nothin' about no murders. We was only tryin' to hold up the train. We needed some cash to make our way out to California. We didn't even aim to really hurt this feller. He just got in our way."

"Well, you admit to that, at least," the constable threw back. "That alone should make the circuit judge's trip worth his while. But your companion there ain't uttered a word yet, and you'll have to do some pretty fast talkin' to convince the judge the three of ya weren't the ones to kill Cahill Alexander."

"I'll tell you again and again, we didn't kill nobody," the redhead growled.

"Yeah, yeah. That's just what I'd expect you to say. I'd probably say the same if I were lookin' at swingin' from a hangman's noose."

Magnolia felt the scrutiny of their masculine partner, and she cringed as she met his gaze through the wall lantern's flickering shadows. He evaluated her in a most forward and lewd manner. . .in a manner that suggested he had seen her before. . .in a manner that made her thankful the good Lord had prevented her from being at the farm the day of her uncle's murder. Certainly, this dastardly creature must have been the ex-lawman her uncle mentioned. There could be no other explanation.

"Circuit Judge Hamilton should be through here in a couple of weeks, Levi," Parker said. "The trial shouldn't take long. I'm assumin' you're planning on being in these parts till then?"

"Yes."

The evil man's lecherous perusal added to the evilness radiating from the lawless trio and thoroughly repulsed Maggie. She rushed back into the outer office. The revolting odor following her, Magnolia hurried past the constable's desk to the front door. Flinging it open, she stepped outside and inhaled great gulps of the warm morning air. The resignation that she would soon be forced to share Uncle Cahill's humiliating secrets only added to her distress.

Who was this ex-lawman turned bad? Uncle Cahill said he no longer went by the name Dallas Blankenship. Was that the name on his "Wanted" poster? She debated how best to inquire of the constable concerning these matters without giving away her uncle's disgraceful history.

"Are you all right?" Levi asked from close behind. The light hand on her left shoulder spoke of the concern in his voice, a concern that broke through all of Magnolia's tumultuous musings. Levi. Levi Campbell. He was a kind man. A considerate man. A man who would willingly take her heart, were she to extend it. Should she confide in him? Should she burden his broad shoulders with her growing problems? Would he indeed reject her as she had previously assumed?

The morning's humidity combined with the tornado of varying, tumultuous thoughts caused her pulse to pound in her temples, and she passionately hoped this wasn't the beginning of one of her blinding headaches. *Oh, Lord, guide me. Please show me the right thing to do,* Maggie pleaded as she turned to face Levi.

"Fine. I'm fine," she answered. "The whole thing just got to be too much for me."

"If that rascal wasn't behind bars, I'd have thrashed him," Levi said through clenched teeth.

Maggie's cheeks heated at the thought that Levi understood what the horrid man had been thinking. Not daring to raise her gaze above his shirt's top button, she muttered a polite, although embarrassed "thank you."

Constable Parker arrived at their side. "I'm sorry if that was too much for ya, Miss Maggie," he said, a father's concern in his eyes. "But I had to know if you might recognize that man."

"To my knowledge, I've never seen him before," Maggie replied, groping for any natural way to inquire about seeing the man's "Wanted" poster. "But. . . I was wonderin'. . . ," she hedged.

The constable raised his bushy, graying brows.

"Would it be possible for me to see his 'Wanted' poster. It might. . .might give me a better. . .better idea of his features. The cell was rather shadowed, and. . ." At least that was true. Perhaps she might recognize him once she saw a clear drawing. Groping for any possibilities, she held her breath as Parker produced the "Wanted" poster.

"Here 'tis," the constable said as he stepped onto the boardwalk.

Anxiously, she pored over the unfamiliar image, then traced her finger along the list of six aliases. The name "Dallas Blankenship" was not mentioned. However, the fact that he had used six other assumed names left her concluding that he must have dreamed up a few pseudonyms that were left off the poster.

Feeling the men watching her, Magnolia shook her head. "I can't say that I've ever seen him before, Constable." Cautiously, she glanced at the lawman, who suspiciously eyed her. Maggie, fatigued from the whole ordeal, turned her back on the office. Lifting her moiré skirt, she stepped off the boardwalk and headed toward the doctor's black carriage.

The men's congenial adieus did little to disrupt Maggie's heavy deliberation. Never had she been so trapped between decisions—decisions that would alter her life and the life of another. Pausing by the doctor's hooded buggy, she contemplated her options. If she read Uncle Cahill's letter in court, that man in the jail cell would undoubtedly hang, and Maggie's reputation would hang with him. If she didn't read the letter. . . She squelched the very notion and made her final decision. Magnolia would do what was right, what was lawful. She would read the letter. She would also begin considering the possibilities of leaving Dogwood, for after the trial, she would assuredly be stripped of her glowing reputation.

She began embarking the carriage, only to have Levi gently grip her upper arm. Too emotionally spent to stop him, Magnolia allowed his assistance and settled on the padded bench. When he untethered the horse, Magnolia scolded herself for forgetting that simple task.

"Are you sure you're all right, Magnolia?" he asked. Walking back to her side, he placed the reins in her hands.

Her pulse quickened with the natural way Levi had fallen back into addressing her by her given name. "Yes. I'm fine. I'll be fine."

Levi walked around the buggy, pulled himself up with his good arm, and settled beside her. "We don't have to visit Travis's place just yet. I'm certain the doctor would understand if you—"

"No. My professional obligations lie with Rachel now. I mustn't let Dr. Engle down."

"If only you were as concerned about letting me down," he said, his barely discernible voice taking on the subtleties of poetry.

His words of adoration tugged Magnolia ever closer to the point of casting aside all her perfectly sensible reasons for not capitulating to Levi's romantic intentions. But her momentary vacillation was soon swept aside by her fears. Her fears of trusting. Her fears of his abandonment.

"Mr. Campbell," she snapped, turning to face him. But instead of words of rebuttal, only silence settled between them. Silence, and the enchantment of a man thoroughly smitten. Maggie gulped as Levi's focus hungrily settled upon her lips.

"Magnolia?" he whispered.

Under his hypnotic gaze, Maggie forgot they were sitting on Dogwood's Main Street. And her earlier, immodest musings about what his lips might feel like against hers rushed back, more potent than before. As if an invisible current tugged her toward him, Maggie leaned forward, only a breath of an inch. Levi's eyes widened as he gently reached to stroke her check. An explosion of tingles cascaded down her neck. A new depth of awareness. A sudden realization that shaking Levi Campbell might be much harder than she had ever imagined.

The sound of slowing footsteps jolted Magnolia back to reality—back to the fact that they were, indeed, sitting in clear view of public eyes. When she glanced toward the boardwalk to see to whom the footsteps belonged, the vexed Magnolia wanted to faint with mortification. For the buxom, ruddy-cheeked Bess Tucker gawked as if she had caught Levi actually kissing Maggie.

Compressing her lips, Magnolia tugged the reins to the left, and the horse responded with a jolt. Curtly, she nodded toward Bess and could only imagine what the quilting rings would be saying by the week's end. Skillfully, Maggie guided the carriage past Dogwood's familiar landmarks and into the tunnel of trees that covered the lane leading to the Campbell farm. As a child, Maggie had ridden down this road countless times, nestled by her uncle Cahill's side. Despite the tension still vibrating between her and Levi, a sense of deep comfort settled over Maggie. A sense of knowing that Uncle Cahill would have liked Levi Campbell.

But what does that matter? a pragmatic voice demanded. *Uncle Cahill was a former outlaw who lied to you. You couldn't trust him, and you can't trust Levi!*

But a softer voice suggested, *You have not once prayed about the Lord's will in your acquaintance with Levi. Why not relinquish your fears to God?*

Thus, the conflicting thoughts raged war within Magnolia. As they approached the farm of her childhood, she longed more than ever to feel

Levi's strong arms around her, to share her anxieties with this wounded hero who had attempted to stand between two bandits and the train passengers. Would a man of such valor be the sort to abandon a woman whom he cared for because of her family's scandalous background?

No, but neither did Uncle Cahill seem an ex-criminal! You mustn't trust again!

Overcome with the internal turmoil, Magnolia realized she would be of no use whatsoever to Rachel in her current state of internal upheaval. She needed to calm her raging emotions and resume her professional demeanor before approaching the distraught mother whose infant had died. She knew only one source that could calm her nerves.

"We're. . .we're coming to Uncle Cahill's farm. W–would you mind if we paused there for just a moment?" she stammered. Simply addressing Levi seemed to bring back that moment when he had stroked her cheek. "Travis and Rachel's ranch is just around the bend, and. . .and I would like to seek a moment. . .moment of prayer before approachin' Rachel. I. . .I need nothing short of divine wisdom. I can't imagine what she must feel like."

"Certainly," Levi replied as naturally as if he had never thought of kissing her. "I'd enjoy seeing where you grew up."

At last they reached the scenic lane leading to the Alexander farm, and Maggie guided the horse onto the circular drive. She brought the buggy to a halt between the yard full of pines and the porch on which she had often sat while listening to the pond frogs and whippoorwills' melodious chorus. Before she could gather her skirts to disembark, Levi clamored from the buggy, rounded the back, and appeared at her side, his left hand extended, his gaze as ardent as it had been in town.

Magnolia wavered between accepting his proffered help and unceremoniously scrambling out on the opposite side. But Levi stepped nearer and gently wrapped her hand in the warmth of his. Her grip on the reins relaxed. The flames in her soul glowed ever the brighter. And she regarded only one man. . . one longing. . .one possibility. The man: Levi Campbell. The longing: Maggie desired his kiss, desired the assurance of his strong arms, despite all better judgment. The possibility: Levi possessed every intent of continuing that magic moment that started in town.

As she descended the buggy with his assistance, each second turned to a moment of mystery. A moment of expectation. A moment of enchantment. She stepped to the ground and stood only inches from him. Magnolia peered upward to once more see his gaze trail to her lips.

"Magnolia. . . ," he whispered. "I—"

With the mocking birds frolicking in the pines, she leaned forward but a fraction, yet enough to grant Levi full permission to wrap his arm around her and tug her closer. Maggie felt as if the world itself stopped spinning in that mystical moment. And she sensed. . .she sensed she was coming home. Home, to Levi's open arms.

Gingerly, he tightened his left arm around her, pulling Maggie as close as the sling would allow. "Ah, Magnolia," he whispered against her ear. "How often have I dreamed of this very moment. . .of holding you. . .of the softness of your hair against my cheek. . . ," he uttered as if he were reading the most elegant of poems. "And. . .and I know you—for whatever reason—you have become unsure of me."

Magnolia swallowed hard, her eyes filling with the warm waters of misgivings. "I'm just so scared," she rasped.

"Yes, I know. I see it every time I look at you, but if you could just bring yourself to tell me why, I—"

Abruptly, she tore herself from his embrace. And with a broken sob, Maggie ran. She ran from the dread of telling Levi the truth. She ran from the horror that he might reject her once he knew of her uncle's dishonorable past. She ran from the gentle voice that again insisted she should pray and trust. . . trust and pray. Yet her distant point of destination ironically became the apple orchard, the one place of solitude where she had met the Lord on many glorious occasions. Perhaps that gentle voice was right. Perhaps Maggie's answer to all of her turmoil lay in the embrace of Jesus.

However, the presence of a lone horseman, cantering up the lane, distracted Maggie from her goal, and she immediately stopped. Biting her bottom lip, she forced the tears into abeyance and scrubbed against her cheeks, attempting to gain control of her raw emotions before addressing Jed Sweeney.

Chapter 10

I was hoping I'd find you here, Miss Alexander." Jed Sweeney reined his ebony steed to a restless stop within feet of Magnolia. His shoulder-length black hair hung in feathery wisps under a black derby that rested lightly over his brow. Sweeney was a tall, lean man with broad shoulders. In his white, starched shirt and black riding britches, he could have easily been taken for a banker or lawyer, save the length of his hair and the measured way he bit into the ever present pencil-thin cigar.

With her hand, she shaded her eyes against the midmorning sun and noticed Sweeney's keen eyes taking in the carriage and Levi. He most certainly had seen Maggie running, and she couldn't help but wonder what he must think. Swiftly, her mind trailed to Louella. . .to her plight. . .to the cold-hearted manner with which Jed Sweeney had dismissed her.

"What can I help you with, Mr. Sweeney?" Magnolia asked, her defensive tones reflecting her displeasure of his interactings with Louella.

Sweeney's right brow arched. "I simply wanted to discuss my former offer to buy your estate," he said precisely.

"I'm not sure. . .not sure I still. . .still want to sell it." *Especially not to you,* she added to herself. The fact that the man owned a string of saloons had certainly been a mark against him. But the longer Magnolia considered his kicking out the destitute Louella, the more she wanted to find another buyer.

"Miss Alexander, have I in some way offended you?" Sweeney leaned against his saddle horn, his lips twisting with a hint of mockery.

The crunch of Levi's footfalls just behind Maggie preceded his supportive hand on her shoulder by only seconds. His touch gave her the courage she needed to defend Louella. "No, you have done nothing to me personally, but you certainly offended a friend of mine—Louella Simpson."

Once more his brow arched, and he took a long draw on the cigar before removing it from his teeth. As he studied the smoking tip, he exhaled a thin stream of smoke past thin lips.

"From what I understand," Maggie continued as the pungent odor of cigar smoke encircled her, "you dismissed her on the spot without so much as giving her the money she was rightly due." Fully expecting a heated retort, Magnolia braced herself, and Levi's grip on her shoulder increased.

Sweeney looked up from the cigar, a calculating, although humorous, gleam in his eyes. "So if I pay Louella Simpson, will you reconsider my offer?"

"I. . ." Never expecting Sweeney's ready cooperation, Maggie stared at him in disbelief. "I. . ."

"I'm a fair man, Miss Alexander," Sweeney said. Taking a final draw on the cigar, he tossed it onto the road and exhaled the smoke toward the west pasture. "The problem with *Mizz Louella* was that she and that weak-kneed manager of mine had hidden her pregnancy from me for months. I don't come through often, and she had managed to stay behind that bar when I was there. But I have a few rules concerning the people I employ—and my rules don't allow *pregnant* women. It ain't right for a pregnant woman to be working in a saloon. It's bad for her and bad for business."

A bit flustered with his improper use of such a word, Maggie looked at his horse's well-manicured hooves and couldn't believe for one second that Jed Sweeney cared at all about Louella's well-being.

"Excuse me for interrupting. . ." Removing his hand from her shoulder, Levi stepped to Maggie's side, his tone suggesting he didn't appreciate the saloon owner's language any more than Magnolia did. "But I am now considering the purchase of Miss Alexander's property. I'm sure she will let you know if she reconsiders your offer."

Shocked by Levi's words, Magnolia forced herself to stare at her fingers, now intertwined in a tight knot.

Silence followed. The kind of silence that suggests mute fury. Maggie looked up to see Sweeney's eyes narrowed to thin slits. All humor, all mockery were replaced by rage. "I offered first," he growled.

"Mr. Sweeney, I never promised I'd sell to you," Maggie claimed.

As slow as a listless copperhead, Sweeney reached into his breast pocket and pulled out a brass money clip, holding a thick stack of bills. With the flip of his wrist, he coldly tossed a ten-dollar bill onto the ground between them. "That's more than enough to make *Mizz Louella* happy," he said in an expressionless tone, which belied the anger, still stirring his eyes. "I'll be by the boardinghouse Monday in hopes that you'll change your mind about the estate." He disdainfully observed the injured Levi. "Takes money to buy a spread like this, Miss Alexander, and many times a hopeful buyer can't pull together the funds. Might better reconsider my offer while I'm in the buying vein." Without another word, he yanked the stallion's reins to the left and galloped back toward the road.

"We need to continue our journey to your brother's ranch," Magnolia said, grabbing the ten-dollar bill and marching toward the buggy before Levi had a chance to so much as utter one word.

❖

Narrowing his eyes, Levi watched her stiffly mount the buggy and turn an expressionless, blue gaze his way, as if she were impatiently awaiting him to follow. So much had happened in this journey with Magnolia that he felt as if he needed at least two nights on the range to sort it all out. He thought about that blasted wall she had erected between them. Somehow, that little lady had managed to get scared stiff of any kind of a relationship. She had only made vague references of something to do with her family. Levi wondered if it all related to her uncle's murder.

Nevertheless, he recalled the moments she had let down her guard. She had enjoyed his winking at her that very morning. Levi reveled in the memory of her in his arms, and his pulse quickened with the expectation of a possible commitment in the future. For during all those long hours Levi had lain in that doctor's bed, he had prayed. He had prayed as he had never prayed in his life. And, he at last came to the conclusion that Miss Magnolia Alexander was the answer to his prayers for a godly wife. But Levi had also felt a heavenly caution that these things take time. He shouldn't rush Magnolia. He *wouldn't* rush Magnolia. Levi would continue praying, continue chipping away, bit by bit, at that wall of hers. Continue in tenacious persistence. Magnolia might not realize it, but Levi Campbell had chased stray doggies across the plains longer than he had chased her.

He produced what he hoped was his most engaging smile and stepped toward Magnolia, perched upon that buggy. But he paused and glanced back toward the lane, toward the place where Jed Sweeney had disappeared from view. With a knot of dislike forming in his gut, Levi decided he would purchase this place before allowing the likes of that hardened saloon owner to buy the home where Magnolia grew up. And what that Sweeney fellow didn't know was that Levi had more than enough money in his trust fund to pay for the estate. The plan hatching in his mind left him smiling all the broader. He would buy Magnolia's old home place. Then, he would win her heart.

During the fifteen-minute journey to Travis and Rachel's ranch, Levi chose to remain silent. He stared straight ahead at the rutted lane. He never once gave Magnolia cause for discomfort, although Levi felt her discomfort—felt it as thick as that bitter brew he and Dr. Engle enjoyed that morning. Only one fact stopped Levi from drowning in confusion over Magnolia's vacillating responses to him. She *did enjoy* his embrace. Levi only had to somehow break through that stone bulwark she continued to erect between them.

"There's Travis and Rachel's place—just up ahead." Maggie pointed toward a new white barn rising above the pasture where four Appaloosas grazed. Near the barn, Levi caught glimpses of a ranch house with a broad front porch.

"Travis wrote us about the barn burning and all the trouble Rachel had with that horrible neighbor. But looks like they did a fine job of buildin' a new barn." Thankful for any topic of conversation that he could share with Magnolia, Levi admired the lush, green countryside and rolling pastures. "You know, in Travis's letters, he said the place looked like a green paradise, but it's mighty strange to see rolling hills and all these trees in Texas. Around El Paso, all we have are flatlands."

"Local folks have reason to boast about the scenery." As she turned the horses onto the lane leading to the ranch house, now clearly in view, Maggie thoughtfully appraised the land, a faint wisp of indecision flitting across her features. "I do love the home where I grew up," she said wistfully. "I only wish I had the skills to run a ranch. . . ."

"I meant what I said back there, Magnolia," Levi said. "I would be honored for you to sell your uncle's property to me."

Startled, she observed him as if she were searching for any traces of teasing. "But there's over two hundred and fifty acres there. . .and all the cattle. . . and the crops and the whole thing is worth. . .is worth. . ."

He shrugged and produced the most flirtatious smile he could conjure up. "I've lived with cows most of my life, remember? Two hundred and

371

fifty acres is a drop in the bucket compared to the size of my pa's ranch, and—"

A spark of ire flashed in her eyes.

"I'm not trying to belittle your holdin' in any way, now. It's a simple fact, that's all. And another simple fact is, I'll pay you top dollar. I can have the cash here by next week. There's nothin' I'd love more than ownin' a little east Texas ranch right next to my big brother's." Even as the words left his mouth, Levi wondered at his meaning. Two years ago, the last thing he would have ever wanted was to live by his older, "perfect" brother. But perhaps during this trip the Lord was helping him come to final terms with the remaining traces of jealousy left over from childhood. Even if their father couldn't quiet understand Levi's bent to poetry, his need for quietude, his desire to pen his own poems and essays, he and Levi had grown closer in the year since Travis's absence. A closeness that had resulted in the elder Campbell bequeathing Levi an equal share in the Campbell ranch with Travis.

As if Levi had never made the offer, Maggie silently guided the carriage to a stop near the expansive, white barn. With Travis trudging toward them from the rolling pasture, Levi hoped her silence stemmed from surprised consideration of his earnest offer and not from a bent to reject him.

Levi disembarked the carriage as a red-eyed Travis approached his brother's side. The only other time Levi had ever known Travis to cry was at the death of their grandfather. Truly, the loss of that baby must be eating him up. Levi's own eyes stung at the sight of his elder brother's pain. Once again, an ocean of guilt lapped against the sands of his soul. The news of the miscarriage had come on the heels of a round of envious thoughts concerning Travis, the same types of thoughts that had plagued Levi his whole life. Yet Travis had never done anything to purposefully evoke Levi to jealousy. Levi didn't even think Travis knew about the resentment. And at that moment, standing beside his elder brother, Levi vowed that with God's help he would forever divorce himself from the mental rivalry that had plagued him since birth.

"Miss Maggie." Removing his straw hat, Travis nodded toward the lady as Levi assisted her descent with his free hand. "Thanks for coming out. I know Rachel will enjoy your company. Her cousin, Angela Isaacs, is here now—"

"Yes, I know Angela well," Maggie said respectfully. "I don't know that there's much I can do. . .or say, but you and Rachel have been such a great source of support for me during my own loss, that I feel I just have to be here for you."

"We appreciate you more than you can ever know," Travis said.

She dimpled into a supportive smile. "Well, if you'll excuse me, then. . ."

With admiration flooding his every fiber, Levi watched Maggie cross the farmyard, gather her skirt, and climb the three steps onto the porch. The moment the creaky front door closed behind her, Levi turned to his elder sibling to catch an inquisitive glint in Travis's eyes, still hazy with grief.

"So the rumors around town are right?"

Magnolia faintly tapped on Rachel's closed bedroom door. "Hello, Rachel?" she called gently. "It's me, Maggie. May I come in?"

A familiar face appeared on the other side of the door. "Rachel's asleep right now," Angela Isaacs whispered, "but do come in." Her chestnut-colored hair and freckled nose attested to Angela and Rachel's kinship. But that's where the cousins' similarities ended. While Rachel was fiery, Angela had always been more reclining. Angela, slender and tall, carried herself gracefully, but seemed to dwarf the petite Rachel when the two stood side by side.

Magnolia stepped into the room to see the lace curtains waving in front of the numerous bedroom windows. The large wicker fan lying on the foot of Rachel's bed attested to Angela's having fanned her cousin while she slept.

"How is she doing, Angela?" Maggie asked.

"Well, she cried herself to sleep." Angela paused to blink back the tears. "But I believe the elixir Dr. Engle left this morning has helped her sleep in peace now for the first time since the labor started last night. She's been asleep a couple of hours now."

"Bless her," Maggie said, astounded at how drawn Rachel's pale face appeared. And the bright sunshine spilling through the windows only highlighted the dark circles marring her eyes. Once again, Maggie was reminded that she didn't hold the exclusive rights to trouble. About a year ago, Rachel's father had died, leaving her alone to tend to this expansive land. Now, she and Travis had lost their first child—a little girl, according to Dr. Engle.

"Is there to be a funeral?" Magnolia asked.

"No. Travis and Dr. Engle buried the baby this morning, out in the pasture, under one of the trees."

"And Rachel? Did she see the baby?"

Angela nodded, her eyes filling with tears.

The patient stirred, and Magnolia stepped to her side to notice dots of perspiration along Rachel's forehead. "Are there some damp cloths for her face? She looks terribly hot."

"Yes," Angela said, moving to the door. "Travis just brought in a fresh bucket of cold well water not long ago. I'll go get some of it and bring some fresh cloths as well."

"Magnolia?" Rachel breathed, restlessly stirring.

"Yes, I'm here." Maggie knelt beside the feather bed and encircled Rachel's hand within her own.

At last, Rachel opened her eyes to look up at Maggie with doelike agony. "It w–was a little. . .little girl," she said, tears dampening her cheeks.

Remembering her own mother's pain-filled inscriptions about the deaths of her twin sons, Maggie nodded. Somehow, being with Rachel at this moment gave Maggie a sense of connection with the mother she had never known.

"Dr. Engle has–has been like a–a father to me." Rachel's voice cracked as she wrinkled her brows.

"I think he's like a father to most of Dogwood, Rachel," Maggie said. "He's a wonderful, wonderful man."

"Yes. . .but I–I can tell when–when he's withholdin' bad news. I'm afraid there's somethin' t–terribly wrong. That–that perhaps I won't ever be able–able to have children. It's just this h–horrible feelin' I have that I can't—I can't get over."

Wondering what she should say, Maggie grappled with an appropriate reply. As usual, the stirrings of inadequacy plagued her. *How much should I tell her? Exactly how sure is Dr. Engle that Rachel mustn't try to bear children?* At last, Maggie decided that now was certainly not the time to share more disheartening news with the devastated Rachel.

"I'm not as. . .as experienced with these types of things as Dr. Engle, but. . .but he wouldn't have left you this morning if he didn't think you were going to be fine. He'll be back out to check on you before dark this evening. You can tell him your concerns then. I'm sure he'll be glad to answer all your questions. Right now, you just need to focus on recovering." Maggie gripped Rachel's hand all the tighter and hoped the patient didn't push for more information concerning the dim prognosis.

Spiritlessly, Rachel stared out one of the open windows. "I know I sh–shouldn't doubt the–the Lord, Maggie," she said, her voice gaining strength the more she talked. "But I think I must be the worst doubter in the world. Sometimes I just don't understand why He allows all the sufferin' and. . .and death. I didn't think I'd ever get over Pa's death. Now. . .now this!" She turned imploring eyes to Maggie. "Doesn't the Lord think we would make good parents? Is there something I've done wrong? I want a baby more than anything. And if. . .if—just supposin' I can't—I'll feel as if I've let Travis down in the worst of ways."

"Yes, I understand, but. . .I'm sure the Lord will somehow. . ." Maggie didn't know what to say. So fresh were her own questions about God and life that she could do nothing but hold Rachel's hand and silently support this childhood friend. "I'll certainly keep you in my prayers," Maggie encouraged. "If. . .if you'll remember me as well."

Rachel nodded in understanding. "We can be a support to one. . .one another." Her head tilted to the side. Her heavy eyes closed. And her breathing became more steady.

Praying for Rachel's strength and her own wisdom, Magnolia thoughtfully observed her friend slipping into the folds of sleep. And with the cattle's soft lowing flowing through the opened windows, an idea, like a tiny cloud, presented itself on the horizon of her mind. At a breathtaking pace, that cloud gained size. . .size and definite plausibility.

Louella Simpson was due to give birth very soon. She had no idea what she was going to do once the baby arrived. She had no means of supporting the child. She even said that returning to her hometown would heap ridicule upon her mother and herself. So she couldn't even go back home. But just suppose. . .just suppose Louella loved her child so much she would be willing to place it in Rachel's welcoming arms? Precious few people in Dogwood knew about Louella. Only key people had privy to the fact that Rachel had even miscarried. Rachel and Travis could very easily accept Louella's baby as their own, and the child would never bear the shame of the label "illegitimate." No one in Dogwood need ever know the child was adopted.

The sound of Angela entering the room disrupted Maggie's thoughts, but by no means dismissed the exciting possibilities. . .if only Louella would agree.

"I'm sorry it took so long," Angela said in her usually tranquil tones. "But Travis and his brother. . .um. . ." She squinted as if she were searching for his name.

"Levi," Maggie supplied while Angela poured the cool water into the stoneware washing bowl on the bedside table.

"Yes, Levi." Angela's brown eyes glittered with the romantic speculations that Magnolia had seen all over town. Was no one in Dogwood left without knowledge of Magnolia's personal life? "The two of them were inquiring concerning Rachel," the schoolteacher said. Her words, as precise as always, reflected her studious nature and the academic excellence to which she pushed her students.

"I'm so hot," Rachel muttered, stirring from her light sleep.

Maggie dipped one of the clean, although stained, cloths into the well's icy water and gently patted Rachel's forehead.

"Thank you," Rachel mumbled. Taking the cloth from Maggie, she stroked her neck and cheeks as well. "It's so p–powerfully hot today." She produced a languid smile, which hinted at her usually playful nature. "I heard you. . .talking about Levi," she said, her voice once more gaining strength with each word she spoke. "Angela, Levi is c–courting Maggie. Did you know?"

Shocked, Magnolia glanced from Rachel to the speculative Angela and back to Rachel.

"We're–we're going to be sisters-in-law, I think," Rachel continued.

"Yes, that's what I hear," Angela said in a scheming voice. "Yesterday at the quilting bee—"

"We *aren't courting,*" Maggie blurted, recalling Levi's brief embrace, which suggested the opposite.

"Then may. . .maybe he'll court Angela." Rachel's feeble wink left Maggie glad to see some of the redhead's spunk, although her chagrin increased all the more.

"Even from her sickbed, she torments me," Angela said. "I'm an old maid, and I will remain that way all my years. I'll probably go to my death before trusting a man again."

"Ah, Angela, one d–day somebody as good as my Trav's gonna come along and. . .and make you forget you ever said that." Rachel raised her head, and Maggie automatically placed another pillow behind her. Perhaps the patient would even feel like sipping some broth for her noon meal.

Glancing toward the blanching Angela, Maggie recalled the tragic story beneath the sudden stoniness in her eyes. She had been jilted ten years before, when Maggie was still in adolescence. Now thirty, the mildly attractive schoolteacher stood little chance at matrimony, and spinsterhood apparently suited her.

Trust. Trust. Trust. The word reverberated through Maggie's mind like an annoying chant. In recent days, she had experienced much of what she now saw in Angela's eyes. Disillusionment. Betrayal. Suspicion of all mankind. But was that any way to live? In the deepest recesses of her soul, a still, small voice urged Maggie to relinquish all the anger, all the betrayal, all the uncertainties to the Lord.

Chapter 11

After the noon meal, Maggie guided the sorrel mare toward Dogwood, past Uncle Cahill's estate, past neighboring farms, across the lush, rolling hills. Maggie didn't say a word to Levi, who likewise maintained a distant silence. The tension of their other encounters seemed to have eased into companionable serenity. Certainly, Magnolia was beginning to comprehend that she must come to terms with some of the negative feelings that had flooded her soul upon learning of her uncle's betrayal. But even now, her heart burned with anger at the man who had raised her in the bowels of deception.

As they approached the lane leading to the Dogwood community church, she turned to her quiet traveling companion. His drawn face attested to the seriousness of the wound from which he still recovered. "I know you are tired, Levi, but could we pause for just a moment so I can visit Uncle Cahill's grave? I. . .there are some things I feel I need to talk to the Lord about."

"I think that's a good idea." His expectant gaze caressed her as a hint of a smile played on his face. "After your delicious lunch and that catnap, I'm feeling fit as a fiddle."

"Are you sure? You're looking a bit tired."

"I'm fine. You just do whatever you need to do." His grin increased to the dapper variety, and Magnolia wondered if he might be going to wink at her again.

The serenity they had just shared was dashed aside by the fresh tension now wedging itself between them. Maggie relived their brief embrace from only hours before. All the yearning, which had built from the moment she met Levi, descended upon her with renewed intensity. Before discovering Uncle Cahill's deception, Maggie had vaguely wondered if God were placing Levi in her life. But as late as this morning, Maggie had doubted Levi's constancy, were he to learn of Uncle Cahill's shameful past. Immediately, Angela Isaac's stony, distrustful face ingrained itself upon Maggie's mind. Was that the kind of lonely life she wanted? As she steered the mares toward the white, steepled church, she accepted the fact that she needed God's guidance, His healing, as never before.

A hushed tranquillity enveloped the churchyard when Maggie pulled the horse to a halt. The white house of worship thrust its steeple toward the cloudless blue sky as if to point all who passed to the holy creator. A warm breeze stirred the summer heat and wafted the smells of bitterweeds and pines across the green hills. Intent on soaking up the peacefulness, Maggie gazed toward the church where she had worshipped as a child. Now, she attended one of the churches in Dogwood, but this small sanctuary had been so much more than just a place to be on Sundays. This house of God had been the grounds on which Maggie's firm devotion to the Lord had taken root.

Uncle Cahill had made certain Maggie attended every service. Uncle Cahill had encouraged her to read the Bible. Uncle Cahill had begun every day on his knees in prayer. Despite the fact that the man was actually no kin to Maggie, he had followed closely to the Lord and had shown Maggie the way.

From the left, Levi cleared his throat. Startled from her concerns, she looked down to see Levi standing, his left hand extended toward her. She had been so engrossed in her musings that she failed to hear him disembark the carriage. And now he stood, ready to assist her descent. This morning he had likewise extended his hand. This morning his fingers had covered hers as she stepped from the buggy. This morning he had embraced her and pleaded that she tell him the reasons for her impassioned aversion to his courting her. Would Levi repeat the embrace from only hours ago?

❖

Magnolia, her blue eyes stirring with confusion, placed her hand into Levi's. As much as he wanted to feel her in his arms, Levi backed away to give her plenty of space to disembark. She stepped onto the dusty churchyard, and Levi couldn't resist holding her hand several seconds longer than necessary, pausing in appreciation of her beauty. That blond hair, with wisps forever curling around her face. The fires of faith burning in her soul. The way those dimples formed when she smiled. Magnolia returned his appraisal, and for the first time since she erected that wall of ice between them, Levi perceived that it might very well be melting. He had been transparent in his desires to court her. Perhaps she was coming to terms with the unexplained fears that sprang between them.

Turning her face toward the graveyard, she removed her hand from his.

"I'll wait in the church," he said.

Nodding, she walked the short distance to the cemetery, the summer wind swishing her skirts around her ankles. Levi tethered the horses to a nearby tree, then paused with his hand on the stair rail leading into the clapboard building. Pensively, he watched Maggie kneel beside a fresh grave. *Oh Father*, he pleaded silently, *help her.*

Entering the country chapel, Levi's footsteps echoed across the empty sanctuary. Through the dozen tall windows lining the room, spears of sunlight warmed the air, which smelled of musty hymnbooks. The sound of Levi's boots against polished wooden floors echoed off the ceiling as he walked down the center aisle. He stepped between the pews only long enough to open several of the windows in an effort to circulate the hot, stale air. At last, he reached the point of his destination. The well-worn mourner's bench. Bracing himself with his left arm, Levi knelt in front of the tear-stained altar and wondered how many men before him had sought the Lord for divine guidance here.

In an attempt to gain a comfortable position, he adjusted the Colt .45 Peacemaker encased in its soft leather holster, which Travis had returned during their visit. Oddly, the firearm he had worn as an extension of himself now left him a bit awkward after days without it. For several long minutes, Levi rested on his knees. Soaking in the stillness. Focusing his thoughts on nothing in particular. Feeling peacefully at ease. This trip to Dogwood, which started as a harmless journey to visit his elder brother, had turned into a life-changing event. For the first time in his life, Levi had been shot. For the first time, he had met a godly woman with whom he had shared a reciprocal attraction. For the first time, he had offered to buy his own ranch. A ranch that belonged to the woman of his dreams. Surely, Levi required divine guidance now more than ever.

Accompanied by the sounds of a distant woodpecker pounding his way into a tree, Levi began his prayer. "Lord. You promise to give wisdom to anyone who asks, and I'm asking You now. What would You have me do? You know I've prayed about this before, but I'm asking now if maybe my human desires are jumping in the way of Your will. I think I know myself well enough to say that I'll do whatever You ask of me— only show me, Lord, what that might be."

A wisp of a breeze seemed to carry his words heavenward as he continued his petition. "I'm not skilled enough in the ways of women to understand what's going on in Magnolia's heart. But You created her. You must know what she needs. I'm begging You, Father. Show me Your will! Give me wisdom in dealing with her."

Once again, Levi allowed his mind to drift aimlessly. He looked out an open window to the shaded cemetery situated on the churchyard's western slope. Maggie's huddled form crouched beside her uncle's fresh grave. Her shoulders shook with inaudible sobs.

"Lord," Levi prayed. "Please put your arms around Magnolia and draw her near to You." He paused, then slowly said, "And if I am *not* the one to help in her healing, won't You bring another man into her life that she can trust to help carry her burdens." The last words were some of the hardest Levi had ever prayed. Even though he had talked to the Lord many an hour while in that bed of recovery, and even though he had felt nothing but a deep peace that Magnolia's presence was something the Lord had planned, Levi experienced a new release from the whole situation. A release he had not known since the first time he began to grasp the dream of courting Miss Magnolia Alexander. Certainly, Levi was placing his "angel of mercy" into the hands that had created her and abandoning himself to God's sovereign will. Whether that be marriage to Maggie or life alone on a west Texas ranch, Levi would accept God's plan.

As he once more observed Magnolia's battling her overwhelming grief, a compulsion to wrap his arms around her in comfort overtook Levi and bade him to approach her. Purposefully, he rose from his place of prayer and retraced his earlier steps. After closing the windows, he left the church and took determined strides across the yard as the urgency to be with Magnolia grew.

Her sobs, accompanied by that persistent woodpecker, echoed through the tombstones as Levi neared. At once, Levi second-guessed his decision to intrude on this private moment. But the former desire to comfort her pushed him forward once more.

"Uncle Cahill, w–why weren't you h–honest with me from the b–beginning?" Magnolia demanded through broken sobs.

Levi stopped again as he considered the meaning of her painful outburst.

"This would all be so much easier if I had dealt with it when you were still alive."

Gently, Levi laid a supportive hand on Magnolia's shoulder and knelt beside her.

Covering her face, she turned into his embrace, her wrenching cries now muffled against his shirt. In silence, Levi rested his head atop hers and groped for a way to comfort the seemingly inconsolable woman.

"What has you so troubled, Magnolia? Won't you please tell me? There seems to be more to your grieving than your uncle's death. And I can't help you if I don't know what's wrong."

"Oh, Levi," she said, pulling away to expose him to tear-filled eyes. "Uncle Cahill was nothing but a fraud and a liar and a coward to boot! It wasn't until he was faced with his death that he had the courage to write a letter and confess the truth to me." And Magnolia poured out the full story of what she had so recently learned: James Calloway, alias Cahill Alexander, was an impostor.

On a shuddering breath, she finished her sorrowful report. "And now I'm going to have to witness in court against that horrible man in jail and the whole county will know I was raised by an outlaw. It's going to ruin me! No one will want to walk on the same side of the street with me. No upright man would ever marry me!"

"Is *this* the reason you keep pushing me away?" Within Levi's heart, a blossom of exultation sprouted where only confusion had once grown.

"Yes, partly," she said, brushing away the final tears.

Spontaneously, Levi threw back his head and laughed as if he were alone on the west Texas range.

"This is not funny!" She stood to her full height, placed hands on hips, and stamped her foot.

"Oh yes, it is!" he said, shaking his head as he stood. "Long ago I think my mother decided I was a hopeless cause in the ways of society. When I wouldn't follow Travis's footsteps and be shipped off to that stuffy law school in Boston, I think they just 'bout gave up on me.

" 'What will people think?' I heard my mother say that more times than not. But, I'd always just shrug my shoulders and ride onto the range with my poetry books and journal."

"You write?" Magnolia asked, blinking in surprise.

"Of course." He winked jauntily and watched with delight as her cheeks flamed to that enchanting shade of crimson. "I've even been guilty of composing a few poems for one pretty little lady in Dogwood."

Her cheeks grew all the redder, and she stepped away from him.

"That's all fine and good, Mr. Campbell," she said formally. "And you can make light of my concerns all you want, but—"

He closed the few feet that separated them and gently grasped her upper arm. "I'm tellin' you, Magnolia. I don't care what your uncle was or wasn't. I'm interested in getting to know *you*."

"But people will—"

"I'm not the kind of man to put stock in what anybody thinks. Didn't you hear what I just said about my mother?"

She searched his face as if she were searching for any signs of falsehood.

"I understand the reason you would think that about me," he said diplomatically. "There are some people who—who are so bent on what others think they'd throw away their own lives for the sake of pleasing the world. But that's not the kind of man I am, Magnolia." He stroked her cheek with the back of his fingers and cherished its softness. "All I'm asking is that you consent to givin' the two of us time to get to know one another. Will you let me call on you?"

Staring down at her knotted fingers, she hesitated. "There's more to it than just that." She raised her chin and boldly held his gaze. "How do I know I can trust you?" she blurted. "The one man I thought would never betray me has done exactly that!" Maggie pointed toward the grave, covered in red dirt. "He wasn't even who he *said* he was."

Levi blinked with the vehemence of her words as a heavenward plea formed in his soul. A plea for wisdom. "I guess," he finally said, "you'll just have to give me the chance to prove I'm trustworthy. At least I am who I say I am, you know that much. You have Travis's word on that."

"And you would stand by me through public disgrace?"

"Every minute of it."

"And you wouldn't care that people might say you are the same kind of man Uncle Cahill used to be?"

"No. I am who I am in Christ. And He's teaching me not to lean so much on what everyone thinks." Levi hesitated before expounding on this new vein of contemplation. With another heavenward cry for help, he continued, "And I think that's something your Uncle Cahill learned as well. There's a verse that I've clung to many a nights out under the stars: 'Therefore if any man be in Christ, he is a new creature: old things are passed away; behold, all things are become new.' "

Her pale blue eyes flashed with the sparks of astonishment. Astonishment and a glimmer of understanding. Understanding and eagerness. An eagerness to hear more of what Levi was saying.

"Sounds to me like your uncle made some wrong decisions, even after he accepted Christ. But he still followed the Lord and raised you to know Him. He *did* become a new man in Christ. Just like we have.

"I think when your uncle found you, he was forced to make some pretty tough choices in a few moments' time, and he did the best he could under the circumstances. He didn't do so bad by you, did he? Would you have rather he turned you over to the crooked lawman to be carted off to some orphanage? He probably regretted not telling you the truth a million times. But do you know a single soul who lives without some regrets?"

Levi adjusted his right arm in the sling as a slow throb began to emanate from his injured shoulder.

Magnolia's skilled eyes noticed his discomfort. "Perhaps we should—"

He held up his hand and captured her gaze with his own. Deliberately, he winked again and smiled in a fashion he hoped left his musings clear. "But you haven't said I could court you yet. Do you honestly think I'm going anywhere until you agree?"

Solemnly, Magnolia held his gaze until the beginnings of a smile nibbled the corners of her mouth.

"I'm not asking for your hand in marriage. We haven't known each other anywhere long enough for that. But I would like the opportunity to better make your acquaintance. . .to sit beside you in church. . .to find out your likes and dislikes. . .to maybe even. . .fall in love," Levi said, reciting a few of the lines he had mentally composed after meeting Magnolia.

As the smile increased, she looked down and bit her bottom lip. "I think your parents were right. You should have been a lawyer. You would have won every case, for sure."

With a whoop, Levi picked her up with his good arm and twirled her around.

"Stop this! Stop this now!" she insisted, clamping her hand over her petite, black hat. "You're going to hurt yourself, and Dr. Engle's going to—"

Abruptly, he deposited her back on the ground with a decided thud. Grimacing, Levi clutched his shoulder as the pain tore down his right arm.

"I told you! I told you to stop that nonsense. Now look what you've gone and done to yourself! Dr. Engle will have your hide. . .and mine too," she fussed, tugging him toward the buggy.

As Levi struggled to climb onto his seat, his smile transcended.

❖

While Maggie drove the short distance back to Dogwood, an image of Uncle Cahill bore upon her mind. She envisioned his laughing eyes—eyes that had always revealed the goodness and love of Jesus. She saw once again his carefree smile. She recalled his undying love for his "niece." Even though Magnolia wasn't certain the Lord had delivered her from every vestige of dismay and distrust, she knew He had spoken especially to her there by that gravesite. The verse Levi quoted was the very one that had haunted her the past few days. Perhaps the Lord was trying to teach her to focus more solely on Him and less on what others thought. Uncle Cahill became a new creature in Christ. But, so had Magnolia. And. . .so had Levi.

Furtively, Maggie eyed Levi from beneath her lashes. Even with the evidence of pain marring his face, the man's finely chiseled features spoke of both character and compassion. Yet despite all that he said—and all that she knew was right—a tendril of distrust twisted in her midsection. Certainly, the wrenching betrayal from Uncle Cahill's admission would take time to heal, but Magnolia would trust the Lord to help her trust Levi. She would not, she *could* not rush into anything as serious as marriage. But Maggie would grant to Levi what he had requested. The two of them would certainly get to know one another better.

Once they entered the outskirts of Dogwood, the horse turned instinctively down Main Street and through the bustling town. She pulled the carriage to a halt in front of the boardinghouse, and Levi stifled a groan as he descended.

"You go up to your room, *now*," Maggie admonished in her disapproving nurse's voice. "I'm going to send for Dr. Engle."

He flashed her one of those impish grins, which Maggie was hastily coming to expect at the most inopportune moments. "So my angel of mercy carries a whip."

Before Maggie could formulate a rebuttal, Widow Baker opened the beveled glass door, and Louella Simpson eased her swollen form over the threshold, onto the porch. Wincing, Levi attempted to tip his hat at the ladies as they descended the stairs.

"Miss Maggie, wait! I'm so glad you're here." Sarah Baker, typically the epitome of aplomb, nervously fidgeted with her embroidered hanky. "Miss Louella is. . .is feeling dreadful since we took her to visit Dr. Engle earlier today," she whispered, casting a frenzied glance over her shoulder as Levi entered the boardinghouse. "I'm afraid the child is soon to appear. Luke—" She cleared her throat and glanced downward. "I mean, Dr. Engle said she could deliver any time. Would you mind terribly if we rode with you over to his office? Luke—Dr. Engle insisted on her delivering there. She will have no privacy here whatsoever. And—and she wants me with her at the time."

"Of course I'll take you," Maggie said, but her mind raged with curiosity, with astonishment. *Luke?* The Widow Baker had called Dr. Engle *Luke!* Since the mysterious rift in their relationship, Maggie had never known Sarah to refer to the doctor as anything more than a formal "Dr. Engle," a disdainful "That *Engle* Man," or a frustrated "That *Stubborn* Doctor." As Louella and Mrs. Baker mounted the buggy, Magnolia speculated that the Dogwood rumor mills might soon be humming with more than one romance.

Chapter 12

In a matter of minutes, Maggie had ushered Louella and Mrs. Baker into the outer office and changed the linens on the bed Levi had vacated only that morning. Certainly, as Dr. Engle ascertained, these were busy days for the medical profession. But as Magnolia dashed around the small, austere room making certain all was spotlessly clean, one word drummed out a tattoo in her mind.

Adoption. Adoption. Adoption.

Would Louella? Would Travis and Rachel? Would God. . .could God have placed this hopeless young woman in the most unlikely of towns for the definite purpose of miraculously giving a newborn to a heartbroken couple?

The potential of such a match so filled Maggie with joy that, for the first time since her uncle's death, she forgot the burden of her own heartache. Someone stirred in the kitchen across the hallway, and Maggie fully expected to find the doctor. Humming a lullaby, she rushed toward the kitchen, dropping the linens near the washtub just inside the door.

"Dr. Engle!" she whispered.

The groggy doctor, turning from his pursuit of concocting more of that horrid coffee, attempted to stifle a yawn. "Excuse me, Maggie. I just woke up. I wasn't asleep long this morning when Sarah—I mean, Widow Baker arrived with Miss Simpson."

Sarah! Despite her valiant attempts to hide the conclusions at which she was swiftly arriving, Maggie's eyebrows rose.

Dr. Engle chuckled. "You look like none other than Bess Tucker."

"Doctor, *please*," Maggie gasped, appalled that her lifetime friend would insinuate she could in any way resemble that nosy store owner.

"You're just like the rest of 'em, Maggie, whether you want to admit it or not. Just as interested in the latest gossip as everybody else around this town."

"And you're not?" she asked. "If I recall, you've looked at me rather oddly a few times lately."

"Well who wouldn't with the sparks flyin' between you and that Campbell man?"

With a faint gasp, Maggie covered her mouth. "I almost forgot! You need to pay a visit to Levi at the boardinghouse. He. . ." She glanced out the window as she recalled the delightful moment Levi twirled in triumph. "He seems to have injured his shoulder."

"I told him to take it easy. What'd he do? Go chasing after a cow or something?" he said, his eyes dancing as they hadn't since. . .since the last time he courted Widow Baker.

"No. . . ," Maggie hedged as the doctor finished filling the coffeepot with grounds. "But before you go check on Levi, you'll need to speak with. . . *Sarah* in the waiting room."

"She's here? Now?" He dropped the lid to the coffeepot.

"Yes. With Louella. I fear Louella's time is upon her. But—" Maggie bit her lip and hesitated only a moment before plunging into the subject that left her heart beating with anticipation. "When I was out visiting with Rachel today, I began to wonder. . . . Dr. Engle, do you think Travis and Rachel would adopt Louella's baby? The poor girl has no place to go with a child. She can't go back home because—but if she were to allow the child to be adopted, she could go return to her ma—and no one would ever know. I just started thinking that—"

"No, Child." Dr. Engle laid a fatherly hand on her forearm. "You weren't thinking. God was speaking to you."

Maggie's eyes misted. Her pulse accelerated. Her mind careened with the doctor's words.

"He has spoken to me as well. I have thought of almost nothing else since I examined Miss Simpson this morning."

"Rachel could even nurse the baby." Magnolia shook her head in wonder as a tear of exultation dropped to her cheek. During the last week, she had shed so many tears of sorrow that this moment of happiness seemed to somehow initiate the cleansing of her soul.

"I will go and examine the young lady again." Dr. Engle removed his wire-rimmed spectacles to press against his own reddened eyes. "If you will join me, perhaps the two of us could present the idea to Miss Simpson."

"And do you think Rachel and Travis—"

"I think Mr. and Mrs. Campbell will bless God all their remaining days."

❖

Magnolia cradled a newborn boy in her arms and stood on the Campbells' front porch with Levi and Dr. Engle, impatiently shifting their weight from foot to foot. The doctor hammered away at the door again and muttered under his breath. "I sent a message to Travis last night saying we'd be here by six-thirty. I don't know why he's not up and at 'em."

Joy bubbles gurgled from Maggie's soul, forcing her to suppress the giggles akin to those of a child on Christmas morning. As a mockingbird serenaded the morning, the sun's pink fingers grandly stretched themselves across the eastern horizon. Surely, nature itself was celebrating this amazing moment.

As Dr. Engle pounded on the door even more ferociously, Levi bent to gently pull the thin blanket away from the sleeping, redheaded infant. "I can't believe his hair's the same color as Rachel's," he whispered. "It just all seems too good to be true." Levi peered into Magnolia's eyes as if his meaning weren't limited to the adoption.

"It's all in God's plan," she said. "There's no other explanation." As he solemnly agreed, Magnolia fleetingly hoped Levi proved as steadfast as she wanted to believe. Throughout Louella's uncomplicated childbirth, Maggie had experienced intermittent spells of panic, due to the fact that she had actually agreed to Levi's courting her. But laced with the panic was always the same trace of peace. . .peace and a flurry in her midsection. Truly, Levi's dashing smile and candid nature touched a chord in Maggie that no man had yet stirred. She prayed, oh how she prayed, that she could learn to trust again with the same sweetness she once had known.

At last, a bleary-eyed Travis opened the door, his pullover shirt hanging outside his denims. "We were so excited, we didn't get to sleep until well after three. We—" He stopped and gazed at the infant in awe.

"Congratulations! It's a boy!" the doctor announced.

"A redheaded boy!" Levi beamed.

Unable to suppress the giggles a moment longer, Maggie extended the baby to his father. "Congratulations," she echoed, her eyes suddenly misting all over again.

Gingerly, Travis took the child. "My son," he said with wonder, staring into the infant's wrinkled face. On the heels of a yawn, the baby whimpered and squirmed.

"I think it's time for his feeding," Maggie said discreetly as they entered the house. "I can take him into Rachel, if you like, and assist her."

"Yes, yes, Maggie," the doctor insisted. "I don't know what I'd do without you. Don't know what I'd do."

"Would you mind if I carry him into Rachel?" Travis asked.

"No, not in the least." Meeting the sagacious gaze of the doctor, Magnolia waited near Levi as Travis cradled his son and strode down the short hallway.

Cloaked in respectful silence, Maggie and her companions settled upon the horsehair sofa and awaited Travis's return. When half an hour elapsed with no signs of Travis, the doctor suggested Maggie discreetly peek in on them.

Cautiously, Magnolia crept up the hallway to pause outside their opened bedroom door. The peaceful scene that greeted her could have been nothing but God-ordained. Father, mother, and baby. . .all dozed. The newborn child, his stomach assuredly full, rested peacefully against Rachel's chest. Tears of rapture still dampened Rachel's cheeks, and Travis radiated nothing short of jubilation, even in his sleep.

Louella had requested that she be allowed to spend the night with her baby before sending him to the arms of his new mother, and Dr. Engle had granted her supplication. The young mother had shed a good number of tears when placing the child in Magnolia's arms one last time. She had even watched from the boardinghouse window as Magnolia and the baby rode away with the doctor and Levi. During those moments of departure, Maggie had wondered if they should have arranged to separate baby from mother, despite the hardships the two would face together. But with the morning's weak light gently spilling upon the scene before her, Magnolia knew she and the doctor had done the right thing—the thing God Himself had willed. And Louella. . .Louella would receive a full description of this touching scene, and God would bequeath to her His eternal peace.

❖

As the sun approached the western horizon, Magnolia and Levi stepped onto the porch of her childhood home. The two had stayed with Rachel and Travis all day long—Maggie, as Rachel's assistant; Levi, as Travis's confidant and brotherly supporter. In Travis's borrowed buggy, they were traveling back into town when Maggie requested they stop by the homestead.

Some invisible force seemed to be pulling her back to the place of her childhood. After learning all the truths about Uncle Cahill, Maggie had embraced the notion of selling the old ranch to anyone. . .*anyone*, even the likes of Jed Sweeney. But as the days melted into one another and the rawness of her pain lessened, Magnolia began to toy with the idea of keeping the place—keeping it and hiring someone to manage the estate, to do the job of her uncle Cahill.

With a wistful sigh, she settled onto the porch swing and pushed against the porch with her feet. The sound of two courting whippoorwills echoed throughout the piney woods, and Magnolia toyed with the pleats in her pink cotton skirt. Despite the fact that her mourning period was not officially over, Maggie was sick to death of those hot black dresses. As the swing creaked beneath her, she wondered how many times she and Uncle Cahill had sat in this spot until the last rays of light slipped below the horizon. Even the squirrels, chasing among a nearby cluster of oaks, seemed as constant a part of the scenery as was the swing.

"Are you having second thoughts about selling the place?" With the swing still in motion, Levi clumsily claimed the spot beside her.

"Yes. I—" Spontaneously, she turned to Levi. "Instead of buyin' the place, would you be interested in living here as the manager for awhile. . . until I begin to feel more like making a final decision?"

"Yes," he said as if the decision were already made for him. "I'd be glad to."

A surge of relief swept over Magnolia. "Then I could take my time about deciding whether or not to sell out. Last week I was so disgusted I was ready to sell everything, furniture included, to the first person who'd have it. But as disappointed as I've been over Uncle Cahill's deception, he was still. . .he was still—"

"He was the only father you ever knew," Levi said with wisdom. "And I think it's best for you to wait before making any big decisions—*any* decisions," he added, his meaning clear. "I was only offering to buy the ranch so soon because I thought maybe you *had* to sell, and I didn't want you to be forced into selling to that saloon owner."

Thoughts of Jed Sweeney left Magnolia suppressing a shudder, despite the evening heat. The only good thing she knew that man had done was to give Louella enough money to go back home. And that gesture was most likely done to soften Magnolia's resolve not to sell to him.

A resounding thud reverberated from inside the house, jarring Magnolia from her reverie. She exchanged a nonplussed stare with Levi.

"Are your hired hands supposed to be in your house?" he asked.

"No. And they should have gone home by now."

"Do you think a tree limb fell on the roof or—"

Another thump annihilated Levi's speculations and soon a shadowed figure moved behind the parlor window.

"Levi." Maggie gripped his arm. "I just saw a shadow. Somebody's in—"

"I saw it, too." Levi stood and touched the Peacemaker, holstered on his left thigh.

"Can you shoot left-handed?" Maggie whispered, feeling anything but protected at the moment.

"We'll see," he replied, drawing his weapon.

But the front door banged open, and Jed Sweeney stared at them down the barrel of his raised Winchester rifle. "Drop the gun," he growled, his ever-present cigar clamped firmly between his yellowed teeth.

Levi hesitated.

"Drop the gun *now*."

Her upper lip beading in perspiration, Maggie's stomach clenched into a tight knot as Levi obeyed the snake-eyed saloon owner's command.

"Both of you get in this house," he snarled, waving the gun toward the door.

Immediately, Maggie recalled that lecherous man in the jail cell. She remembered the lady bandit saying they hadn't murdered anyone. She reflected on her uncle's letter. Could Jed Sweeney also be a former lawman? If he were. . .and if he did kill Uncle Cahill. . .why would he offer to buy her property?

With Jed pointing that rifle at their backs, Maggie preceded Levi into the room that had witnessed many nights of familial pleasantries. But Sweeney had overturned every piece of furniture, had even gutted the red velvet settee and matching chair. As the cigar-smoking scoundrel slammed the door behind them and slid the bar lock into place, Maggie strained to see into her uncle's bedroom, only to witness the same chaos in his room as in the parlor.

"I waited until those stinkin' hired hands left before coming after it," he declared, the hardness in his glittering eyes as dense as granite. "But I'm determined to get my hands on it, even if I have to kill the two of you."

Levi stepped between Maggie and the gun, and her heart hammered wildly as she attempted to fathom Sweeney's intent. What exactly was he after? Was it so valuable that he would offer to buy the whole estate? So valuable that he would kill Uncle Cahill?

From behind Levi, Maggie peered over his shoulder and into

Sweeney's murderous countenance. "You killed my uncle," she muttered in stunned disbelief.

Sweeney produced a chilling smile. "Of course," he said menacingly. "Now, I'm looking for the gold he cheated me out of twenty years ago." He laughed wickedly. "That stupid Calloway thought that just because I was in the sheriff's office that day that I was the lawman. Truth was, my brother was the lawman. I just happened by. Turned out to be my lucky day. I lied about my name, and the two of us struck a deal: I'd let him go free and he'd hand over the loot. I didn't find out until a year later from my own brother that there'd been a chest full of gold coins on that stage-coach Calloway robbed. I decided right then and there that I'd catch up with him one day. Imagine my surprise when I ran into him in this dumpy little town. Now, you two, all you have to do is hand over the gold. I promise. . ." He smiled like a demon. "I won't kill you. I'll just tie you up so you can sit tight while I have time to get out of the county."

"If there's any gold, Magnolia, give it to him," Levi said, glancing over his shoulder.

"There's no gold," she said, her voice ringing with a certainty that surprised even her ears. "Uncle Cahill l–left me a letter before his death. He said there was no gold."

Jed's intense stare, like a dagger of ice, pierced her to the base of her soul. The man had no feelings whatsoever. . .no feelings for anyone. "I told that stinkin' James Calloway I'd turn him into the law if he didn't either tell me where the gold was or pay me the equivalent in cash. He finally told me the gold was buried. I gave him a day to dig it up. When I came back, he tried to kill me. . .didn't work." His lips twisted wickedly.

"Now, by Calloway's own admission, I know there's gold here. If you do not tell me where it is, I will kill you, too," he said in measured tones.

"He means it," Levi said, his voice shaking.

Magnolia's mind raced with any possibilities, but she came up completely without options. She also believed there really was no gold. Maggie remembered the numerous years when the cotton crop had failed or the winter had been harsh and they had suffered financially from the loss of crops or cattle. If Uncle Cahill had been hiding gold, he would certainly have delved into it during the lean years. Instead, they had struggled past the seasons of financial difficulties until the profitable ranch now thrived. Perhaps her uncle did tell Sweeney he would dig up the fictitious gold in order to buy time. With that gun pointing in her face, Magnolia would almost tell Sweeney anything he wanted to hear, as well.

"Let's go to the barn and get some shovels," she said, sounding much calmer than she felt. With Sweeney's gun in their backs, they walked through the kitchen, to the spacious back porch, and onto the dusty barnyard. All the while, Maggie prayed. She prayed as she had never prayed in her life. She wanted a husband and children. . .a life. Furtively, she glanced toward Levi, his intense eyes reflecting her own inner turmoil. Assuredly, Maggie perceived that if something didn't happen soon, Sweeney would kill her and Levi, gold or no gold.

With the waning sun inviting evening's shadows to creep alongside the trees and hills, Maggie pushed against the massive barn door. The hinges produced a faint squeak—a squeak that reflected the hopeless whimpers floating from Maggie's soul. *Please, God, please do something! Don't let this evil man kill us!*

The rivulets of light seeping through the hayloft's ajar door provided precious little illumination for the dark building. With the smells of hay and horse manure engulfing her, Maggie stepped into the unlit building and halted, giving her eyes a chance to adjust.

"Keep walkin'," Sweeney demanded from behind Levi.

Maggie glanced to her left, and noticed the two shovels for which she came. Darting a prayer heavenward, she quickly stepped toward them, grabbed one, raised it over her head, and held her breath as first Levi, then Sweeney stepped into the barn. With a rush of strength, she crashed the shovel blade against Sweeney's temple. Only a muffled grunt passed his lips before he dropped like a bag of feed, his Winchester spinning across the dirt floor.

Levi, quick to action, retrieved the rifle and pointed it toward the murderer.

Shivering in horror, the dazed Magnolia gaped at the unconscious man sprawled at her feet. How had she conjured the courage and strength to render him powerless? But Maggie knew, even as the question of awe rushed upon her, that the strength, courage, and power had not been her own. The Lord Himself had divinely intervened.

In the distance, the pond frogs voiced their nightly chant. The bobwhites whistled their simple message. A mare, resting in her stall, whinnied uncertainly. And Levi looked at the trembling Maggie, a glimmer of admiration in his eyes.

"You're my kinda woman, Magnolia Alexander," he said with one of his untimely winks.

Epilogue

Two years later, Maggie again settled on the porch swing and pushed against the porch with her foot. A tiny bundle claiming her arms, she smiled with a contentment only Jesus Christ could impart. The six-week-old Sarah Louella yawned and rubbed her eyes with a tiny fist, and Maggie bestowed a tender kiss against the baby's forehead. Sarah Engle, no longer the Widow Baker, and Rachel, busy with her two year old, had been such a help to Maggie during these first weeks of the baby's life. Dr. Engle had insisted his wife leave her duties as his nurse to stay with Maggie at least one day a week. And Travis had likewise persisted in making certain Rachel assisted their new sister-in-law. Maggie certainly couldn't have survived without the two women.

Already, the first stars appeared against the twilight sky, and Magnolia waited for Levi to join her for their nightly prayers and Bible reading. His worn, black Bible in hand, Levi strode from the house, and Maggie slowed the swing to let him claim the spot beside her. "I thank God every hour of the day for Sarah. . .and you," he said, brushing his lips against her forehead.

"I feel the same way," Maggie said. "Two years ago, I never dreamed I could be so happy."

"The Lord's healing is a marvelous thing. . .a marvelous thing."

"Yes, I think I'm learning that no matter how people might betray us, the Lord is always steadfast." Maggie reflected over the slight tinge of pain, still present when she thought of Uncle Cahill's deception. Ironically, the very man who passed onto her a legacy of trusting the Lord had himself covered the whole truth. But despite all his mistakes, she would certainly extend her uncle's legacy of faith to the next generation. With Jed Sweeney having been convicted and hanged, Maggie was putting her past behind her. Levi was steadfastly proving to the township that he and his wife were indeed worthy of respect, regardless of Cahill's scandalous past. And Maggie, day by day, was growing in her reliance on the constancy of a godly man.

Texas Angel

with Robert Osborne

Dedication

For my own little angels—Brett and Brooke.

$\mathscr{P}rologue$

(Taken from *Texas Lady*)

Dogwood, Texas. June 1886.

M agnolia faintly tapped on Rachel's closed bedroom door. "Hello, Rachel?" she called gently. "It's me, Maggie. May I come in?"

A familiar face appeared on the other side of the door. "Rachel's asleep right now," Angela Isaacs whispered, "but do come in." Her chestnut-colored hair and freckled nose testified to Angela's and Rachel's kinship. But that's where the cousins' similarities ended. While Rachel was fiery, Angela had always been more reclining. Angela, slender and tall, carried herself gracefully, but seemed to dwarf the petite Rachel when the two stood side by side.

Magnolia stepped into the room to see the lace curtains waving in front of the numerous bedroom windows. The large wicker fan lying on the foot of Rachel's bed attested to Angela's having fanned her cousin while she slept.

"How is she doing, Angela?" Maggie asked.

"Well, she cried herself to sleep." Angela paused to blink back the tears. "But I believe the elixir Dr. Engle left this morning has helped her sleep in peace for the first time since the labor started last night. She's been asleep a couple of hours now."

"Bless her," Maggie said, astounded at how drawn Rachel's pale face appeared. And the bright sunshine spilling through the windows only highlighted the dark circles marring her eyes. Once again, Maggie was reminded that she didn't hold the exclusive rights to trouble. About a year ago, Rachel's father had died, leaving her alone to tend to this expansive land. Now, she and Travis had lost their first child—a little girl, according to Dr. Engle.

"Is there to be a funeral?" Magnolia asked.

"No. Travis and Dr. Engle buried the baby this morning, out in the pasture, under one of the trees."

"And Rachel? Did she see the baby?"

Angela nodded, her eyes filling with tears.

The patient stirred, and Magnolia stepped to her side to notice dots of perspiration along Rachel's forehead. "Are there some damp cloths for her face? She looks terribly hot."

"Yes," Angela said, moving to the door. "Travis just brought in a fresh bucket of cold well water not long ago. I'll go get some of it and bring some cloths as well."

"Magnolia?" Rachel breathed, stirring restlessly.

"Yes, I'm here." Maggie knelt beside the feather bed and encircled Rachel's hand within her own.

At last, Rachel opened her eyes to look up at Maggie with doelike agony. "It w–was a little. . .little girl," she said, tears dampening her cheeks.

Remembering her own mother's pain-filled inscriptions about the deaths of her twin sons, Maggie nodded. Somehow, being with Rachel at this moment gave Maggie a sense of connection with the mother she had never known.

"Dr. Engle has. . .has been like a. . .a father to me." Rachel's voice cracked as she wrinkled her brows.

"I think he's like a father to most of Dogwood, Rachel," Maggie said. "He's a wonderful, wonderful man."

"Yes. . .but I. . .I can tell when. . .when he's withholdin' bad news. I'm afraid there's somethin' t–terribly wrong. That. . .that perhaps I won't ever be able. . .able to have children. It's just this h–horrible feelin' I have that I can't. . .I can't get over."

Wondering what she should say, Maggie grappled with an appropriate reply. As usual, the stirrings of inadequacy plagued her. *What do I say? How much should I tell her? Exactly how certain is Dr. Engle that Rachel mustn't try to bear children?* At last, Maggie decided that now was certainly not the time to share more disheartening news with the devastated Rachel.

"I'm not as. . .as experienced with these types of things as Dr. Engle, but. . .but he wouldn't have left you this morning if he didn't think you were going to be fine. He'll be back out to check on you before dark this evening. You can tell him your concerns then. I'm sure he'll be glad to answer all your questions. Right now, you just need to focus on recoverin'." Maggie gripped Rachel's hand all the tighter and hoped she did not push for more information concerning the dim prognosis.

Spiritlessly, Rachel stared out one of the open windows. "I know I sh–shouldn't doubt the. . .the Lord, Maggie," she said, her voice gaining strength the more she talked. "But I think I must be the worst doubter in the world. Sometimes I just don't understand why He allows all the sufferin' and. . .and death. I didn't think I'd ever get over Pa's death. Now. . .now this!" She turned imploring eyes to Maggie. "Doesn't the Lord think we would make good parents? Is there something I've done wrong? I want a baby more than anything. And if. . .if just supposin' I can't. . .I'll feel as if I've let Travis down in the worst of ways."

"Yes, I understand, but. . .I'm sure the Lord will somehow. . ." Maggie didn't know what to say. So fresh were her own questions about God and life that she could do nothing but hold Rachel's hand and silently support this childhood friend. "I'll certainly keep you in my prayers," Maggie encouraged. "If. . .if you'll remember me as well."

Rachel nodded in understanding. "We can be a support to one. . .one another." Her head tilted to the side. Her heavy eyes closed. And her breathing became steadier.

Praying for Rachel's strength and her own wisdom, Magnolia thoughtfully observed her friend, slipping into the folds of sleep. And with the cattle's soft lowing flowing through the opened windows, an idea, like a tiny cloud, presented itself on the horizon of her mind. At a breathtaking pace, that cloud gained size. . .size and definite plausibility.

Louella Simpson was due to give birth very soon. She had no idea what she was going to do once the baby arrived. She had no means of supporting the child. She even said that returning to her hometown would heap ridicule upon her mother and herself. So, she couldn't go back home. But just suppose. . .just suppose Louella loved her child so much she would be willing to place it in Rachel's loving arms? Precious few people in Dogwood knew about Louella. Only key people had privy to the fact that Rachel had even miscarried. Rachel and Travis could very easily accept Louella's baby as their own, and the child would never bear the shame of the label, "illegitimate." No one in Dogwood needed ever to know the child was adopted.

The sound of Angela entering the room disrupted Maggie's thoughts, but in no means dismissed the exciting possibilities. . .if only Louella would agree.

"I'm sorry it took so long," Angela said in her usually tranquil tones. "But Travis and his brother. . .um. . ." She squinted as if she were searching for his name.

"Levi," Maggie supplied while Angela poured the cool water into the stoneware washing bowl on the bedside table.

"Yes, Levi." Angela's brown eyes glittered with the romantic speculations that Magnolia had seen all over town. Was no one in Dogwood left without knowledge of Magnolia's personal life? "The two of them were inquiring concerning Rachel," the schoolteacher said. Her words, as precise as always, reflected her studious nature and the academic excellence to which she pushed her students.

"I'm so hot," Rachel muttered, stirring from her light sleep.

Maggie dipped one of the clean, although stained, cloths into the well's icy water and gently patted Rachel's forehead.

"Thank you," Rachel mumbled. Taking the cloth from Maggie, she stroked her neck and cheeks as well. "It's so p–powerfully hot today." She produced a languid smile, which hinted at her usually playful nature. "I heard you. . .talking about Levi," she said, her voice once more gaining strength with each word she spoke. "Angela, Levi is c–courting Maggie. Did you know?"

Shocked, Magnolia glanced from Rachel to the speculative Angela, and back to Rachel.

"We–we're going to be sisters-in-law, I think," Rachel continued.

"Yes, that's what I hear," Angela said in a scheming voice. "Yesterday at the quilting bee—"

"We aren't courting," Maggie blurted, recalling Levi's brief embrace, which suggested the opposite.

"Then may–maybe he'll court Angela." Rachel's feeble wink left Maggie glad to see some of the redhead's spunk, although her chagrin increased all the more.

"Even from her sick bed, she torments me," Angela said. "I'm an old maid, and I will remain that way all my years. I'll probably go to my death before trusting a man again."

"Ah, Angela, one d–day somebody as good as my Trav's gonna come along and. . .and make you forget you ever said that." Rachel raised her head and Maggie automatically placed another pillow behind her. Perhaps the patient would even feel like sipping some broth for her noon meal.

Glancing toward the blanching Angela, Maggie recalled the tragic story beneath the sudden stoniness in her eyes. She had been jilted ten years before, when Maggie was just past adolescence. Now thirty, the mildly attractive schoolteacher stood little chance at matrimony, and spinsterhood apparently suited her.

Chapter 1

Rusk, Texas. September, 1888.

The faint ticking of the worn clock hanging on Sheriff Garner's office wall wormed into Noah Thorndyke's brain until his head throbbed with an incessant ache. Suddenly the clock's hammer tolled ten doleful times. *One for each hour I have to live,* Noah thought. *Oh God, help me!* he despaired, his soul feeling as if it would rend in twain.

The jail cell smelled of sweaty, straw-filled mattresses. Mildew clung to the walls like the sooty cloak a hangman wears. A lone window on the opposite side of the cell admitted a few lonely night sounds: crickets, a dog barking at some menace, and owls hooting in the east Texas woods. Noah, condemned to die, sat on the edge of a cast-iron bunk and gazed in despair at the wrinkled "Wanted" poster that bore his exact likeness. However, the name beneath the image was Rupert Denham, not Noah Thorndyke. Meager light from a candle, sputtering in protest over the inferior tallow, cast a pale glow of dappled light across the poster. As Noah had wondered a thousand times, so he wondered now, *Who is Rupert Denham, and why does he look so much like me?*

Noah's eyes burned with a combination of fury and foreboding, and the tension in his gut testified to his soul's despair. He and this Rupert Denham shared the same square jaw line. The same dark hair and eyes. The same straight nose and prominent brows—like that of a Greek sculpture. The only difference between Noah and this Rupert was the scraggly mustache that made his counterpart appear villainous. Noah always kept himself cleanly shaven.

He ran long, artistic fingers through his neck-length hair, then slapped his knee, crumpled the poster, and stood. As he had all day, Noah wondered how his call to preach had culminated in such a tragic and unfair ending. *Sentenced to hang. . .I have been sentenced to hang.* The facts seemed less the product of reality and more the results of a tortuous nightmare.

Room for only two steps in either direction made pacing difficult. But confinement tortured him, so persistent movement provided some measure of relief. Nagging thoughts of the next few hours crumbled in a useless heap. The candle's flame dwindled. Ghostly shadows lost their outlines and mingled with the uneven texture of the rock walls.

Fatigue bore into his every muscle, producing a nervousness impossible to calm. He stopped walking and with sweaty palms gripped the bars on the cell door. The cold bars, smooth from the wear of calloused skin on iron, seemed a metaphor for the chill in Noah's spirit. Many others must have experienced the despair of lonely hours waiting for rough hemp to squeeze the last breath from their throats. The candle popped a final time, then lost its battle with the darkness. A darkness that settled around Noah. A darkness that seeped into his soul like the kiss of death itself.

Oh Lord, Noah's soul cried in anguish. *Oh Father, you've got to save me!*

"Jailer!" he called, desperate for relief from the inky darkness. "My candle has gone out. Please, bring another."

The silence persisted.

"Jailer!" the prisoner shouted again and shook the door of his cell until it clattered like a collection of tin cans in a feed sack.

The creak of a swivel chair and feet hitting the floor preceded a grumble and the turn of a key in the office door. As the door opened, a shaft of weak light penetrated the darkness. "Wha-da-ya-want?" the jailer inquired, his voice slurred with sleep. He squinted toward Noah, his thinning, gray hair rumpled from the long night.

"My candle is out."

"Go to sleep then." The old man rubbed his face, shadowed from need of a shave.

"Could you sleep, Lester, if you were waiting to be hung?" The words left Noah nauseous, and he wondered if his mother would ever learn what had happened to him.

"You're gettin' what you deserve. Shootin' our banker!" Lester eyed Noah with a condescending glare. "No better man ever lived than William Frank. They can't hang you quick enough for me!"

"Like I told the judge, I didn't have anything to do with that murder," Noah argued, a fresh surge of frustration rushing upon him as he recalled that horrid trial. Never had Noah been so aghast at how lies could sound so truthful.

"I've heard that plenty of times from men standin' right where you are, and it don't make no difference. I'll get your candle," he ground out. "But it's just 'cause I'm tired of yer bellowin'. Otherwise, I'd say get used to the dark. The place you're goin' is blacker than night, or so I've been told."

"Would you get me a deck of cards too?" Noah asked, hating to resort to the deceptive plan that was slowly inching its way into his thoughts. But at this point, Noah felt he had no choice. He could wait for an unjust death or use artifice to gain his freedom.

"What?" Lester's bushy brows rose. "You been tellin' everybody you're a preacher man. How do ya square that with card playin'?"

"Just a little solitaire to keep my mind off. . .you know." Noah shrugged.

"Humph. Figures," Lester growled. "There's some cards in the sheriff's desk. Anything to keep you quiet so I can get some shut-eye." He yawned and rubbed his balding head. "I'll be back in a minute."

Lester clicked the door closed, then turned his key in the lock with the squeaking sound of metal against metal. The noise reassured Noah that Lester carried his keys with him at all times. His plan for escape might work, and work well. He busied himself thinking through each step until the rusty lock once more protested against Lester's key.

Holding the flickering candle, the jailer passed Noah the cards. He walked toward the window across the room, removed the spent candle from its tin holder, and dropped the stub on the floor. In seconds, he forced the fresh, burning candle into the holder and turned to face Noah, the glow of the lone flame behind him.

"Do I get any food?" Noah asked. "I didn't get dinner or supper, and breakfast was lean as well, for that matter." His stomach growled as if to punctuate his plight. No one in these parts seemed too concerned about the livelihood of a prisoner whom they were certain was a murderer.

"Not 'til morning. And don't expect much then. Where you're goin' you won't need much to eat!" the jailer barked, walking toward the door.

Smiling, Noah spoke as kindly as he dared. "Say old-timer, do you like card tricks?" He expertly shuffled the deck and put the cards through a battery of fancy moves.

"Devil's work! And if you was any kinda preacher, you wouldn't be so familiar with that deck." Lester hitched up his droopy britches with one hand and suspiciously eyed Noah. "Where'd ya learn to do all that, anyway?"

"I spent a lot of time on the river when I was a kid." Noah continued the shuffling, all the while hating the feel of the cards in his hands. Years had passed since he had shuffled a deck. Years. . .but the skill came back to him as if he had played poker only yesterday.

"I know'd you weren't no preacher!" Lester sneered.

"A man can change. That's what the Bible teaches." The cards pattered together in a patterned cadence, and Noah shuffled them again.

"Didn't work for you," the jailer grumped and started for the door.

"Watch the ace of spades disappear." Noah's toes curled inside his boots. If this plan worked, he would be free in a matter of minutes. Free, to prove his innocence.

The old man looked back, a hint of curiosity in his faded, gray eyes. Noah fanned the deck with only the ace of spades staring at the jailer. He closed the fan very slowly. When he reopened the deck, the ace had disappeared.

"Gimme them cards!" The old man stepped forward and carefully inspected each one. Noah expertly inserted the ace into the man's pocket. "Where's that ace?"

"Look in your shirt pocket," Noah said smugly.

Lester reached toward his pocket, his double chin bunching under his neck. He fumbled in the folds of his shirt and pulled out the ace of spades. "Glory be! How'd you do that?"

"My secret," Noah said with a grin. "Now, here's another trick, but you've got to come close."

Mesmerized by Noah's slight-of-hand, the simple jailer pressed into the bars, his gaze fixed on the cards. In one deft move Noah reached through the rungs and slipped the jailer's pistol from its holster. Dropping the deck, he gripped the jailer's belt. Yanking him up to the bars, Noah spoke softly but firmly. "Ease over to the door, and you'll unlock it, right?" His heart pounding, Noah wondered what he would do if the old man refused. He certainly would never use the gun.

Lester's baggy eyes bulged like a frog's. His lips trembled. His breath came out in short, wheezing bursts. "Of. . .of course," he stuttered and shuffled toward the door. He slipped the key into the lock and turned the shaft. With a metallic grunt the bolt moved and the bars swung out.

Noah released his grip. "Get in here," he commanded, loathing the taste of every word. Stepping aside, Noah allowed Lester to move into the cell. "Take off your shirt and tear two strips from the bottom."

The old man, whimpering like a pup, began the tedious task. The sound of tearing fabric reflected the ache in Noah's soul. He detested having to play the scoundrel. Noah Thorndyke was a man of God, not some ruffian. *Oh Lord, forgive me,* he prayed. *Forgive me if I am doing wrong, but I don't want to hang. You know as well as I do that I'm not a murderer.*

As the old man tore the final strip from his shirt, Noah recalled his musings as he prepared for the journey from Louisiana to Tyler, Texas, mere weeks ago. He had prayed that, perhaps, this trip would introduce him to the woman whom God intended him to marry. Noah was so tired of his lonely existence. He hungered for the completeness only a godly wife would bring to his life. Ironically, instead of a woman of God, Noah had encountered a sentence of death.

The jailer finished his task and helplessly stared at his prisoner.

"Stuff one strip into your mouth," Noah ordered. "Tie the other around your head to hold the gag in." He waited while the jailer complied. "Now we're going to the office nice and quiet." Waving the gun barrel toward the door, Noah allowed the jailer to precede him.

Once through the door, Noah spotted a pair of handcuffs, blotchy with rust, hanging from a spike in the wall. "Get those cuffs," he growled, then waited as Lester, his shoulders slumped in defeat, obeyed the command. If only the old man could detect just how severely Noah was shaking and how reticent he was to place his finger against the trigger, Lester would have never complied. Noah prayed like a madman that he could continue this facade until he secured his freedom.

"Now, walk back toward the cell, nice and slow," Noah said.

As if he could read Noah's mind, Lester cast a speculative glance toward his captor.

"Now!" Noah snarled.

The old man jumped and grunted, then shuffled toward the door.

Within minutes, Noah fettered Lester's hands behind his back and locked the jail cell. He paused before making his exit and spotted a worn Bible lying on the thin mattress. "I'm sorry to do this to you old fellow. I really am. And if it makes you feel any better, I wasn't lying when I said

I am a man of God. I'd have never shot you, and I want you to know how much I appreciate your cooperation."

Lester, glaring at Noah, produced a long string of grunts that sounded strongly like cursing.

"The Lord can sure help you with your feelings over all this," Noah said through a perverse, wobbly chuckle. "And I'll point you to that Bible the sheriff lent me. It will guide you down the right paths." He nodded toward the leather-bound book, lying on the mattress. "Meanwhile, I'll put your pistol on the sheriff's desk. Don't want to run off with anything that doesn't belong to me. You'll find your keys with the pistol."

Noah retreated, stepped through the office doorway, and closed the door behind him. As the weight of what he had done settled around his shoulders, Noah's heart thudded like the steady pounding of wild horses, galloping upon a path, well trodden. Even during his years of adolescent rebellion, Noah had never broken the law to this degree. "But it was break the law or have my neck broken by the hangman's rope," he muttered, despising the choice he had been forced to make.

He stepped toward the cluttered desk and deposited the pistol and keys on it. Trying to run from the guilt that plagued his spirit, Noah rushed toward the front door, eased it open, and peered onto the street. Behind him, the Seth Thomas produced a broken chime, announcing that ten thirty had arrived.

Noah scanned the shadowed road, deserted except for a group of horses, three hundred yards away, tethered outside the saloon. Clanking piano music, raucous laughter, and faint, feminine squeals floated from the saloon. His hands producing a thick film of sweat, Noah stepped onto the boardwalk. He needed only to gain entrance into the horse livery up the lane, reclaim the steed that was rightfully his, and make his escape. *Lord, please extend Your grace but a few minutes more,* he prayed as he raised his collar, hunched his shoulders, and began the brief journey toward the livery, toward his freedom.

Chapter 2

Dogwood, Texas

A ngela Isaacs winced as she tugged her brush through long waves of tangled hair, the color of chestnuts. Despite the relentless snags, her persistence won, resulting in a gleaming cascade of silky tresses reaching her waist. She gazed at her own reflection in the mirror and noted the few crows' feet that were forming around her eyes. The lamplight, flickering from her bedside table, accented her best feature—the deep, auburn hair, so like her mother's.

She recalled many nights brushing her mother's long, flowing curls. During those hours away from the prying ears of her elder brothers, Angela asked many womanly questions and begged for the tales her mother recounted with fiery passion. Some stories reflected memories from childhood. Others were fairy tales. Then, there were the Bible stories, which especially lit her mom's face with the glow of faith and love. But that was long ago. The demanding duties of Angela's teaching, coupled with the disappointments of the past, left her spending less and less time with God. Certainly, Angela attended church. That was part of the fulfillment of her contract as a schoolteacher. But for Angela, an intimate relationship with the Lord now settled as a pale memory on a distant horizon.

The early September breeze now dancing through the opened window promised cooler days to come. Angela stepped toward her bed's fluffy feather mattress, lowered the lamp's wick, and settled against the down pillow. With the sound of crickets shrieking near her window,

Angela watched the shadows dancing on the ceiling. Shadows that seemed a specter of her past.

Visions of her childhood blended with vague forms projected by the dim light. There were happy faces: her father, playfully tugging at her mother's apron strings and kissing her neck, just below her ever present bun; her brothers, begging their dad to forego the day's work and take them hunting for rabbits and squirrels; a mother's careful needlework, which produced the lovely dresses few other girls of Angela's station could afford. The images spoke of security and warmth. Warmth and love. Love and promise.

But the promise of childhood had faded in the light of the grown-up reality. A dark, leering figure from twelve years ago broke into her memories. Angela, desperate to block out the image of her former fiancé, closed her eyes, and coaxed herself to relax. As in the past, she buried her pain in the deepest recesses of her soul until she eventually found escape in the arms of slumber.

But this night, as with many others, the recollections of her deepest heartache—a heartache that left Angela determined to never again trust a man—were vividly reenacted in her dreams. . . .

❖

Jason Wiley rode into Dogwood with saddlebags full of law books and a story of an eastern education. He attended church every Sunday and finally picked Angela as the girl he liked best. She never uttered a prayer without thanking God for this wonderful man. There were picnics and square dances and hints of marriage. Sitting by Jason during the church service elicited dreams of a home and children.

But on the Tuesday before Christmas, Angela's six months of bliss turned to ashes. She drove the family buggy into town that afternoon and purchased some last-minute items for the special meal her mother always made on Christmas Eve. Jason had bought a new suit and would sit across the table so his eyes could melt her heart again. She knew for certain that he planned to speak with her father that night. Along with Angela, the whole town had fallen for Jason with his dark hair and sparkling blue eyes. Consequently, his law practice grew each day. Jason's success would encourage Papa to bequeath his consent for his daughter's matrimony.

Although knowing she might interrupt a client, Angela *had* to drop by his office that Tuesday. She decided that if she could not steal one of his warm, tender kisses, she would discreetly blow him one from her fingertips. The bell jingled merrily as she stepped through the door and into the small, outer office. An uneasy silence settled about the quarters like the faint gasp of an insulted matron. Muffled noises, oozing with the nuance of impropriety, drifted from Jason's main office. A rolling chair, gliding across the hard wood floor, accompanied a suppressed giggle.

"Jason?" Angela called. "Are you there?"

"Just a minute," he shouted.

The caution in his voice left Angela's stomach churning with misgivings. "Is everything all right?"

A second giggle brought a tingle to the back of Angela's neck and left her legs weak. Jason's oak office door stood open by only inches. As if propelled by some unseen force, Angela stepped around the secretary's desk and approached the door. Her fingers shaking, she pushed against it. Complaining with a coarse creak, the door swung inward to reveal a faded couch in the room's shadowy corner. Leah Marsh, the barmaid at the saloon, sat in a disheveled heap. A silly smile adorned her painted face. Jason stood by the window trying to get his shirt buttoned. Traces of lip rouge left their telltale prints around his mouth, cheeks, and even on the right earlobe.

"Angela. I. . .I can. . .explain," he stammered.

"Explain!" Angela gasped, feeling as if her soul had been ripped out and trampled by a thousand stampeding stallions. "Explain!" she erupted again, choking back a disillusioned sob. "This scene does. . .doesn't need any. . .any explanation. You won't *ever* ex–explain anything to me. . .me *again*." She stumbled back, grasped the knob, and slammed the door shut. The sound made a thud in her heart like a steel curtain dropping on the stage of her life.

The few feet to the front door felt like a day's journey through a dense, briar-filled forest, infested with vipers and carnivorous beasts. Angela trudged past the thorns of depression, the pits of heartache, the crags of worthlessness, before finally gripping the knob that would lead her to the boardwalk, to her waiting horse and buggy. Confusion, dense as a cold fog, descended upon her as she clambered onto the driver's bench.

Forgetting other errands, Angela wheeled the buggy around and headed for home. Once out of town, the sobs tore at her soul, seeming to shred her spirit with every eruption. The road turned into a watery blur while the gray mare strained forward in abeyance to her furious urging. As they neared her parents' homestead amidst flying dust and a creaking buggy, Angela, at last, slowed the exhausted animal. The buggy rolled to a shuddering halt, and Angela plunged into the house, racing directly to her room. Her bitter crying lasted well into the night.

The day after Christmas, Angela's father called on Jason's office. The next day, her three brothers paid a visit of their own. By the first of the year, Wiley left town, and no one ever saw him again. Although everyone was kind, weeks of personal anguish and months of public humiliation dogged Angela. In spite of her parents' spiritual support and her questioning prayers, the bitterness of betrayal severely hindered her healing process. God had seemingly given Angela the man of her dreams, only to allow him to be yanked away. Jason Wiley had played a cruel trick on her. Her scarred heart never beat as softly again.

Mother and Father sacrificed to make a new life possible for Angela. Three days after her twentieth birthday they sent her to Houston College for Teachers. Her wounds closed but never completely healed. The delights of watching her pupils learn slowly became the focus of her life. The happy faces of her current students paraded across the field of her dreams, each busy at spelling, reading, or math. . . .

❖

The pain of her past bubbled to the surface again and tore her spirit with new rivers of tears. "No. . .no. . .no. . . Why, Jason, why. . . ," she muttered, shifting from side to side until she gradually gained consciousness. Her hair, damp with tears, clung to the sides of her face, and the sheet and quilt tangled around her legs as if she had been running in place. Angela, sitting up, gazed around the simple room, rubbed her eyes, and wondered when these horrible nightmares would cease. During the past years, they had reduced themselves to only two or three times a year, but Angela was tired of even that much. Frustrated, she dashed aside the disheveled covers and stood.

The light of the full autumn moon sent rays of golden honey flooding into Angela's room through an open window. She padded across the floor and stilled the fluttering curtains long enough to pull the window shut against the cool September breeze. Rubbing her arms, Angela walked toward her dresser and picked up the watch she wore on a chain around her neck. Squinting, she tilted the watch toward her window and saw the eleven o'clock hour swiftly approaching. She could not have been asleep more than half an hour.

With a faint groan, Angela deposited the watch back on the tatted doily and walked to her bed. In defeat, she lay on the feather mattress, sinking deeply into its folds as she sank into an equally deep despair. During the light of day, Angela could convince herself that she was completely over Jason Wiley. Even now, she conjured images of him in her mind and was pleased with the lack of romantic notions his form evoked.

Perhaps Angela's problems lay less with leftover love for Jason and more with leftover agony from the wounds he inflicted.

Her adolescent dreams of true love now seemed nothing but a mockery. At age thirty-two, those fantasies had dimmed to infrequent moments of hope, followed by fearful doubts. Occasionally, brief longings for the love of an honest man did flood Angela's heart, but the visions usually wandered down the misty road of "never mind." She looked toward the vacant spot beside her and wondered if she really wanted to grow old alone. Then, the anguish rose from the pits of her soul once more. *Alone. . .yes, alone is better than risking more heartache.*

The thought of agreeing to marry a man left Angela drowning in panic. Her younger cousin, Rachel Campbell, had recently told Angela that the Lord could help remove the haunting shadows from her eyes. But Angela was not sure she *wanted* them removed. She had hidden behind those haunting shadows and thus kept her heart safe for many years. So Angela clung to the shadows. They would continue to shield her for decades to come.

With a defeated sigh, she placed her hands behind her head. Tomorrow was Friday, filled with reports, testing, and lessons. But before school, she needed to check the pumpkins, sweet potatoes, and other vegetables in her fall garden. Alone. . .Angela would check the garden alone.

❖

In Rusk, Noah hurried down the shadowed boardwalk and paused at the corner before crossing a pathway, which led to an alley between the buildings. After five easy strides, he mounted the next wooden walkway and continued his hurried mission toward the livery, toward his horse. At last, the livery stable came into sight. Noah, his mind whirling with prayers and panic, sprinted from the boardwalk and neared the structure that appeared to be a small, red barn with closed double doors.

Surreptitiously, he glanced over his shoulder before testing the door. It swung inward with a faint sigh, exposing Noah to the smells of horseflesh and hay. His pulse pounding in anticipation, Noah entered the structure and strode straight toward the row of stables lining the back wall. He had placed his horse here two days ago and told the owner he would only spend one night in Rusk. Then, the first morning in town, he had been nabbed for murder.

Frantically, Noah peered into each stable, desperate for any sign of his coal black gelding. His boots shuffled against the hay-strewn floor and seemed to produce enough sound to awaken the whole town. *Oh Lord*, he prayed while finding a dappled gray in the next to the last stable, *tell me that man didn't sell my horse when he found out I was supposed to hang.* Only one stable remained, and Noah pondered his limited options should that stable not hold his steed. He could either steal one of the horses or see how far he could get on foot. As Noah approached the final stable, he decided he really did not have a choice. Noah could not steal a horse. Breaking from jail had been bad enough—but he was innocent. Noah would not turn to horse thievery. Holding his breath, he peered into the stable to see the great, dark eyes of his ebony mount gazing back at him. Midnight whinnied and knocked an anxious greeting with one hoof against the stall's floor.

Noah suppressed a shout of victory. "Hello, Boy. Miss me?" he whispered instead, extending his hand to stroke the horse between his eyes. The horse huffed out his nose and raised his head, his ears pricked. Noah turned the wooden latch and the door swung outward. "Listen," Noah said under his breath. "I need you to run like you've never run in your life. Understand, ol' boy? We don't have a second to spare."

Noah retrieved his saddle, which hung on the wooden rail, and silently slipped it on the horse's back. Midnight pranced restlessly as if he were anticipating his mission. At last, with the saddle fastened and Midnight's bit in place, Noah led the horse across the spacious livery, toward the slightly ajar front door.

"We've almost made it," he soothed, his mouth as dry as Texas dust. "Almost. . ." He opened the door, led Midnight into the shadows, and mounted his steed. As he swung the animal around, he could almost taste victory. Then, a voice from within the livery bellowed, "Horse thief!"

His victory turning to despair, Noah rammed the heels of his boots into the gelding's sides. In response, Midnight bolted up the street.

"Horse thief! Horse thief! Help!" the man roared, and a hound joined in with a course of offended barks.

"Come on, come on, Boy, run!" Noah urged, jamming his boots even deeper into the horse's side. His ears back, the horse surged forward, ever faster.

But the steed was not fast enough. Before Midnight galloped thirty yards, the loud report of a pistol attested to the livery owner's fury. A searing pain tore at Noah's side, and he gripped the saddle horn to keep his balance. "Oh dear Lord, I've been shot," he ground out. "Save me!"

Another bullet whizzed past his head, and a turn in the road could not have come at a better moment. Noah, leaning forward, clung to the saddle horn with one hand, and clasped the reins in the other. The horse continued its northward journey, and every breath racked Noah's body with a jagged blade of pain. A warm ribbon of blood inched its way across his waist and down his thigh as a growing fog seeped into his brain.

Time blurred as Noah pushed Midnight to the end of his endurance. The longer they traveled, the more Noah leaned upon the horse. At last, his cheek pressed into the gelding's damp hair, and the animal's exhausted wheezing seemed an echo of Noah's own labored breathing. After several miles of galloping, the horse reduced his rate to a canter. When the hours of morning approached, Midnight slowed to a walk. Eventually, his steps grew shorter, until he stopped and seemed to quietly estimate which of them would move next.

Struggling to think, Noah rubbed his gritty eyes and peered at his surroundings. The eastern horizon, pale from the approaching sun, produced faint illumination but not enough to penetrate the shadows. All Noah's foggy mind could acknowledge was that somewhere in their journey, they had wandered off the road and into what might be someone's garden.

Midnight shifted his weight as if he were weary to the bone. "I'm sorry, Boy," Noah muttered, his tongue thick. "So, so sorry." The blackness in his mind pushed back the feeble light of concentration. The combination of pain and loss of blood, along with lack of food and water took their toll upon Noah. He loosened his hold on the saddle, slowly collapsing onto a bed of cool, damp vines. Inky darkness wrapped its heavy cloak around his troubled spirit.

Chapter 3

S hortly after dawn, Angela stepped out her back door and fitted the calico bonnet on her head. In seconds, she fashioned the ties into a snug bow under her chin and looked toward her fall garden. A heavy autumn dew covered the piney, east Texas hills and attested to the cool night temperatures which bore the kiss of autumn. By noon, Angela fully expected the hint of summer heat. But for now, she would enjoy the cool air.

She retrieved the small, sharp hoe from near her back door and walked toward the fall garden, full of pumpkins, tomatoes, turnips, and sweet potatoes. In the distance, a whippoorwill serenaded the rising sun that created a rainbow of colors on the eastern horizon. At the garden's edge, Angela paused to savor the morning smells clinging to her work dress: the scent of earth, the freshness of her garden, the aroma of coffee.

Angela's expectant cat, Grey, produced a faint meow and rubbed against her ankles. "Hello, Kitty," Angela said, bending to scoop the animal into her arms. Grey purred and rubbed her face against Angela's. The cat had been a great companion for Angela during the last few weeks. She had arrived on the teacher's steps in August, and Angela eventually realized the cat would soon produce a few more "friends."

"Did you come to help me work?" Angela asked, depositing the feline at her feet. With a disinterested air, the cat trotted toward the house as if to incite Angela to provide her usual saucer of milk.

Smiling, Angela gripped the hoe and stepped into the garden, ready to tackle the weeds that had arrived in the last few days. A classic folk song she planned to teach her students poured from her rich, alto voice.

The tune danced among the brittle shafts of corn, left over from summer, and echoed against the deep orange bowls of ripening pumpkins. Angela gently hoed out the weeds and examined the growing autumn vegetables for signs that they were ready to harvest.

The fall tomatoes, toward the center of the garden, pled for her attention. The obnoxious grasses, vying for nutrition, seemed to have sprung up overnight. Angela viciously applied the hoe to the weeds, while noting with satisfaction that she would have ripened tomatoes within the week. She continued her song, digressing to a merry yodel from time to time.

Her hoe, striking against a reddish rock, produced a heavy clank, but another noise, like a swishing in the dried cornstalks, diverted Angela's attention. Pausing, she straightened and strained to listen, but heard only the faint breeze. She turned back to her task and took two more steps before the rustling in the corn stalks stopped her again. Angela's demanding schedule had prevented her from removing the stalks from the corner of her garden after the corn had stopped producing. Now, something was awkwardly moving through the weed-infested stalks. That something was, most likely, a raccoon.

With the hoe poised, Angela cautiously edged toward the quivering stalks. She had never killed a coon. They reminded her too much of cats, and she loved cats. But Angela certainly held no qualms about scaring the daylights out of any coon. She stopped within inches of the corn and weeds, raised her hoe and yelled, "Get out of here, you nasty varmint!" Angela drove the hoe against the ground to produce a pounding threat, sufficient to scare the most daring of coons. The hoe hacked aside a layer of weeds to reveal the face of a man—not a coon.

"P–please," the man faintly begged. "I've. . .I've b–been shot. H–Help me." The man's face contorted into a painful grimace.

"What are you doing here?" Angela gasped, her mind whirling with shock.

"They. . .they w–were going to. . .to hang me in. . .in Rusk. I–I'm innocent," he said, panting with every word. "C–couldn't. . .couldn't let them h–hang me." He swallowed hard. His dark brows knitted together. He squinted as if concentrating were a monumental task.

Angela weakly leaned on her hoe and suspiciously scanned the countryside. The hair on the back of her neck prickled as she pondered the possibilities. This whole situation might be a trap of some sort. Her gaze settled once more on the man, whose face had fallen against his arm. *But what if he's telling the truth?* Angela wondered what it would feel like to be falsely accused of murder: the panic, the horror, the terror.

"W–water. . .I need. . .need water," the man rasped, reaching toward her laced work boot. "P–please. . .p–please help. . .help me." He gazed upward, his dark eyes full of pain. Pain and questions. Questions and desperation.

Impulsively, Angela knelt beside him and pushed away the intruding weeds, only to discover that they were smeared with blood along his right side. "You *have* been shot," she muttered, examining the tattered shirt, stained red.

"Y–yes."

With shaking fingers, Angela gently pulled away the shredded shirt to see what appeared to be a deep flesh wound, still oozing with blood. She winced as the man moaned. "I'm. . .I'm sorry."

"I–I need. . ." He trailed off, and a final look into his agonized eyes prompted Angela to make a decision. The strong lines of his square jaw, shaded with whiskers, suggested a man of honor who, at the moment, required assistance. She would aid him. Then, she would most likely notify the authorities. If he were indeed innocent, he should somehow prove that to the sheriff. Meanwhile, Angela's compassionate nature left her no choice. The same woman who took in an expectant, stray cat. . .the same woman who sat up late sewing dresses and shirts for students in need. . .the same woman whose heart would not allow her to kill a coon. . .that same woman would help this ailing stranger.

"I'm not sure I know what to do with you," Angela said, as if she were talking with herself. "I've never treated a gunshot wound before. Maybe Dr. Engle—"

"No." His firm refusal came with more spunk than he had yet expressed. "If. . .if you can j–just give me. . .give me food. . .food and w–water and. . .and a b–bandage. . . and a night's. . .night's rest. . .I'll. . .I'll be on my. . .on my way."

The liquid brown eyes now beseeching Angela seemed full of anything but murderous intent—only gentleness and goodness, touched with distress. The vertical lines between his heavy brows spoke of a man of thought, a man of quiet but intense power. The curve of his lips suggested a sensitive spirit. Something in his voice urged her to give him a chance. . .to trust his word.

But her rooster's raucous crow from near the schoolhouse seemed an echo from Angela's recurring past. Once she *had* trusted a man. Trusted with all her heart. That trust had resulted in her betrayal, heartache, devastation. *You are crazy to even consider helping this man!* a rational voice urged. *He probably is a murderer. Leave him here! Wait until the schoolchildren arrive, and have one of them go for Constable Parker.*

"J—just one day. . . ," he gasped. "One d–day of your. . .your time. That's. . .that's all I'm. . .I'm asking. But. . .but, please. . .please don't. . .don't turn me in," he said as if he could read her mind.

Her stomach clenching with indecision, Angela did something she had not done in years. She shot a brief prayer heavenward, beseeching the Lord to direct her decision. Torn with anxiety, she at last settled upon the first plan. Angela would at least treat this human being with the dignity she had bestowed upon her stray cat. She would give the man water and food and tend his wound. After that, she would face the other decisions to be made.

"Can you walk?" she asked as another doubt nagged her. One of the conditions of her teaching contract involved Angela's not allowing men into her home unless they were escorted.

"M—maybe," he said, relief evident in his relaxing shoulders. "If. . .if you'll help. . .help me."

Nervously, Angela looked to the east and noted the sun's position. The children would arrive within an hour. She had precious little time to spare if she was going to successfully hide this man in her home before anyone arrived. No one—*no one* must ever suspect that the Dogwood schoolmistress was housing a lone gentleman. That would mean the end of her job.

"We don't have much time to spare if I'm going to get you settled. I am a schoolteacher. Within the hour, the children will start arriving for school." Leaning on her hoe, Angela grabbed his arm.

"What. . .what about your h–husband? H–he should. . .should help."

"Don't have a husband," Angela said in the brusque voice she often used to hide her vulnerability.

"Me either." His irrational comment spoke of his confusion as well as his marital status. And the fact that this desperate human being was also without a wife left her in an even more compromising position.

"Here," she commanded, taking his chilled hand in hers. "Use the hoe handle to pull yourself up." She placed his hand on the hoe, and he gripped it.

After several failed attempts at righting himself, the man dragged himself to his knees. Angela, her pulse pounding, apprehensively glanced across the school yard and up the dusty road. Still, no sign of a living soul. Accompanied by the sound of her rooster's persistent squawking, Angela gritted her teeth and tugged on the man's arm while he stumbled to his feet. Pausing, he gripped the wooden handle with both hands as if it were his lifeline.

"Haven't. . .haven't eaten since y–yesterday m–morning." He swallowed as if his mouth were full of dust. "N–need some water t–too."

"Yes. . .yes. But, we've got to get you into the house first." Angela stepped to his good side and placed his arm along her shoulders. "Now, lean against me," she commanded, offering her shoulders for support.

"Don't. . .don't want to knock you o–over, Lady," he said as if he were truly concerned for her safety.

"I'll be fine," she countered with spunk as he relaxed against her. A tall woman, Angela found this man's unusual height a surprise. Many men were shorter than she.

Bit by bit, the pair hobbled out of the garden and toward the cottage. All the while, Angela scanned the yard and surrounding countryside, feeling as if the entire community were watching. But the only eyes observing her belonged to her two horses and the one milk cow, watching them from the north pasture.

The faint smell of leather and horseflesh clung to the man. That, coupled with his warmth, left Angela all too aware that twelve years had lapsed since she had allowed a man this close. Her face flushed with the turn of her thoughts, and she was thankful for the physical exertion that covered any reason for the blush.

As they neared her back door, Angela worriedly glanced over her shoulder to see only the ancient barn and a few hens, pecking here and there. Nonetheless, her feelings of being watched persisted. She glanced toward the face, whose narrow set eyes and long, straight nose reminded her of a Greek sculpture, honed in fine marble. But now, that face blanched with pain. "Are you going to make it?"

"Yes. . .just a few more. . .more feet," he said through puffing breaths.

Angela, her mind whirling, tried to devise a plan for hiding the man during the next day. The thought of someone finding him in her home and her subsequent dismissal from her job left her wondering if she should reverse her decision and turn him in to the authorities. But Angela recalled the flickering light in his deep, serious eyes. In spite of his condition, the spirit she saw melted her heart and made him seem more like a crippled deer rather than a gunshot murderer.

Nonetheless, the face of Jason Wiley flashed across her mind. *He had beautiful eyes—eyes that made me want to melt.* She dashed a glance at the victim, then looked at her back door, only feet away. *I'm crazy!* she thought in panic and coerced herself not to jump away from him. The winds of indecision once more accosted her, like an angry hurricane, yanking a lone ship from one watery, mountainous crest to another. Her pulse pounding all the more urgently, she continued her journey until the back door was within reach. Angela, rigid with fear, stopped in her tracks and stared at the metal doorknob as if it were a coiled copperhead, so prevalent during east Texas summers.

Gasping for air, the man seemed to relinquish a new portion of his weight upon her shoulders with every minute that passed. Her spine and neck ached, and Angela fought back the tears of doubt that pushed against her soul. She felt the man's curious appraisal and darted a glance into his eyes. A current of silent communication flashed between them, and Angela voiced her misgivings.

"If anyone finds out I'm hiding you, I'll lose my. . .my job." She gulped and forced the tears into abeyance. "And. . .and if you're lying to me, Mister—"

"I'm t–telling you the. . .the truth," he said feebly, his face seeming to grow more ashen with every word.

Across the yard, that persistent rooster produced another hoarse crow, and Angela jumped. Then, a dove's soft cooing brought back memories of her brother, Eric. Even as a child, he had loved to sit outside and listen to the doves. But Eric was in heaven now. He had arrived at the pearly gates as a young man because he had been falsely accused of a heinous crime. This man, leaning upon her, claimed a similar fate.

Without another thought, she reached for the doorknob, twisted it, and allowed the creaking door to swing inward. As her cat scurried into the kitchen, the sound of the door's unoiled hinges sent a chill across Angela's spirit. She cast another indecisive look at the man and held his tormented gaze. Something in the center of her being shuddered in reaction to his rugged, masculine appeal. Even with his features twisted in pain, this tall man, so close to Angela, left her recalling the nights she had pondered the possibilities of allowing herself to fall in love once more. These unexpected thoughts made Angela want to run all the more.

"P–please, Lady, don't. . .don't desert m–me now," he stammered as if he could read her mind.

"I have precious little choice at this point," she said with practical resignation, although images of Eric left her feeling far from practical. "I can't exactly leave you sitting on my porch steps." Angela, accepting this very truth herself, placed her foot on the first of three short steps leading up to the back door. "If you can make it into the kitchen, I think I have the perfect spot for you," she said, thinking of the storm cellar underneath the braided rug.

"Oh?" he said, a note of caution in his voice. "D–do you. . .you plan to. . .to boil me in. . .in oil?"

Angela turned widened eyes toward the man to see a spark of humor tilting the corners of tight lips and trailing through his dark, limpid eyes. "No indeed," she answered, refusing to smile. "My father and brothers dug out a storm cellar under the kitchen a year ago after a tornado helped itself to my roof. I keep a mattress, lamp, and bedding down there—just in case."

The two of them struggled up the three wooden steps, only to have the man stumble over the door's threshold and collapse just inside the kitchen. Angela, still gripping onto her charge, joined him in a heap on the floor, her knees and right hip stinging with the jolt of the fall.

A low groan erupted from the man.

"I'm sorry," Angela panted while trying to disentangle herself from his long arms. Her face heating anew, she evaluated the impropriety of her position and ascertained that if the facts concerning the activities of the morning fell into the right hands, she would be unemployed by sundown. Forcing herself to remain calm, she determined to place as much distance as possible between her and this stranger who had been dropped into her life. Angela wrenched the bonnet from her head, cast it aside, stood, and reached for his legs. She swung them into the kitchen and shut the door with a decided click. The shadows that engulfed them seemed the cloak of finality. Angela had made her decision. She hoped she did not live to regret it.

Chapter 4

Thirty minutes later, Angela stood at the top of the ladder, which led into the storm cellar. She paused, brushing aside the beads of perspiration on her forehead that resulted from her labor and distress. Getting the man down the ladder and onto that mattress had been an adventure, to say the least. Already, Angela felt as if she had worked from sunup to sundown. Darting repeated glances toward the window, she took a deep breath and clutched the mug of herbal tea and extra quilt she planned to deliver to the man. The first pupils had begun to arrive. Soon, they would wonder where she was.

Angela carefully picked her way down the steep steps and into the coolness of the dark earth, illuminated by only the flickering flames of twin candles and the pinpoints of light seeping through the cracks in the kitchen floor. The man lying on the feather mattress amidst the shadows observed her with gentle eyes. "Thanks for the water and soup," he said, his voice and breathing less strained. "I. . .I think I'm already improving."

Before her last trip to the cellar, Angela had retrieved last night's soup from the spring house. Upon presenting the man with some sustenance, he had attacked both the water and warmed-up soup so ferociously that she made him slow his intake. "I'm glad they helped. I brought you some of Dr. Engle's special tea." She extended the warm mug, and he propped himself up to receive it. "He gave it to me last spring when I wrenched my ankle. The tea will help you sleep and take some of the edge off the pain."

As he greedily drank the liquid, Angela moved about in silence,

424

spreading the extra blanket across the man's form. She planned to place a chamber pot in the room before leaving for school, a distasteful, yet necessary task. She felt Noah watching her and that left her all the more uncomfortable. *Oh Lord*, she prayed to herself. *I know I haven't been the best at keeping up between me and You, but if You could just assure me that I haven't made a mistake concerning this man. . .and. . .and get me out of this situation without anyone discovering what I've done.*

"The children are arriving," she said formally. "I must tend to my duties."

"Yes. . .of course," he said politely as he set the empty mug on the floor beside the bed.

She reached toward the stoneware basin sitting next to the mattress and picked up the white cloth lying in the cool water. The sounds of dripping liquid accompanied her wringing out the makeshift bandage. "I'll remove the other cloth and place this new one on your wound. Hopefully, by the time I come back to check on you, the water will have dissolved all the dried blood and we can get a better idea of how bad off you are. Right now, I think it's just a deep surface wound."

"Hurts like half my side is gone."

"I can only imagine," Angela said. She pulled back the covers and tugged aside the first cloth, already stained red.

He winced and produced a pain-filled gasp.

"Sorry," she said. "I think the bleeding has about stopped altogether, if that makes you feel any better."

"I feel better than—than I have in days," he said as she laid the damp cloth on the wound and replaced the covers.

With the sound of children squealing in the school yard, Angela paused for a moment to search the man's eyes. The appreciation and admiration flowing from his dark orbs left a tendril of respect twining its way through her spirit. An unexpected question scurried through her mind: *Would a convicted criminal be so polite and thankful?*

"I think you just saved my life, Lady," he said, gratitude oozing from his words. "Do you, by chance, have a name?" Again, a faint smile attested to a sense of humor, not far beneath the surface of the pain and drowsiness.

"Miss Isaacs. Miss Angela Isaacs," she replied, never taking her gaze from his. "And yours?"

"Reverend Noah Thorndyke."

Her brows shot up of their own volition.

"Surprised?" he asked, his eyelids drooping. "They think I'm a killer named. . .named Rupert Denham. It would seem that we look alike. I was scheduled to hang this morning. Instead, looks like I met an angel." He lazily observed Angela.

She flinched as his words brought back unpleasant childhood memories.

"I'm sorry. I have offended you," Noah said with concern.

Sighing, Angela shook her head. "It's nothing. I took no offense." During her school days, some of Angela's classmates had tormented her by dubbing her "Angel." She had always been taller and thinner than the other children and often she was assigned the part of an angel in Christmas plays. Soon, several of the bratty boys had shortened "Angela" to just "Angel." The nickname stuck, especially when her classmates learned she detested the moniker.

The clanging of the school bell announced the arrival of the Johnson twins. Those two third-graders apparently didn't believe they could survive one day without ringing the bell loudly enough to be heard across the county.

"Sounds like they're ready for you," Noah said, eyeing her with a mixture of uncertainty, distrust, and fear.

"Yes. I must go now. I'll check on you as soon as I can." Gathering her skirt, Angela stood.

"Please, Miss Angela. Promise me. Promise you won't turn me in?" Noah asked, his face full of apprehension.

Chewing her bottom lip, Angela again debated her predicament. "I could lose *my job* over having you here," she said. "It would be incriminating enough if you were a gentleman. But the fact that, by your own admission, you're a convicted criminal—"

"And innocent. I could lose *my life*." He grimaced as if the very words increased the pain in his side.

The bell continued its incessant clanging, and Angela moved toward the ladder only a few feet away. She weighed his potent comments. His life was certainly more valuable than her job. *But what if he isn't innocent?* As she gripped the ladder, a new thought struck her. This man said he was a preacher, but could he prove it? She exposed him to a piercing gaze and stated, "Quote the Twenty-third Psalm."

"Excuse me?" He squinted as though he were straining to catch her meaning.

"The Twenty-third Psalm—can you quote it?"

"Yes, but—"

"You say you're a preacher. Do you know your Bible?"

Immediately, he began to slowly, deliberately, quote the well-known passage.

When he finished, Angela blurted, "What about Genesis 1:1?"

"In the beginning God created the heaven and the earth." He held her gaze and continued, a firm edge to his otherwise sleepy voice. "And the earth was without form, and void; and darkness was upon the face of the deep. And the spirit of God moved upon the face of the waters. And God said, Let there be light: and there was light. And God saw—"

"And can you recite the story of the birth of Jesus from Luke?" Angela asked, now expecting him to meet her request.

His gaze never wavering, he obliged her. Three verses into his recitation, he stumbled across several words and knitted his brows as if the effort were taxing his strength.

"That's fine," Angela said, her voice reflecting her growing distress. If he were indeed telling the absolute truth about his predicament, that left her in a precarious situation. She could not, in good conscience, turn out an innocent man to be hanged. The potential tragedy left her reeling with a new sense of moral obligation. Fresh memories of Eric's cruel death flooded her as Angela chose one last test to prove Noah Thorndyke's Bible knowledge. "And what about Malachi six-twenty?"

"There's. . .there's no s–such chapter," he said, as if each word required increasing effort.

Something in the deepest recesses of Angela's soul confirmed that the man was very likely telling her the truth. Her chilled fingers, gripping the ladder, shook against the rough wood. The dank smells of earth seemed at once suffocating. The lantern, flickering near Noah's mattress, accented his distraught features. And all Angela could think was, *Dear Lord, what have I gotten myself into?*

The school bell, which had ceased for a season, began ringing all the louder. "I'll be back as soon as possible," she said.

Noah nodded, his eyes closing as if he could no longer hold them open. "And. . .and you won't. . .won't tell?" he slurred, but before Angela could answer, his rhythmical breathing attested to sleep's claim.

Her stomach churning, Angela raced up the ladder and retrieved the chamber pot. After setting it in the corner, she ascended back into the kitchen, closed the cellar door, and covered it with the woven rug. She rushed to her bedroom and examined her appearance in the dresser mirror. A cobweb graced her hair, along the edge of her bun. Dirt smudged her nose. And the expression in her brown eyes spoke of a woman deeply troubled.

Angela schooled her features into her schoolmistress mien, dashed away the cobweb, and stepped to the washbasin. She thoroughly scrubbed her hands and splashed her face with cool water. She dried her face on the way to the kitchen and dropped the cotton cloth on the rough-hewn, oak dining table. When she stepped onto the short back door steps and looked down, Angela spotted the imprints of a man's boots in the dust, near her cottage. Violently trembling, Angela dashed back inside, grabbed her worn broom, and rushed outdoors to brush furiously at the footprints until they were no more.

She propped the broom by the back door and rushed toward the group of mischievous boys gathered around the school bell.

"Teacher! Here comes Teacher," one of them squawked before all raced toward the schoolhouse.

Frowning, Angela followed in their wake, up the short flight of steps, and opened the door leading into the one-room haven of learning that resembled a small chapel. With the change of every season, Angela meticulously changed the schoolroom's look. Through the years, she had collected a wide array of colored material and used it to create an aura pleasing to the senses. Presently, the walls on either side of the chalk-board were covered with cloth the color of pumpkins. Angela had used the tiny nails that held the material in place to tack leaves and branches of pine needles upon the fabric. The two bookcases, large globe, and printed multiplication tables added to the room's aura of learning.

Presently, all twenty-five of Angela's students rigidly sat in their worn desks, facing the chalkboard. She pondered the necessity of taking the boys to task over the bell ringing but decided not to. Given all that had happened this morning, Angela had precious little strength left to chide children, despite their deserving it.

"Let's get our morning underway," she said, briskly stepping into the schoolroom. She started to close the door behind her but hesitated as the sound of horses' hooves pounded into the school yard. Angela, glancing over her shoulder, caught sight of one symbol amidst the flurry of horses: a sheriff's badge. Approximately twelve men accompanied a lawman, whose scowl spoke of hours in the saddle and a determination to accomplish his goal.

Immediately, Angela realized the men were looking for the person under her kitchen floor. Feeling as if she would lose her breakfast, Angela barked out the commands to her students. "First graders, work on your alphabet and making capital letters. Alex, you and Jenny call out the multiplication tables to each other. Grades six and seven have reading assignments. Grades eight and nine, study your world maps; there will be a test on European countries this afternoon. Lea Ann, read over your essay and check for any errors. I want to go over the grammar with you in a few minutes. Now, did I miss anyone?" No hands went up. "All right, everyone, busy now!"

Behind her, a faint knock on the door, which still stood ajar, sent a compulsive jump through Angela. Although she had fully expected one of the men to approach, his presence seemed to bring with him images of Noah Thorndyke. She turned to stare up into the sheriff's intense, gray eyes that suggested he tolerated no compromise. Under a dark, bushy mustache, his lips drew into a tight line. A bright, silver star occupied a prominent place on the pocket of his black vest.

"Yes, may I help you?" Angela asked, relying on her years of experience at maintaining composure under the direst of circumstances.

"Mornin', Ma'am," the lawman offered. "May I have a moment of your time?"

"Of course," Angela said. "Children, I am closing this door momentarily, but I will be right on the other side. I don't want to hear a peep from any of you." They dutifully continued their work. Angela, her throat constricting so tightly she could hardly breathe, stepped onto the top step and closed the door behind her. She knew before the lawman ever spoke what his inquiry would consist of, and she had no idea how she would answer.

"I'm Sheriff Garner from Rusk. We're out lookin' for this criminal." With that persistent rooster crowing from Angela's yard, the sheriff held up a "Wanted" poster. Angela examined the poster to discover the almost exact image of the man who now lay under her kitchen floor. The same dark, heavy brows. The same close-set eyes. The same prominent nose and square jawline. The name "Rupert Denham" was printed under the likeness.

Her mind whirling with a fresh onslaught of misgivings, Angela relived the events of the morning up until minutes ago when Noah Thorndyke told her they thought he was Rupert Denham.

"Have you seen a rider bearing this resemblance pass here in the last couple of hours? We're chasin' this killer. He's dangerous. He broke out of jail by duping my deputy with card tricks. We found his horse 'bout a mile up the road, near a stream."

Angela, gulping in fear, glanced toward the group of men in the school yard. Their grim faces bore the identical question, the same determination, the certainty that they would snare their prey. Angela's face chilled with the implications of her predicament. Within the last hour, she had broken her teacher's contract and possibly housed a criminal. *What must I have been thinking?* Nervously, she toyed with the watch hanging around her neck.

"Don't mean to scare you none, now, Ma'am," the sheriff said, his voice softening. At last remembering his manners, the lawman removed his hat and held it at his side as if he were attempting to hide the imposing Colt Peacemaker attached to his hip. "We're just trying to do our job. And it's very likely that there's a dangerous killer in your area. If you happen to see him. . ." Pausing, the sheriff gazed across the countryside, and Angela remembered the dried blood on the weeds in her garden.

She opened her mouth, ready to do what she should have done when she first saw the sheriff—blurt the location of Rupert Denham. But some insistent impression deep within her soul stopped the words before they left her lips. The man in the cellar said his name was really Noah Thorndyke. *Reverend* Noah Thorndyke. His quoting of scripture had even backed his claims of being a preacher. Most killers could not quote scripture like Noah had—but, then again, most preachers did not skillfully play with cards. And Sheriff Garner had said he tricked the deputy with cards.

Her palms sweating profusely, Angela rubbed them against the sides of her skirt and licked her lips. *Dear God, what do I say?* she pleaded, feeling the sheriff's scrutiny. Lips quivering, Angela could only stare at the image on the "Wanted" poster and flounder for a proper response while tears of anxiety blurred her eyes.

"Ma'am, it looks like I've scared you out of a year's growth," Garner said. "Wasn't my intent. But you and the children need to be mighty careful. Might not even hurt to close the school down for the day—just 'til we can find our man. This rat killed a banker in our town, and he was supposed to be hanged and dead by now. So he's desperate to get away. I wouldn't put it past him to kill or cheat or lie. . .whatever he has to do to get out of facing that rope he deserves."

Lie. . .lie. . .lie. . . The word echoed through Angela's mind like a chant, bent on proving Noah Thorndyke really was Rupert Denham. She opened her mouth to disclose the truth, but once more, that insistence deep in her soul stayed her words. "I'll send all the children home," she said.

"Good idea, Miss. . ."

"Isaacs. Miss Angela Isaacs." Keeping her eyes downcast, Angela extended her hand, hoping the sheriff interpreted her demure actions as those of a lady, following the rules of propriety.

"If you can round up your young 'uns quicklike, I'll get my men to escort them home."

"Yes. . .yes, of course," Angela agreed, relieved to be free of her duties. The upheaval of the morning had left her so addled, she felt anything but capable of teaching a room full of children. Furthermore, she wasn't certain a man in Noah Thorndyke's condition needed to be left to his own upkeep for the duration of a school day. He would need more water and food. In her haste, Angela had left no extra provisions for the man who claimed to be innocent.

She opened the door wider and extended a hand for the sheriff to enter. Turning on her heel, Angela walked to the front of the classroom and faced them. "Children, there has been a turn of events in our day," she said succinctly. "It seems there is a man at large who might be a danger to us. Sheriff Garner and his men have offered to escort each of you to your homes."

A collective gasp went up from the children. As one, they turned toward the sheriff, towering in the back of the schoolroom.

"Arc they looking for a murderer?" Lea Ann Turner asked. At fourteen, Lea Ann seemed more a young lady than a schoolgirl, and her questions usually reflected the intuitions of a full-grown woman.

"That's neither here nor there, Children," Angela snapped, not wanting to alarm her students any more than they would be under such odd circumstances. Besides, Angela well knew where the supposed convict resided and thoroughly believed the students were not in danger. However, she also knew she must behave in a logical manner with the sheriff; it was logical for a schoolteacher to allow her students to be escorted home. "Now, all of you gather your things and do as Sheriff Garner tells you." Gripping her hands behind her, Angela leaned back against her oversized desk ever so slightly—just enough to maintain her balance. Otherwise, she was certain her knocking knees would buckle beneath her at any given moment.

The students, bustling with excitement, grabbed their books and papers and hats and approached the sheriff. Angela, calling out instructions for proper conduct, followed in their wake. In a matter of minutes, the sheriff and Angela had assigned the sheriff's twelve men to their respective children and given out directions to the children's homes. Angela, hovering near the bottom step, watched as the children frolicked toward their homes, the horsemen close beside. Squeals of delight erupted across the countryside, belying the gravity of the moment.

Feigning composure, Angela compressed her lips and nodded toward the sheriff, standing nearby. After a brief thank you, she walked up the short flight of steps and back into the schoolroom. The smell of chalk and musty books enveloped her and at once seemed the stifling pall of accusation. Angela rushed toward her meticulous desk, plopped into her straight-backed chair, propped her elbows atop her handmade desk calendar, and covered her face with her hands. Every nerve in her body quivered in reaction to the mammoth problem that lay before her. With every passing minute that Angela did not speak the truth to the sheriff, she dug herself deeper and deeper into the pit of Noah Thorndyke's predicament. If anyone learned the truth of what she had done that morning, she would most certainly lose her job and probably every scrap of her flawless reputation.

For some reason, the image of Jason Wiley swam before her mind's eye. That man had been nothing but a lying, two-faced womanizer who looked as innocent as a lamb. He could also quote numerous scriptures from memory and produced enough "amens" during Sunday morning worship to impress most of the countryside. In light of Jason's convincing performance, Angela wondered if she had been a fool to let Noah Thorndyke's knowledge of Scripture influence her into actually believing him. She had trusted one man and vowed never to trust again. *Have I lost my mind?*

Noah's dark, honest eyes, like twin pools of ink, flashed through her mind. His tousled hair, the color of teak. His square jaw, shadowed with need of a shave. His insistence that he was innocent blended with memories of the man's masculine appeal. Noah Thorndyke was by no means as handsome as that Jason had been, but he had pulled at Angela's heart from almost the moment she saw him, helplessly lying in her garden.

Perhaps Angela's years as a spinster had finally caught up with her. For, despite her vows of avoiding all men, her lonely heart now seemed to be making decisions for her.

Angela Isaacs was lonely. Yes, lonely. She had never admitted that truth to a living soul. And even pondering the reality this morning left her traitorously wanting to walk back to her home and check on the man in the cellar. She shook her head in disgust, defeat, and distress. *If you are not guilty, Noah Thorndyke, then my helping you is the only honorable choice. But if you really are a murderer, then I am the biggest fool in Texas.*

The sound of the school door's opening interrupted her thoughts, and a quick upward glance confirmed the worst: Sheriff Garner had returned. His hat in hand, he speculatively observed Angela. Although a good twenty feet separated them, Angela felt as if his keen, gray eyes bore into her very soul. The suspenseful silence that settled around them seemed to drop a bucket full of cold, jagged rocks into Angela's stomach.

"Sorry to bother you again, Ma'am," the sheriff said in a measured voice. "But I just wanted to say that. . .let's just say that if a young woman was to happen to find that criminal and was to think of helpin' him. . ." He paused as if he were carefully considering every word. "The penalty for such ain't really appropriate for a lady like yourself."

"Sheriff, *please*," Angela gasped, so shocked she could think of nothing else to say.

The conviction in Garner's eyes wavered, and he glanced at the wooden floor. "Sorry, Ma'am," the tall lawman said. Squinting, he looked back at Angela as if he were still gauging her response. "It's just that one of my men had to get off his horse and chase after them twin boys. They ran into your garden, and my deputy came back to say he seen some blood near your dried-up corn stalks. I went over there, and the weeds are pressed down like somebody's been layin' in 'em."

Her face growing cold, Angela stared wide-eyed at the lawman. She had absolutely no words to respond to the man's direct inquiry. *Dear God, help me!* was all her mind could conjure.

Garner, a brawny man with hands the size of bear paws, cleared his throat as if he were highly uncomfortable with Angela's scrutiny. She had witnessed the exact same response out of more than one overbearing father, thwarted in his attempts to intimidate his son's teacher. "I suppose. . .I've jumped to a wrong conclusion. There's always the likelihood that an injured deer spent the night in your garden. I don't suppose that a lady in your position—"

"Thank you, Sheriff," Angela said firmly. Standing on wobbly legs, she did what she had done throughout her teaching career. Angela, sensing she had gained her bluff, took every measure to maintain the advantage in this interaction. She placed her palms against the top of the desk, drew upon every scrap of composure she could muster, and observed the overgrown sheriff as if he were a truant schoolboy.

"Would you like me to escort you somewhere?" he asked, as if he were genuinely sorry for his assumptions.

"No. . .no, that's all right," Angela supplied evenly. Straightening, she rearranged the neat row of pencils on her desk. "I have work to do here and in my home." *As in, deciding what I'm going to do about Noah*

Thorndyke! "And I can securely lock the schoolroom and my cottage. I, um, also know how to use my papa's old shotgun if the occasion arises."

"Well, we've already given this area a good lookin' over. Even if he *did* spend the night in your garden, I'd say he has moved along."

Choosing not to respond, Angela held the lawman's gaze as he nervously fingered his Peacemaker, then hedged his way toward the door. "Mighty nice makin' your acquaintance, Ma'am," he said with a nod before taking his leave.

When the door clicked shut, Angela expelled her pent-up breath and collapsed back into the chair.

Chapter 5

For hours, Noah drifted between the awareness of the dank, dimly lit cellar and the sensation of lying encased in a tomb. The dull pain in his side seemed a mere remnant of the sharp tormentor it had been. However, Noah tossed on the mattress, encased in the grips of sporadic and fitful slumber. Scenes from his youth played in the shadows of his mind like vague specters of the past. Images came and stood in the distance, their edges blurred and colors distorted, running together in whirlpools surging to the center. He strained to hear the voices, but their whispers only tantalized his ears with sketches of familiarity.

Once he thought his mother passed by. She appeared to hold out her arms and call to him, but the words were garbled; then she was gone. How he wished to speak to her and explain   no, ask forgiveness for leaving home, breaking her heart. Yet, even in his confusion, Noah remembered a time when he had already done exactly that. . . .

Then the phantom of a huge raft floating in a shoreless river moved toward him. The deck held scores of men—brawling and cursing—trying to grab Noah while the ship glided by. As the stern came abreast of Noah, a man in a long coat and beaver hat held up a pair of dice and a deck of cards. He dropped the pack and turned to a black and red wheel behind him. Thousands of numbers dotted its surface. Noah grasped the side of the boat and tried to pull himself aboard. But the well-dressed man stomped his hands and spat on him, mumbling in derision of the boy's skills. Guns barked. The gambler fell into the water, dragging Noah with him. The boy fought for air; then everything went black. . . .

But from the pits of that blackness came the faint smell of warm wax, the feel of a soft, homespun quilt, the distant caw of a crow. With great effort, Noah allowed his eyelids to admit the tiniest bit of light. The yellow glow from candles burning on a ledge across the room gave a momentary illusion of sunrise. He fully opened his eyes and surveyed the dark corners of his cell. As in his muddled dreams, Noah's mind raced with panicked thoughts that perhaps he was in a tomb—buried alive after a failed hanging. Desperately, he glanced from side to side in hopes of discovering his location. The erratic dance of the flames only increased the tomb's eeriness, and Noah's heart violently thudded.

Then, Noah remembered. . .he remembered a woman, tall and lithe, with hair the color of chestnuts and brown eyes as soft as the velvet coat of a newborn colt. Angela—her name was Angela. For some reason, she did not like his calling her an angel. Relaxing, Noah closed his eyes and the faint sound of a woman's footsteps above him increased his feeling of security. Before the doctor's tea gained control once more, Noah reminded himself that he owed that angel his life. . . .

Yet, again, a dreary plodding dream overtook Noah's mental images, and his steps led to a cottage deep in a grove of massive oaks. The roof tilted in a steep angle and grew spots of green moss on the south side. The walls were half river stones and whitewashed above. A mirror hung on the wall, and on the lawn a child played in front of the mirror. He rolled a ball in a tight circle with his foot. But another child in the mirror attempted to chase the ball and kick it away. Repeatedly the boy on the lawn laughed and called to the other to come out of the mirror and play with him. But the mirror child frowned and doubled his fists, then turned away. Thunder rumbled in the distance, and a cool breeze blew across the landscape. Suddenly a light burst against the horizon, momentarily distracting Noah. As the light continued its soft glow, a voice called his name several times.

He opened his eyes and squinted. The angel stood before him—the woman who had said her name was Angela Isaacs. Behind her, the cellar door emitted a wide shaft of light. In her hands, she held a tray of food that smelled as if it came straight from the corridors of heaven. The light from the door and the candlelight, flickering behind her, created a halo effect around her disheveled hair. Her ethereal image left the groggy Noah wondering exactly how long her tresses were and exactly how they would feel beneath his touch.

"I'm glad to see you're awake," Angela said quietly, her soft eyes kind yet worried. "It's almost two in the afternoon. You've been asleep since this morning when I left."

"Are you through with your school duties?" Noah asked as the memories of his predicament plopped into his mind, piece by piece.

"Yes." She knelt beside him, placed the tray on the floor, and busied herself with the arranging of dishes filled with food. "The sheriff arrived first thing this morning, saying he was looking for a convicted criminal named Rupert Denham." Pausing, Angela exposed him to a gaze full of fear and questions.

A tight knot as cold as a gun barrel formed in the pit of Noah's stomach. His tongue thick, he swallowed against a throat dry from sleep.

"And?" he asked nervously.

"He suggested that his men escort the children home, and I let him," she finished.

"So, you didn't—"

"No." She shook her head. "Not a word."

The knot in his stomach dissolved. "Thank God," he breathed.

"Do you feel like you can sit up and eat?" she asked, avoiding eye contact. "I have a small stool I can bring down to sit the tray on."

"Yes, thank you," Noah said, attempting to put as much honor and respect into those three little words as humanly possible. "I owe you my life," he added, repeating the sentiment he had already expressed before his long slumber.

As if she were overwrought with the burden of her charge, Angela's lips trembled and she produced but a faint nod. "How's your side?" she asked, standing.

"Better. . .thanks to you."

"Good," she said simply. Turning toward the pair of candles on the ledge, she removed a fresh taper from her apron pocket and replaced one of the spent candles.

Noah, gazing up at her, decided that Miss Angela Isaacs was by far the most enchanting specimen of femininity that he had ever encountered. The gentle turn of her lips and the hint of vulnerability in her eyes coupled with her spirit's serenity and strength began to render Noah almost giddy with the magnitude of his good fortune. Somehow, the Reverend Noah Thorndyke had gotten himself sentenced to hang, then escaped from jail, and landed in the hands of a woman of virtue who had snatched his life from the jaws of death. And the thought that sprang upon him left him breathless: *Is this whole predicament the product of good fortune or the result of God's handiwork?* His mind rushed back to the night before he left on his journey from Louisiana into east Texas. That very night, Noah had prayed that God would somehow use the trip as a means to provide him a wife, a suitable helpmate for his ministry. *Could it be?* he mused, then dashed aside the notion.

At once, Noah forced himself to turn his thoughts away from such alarming and unlikely matters. He had other concerns besides the woman whose skirts produced a delightful swish as she ascended the ladder. His life was in jeopardy!

Abruptly, Noah propped himself up on his elbow, only to produce a moan of protest when his wounded side complained. Angela immediately postponed her upward journey and rushed to his side. Kneeling nearby, she placed her arm behind Noah's shoulders to lend support while she stuffed an extra feather pillow beneath his shoulder blades. Noah, enveloped in a sweet, floral scent, observed Angela's concerned face and wondered if her cheeks were as soft as they appeared. His gut clenched, and he decided not to tell her that he felt capable of sitting up alone, despite the protest in his stiff side.

"Is that better?" she asked, trying to pull away from him. But something stopped her short, and she produced a frustrated groan as she looked downward. Noah followed her gaze to see that the chain of the watch she wore around her neck had somehow tangled in a button on his shirt. Her fingers shaking, she tried to maneuver the chain but only tangled it worse.

"Here, let me help you," Noah said as she fumbled with his button. He reached for the chain, but instead found his fingers closing around her hands. Her trembling fingers stilled within his grasp. Noah's gaze slowly traveled up her arm, across her shoulder, and found refuge in the softness of her brown eyes, as tender as an adolescent's when she's courted by her first beau.

A thrill of attraction zipped through Noah and reflected itself in Angela's eyes. His reaction, so confusing and unexpected, left him breathless with its potency. Noah's focus, bent on betraying him, trailed to her quivering lips. The inappropriate desire to kiss this woman surged through him, and he severely restrained himself with memories of his profession.

As if Angela could read his every thought, she pressed her lips together, disentangled her hands from his, gripped the chain, and ripped it away from his shirt, dislodging the button in its wake. Standing, she spun on her heel and marched back toward the ladder. "I'll return shortly with your stool," Angela ground out. Her words, as cold as jagged rocks, left Noah with no questions about her disapproval.

"Please don't be angry with me, Miss Isaacs. I guess. . .I guess. . .you saved my life," he repeated the amazing truth. "I think it's most natural for a man to. . .to feel grateful and. . .and want to express that."

Her back to him, Angela paused at the ladder, as if she were waiting for his further words. However, the sound of someone knocking on a door penetrated the cellar, and a woman's muffled voice called out Angela's name.

She gasped and whirled to face Noah. "That sounds like my cousin, Rachel." Her eyes wide with apprehension, she peered at Noah as a silent, panicked communication flashed between them. "Do the best you can to eat your meal. I know you must be hungry, but eat *quietly*. I'll check on you as soon as I get rid of—um, I mean, as soon as Rachel leaves."

"Yes, please do," Noah said with a faint smile. Perhaps his own precarious predicament was leaving him delirious, but Angela's bluntly saying she would "get rid of" her own cousin left Noah responding with humor. Her matronly scowl, obviously meant to put him—and *keep* him—in his place, only increased Noah's grin.

After a final glare, Angela tromped up the ladder, and climbed into the kitchen. Noah's perverse humor demanded that he release a faint chuckle. Before closing the cellar door, she produced a glower fierce enough to stop a rabid bull in his tracks. "There is absolutely nothing funny about this," she hissed. "You're a wanted man, and I'm an accessory. Do you have any idea what will happen if you're caught in my house? My reputation and my job will be ruined."

"Angela? It's Rachel! Are you here?" the feminine voice called again.

"I'm sorry, Ma'am," Noah said as meekly as he could. "No harm intended. It's just that—well, if you don't mind my saying, you are a sight when you're riled."

"Yes, that's what they tell me," she whispered, her eyes glaring bullets at him. Without another word, Angela lowered the cellar door and left Noah to his own devices.

Yes, you're a sight, Miss Isaacs. A sight for sore eyes. A beautiful sight, indeed. The vision of an angel. Noah reached for his food tray and scooted it closer.

Weak with apprehension, emotional fatigue, and a blazing dose of ire, Angela quietly closed the door in the floor. Within seconds, she scooted the woven rug over the door and strategically placed one of the pine dining chairs atop the rug. Rachel produced another round of knocks, and Angela blindly brushed at her disheveled hair, hoping there were no cobwebs gracing her locks.

She rushed the few feet across the tiny cottage's parlor to open the front door and find a worried Rachel looking at her in exasperation. "You scared me to death, Angel. I thought he'd already gotten you!"

"Who?" Angela asked, wondering if Rachel would *ever* stop calling her Angel.

The petite redhead turned and waved to a man sitting on the driver's bench of the work wagon. "I don't have but a minute," Rachel said, brushing past Angela. "Travis is at home with Little Trav. We decided I needed to come get you, and Travis wouldn't hear of my coming alone, considering the escaped criminal that's on the loose. So he sent one of the hired hands with me. He would have come himself, but we decided that I'd have a better chance of getting you to come home with us, considering your stubborn streak—" Her pale brown eyes widening, Rachel covered her lips and stared up at her cousin while a silent "oops" seemed to ricochet around the room.

Angela bit her lips to stop the burst of laughter that threatened to spew forth. Apparently, Noah's warped sense of humor had rubbed off on her. Or perhaps the desire to laugh was just a way to expend some of the emotions that had churned through Angela since she found Noah in her garden. At once, she understood Noah's own chuckles and immediately forgave his inappropriate humor. He must be under more pressure than Angela could ever imagine. Even though her job was at stake, Noah's life was on the line. If Sheriff Garner found him, Angela had no question that the lawman would execute his immediate hanging.

"I'm sorry," Rachel said after the weighty, lengthy pause. "I didn't mean to. . ." Rachel nervously rubbed the band of freckles that had claimed her nose since childhood—freckles so like Angela's.

"It's okay," Angela said over a chuckle. "You're right. I'm as stubborn as a mule—at least that's what Papa always says. But then, so are you," Angela said, pointing her finger at Rachel's upturned nose. The cousins shared companionable laughter.

Although Angela was a full decade older than her younger cousin, the two had been close friends since Rachel's adolescence—a friendship which deepened after Rachel experienced a miscarriage and the Lord provided a redheaded newborn for them to adopt. But while the cousins shared the same stubborn streak, their personalities varied. Rachel had always been more spontaneous while Angela was more certain, thoughtful, and precise. Other than their similar coloring of red hair, freckles, and skin tone, their appearance contrasted as widely as their personalities. While Rachel was petite and cute, Angela had always been ganglier and in her opinion, plain, despite the glow of admiration she had seen in the eyes of more than one man.

Angela tried to make up for her lack of classic beauty with an air of composure and dignity. That demeanor reaped respect from her pupils and their parents. *What would they all think if they knew I was housing a criminal?* Angela's strained mind raced in panic.

Rachel produced a resigned sigh as she nervously rubbed her hands against her full skirt. "I came to take you home with me. Are you going to come? Travis and I are really worried about you here by yourself. If you would just consider coming to the ranch, we—"

"No," Angela said gently but firmly. "Earlier this morning, Papa and Momma sent one of their hired hands for the same reason, but I've chosen to stay here. I have schoolwork to catch up on, and I am perfectly safe. That criminal has probably holed up somewhere by now, anyway." *And you just don't know how truthful that statement really is,* Angela thought as a new surge of irrational laughter bubbled up within her. Images of Noah lying only feet away and undoubtedly hearing every word left Angela feeling as if her features must scream "guilty." That realization dashed aside every nuance of laughter.

"Listen, Angel—"

"I really wish you'd stop calling me Angel," Angela snapped, reacting from the overwhelming agitation that coursed through her veins.

Taken aback by her cousin's sudden rudeness, Rachel once more stared up at Angela in round-eyed scrutiny. "I'm s–so sorry. I didn't. . .didn't realize you disliked being called that. I've always thought of it as an endearment of sorts." Rachel's limpid eyes reflected her affected feelings, and Angela felt like a shrew.

"I'm sorry I snapped at you," she said, placing a consoling hand on her cousin's shoulder. "Really. . .it's just that. . ." *It's just that there's a man hiding in my cellar. A man who says he's innocent. A man whom I just had the most shameful desire to kiss. I'm overwrought, to say the least.* But Angela voiced none of these thoughts. Instead, she silently appraised her younger cousin, who eyed her as oddly as if she had just sprouted spiraling horns from the top of her head.

"Are you feeling all right?" Rachel inquired delicately. "You look a bit pale and. . .and maybe overworked. If there's something I can do for you. . ."

"No. . . No. . ." Angela, forever honest, had never been good at duplicity, and the pressure of her situation left her feeling as if a band of deceit were forever tightening around her heart. Inch by precarious inch,

Angela Isaacs was being dragged ever deeper into the pit of Noah Thorndyke's predicament.

Like the grinding jaws of a trap, a new rush of panic clamped onto her soul. Angela's family trusted her. Her students trusted her. Her neighbors trusted her. Yet, she was breaking their faith by housing a convicted murderer.

Images of Noah Thorndyke, with his honest face and gentle, cultured voice, invaded her thoughts. He said he was innocent. With every hour that progressed, Angela became more convinced that he was indeed telling her the truth. For some unexplained reason, she was slowly doing what she had vowed never again to do—trust the word of a man.

Awkwardly, Rachel cleared her throat. "Well. . . ," she said as if she were at a total loss for words. "I guess, then, that's your answer." She reached for Angela's arm. "If there's anything I can do—I guess I'm trying to say that, whatever it is that's bothering you—you know I'm here for you."

"I know," Angela said, covering her cousin's hand with hers. "I know."

Clearly troubled, Rachel reluctantly left the cottage. Angela heartily waved at her cousin as her work wagon rolled away, up the dusty road lined with pines. The emotions tumbling through Angela left her teary with relief, with anxiety, with a deeper awareness of the magnitude of her assisting Noah Thorndyke.

Stifling several telltale sniffles, Angela stumbled into the parlor, collapsed onto the velvet settee, and covered her face with her shaking hands. "Oh Lord," she breathed as a new rush of panic swept through her soul. "What have I gotten myself into? You've got to help me." Instinctively, Angela reached for the worn Bible lying atop a doily on the walnut end table near the settee. She had placed the Bible beside the shaded oil lamp as part of the decor of the meticulous home. Angela knew that the sight of the Word of God, so prominent in a teacher's parlor, brought a sense of comfort to any parent who might frequent her quarters. But only Angela knew that the Bible was there for appearances. Over the years, she had allowed one thing and then another to crowd out her time with the Lord. Furthermore, the various heartaches of life, including Jason Wiley's breach of faith and her brother's unfair death, had somehow seemed a direct betrayal from her Lord.

But this afternoon, Angela was more desperate than she had ever been in her life. Only feet away, beneath the floor of her petite kitchen, lay a convicted criminal, eating a meal Angela had prepared for him. Distraught for some comfort, Angela turned to Proverbs. If ever she needed Solomon's heavenly wisdom, it was today. Even after all the years of not reading the Word as she should, Angela still knew her Bible well. Her mother had made certain that all her children held a solid knowledge of the Word of God.

Hungrily, Angela read the Scripture, searching for any phrase or thought, no matter how minuscule, that would bequeath her equilibrium. Upon arriving at Proverbs 3, Angela's gaze fell upon verses five and six. *Trust in the LORD with all thine heart; and lean not unto thine own understanding. In all thy ways acknowledge him, and he shall direct thy paths.* A rush of tingles swept up Angela's spine, leaving her breathless in its wake. A new surge of tears, accompanied by a muffled sob and ample sniffles, preceded the questions that bombarded her soul. *How long has it been since I trusted the Lord with my whole heart? How long since I leaned upon His understanding? How long since I acknowledged Him in all my ways?*

The disturbing questions left Angela reeling with their impact. Immediately, she snapped the Bible shut and plopped it back in its spot on the table. Rising, she took three steps toward the kitchen, then stopped, as if she had come against a wall of stone. Only feet away lay a man whose life rested in her hands. He said he was innocent, and his dark, liquid eyes suggested he was telling the truth. Angela thought of her younger brother, Eric, of the night he had been shot and killed by an angry, drunken father who accused him of the worst kind of indecency against his daughter. Months later, Eric's name had been cleared, but that was too late. Eric had already lost his life because of a lie, and by the time the father could have been held accountable, he had died in a drunken stupor. Only three years had passed since that wretched ordeal, and having Noah Thorndyke dropped into her life repeatedly brought those images back, with the full weight of their tragedy.

"Miss Isaacs?" The soft, masculine voice floating from beneath her kitchen left Angela biting her bottom lip. "Miss Isaacs," Noah called again, concern in his voice. "Is everything all right up there?"

Angela walked toward the braided rug in her kitchen. She dashed it aside, and inserted her fingers into the hole shaped like a half-moon. However, she stopped before pulling upward on the cellar door. The last time she was with Noah Thorndyke, her chain had caught in his button, and he had looked at her with a longing that Angela had felt many times.

A longing to end her loneliness. A longing to be embraced by that special someone. Over the years, when those desires came upon Angela, she forced herself to remember Jason Wiley and her vow never to trust again. But now, Angela could not quite decide if that vow had been a wise one.

"Miss Isaacs?" Noah called once more.

Angela lifted the cellar door to see Noah standing at the base of the ladder, clutching it as if he were about to collapse.

"You shouldn't be up," Angela scolded, and rushed down the steep steps toward him.

When she stood at his side, Noah observed her with drawn brows. "I thought I heard you crying," he said like a true gentleman.

Guiltily, Angela rubbed the corner of one eye. "I was just. . .just overwhelmed with the pressure of my encounter with Rachel."

"I heard everything," Noah said, the flickering candles making his pained face seem all the paler. "Thank you so much. There's no way I can ever repay you—and you don't even know me. . . ."

"Yes, I have had similar thoughts," Angela said dryly, nudging him toward his mattress. "I see you enjoyed your meal." She nodded toward the empty dishes on the tray as he lowered himself onto his bed.

"Every bite of it." Noah looked up at her as if he were an adolescent boy who had developed an outrageous attachment to his teacher.

Her cheeks warming, Angela busied herself with the tray. Schooling her face into a firm mask, she picked up the tray and turned toward the ladder. Despite her better judgment, Noah's blatant admiration left a warm rush of pleasure sprouting from her midsection. She should not—*should not*—react in such a way to a man she just met, and especially a man with a more than questionable background. The memory of her chain getting caught in his button once more wove its way through her mind and left Angela remembering her own shameful desires. She had lived a life of solitude too long—simply too long—and her emotional solitude had left her vulnerable, despite her better judgment.

"So, have you decided whether or not you really believe me yet?" Noah asked softly.

Angela stopped, and the various dishes rattled. "That's neither here nor there," she mumbled over her shoulder before balancing herself on the bottom step.

"Wouldn't you like the details of my predicament before making your final decision?"

The word "no" posed itself on Angela's lips, but she failed to voice it.

Instead, her mind whirled with curiosity. Silently, she walked up several steps and slid the wooden tray onto the kitchen floor, then descended the ladder once more. Adjusting her skirts, Angela sat on one of the ladder rungs and scrutinized Mr. Thorndyke with a ponderous gaze. "Yes, I think that would be good."

Chapter 6

Noah silently observed Angela and noted that she seemed to appear more disheveled with every passing moment. The dark circles under her red-rimmed eyes attested to her emotional and physical exhaustion, and Noah hated to think that he was the cause of such distress. But really, he had no choice but to throw himself upon her mercy. As much as he disliked bringing discomfort to a lady of Angela's quality, Noah's desire to escape a hangman's rope proved the most eminent concern.

"I will begin by saying that I believe that God brought me to you. I'm praying that He has a plan to see me through this alive, and I think perhaps you are the instrument He intends to use."

"Are you *really* a preacher?" she blurted. Her fingers, nervously picking at her heavy cotton skirt, revealed her increasing agitation.

"Yes." Noah held her gaze, determined to beam forth an expression of consummate honesty. "When all this happened, I was on my way to Tyler as a candidate for pastor at a congregational church."

"But Sheriff Garner mentioned your tricking the jailer with cards, and you even talked about gambling in your sleep," she said, a faint edge of accusation to her words.

The light, spilling through the opened cellar door, highlighted her coppery locks and flushed cheeks, and Noah recalled the long hours when he had beseeched the Lord for a companion. *Could it be?* The question nibbled at the corners of his mind and left him a bit flustered. The moment her watch chain tangled itself in his shirt button flashed through

Noah's mind, leaving in its wake the inappropriate longing to feel his lips upon hers.

Noah disciplined himself to keep his thoughts on the issues at hand, on her searching gaze, which seemed to probe the corridors of his mind in quest of the absolute truth. Shifting uncomfortably, Noah debated whether he should tell Angela of his past. Even among his close friends, he had yet to become completely comfortable with relating the story of his rebellion against godly parents, of his sinful past, of his own running from God. Noah had just met this lady and certainly was gripped in the talons of discomfort in relating such intimate, although ghastly, details. However, these wretched circumstances certainly insisted upon levels of intimacy that would normally be considered highly unsuitable. And something in the recesses of Noah's soul suggested that if he expected this angel to continue ministering to him, she needed the whole miserable story, a story that must start at the beginning.

"My parents tell me that when I was about three, they found me one Sunday morning, crying on their doorstep. Around my neck was tied a piece of paper with only the name 'Noah' written on it." He intently studied the texture of the dirt walls as he spoke. "I was really sick, and they weren't sure I was even going to live. But soon, my health returned, and they realized nobody was coming back for me. After several months, they decided to legally adopt me, but I don't remember any of that. Every memory I have is wrapped up in the parents who raised me. I have no idea what might have happened to cause me to arrive on their porch. But, I do know that my mother had been praying so desperately for a baby. She and my father had been married fifteen years at that time, and she has told me over and over again that I was her special gift from God."

"So you were adopted," Angela mused.

Noah nodded.

"My cousin who was just here—Rachel Isaacs—and her husband adopted a baby boy two years ago."

"I think adoption is a good thing," Noah said. "But then, I guess I would naturally think so." A vague smile played at his lips as images of the strange, plaguing dream again filled his mind. The cottage, deep in a grove of massive oaks. The boy, playing in front of a mirror. The conflict between the child in the mirror and the "real" boy. Recalling the dream made Noah feel as though he swam in a sea of confusion, and he was hard-pressed to maintain his concentration.

He closed his eyes as fresh sorrow issued from his soul. "I told you about my parentage to underscore just how wretched my choices were. Everything my parents did for me makes what I did to them all the more detestable. By the time I was thirteen, I decided I was tired of hearing about the Bible. My father is a Methodist minister who doesn't mince any words when it comes to the Word of God.

"Anyway. . . ," he slowly continued, placing his hand between the pillow and his head. "I ran away from home one night after my father had thoroughly thrashed me."

"Was he terribly mean to you?" Angela asked, a hint of concern in her voice.

"No. I had it coming," Noah replied practically. "And that's the only time I can remember Father really tearing into me. But by that time, I was taller than my mother, and, in my father's absence, I had looked down on her and told her just how smart I was and how ignorant she was. When my father came home and found my mother crying. . ." Noah left the rest unsaid. Although twenty years had passed since that pivotal day, his gut tightened with the memory of his own youthful stupidity. He stared up at the kitchen floor with its slits of light seeping into the cellar and thanked God he had come to his senses. "I guess my story is the prodigal son's all over again," he continued. "After I ran away, I wound up living on the Mississippi—gambling, stealing—doing whatever I had to do to survive. That's where I learned how to handle cards," he said, eyeing Angela to gauge her response.

Silently, she observed him, her expression schooled into a bland mask. Feeling as if he were on trial all over again, Noah continued, "I was out in the world about five years when I came to my senses and crawled back home. My parents welcomed me back with opened arms. . .so did God," he added, shifting his position. His side produced a dull ache that seemed but a reflection of the searing pain that had accosted him when the bullet tore at his flesh last night. Last night? Had he escaped from jail less than twenty-four hours ago? An eternity seemed to have slipped by since Noah had been facing death.

"And then?" Angela asked, her right brow slightly raised.

"Then, the Lord called me to preach within a year. After helping me catch up on my academics, my father enrolled me in seminary and stood by me while I prepared for the ministry. I've been pastoring now for about eight years. About six months ago, I received a letter from a deacon, Miles Norman, in the First Congregational Church of Tyler, requesting that I come preach for them. At first, I declined." He shrugged. "I'm content with my congregation, and my parents have retired and are now members of my church. But when Mr. Norman continued to correspond, I eventually decided to visit them and prayerfully consider their invitation. Besides, I—my life lately seems to need a change." Noah stopped short of mentioning his deep desire for a wife. Instead, he examined the worn, patchwork quilt covering him.

"I consulted a fellow pastor—Dan Wilson—in Timpson. He encouraged me about the opportunity and even suggested that I could always move my parents with me. When they agreed to the possible opportunity, I decided to take the trip. Everything went fine at first. Then, when I pulled into Rusk, I decided to treat myself to a night's sleep in a real bed. When I placed my horse at the livery, the owner offered to rent me the spare room at the back of the stable. It was cheaper than a hotel, and I figured the Lord was smiling on me. But sometime during the night, a couple of men broke into my room, gagged me, tied me up, and hauled me away."

Angela's eyes sparked with interest and alarm.

"They wore bandannas, and there was so little light I have no idea who they were. Oddly enough, they knew me, even called me by name. They threw me in front of the sheriff's office and knocked me out cold. When I woke up, it was close to dawn, and the sheriff was standing over me. The next thing I knew, I was thrown in jail, tried for murder, and sentenced to hang."

"Someone is framing you," Angela muttered, her eyes wide.

A wave of fury washed upon Noah. "I know! Everyone who witnessed against me at the trial was convinced I was Rupert Denham and had killed their banker."

"Have you seen Denham's picture?" Angela asked.

"Yes. They shoved a "Wanted" poster in my face the first chance they got."

"The two of you look almost exactly alike."

"I know. But I'm *not* Rupert Denham, and I have *never killed* another human being," Noah rushed. "Even during my prodigal years, I never stooped to murder."

"I believe you," Angela whispered, her tumultuous eyes seemingly tormented by her own admission.

Noah, breathless with her words, silently stared at Angela as a renewed sense of gratitude descended upon his soul. If Noah hadn't been injured, he would have twirled her around the room. "Thank God," he uttered.

Angela, tears burning her eyes, stood and walked toward one of the candles. She nervously toyed with the curved handle on the flat, tin holder and produced a sniffle.

The Bible verse that she had recently read became a recurring chant in her mind, *Trust in the LORD with all thine heart; and lean not unto thine own understanding. In all thy ways acknowledge him, and he shall direct thy paths.* This verse had sprung from the pages and branded itself upon Angela's spirit only minutes after her heavenward plea for help. The very first word of that passage was "trust"—the one word that had been Angela's bane for over a decade. In three little words, *I believe you* Angela had extended trust in Noah Thorndyke and his word. But she did believe him. Somehow, she saw Eric's horrible situation all over again in Noah Thorndyke. Furthermore, something in his dark eyes left no room for doubt—something that spoke of honor and righteousness and valor. Although Noah and Eric looked nothing alike, that same flame of honor now burning in Noah's eyes had once burned within the blue eyes of her brother.

Yet, despite what her heart whispered to her, Angela's extending the trust she had so long held at bay scared her beyond reason. As the tears silently trickled down her cheeks, she touched the candle's soft, warm wax, dripping down the taper's sides. And she knew without doubt that if Noah Thorndyke were not innocent that she was the biggest fool alive. Before that morning, she had never even seen this man. Now, she had placed her job and reputation on the line for him. The need to protect her own vulnerability left Angela pressing her lips together and whirling to face Noah.

"I do believe you, Mr. Thorndyke," she said. "But if I find out you're lying to me, I'll—I'll—"

He raised his brows.

"I'll turn you in faster than that bullet tore into your side. Do you understand me?" she asked, shaking her finger at his nose as if he were a truant school boy.

"Yes," he said solemnly. "But I can assure you that I *am* innocent, and I have *no idea* who Rupert Denham is."

"And, one other thing you need to understand," she continued as if he had never spoken. "I *will* help you get back on your feet and help all I can to get you back to your home, but that gives you no license to. . ." The memory of that intimate moment when his gaze trailed to her lips left her cheeks as warm as the candle wax clinging to her fingertips. Despite her own verbal spewing, Angela looked toward Noah's lips and wondered what she had been missing all these years. The heat in her cheeks rushed down her spine.

"Would you allow me to beg your humble forgiveness, Miss Isaacs," he said, his dark eyes spilling forth genuine repentance. "I have not been myself these past few hours. And well, if you must know. . ." Noah looked away and restlessly shifted, as if he were afraid of his own words. "I promise to behave as the consummate gentleman from henceforth during our association which, I hope, for your benefit, will remain brief," he said, his attention on the ladder.

Surprisingly, Angela felt none of the relief she had experienced throughout the years when one man or another attempted to court her and at last gave up. Instead, a tendril of disappointment sprouted deep within her heart.

"Thank you," she said dispassionately as she hurried toward the ladder. "The afternoon is waning, and I have numerous chores to which I must tend. If you'll excuse me, please." Without looking back, Angela climbed the steep steps and began to close the cellar door.

But before the door settled into place, she heard Noah's soft words, like a warm spring breeze upon branches, left barren by winter's chill. "And what, fair lady, does your past hold?"

Rupert Denham mumbled to himself and stroked his dark mustache. Impatiently, he grabbed for the scabbard at his side. With one deft move he whipped out a heavy knife and jabbed it into the tabletop. His thin-faced stepbrother, sitting across the dilapidated table, snatched his hand out of the way.

"Do that again, and you'll be sorry," Mark snarled.

"Well, he done ripped the bottom outa my plan!" Rupert shot back. "And you ain't done a thing to help."

Mark, eight years his brother's junior, wiped his face with a dirty sleeve and glared at his sibling. "What am I supposed to do but report what I learned? Would ya have me lyin' to ya?"

Denham, disgusted beyond reason, grabbed the knife's handle and maneuvered it in a slow circle until the tip loosened. He raised the knife and fiercely stabbed the table again. "No, but you could try killing Noah Thorndyke! I had him right where I wanted him, and now you've lost him!"

As if he were searching for a weapon of his own, Mark glanced around the shabby, abandoned cabin that was nestled deep in the east

Texas woods. "You got no right blamin' me," he growled. "If you want Thorndyke dead so bad, why didn't you go after him on your own?"

Denham glowered at his brother and knew he could produce no reply. Since the start of his mission to end Noah's life, Rupert had taken no chances on being identified. If and when Noah was dead, then Rupert would be dead—according to the law, anyway. And that meant freedom. Rupert scratched at his scraggly beard, grown in an attempt to disguise his appearance. That, plus the shoulder-length, bushy hair made him look more like a bear than a man. However, until Noah was dead, Rupert was taking precious little risk of discovery.

With renewed frustration, Rupert sent a tin pan and fork sailing into the wall. The pottery mug, half full of cold coffee, tipped from the table and landed in Mark's lap. "We got no food except some stinking beans and a piece of hog belly. I gotta come up with a new plan."

Standing, Mark Denham placed flattened hands on the graying table and lowered his face toward his elder brother. The afternoon sunshine, filtering through the milky windows, cast a glow upon his hard, gray eyes making them seem more like granite. "You ain't gonna have me in them plans if you don't stop treatin' me like the dirt under your feet. I'm sick of it!" He grabbed a handful of Rupert's shirt. "I'm doing the best I can to help you, and yer actin' like a bear! Now, you've got a choice, big brother," he sneered. "You can either stop yer stupidity or you can dig your way out of this one alone."

Rupert, shocked speechless, stared at his kid brother in disbelief. Never had Mark stood up to him so vehemently. And, for the first time Rupert saw Mark as a man, not the kid he had helped raise. However, he could never let Mark get the upper hand. Standing, he jerked his brother's hand from his shirt and tightened his grip on his wrist. "Don't threaten me, *Boy*," he growled. "If you leave me high and dry and I get caught, I'll tell every lawman who'll listen just how big of a help you've been in all our little projects. Understand?"

The edge in Mark's eyes dulled a bit, but the steel remained. "That ain't so, and you know it."

"Well, I've been lookin' for Noah ever since Pa told me about him on his deathbed! Now that I've found him, I'm not gonna let you ruin it for me! Pa might have spoiled you rotten, but I ain't yer pa! And I'll turn you in quick-like if you back out on me."

The two embarked upon a silent contest of the wills, a contest Rupert won when his brother looked away. "Go get us some firewood for tonight," Rupert snarled.

His mouth set in a rebellious line, Mark walked outside and slammed the door behind him.

Rupert ground his teeth together and kicked at the rickety chair he had just vacated. It toppled onto the grimy floor just like his well-laid plan that had shattered at his feet. As bad as he hated to, he was going to have to involve Quincy in this deal. But Quincy never came cheap. The help of that crooked lawyer would probably cost Rupert every piece of the gold he and Mark had lifted from that bank in Rusk. However, the scheme would most likely insure Noah's death and Rupert's freedom. He could always replace the gold through another robbery. But his freedom was priceless.

"Mark!" he yelled. After striding toward the dilapidated door, he flung it open. "Mark! Come here! I want you to make a trip to town!"

Chapter 7

Saturday morning, Angela hitched her horse and buggy near Dogwood's general store and cringed at the thought of having to make her way through the town, already bristling with the usual rush of Saturday traffic. Everywhere she turned, Angela saw farmers trading cattle; wives rushing here and there to stock up on provisions; children chasing and squealing along the boardwalks. Even though no one should suspect Angela was housing a supposed criminal, she felt as if her every expression announced the fact to the world.

She would not have come to town except that she did need a few supplies, and her patient had discreetly requested a bath. Angela, feeling as if she were taking a grave risk, had agreed to Noah's leaving the cellar while she was gone. After securely closing all curtains and shutters, Angela had left her metal tub full of warm water in the kitchen.

Fortunately, she had just finished sewing and mending some clothing for a man whose wife had died while giving birth to her tenth child. Since several of the family's children were her pupils, Angela had offered to assist the poor father in some of the housekeeping duties his wife had once performed. With a spirit of thankfulness, the struggling dad had given Angela three feed sacks full of torn clothing that needed mending—belonging to both him and the children. She had retrieved a pair of the man's overalls and a shirt for Noah to wear until she could wash his clothing.

With a deep breath, Angela screwed up every ounce of bravado she could muster and opened the store's door. The bell's cheery tingle greeted her as she stepped over the threshold. Instantly, the smells of coffee beans, peppermint, and leather assailed her. A number of customers milled around inspecting the various items, from horse harnesses to material for clothing to bags of cornmeal. Angela, keeping her face impassive, went to work gathering the sugar and coffee she needed. Next, she chose several spools of thread and a new package of needles, then examined the light cotton, perfect for making fresh bandages. This morning, Mr. Thorndyke had moved more freely. She had even discovered him at dawn, standing near one of the cellar's narrow air vents, peering out for a limited view of the surrounding countryside.

At last, Angela had accumulated her supplies and stacked them by the cash register. The buxom Bess Tucker, the town busybody, stopped her usual round of gossip with one of the locals and made her way to the cash register, where she began ringing up Angela's bill. Jars of candy lined the wall behind the counter, and Angela recalled the awkward conversation she and Noah had exchanged last night when she delivered his supper. During their stilted words, he had mentioned loving licorice since he was a child. Perhaps the reason for their trivial conversation had been the increasing tension that seemed to simmer beneath the surface of their every encounter. If Mr. Thorndyke's liquid brown eyes were any indication, the man found Angela immeasurably pleasing. But now that Angela had decided he really was innocent, there was nothing left for them to discuss. *Nothing.* As she had promised, Angela would help him, and when he rode out of her life, she would dismiss him from her thoughts. For despite Angela's step of faith in believing his story, she would never trust her heart to another man. *Never.* The light of resignation in Noah's eyes suggested that he saw and understood more than Angela had ever stated.

"And will that be all?" Bess asked absently. Distracted by the increasing crowd, the fiery redhead gazed around the store.

"Um. . .add two cents worth of licorice to my order, please," Angela said as nonchalantly as she dared.

Bess looked at her quizzically. "Why Miss Isaacs, I thought you deplored licorice," she said, her brassy voice rising above the hum of the patrons. "Acquiring a new taste?"

A lull in the customers' various conversations made Angela feel as if all attention focused on her. Feigning an air of assurance, she chose to ignore Bess's question and simply paid her bill. A discreet glance over her shoulder proved that no one was interested in whether she hated licorice or ate sixteen pieces a day. Nonetheless, Angela's heart pounded as if she were on trial. And the realization of the magnitude of the risk she was taking hit her anew.

Bess stacked Angela's purchases in the crate she had brought with her. Scooping up the crate in her arms, Angela turned toward the front door, certain she could not leave the store soon enough. A tall, wiry man standing near a display of Stetson hats in the front window turned to face her. A man who happened to be Constable Parker. With a kind smile, he opened the door and followed Angela onto the boardwalk.

Trembling, Angela produced a composed nod and stepped toward her horse and buggy.

" 'Scuse me, Miss Isaacs," Parker said politely. "But may I have a word with you in my office?"

Feeling as if she were caught in the direct path of a Texas twister, Angela swallowed hard. *What could he want with me?* her mind raced. *He knows I'm housing a criminal! But he can't know! How could he know? He must want something else. But what?* "Of course, Constable Parker," she said, amazed at her own dignified air.

He relieved her of the crate and motioned for her to precede him down the covered boardwalk, toward his office. Dust kicked up by wagons and stock attested to the need of another autumn shower. Angela, thankful that today's temperatures were cooler than yesterday's, raised her skirts a couple of inches to protect the hem. Several children called her name and waved. Angela, emulating her usual stoic yet amiable air, returned their greetings. However, every word she spoke seemed to hold an undercurrent of duplicity. No trip to town had ever made her feel more conspicuous. Stepping up on the opposite walk, she shook her dress, then allowed Constable Parker to open the door to his office—a shadowed, windowless room, whose stone walls assured a cooler temperature during Texas heat waves.

Once inside, the constable turned up the lantern and offered Angela a rather unstable armchair. "Sorry, Ma'am," he said, dropping his hat on the corner of his desk. "The county don't give us a lot for furnishin's."

"That's perfectly fine," she answered, primly lowering herself into the chair that wobbled with her weight. Yet all the while Angela's stomach knotted into an ever tighter wad of tension.

Parker shuffled through the disarray of papers on his desk and drew out an oversized poster. "Ever seen this feller?" he asked casually.

Her worst fears confirmed, Angela forced her stiff fingers to accept the rough, printed paper from the lawman. Her free hand clutched the chair's arm and she felt as if the constable were scrutinizing her every move. "Sheriff Garner asked me the same thing yesterday morning, Constable," Angela said evenly.

"So you already know what the man looks like?"

"Yes," Angela said, deciding the best course of action was to look the lawman square in the eyes. She had learned through the years of dealing with children that the ones who made eye contact were usually the ones with the least to be ashamed of.

"Reason I'm askin' is, the sheriff found his horse not far from your place and a spot in your garden that looked like somebody might have spent the night there."

"That's what he told me yesterday morning," Angela said.

"Blast that man," Parker growled. "He told me they escorted the kids home but never once mentioned showin' you the "Wanted" poster. Now I've done gone and wasted your time—"

"It's quite all right," Angela said with a kind smile, feeling as if she would swoon with relief. "You're just trying to do your job. The sheriff was probably so tired from riding all night that he failed to report all the details to you."

"Thanks for your understandin' spirit, Ma'am." With an apologetic smile, Parker reached for the poster. "The man's a killer, and I just want you ta be safe. The sheriff says he's a master at lyin' and is even trying to pass himself off as a minister."

"Oh?" Angela asked, her face growing cold.

"Sure thing. That horse he was on wound up bein' Denham's. At first, the sheriff thought he had stole it, but come to find out, it was his own. Anyway, he told the sheriff from the start that he wasn't Rupert Denham, but a preacher man from Louisiana by the name of Noah Thorndyke. Sheriff says the criminal had tried to get them to look in his saddle bags, but both the sheriff and the town was so convinced he had to be Denham that he didn't see no sense in it."

"Yes?"

"Well, we decided it might be best to go through them saddle bags and discovered some letters from a First Congregational Church in Tyler, Texas, addressed to a Reverend Noah Thorndyke, for sure."

Angela's attention remained riveted upon the graying constable as he stroked his wide sideburns and placed an elbow on the desk.

"But the best the sheriff and I can figure, there ain't no such church there. The sheriff's folks lives in Tyler, and there just ain't no such church."

Angela's hands shook as if *she* were the one accused of murder. She tightly wrapped her fingers around the velvet reticule lying in her lap, all the while praying that the constable did not notice her rapid pulse pounding against the base of her neck.

"And along with them letters and a mighty fine gold watch with the name 'Denham' engraved on the back, there was one of them "Wanted" posters, all crumpled down in the bottom of the bag. So, the sheriff and I have done put it all together and decided the killer is tryin' to use them letters to somehow prove he's a preacher."

"Really?" Angela rasped, her mind spinning with questions: *Why was Noah carrying a "Wanted" poster? He claimed he knew nothing about Rupert Denham before entering Rusk. And while the letters match his story, there's no such church. What does that mean other than he made up the whole story? His being in possession of that poster and watch suggests that he* is *Rupert Denham! Have I been duped? Have I allowed my brother's tragic story to blind me to the truth?*

Thoughts of Jason Wiley stomped through Angela's mind, and she felt as though every breath had been snatched from her. The licorice residing in the crate on the constable's desk at once became symbolic of a long, ebony serpent, bent on poisoning Angela's life; a serpent, dwelling in the heart of the man who had tried his best to trick Angela; a man her heart had secretly wanted to please with the licorice, despite her mind's resolution to keep him at arm's length.

She opened her mouth, ready to blurt the exact location of Rupert Denham, but a flash of anxiety assaulted her spirit, and that Bible verse from the day before swept, once again, through her mind. *Trust in the* Lord *with all thine heart; and lean not unto thine own understanding. In all thy ways acknowledge him, and he shall direct thy paths.* Upon the heels of that verse came another disturbing thought. *Perhaps you should pray about this decision. . .pray, as you haven't prayed in years.*

"Well," the constable continued, "I guess I've taken enough of your time. Just keep your eyes open the next couple of days, Miss Isaacs. You're a woman alone out in them parts, and I don't want no harm to come to ye," he said with an assuring nod.

"And what of my students?" Angela asked, her voice sounding strained, even to her own ears. "Should we continue with school on Monday?" The question seemed insane, considering she was housing the supposed criminal, but Angela knew it was one she should ask.

"Might not hurt to wait till midweek," Parker replied, pushing back his chair. "Have the preacher to announce in tomorrow's service that I asked you to hold off. By Wednesday, I look for that criminal to be out of

Cherokee County—if he's as smart as he looks so far. Accordin' to the sheriff, Denham's injured, but he ain't injured too bad, or he'd have never given us the slip so soundly."

Angela stood on shaking legs. Never had she been so torn concerning what to do. Just about the time she had embraced Noah's innocence as fact, she was slapped with another round of incriminating evidence. Without a doubt, she did need to pray. Pray as she hadn't prayed in years.

"Thank you for your time, Ma'am," Parker said, standing. "Can I get the crate for you? I hate that I done hauled you off up the street so far from yer buggy."

"No. That's fine," Angela rushed, reaching for the crate. "I can manage it. I'm sure. . .I'm sure you have many more pressing tasks."

As if to punctuate her remark, the office door banged open and a harassed-looking man entered. "There's a fight in front of the saloon," he barked out, and the constable dashed out the door before Angela had time to even gather her wits enough to walk.

Within minutes, she sprinted up the boardwalk and to her buggy. Angela deposited the crate behind the driver's bench. Placing one hand atop her conversation hat, decorated in plumes the color of evergreens, she embarked the buggy and gave the bay mare a gentle slap with the reins. The dependable creature trotted up the busy street and away from Dogwood.

Angela, burdened with the weight of the constable's news, held herself erect, her emotions in check, her mind in firm control. For if she allowed herself to slip in one area, she knew she would lose control in all areas. Although she left Dogwood's teaming streets behind, Angela felt as though the whole town still watched her, still speculating, still suspicious. And she *would not* give them reason to imagine that the conversation with Parker had in any way upset her.

Fifteen minutes into her journey, Angela's emotions would no longer remain in check. As the sight of a thick grove of pines came into view, she was reminded of a similar grove near her parents' homestead several miles south of Dogwood. A grove such as this had been her special sanctuary and haven of prayer during her younger years—a place where she met the Lord and He directed her path. It was among fragrant evergreens such as these that she learned to turn her heart toward her heavenly Father and seek His ways.

Her soul heaved like a tumultuous sea, tormented by the breath of a livid hurricane. And Angela pulled the small carriage to a stop, allowing the reins to inch from her fingers. Her hands quivering, she covered her face and welcomed the pent-up tears. Tears of panic. Tears of tension. Tears of repentance.

"Oh Father," she said over a sob. "I don't know what. . .what to do. Please. . .please forgive me for. . .for waiting until such a dark m–moment to turn to You. But. . .but I so desperately need Your wisdom." She tried to catch her breath but only produced a strained hiccough. "Please direct my path, and. . .and show me. . .me whether I should turn in Noah or continue to help him. If he *really is* Rupert Denham. . ."

The repetitive, soft cooing of a dove on a distant, piney hill penetrated Angela's agitation and gradually wove an aura of peace around her spirit. After almost half an hour of quiet reflection amidst the lush countryside touched in gold, Angela understood that, for whatever reason, the Lord did not want her to report Noah's location to the authorities. A gentle assurance deep in her soul confirmed that Angela had been right in not blurting all to Constable Parker.

However, the confusion still remained over why Noah had been in possession of a "Wanted" poster and a gold watch with "Denham" on the back. As Angela picked up the reins and began her journey anew, she purposed to tell Noah what Constable Parker had shared with her. Both the poster and watch incriminated Noah and made him look as if he had lied to her. But Angela felt that the Lord was urging her to at least give him a chance to explain.

For the first time in over a decade, Angela Isaacs had begun the journey of allowing God to direct her path, of setting aside her own understanding, of trusting Him, even in the face of opposing logic.

But will you allow Me to heal your hurts? The thought pierced through her soul like a pinpoint of light, penetrating a pit as black as night. Angela recoiled from the notion. She had clung to the shadows of her painful past for so many years that they had become a symbol of security. As long as she hid behind the shadows, she took no risks with her heart. Releasing her heartache to God would result in His breaking down the wall that separated Angela from the rest of the world, a wall that prohibited her from developing intimacy in any new relationships—especially with the opposite sex.

Angela thought of Noah Thorndyke, of how he obviously admired her, of how she had enjoyed the presence of a man in her home, of how poignant her lonely existence now seemed. But the idea of releasing her past, even for someone like Noah, left Angela emotionally terrified.

❖

Deep in the east Texas woods, Rupert stood waiting beside the cabin's milky window. At long last, two horsemen approached through the thick, brushy woods. Rupert had waited all morning for their appearance.

Yesterday evening, he had sent Mark into Jacksonville, the town between Rusk and Dogwood, with the purpose of making Quincy Brown an offer. Hopefully, Quincy's accompanying Mark meant that the crooked lawyer had gleaned the information Rupert so desperately needed.

With jittery fingers, Rupert scratched at his beard. He would never let on, but Quincy made him nervous. While the lawyer and Rupert both made a profession of separating people from their money, Quincy knew how to do it legally. His sly use of the law left Rupert feeling at a disadvantage. The outlaw suspected that during one or two of their dealings, Quincy had dealt him a raw deal. But Rupert had no choice in using him this time.

He settled onto the musty cot against the wall, feigning an attitude of nonchalance. But inside, he was wound tighter than a coiled watch spring. He reflected upon the last year. . .upon his learning from his dying father that he had a twin brother. . .upon his tracking down Noah in Mansfield, Louisiana, only to discover he was a stinkin' preacher. That within itself made destroying Noah all the more rewarding. For some evil serpent deep within Rupert hated the very thought of God and religion. He chuckled to himself as he recalled his scheme of enticing Noah to Texas—through fictitious letters from a fictitious church in Tyler looking to fill a fictitious pastoral position.

The door slowly creaked open, and Mark entered with Quincy on his heels. The erect and "dignified" lawyer discreetly practiced his deceit with anyone willing to produce his exorbitant fees. While many prominent citizens in the county paid respectful homage to Quincy, Rupert and his kind understood that the lawyer valued one thing above all others. Money. And lots of it. Quincy would stoop to any fraud, treachery, or cruelty for another dollar to bolster his burgeoning fortune.

The physical contrast between Mark and Quincy belied the similarities of their intents. While both were tall and lean, Mark looked the part of the typical dark-headed, buzzard-eyed, unshaven outlaw. Quincy, on the other hand, appeared as if he should be sitting in a tea parlor among the most dignified of society. The lawyer's freshly shaven face and long-tailed suit made Rupert want to gag. Only his keen, green eyes suggested he had the heart of a cobra.

"What do you need?" Quincy asked, peering at Rupert with an air of distaste.

"I'm in the middle of a killin'," Rupert drawled, never bothering to move from his reclining position. "Or haven't you already figured that one out?"

Quincy Brown's blond brow rose.

"What did you expect me to be needin' you for," Rupert growled, "to invite you to a ladies' quiltin'?"

"Mark only said you wanted any clues to where the law thought you were hiding."

Rupert produced a harsh laugh. "That's exactly what I wanted!"

Brown, his eyes narrowed, studied Rupert. "From what I gather, there was a rope awaiting you in Rusk, and you sprang jail," he said in precise English.

"Think again," Rupert's voice taunted. The blond lawyer's jaw clenched, and Rupert knew his flippant air was having the annoying effect he desired. "Wasn't me in that jail cell. 'Twas my twin brother," he said with a satisfied smirk.

The astonishment in Quincy's eyes was almost worth every ounce of trouble this whole ordeal had cost Rupert. In all their dealings, the outlaw had never felt as if he possessed the upper hand with Quincy. The surge of power left him almost giddy with triumph. He casually stood and eyed Mark, who stirred the coals in the rock fireplace, then laid a couple logs atop the red embers.

Quincy, crossing his arms, scrutinized Rupert. "Are you going to give me the details of this scheme or not?" His question held the nuance of a command.

Purposefully pausing, Rupert walked to the empty coffeepot and handed it to his younger brother. "Make some more," he said. Noting the flair of resentment in his brother's eyes, Rupert decided Mark was long overdue a beating.

"My plan," Rupert said, straddling the rickety, wooden dining chair and dropping into it, "is to get my twin brother hanged so I can go free. The whole plan was workin' like a charm 'til that rat broke outa jail."

"I didn't even know you had a twin," Quincy said as Mark left the cabin in quest of some well water.

"Neither did I 'til 'bout a year ago. My pa told me all about him the day 'fore he died. My ma died when we was just babies. I was the healthy one of the two. Seems Noah couldn't stay well, and Pa was sure he was gonna die if he didn't get some medical care, but he didn't have no means to do that. So when he was passing through Mansfield, Louisiana, he left Noah on the porch of the local parson, named Thorndyke. My pa was the decent sort." Rupert produced a calculating smile. "The day 'fore he died, Pa told me I had a twin. He seemed to think that with him and Mark's ma both gone, Mark and me would like to know about another relative. But I had a better idea for my twin brother."

Mark tramped back into the cabin, carrying the gray, rusted coffeepot full of water.

"I figured if I could somehow lure him into east Texas, I could get him arrested and hanged as me." Rupert observed Mark, dumping enough coffee into the pot for sixteen cups. "Not so much," he demanded. "It'll be so stiff we can't stomach it."

Clenching his jaw, Mark glowered at his brother. Without a word, he dropped the pot and the coffee bag on the table, then stomped outside.

"Looks like your biggest fan is ready to brawl." Quincy pulled a long, thin cigar from his sorrel coat's inside pocket, smirking as if he relished the tension between the Denham brothers. The lawyer placed the cigar between even, white teeth and leaned toward the lantern, which gleamed from the table's center. He removed the sooty globe and inserted the tip of the cigar into the flame, puffing it until the end glowed and the room smelled of acrid smoke.

"He ain't nothin' but an overgrown boy," Denham said. "And he's long overdue a beatin'."

"That would be something to see," Quincy said, his eyes narrowing as he sucked a long draw on the cigar.

"Meaning?"

"He's as big as you are. Or haven't you noticed?"

"I didn't ask you to come out here to tell me what ya think of me and my brother," Rupert said evenly. "I want to know what you found out about where I'm s'posed to be hidin'."

"Oh, I found out a thing or two," Quincy said, brushing at his impeccable coat sleeve.

"And?" Denham asked, abruptly standing.

Quincy Brown stiffened as though ready to draw his sidearm at any given moment. Rupert hid his smile. He liked knowing Brown was on edge. Feigning nonchalance, Denham grabbed the warped, metal poker and stabbed at the crackling logs, all the while keeping his eye on the lawyer.

"I'll tell you everything I know as soon as you tell me where the gold is hidden. That was the deal Mark offered."

"Okay," Rupert said. "You'll find it 'bout fifty yards behind this cabin, under a big rock. As soon as you give me the information, you're free to go get it." The outlaw glanced out the cloudy window. "Hope you brought your big saddlebag."

"I came sufficiently prepared," Brown snapped.

"Great," Rupert said, chuckling to himself. Neither Quincy nor Mark knew that Rupert had dug up that gold last night and hid half of it in the cabin's attic. Quincy thought he was getting the whole cache. "Now what did you find out?"

"After Mark arrived, I wired a note to my contact—one of Sheriff Garner's deputies."

Rupert impatiently nodded.

"We agreed to meet last night, halfway between Jacksonville and Rusk. For a few pieces of gold, he told me that they found what they thought was your horse close to the schoolhouse just north of Dogwood, and they found signs of your spending the night in the school mistress's garden. There was blood smeared in the weeds as well as the outline of a man. The deputy said you took a bullet on your way out of town."

"But it warn't me," Rupert said, slowly tucking his soiled shirttail into his britches. Quincy noted the outlaw's every move. Just for meanness, Rupert picked up his pistol lying near the lantern and inserted it between his waist and his britches band.

"No, it wasn't you," Quincy said, the cigar still firmly between his teeth.

"And what else?" Rupert asked, recalling the location of that particular schoolhouse, about fifteen or twenty minutes east of his present location. Denham had actually lifted a few heads of cattle not far from there the year before last.

"That's it. They think you've given them the slip."

Rupert, his mind whirling with possibilities, stared at the blazing logs. "And what about that schoolmarm? Ain't nobody questioned her 'bout whether or not she seen or helped a criminal?"

"Of course," Quincy said. "The deputy says she's not the kind to assist a criminal. She's the uptight, proper variety."

Squinting in calculation, Rupert held Quincy's snake-eyed gaze. "They think they're chasin' me, and they know I've given 'em the slip before, but I don't believe for one second a preacher-man would have enough weasel in him to put such a slip on the law, especially if he was injured." Rupert paused as his mind began piecing together the mystery. "And you know somethin', without my beard and all this hair, I'm a good-lookin' devil—or so the ladies have told me." Denham produced a lascivious grin. "I just wonder if maybe that schoolmarm might be more open to a man's company than she's lettin' on."

"I doubt it," Brown growled.

"Well, I aim to find out," Rupert replied. "I'm a wanted man, and I'll do anything to get my freedom—even if it means roughin' up a prude till she talks."

Chapter 8

Noah, enjoying his bath, soaked in the warm water as long as he dared. Finally, he got out, dried himself off, and was able to redress his wound, thankful that his side showed signs of healing. Nonetheless, Noah had barely donned the faded overalls and flannel shirt before exhaustion set in. He was certainly improving, but needed a few more days before he could travel. Already, Noah's thoughts were turning toward the possibilities of beginning his journey home under the cover of an inky night.

He stepped onto the ladder and descended the steps into the cellar. Welcoming the feel of the mattress beneath his back, Noah snuggled under the covers and closed his eyes. A sweet sensation of release washed over him as he dreamed of the woman of light and beauty who came to minister to him—his own angel. He relived the softness of her touch and the gentle manner in which she dressed his wound. He reached to touch her auburn hair only to have the breeze of his fantasy blow her away and bring with it a gray mist. . . .

❖

A child's voice whimpered in the middle of the mist. Noah stepped forward. As he walked, the fog parted and the voice became more distinct. The vision of the previous dream swam before his eyes: an expansive, green lawn shaded by huge trees, the rock cottage, the oppressive mirror with its heavy baroque frame, and the little boy looking forlorn and lost. The child stood before the glass, his arms outstretched, and the mirror boy taunted him with grotesque facial expressions. A man of coarse appearance but loving countenance scolded the mirror boy for his behavior. He then regretfully looked at a gleaming, gold pocket watch and turned beseeching eyes to Noah. With a glimmer of remorse in his eyes, he stepped from the mirror and picked up Noah, who had somehow become the toddler outside the mirror.

Feeling as if his heart were torn asunder, Noah clung to the rugged man whose face was moist with his own tears. A thick cough ravaged Noah's body and interrupted his tears. His eyes burned from fever. His head pounded as if someone were assaulting him with a hammer.

"No. . .no. . .no. . . ," he wailed in the voice of a child.

However, he was spun from the man's arms and plopped onto the banks of the Mississippi. Now, he was in his teen years, yet still his soul was crying, "No, no, no!"

Agitated, Noah struggled to sit up from the bank of the river, only to have someone pushing him back down into the warm, comfortable mud. He hollered out, struggling against his antagonist, only to feel a sharp tingle against his cheek. . . .

❖

Noah's lids popped open, and he stared straight into a pair of beautiful brown eyes—the eyes of his angel. "M–Miss Isaacs?" he whispered, looking around the dirt cellar in confusion.

"I'm sorry," she said, and her eyes widened to emphasize her true remorse. "But I just slapped you."

"Yes." Noah gingerly touched his stinging cheek.

"I couldn't get you to wake up," she said, leaning away from him.

"What—what time is it?"

"It's supper time. I came down to tell you I have your tray prepared, but you were having a horrific nightmare. You were waving at the air, screaming 'No, Papa, no' at the top of your voice—but you sounded more like a young child than a man." She shuddered, and her expression reflected the very trauma that still left Noah's soul reeling with the devastation of pain. . .the pain of a child being abandoned by his father.

"Oh, no," Noah groaned, covering his face with trembling hands. All these years his past had seemed an enigma. Now, he felt as if the past were swallowing him alive. Never, until this very moment, had Noah linked his rebellious years on the river to the cry of his heart as a toddler.

Perhaps. . .just *perhaps* Noah had been searching for his father all those years on the Mississippi, searching for the teary-eyed man who had left his sick child upon the mercies of another family.

"Your dream—you were so—so disturbed," Angela said. "Are you okay?"

"It's the second time since yesterday I've had that dream," Noah said, staring blindly toward the ladder. "I keep dreaming about two boys. One is in a mirror; the other one is looking into the mirror. They're identical. But today—just now, I dreamed about a man with. . .with. . ." Noah strained to recall the details as he struggled to sit up. Quickly, Angela stuffed an extra pillow behind his shoulders. "The man was holding a gold watch. He kept looking at it, and—"

"A gold watch?" she asked, her face paling as if an apparition had sashayed between them.

"Yes—yes, a gold watch. He was crying. He stepped out of the mirror and picked up the little boy outside the mirror. But the boy was me now, and I was screaming, 'No, no, no.' Then I landed on the banks of the Mississippi, and you slapped me."

"Have you ever had these dreams before now?" Angela asked.

"No, never," Noah said, shaking his head in confusion.

"Do you think that the Lord is somehow trying to show you something?" Angela peered deeply into his eyes.

"As in?"

"Constable Parker asked me to come to his office today and showed me that "Wanted" poster. He didn't know Sheriff Garner had already asked me about you."

"And what did you say?" Noah's fingers curled into a fist.

"I just told him that the sheriff had already asked me if I had seen you, and the constable never pursued the subject."

Noah let out his pent-up breath, and Angela eyed him, a new hint of suspicion tugging at the corners of her lips. "But Parker did tell me that they went through your saddlebags and found a gold watch with the name 'Denham' engraved on the back."

Noah, astonished by her words, gripped the covers, and felt as if the gold watch from his dream was dangling before his eyes. "And I dreamed about a man with a gold watch," he rasped.

"Yes, and a mirror image of two boys."

He nodded.

"Have you ever contemplated the notion that you might have a twin brother, Mr. Thorndyke?" Angela swept aside a strand of hair from her eyes. The sagging bun atop her head had allowed numerous wisps to escape and fall in an attractive array around her face.

"A twin?" he whispered, feeling as if they were stumbling upon a definite possibility.

"It would make perfect sense. This Rupert Denham looks too much like you to be a mere look-alike."

"The boy in the mirror. . . ," Noah muttered, his heart pounding as if he were in the grips of the dream once more. "But how did that watch get into my saddlebag?" he asked, studying Angela's countenance, desperately searching for any sign that she might set aside her new suspicions and continue to believe in him. He saw the questions churning through her eyes; questions that suggested a gold watch in his saddlebag with "Denham" on the back would logically incriminate him.

"The constable said they also found the letters from the Tyler Congregational Church that you mentioned."

"Yes," Noah rushed. "I carried them with me as evidence that I was the man with whom they had been corresponding."

"Constable Parker says there is no First Congregational Church in Tyler. Sheriff Garner's folks live in Tyler. There's no such church, and. . .and. . ." She fidgeted with her dress's fringed neckline. "They also found one of those posters with Rupert Denham's picture on it," she said softly, her gaze seeming to probe the very recesses of his heart.

His palms grew clammy, and Noah shook his head. "But how can it be? I never even *saw* that poster until they shoved it in my face after locking me up, and I corresponded with that deacon—Miles Norman—for months."

"Do you think the whole thing was a setup?" Angela asked slowly, the momentary doubt in her eyes fluttering away.

The pieces of a puzzle seemed to be plopping into place one by one. "If I have a twin, and he's wanted for murder, and I'm killed in his place, then he goes free."

She nodded.

"Miles Norman probably doesn't even exist. And this Rupert Denham must have put the watch and the poster in my saddlebags—just in case." Noah felt as if he were sinking into the grips of a muddy pit, bent on smothering the very life from him. "Rupert might very well have been the one who knocked me unconscious and dropped me outside the sheriff's office." A wave of terror washed upon the shores of Noah's soul. The truth at once became as clear as the waters of a chilling spring, bubbling from the side of a jagged mountain. "Dear Lord, save me, could I have been framed by my own brother?"

"How do you feel?" Angela asked, standing. "Is there any way you could travel tonight?"

"Trying to get rid of me?" Noah asked with a teasing smile.

"I'm trying to arrange for your quick and efficient escape, Mr. Thorndyke," Angela said as if he were a hardheaded student. "If our theory is correct and this Rupert Denham is indeed after you, then he might very well be lurking in these woods, waiting on you to show yourself. The sooner you can get out of here, the better."

"I don't think I could make it very far tonight," Noah said. "That bath wore me out."

"Then we'll have to try for tomorrow night," Angela said practically. "Constable Parker asked me to announce in church tomorrow that there will be no school until Wednesday, in order to give you time to get far out of the area." Pausing, Angela produced a faint, although ironic, grin. "If I have to, I'll hide you under some quilts in the back of my buggy and try to get you as far south as possible before leaving you on your own with my extra horse. Of course, I would need to be back before dawn, so no one would suspect that I had been away." She turned for the ladder, her full, cotton skirt producing a delightful swish. "I'll be back with your supper."

Noah, deeply touched by her continued willingness to assist him, could not help but ponder just how devoid his life had been of feminine intimacy. During all his interactions with this angel, just beneath the surface of his pressing thoughts of survival, Noah had wrestled with the possibility that God very well could be trying to answer his prayer for a mate in the personage of Miss Angela Isaacs. However, the two of them had only just met, and the way things were progressing, Noah might very well escape in the night and never see her again. These facts left Noah feeling as if he were twirling in a whirlpool of distress, and he decided that he must—*absolutely must*—address the issue of their possible relationship. Who knew if he would have a better opportunity before his leaving tomorrow evening?

"Miss Isaacs," he said softly as she prepared to climb the ladder.

Raising her brows, she turned to face him, her expression still schooled into a firm mask that suggested a certain disinterest in Noah's plight. Yet, the stirrings of compassion and worry, churning through the velvety softness of her eyes, suggested that Miss Angela Isaacs was far more disturbed by his unfortunate circumstances than she was admitting.

"It's often during such an unusual state of affairs such as ours that people perhaps. . .breach. . .the norms of decorum. With this in mind, I would like to ask your forgiveness for what I am about to say. However, I feel that it must be said." Noah pushed aside the covers and moved his

470

stiff body to the sitting position. While the bath had seemed to ease his aching side, now that he had lain dormant for several hours, the stiffness had reclaimed his right side with renewed vengeance. However, Noah persisted in standing, even in the face of Angela's protests. Noah simply would not address such monumental issues with a lady while he was on his back. He would not.

"As I was saying, Miss Isaacs," Noah continued, moving to the ladder to grip it for support. "Before I started this journey, I prayed that the Lord would somehow use my trip to introduce me to the woman He has chosen for me."

Her sudden intake of breath and astounded expression attested to Angela's full comprehension of Noah's intent. "Mr. Thorndyke, *please*," she gasped. "We only just met, and I certainly couldn't imagine that you would dare *suggest*—"

"I am suggesting nothing, Madam," Noah said gravely, his stomach fluttering as if he were sixteen and courting his first belle. And just as he had yesterday when her watch chain entangled itself in his shirt's button, Noah's traitorous mind pined to feel her lips against his, longed to feel her warmth in the circle of his arms. "I am simply asking your p–permission. . ." His voice's telltale wobble revealed the uncontrollable shaking of his legs. "I am asking your permission for me to correspond with you in the coming months, should—should I be fortunate enough to escape this wretched situation and find refuge in my home." Despite his better judgment, Noah's gaze trailed to Angela's lips; lips the color of summer's first peaches; lips that were quivering as if he had just kissed her.

Noah dared to reach toward her cheek and stroke its softness. All vestiges of the controlled matron vanished, replaced by a vulnerable woman who now returned Noah's warm appraisal. "I must admit that I have found in you the most becoming woman I have yet to make the acquaintance of. The thought of my departing—without ever stating my thoughts—leaves me somewhat in a panic. I have lain here and planned the whole thing. I was thinking that I would adopt a pseudonym for the purpose of our writing. That way, the law would never suspect we were writing to one another. I pray that you'll forgive my forward overtures, but, as I already said, the duress of our unusual circumstances leaves me no choice."

The moment, fraught with expectation, extended an eternity, and Noah could only pray that Miss Isaacs would agree to his petition. However, instead of answering, she looked away, fidgeted, pressed her lips together, and dashed up the short ladder without so much as a backward glance.

"Miss Isaacs?" Noah called in alarm.

Her back rigid, Angela stopped near the top and never even glanced over her shoulder. "Mr. Thorndyke," she said, her voice vibrating with the tension of the moment, "I find your overtures highly inappropriate and shocking to the point of disbelief. I will assist you back to your home all that I possibly can, but *please*, do not mention your fantastical musings again." Without another word, she ascended the remaining space and prepared to step off the ladder.

A veil of bafflement settled upon Noah's mind. "You are risking your reputation and job to help me, yet you are scandalized by my overtures?" his perplexed tones reflected his complete confusion.

Her back still to him, Angela halted once again. "My assisting you has nothing to do with any hopes on my part of romantic involvement," she said in condescending tones that suggested she was growing increasingly offended with each passing word. "I have prayed about this whole situation and feel that the Lord is directing me to assist you. That is all there is to it."

"So, you are as much a woman of God as I presumed you to be."

These words instigated her pivoting to face him. "I would love to tell you that you have presumed correctly," she said, a note of regret in her voice. "But I have spent many—many. . . ," she cleared her throat, "many years not. . .um. . . your present situation has driven me to my knees in a way that I have refrained from in years."

Noah, surprised by her admission, raised his brows, and she looked away as if the disclosure brought her deep shame. As the seconds ticked by, Noah mused about what must have caused a woman who knew her Bible so well to distance herself from its author. The vulnerable twist to her lips and her continued insistence to keep Noah at arms' length suggested a heart torn asunder. Yesterday, Noah had asked her about her past, never once expecting a reply. But today, the past he had inquired about became the inevitable deduction of a sharp mind. "Who was he, Angela?" Noah dared to say, hoping all the while his assumption was indeed the correct one. "Who was the one who broke your heart?"

With another faint gasp, Miss Isaacs clamored into the kitchen, knelt beside the cellar door, and peered down at Noah. Her eyes, sparkling with unshed tears, reminded him of gleaming, mahogany-colored stones under the surface of a mountainous brook. "First, I will have you remember, *Mr. Thorndyke*, that I have yet to give you permission to address me by my given name. Second, while your previous comments were fantastical, your present remarks are beyond reprehensible," the word squeaked out,

472

attesting to her rising irritation, as did her delightfully flushed cheeks. *"Please*, keep your inappropriate remarks to *yourself!"* She rose and stomped away, leaving Noah feeling as if he had been verbally slapped.

So much for my schemes, he thought. His heart heavy, Noah slowly walked back toward the makeshift bed and lowered himself onto the mattress. Despite the strain of the current situation, the smells of the evening meal wafting through the cellar door left his stomach complaining about its empty status. Yet, his heart felt just as empty. At long last, he had met a woman who seemed to be a potential lifetime companion, and she was so wrapped up in her past that she was blind to the present.

❖

Angela rushed to her bedroom, closed the door, and collapsed onto her bed. Covering her face, she allowed the tears to flow while stifling any noises that would suggest she was crying. She relived the moment that Noah touched her face, a moment that brought back a wave of emotion she had not experienced in years. She dared to ponder the possibilities of love, of joining her life with a man of honor. Her traitorous mind filled with images of Noah—the warmth of his touch, the velvet softness of his eyes, the expectation in his voice when he asked if she would correspond with him. His words, so imploring, had charged her soul and fanned the flame of attraction which had begun a slow burn in that moment when her watch chain tangled in his button.

The potency of these emotions terrified Angela, terrified her beyond reason. Shivering, she buried her face into the homespun quilt that smelled of lye soap. Angela, paralyzed by anxiety, contemplated the potential for her heart to be broken again. And she knew that, despite her reaction to Mr. Thorndyke, she could never allow him to court her—either in person or by mail.

Yet, a psalm she memorized in childhood waltzed among her troubled thoughts to suggest a new manner of introspection. *I will lift up mine eyes unto the hills, from whence cometh my help. My help cometh from the LORD, which made heaven and earth.* As if drawn by a power greater than herself, Angela dried her eyes on the edge of the quilt and looked out her opened bedroom window, toward the surrounding east Texas hills. The sun's last rays illuminated the countryside, touched with a hint of autumn's gold. A dove, softly cooing, wove an aura of tranquillity upon the whole scenic view. The small schoolhouse that sat about a hundred yards away tugged at Angela's heart. That schoolhouse represented her whole life. She had never once hesitated to weave every fiber of her heart into the lives of her students. Her past pain, her horribly humiliating experience with Jason Wiley, had left her no choice but to isolate herself from romance, but Angela had never once isolated herself from interacting in the lives of her pupils.

But the love of a noble man would make life so much more fulfilling. The thought left Angela blinking, and on the heels of that thought came the psalm once again. *I will lift up mine eyes unto the hills, from whence cometh my help. My help cometh from the LORD, which made heaven and earth.*

I will heal your heart, if only you will lift your eyes to Me and let Me help you. The words swirled through her soul, sending a rush of tingles down her spine, and Angela knew that God was nudging her toward relinquishing her past. But the past was her shield, her protector, her whole identity. Newly terrified, Angela covered her face again and doubted that she even knew how to release her past.

Chapter 9

T he next morning, Angela pulled her carriage into the country churchyard and noted the group of people standing in front of the white, one-room church. The numerous, tall windows and white steeple seemed as much a part of the fabric of Angela's life as did her parents' own farmhouse, south of Dogwood. The autumn morning's brisk breeze chilled the air even more than yesterday. Angela's nose tingled as that cold breeze, rustling the surrounding pines, scurried around her Sunday hat. However, that cold wind felt as if it blew from the very portals of Angela's soul.

This morning, as she had yesterday evening, Angela delivered Mr. Thorndyke his meal, along with a thick helping of stony silence. He never said a word, but Angela felt his ardent gaze upon her. Already, she anxiously awaited tonight, when she would assist the man in leaving the premises. Even if she had to squeeze him behind the carriage's driver's bench, cover him with quilts, and drive all night long, Angela would do anything to remove his troubling presence from her home.

After her silent yet potent cry yesterday evening, Angela had hardened her heart all the more against the notion of God's helping her recover from her past pain. In short, the longer she thought of releasing her past, the more apprehensive she grew. Trying to focus on the task at hand proved a convenient means to escape her troubling thoughts. Angela pulled in among the eclectic array of buckboards, wagons, buggies, and the Griffin's carriage brought all the way from Dallas by a neighbor's well-to-do cousin.

She spotted Rachel and Travis, standing under a big sycamore talking to Travis's brother, Levi, and his wife, Magnolia. In her arms, Magnolia held their baby daughter. The blissful blush on her cheeks attested to her happiness with life. While Rachel cooed over Magnolia's baby, her red-headed toddler, fondly dubbed Little Trav, hung on Rachel's emerald-colored skirt and tried to play peek-a-boo with a disinterested squirrel. Angela would never stop marveling at God's providing an adopted child for Rachel and Travis immediately after they lost their firstborn. And Little Trav, with his red hair like Rachel's and green eyes like Travis's, looked as if God had designed him especially for them.

Rachel, recognizing her cousin's buggy, waved to Angela, scooped up Little Trav, and excused herself from the discussion. As Angela stepped down from her carriage, Rachel gripped her arm and smiled into her eyes as if she were searching Angela's expression for any traces of Friday's strained conversation.

Angela, determined to place her younger cousin at ease, returned Rachel's smile and tried to put forth as relaxed a manner as was humanly possible under the present circumstances.

"I'm so glad to see you," Rachel whispered with excitement. "Travis worked half the night on his sermon, and I think I'm as nervous as he is. Since this is his first time to preach, he needs our prayers."

"I forgot that Pastor Eakin asked him to fill the pulpit today," Angela said. The recent distractions of her had left her almost forgetting her own name. "Rumor has it he's out preaching at another church in lieu of a call. Have you heard?"

"Yes," Rachel said, pushing a strand of auburn hair away from her face. "That seems to be true. Brother Eakin told Travis when he asked him to fill the pulpit today that he feels the Lord is asking him to move to this new church—just outside Dallas. We all can't imagine what it's gonna be like without him, but the Lord will provide. Meanwhile, Travis is really nervous. He's already planning to head up a pulpit committee and find a preacher soon. I think he did enjoy preparing today's sermon, but the thought of having to fill in until we find a pastor. . ." Rachel left the rest unsaid.

"It's hard to picture Travis being nervous," Angela continued with her usual assurance. "With his oratory skills from law school and knowledge of Scriptures, I'm sure he'll do exceptionally well and would continue to do well long-term, if the need arose."

Rachel gently squeezed Angela's hand. "I wouldn't share this with anyone except you, but last night Travis prayed over the sermon 'til he almost cried. When we prayed together, he said he feels as if the Lord has given him a message for a specific person today."

"Travis is a wonderful man," Angela said absently, her mind drawn to Noah. He too seemed sincere and wonderful, and Angela prayed he wouldn't needlessly lose his life. She scanned the countryside, wondering if Rupert Denham might be lurking behind one of the myriad of trees, covering the rolling hills.

For the first time since her petulant verbal outpouring, Angela felt mean-spirited for her waspish response to Noah's humble request to correspond with her. Her resolved desire to see him gone wavered in the memory of her own rudeness. Angela extended her arms to Little Trav, who gleefully fell into her embrace. With Rachel at her side, she turned toward the church. But the closer she walked to the house of God, the more she felt the Lord's gentle tug on her heart. For the last several years, Angela had attended church as a necessary duty, required by her teaching contract. But today's pending service already felt different—as if Angela were embarking upon a new spiritual journey. Even now, she sensed the Lord's holy scalpel applying pressure to the cancer of her emotional wounds, and Angela wondered if perhaps she were the one whom Travis's sermon would touch.

Noah finished the breakfast that Angela had silently served him before her departure for church. His heart heavy, he gripped the mug of lukewarm coffee and stood to walk to the air vent of his cellar abode. Although his side was still stiff, Noah felt much better this morning, much better than he had felt even last night. He peered through the air vent and drank in his limited view of rolling, east Texas hills. In the distance, a rooster crowed, hens clucked, and a woodpecker hammered against a tree.

The plan that had begun to nibble at the corners of Noah's mind last night, before he fell asleep, now resurrected itself. Ever since Noah had dared to ask Angela about the possibilities of their corresponding, she had turned into nothing short of an ice maiden, ready to freeze his soul with her very presence. Without doubt, the woman was ready to be rid of Noah. And, if that were the case, perhaps Noah should grant her the wishes of her heart. He had assumed she would attend church this morning; his assumptions proved correct. All Noah needed to proceed with his plan was a bonnet, a house robe, and hopefully, a horse. Miss Isaacs had mentioned an extra horse when she spoke of assisting him in his getaway.

"Well, it looks like I'll save you the worry, my dear Miss Isaacs," Noah muttered irritably. He took a final swallow of the strong, black coffee and decided to enact his plan. All he needed to do was make a trip to Angela's bedroom and borrow the items of clothing and find a pen and ink along with paper. Noah would take her horse but assure her he would send the money to cover the purchase of a new one as well as provide for the missing clothing.

With his decision made, Noah set his coffee cup on the tray beside his mattress and swiveled to face the cellar ladder. Yet, a melancholic veil draped across his spirit, a veil that seemed as thick as the despondency that had visited Noah after those wretched dreams. For the first time in his life, Noah had tasted the despair of being abandoned as a sickly child. However, experiencing that pain had somehow breached a gap in Noah's soul, a gap that had held a mystery. Likewise, Noah's tasting the possibility of developing a relationship with a delightful woman had left him longing to fill the gaping hole in his life marked "wife and family"—the hole he had pleaded with the Lord to fill. But Miss Isaacs was not the least bit interested, or so she said. Noah wasn't blind. He sensed that she found him alluring, but that seemed to matter little to Miss Isaacs.

Pressing his lips together, Noah ascended the ladder and pushed open the cellar door. If he left now and traveled north, he could cross over the Louisiana border, hopefully by midnight, before heading south, toward his home. As he stepped into the kitchen, his side caught, and Noah winced against the sharp pain, shooting toward his ribs. *Dear Lord*, he prayed. *You preserved my life this far. Please go with me now.*

❖

Rupert and Mark hovered in the woods behind the schoolhouse until the teacher's buggy disappeared up the dusty, narrow road. Then, they traipsed through the woods and neared the teacher's house.

Rupert, gripping the binoculars, sensed Mark's resentment growing out of proportion. However, Rupert firmly maintained the upper hand, never once showing a sign of weakness.

They paused on the edge of the woods, and Rupert scanned the two-hundred-yard space between their location and Angela's house. Next, he glanced across the countryside one more time, just to ease his quivering nerves. No other houses were in sight, and the countryside appeared uninhabited as far as the eye could see. He and Mark had specifically planned to begin the hunt for Noah on Sunday morning, when the teacher would hopefully leave for church. If they didn't find Noah at the teacher's, they planned to methodically break into every house in the vicinity until they found him. By starting with the teacher, they were simply playing a hunch and following the lead that Quincy had given them.

"Okay, here's the plan," Rupert whispered. "We run to the back door and pry it open with that poker you're carrying. I want us in and out as quick as possible. If we don't find no signs of him, then we go to the schoolhouse and make sure he ain't there. From here, we'll go north and hit the next house we come to—if 'n they're at church too. Got it?"

"I got it back at the cabin," Mark said, his mouth in a sullen line.

Rupert, his patience wearing thin, grabbed a handful of Mark's smudged shirt and yanked him close. "Listen, *you*, I don't know what burr you've got under your saddle lately, but it's time to straighten up," he growled, his gut tight.

Mark squinted, and his right eye twitched. Clenching his teeth, he deliberately pried Rupert's hand from his shirt. "I know you didn't give Quincy all that gold," he sneered. "I saw him dig it up, and it was only half what you got from the bank."

"What are ya gettin' at?" Rupert said, surprised by Mark's power of observation.

"I *mean*. . .you're trying to make me believe you ain't got it." A rooster crowed from near the outhouse as if to punctuate Mark's claim. "And I don't think it's the first time, either."

"I'll wind up payin' for yer upkeep anyway," Rupert said.

"I'm tired of you payin' for my upkeep. I'm a grown man. I ain't no stinkin' kid anymore, and I deserve—"

"Shut up about what you *deserve*," Rupert snarled as a cool breeze scampered across the branches, decorated in gold-touched leaves. "From the time Pa first took sick ten years ago up 'til today, I've taken you under wing. Now you act like I owe you somethin'."

"Well, I—"

"Shut up," Rupert snapped. "Just shut up, and let's do what we came to do. After this is all over, if you want to be on yer own so bad, then I'll give you half of what's left of that gold, and you can hit the trail. You're gettin' to be more trouble than yer worth." Rupert fingered his pistol, safely tucked in his holster, and hoped he didn't have to pull it on Mark. He wouldn't shoot the boy out of anything but self-defense. But presently, the resentment in Mark's eyes bordered on hate, and Rupert no longer trusted him. Once they found Noah and saw him safely hanged, Rupert would be glad for Mark to set out on his own.

He prepared to step from the edge of the woods and motioned for his brother to follow. However, a woman, dressed in a bonnet and a frilly dress of sorts, walked out of the back door and toward the small barn, north of the teacher's house. But the longer Rupert watched that woman, the more he noticed that she really walked like a man—an injured man

❖

Angela held Little Trav closely and followed Rachel up the few steps leading to the church door. While Rachel continued a lighthearted banter, Angela playfully intercepted the baby's chubby hand as he reached for her plumed conversation hat. His green eyes sparkled as he charmingly tried to say "hat," but much of the toddler's allure was lost on Angela.

Instead, yesterday's prayer time, among that grove of pines, invaded her thoughts. She had leaned upon the guidance of the Lord to determine Noah's fate. Now, for the first time since her heated rejection of Noah's romantic overtures, Angela wondered if she should dare ask the Lord to guide her decision about Mr. Thorndyke's correspondence. She had never once prayed about God's will in her interacting with Noah.

"Is that all right with you?" Rachel asked, turning at the door to face Angela, her brown eyes alight with the reflection of a woman in love with life, with her husband, her child, and her Lord.

"What?" Angela asked.

Before Rachel repeated her question, she eyed Angela, a cloak of apprehension settling upon her features. "You seem so distracted," she said softly. "Just like Friday. This is not like you. Are you sure you're all right, Angel? There's just. . .just something. . .some shadow in your eyes that. . .that. . .it's almost scary—almost as if Dr. Engle has given you a horrible diagnosis or something."

Angela swallowed hard and wondered why she ever thought she could hide anything from Rachel. Even though Angela was a full decade older than her cousin, Rachel possessed a spirit of discernment that increased as she matured. "I'm sorry," Angela said. "There's a lot on my mind. What was your question?"

Her heart pounding, she contemplated telling Travis and Rachel about Mr. Thorndyke's predicament. Travis would assuredly be better equipped to assist Noah out of the state than would Angela. She considered afresh the impact such an escapade might have on her teaching position. Were Angela discovered out alone during the night, her actions would be viewed as outrageous. Indeed, the whole countryside would be aflame with gossip before the next sunset. Furthermore, if anyone found out that a man was involved, Angela would be dismissed from her teaching post immediately. In order to minimize the chances of anyone discovering her nocturnal journey, she would be forced to be back home before dawn. However, Travis could travel all night and spend most of the day tomorrow getting back home. Given Travis's duties at the ranch, he had ample reasons to be gone overnight.

A group of church members ambled up the steps, and Angela followed Rachel into the quaint, country church. The hardwood floors gleamed in the morning's light, spilling through the windows that spanned five feet tall. The polished pews were already filling with church members, and Rachel scanned the last few pews. "When we were outside, I was just asking if you would mind sitting on the back pew with me," Rachel said. "Travis will need to sit up front, and Little Trav has a way of distracting everyone if I sit up there."

"Of course, I'll sit with you," Angela said as Little Trav squirmed in her arms. His blue striped jacket, made of wool, had suddenly become too confining for him, and he tugged at the sleeves as if he were a caged animal.

"Here, let me have him," Rachel said, reaching for her son. "He's so hot-natured." Immediately, the young mother found a spot on the last pew and began tending her baby.

Angela settled on the hard pew beside her cousin, and something in the pit of her stomach twisted as she observed the unbreakable bond between mother and child. Fleetingly, she wondered what it would be like to have her own child. Over the years, Angela had channeled all maternal instincts toward her students, but a new longing swept over her, a longing to have a family of her own. Yet, that longing could only be fulfilled if she were willing to take another chance on love. *All Noah Thorndyke asked was permission to correspond. What is that going to hurt?* she thought. Angela's lips trembled with indecision. Her eyes stung, and unexpected tears seeped from the corner. Shamefully, she dashed aside the tear, hoping no one noticed her display of seemingly irrational emotions.

However, Rachel noticed. She once again observed Angela, a grave concern spilling from her countenance, a concern that said, *Please tell me what is wrong. I'll help you all I can.*

But the service began, the music started, and Angela mechanically mouthed the first stanza of the opening hymn. The voice of the organ exploded in her ears like the crashing of trees in a landslide. Songs, prayers, and announcements marched in succession while visions of Noah, forlornly locked away in the cellar, played upon Angela's mind. *All Noah asked was permission to correspond*, she thought again and again and again, while reliving her harsh treatment toward him. Slowly, a veil of anxiety cloaked itself around Angela's soul and left her debating her quick and definite "no" to Noah's overtures. Furthermore, the Lord seemed to whisper to her soul that this should be a matter of prayer. She had trusted God's guidance concerning Noah's innocence; perhaps the time had come to begin the journey from behind the shadows of her past and into the sunshine of the present and future. Yet with these very musings, Angela's heart constricted in alarm.

Finally, Travis Campbell stood, and the entire congregation, including Little Trav, focused solely on the tall rancher. He approached the well-used pulpit and awkwardly rustled the pages of his worn Bible until he found the proper page. His fingers moved to the designated spot in the text.

"Da Da!" Little Trav exclaimed and the whole congregation produced a group chuckle.

Rachel, her cheeks reddening, tried to cover the baby's mouth, but he wiggled out of her reach and hollered all the louder, "Da Da, Da Da *Da Da!*"

More laughter rose from the group, and Angela couldn't contain the bubble of joy mounting in her soul.

Travis, his eyes glowing with love, gazed toward his wife and child. "At least I have one fan in the crowd," he said, and the congregation burst into a round of applause, mixed with new guffaws.

"Excuse me," Rachel whispered, her expression a mixture of motherly exasperation and humored adoration. "But I'm going to have to take him out." She rose, and Angela moved her legs to the side so her cousin could exit. Once Rachel passed, Angela arranged her skirts and prepared to open her Bible.

Upon the heels of Rachel's departure and Little Trav's persistent calls, the congregation turned its sole focus to Travis, and he cleared his throat. "I'll be reading two passages today. The first one is found in Proverbs 3:5–6." Angela compulsively gripped her Bible without ever opening it. She gazed at the top of the pew in front of her and held her breath as Travis read the words, so fresh in her memory. "Trust in the LORD with all thine heart; and lean not unto thine own understanding. In all thy ways acknowledge him, and he shall direct thy paths."

Travis paused and glanced over the congregation as if he were searching for the one person whom these Scriptures would touch. "The other passage that the Lord has laid upon my heart is Psalm 121." He looked downward and began reading once more. "I will lift up mine eyes unto the hills, from whence cometh my help. My help cometh from the LORD, which made heaven and earth. . . ."

Immediately, Angela felt as if the whole church were empty. . .empty of everyone but her and the Lord and a mellow voice, reading a divine message, especially for her. Her eyes pooled in tears as wave upon wave of God's love rushed into the caverns of her hollow soul.

"He will not suffer thy foot to be moved," Travis continued, "he that keepeth thee will not slumber. Behold, he that keepeth Israel shall neither slumber nor sleep. The LORD is thy keeper: the LORD is thy shade upon thy right hand. The sun shall not smite thee by day, nor the moon by night. The LORD shall preserve thee from all evil: he shall preserve thy soul. The LORD shall preserve thy going out and thy coming in from this time forth, and even for evermore."

As Travis began expounding on the verses, Angela's heart poured out a cry to her holy creator. *Oh Lord*, she pleaded, the Bible trembling as if it were an extension of her own hands. *I desperately need You to help me and to—to preserve my soul. Show me how to acknowledge You in all my ways—even when it comes to the possibilities of courtship. I'm so out of practice in acknowledging You. I'm not even sure if I know how. And then there are these shadows from the past, from—from what Jason Wiley did to me. Oh Lord, show me how to let them go.*

Chapter 10

Peering at the lone, ebony horse residing in the north pasture, Noah continued his swift trek toward the tiny, shabby barn. Even though there was no sight of anyone in the area, he felt as if every eye in the county were upon him. Despite the cool temperatures, Noah perspired from anxiety alone. He dashed aside the thin film of sweat that was forming where the bonnet met the sides of his face. A walk that took only two minutes felt as if it spanned two hours.

At last, Noah stepped into the shadowed barn that smelled of horse oats and straw and allowed his eyes to adjust to the difference in light. The barn was equipped with the usual garden tools, a few bales of hay, and even several small crates that appeared to hold various teaching tools as well as material. Two stalls took up most of the far wall. On one of those stalls hung a saddle. Noah trudged toward the saddle, the pain in his side gradually increasing with his every move.

Perhaps this idea wasn't such a good one, he thought as he strained to pull the saddle from its position. A large part of his desire to leave stemmed from embarrassment and injured pride laced with exasperation over Miss Isaacs's rejection of his overtures. Momentarily, Noah hesitated and wondered if his leaving in such fashion was either gracious or polite. *But on the other hand,* he reasoned with himself, *she acts as if she will be thrilled when I do leave. And my leaving is inevitable.*

Once more he saw the merciless eyes of the jury and heard the cries of excitement in the packed courtroom when they read the verdict. *Guilty!* The word had seemed to squeeze the very breath out of Noah, as if the noose were already tightening around his neck. *If they catch me again, they will undoubtedly hang me on the spot.* That fact alone spurred him forward. Gritting his teeth against the dull ache in his side, Noah hoisted the saddle onto his shoulder and trudged toward the barn door, all the while praying that the Lord would protect him until he safely arrived home. But just as Noah stepped out of the barn, a sharp blow met the back of his skull. He cried out in pain, then everything went black.

❖

After church, Angela wasted little time driving her carriage the brief distance back to her cottage. She stopped her dappled gray mare near the aging barn and made short work of releasing the horse from her harness and leading her into the pasture, where she was greeted by the ebony stallion. Angela had bought the stallion only two months before as an investment. She hoped the two horses would soon produce a colt that she could possibly sell for a profit.

Within minutes, Angela laid the heavy harness and accompanying paraphernalia in the barn. On the way out, she noticed one of her yellow summer bonnets, lying crumpled, just inside the door. Perplexed, she picked up the bonnet. Angela thought she remembered pushing aside the bonnet that morning when she reached for her felt church hat, the color of cedars.

Gripping the bonnet, Angela chose not to puzzle over the diminutive mystery. Instead, she focused on the task ahead of her, a task that left her palms sweaty and her heart racing. There were several items of business she needed to address with Mr. Thorndyke. First, Angela felt that the Lord was showing her she owed the gentleman an apology and an explanation for her rude behavior.

Travis's soft, yet potent sermon had affected Angela on numerous levels. Although she still wasn't certain she was indeed ready for any romantic involvement, Angela had decided to tell Mr. Thorndyke that he was welcome to write her, once he arrived safely home. The prospect left her both giddy with anticipation and timorous beyond expression. However, the same thought that had begun a chant during that church service once more became her companion: *I'm not agreeing to marry him. What harm can come from corresponding with the man? If I feel too terribly uncomfortable, I will just tell him to stop writing.*

Along with the issues of their correspondence, Angela also needed to discuss Mr. Thorndyke's pending escape that very night. She wanted to ask his permission to request Travis's assistance. When she fervently shared with Travis just how much she enjoyed his sermon, Angela had been tempted to take him aside and request his services then, but she had stayed her request. Angela did not want to make her final decision before discussing the possibility with Noah. She hoped Travis would take her and Noah's word concerning his innocence, but there was a certain risk that Travis would not believe Noah's story.

Still gripping the yellow bonnet, Angela opened her back door and allowed Grey to slip in ahead of her. The house cat meowed pitifully, as if she hadn't eaten in weeks. Smiling in her direction, Angela said, "I'll get you another bowl of milk in just a—" Angela stopped. The cellar door gaped open, and she wondered why Mr. Thorndyke would open the door in her absence.

"Mr. Thorndyke?" she softly called into the dark cellar. When silence greeted her, Angela said his name again. A nauseous knot formed in the pit of her tightened stomach, and she gazed toward her small parlor in hopes of catching sight of her patient there. Her heart wildly pounding, Angela dropped her reticule and the bonnet on the kitchen table. That's when she saw the edge of a note, peeking from beneath the straw mat where she took her meals. Only the words *Miss Angela Isaacs* were visible on the beige paper.

Her hands trembling, Angela pulled the paper from under the mat and glanced at the signature at the bottom to see the words, *Admirably yours, Rev. Noah Thorndyke* scrawled beneath several lines of script. Her eyes misting, Angela sank into the nearby kitchen chair and swallowed against the lump in her throat. Dreading what the note might say, she closed her eyes and took several steadying breaths. At last, Angela forced herself to focus on the letter.

Dear Miss Isaacs,

Please allow me to beg your forgiveness for intruding upon your privacy the last few days. However, I must admit that you were an answer to my prayers. Thank you so much for believing in my innocence and coming to my aid.

I would also like to beg your forgiveness for my effrontery in suggesting that perhaps you were an answer to my prayers in other areas as well. Never did I suspect that my propositions of correspondence would insult you so severely. Had I understood the level of your delicate and sensitive nature, I would have never broached such a subject.

In order to relieve you of further pains, I have decided to test my fortune and God's providence and set out for home this

*morning. I borrowed one of your yellow bonnets as well as
your frilly house robe—the one lying at the foot of your bed. I
am disguising myself as a woman in hopes that I will be able
to arrive safely at the Louisiana border by midnight. You will
also notice your other horse missing as well. Please understand that, as soon as I arrive safely home, I will forward sufficient money to cover the cost of your clothing and horse, as
well as enough to reimburse you for my upkeep these last few
days.*

   *Please pray for me, Miss Isaacs, that I will arrive safely to
my home.*

Admirably yours,
Rev. Noah Thorndyke

Her emotions tilting beyond all realms of logic, Angela covered her
face with quivering hands and produced several trembling gasps. *Oh no!
What have I done?* she thought, reliving the stony silence to which she
had exposed Noah. Lambasting herself, Angela took complete blame for
driving Noah to risk his life by leaving during the day, rather than waiting
until nightfall. "If he gets killed, I will never forgive myself," she rasped
against a shower of tears, drenching her cheeks.

   But an image, completely detached from the moment, swam before
her mind's eye—an image of an ebony stallion that greeted the dappled
gray mare. *But I thought Mr. Thorndyke said he took the stallion!* Her
mind racing, Angela grabbed the note and reread the second paragraph to
confirm that her memory was not deceiving her. Indeed, she had remembered correctly.

   Next, Angela gazed dumbfounded at the crumpled yellow bonnet
lying nearby. Her eyes widened. She held her breath. And the room
seemed to spin around her. For the back of that bonnet was smudged with
something Angela had failed to notice before now, something red, something that suspiciously resembled a blotch of blood. She grabbed the bonnet and inspected it more closely, to have her contemplations confirmed.
There is *blood on the bonnet!*

   Her pulse pounding in her temples, Angela abruptly stood, knocking
over the ladder-backed chair and causing Grey to race across the kitchen,
her tail straight up. In desperation, she stumbled out the kitchen door,
across the yard, and back to the barn. She threw the door open and
searched for the horse's saddle, where she always left it—hanging over
the side of the stall. But it was gone. Puzzled, she glanced across the rest

of the barn, to see the saddle, lying askew against the front wall. As if to confirm her worst fears, Angela stepped outside the barn and saw an image in the dust that left her mouth dry—drag marks, as if someone had pulled a lifeless body outside the barn. The dust also bore numerous boot prints, and Angela followed them with her eyes until they were lost amidst the grass.

"They found him," she whispered in disbelief, shaking her head. *But was it the law or the one who framed him?* Angela, not certain of the answer to that question, knew she had precious little time to spare. Regardless of the identity of Noah's captors, she needed to consult with Travis. She had no choice. This whole ordeal was bigger than anything Angela could possibly handle.

❖

Noah jolted to consciousness when his backside met what felt like a hardwood floor. However, the dark hood over his pounding head blocked out any view of his surroundings. The sudden jar left his head thudding all the more. Spears of pain shot from his bound wrists and up his arms.

"You can take the hood off now, Mark," a masculine voice snarled. "What Denham sees from here on ain't gonna make no difference."

Someone untied the strings of the black cotton sack and pulled it away.

Noah, thankful for the cool air that rushed upon his head, breathed deeply and glanced around the dingy, cluttered cabin that smelled of stale coffee. "I'm not Rupert Denham," Noah insisted, his tongue thick. He swiveled from his spot on the floor to face a man with brown eyes, stringy, dark hair, and a bushy beard to match.

" 'Course you ain't," the man sneered. "That would be me, now, wouldn't it? Surprise!" he mocked. "You just got yourself a twin brother."

At once, images of that troubling dream raced upon Noah. The mirror boy had made faces at Noah, as if to accuse him of some wrongdoing.

Noah took in the sharp angles of Denham's cheeks, the long, straight nose, the close-set eyes with heavy brows. Even though the hairy person before him looked more like a bear than a human being, Noah could detect the features that were very much his own.

For a flickering moment, the two sets of mirrored eyes held each other in soul-searching scrutiny. In that brief second of reunion with his twin, Noah caught a waver, a softening, in the evil-hearted Rupert.

"I. . .I speculated about having a twin, but I wasn't completely. . .completely sure," Noah said, his mind numb. He continued to search his brother's eyes, clinging to the hope that he could employ this uncanny sense of bonding and talk Rupert out of his devilish schemes.

However, with two quick blinks and a shake of his head, a fresh glaze of hate blazed from Denham's soul and he snarled, "Well, you got more than a twin. You also got yerself a half-brother, too." Denham jerked his head toward the one he called Mark.

The young man observed Noah with a spark of speculation. "After your ma died, your pa married my ma. They soon had me. My ma died when I wasn't but eight."

"Pa died last year," Rupert said with a scheming edge to his voice. "Told me all about you 'fore he took his last breath. Told me you was so sick he feared you was gonna die, so he left you on the porch of a parson named Thorndyke." Rupert walked toward the rock fireplace and threw a couple of logs on the glowing embers.

"S—so you just. . .just decided to. . .to find me and. . .and let me hang instead of you. Is that it?" A warm trickle of blood oozed down the back of Noah's hand, and he winced with the pain of the ropes on his wrist.

"Yer a right smart one," Denham said, placing his booted foot in one of the rickety, gray dining chairs that squeaked its protest. "Smart enough to break jail once, and I don't 'magine I'm gonna let you have the chance agin."

"What's that supposed to mean?" Noah asked, his voice cracking.

"Soon as night falls and I can work under the cover of darkness, I'm fillin' you full of bullets and special deliverin' you to Sheriff Garner." His malicious smile revealed crooked, yellowed teeth.

Noah stared up at his brother, astounded that one who shared his looks could carry within him such a heart of darkness. Then, Noah recalled his own years on the river, years of gambling, years of stealing, years of rebellion against God. Looking back, Noah knew that corrupt lifestyle had nearly sucked him under. Only by the grace of God was he a righteous man today.

"Get busy makin' some coffee," Rupert growled in Mark's direction. The younger man, who shared Noah's coloring and heavy brows, glowered at Rupert. And Noah felt an undercurrent of bitterness flash between the two. However, Rupert ignored the younger man and focused his attention on the whiskey bottle he pulled from beneath the cot.

"Mark, would you please get me a drink of water," Noah said, trying to sound as polite as possible. Already, Noah was trying to form a means of escape. Getting Mark on his side might prove the only method.

❖

"Angela!" Rachel exclaimed. As she opened the door to the ranch house, it brushed against her full skirt, the color of rich coffee.

"Hello," Angela said forlornly. "Might I have a few minutes of your and Travis's time?"

"Of. . .of course," Rachel said, stepping aside to allow Angela to enter. "We just finished our noon meal. Have you eaten?"

"No."

"Is everything all right?" Rachel rushed. "You look terribly pale, and—"

"Everything is far from all right." Angela gathered up the skirt of her deep green church frock and stepped into the homey ranch house. Resolutely, she forced her emotions under control. The smells of beans, cornbread, and peach cobbler did little to ease the nausea churning in her midsection.

"Travis is in the parlor with Little Trav," Rachel said, flipping her waste-length, auburn braid over her shoulder. A toddler's delightful squeal erupted from the direction of the parlor, and Rachel led Angela the few paces into the room. Travis, on the floor with his son, looked up and produced a tired smile.

"Angela! What brings you here?" he asked. Respectfully standing to acknowledge the presence of a lady, he fumbled with the tail of his shirt, trying to discreetly tuck it back into his trousers.

Angela, gripping her reticule between stiff fingers, gazed around the room—to the horsehair sofa, the worn rocking chair, the massive rock fireplace—she wanted to look anywhere but in the eyes of her relatives. At last, Angela screwed up the courage to state her mission. "I have some rather alarming news for both of you," she said in her schoolmistress voice, then looked directly into Rachel's apprehensive eyes.

"Since Friday, I have been. . .I have. . ." Angela cleared her throat. "I. . .um. . ." Her mind raced with the possibility that the two of them would not believe that Noah was innocent, that perhaps they would think she had been a fool. But Angela knew different. Noah Thorndyke was not a murderer, and Angela had been far from a fool. She had to take the chance of Travis and Rachel thinking she was daft. "Friday morning, in my garden I discovered the man for whom the sheriff and constable have been searching. I have been hiding him in my storm cellar for the last two days," she blurted.

"What?" Travis burst, his eyes wide.

"Oh, dear Lord, help us," Rachel whispered, lowering herself to the sofa, as if she no longer had the power to stand.

"Angela, that's considered aiding and abetting a criminal," Travis said. "You could face serious charges! And what about your safety? He hasn't tried to harm you, has he?"

"If the two of you will just listen to me," Angela said, sounding far more composed than her sweaty palms depicted. "The man I am—have been housing is not the criminal. His name is Noah Thorndyke. He has been terribly mistaken for Rupert Denham and, out of sheer desperation, he escaped the night before they were going to hang him. He is really a minister from Mansfield, Louisiana."

"Do you have solid proof of all this?" Travis asked.

Angela looked down at Little Trav, who toddled from his place in the middle of the rug toward his mother. "Yes," Angela said anxiously. "I have his word, and I have the guidance of the Lord that he speaks the truth." She imploringly gazed at Travis, who dubiously observed her.

"That won't hold up in any court of law," he said, shaking his head as if he could hardly believe his ears. "And Angela," he continued gently, "you need to understand that most criminals will swear they're innocent." Travis, turning from her, scrubbed his fingers through his tawny hair as if he wanted to pull it out by the roots.

"You don't believe me!" Angela cried, her insides feeling as if they were full of cold bricks.

"Angela. . . ," Rachel said uncertainly.

"That man supposedly shot and killed a banker in Rusk," Travis said, spinning to face her. "It's a wonder he hasn't slit your throat."

"Will the two of you listen to me?" Angela demanded, stomping her foot. "The point of this whole trip is that he's gone! Someone came and dragged him off, and his life might very well be in danger. I've got to have help!" she choked out, covering her face with her trembling gloved hands.

The sound of Rachel's skirts swishing against the wooden floors attested to her nearing. Soon, a consoling arm settled around Angela's shoulders, and the reassurance gave her the strength to continue.

"I don't know if the law has come and gotten him or if it's Rupert Denham," she said, blotting at the tears on her cheeks. "Mr. Thorndyke and I speculated that perhaps this Denham had framed him. They're exact look-alikes, and Mr. Thorndyke even suspects that they might be twins.

His father abandoned him when he was only three, and he was adopted by a parson and his wife in Mansfield, Louisiana."

Travis neared and stopped within inches of Angela. At the same time, Little Trav produced an irritable cry, and Rachel bent to pick him up. Angela dared look into Travis's eyes, churning with enough misgivings to fill the sky with storm clouds. "Angela, I'm sorry," he said. "But this whole story sounds too fantastical for belief."

"Well, if it's any consolation," she snapped, vexed beyond the determined self-control she normally exhibited, "it's *your* sermon that helped me come to terms with part of what has happened this weekend." She pointed her index finger at his nose.

Blinking in astonishment, Travis held her gaze.

"*You're* the one who waxed eloquently this morning about letting the Lord guide you and trusting Him to help us, even with life's most difficult moments," she said, mimicking his voice's inflections. "Now, have you or have you not prayed about the snap decision you just made?" Angela asked, resorting to the same stern look to which she had exposed the sheriff two days before. The expression produced the exact same effect on Travis as it had the sheriff.

"Well. . . ," he said sheepishly.

"I think she has a point, Travis," Rachel said.

"Exactly what did you want me to do?" Travis asked.

"I was thinking that perhaps you might agree to go into town and ask the constable if there had been any word about Noah—I mean, Mr. Thorndyke's capture. It would be natural for you to go, and I don't want him suspicious about why I'd ride into town and ask. I just talked with him yesterday, and he told me then to call off school until Wednesday or until he told me otherwise. I just don't want to do anything to make him suspect. . . ." She left the rest unsaid.

"I'm sure the sheriff would wire the constable the minute Noah is caught," Angela said. "If he hasn't been captured by the law, then we can only assume that someone else has gotten him."

"How do you know he didn't just ride off?" Travis asked, his voice still indecisive.

"He—he *did* leave me a note to that effect," Angela said. "He told me in the note that he was taking my yellow bonnet and house robe, so that he would be disguised as a woman. He also said he'd be taking my ebony stallion and that he would send me money to cover the cost of everything he took. But the horse is still in the pasture. The bonnet, I found in my barn, with. . . with blood on it. And there are marks in the sand that look as if someone has been dragged through the dust."

Travis exchanged an increasingly urgent glance with Rachel. "I'll ride into Dogwood and see if the constable has word. Then, I'll swing by your place on my way home and give you a report," he said.

Rachel nodded, and Angela released a pent-up breath.

Chapter 11

Noah's body ached all over. He had been sitting propped against the wall for the better part of an hour while Rupert took several swallows of whiskey, then fell into a light sleep. The ropes binding Noah's wrists felt as if they were cutting tiny furrows into his flesh. Occasionally another trickle of blood oozed from the lacerations, and the stinging increased all the more. The wound in his side produced an infrequent jabbing pain that only added to his discomfort.

Noah prayed until his mind was numb. He repeatedly quoted the Twenty-third Psalm to himself. And he thought of Miss Isaacs, his own guardian angel, who had taken a risk on believing his word. Furthermore, Noah decided that if he survived this ordeal, he would frequently write to Miss Isaacs, only stopping if she forbade him to continue with the most severe and continual reprimands. The longer Noah thought about her, the more he believed that she might very well be an answer to his prayers. Only time would tell, but Noah would not take just one "no" as an answer from her. *You will have to tell me "no" at least six times before I will stop writing you, Miss Isaacs*, he thought with resolution.

Mark entered from outside and tossed another log on the fire. He glanced at the sleeping Rupert and walked toward Noah. From a sheath strapped to his thigh, the younger man whipped out a knife with a long, gleaming blade. Noah's gut tightened in dread of Mark's next move.

The young man bent over Noah's feet and cut the cord binding his legs. "Get on your feet," Mark whispered. "We're going for a little ride."

Shocked, Noah began struggling to his feet. As often as possible in their brief acquaintance, Noah had smiled at Mark, been polite, and tried to show the young man the respect Rupert was far from exhibiting. Noah's soul filled with a rush of hope. Perhaps his plan was working, and Mark had decided to help his half-brother escape.

However, the first step in that process included Noah's standing—a step that proved more difficult than he ever imagined. He was stiff from the cramped position, and the wound in his side produced intermittent stabs of pain. Silently, he pleaded with his muscles to provide enough strength to rise. At last, Mark reached down and grabbed his arm, supplying Noah with the appropriate support to gain his footing.

"Head for the horses outside," Mark said under his breath.

Noah didn't waste a moment arguing with him. As quietly as possible, he walked to the door, only pausing long enough for Mark to open it for him. Noah glanced over his shoulder to see Rupert stirring in his sleep, and he hastened out the door. Silently, Mark shut the door and, without a word, cut the ropes binding Noah's raw wrists. Immediately, Noah pulled his aching arms in front of him and gingerly touched his chaffed wrists.

"I'm going to get on the bay. Get on behind me after I mount," Mark whispered from behind.

Noah looked toward two horses—one a bay, the other a palomino—both tethered to one of the numerous trees. His mind racing with anticipation, Noah nodded his ready agreement. In seconds, Mark assisted him atop the bay gelding, and he hung onto the saddle's back rim as the horse trotted up the worn trail, winding through the woods. The sun, inching its way toward the western horizon, suggested the hour was between three and four. Noah wondered whether Miss Isaacs had spent the afternoon regretting his departure or reveling in relief that he now was gone.

"Where are we going?" Noah whispered, his head still pounding with every word he spoke.

"Wherever you want to go," Mark said, glancing over his shoulder. "We're only about twenty minutes from where we got you. Do you want to return there?"

Noah thought of Miss Isaacs, of her probable discovery that he had not taken the ebony stallion after all. He wondered if she suspected that he had been kidnapped during his attempts to leave. Noah would like to speak to her one last time before trying to make it to Louisiana. Perhaps the smartest thing would be to ask her permission to stay in her cellar until nightfall. For, after the recent turn in circumstances, Noah did not feel physically capable of striking out on his own. Miss Isaacs had once mentioned driving him part of the way, and Noah wondered if her offer still stood.

"Yes, let's go back to where I was," Noah said, pausing before posing his next question. "Why are you doing this?"

"Because you're innocent and don't deserve to die, and I've put up with Rupert all I'm goin' to. I'm cuttin' out on him. I never did take to all his stealin' and connivin'. I'm tired of being on the edge of it all. Our pa might not 'a' been perfect, but he shore didn't raise us to be robbers and murderers."

"I know Rupert is wanted for murder. Are you?" Noah asked, hoping for a negative answer.

"Nope," Mark said. "I ain't never killed a person in my whole life. Don't ever plan to either. And as far as the stealin'. . .I only done what I was forced to do."

A sudden rush of camaraderie blanketed Noah and his half-brother. There was something very decent in the sound of Mark Denham's voice. Even though this man in front of him had assisted in his capture, he *was* Noah's brother and he *was* aiding in his escape. "Tell me more about our father," Noah said.

However, Mark's reply was cut off by the explosion of a bullet and Rupert's raucous cursing, echoing through the woods.

"Hang on!" Mark commanded before burying his spurs into the horse's flanks. The animal bolted forward, and Noah's side protested against the sudden lurch. Another gunshot rang out, and a bullet whizzed past Noah's head. He joined Mark's instinctive duck as even more bullets pelted the trees. And Noah relived another such ride only two days before—a ride that left him lying in Miss Isaacs's garden, a wounded and desperate man.

❖

Angela, exhausted from fatigue, lay on her velvet sofa and watched the fireplace's glowing embers. Anxiously, she waited for word from Travis. Angela looked at the watch hanging on the chain around her neck and noted that three-thirty was swiftly approaching. Travis should arrive any moment with a report from Constable Parker. Once again, Angela rose from the couch to pace her living room. With each pace, she relived her harsh treatment of Mr. Thorndyke and cringed with the recall of every word. *How could I have been so calloused?* She could only pray that Noah would not die before she had the chance to beg his forgiveness. Angela, tightly gripping her hands, beseeched the Lord to protect him, wherever he might be.

A muffled shot rang out, and Angela jumped. She raced to her parlor window to see no signs of an intruder. Yet, an even closer shot attested to the presence of a nearing gunman. Angela, her heart palpitating, ran to look out the window in the kitchen. From this vantage point, she could see a horse galloping toward her house at breakneck speed. Upon its back sat two men. One of them appeared to be Noah. "Jump!" the man in front hollered, and Noah lunged from the horse as it sped away from the house. Angela, gasping for air, watched as Noah hit the ground to roll several feet and stop near her back steps. Another shot rang from the woods before a second horseman galloped from the forest and into the clearing. Flinging open the back door, Angela grabbed Noah's arm and assisted him as he struggled up the steps, to collapse into her kitchen. She slammed the door and slumped against it. But when a bullet pierced the wood just above her head, Angela hit the floor beside Noah.

"It's Rupert Denham," Noah gasped, his face contorting in pain. "Mark. . . Mark and I were h–hoping he wouldn't see me jump, and. . .and would continue to chase Mark."

"Looks like that plan didn't work," Angela ground out.

"Rupert *is* my t–twin, and he wants me d–dead!" Gripping his right arm, Noah groaned.

"You've been shot again!" Angela cried, as she noticed the sickening blotch of blood oozing from beneath his hand.

"Lock the door!" Noah commanded, scooting himself farther into the kitchen.

Angela scrambled to secure the wooden bar firmly in place only seconds before the sound of pounding horse's hooves stopped outside the door. "I'm going after my shotgun," Angela said, racing toward her bedroom. She grabbed a handful of bullets from the top drawer of her chest of drawers, then reached for the loaded shotgun standing beside her bed. Her father had insisted upon Angela's expertise with a firearm when she moved to the cottage. And every month, the aging gentleman paid a special visit to his daughter for the sole purpose of shooting. Now, she stumbled back into the kitchen and gulped for air. As Angela gripped the gun, the door's wooden bar bulged against the strain of the man slamming his body into the door. She hoisted the shotgun and prepared to pull the trigger, thankful that her father had never missed one of their marksman appointments.

As she suspected, the door at last crashed inward, and a tall man with a wiry beard and eyes like a demon stumbled into her kitchen. Angela gave him no time to gain his balance. She pointed the gun at his legs and pulled the trigger. He howled and lunged forward, falling at her feet as if he were a felled tree. His revolver flew from his hand and spun across the kitchen floor. Angela automatically inserted another bullet into the gun's chamber, snapped it shut, and braced it against her shoulder.

"If you try anything stupid, I'll be forced to shoot you again," she said precisely, yet her legs trembled so violently she feared she would collapse.

The smell of gunpowder permeated the kitchen, and the man on the floor writhed. Angela suspected he would be incapacitated for quite some while.

"You. . .you saved my life a–again," Noah gasped, pulling himself to a sitting position. "How can. . .can I ever repay you?"

Travis's firm knock resounded through the cottage. "Angela! Angela!" he yelled, then rattled the front door. "Are you in there? Angela? I heard gunshots!"

"Come. . .come to the kitchen door," Angela hollered.

In seconds, Travis rushed into the kitchen. "I heard shots, and—" He stopped short when he saw Rupert Denham lying on the floor, with Noah a few feet away.

Angela, never taking the gun off Denham, bit her lips and choked on a sob of relief. "I. . .I can't believe I've done it, but some–somehow, I managed to cap–capture the criminal," she said.

His eyes round, Travis stared from Denham to Angela to Noah. He pushed back his felt hat, shook his head, and whistled in disbelief.

❖

By noon the next day, all of Dogwood buzzed with the news of Angela Isaacs's heroic capture of the notorious killer. The stories flew high and wide and were so variant in their details that Angela felt certain no one suspected she had housed Noah Thorndyke for two days. Presently, with the exception of Dr. Engle, the whole town seemed to think that the first she had ever seen of Noah was when he crawled into her kitchen seconds before Denham made his entry.

When Angela arrived at Dr. Engle's office to pay Noah a visit, the doctor exposed her to a welcoming smile. "It's a good thing you're here," he said, removing his spectacles to rub his bushy, gray brows. "Mr. Thorndyke has been restless to see ya all morning." The doctor eyed her speculatively, and Angela returned his gaze with as bland an expression as she could muster.

According to Travis, when he delivered Noah to Dr. Engle's office for treatment of the gunshot wounds, the insightful doctor demanded to know who had tended the first injury. Travis swore the doctor to secrecy before telling the whole story of Angela's hiding and nursing Noah.

"Humph," Dr. Engle now said. "To look at you, you'd think you didn't give one flip whether the man lives or dies, but I think I know different," he continued with an audacious wink.

"Has he had a good morning?" Angela asked, purposefully maintaining her composure.

"Yes, quite good. Fortunately, the bullet wasn't lodged too deep and didn't chip a bone. Looks like the Lord was lookin' out for that man on all sides. The whole town is talkin' about the way he escaped jail, and word has it Sheriff Garner is supposed to appear sometime today to present a formal apology."

"He should," Angela said with gravity.

A bell's demanded ring sounded from the patient's room. "Well, go on in," the doctor said, jerking his head toward the room. "He's waitin' on you and is about to drive me to distraction with that bell." The doctor walked toward his kitchen, all the while mumbling, "I'll be, if there ain't another romance brewin' in that room. Seems like every time a man gets himself injured in these parts, he winds up in that bed and next thing you know—boom—he's hitched."

Angela, smiling slightly, remembered when Dr. Engle's nurse, Magnolia Alexander, wound up marrying one of her own patients, who also happened to be Travis Campbell's brother. Yesterday at church, Magnolia and Levi had seemed more like newlyweds than a couple married two years who now had a baby. Because of Magnolia's marriage to Levi, the doctor lost a nurse to matrimony, but wound up gaining a wife himself, Sarah Douglas, who now served as his part-time nurse.

Dismissing these thoughts, Angela walked across the rustic outer office that smelled of kerosene and antiseptic. She paused outside the room's door long enough to straighten her hat and rub her damp palms across her full, indigo skirt. With as much dignity as she could muster, Angela opened the door and stepped into the room. Noah's slow smile, laced with pleasure, left her heart beating far past the comfort zone.

"I've been waiting on you all morning," he said, reaching for her hand.

Without hesitation, Angela stepped to his side and placed her hand in his. Her face warmed, and she chose to focus on the starched white sheets that swathed the patient. Through the closed window, the muffled sounds of Dogwood's busy streets punctuated the awkward moment. When Noah's hand tightened on Angela's, she shyly pulled it away and turned to walk the brief distance to the wooden rocking chair. Head bent, she sat in the chair, then immediately stood back up. Fidgeting, Angela walked the few inches toward the window and stared at the numerous buggies, wagons, and pedestrians, rushing here and there.

"There's something—" she began, turning to face Noah.

"Miss Isaacs," he said simultaneously.

She produced a smile of chagrin. "Excuse me."

"No, please excuse me," Noah said with a chivalrous nod of his head.

"I was just going to tell you that. . .that. . ." Angela nervously licked her lips. "That I feel I must apologize for my dreadful behavior toward you during your hour of dire need. I treated you in a most abhorrent fashion, and for that, I am deeply ashamed and. . .and hope that you can find it in your heart to extend your forgiveness."

"Would you care to expound upon what I should forgive you for?" Noah quirked one brow, and his dark eyes danced with merriment. "All I remember is a gracious lady who not only rescued me from a posse bent on hanging me but also bore arms against an outlaw trying to take my life."

Angela, her heart pounding all the more furiously, debated exactly what to say. "Well, I. . .I. . .you requested my permission to. . .to. . ." She cleared her throat and gripped her reticule until she was certain it might scream. "To correspond with me, and I—"

"Ah, the correspondence," he said, breaking into an endearing smile. "Of course. Thank you so much for broaching that important subject." His smile increased, and Angela had the uncanny feeling that she had just stepped through a door he held wide open. "It might come as quite a surprise to you, Miss Isaacs, that, as far as I am concerned, the issue of our corresponding has long been settled."

Her heart sinking, Angela assumed that he must have taken her initial negative answer as the final one. Inside, she floundered for an appropriate way to hint that she had reconsidered his offer without seeming brazen. Yet another troubling thought struck her. *What if he has decided he would rather not correspond?* She turned back to the window, pledging to take every possible means to ensure that Mr. Thorndyke did not detect her disappointment.

"Would it terribly upset you to learn that I decided during my brief season of captivity that I would indeed write to you, whether you initially agreed or not?"

Angela, her eyes wide, spun to face him. Her Sunday-best skirt swirled around her ankles, producing a whisper that reflected the delighted gasp escaping her lips.

Noah observed her with the expression of a smitten schoolboy, his eyes pools of admiration, his lips tilted in an uncertain twist. His hand stirred atop the light quilt covering him, suggesting that his emotions were as taut as her own. "You see, I came to the conclusion that a woman of your character was worth pursuing and that, in order for me to not correspond, you would have to deliver unto me a series of severe and continual reprimands."

"Mr. Thorndyke, I don't know what to say," Angela rushed primly, her disconcerted mind reeling with the implications of his admission.

"Well, if you were to say that you would be agreeable to my writing to you, as far as I'm concerned, that would be a highly appropriate reply." Noah shifted in the bed as if he were anxious for her affirmation.

Angela, her palms damp, diminished the distance between them and Noah once more reached for her hand. This time, she didn't pull away when his fingers enclosed hers. Without blinking, Noah held her gaze and tugged her gloved hand toward his lips. Gently, he pressed his lips against the back of her hand and held them there while he implored her with his eyes to eventually give him a chance at more than just correspondence.

Like an avalanche, the melting ice around her heart cracked, and a flood of warmth filled her being. Angela, her eyes stinging, rapidly blinked and experienced an unexpected surge of panic as Mr. Thorndyke removed his lips. The last time she felt like this, the recipient of her admiration scorned her.

"You might find it interesting to learn that Mr. Travis Campbell has already been by this morning," Noah said with pleasure. "It seems that he is heading up a pulpit committee, and he asked my permission to place my name as a possible candidate."

Angela's alarm increased as her mind projected the possibilities of the next few months: Noah moving in just up the road from her; their initial correspondence turning to a full-blown courtship; the minister's subsequent proposal; Angela's being forced to make a decision.

"I'm. . .I'm not c–certain I'm. . .I'm ready for. . .for. . ." Angela cleared her throat and resorted to the outward composure that years of teaching had bequeathed her. "I will agree to our corresponding, Mr. Thorndyke, but I must be honest and tell you that I am not certain I am ready for any kind of long-term romantic attachment," she rushed, gently tugging her hand from his grasp. "If you move here, I hope it is for the sole reason that you feel the Lord's direction, otherwise—"

"Who was he, Miss Isaacs? Who was the one responsible for the painful shadows in your eyes?"

"I'm afraid we haven't known each other long enough to discuss such—"

"The circumstances of our acquaintance have long since circumvented the norms of propriety. Already, you know my life's story. All I ask is that you share your painful experience so that I might better understand you and therefore take the proper precautions in developing our acquaintance."

With a sigh, Angela peered deeply into Noah's eyes and relived the moment she had met him only three days ago. He had invaded her life in the most outlandish state of affairs and instigated Angela's doing what she had vowed to never do again—foolishly trust the word of a man. But somehow, Noah Thorndyke had seemed an exemplary man of reputable honor, even in the face of being an escaped "criminal." Now, despite knowing him only days, Angela decided to share her broken heart.

With as brief an explanation as possible, she detailed the occurrences that led to her intense mortification and left her the subject of sympathetic gossip for months. "I have had a problem with trust since that day," she honestly stated. "And I am only just now coming to the point of considering. . .that is to say that. . .that my agreeing to correspond with you is nothing short of a miracle within itself. However, I still need time to—"

"Yes, of course you do. I heartily agree. And I must assure you that I, in no way, intend to push you into any agreement that would leave you less than comfortable."

Angela reflected on the fact that she had been anything but comfortable since the minute she found Noah Thorndyke in her garden. "Furthermore," she continued, desperate to be completely honest with him. "You seem to insist upon the impression that I am some sort of spiritual woman of virtue of sorts that—"

"Oh, but you are," he insisted. "There are precious few women who would have—"

"No, I'm not," Angela replied. "I feel it highly necessary to emphasize that I have attended church for these past years only as a fulfillment of the terms of my teaching contract. And as I have already told you, it was only the dire straits in which you arrived at my home that drove me back to prayer."

"Well, as long as the end result is gained, that is all that matters.

Nonetheless, Angela. . ." He paused and exposed her to a pleading gaze. "May I address you by your first name?"

She hesitated but a second. "Yes, of course," Angela said, her cheeks warming again.

"And please, don't hesitate to call me Noah," he replied. With a daring gleam in his eye, he reached, once more, for her hand.

Angela bit her lips as she observed the long, slender fingers that covered her hand. "Of course."

"As I was saying, I think that perhaps the Lord dropped me into your life for a variety of reasons—many of which we have yet to realize." He waited but a poignant second before continuing. "And I'm thrilled to hear of your renewed interest in the things of God. Assuredly, you are a woman whose heart He can touch. Otherwise, you wouldn't have been open to His guidance concerning my plight."

"There was a time or two I almost turned you in," she said, candidly watching him for any negative response.

"Yes, I know," he replied without a blink. "I would most likely have wavered just as you did. That is understandable, but in the end, you did the right thing."

"I guess that's all the Lord asks of us, isn't it?" Angela said, reflecting upon the grace that God had extended to her. Grace that had cleansed her disobedience. Grace that was undeserved, yet fully embraced.

Epilogue

One year later, Angela sat on the second pew of the Dogwood Community Church as her husband of three months took his spot behind the pulpit. Before announcing his text, Noah turned a beaming smile upon her, a smile that spoke of his happiness and even a secretive nuance of pride. For it was that very morning that Angela had shared her suspicions with her husband. She discreetly touched the waistline of her navy blue suit and wondered how much longer she would be able to wear the snug-fitting skirt. Soon, she would discreetly announce the news to the school board and alert them that they would need to find a replacement.

Beside her, Mark Denham leaned sideways, fumbling with his large Bible. "What verse did he say?" the former ruffian asked.

"I have no idea," Angela blissfully whispered, smiling at her new brother-in-law. After the trial and hanging of Rupert Denham, Noah had stepped forward to defend his younger brother and had negotiated an acquittal for Mark. Part of the terms of his acquittal involved Noah's agreeing to Mark's living with him. Mark testified to the Lord's working in his life even before he met Noah. Soon after moving into the parsonage with Noah, Mark had readily accepted Christ as his Savior and was flourishing under the influence of his godly brother.

As the service continued, Angela gazed upon her handsome husband and reflected over the preceding months. She and Noah had corresponded only a few weeks when he accepted the call to pastor Dogwood Community Church. Bit by bit, the Lord had worked a miracle of healing within Angela, and she soon gave her whole heart to Noah. Sighing, she smiled with contentment and tried to concentrate upon the words of the man behind the pulpit. But Angela was too enamored with the man himself to contemplate his words.

At last, Noah called for the benediction, then the people visited and dispursed, until only Angela and Noah remained near the back door. Noah, preparing to open the door, paused and turned to his bride. With a soft smile, he reached for Angela, and she gladly leaned into his embrace. Reveling in the pleasurable warmth that spread through her, Angela wrapped her arms around him and soaked in the ardor of his affection.

"I never dreamed that night when I was waiting to be hanged that God was in the middle of working a miracle," Noah said with wonder.

Angela pulled away far enough to gently stroke Noah's face, smooth from his morning shave. "And I never dreamed that I was hiding my future husband in my cellar or that. . ." She paused as an unexplainable joy welled up within her soul and manifested itself with the warm tears pooling in her eyes. Silently, Angela touched her midsection and Noah covered her hand with his.

"That I would be blessed with two angels," he finished for her.

A Letter to Our Readers

Dear Readers:

In order that we might better contribute to your reading enjoyment, we would appreciate you taking a few minutes to respond to the following questions. When completed, please return to the following: Fiction Editor, Barbour Publishing, Inc., P.O. Box 719, Uhrichsville, OH 44683.

1. Did you enjoy reading *Texas?*
   - ❏ Very much. I would like to see more books like this.
   - ❏ Moderately—I would have enjoyed it more if _____

   _____

   _____

2. What influenced your decision to purchase this book? (Check those that apply.)
   - ❏ Cover
   - ❏ Back cover copy
   - ❏ Title
   - ❏ Price
   - ❏ Friends
   - ❏ Publicity
   - ❏ Other

3. Which story was your favorite?
   - ❏ *Texas Honor*
   - ❏ *Texas Lady*
   - ❏ *Texas Rose*
   - ❏ *Texas Angel*

4. Please check your age range:
   - ❏ Under 18
   - ❏ 18–24
   - ❏ 25–34
   - ❏ 35–45
   - ❏ 46–55
   - ❏ Over 55

5. How many hours per week do you read? _____

Name _____

Occupation _____

Address _____

City _____ State _____ ZIP _____

E-mail _____